A GIFT COMES!

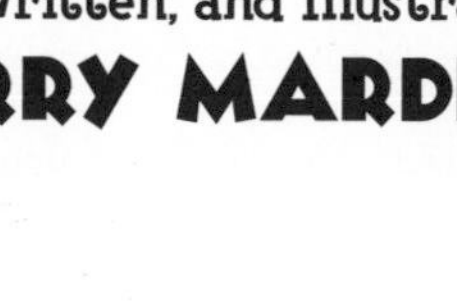

Created, Written, and Illustrated by
LARRY MARDER

DARK HORSE BOOKS®

Dedicated with love to my mother, Babs Marder;
and to the memory of my father, Bernie Marder;
of my grandparents, Larry and Laberda Post;
and of my little brother, Jon. Without their humor,
sacrifice, encouragement, and guidance, *Beanworld*
couldn't ever have existed. I miss them all every day.

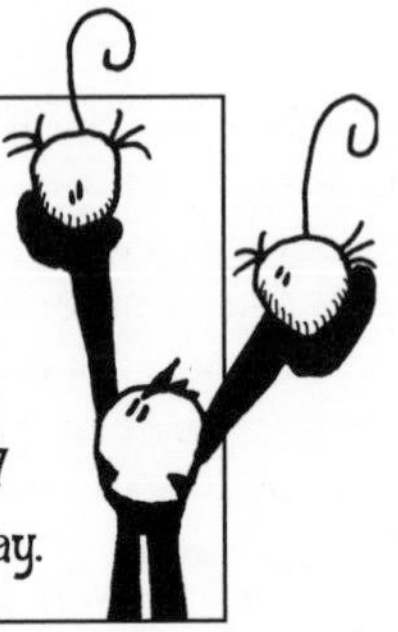

Editor Diana Schutz
Associate Editor Dave Marshall
Assistant Editor Brendan Wright
Book Design Tina Alessi
Digital Production Matt Dryer
Publisher Mike Richardson

LARRY MARDER'S BEANWORLD™ (Book 2): A GIFT COMES!

This volume collects issues ten through twenty-one of *Tales of the Beanworld*,
originally edited by Cat Yronwode.

Published by Dark Horse Books
A division of Dark Horse Comics, Inc.
10956 SE Main Street
Milwaukie, Oregon 97222

darkhorse.com

First Dark Horse edition: July 2009
ISBN 978-1-59582-299-4

1 3 5 7 9 10 8 6 4 2
Printed in China

PREFACE

THIS VOLUME COMPLETES the original run of the *Tales of the Beanworld* comic book. The stories in this volume encompass events with huge implications—not only for the Beans—including their first interaction with other inhabitants in adjacent realms of the Big·Big·Picture.

Major new characters like Mr. Teach'm and Heyoka are introduced. And the reader learns a lot about the Goofy Jerks' Reproductive Propellant Delivery Service. We experience the ever-expanding blossoming of the relationship between Beanish and his secret friend Dreamishness. Big chunks about the start of Professor Garbanzo's career are revealed, along with more than a few hefty hints about the origins of Beanworld's mysterious hero, Mr. Spook.

And in so many ways, the catalyst for these exchanges is the "Gift" referred to in the title of this volume: the unanticipated arrival of the next generation of Bean babies. The Pod'l'pool Cuties.

After I graduated from art school in 1973, I slowly, but surely, began accumulating scribbled notes and story fragments about Beanworld. Funny thing, though—almost nothing in my collection of scrawled notes anticipated the Pod'l'pool Cuties. Almost, but not quite.

At my first post-collegial graphics art job, I had a little scrap of a drawing—pinned to the wall next to my workstation— that was unlike the other Beans I was drawing at that time. It was a character study that looked more like a pea than a bean, and it sported the long, curled, single hair that universally symbolizes "baby" in the language of comics.

I'm pretty sure it had its eyes closed to indicate sleep or meditation, and it was definitely at rest under water and surrounded by little bubbles, with some grassy foliage at the bottom. Unfortunately, the drawing itself has managed to disappear into the fog of the passing years, but I never forgot it and how people would often respond to it with a wistful sigh, saying, "That is soooo cute!"

I filed that information away in my memory, and years later that silly sketch served as a prototype for the little Cuties in their Pod'l'pool.

When I folded the Cuties into the *Beanworld* story mix, I had no idea how much fun they were going to be to draw. Plus, I had no idea how popular they would be with *Beanworld* fans. And I certainly didn't understand, at first anyway, how their presence would in many ways take over the direction of the book.

But they did. I shouldn't be surprised. From the very first time I put that initial little drawing up in a public place, the reaction has always been just like that of the Beans themselves: "Awwwwwww."

With a Hoo-Hoo-HA and a Hoka-Hoka-HEY!

Larry Marder
larrymarder.blogspot.com
2009

THE BEANWORLD GLOSSARY

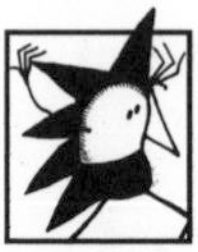

Beanish: Artist. Creator of the Fabulous Look·See Show.

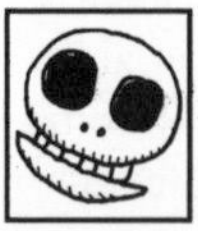

Bone Zone: Skull remains of the Hoi-Polloi Ring Herd located underneath the Four Realities.

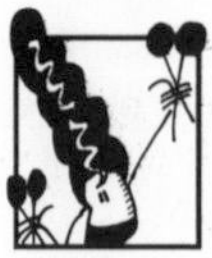

Boom'r Band: A hot trio of Beanworld musicians.

Chow: A dark, stony substance. The Beans eat it, and the Hoi-Polloi use it for money.

Chowdown: The act of consuming food.

Chowdown Pool: Giant tub used by the Beans as a communal feeding place.

Chow Sol'jer Army: They steal Chow from the Hoi-Polloi. Mr. Spook is the leader of the two divisions: Spear-Fling'n-Flank'rs and Chow-Pluk'rs.

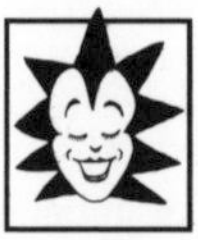

Dreamishness: Beanish's secret friend and muse.

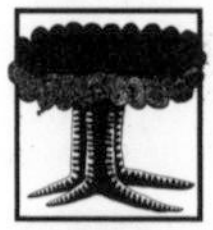

Gran'Ma'Pa: Beanworld's spiritual and culinary guardian. Sole source of Sprout-Butts.

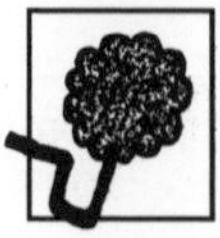

Gunk'l'dunk: All-purpose adhesive.

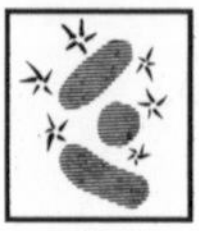

Float Factor: When Twinks get near Mystery Pods, both objects transform into a new entity that floats in the air.

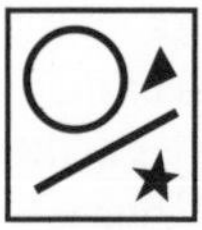

Four Realities: Chips, Slats, Hoops, and Twinks. Easily obtainable raw materials for Beanworld arts and industry. For example, a slat and chip can be manufactured into a spear.

Hoi-Polloi Ring Herd: General adversaries to the Beans. Greedy gambling folks. The only creatures with the ability to process Sprout-Butts into Chow.

Legendary Edge: Departure point from trips to the Four Realities and below.

Notworms: What Mr. Spook's fork is made of.

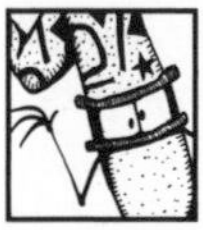

Professor Garbanzo: Toolmaker and thinker.

Proverbial Sandy Beach: Re-entry point from trips to the Four Realities and below.

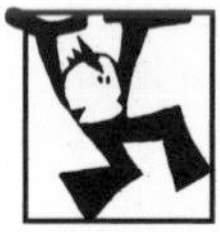

Mr. Spook: Hero and leader of the Chow Sol'jer Army.

Mystery Pods: Powerful objects of unknown origin. Used in Float Factor.

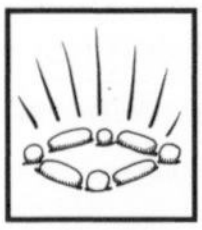

Secret Sketch: Circular Float Factor device that mysteriously transports Beanish to Dreamishness for daily midday visits.

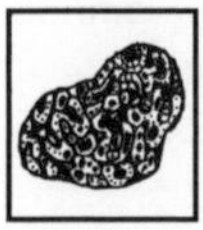

Sprout-Butt: Vocal offshoot of Gran'Ma'Pa. Hoi-Polloi convert Sprout-Butts into Chow.

Thin Lake: Fresh water that covers the Four Realities.

MAP OF THE KNOWN BEANWORLD

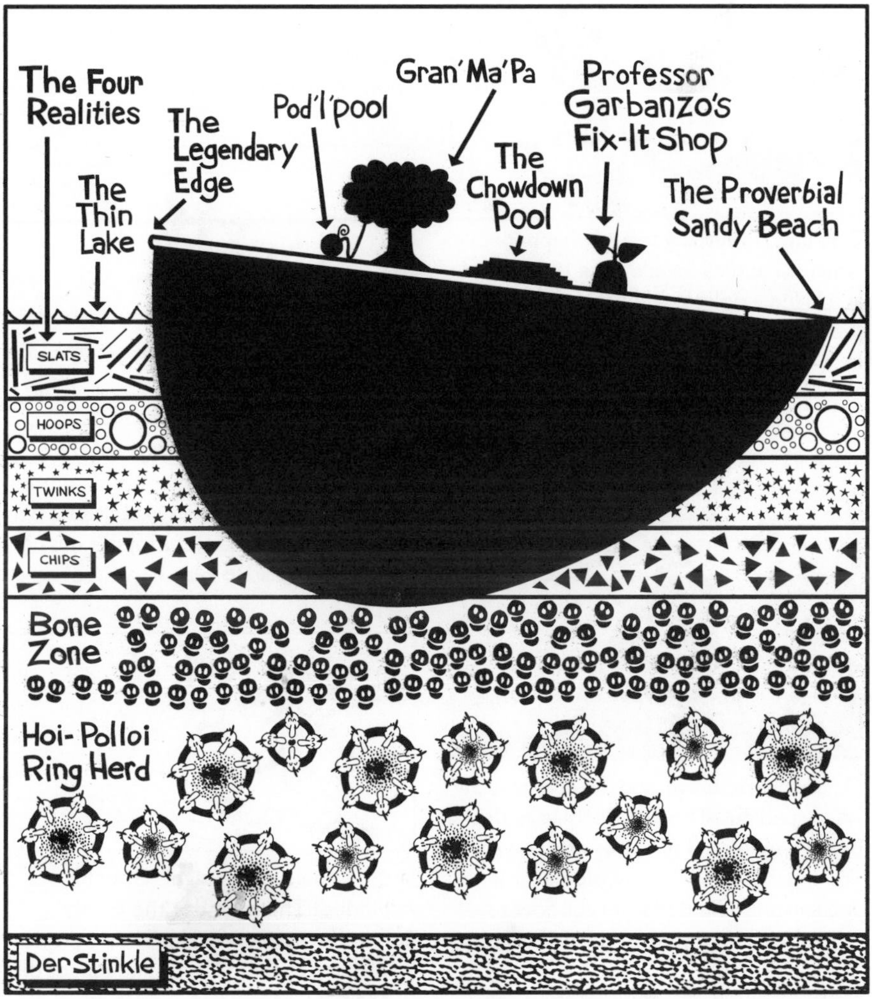
The Four Realities
The Thin Lake
The Legendary Edge
Pod'l'pool
Gran'Ma'Pa
The Chowdown Pool
Professor Garbanzo's Fix-It Shop
The Proverbial Sandy Beach
SLATS
HOOPS
TWINKS
CHIPS
Bone Zone
Hoi-Polloi Ring Herd
Der Stinkle

Hey, what's with this Beanworld anyway?

Beanworld is a weird fantasy dimension operating under its own rules and laws. Beanworld is about the affinity of life. All the characters, whether they are friends or adversaries, understand that ultimately they depend on each other for survival.

One caution:

Please do not search for scientific or magical explanations; you won't find any. Beanworld is a separate reality. It's not just a *place*, it's a *process*. It is what it is—and th-that's all, folks.

WHAT HAPPENED IN BOOK ONE

MOSSY MAMMOTH
LUNCHEON MEATS
BOILED IN BUTTER

One day, something terrible happened! A vicious enemy invaded the Beanworld and killed, cooked, and canned many of the Hoi-Polloi Ring Herd. Fortunately for the Beans, Gran'Ma'Pa provided an awesome weapon: The Flip-Flop Tool.

I THOUGHT WE'D DOWN THIS CHOW PRONTO!
sigh
I HAD NO IDEA IT WOULD TAKE SOOOOO LONG!
ALL WE DO IS EAT & SLEEP! I'M BORED!
Z
WARNING: Too Much CHOW is hazardous to BEANHEALTH.
snore

Mr. Spook was brave, and the enemy Army was wiped out. The Hoi-Polloi gave the Beans a mountain of Chow as a reward. Too much Chow! Beanworld became unbalanced. The Beans forgot how to work. The Hoi-Polloi forgot how to play.

SPOOOT

From out of Der Stinkle, Der Kveen and some creepy bugs got wise to the mountain of Chow, ate the whole thing, and laid Aigs. The Beans couldn't remember where the Aigs came from and called them Mystery Pods. Mr. Spook didn't trust them at all.

YOU MUST NEVER, EVER TELL ANYONE ABOUT ME.
IF YOU DO, YOU WILL NEVER, EVER SEE ME AGAIN.
DO YOU UNDERSTAND WHAT I'M SAYING, BEANISH?
..YES..

One day while using the Mystery Pods' Float Factor to sketch, Beanish made an accidental discovery. His sketch sent him to the sky, where he met a mysterious new friend, but he had to keep his visits a secret.

A GIFT! A GIFT COMES!
A GIFT! A GIFT COMES!

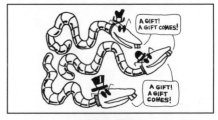

In the middle of the night, Gran'Ma'Pa exploded! The next day the Goofy Service Jerks dropped in. They delivered something to Gran'Ma'Pa and taught the Beans the Gift Song.

Wake-up time!
GASP!
Z
!
?
THE GIFT!
!
Z
Z

Soon the Gift arrived. No one was sure what it was. Then it began to grow.

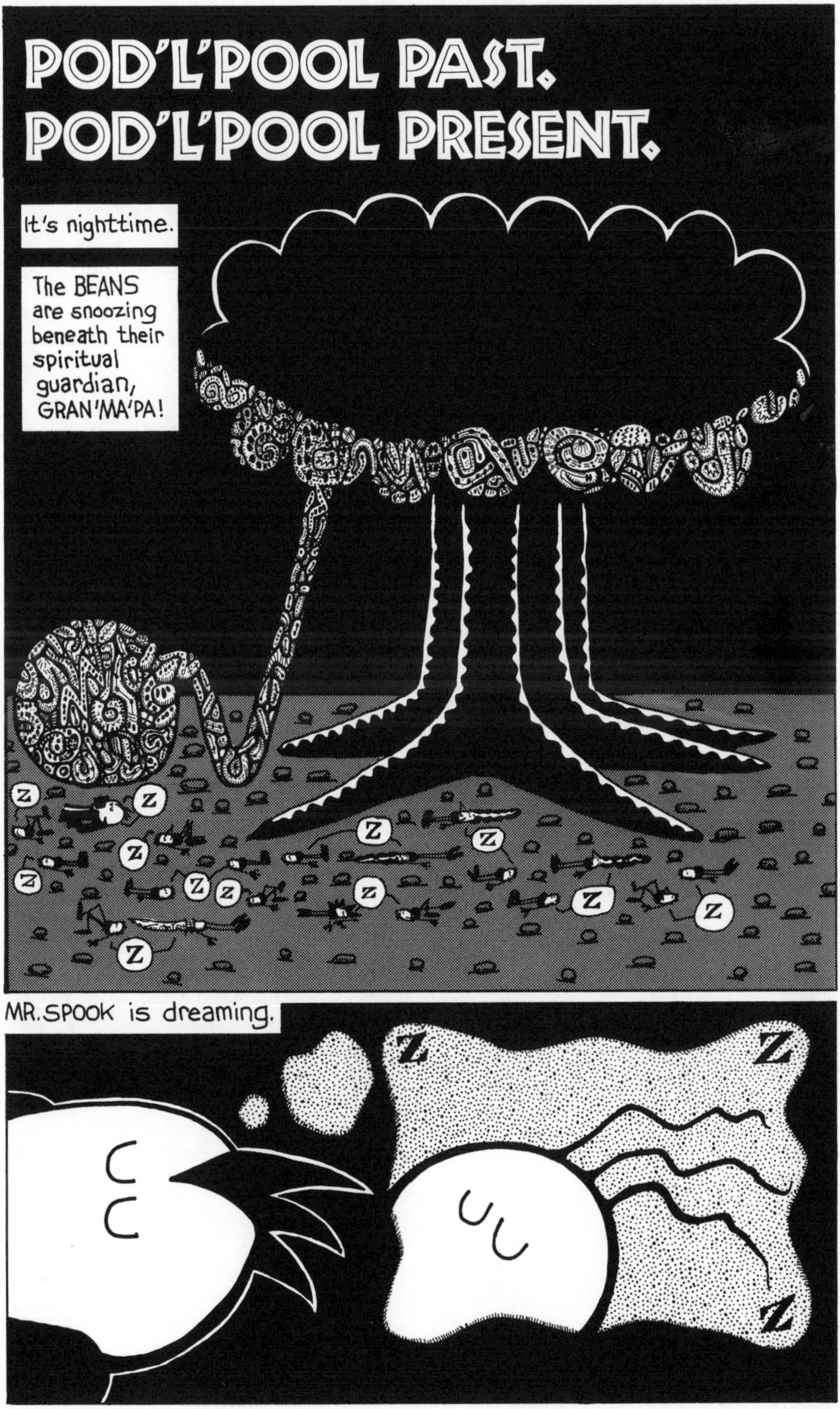
POD'L'POOL PAST.
POD'L'POOL PRESENT.
It's nighttime.
The BEANS are snoozing beneath their spiritual guardian, GRAN'MA'PA!
Z
Z
Z
Z
Z
Z
Z
Z
Z
Z
Z
Z
MR.SPOOK is dreaming.
Z
Z
Z

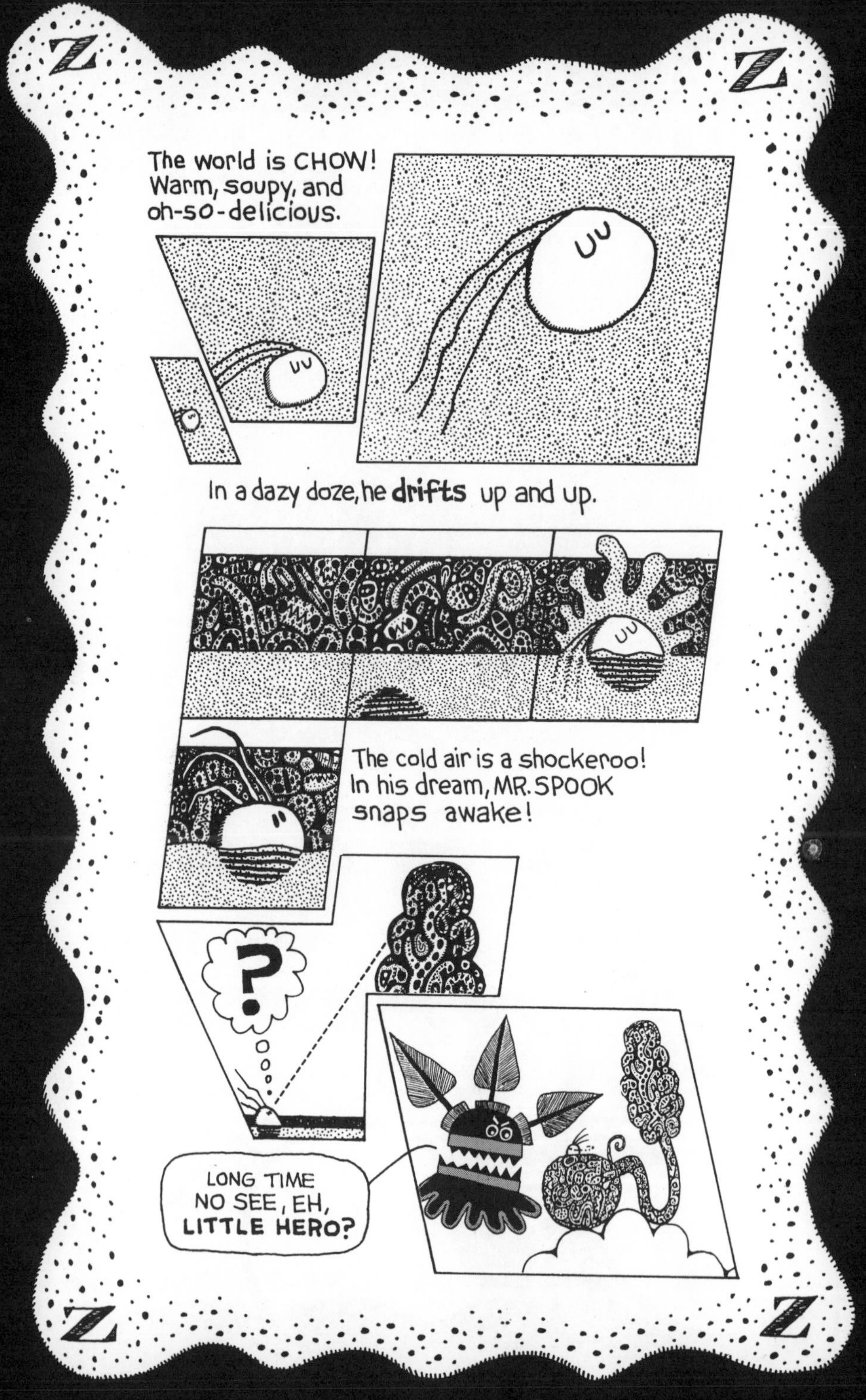

The world is CHOW!
Warm, soupy, and
oh-so-delicious.

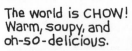
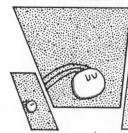
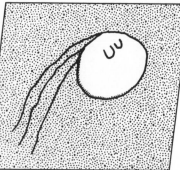

In a dazy doze, he **drifts** up and up.

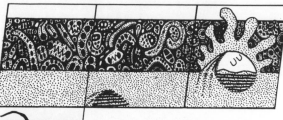

The cold air is a shockeroo!
In his dream, MR. SPOOK
snaps awake!

LONG TIME
NO SEE, EH,
LITTLE HERO?

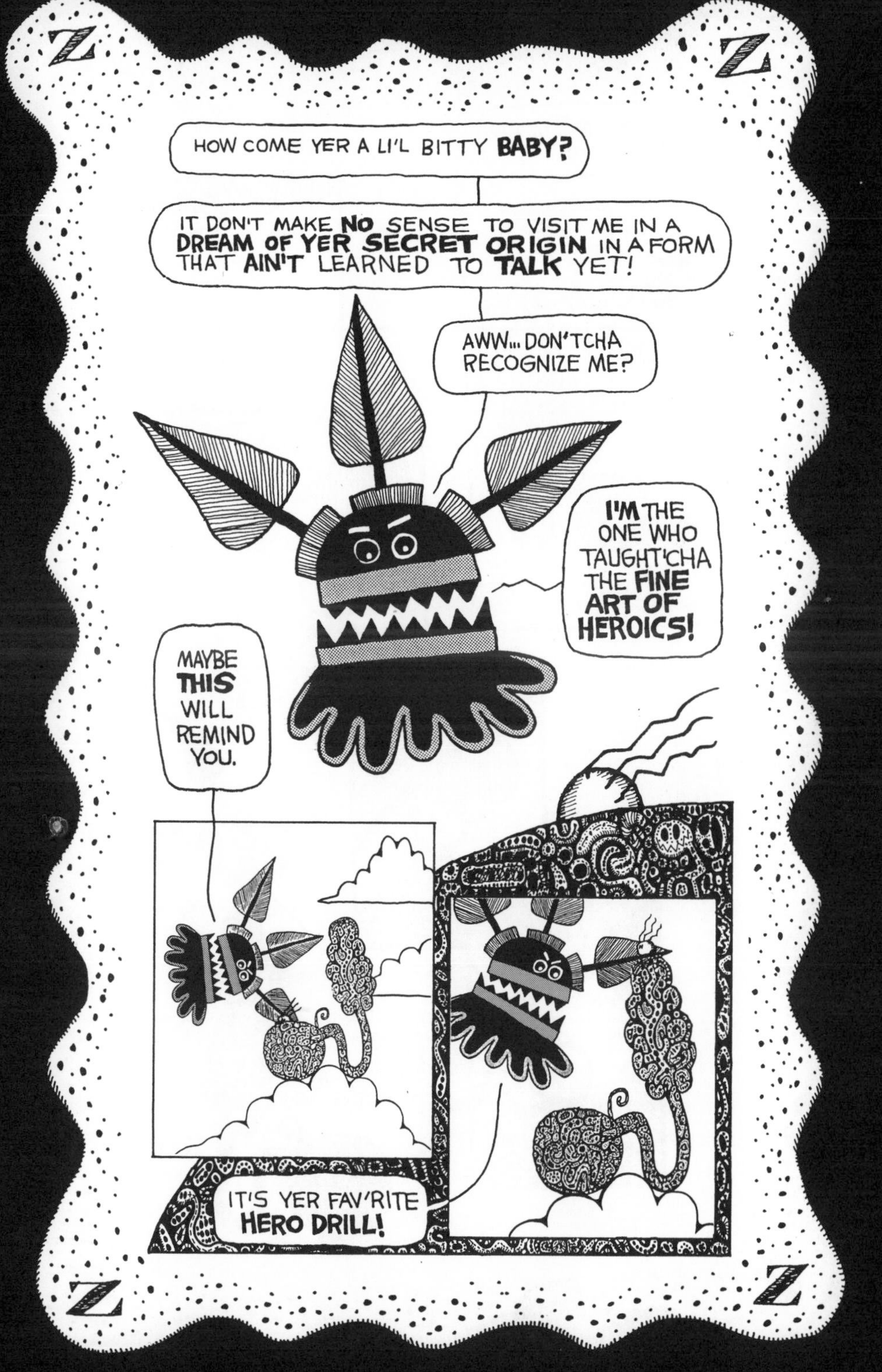
Z
Z
HOW COME YER A LI'L BITTY BABY?
IT DON'T MAKE NO SENSE TO VISIT ME IN A DREAM OF YER SECRET ORIGIN IN A FORM THAT AIN'T LEARNED TO TALK YET!
AWW... DON'TCHA RECOGNIZE ME?
I'M THE ONE WHO TAUGHT'CHA THE FINE ART OF HEROICS!
MAYBE THIS WILL REMIND YOU.
IT'S YER FAV'RITE HERO DRILL!
Z
Z

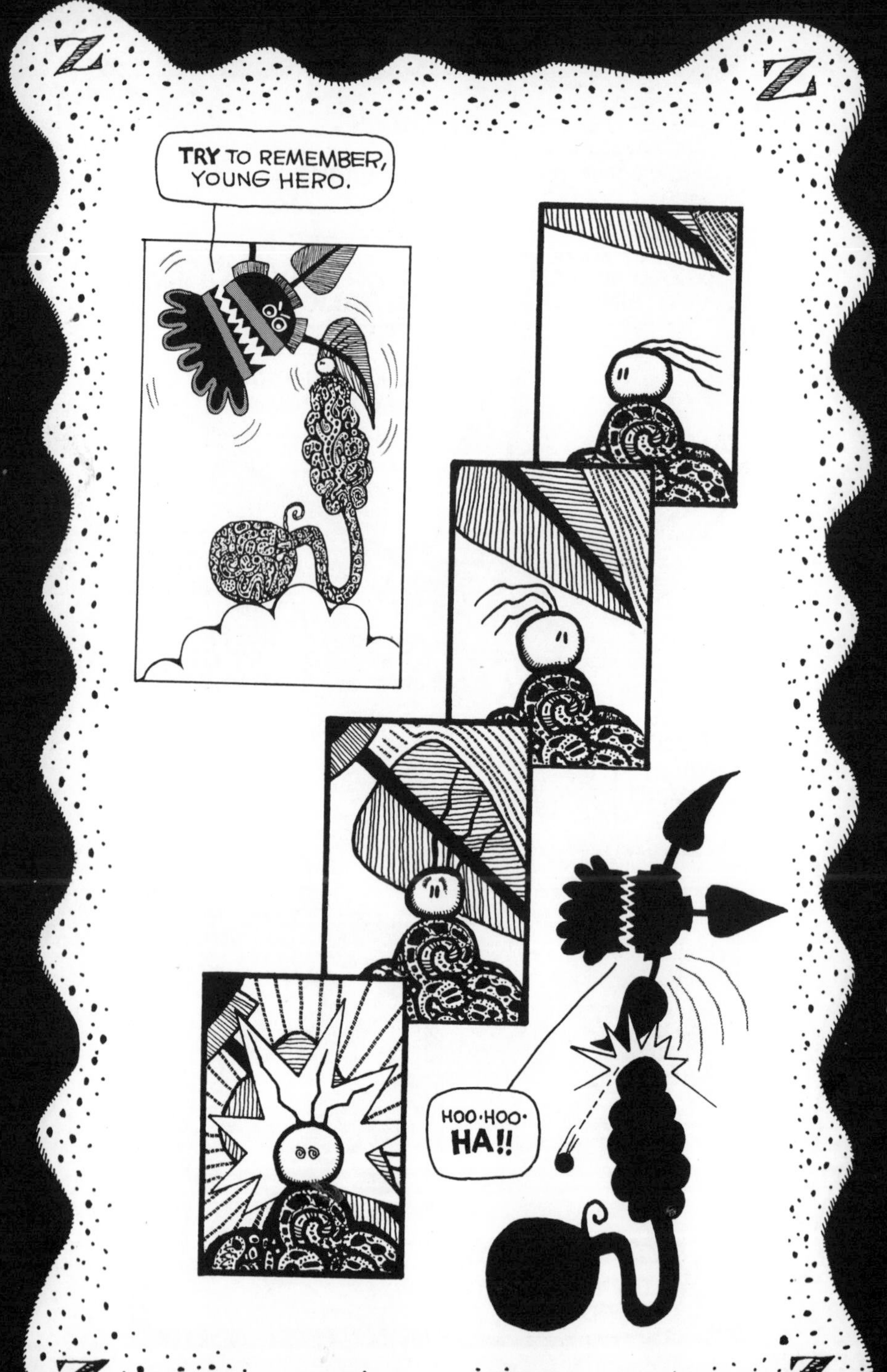
TRY TO REMEMBER, YOUNG HERO.
HOO·HOO· HA!!

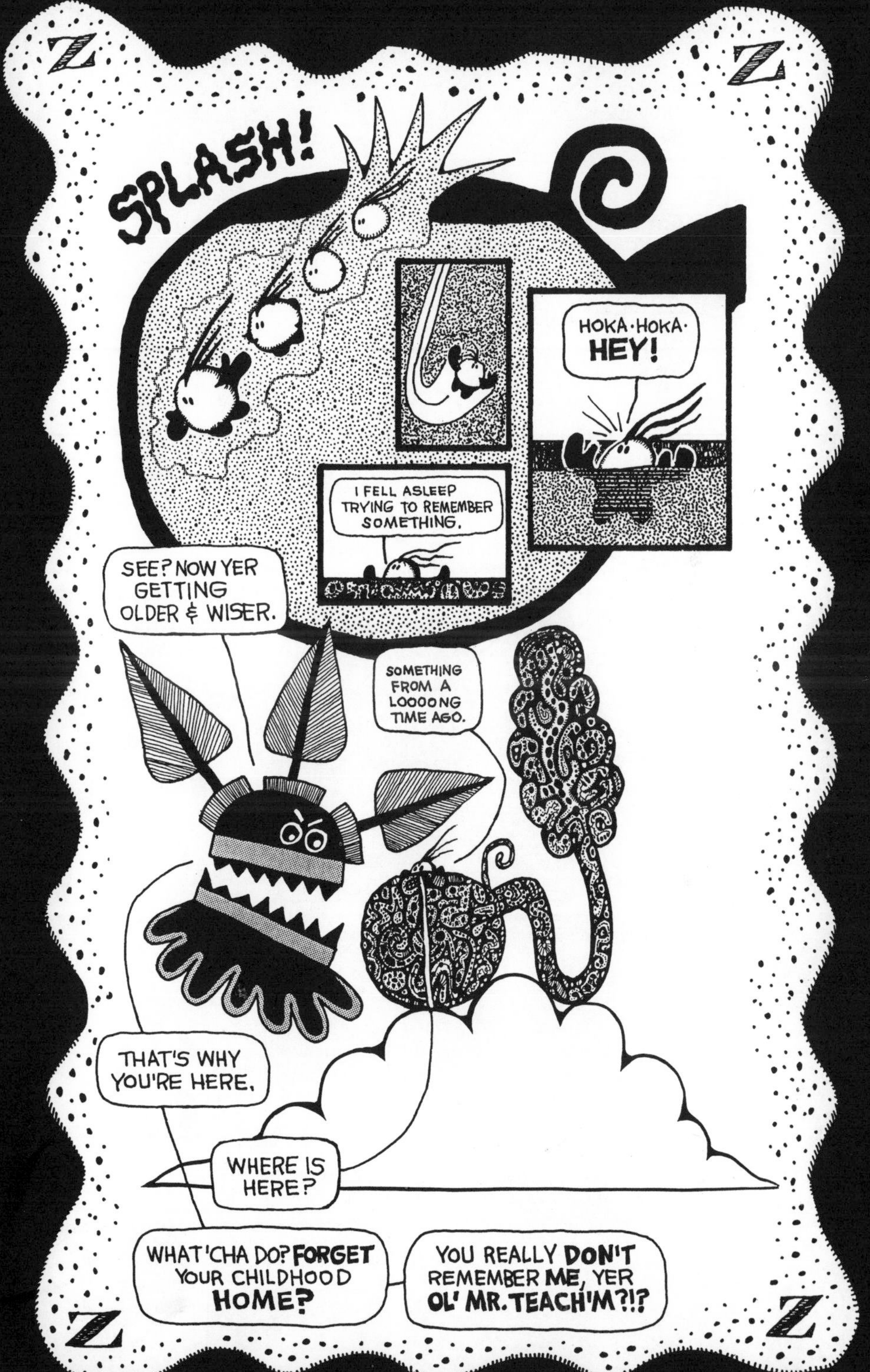
Z
Z
SPLASH!
HOKA·HOKA·
HEY!
I FELL ASLEEP TRYING TO REMEMBER SOMETHING.
SEE? NOW YER GETTING OLDER & WISER.
SOMETHING FROM A LOOOONG TIME AGO.
THAT'S WHY YOU'RE HERE.
WHERE IS HERE?
WHAT'CHA DO? FORGET YOUR CHILDHOOD HOME?
YOU REALLY DON'T REMEMBER ME, YER OL' MR. TEACH'M?!?
Z
Z

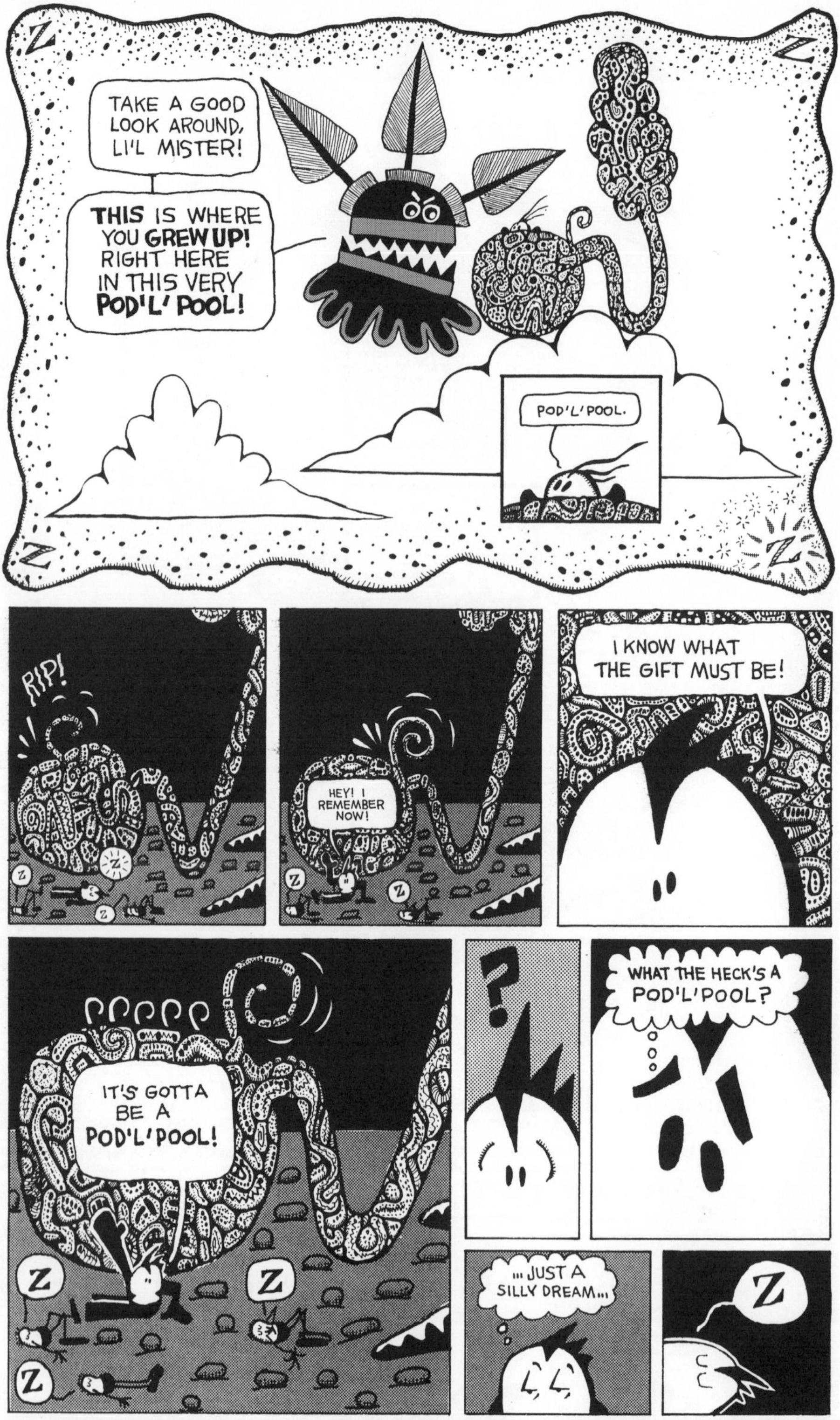

TAKE A GOOD LOOK AROUND, LI'L MISTER!
THIS IS WHERE YOU GREW UP! RIGHT HERE IN THIS VERY POD'L'POOL!
POD'L'POOL.
RIP!
HEY! I REMEMBER NOW!
I KNOW WHAT THE GIFT MUST BE!
IT'S GOTTA BE A POD'L'POOL!
?
WHAT THE HECK'S A POD'L'POOL?
...JUST A SILLY DREAM...
Z

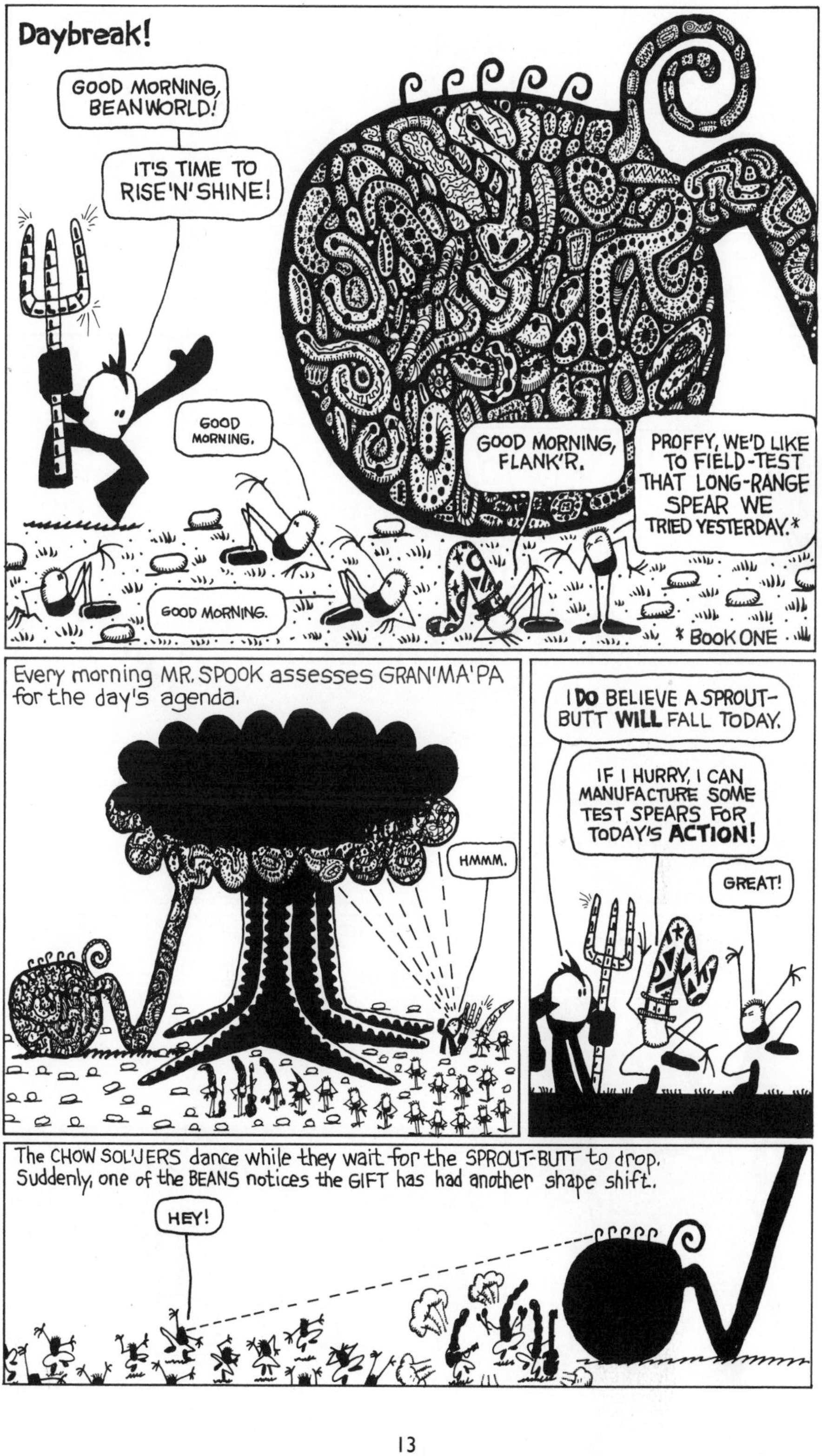
Daybreak!
GOOD MORNING, BEANWORLD!
IT'S TIME TO RISE'N'SHINE!
GOOD MORNING.
GOOD MORNING.
GOOD MORNING, FLANK'R.
PROFFY, WE'D LIKE TO FIELD-TEST THAT LONG-RANGE SPEAR WE TRIED YESTERDAY.*
* Book ONE
Every morning MR. SPOOK assesses GRAN'MA'PA for the day's agenda.
HMMM.
I DO BELIEVE A SPROUT-BUTT WILL FALL TODAY.
IF I HURRY, I CAN MANUFACTURE SOME TEST SPEARS FOR TODAY'S ACTION!
GREAT!
The CHOW SOL'JERS dance while they wait for the SPROUT-BUTT to drop.
Suddenly, one of the BEANS notices the GIFT has had another shape shift.
HEY!

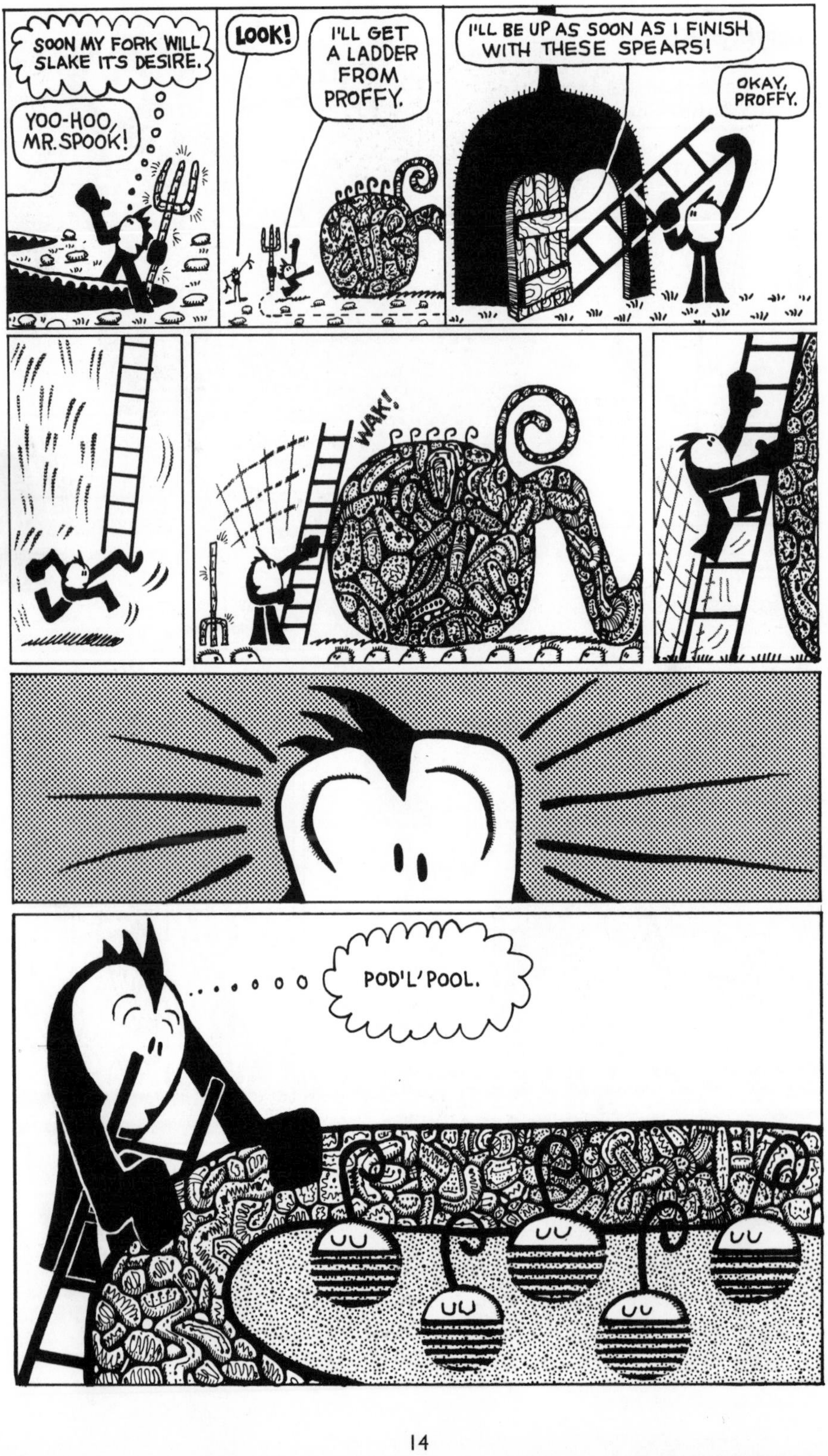
SOON MY FORK WILL SLAKE ITS DESIRE.
YOO-HOO, MR. SPOOK!
LOOK!
I'LL GET A LADDER FROM PROFFY.
I'LL BE UP AS SOON AS I FINISH WITH THESE SPEARS!
OKAY, PROFFY.
WAK!
POD'L'POOL.

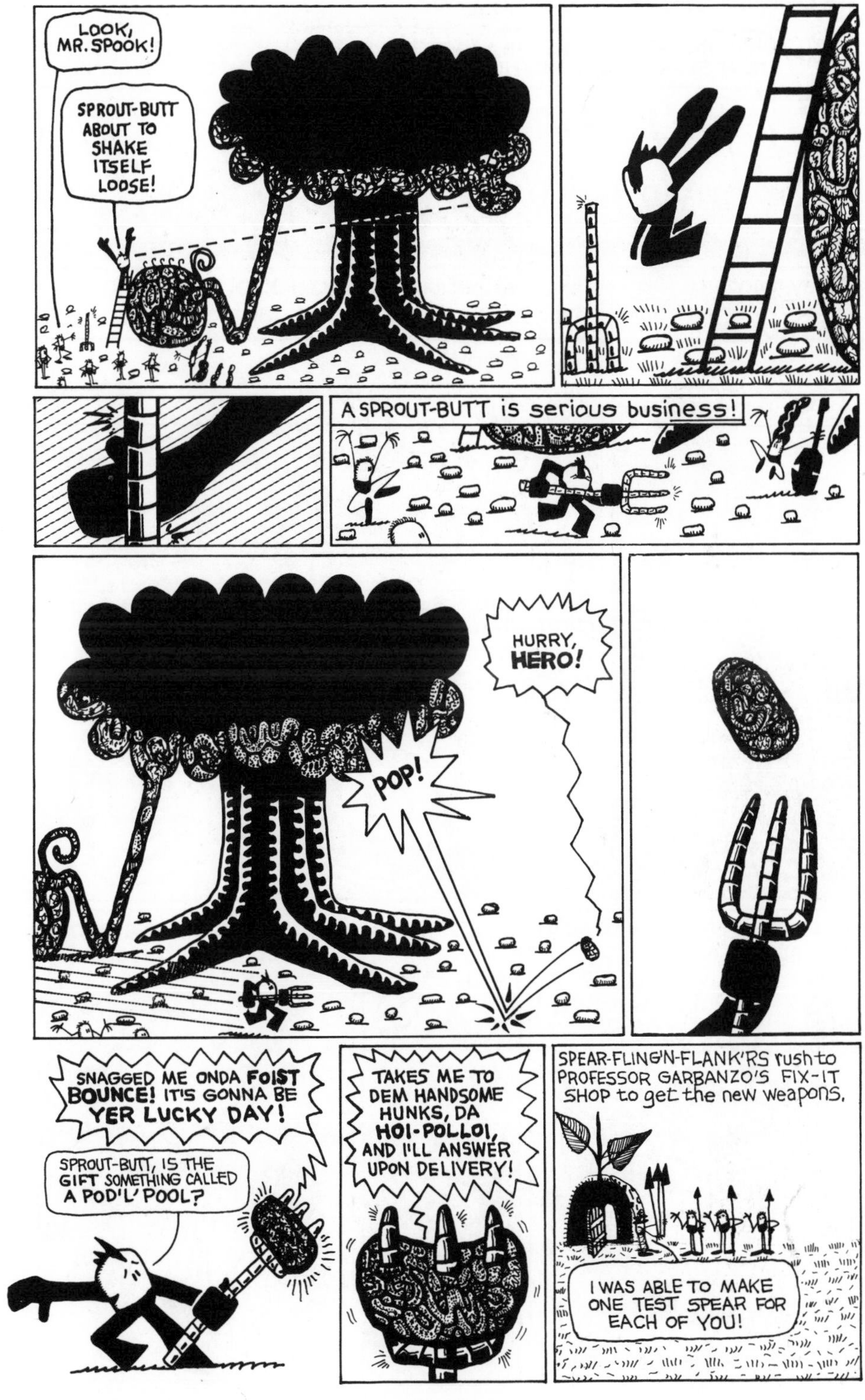
LOOK, MR. SPOOK!
SPROUT-BUTT ABOUT TO SHAKE ITSELF LOOSE!
A SPROUT-BUTT is serious business!
HURRY, HERO!
POP!
SNAGGED ME ONDA FOIST BOUNCE! IT'S GONNA BE YER LUCKY DAY!
SPROUT-BUTT, IS THE GIFT SOMETHING CALLED A POD'L'POOL?
TAKES ME TO DEM HANDSOME HUNKS, DA HOI-POLLOI, AND I'LL ANSWER UPON DELIVERY!
SPEAR-FLING'N-FLANK'RS rush to PROFESSOR GARBANZO'S FIX-IT SHOP to get the new weapons.
I WAS ABLE TO MAKE ONE TEST SPEAR FOR EACH OF YOU!

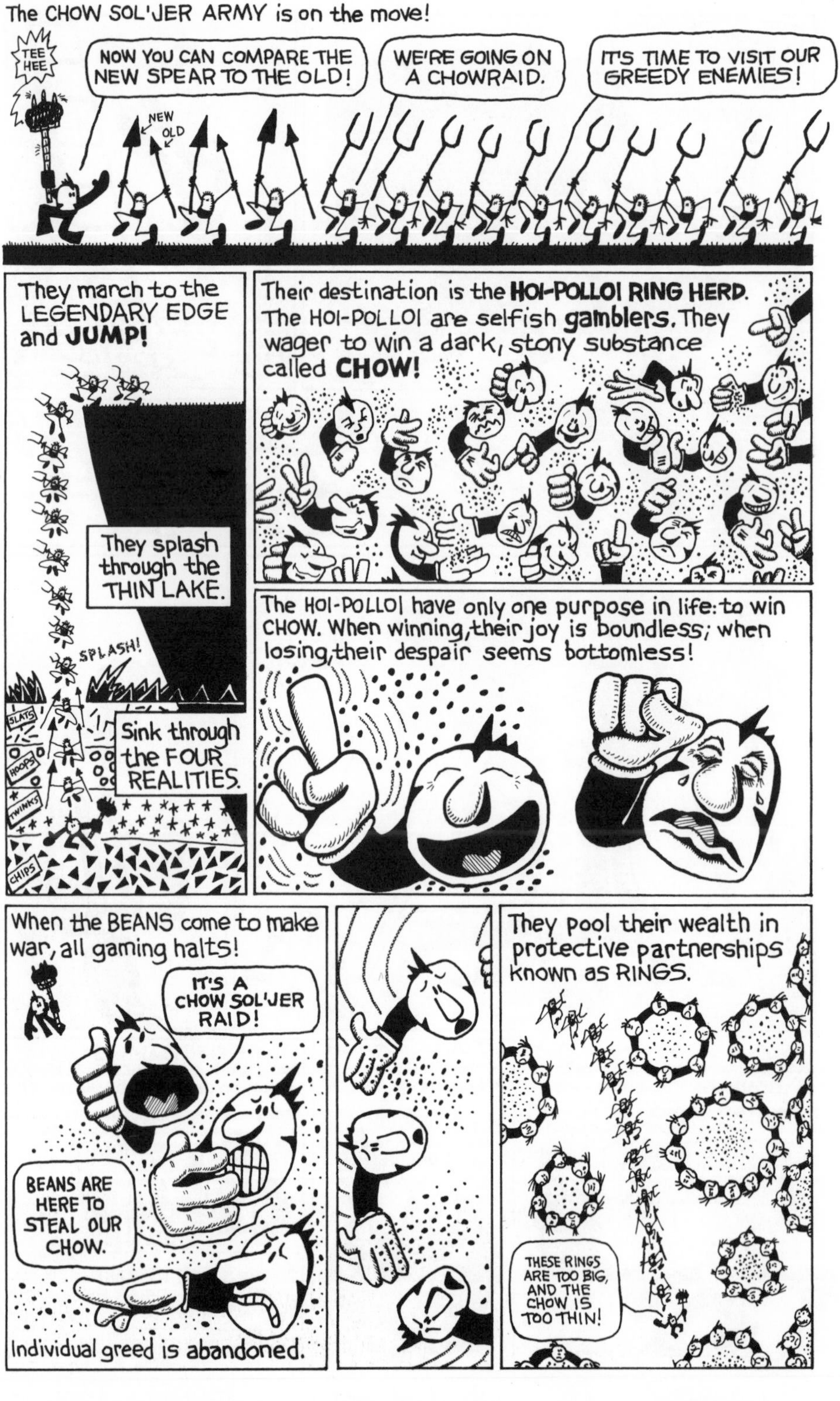
The CHOW SOL'JER ARMY is on the move!
TEE HEE
NOW YOU CAN COMPARE THE NEW SPEAR TO THE OLD!
NEW
OLD
WE'RE GOING ON A CHOWRAID.
IT'S TIME TO VISIT OUR GREEDY ENEMIES!
They march to the LEGENDARY EDGE and JUMP!
They splash through the THIN LAKE.
SPLASH!
Sink through the FOUR REALITIES.
SLATS
HOOPS
TWINKS
CHIPS
Their destination is the HOI-POLLOI RING HERD. The HOI-POLLOI are selfish gamblers. They wager to win a dark, stony substance called CHOW!
The HOI-POLLOI have only one purpose in life: to win CHOW. When winning, their joy is boundless; when losing, their despair seems bottomless!
When the BEANS come to make war, all gaming halts!
IT'S A CHOW SOL'JER RAID!
BEANS ARE HERE TO STEAL OUR CHOW.
Individual greed is abandoned.
They pool their wealth in protective partnerships known as RINGS.
THESE RINGS ARE TOO BIG, AND THE CHOW IS TOO THIN!

While the CHOW SOL'JERS seek war work, the others reason together.

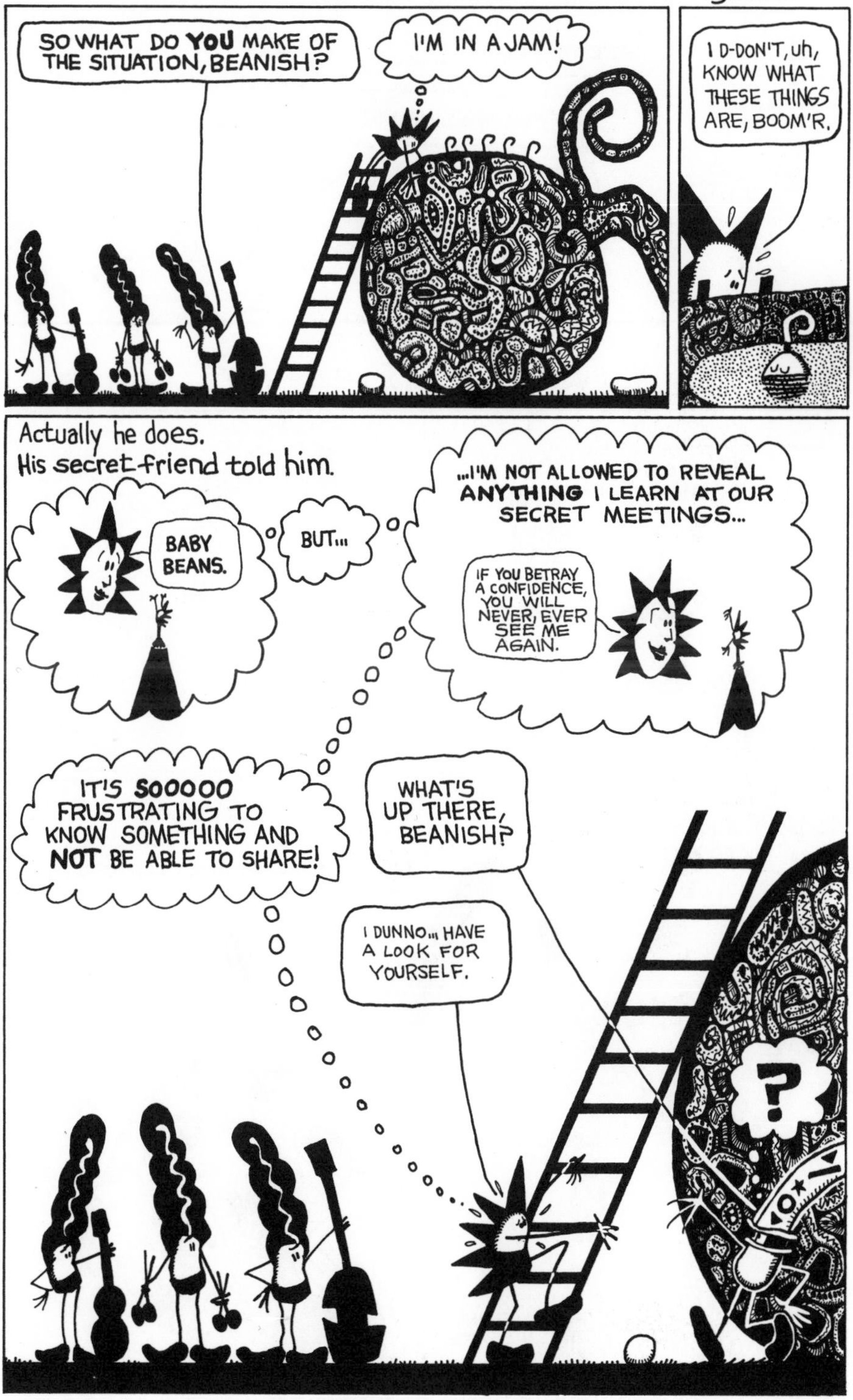

SO WHAT DO **YOU** MAKE OF THE SITUATION, BEANISH?
I'M IN A JAM!
I D-DON'T, uh, KNOW WHAT THESE THINGS ARE, BOOM'R.
Actually he does.
His secret friend told him.
BABY BEANS.
BUT...
...I'M NOT ALLOWED TO REVEAL **ANYTHING** I LEARN AT OUR SECRET MEETINGS...
IF YOU BETRAY A CONFIDENCE, YOU WILL NEVER, EVER SEE ME AGAIN.
IT'S **SOOOOO** FRUSTRATING TO KNOW SOMETHING AND **NOT** BE ABLE TO SHARE!
WHAT'S UP THERE, BEANISH?
I DUNNO... HAVE A LOOK FOR YOURSELF.
?

It looks like MR. SPOOK has found a good war.

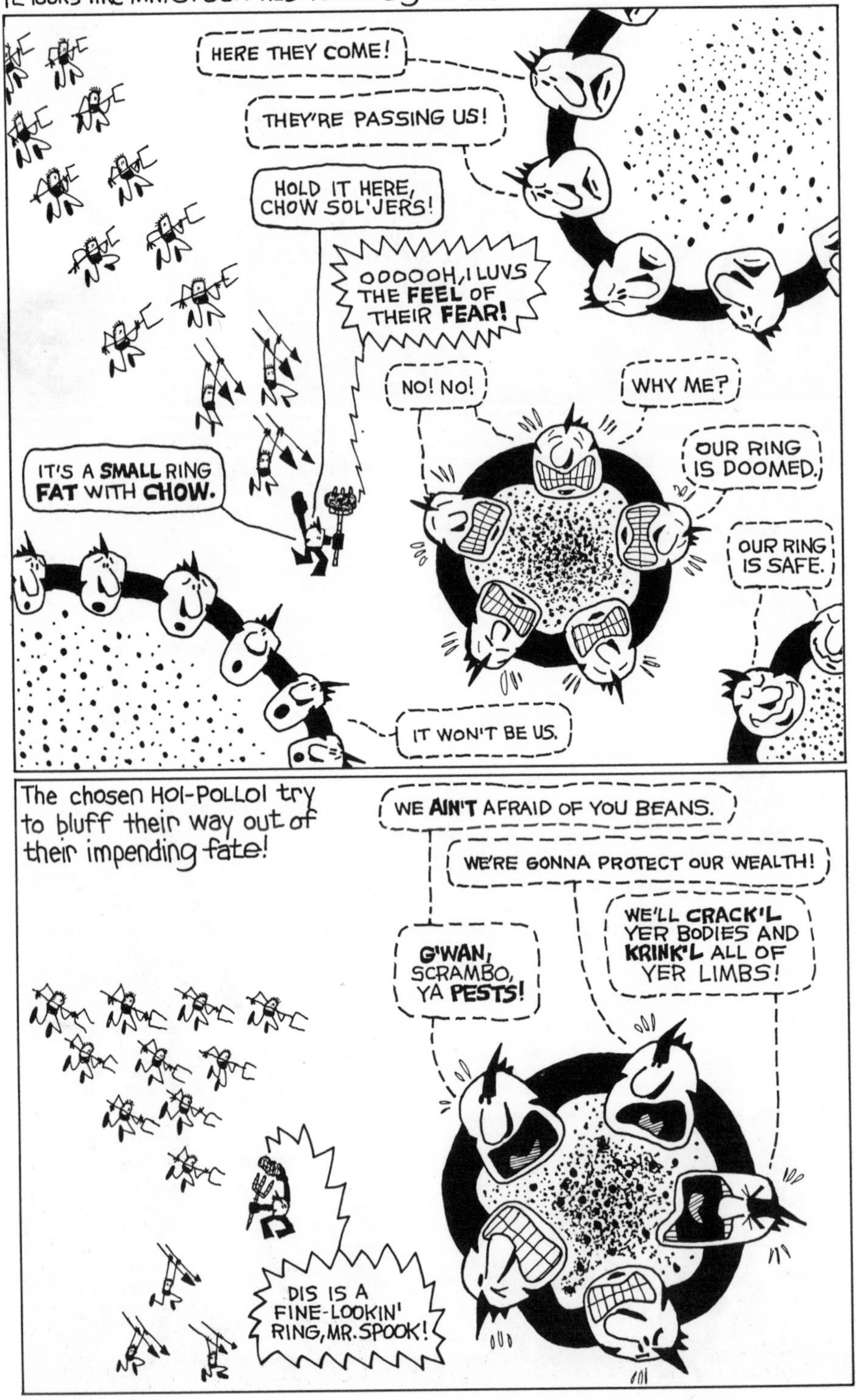

HERE THEY COME!
THEY'RE PASSING US!
HOLD IT HERE, CHOW SOL'JERS!
OOOOOH, I LUVS THE FEEL OF THEIR FEAR!
IT'S A SMALL RING FAT WITH CHOW.
NO! NO!
WHY ME?
OUR RING IS DOOMED.
OUR RING IS SAFE.
IT WON'T BE US.
The chosen HOI-POLLOI try to bluff their way out of their impending fate!
WE AIN'T AFRAID OF YOU BEANS.
WE'RE GONNA PROTECT OUR WEALTH!
G'WAN, SCRAMBO, YA PESTS!
WE'LL CRACK'L YER BODIES AND KRINK'L ALL OF YER LIMBS!
DIS IS A FINE-LOOKIN' RING, MR. SPOOK!

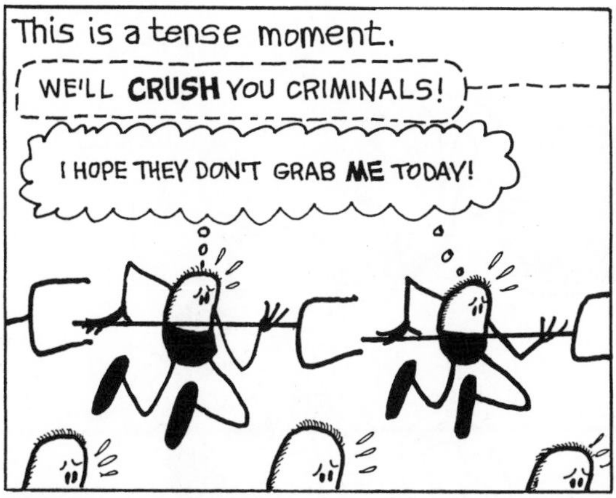
This is a tense moment.
WE'LL CRUSH YOU CRIMINALS!
I HOPE THEY DON'T GRAB ME TODAY!

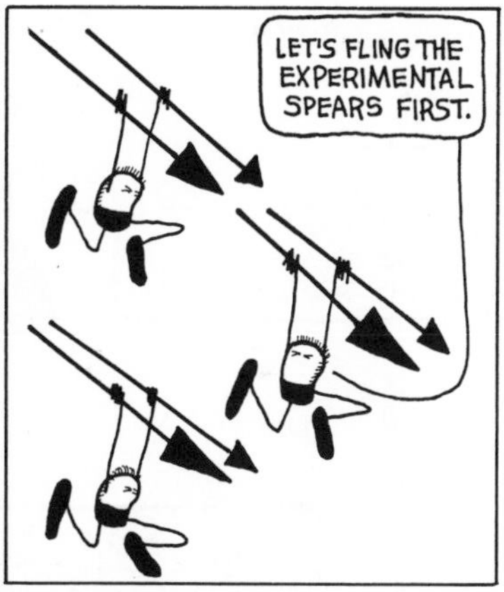
LET'S FLING THE EXPERIMENTAL SPEARS FIRST.

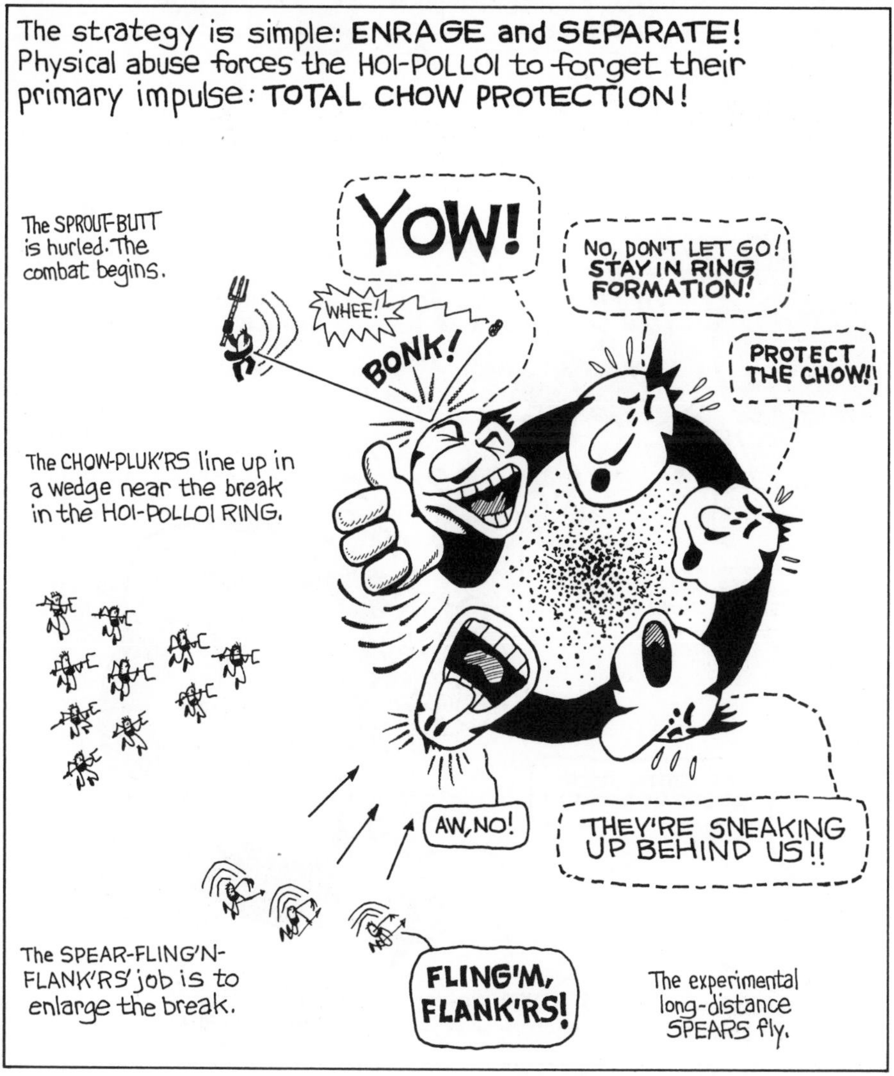
The strategy is simple: ENRAGE and SEPARATE! Physical abuse forces the HOI-POLLOI to forget their primary impulse: TOTAL CHOW PROTECTION!
The SPROUT-BUTT is hurled. The combat begins.
WHEE!
BONK!
YOW!
NO, DON'T LET GO! STAY IN RING FORMATION!
PROTECT THE CHOW!
The CHOW-PLUK'RS line up in a wedge near the break in the HOI-POLLOI RING.
AW, NO!
THEY'RE SNEAKING UP BEHIND US!!
The SPEAR-FLING'N-FLANK'RS' job is to enlarge the break.
FLING'M, FLANK'RS!
The experimental long-distance SPEARS fly.

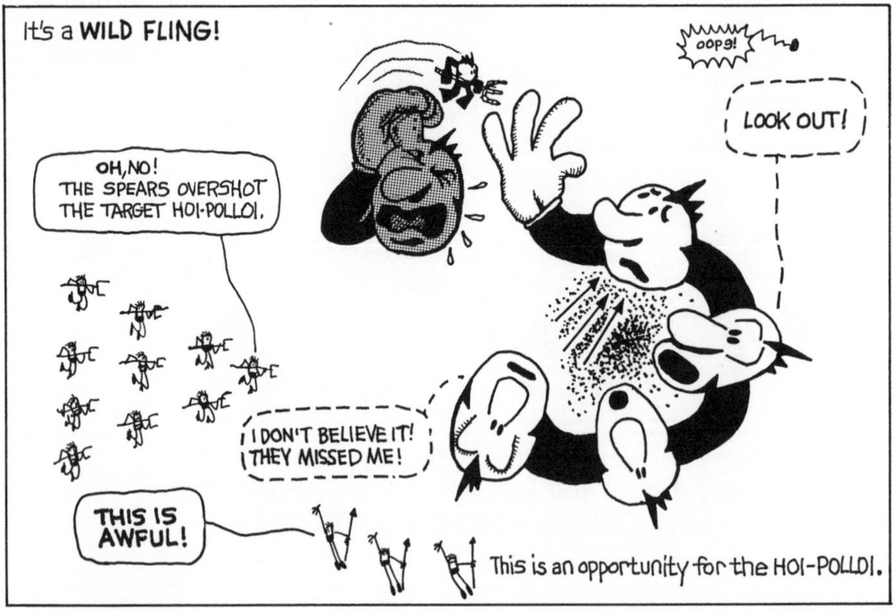
It's a WILD FLING!
OOPS!
LOOK OUT!
OH, NO! THE SPEARS OVERSHOT THE TARGET HOI-POLLOI.
I DON'T BELIEVE IT! THEY MISSED ME!
THIS IS AWFUL!
This is an opportunity for the HOI-POLLOI.

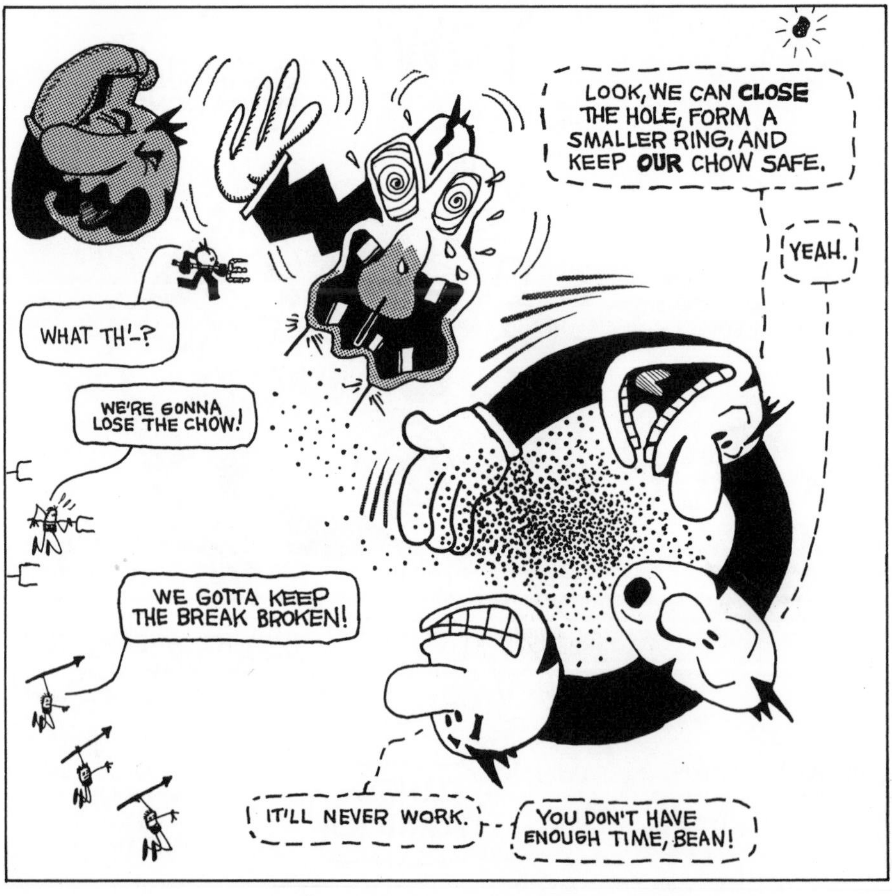
LOOK, WE CAN CLOSE THE HOLE, FORM A SMALLER RING, AND KEEP OUR CHOW SAFE.
YEAH.
WHAT TH'-?
WE'RE GONNA LOSE THE CHOW!
WE GOTTA KEEP THE BREAK BROKEN!
IT'LL NEVER WORK.
YOU DON'T HAVE ENOUGH TIME, BEAN!

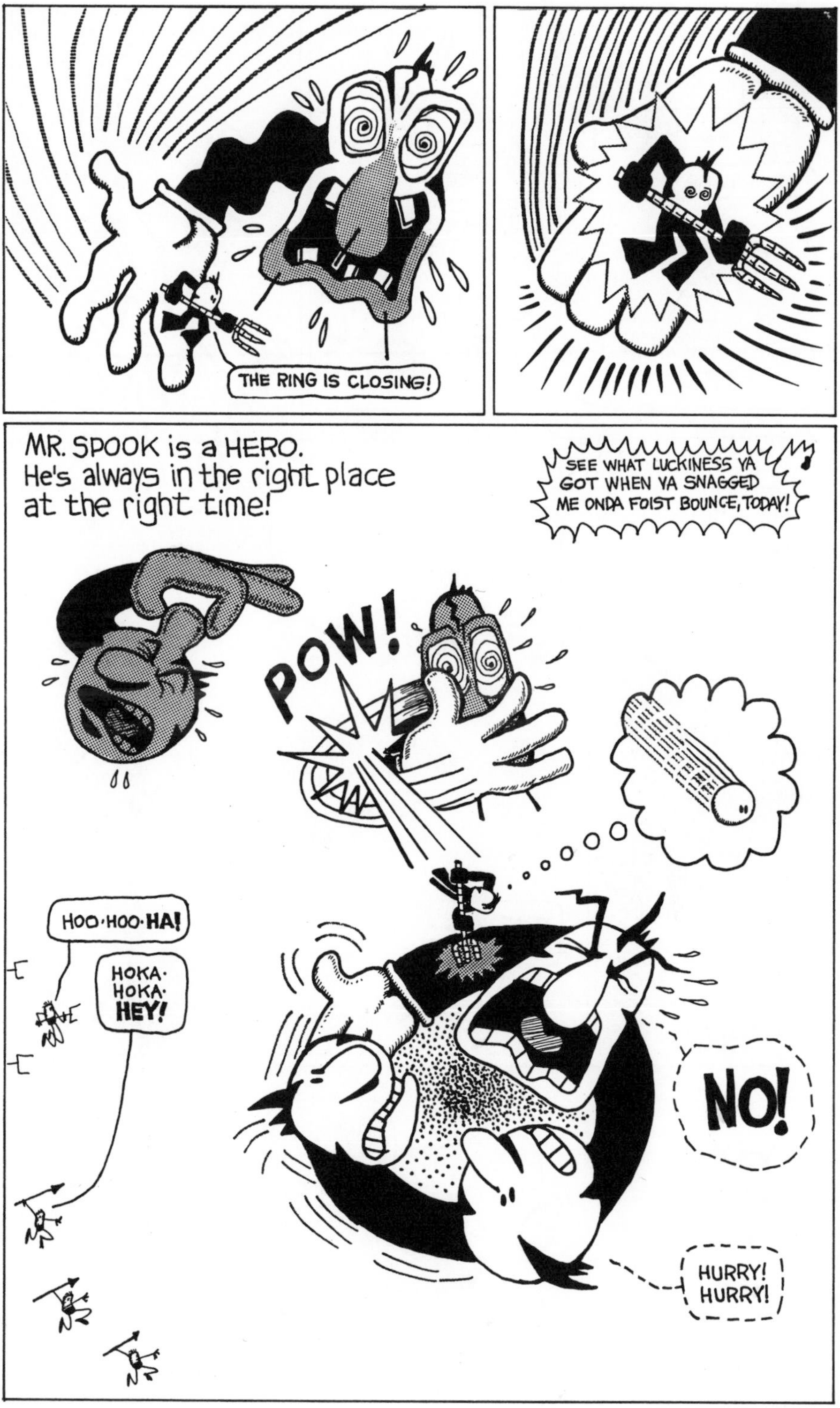
THE RING IS CLOSING!
MR. SPOOK is a HERO.
He's always in the right place
at the right time!
SEE WHAT LUCKINESS YA GOT WHEN YA SNAGGED ME ONDA FOIST BOUNCE, TODAY!
POW!
HOO·HOO·HA!
HOKA·HOKA·HEY!
NO!
HURRY! HURRY!

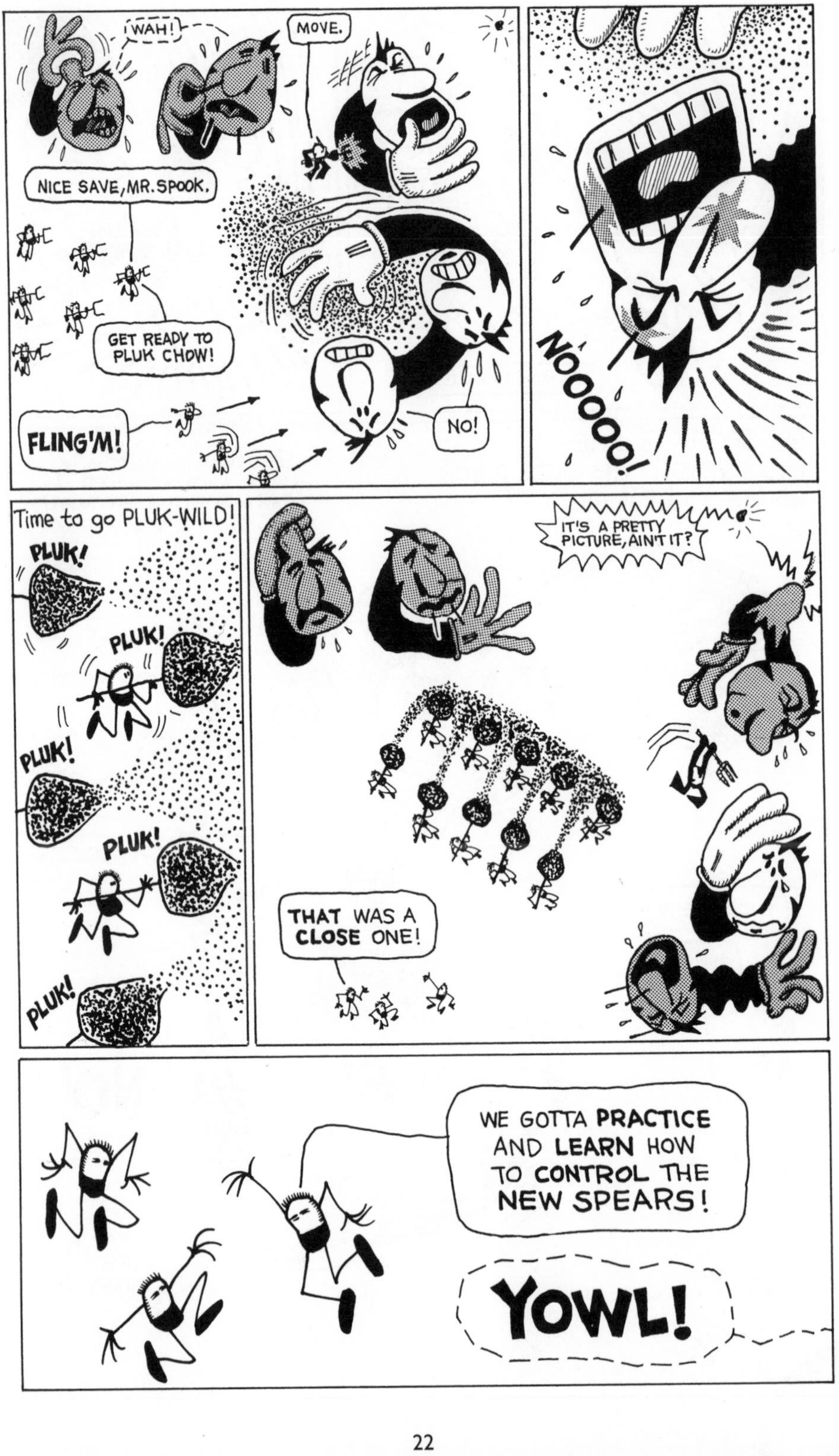
WAH!
MOVE.
NICE SAVE, MR. SPOOK.
GET READY TO PLUK CHOW!
FLING'M!
NO!
NOOOOO!
Time to go PLUK-WILD!
PLUK!
PLUK!
PLUK!
PLUK!
PLUK!
IT'S A PRETTY PICTURE, AIN'T IT?
THAT WAS A CLOSE ONE!
WE GOTTA PRACTICE AND LEARN HOW TO CONTROL THE NEW SPEARS!
YOWL!

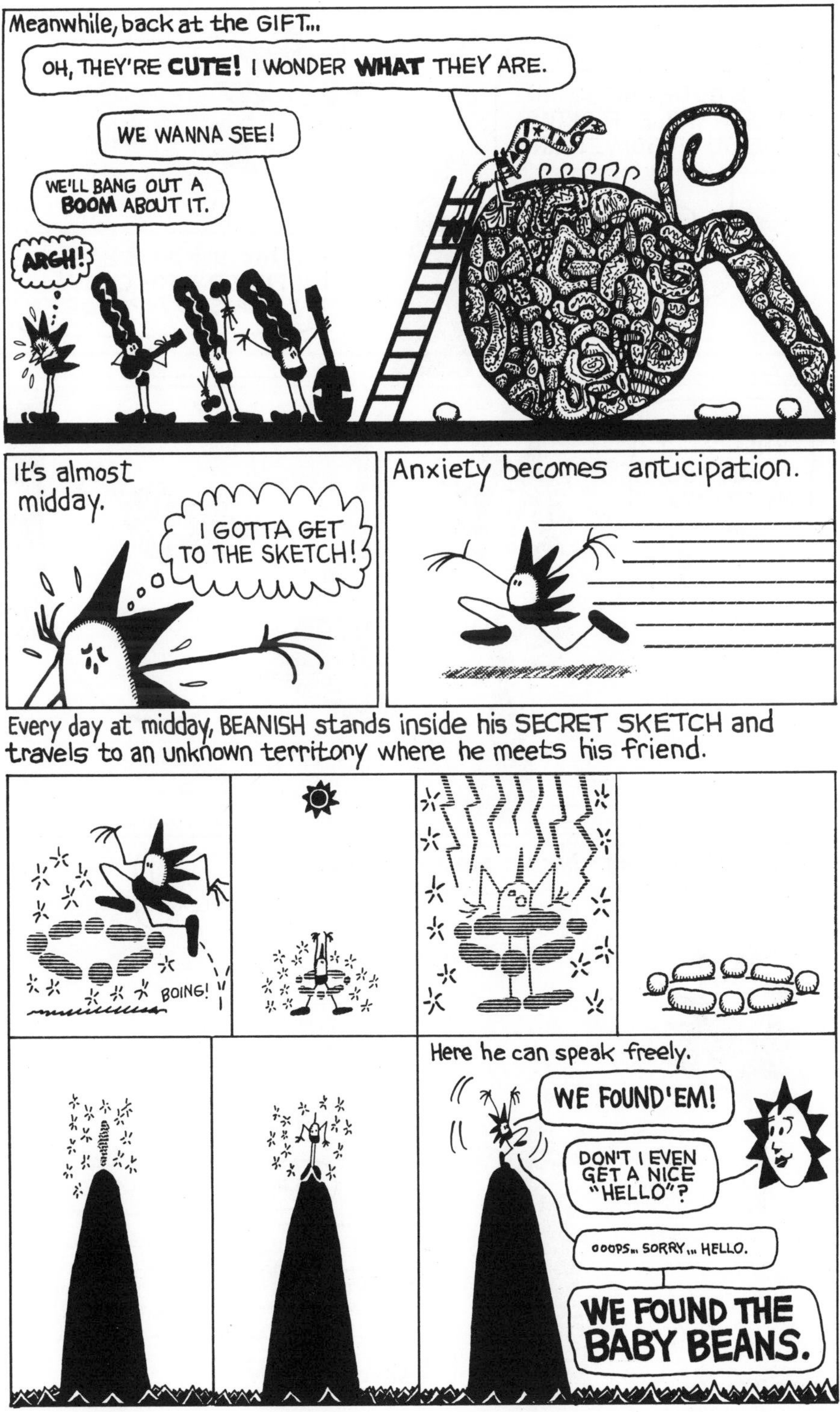
Meanwhile, back at the GIFT...
OH, THEY'RE CUTE! I WONDER WHAT THEY ARE.
WE WANNA SEE!
WE'LL BANG OUT A BOOM ABOUT IT.
ARGH!
It's almost midday.
I GOTTA GET TO THE SKETCH!
Anxiety becomes anticipation.
Every day at midday, BEANISH stands inside his SECRET SKETCH and travels to an unknown territory where he meets his friend.
BOING!
Here he can speak freely.
WE FOUND'EM!
DON'T I EVEN GET A NICE "HELLO"?
OOOPS... SORRY... HELLO.
WE FOUND THE BABY BEANS.

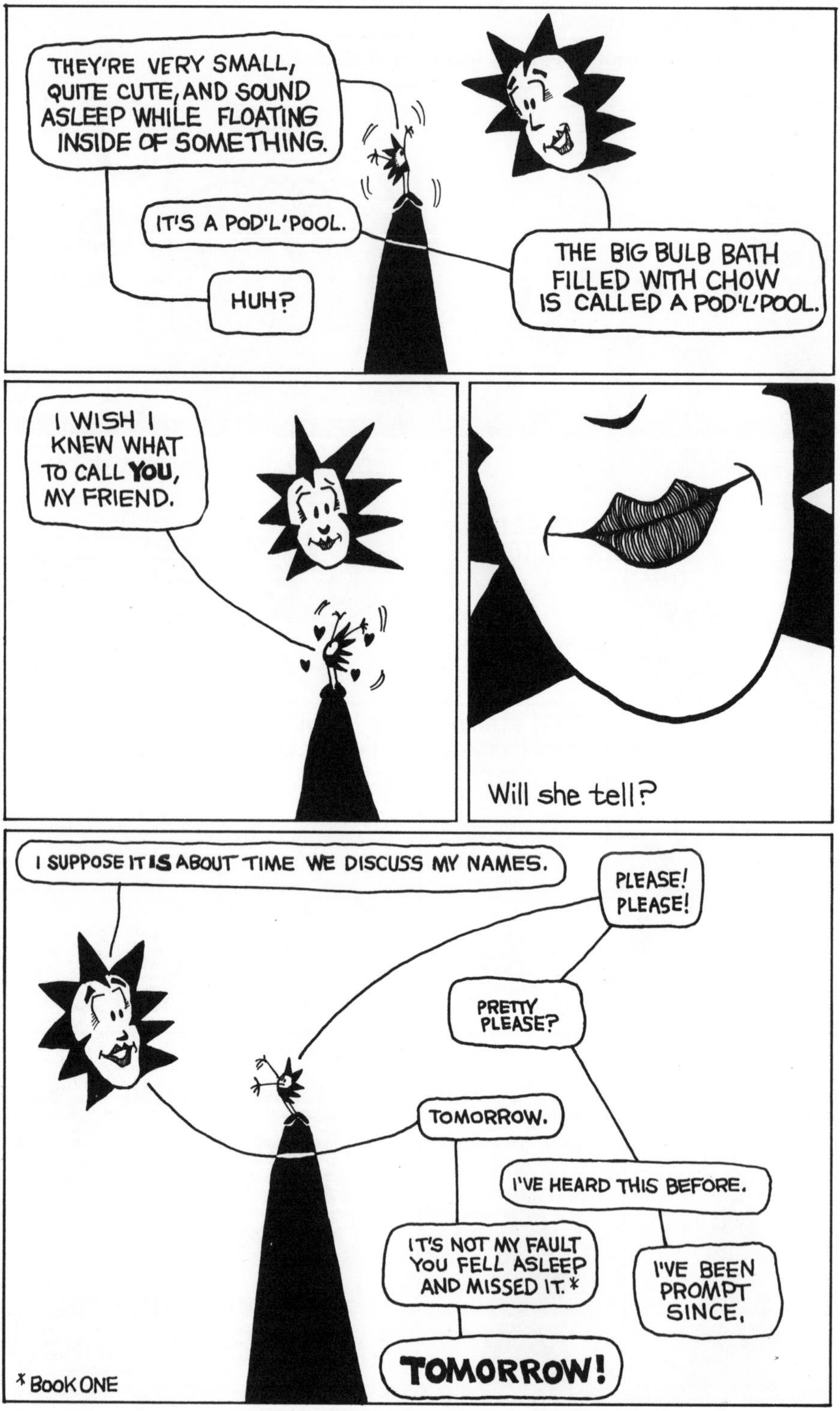
THEY'RE VERY SMALL, QUITE CUTE, AND SOUND ASLEEP WHILE FLOATING INSIDE OF SOMETHING.
IT'S A POD'L'POOL.
HUH?
THE BIG BULB BATH FILLED WITH CHOW IS CALLED A POD'L'POOL.
I WISH I KNEW WHAT TO CALL YOU, MY FRIEND.
Will she tell?
I SUPPOSE IT IS ABOUT TIME WE DISCUSS MY NAMES.
PLEASE! PLEASE!
PRETTY PLEASE?
TOMORROW.
I'VE HEARD THIS BEFORE.
IT'S NOT MY FAULT YOU FELL ASLEEP AND MISSED IT.*
I'VE BEEN PROMPT SINCE.
TOMORROW!
* Book ONE

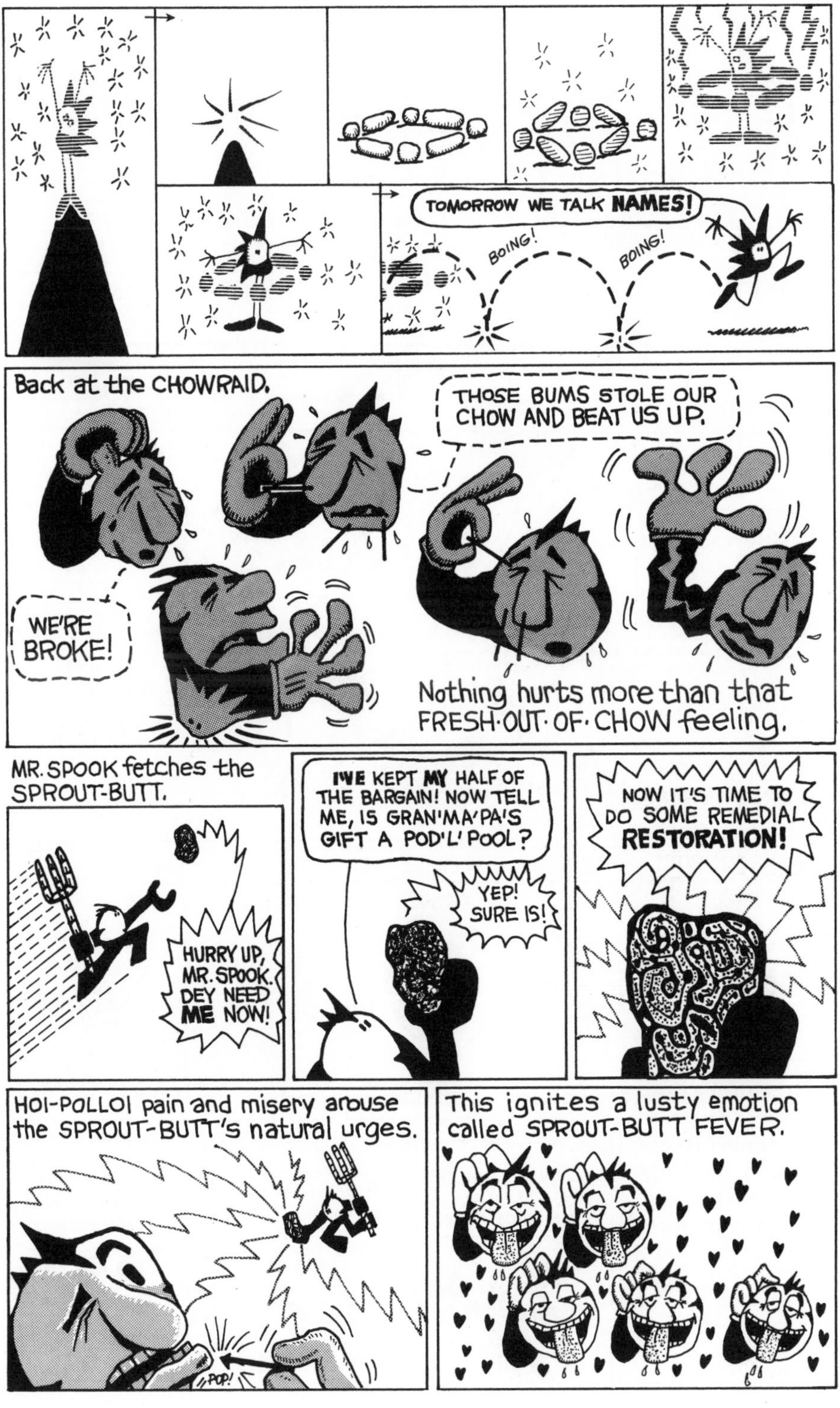
TOMORROW WE TALK NAMES!
BOING!
BOING!
Back at the CHOWRAID.
THOSE BUMS STOLE OUR CHOW AND BEAT US UP.
WE'RE BROKE!
Nothing hurts more than that FRESH·OUT·OF·CHOW feeling.
MR. SPOOK fetches the SPROUT-BUTT.
HURRY UP, MR. SPOOK. DEY NEED ME NOW!
I'VE KEPT MY HALF OF THE BARGAIN! NOW TELL ME, IS GRAN'MA'PA'S GIFT A POD'L'POOL?
YEP! SURE IS!
NOW IT'S TIME TO DO SOME REMEDIAL RESTORATION!
HOI-POLLOI pain and misery arouse the SPROUT-BUTT's natural urges.
POP!
This ignites a lusty emotion called SPROUT-BUTT FEVER.

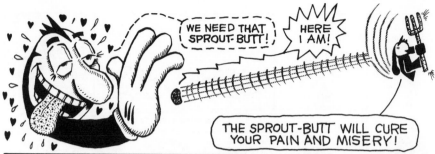

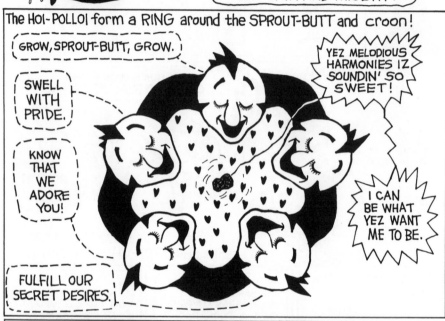

WE NEED THAT SPROUT-BUTT!
HERE I AM!
THE SPROUT-BUTT WILL CURE YOUR PAIN AND MISERY!
The HOI-POLLOI form a RING around the SPROUT-BUTT and croon!
GROW, SPROUT-BUTT, GROW.
SWELL WITH PRIDE.
KNOW THAT WE ADORE YOU!
FULFILL OUR SECRET DESIRES.
YEZ MELODIOUS HARMONIES IZ SOUNDIN' SO SWEET!
I CAN BE WHAT YEZ WANT ME TO BE.
The SPROUT-BUTT will be so overwhelmed with LOVE that it will:
SHIVER...
SWELL...
GROW...
RIPEN...
DISOLVE...
Yes! It will sacrifice its very existence and transform itself into CHOW!
Then the HOI-POLLOI will split the CHOW and resume their crazed gambling.
OF COURSE, SOME DAY, WE'LL RETURN AND STEAL ALL THE CHOW AGAIN.
NATURALLY, WE'LL LEAVE ANOTHER SPROUT-BUTT!
THE LIFE GRAN'MA'PA PROVIDES IS PERFECT, AS LONG AS WE ALL CARRY OUT OUR DUTIES.

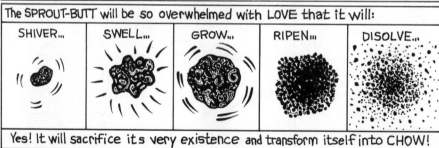

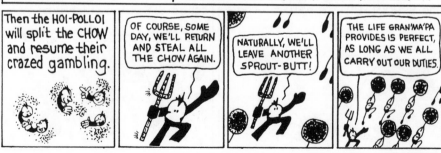

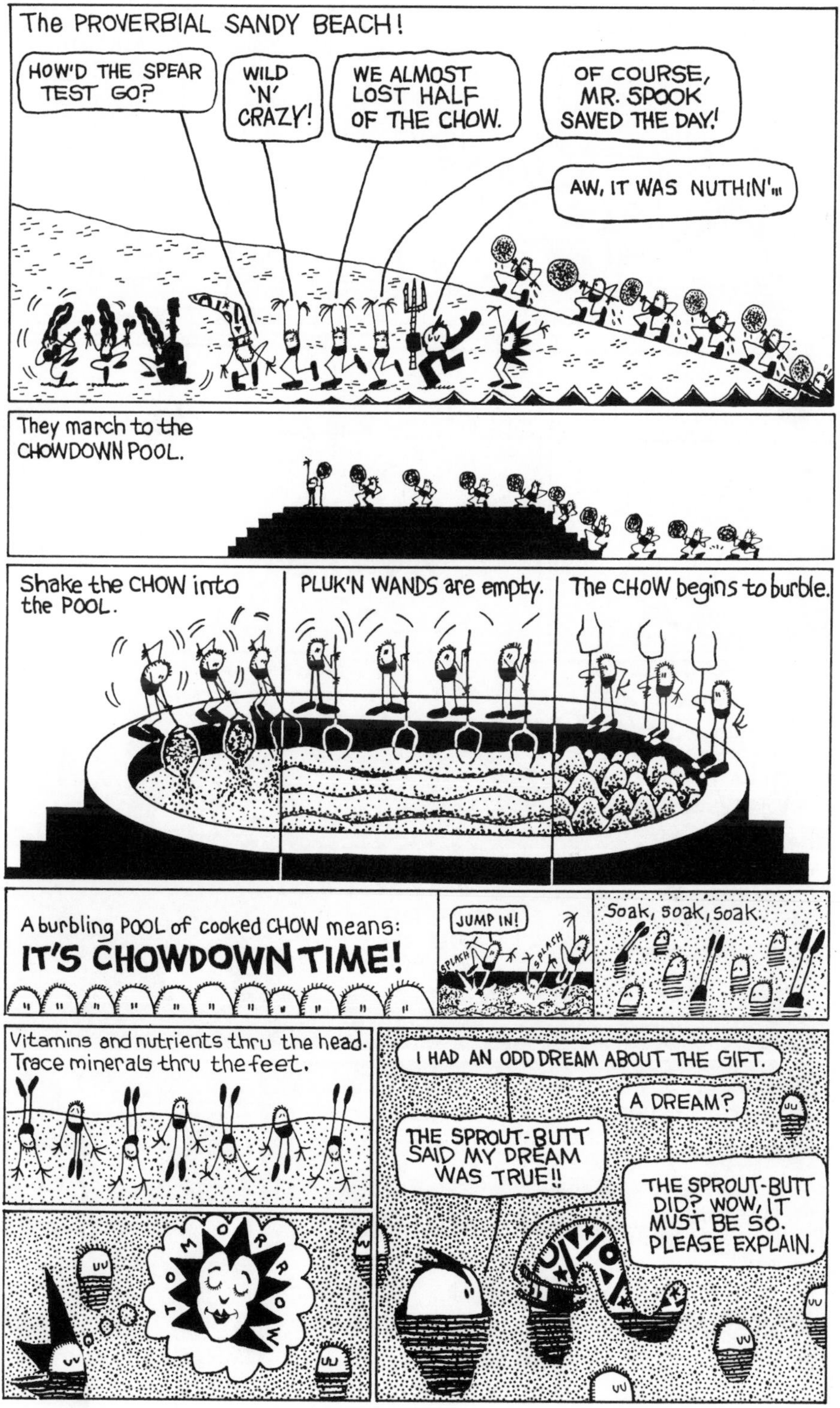

The PROVERBIAL SANDY BEACH!
HOW'D THE SPEAR TEST GO?
WILD 'N' CRAZY!
WE ALMOST LOST HALF OF THE CHOW.
OF COURSE, MR. SPOOK SAVED THE DAY!
AW, IT WAS NUTHIN'...
They march to the CHOWDOWN POOL.
Shake the CHOW into the POOL.
PLUK'N WANDS are empty.
The CHOW begins to burble.
A burbling POOL of cooked CHOW means:
IT'S CHOWDOWN TIME!
JUMP IN!
SPLASH
SPLASH
Soak, soak, soak.
Vitamins and nutrients thru the head. Trace minerals thru the feet.
TOMORROW
I HAD AN ODD DREAM ABOUT THE GIFT.
A DREAM?
THE SPROUT-BUTT SAID MY DREAM WAS TRUE!!
THE SPROUT-BUTT DID? WOW, IT MUST BE SO. PLEASE EXPLAIN.

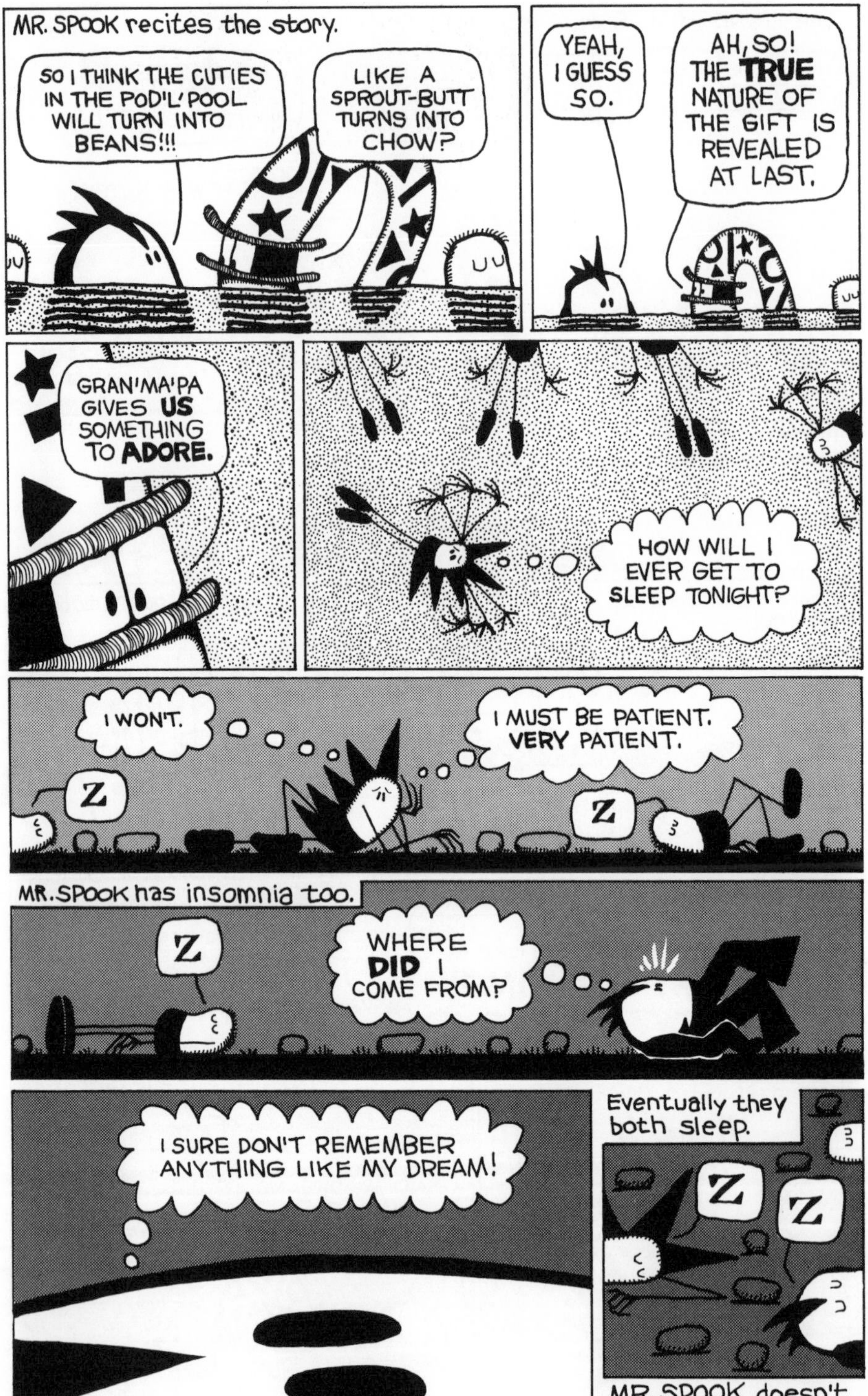
MR. SPOOK recites the story.
SO I THINK THE CUTIES IN THE POD'L'POOL WILL TURN INTO BEANS!!!
LIKE A SPROUT-BUTT TURNS INTO CHOW?
YEAH, I GUESS SO.
AH, SO! THE TRUE NATURE OF THE GIFT IS REVEALED AT LAST.
GRAN'MA'PA GIVES US SOMETHING TO ADORE.
HOW WILL I EVER GET TO SLEEP TONIGHT?
I WON'T.
I MUST BE PATIENT. VERY PATIENT.
Z
Z
MR. SPOOK has insomnia too.
Z
WHERE DID I COME FROM?
I SURE DON'T REMEMBER ANYTHING LIKE MY DREAM!
Eventually they both sleep.
Z
Z
MR. SPOOK doesn't dream again.

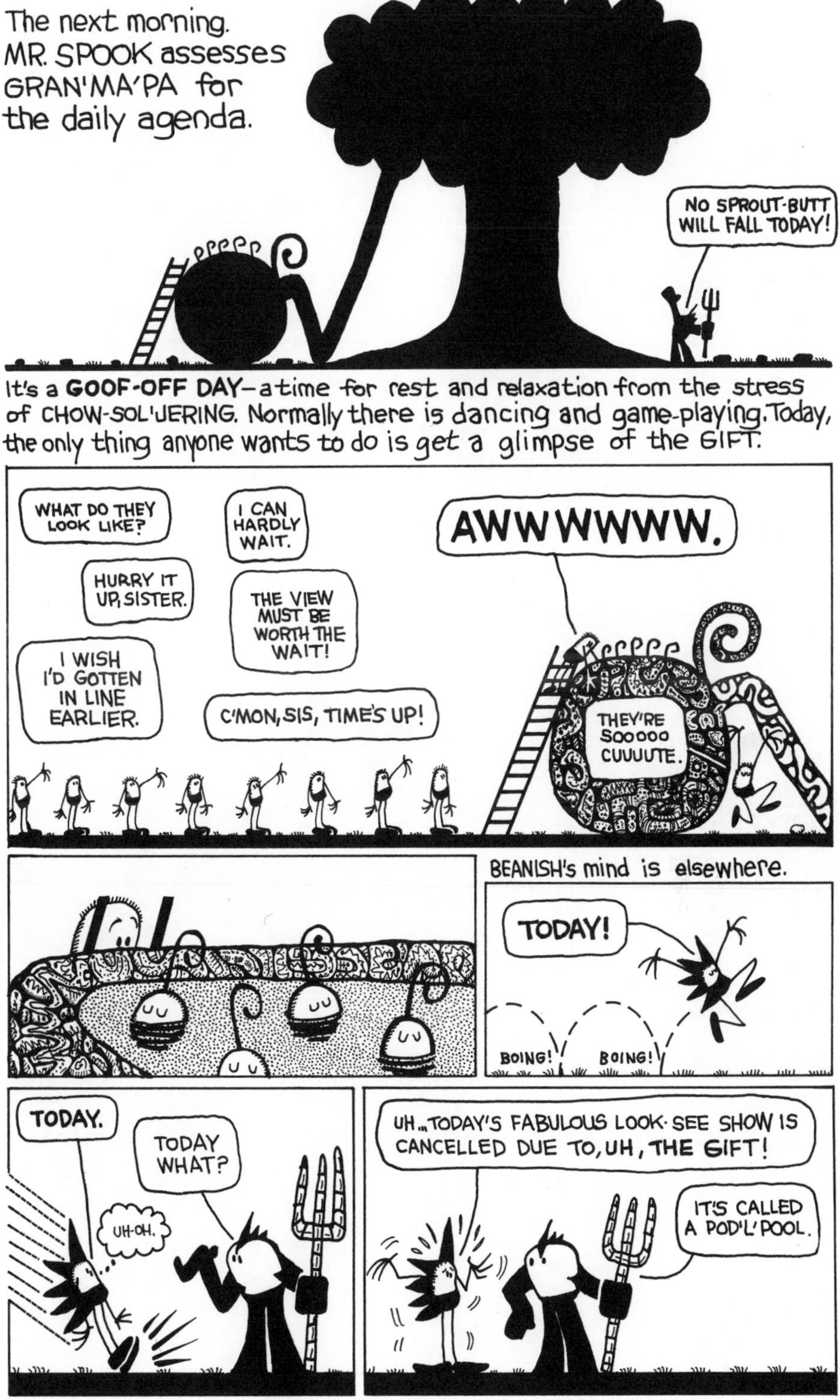
The next morning. MR. SPOOK assesses GRAN'MA'PA for the daily agenda.
NO SPROUT-BUTT WILL FALL TODAY!
It's a GOOF-OFF DAY—a time for rest and relaxation from the stress of CHOW-SOL'UERING. Normally there is dancing and game-playing. Today, the only thing anyone wants to do is get a glimpse of the GIFT.
WHAT DO THEY LOOK LIKE?
HURRY IT UP, SISTER.
I WISH I'D GOTTEN IN LINE EARLIER.
I CAN HARDLY WAIT.
THE VIEW MUST BE WORTH THE WAIT!
C'MON, SIS, TIME'S UP!
AWWWWWW.
THEY'RE SOOOOO CUUUUTE.
BEANISH's mind is elsewhere.
TODAY!
BOING!
BOING!
TODAY.
TODAY WHAT?
UH-OH.
UH... TODAY'S FABULOUS LOOK-SEE SHOW IS CANCELLED DUE TO, UH, THE GIFT!
IT'S CALLED A POD'L'POOL.

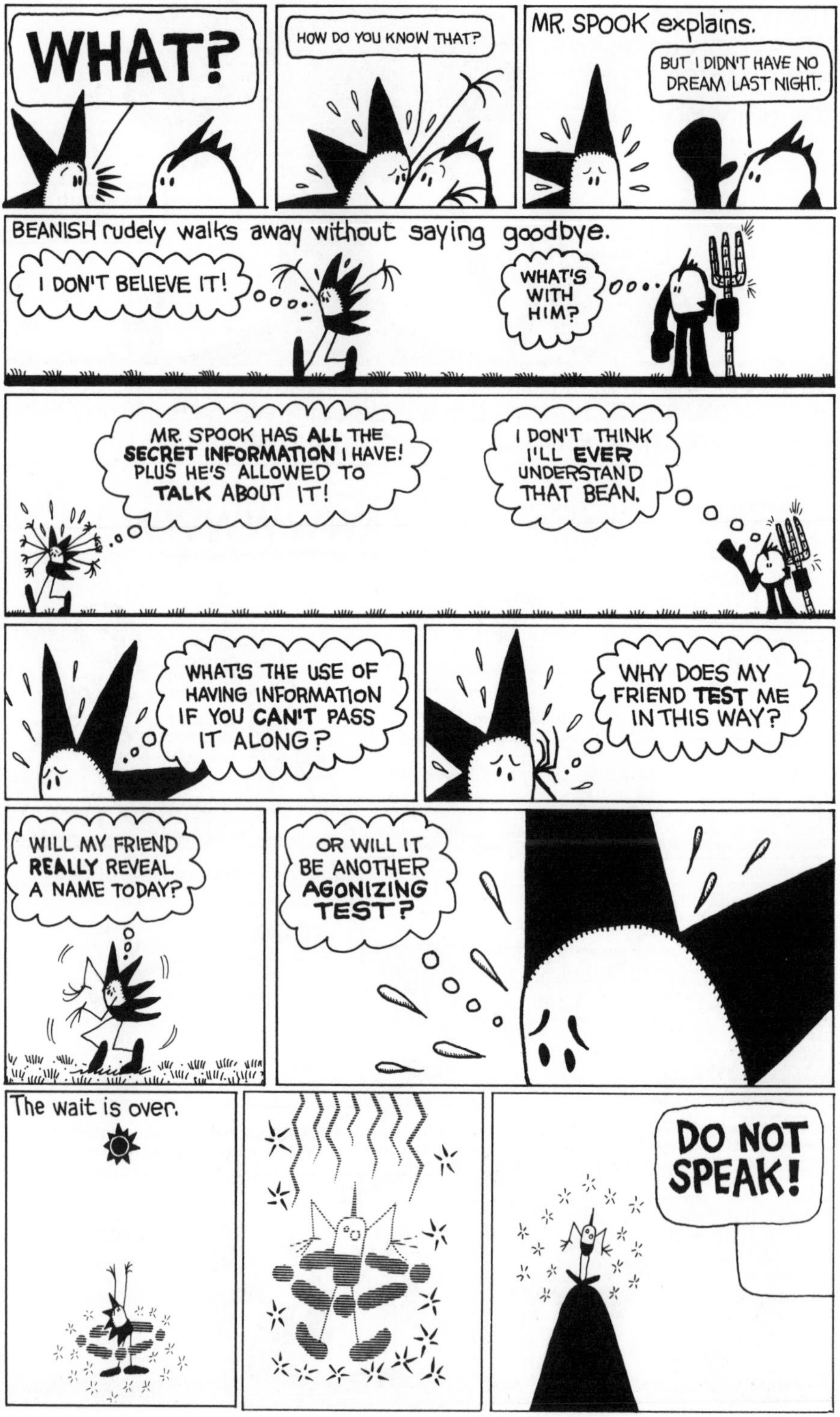
WHAT?
HOW DO YOU KNOW THAT?
MR. SPOOK explains.
BUT I DIDN'T HAVE NO DREAM LAST NIGHT.
BEANISH rudely walks away without saying goodbye.
I DON'T BELIEVE IT!
WHAT'S WITH HIM?
MR. SPOOK HAS ALL THE SECRET INFORMATION I HAVE! PLUS HE'S ALLOWED TO TALK ABOUT IT!
I DON'T THINK I'LL EVER UNDERSTAND THAT BEAN.
WHAT'S THE USE OF HAVING INFORMATION IF YOU CAN'T PASS IT ALONG?
WHY DOES MY FRIEND TEST ME IN THIS WAY?
WILL MY FRIEND REALLY REVEAL A NAME TODAY?
OR WILL IT BE ANOTHER AGONIZING TEST?
The wait is over.
DO NOT SPEAK!

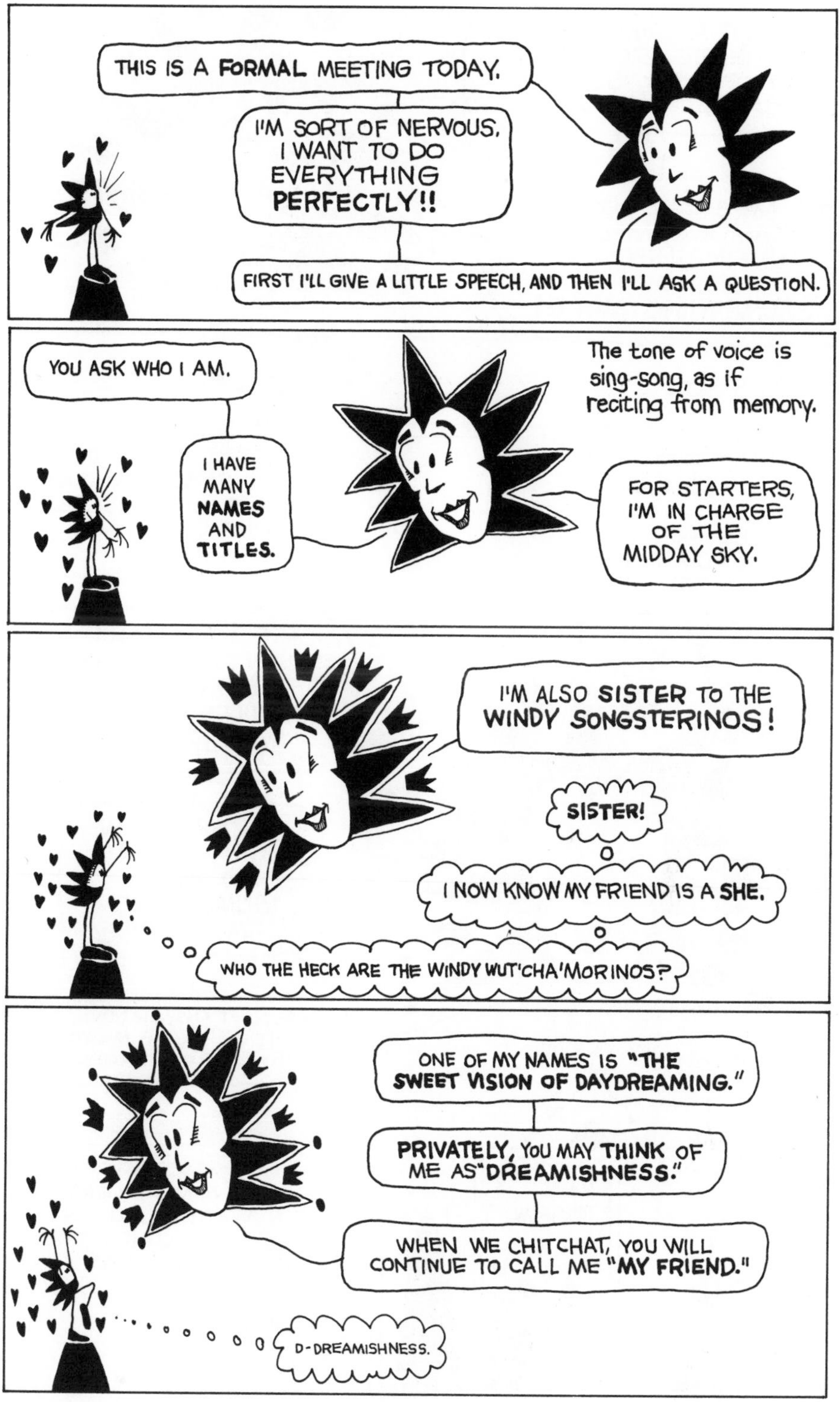
THIS IS A FORMAL MEETING TODAY.
I'M SORT OF NERVOUS. I WANT TO DO EVERYTHING PERFECTLY!!
FIRST I'LL GIVE A LITTLE SPEECH, AND THEN I'LL ASK A QUESTION.
YOU ASK WHO I AM.
I HAVE MANY NAMES AND TITLES.
The tone of voice is sing-song, as if reciting from memory.
FOR STARTERS, I'M IN CHARGE OF THE MIDDAY SKY.
I'M ALSO SISTER TO THE WINDY SONGSTERINOS!
SISTER!
I NOW KNOW MY FRIEND IS A SHE.
WHO THE HECK ARE THE WINDY WUT'CHA'MORINOS?
ONE OF MY NAMES IS "THE SWEET VISION OF DAYDREAMING."
PRIVATELY, YOU MAY THINK OF ME AS "DREAMISHNESS."
WHEN WE CHITCHAT, YOU WILL CONTINUE TO CALL ME "MY FRIEND."
D-DREAMISHNESS.

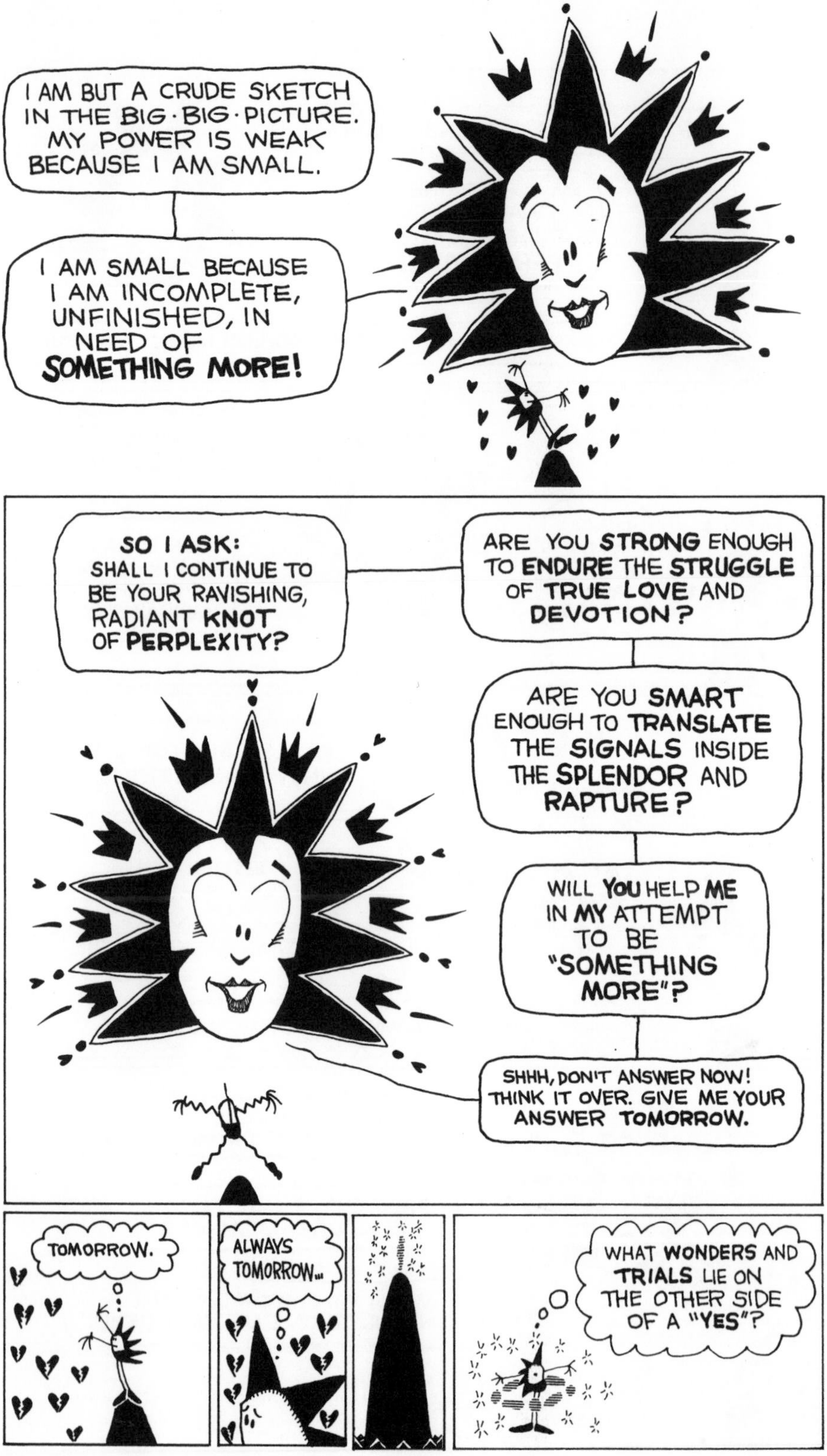

I AM BUT A CRUDE SKETCH IN THE BIG·BIG·PICTURE. MY POWER IS WEAK BECAUSE I AM SMALL.
I AM SMALL BECAUSE I AM INCOMPLETE, UNFINISHED, IN NEED OF SOMETHING MORE!
SO I ASK: SHALL I CONTINUE TO BE YOUR RAVISHING, RADIANT KNOT OF PERPLEXITY?
ARE YOU STRONG ENOUGH TO ENDURE THE STRUGGLE OF TRUE LOVE AND DEVOTION?
ARE YOU SMART ENOUGH TO TRANSLATE THE SIGNALS INSIDE THE SPLENDOR AND RAPTURE?
WILL YOU HELP ME IN MY ATTEMPT TO BE "SOMETHING MORE"?
SHHH, DON'T ANSWER NOW! THINK IT OVER. GIVE ME YOUR ANSWER TOMORROW.
TOMORROW.
ALWAYS TOMORROW...
WHAT WONDERS AND TRIALS LIE ON THE OTHER SIDE OF A "YES"?

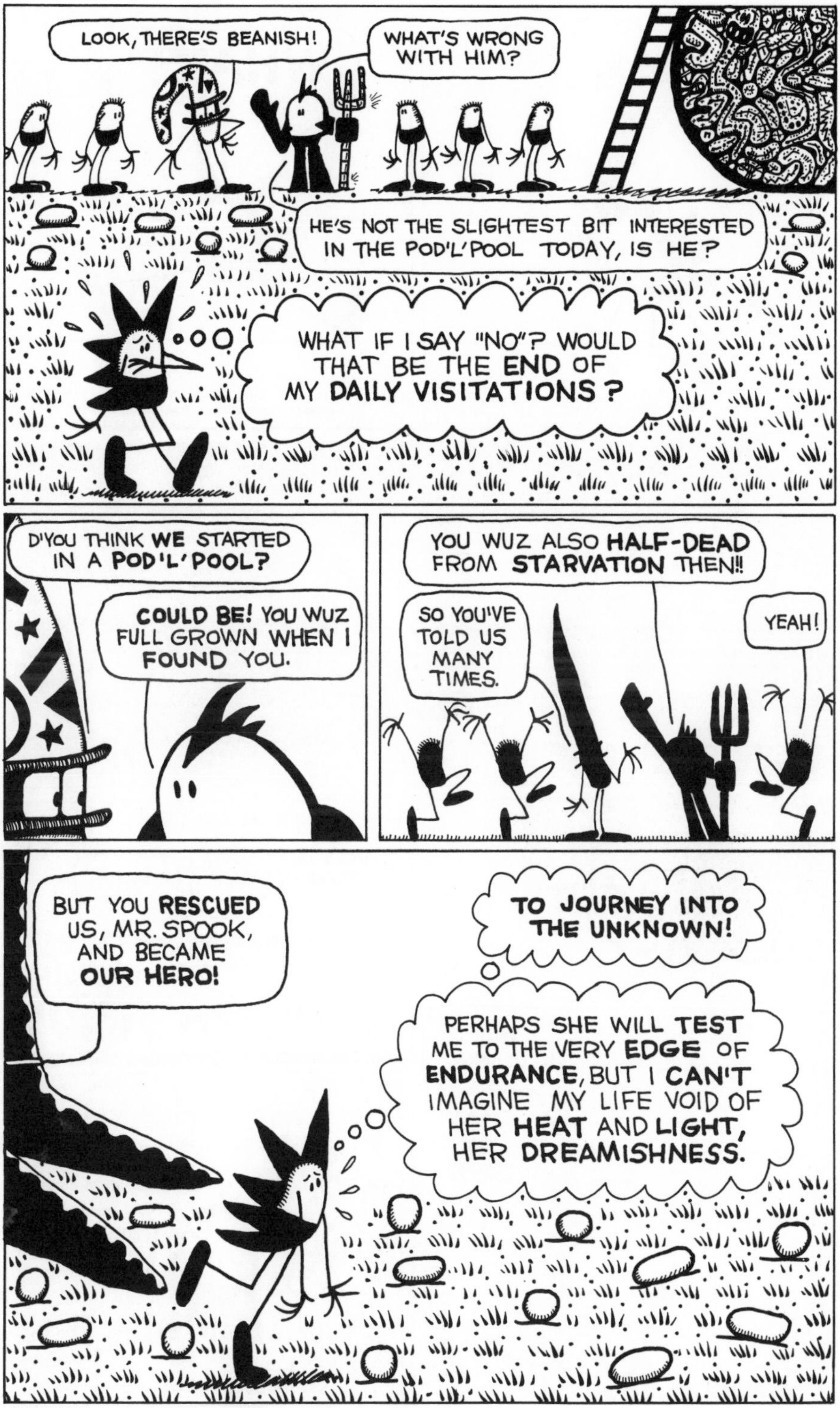

LOOK, THERE'S BEANISH!
WHAT'S WRONG WITH HIM?
HE'S NOT THE SLIGHTEST BIT INTERESTED IN THE POD'L'POOL TODAY, IS HE?
WHAT IF I SAY "NO"? WOULD THAT BE THE **END** OF MY **DAILY VISITATIONS?**
D'YOU THINK **WE** STARTED IN A **POD'L'POOL?**
COULD BE! YOU WUZ FULL GROWN WHEN I **FOUND** YOU.
YOU WUZ ALSO **HALF-DEAD** FROM **STARVATION** THEN!!
SO YOU'VE TOLD US MANY TIMES.
YEAH!
BUT YOU **RESCUED** US, MR. SPOOK, AND BECAME **OUR HERO!**
TO JOURNEY INTO THE UNKNOWN!
PERHAPS SHE WILL **TEST** ME TO THE VERY **EDGE** OF **ENDURANCE**, BUT I **CAN'T** IMAGINE MY LIFE VOID OF HER **HEAT** AND **LIGHT**, HER **DREAMISHNESS.**

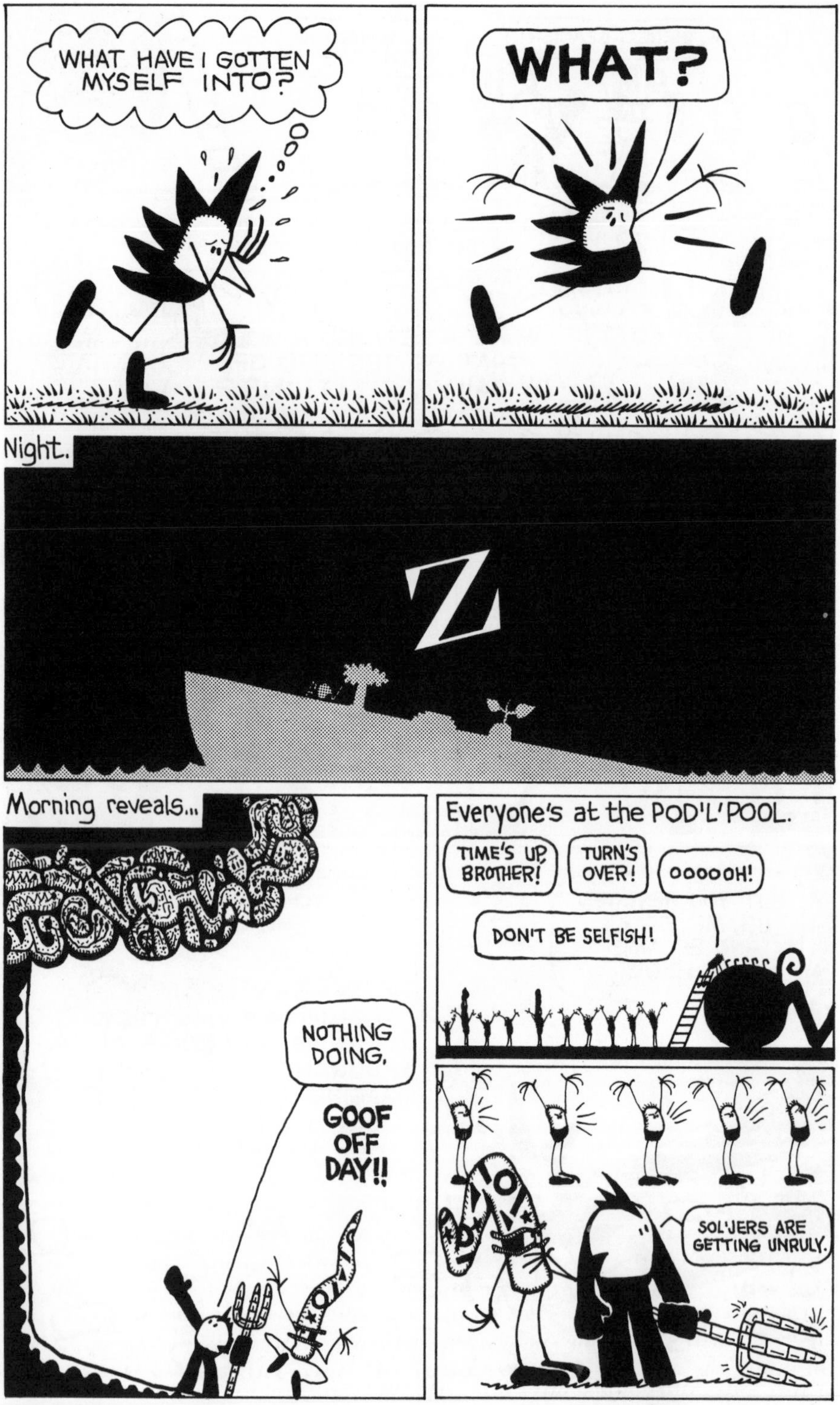
WHAT HAVE I GOTTEN MYSELF INTO?
WHAT?
Night.
Z
Morning reveals...
NOTHING DOING.
GOOF OFF DAY!!
Everyone's at the POD'L'POOL.
TIME'S UP, BROTHER!
TURN'S OVER!
OOOOOH!
DON'T BE SELFISH!
SOL'JERS ARE GETTING UNRULY.

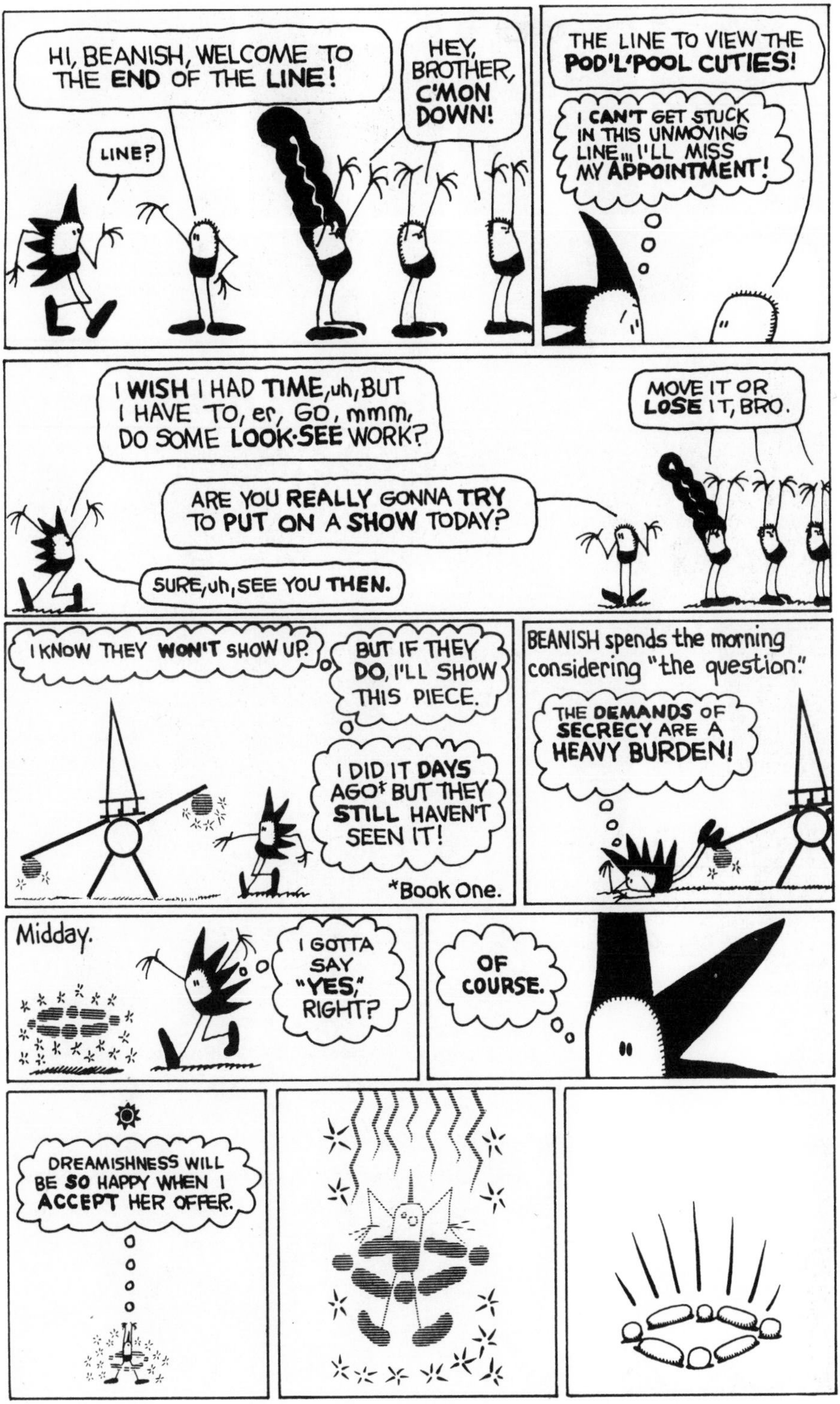
HI, BEANISH, WELCOME TO THE END OF THE LINE!
LINE?
HEY, BROTHER, C'MON DOWN!
THE LINE TO VIEW THE POD'L'POOL CUTIES!
I CAN'T GET STUCK IN THIS UNMOVING LINE... I'LL MISS MY APPOINTMENT!
I WISH I HAD TIME, uh, BUT I HAVE TO, er, GO, mmm, DO SOME LOOK-SEE WORK?
MOVE IT OR LOSE IT, BRO.
ARE YOU REALLY GONNA TRY TO PUT ON A SHOW TODAY?
SURE, uh, SEE YOU THEN.
I KNOW THEY WON'T SHOW UP.
BUT IF THEY DO, I'LL SHOW THIS PIECE.
I DID IT DAYS AGO* BUT THEY STILL HAVEN'T SEEN IT!
*Book One.
BEANISH spends the morning considering "the question."
THE DEMANDS OF SECRECY ARE A HEAVY BURDEN!
Midday.
I GOTTA SAY "YES," RIGHT?
OF COURSE.
DREAMISHNESS WILL BE SO HAPPY WHEN I ACCEPT HER OFFER.

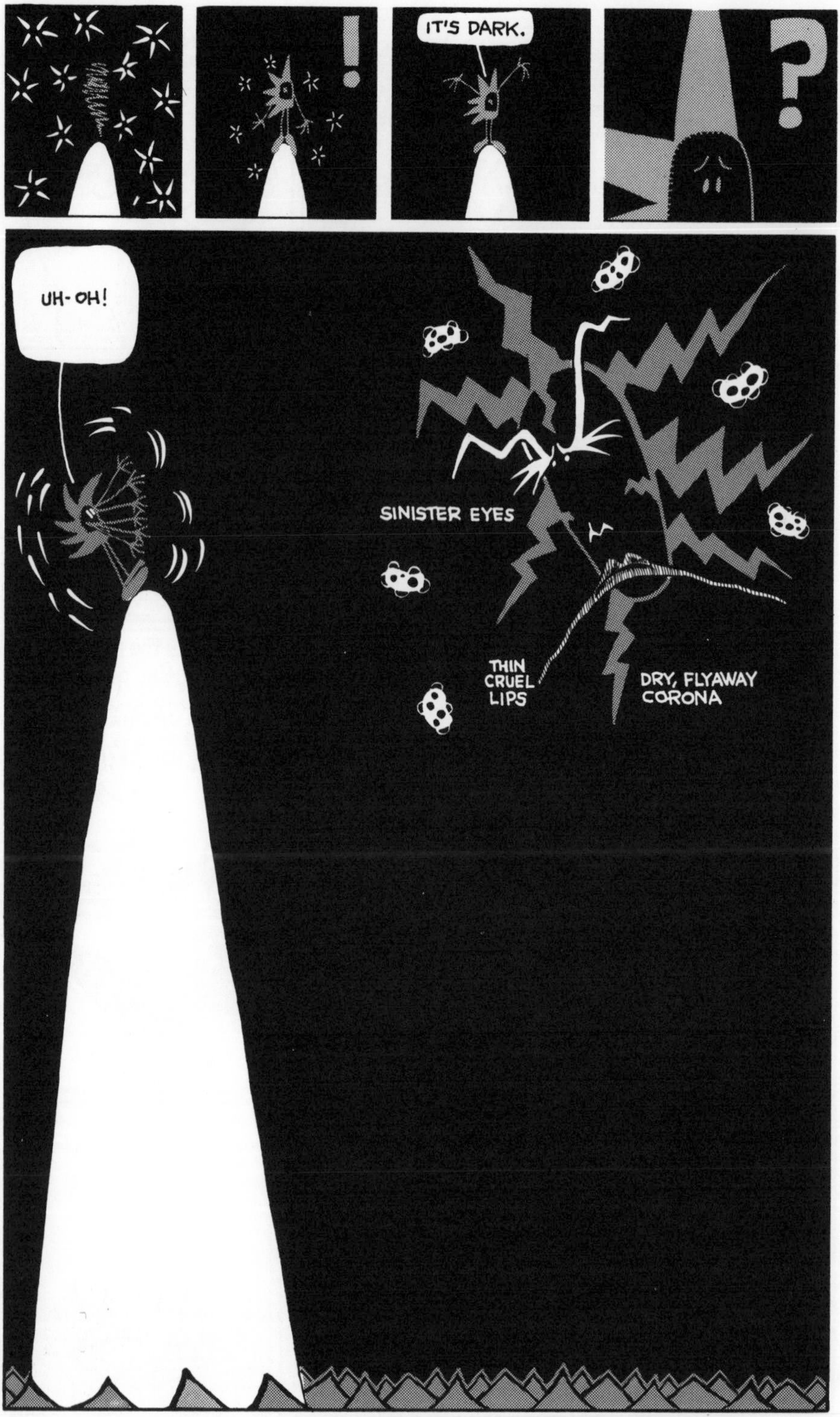
!
IT'S DARK.
?
UH-OH!
SINISTER EYES
THIN CRUEL LIPS
DRY, FLYAWAY CORONA

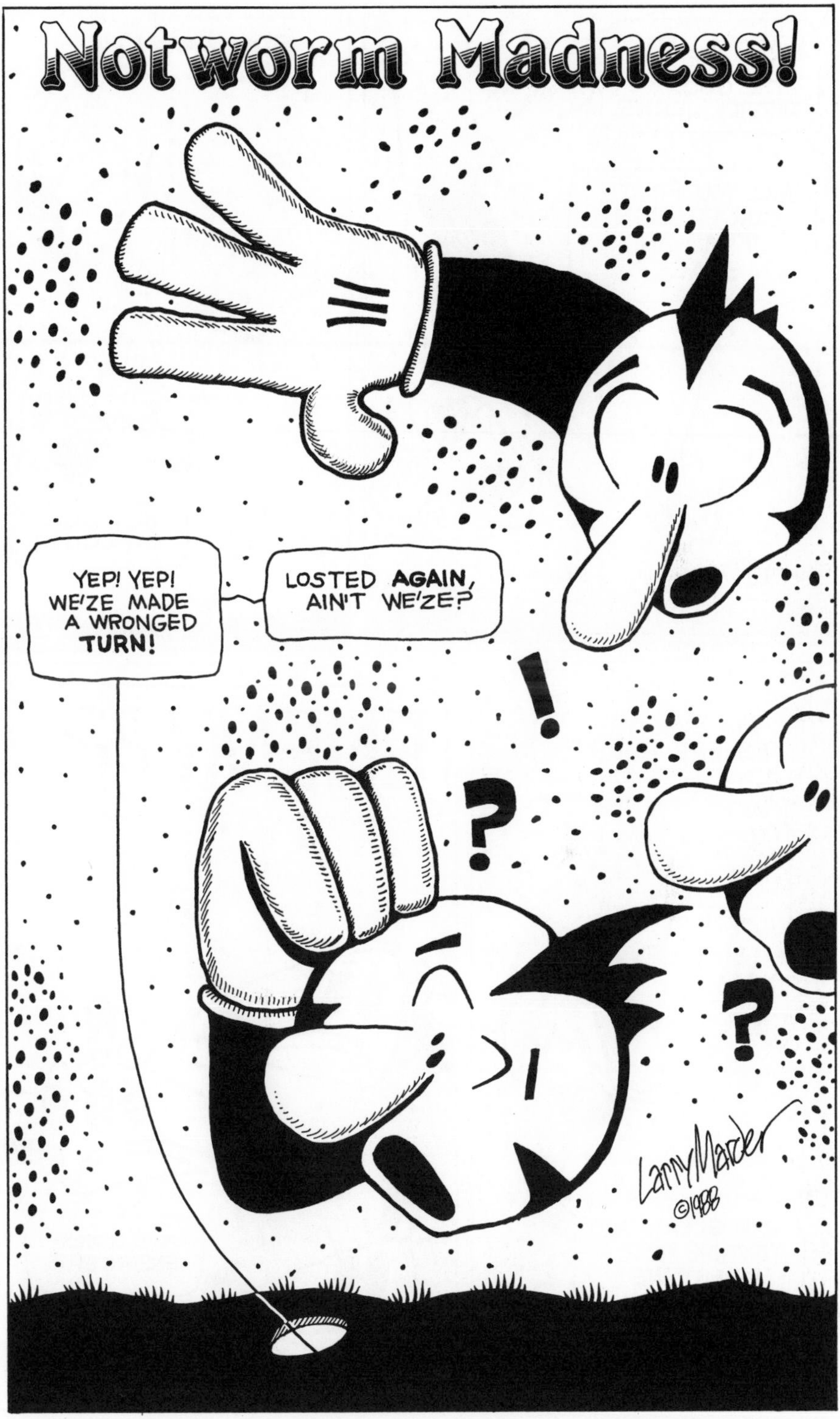
Notworm Madness!
YEP! YEP! WE'ZE MADE A WRONGED TURN!
LOSTED AGAIN, AIN'T WE'ZE?
Larry Marder ©1988

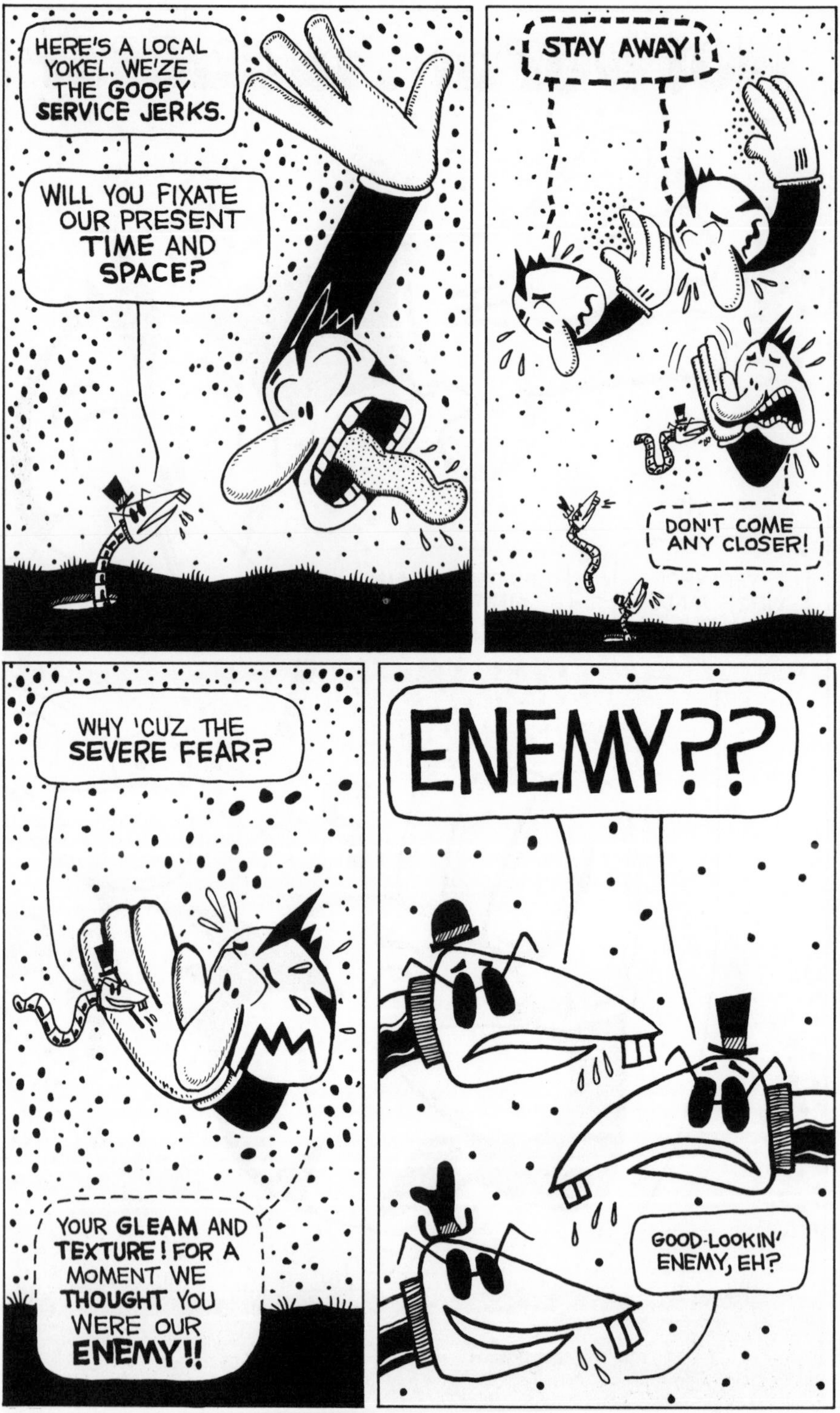
HERE'S A LOCAL YOKEL. WE'ZE THE GOOFY SERVICE JERKS.
WILL YOU FIXATE OUR PRESENT TIME AND SPACE?
STAY AWAY!
DON'T COME ANY CLOSER!
WHY 'CUZ THE SEVERE FEAR?
YOUR GLEAM AND TEXTURE! FOR A MOMENT WE THOUGHT YOU WERE OUR ENEMY!!
ENEMY??
GOOD-LOOKIN' ENEMY, EH?

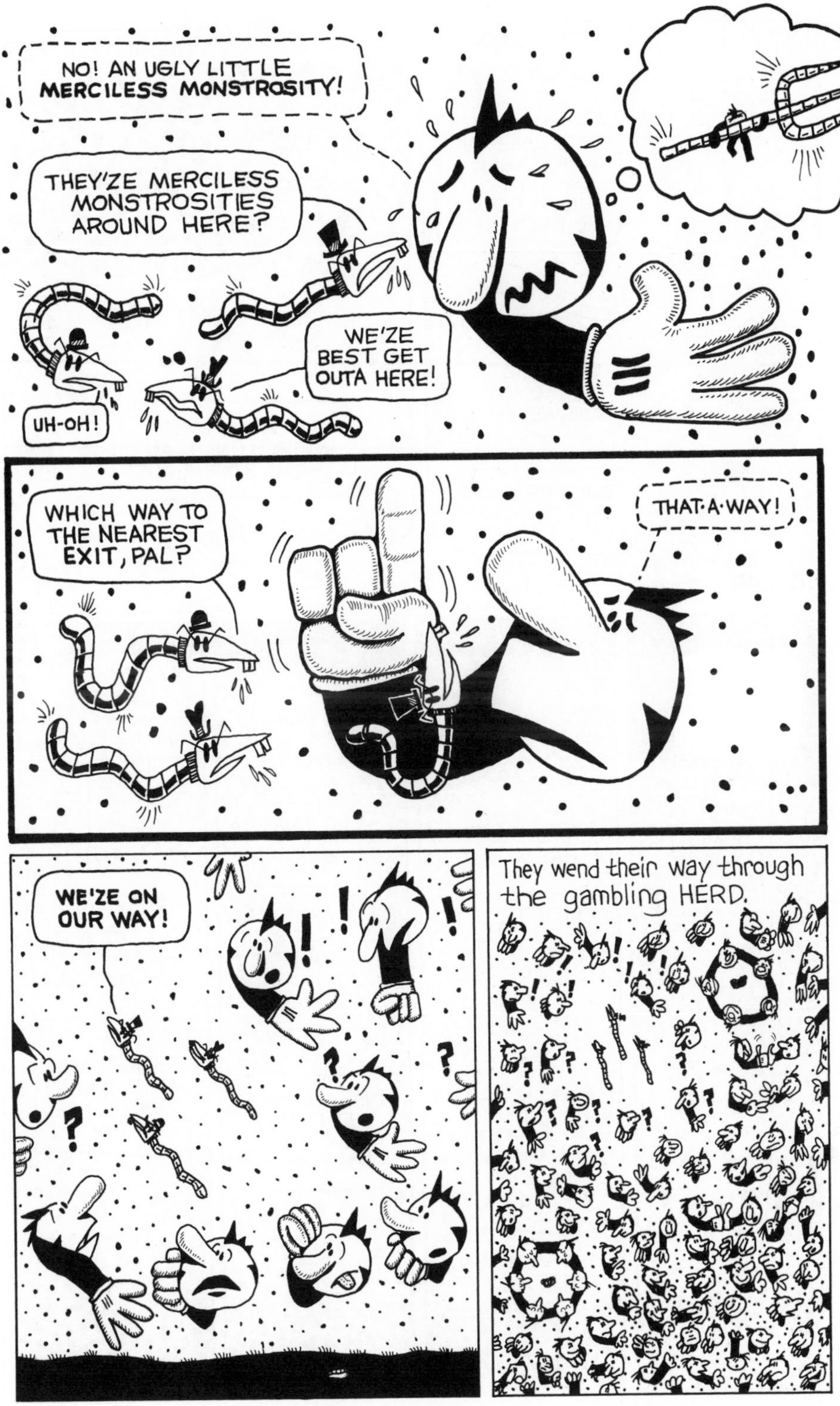
NO! AN UGLY LITTLE MERCILESS MONSTROSITY!
THEY'ZE MERCILESS MONSTROSITIES AROUND HERE?
WE'ZE BEST GET OUTA HERE!
UH-OH!
WHICH WAY TO THE NEAREST EXIT, PAL?
THAT-A-WAY!
WE'ZE ON OUR WAY!
They wend their way through the gambling HERD.

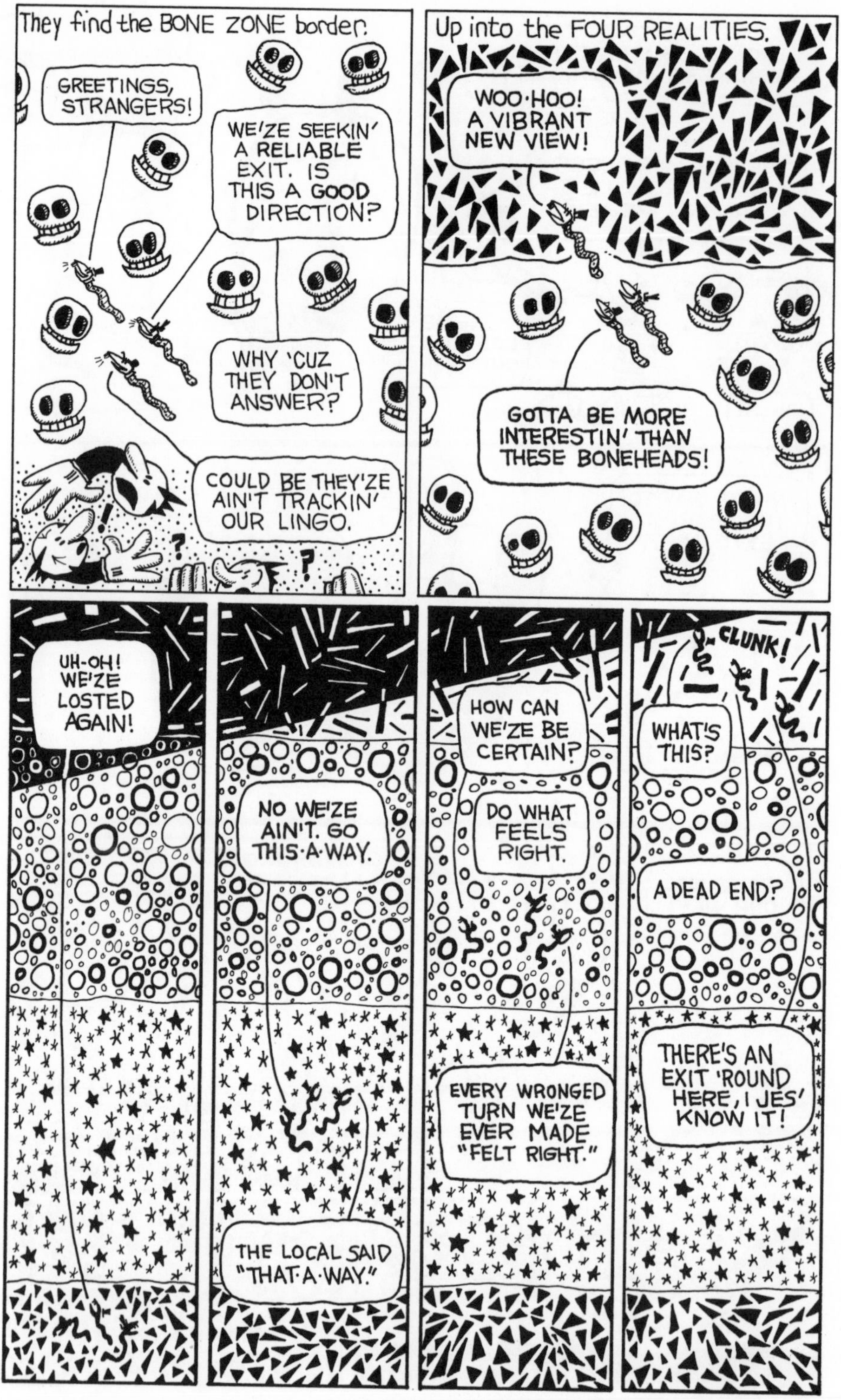
They find the BONE ZONE border.
GREETINGS, STRANGERS!
WE'ZE SEEKIN' A RELIABLE EXIT. IS THIS A GOOD DIRECTION?
WHY 'CUZ THEY DON'T ANSWER?
COULD BE THEY'ZE AIN'T TRACKIN' OUR LINGO.
Up into the FOUR REALITIES.
WOO-HOO! A VIBRANT NEW VIEW!
GOTTA BE MORE INTERESTIN' THAN THESE BONEHEADS!
UH-OH! WE'ZE LOSTED AGAIN!
NO WE'ZE AIN'T. GO THIS-A-WAY.
THE LOCAL SAID "THAT-A-WAY."
HOW CAN WE'ZE BE CERTAIN?
DO WHAT FEELS RIGHT.
EVERY WRONGED TURN WE'ZE EVER MADE "FELT RIGHT."
CLUNK!
WHAT'S THIS?
A DEAD END?
THERE'S AN EXIT 'ROUND HERE, I JES' KNOW IT!

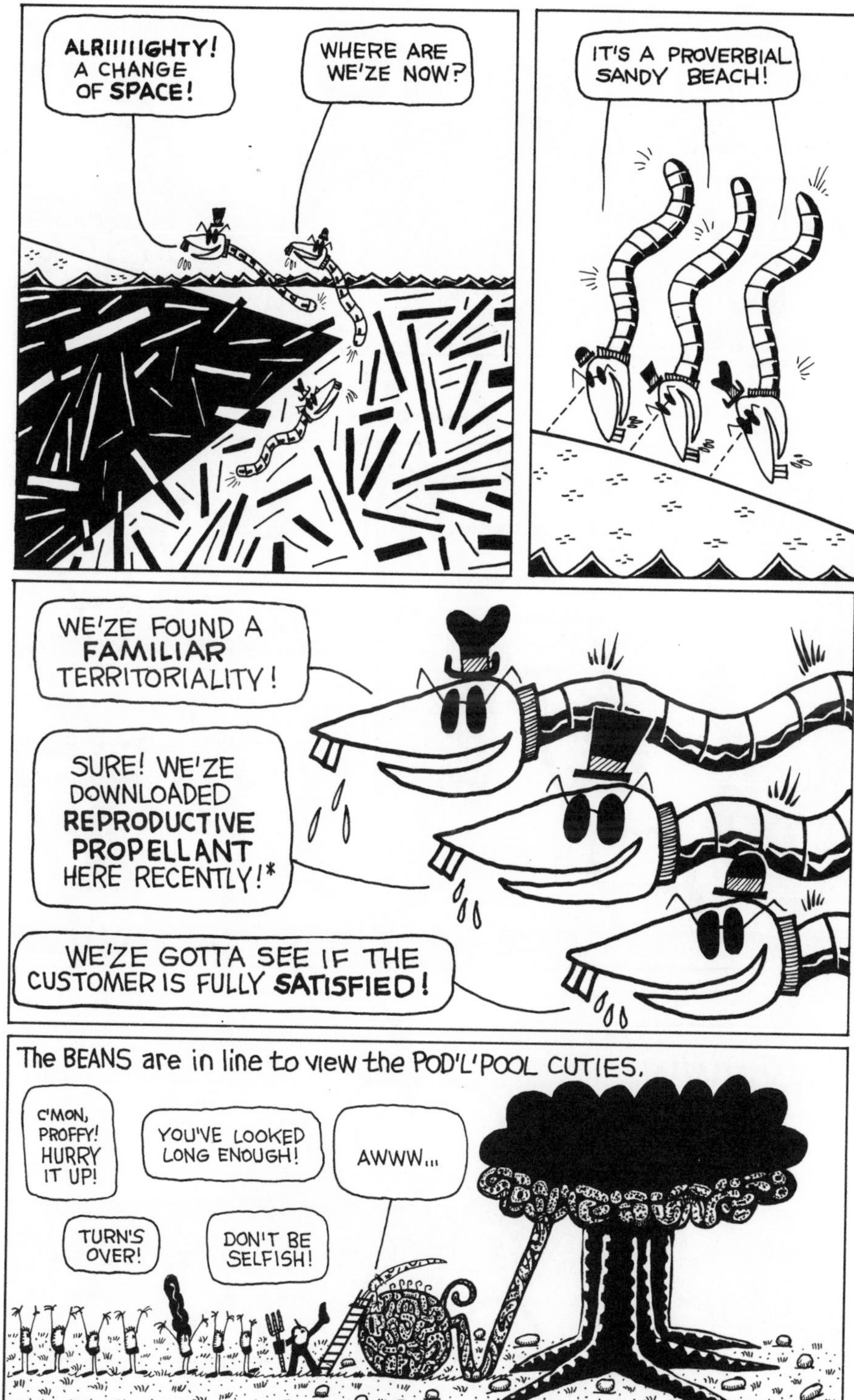
ALRIIIIIGHTY! A CHANGE OF SPACE!
WHERE ARE WE'ZE NOW?
IT'S A PROVERBIAL SANDY BEACH!
WE'ZE FOUND A FAMILIAR TERRITORIALITY!
SURE! WE'ZE DOWNLOADED REPRODUCTIVE PROPELLANT HERE RECENTLY!*
WE'ZE GOTTA SEE IF THE CUSTOMER IS FULLY SATISFIED!
The BEANS are in line to view the POD'L'POOL CUTIES.
C'MON, PROFFY! HURRY IT UP!
YOU'VE LOOKED LONG ENOUGH!
AWWW...
TURN'S OVER!
DON'T BE SELFISH!

*Book One.

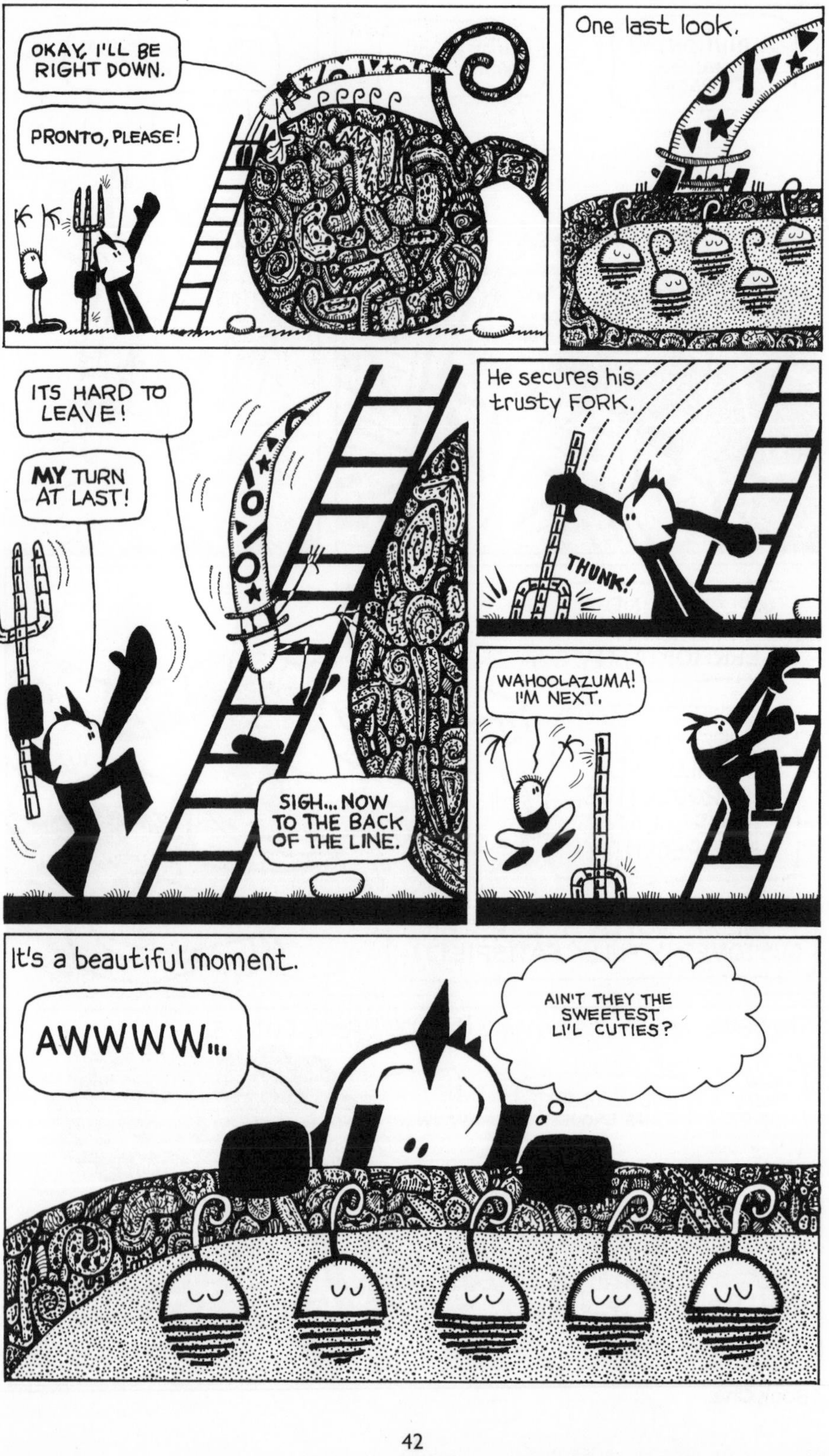
OKAY, I'LL BE RIGHT DOWN.
PRONTO, PLEASE!
One last look.
ITS HARD TO LEAVE!
MY TURN AT LAST!
SIGH... NOW TO THE BACK OF THE LINE.
He secures his trusty FORK.
THUNK!
WAHOOLAZUMA! I'M NEXT.
It's a beautiful moment.
AWWWW...
AIN'T THEY THE SWEETEST LI'L CUTIES?

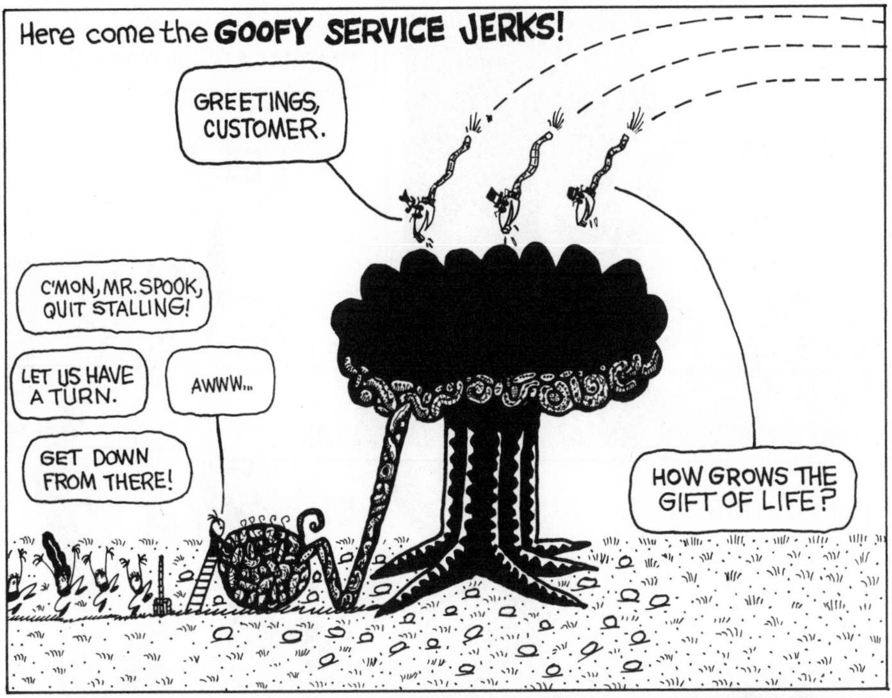
Here come the GOOFY SERVICE JERKS!
GREETINGS, CUSTOMER.
HOW GROWS THE GIFT OF LIFE?
C'MON, MR. SPOOK, QUIT STALLING!
LET US HAVE A TURN.
AWWW...
GET DOWN FROM THERE!

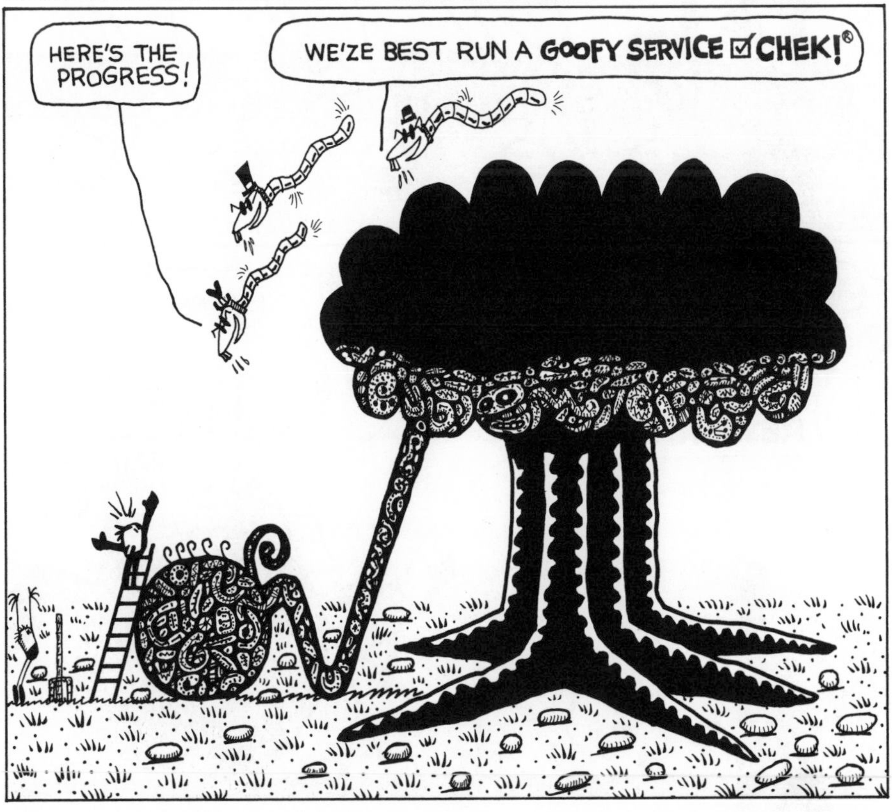
HERE'S THE PROGRESS!
WE'ZE BEST RUN A GOOFY SERVICE ☑ CHEK!®

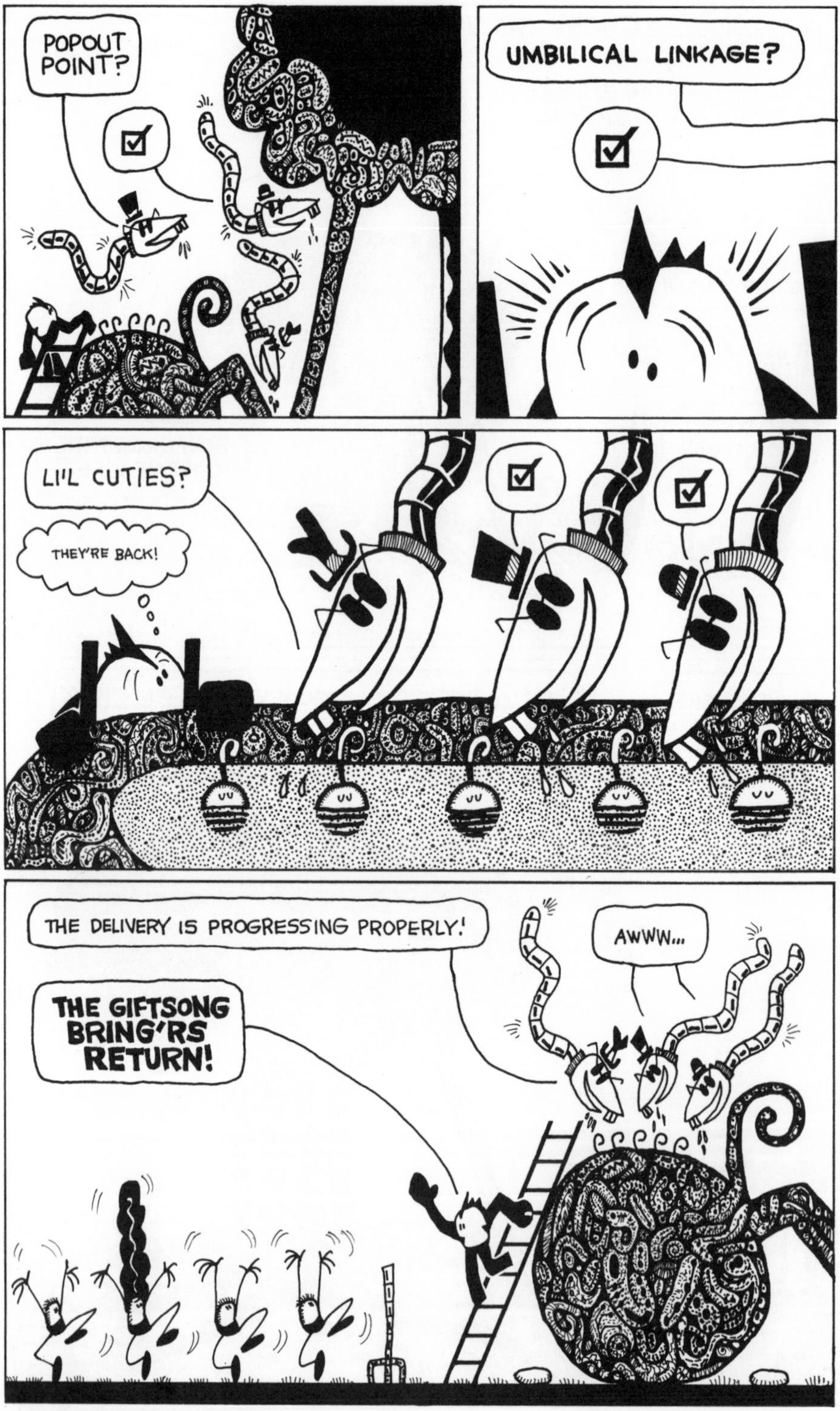
POPOUT POINT?
UMBILICAL LINKAGE?
LI'L CUTIES?
THEY'RE BACK!
THE DELIVERY IS PROGRESSING PROPERLY!
AWWW...
THE GIFTSONG BRING'RS RETURN!

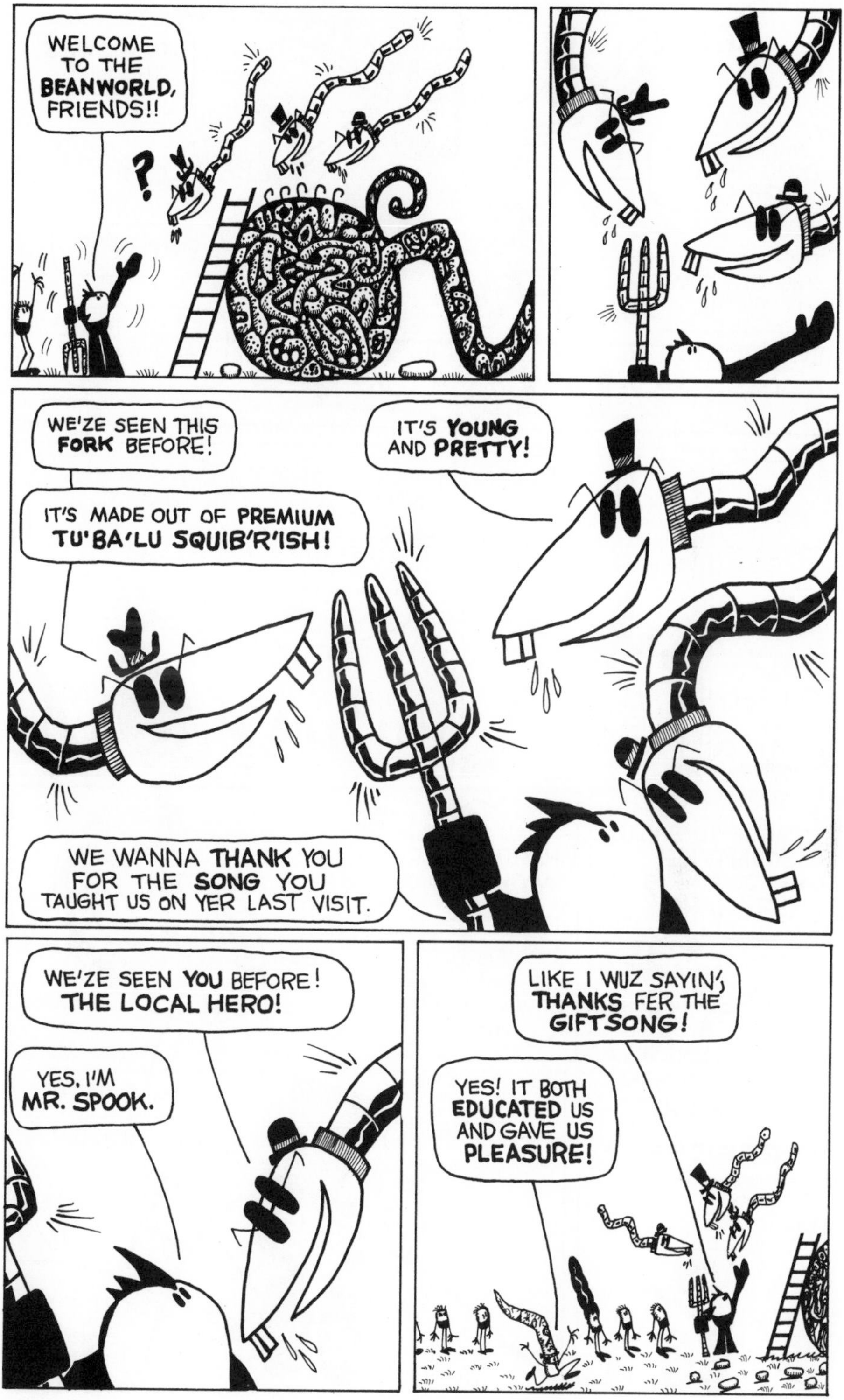
WELCOME TO THE BEANWORLD, FRIENDS!!
?
WE'ZE SEEN THIS FORK BEFORE!
IT'S MADE OUT OF PREMIUM TU'BA'LU SQUIB'R'ISH!
IT'S YOUNG AND PRETTY!
WE WANNA THANK YOU FOR THE SONG YOU TAUGHT US ON YER LAST VISIT.
WE'ZE SEEN YOU BEFORE! THE LOCAL HERO!
YES, I'M MR. SPOOK.
LIKE I WUZ SAYIN', THANKS FER THE GIFTSONG!
YES! IT BOTH EDUCATED US AND GAVE US PLEASURE!

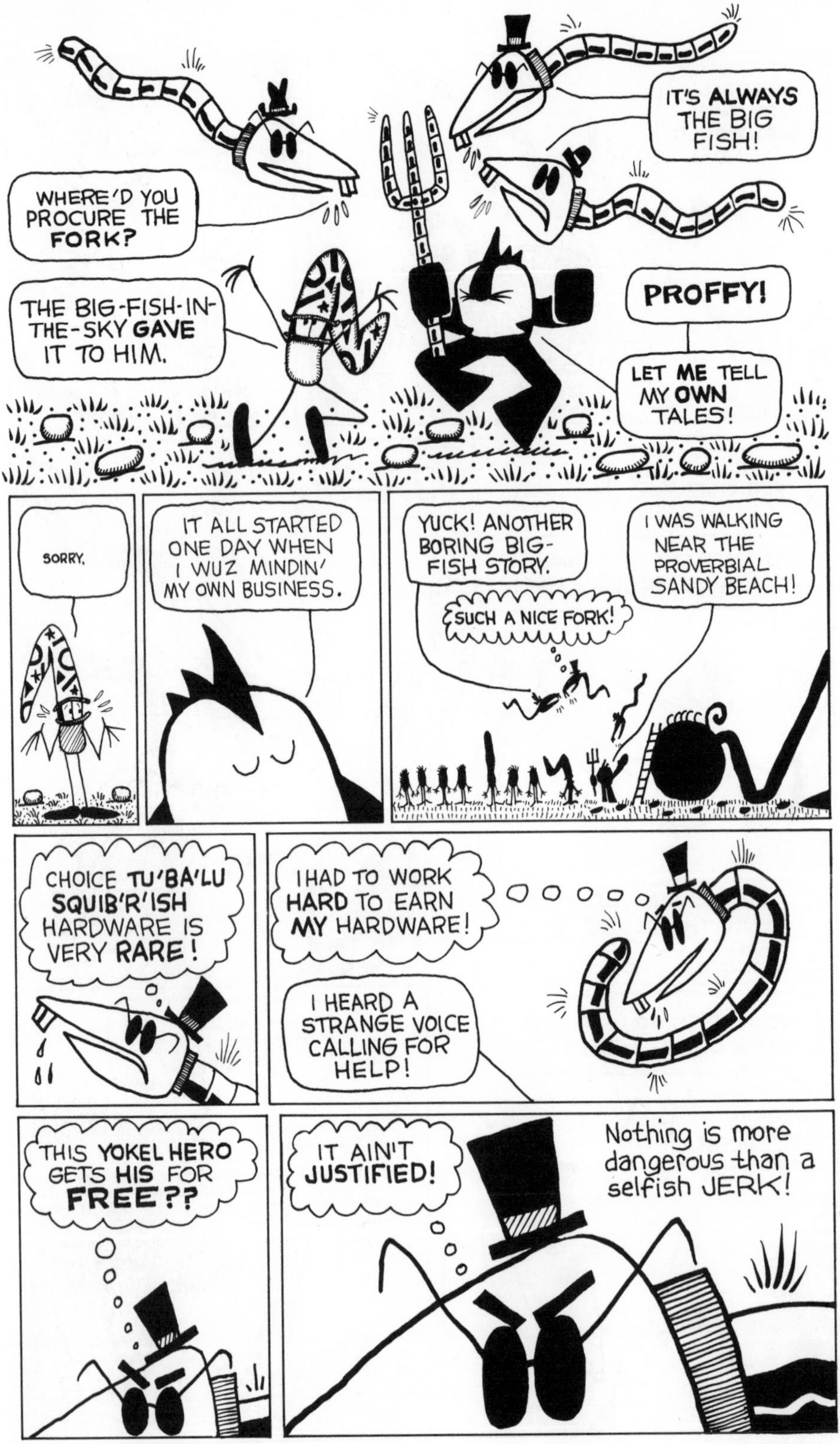
WHERE'D YOU PROCURE THE FORK?
IT'S ALWAYS THE BIG FISH!
THE BIG-FISH-IN-THE-SKY GAVE IT TO HIM.
PROFFY!
LET ME TELL MY OWN TALES!
SORRY.
IT ALL STARTED ONE DAY WHEN I WUZ MINDIN' MY OWN BUSINESS.
YUCK! ANOTHER BORING BIG-FISH STORY.
I WAS WALKING NEAR THE PROVERBIAL SANDY BEACH!
SUCH A NICE FORK!
CHOICE TU'BA'LU SQUIB'R'ISH HARDWARE IS VERY RARE!
I HAD TO WORK HARD TO EARN MY HARDWARE!
I HEARD A STRANGE VOICE CALLING FOR HELP!
THIS YOKEL HERO GETS HIS FOR FREE??
IT AIN'T JUSTIFIED!
Nothing is more dangerous than a selfish JERK!

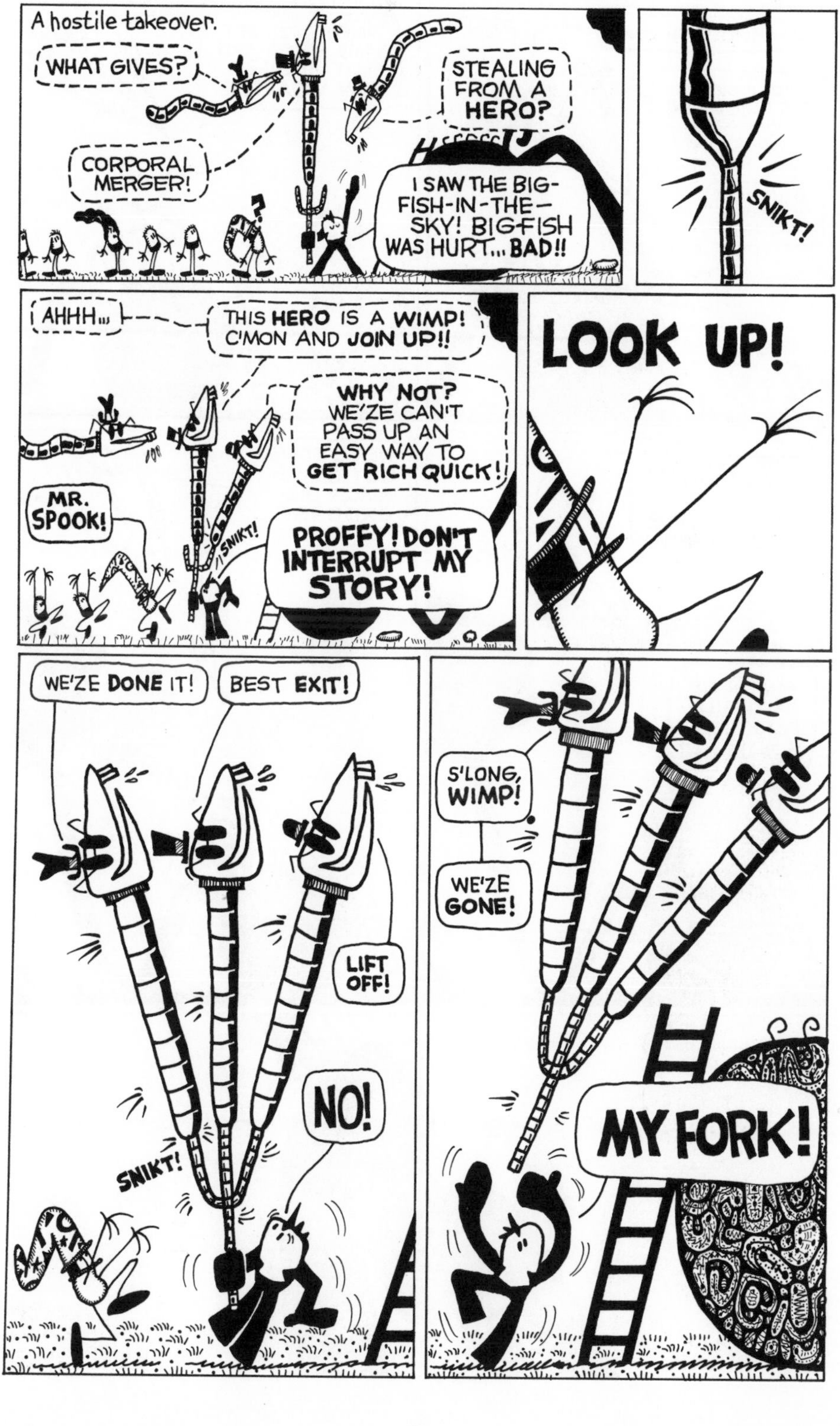

A hostile takeover.
WHAT GIVES?
CORPORAL MERGER!
STEALING FROM A HERO?
I SAW THE BIG-FISH-IN-THE-SKY! BIG-FISH WAS HURT... BAD!!
SNIKT!
AHHH...
THIS HERO IS A WIMP! C'MON AND JOIN UP!!
WHY NOT? WE'ZE CAN'T PASS UP AN EASY WAY TO GET RICH QUICK!
MR. SPOOK!
SNIKT!
PROFFY! DON'T INTERRUPT MY STORY!
LOOK UP!
WE'ZE DONE IT!
BEST EXIT!
LIFT OFF!
SNIKT!
NO!
S'LONG, WIMP!
WE'ZE GONE!
MY FORK!

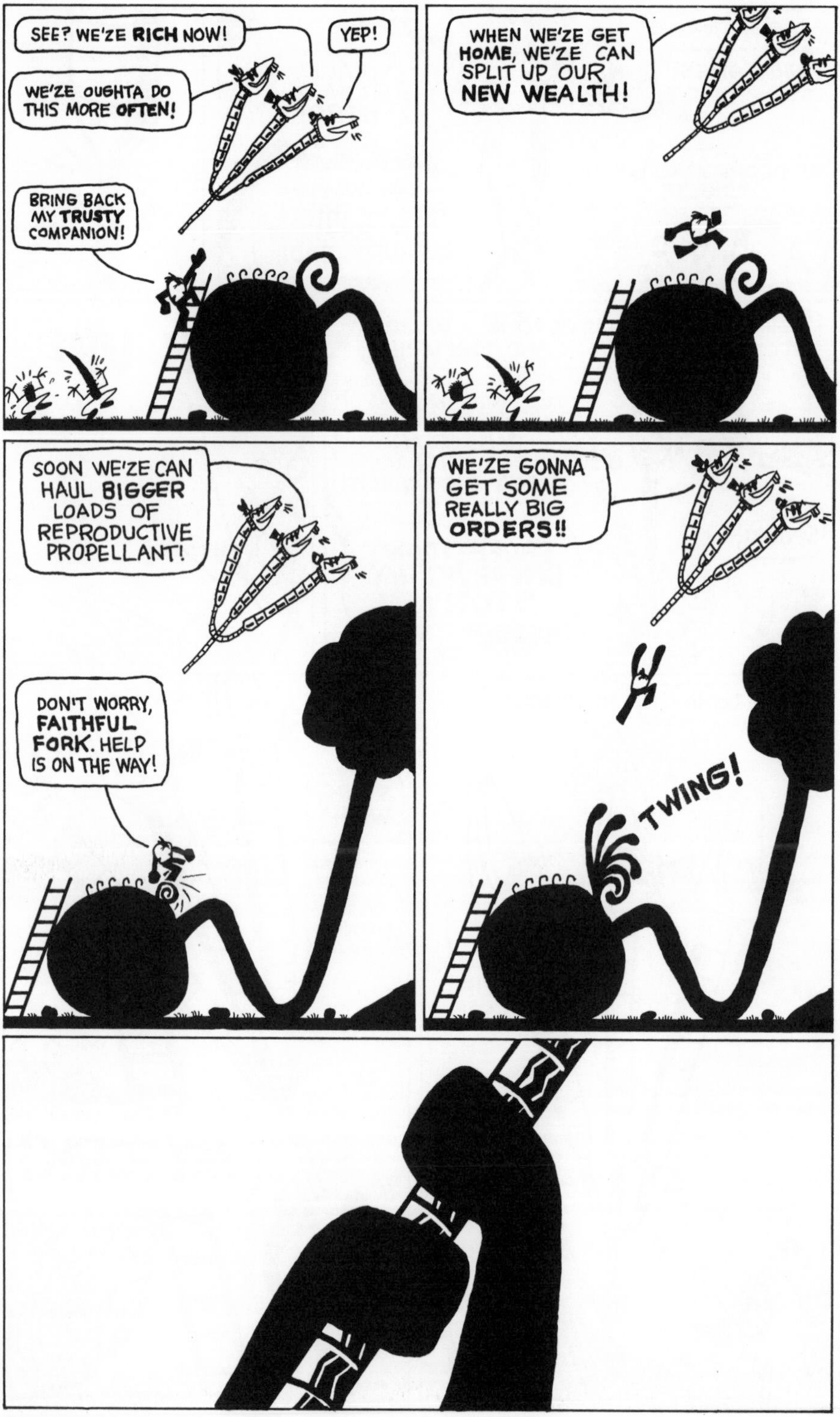
SEE? WE'ZE RICH NOW!
YEP!
WE'ZE OUGHTA DO THIS MORE OFTEN!
BRING BACK MY TRUSTY COMPANION!
WHEN WE'ZE GET HOME, WE'ZE CAN SPLIT UP OUR NEW WEALTH!
SOON WE'ZE CAN HAUL BIGGER LOADS OF REPRODUCTIVE PROPELLANT!
DON'T WORRY, FAITHFUL FORK. HELP IS ON THE WAY!
WE'ZE GONNA GET SOME REALLY BIG ORDERS!!
TWING!

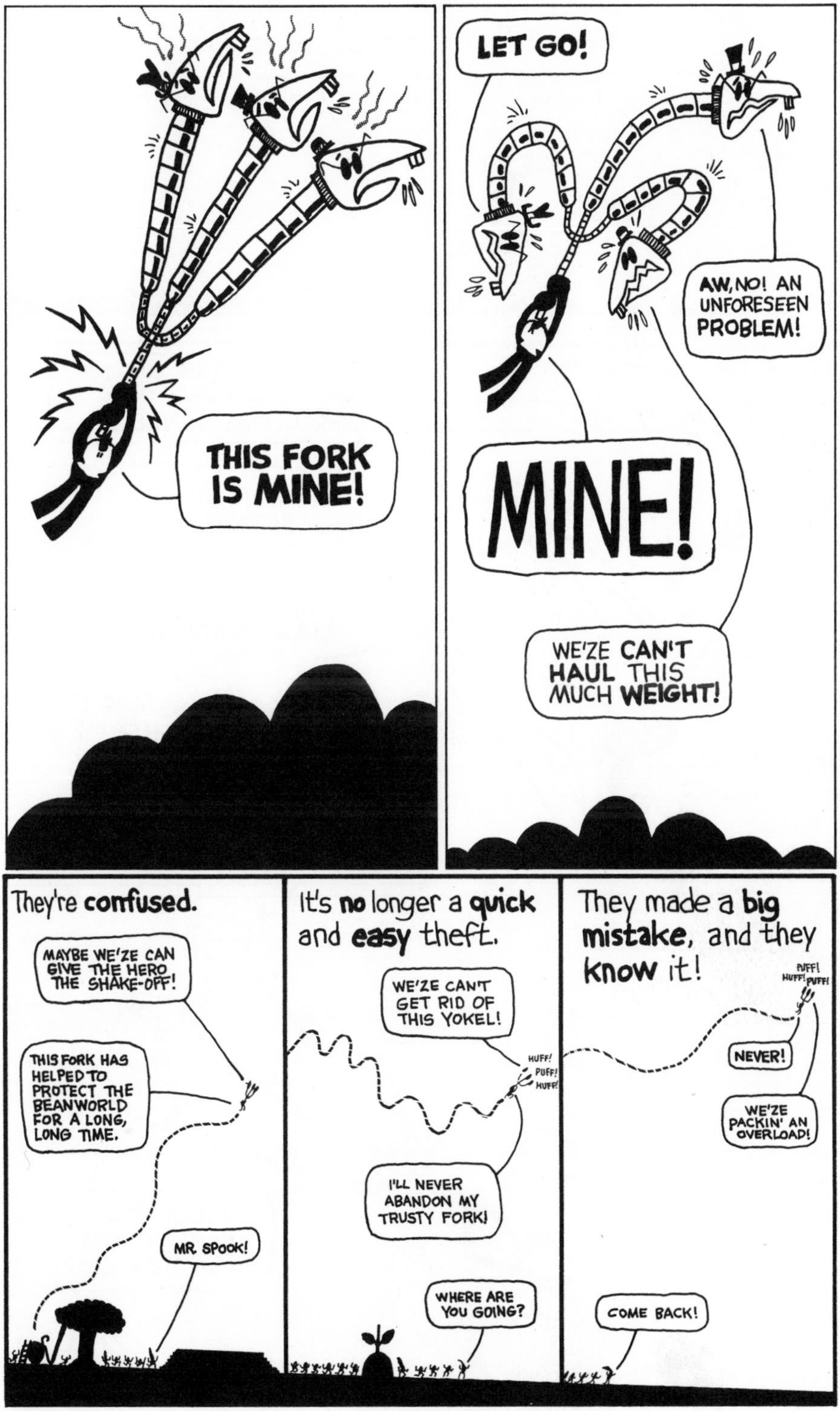
THIS FORK IS MINE!
LET GO!
AW, NO! AN UNFORESEEN PROBLEM!
MINE!
WE'ZE CAN'T HAUL THIS MUCH WEIGHT!
They're confused.
MAYBE WE'ZE CAN GIVE THE HERO THE SHAKE-OFF!
THIS FORK HAS HELPED TO PROTECT THE BEANWORLD FOR A LONG, LONG TIME.
MR. SPOOK!
It's no longer a quick and easy theft.
WE'ZE CAN'T GET RID OF THIS YOKEL!
HUFF! PUFF! HUFF!
I'LL NEVER ABANDON MY TRUSTY FORK!
WHERE ARE YOU GOING?
They made a big mistake, and they know it!
PUFF! HUFF! PUFF!
NEVER!
WE'ZE PACKIN' AN OVERLOAD!
COME BACK!

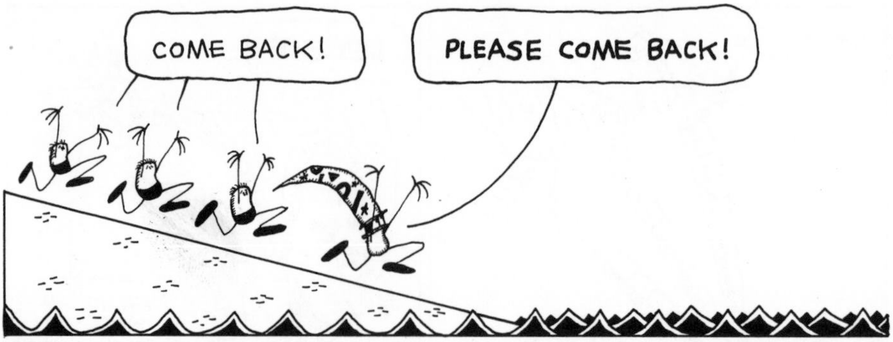
COME BACK!
PLEASE COME BACK!

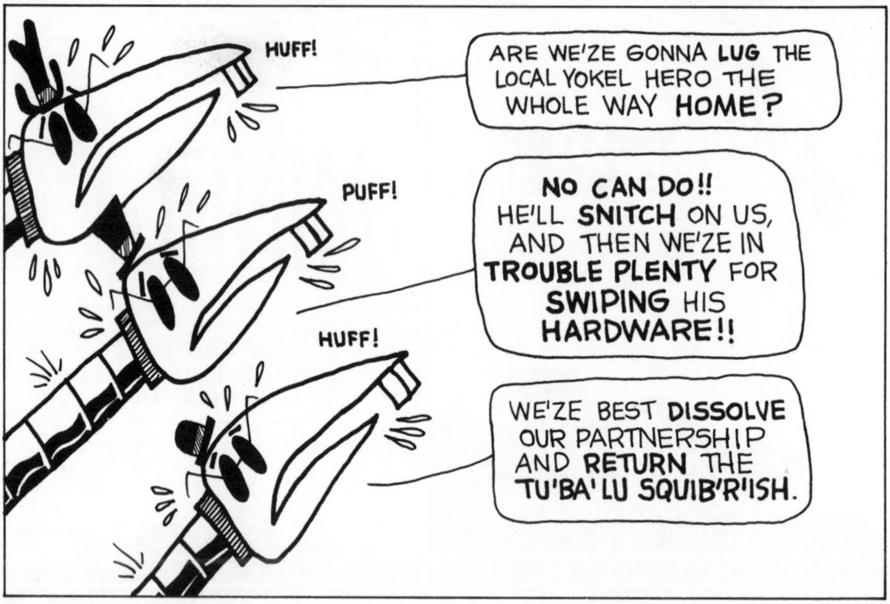
HUFF!
ARE WE'ZE GONNA LUG THE LOCAL YOKEL HERO THE WHOLE WAY HOME?
PUFF!
NO CAN DO!! HE'LL SNITCH ON US, AND THEN WE'ZE IN TROUBLE PLENTY FOR SWIPING HIS HARDWARE!!
HUFF!
WE'ZE BEST DISSOLVE OUR PARTNERSHIP AND RETURN THE TU'BA'LU SQUIB'R'ISH.

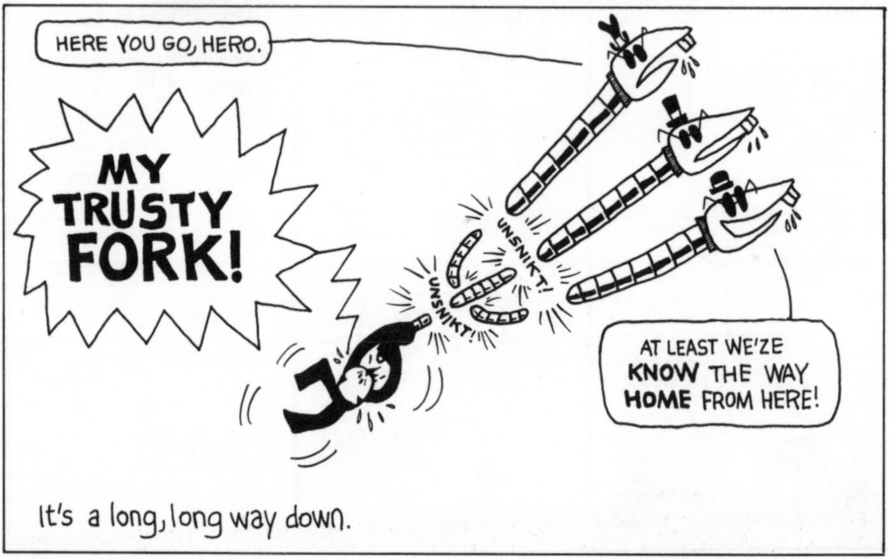
HERE YOU GO, HERO.
MY TRUSTY FORK!
UNSNIKT!
UNSNIKT!
AT LEAST WE'ZE KNOW THE WAY HOME FROM HERE!
It's a long, long way down.

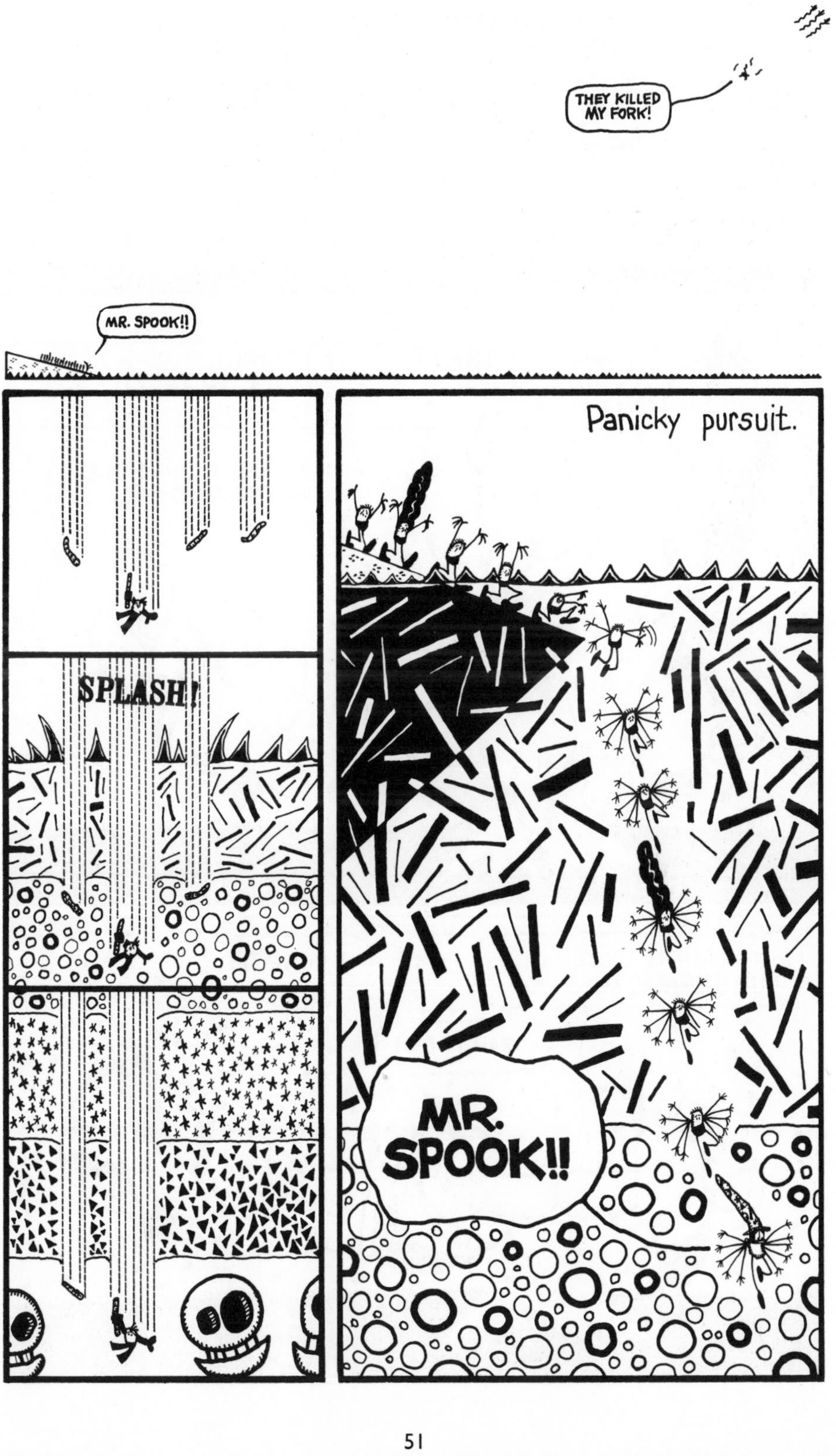
THEY KILLED MY FORK!
MR. SPOOK!!
SPLASH!
Panicky pursuit.
MR. SPOOK!!

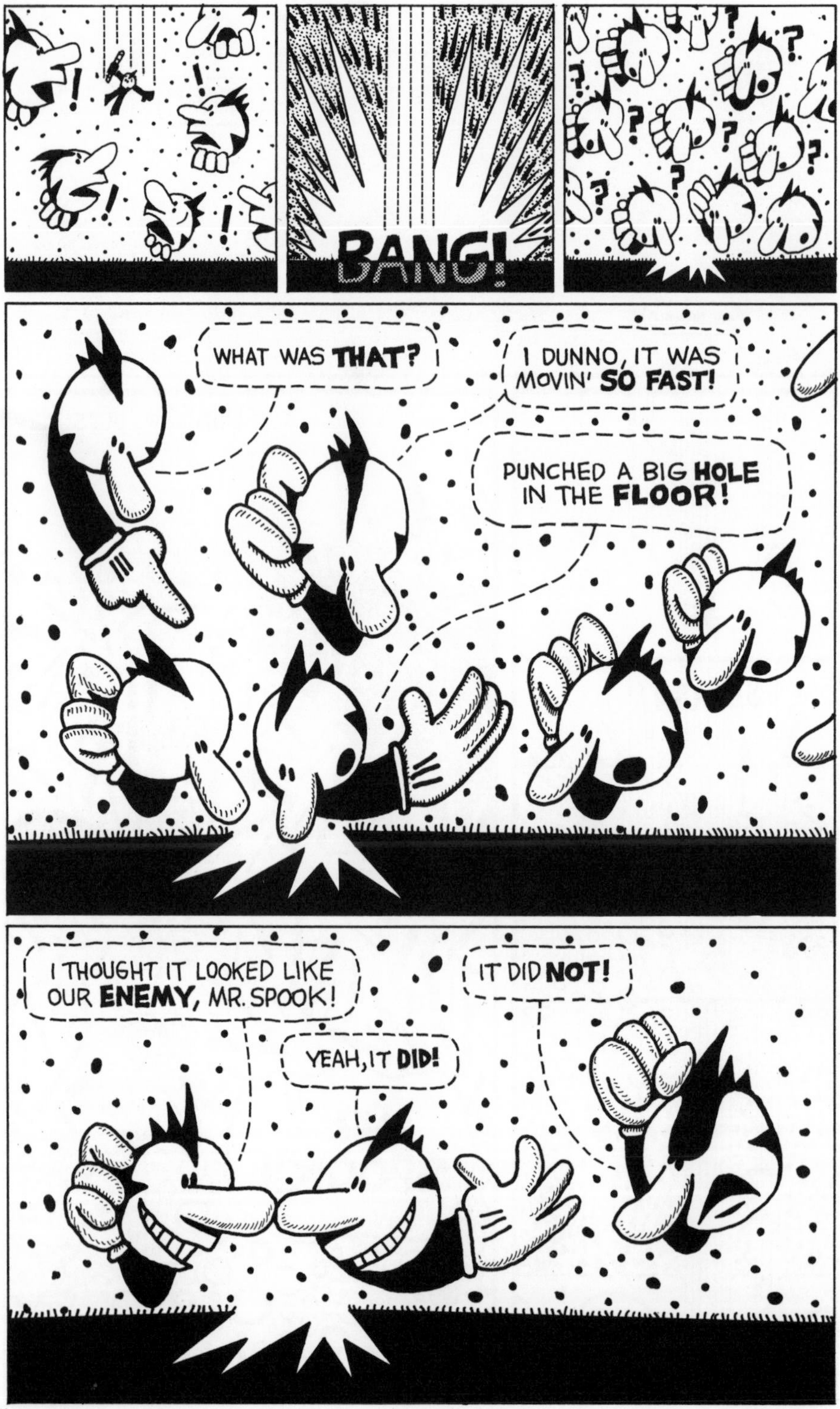
!
!
!
!
!
BANG!
?
?
?
?
?
?
?
?
WHAT WAS THAT?
I DUNNO, IT WAS MOVIN' SO FAST!
PUNCHED A BIG HOLE IN THE FLOOR!
I THOUGHT IT LOOKED LIKE OUR ENEMY, MR. SPOOK!
YEAH, IT DID!
IT DID NOT!

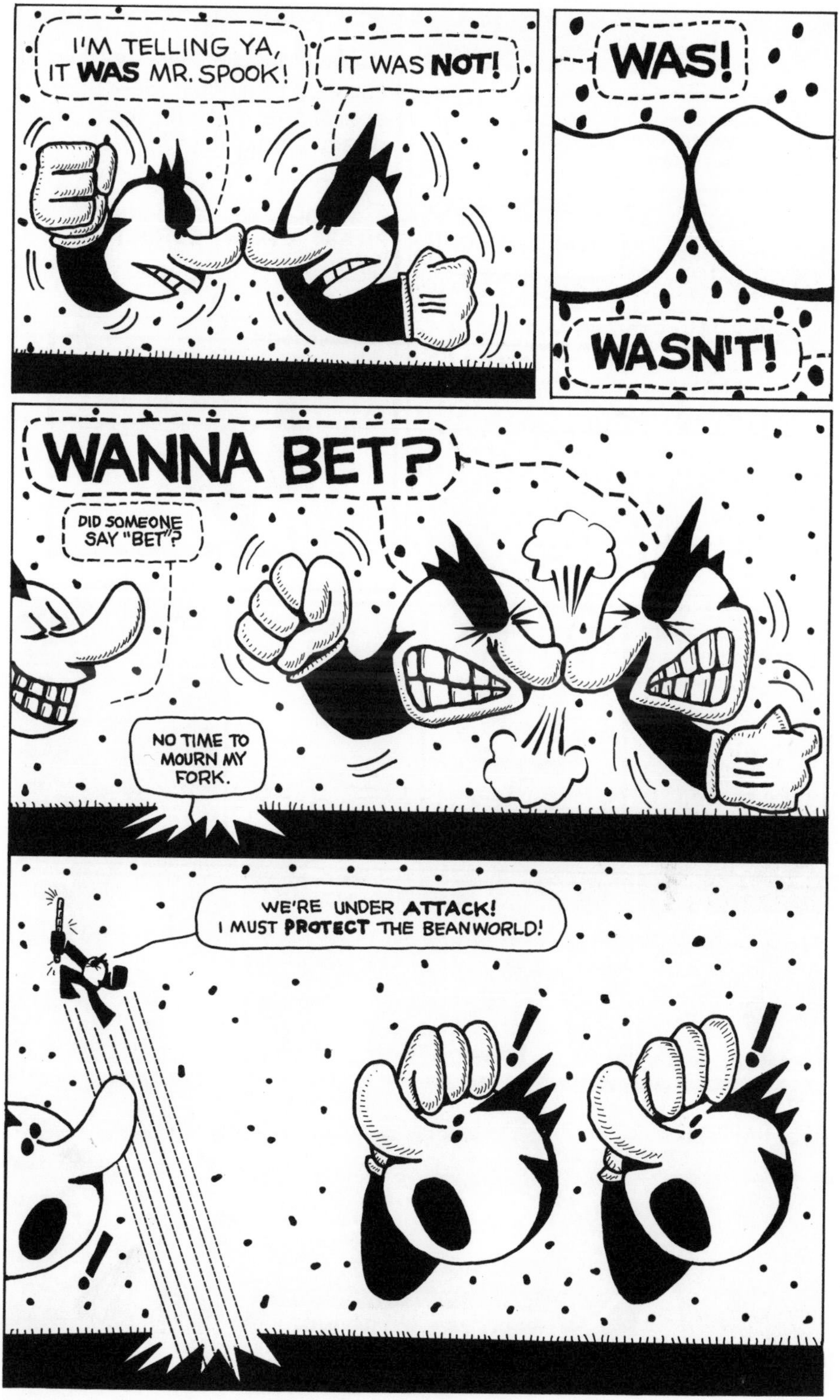
I'M TELLING YA, IT WAS MR. SPOOK!
IT WAS NOT!
WAS!
WASN'T!
WANNA BET?
DID SOMEONE SAY "BET"?
NO TIME TO MOURN MY FORK.
WE'RE UNDER ATTACK! I MUST PROTECT THE BEANWORLD!

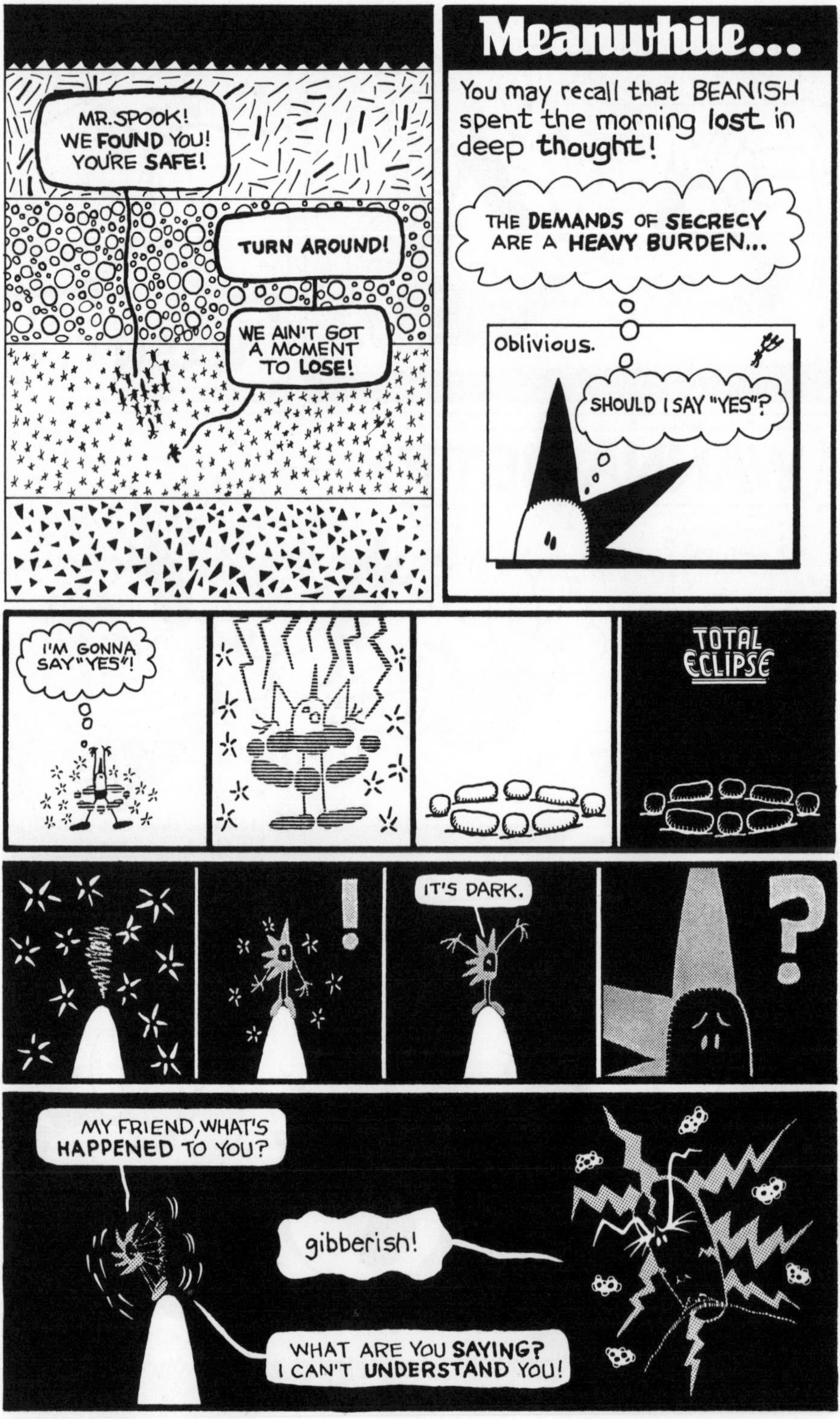
MR. SPOOK! WE FOUND YOU! YOU'RE SAFE!
TURN AROUND!
WE AIN'T GOT A MOMENT TO LOSE!
Meanwhile...
You may recall that BEANISH spent the morning lost in deep thought!
THE DEMANDS OF SECRECY ARE A HEAVY BURDEN...
Oblivious.
SHOULD I SAY "YES"?
I'M GONNA SAY "YES"!
TOTAL ECLIPSE
IT'S DARK.
MY FRIEND, WHAT'S HAPPENED TO YOU?
gibberish!
WHAT ARE YOU SAYING? I CAN'T UNDERSTAND YOU!

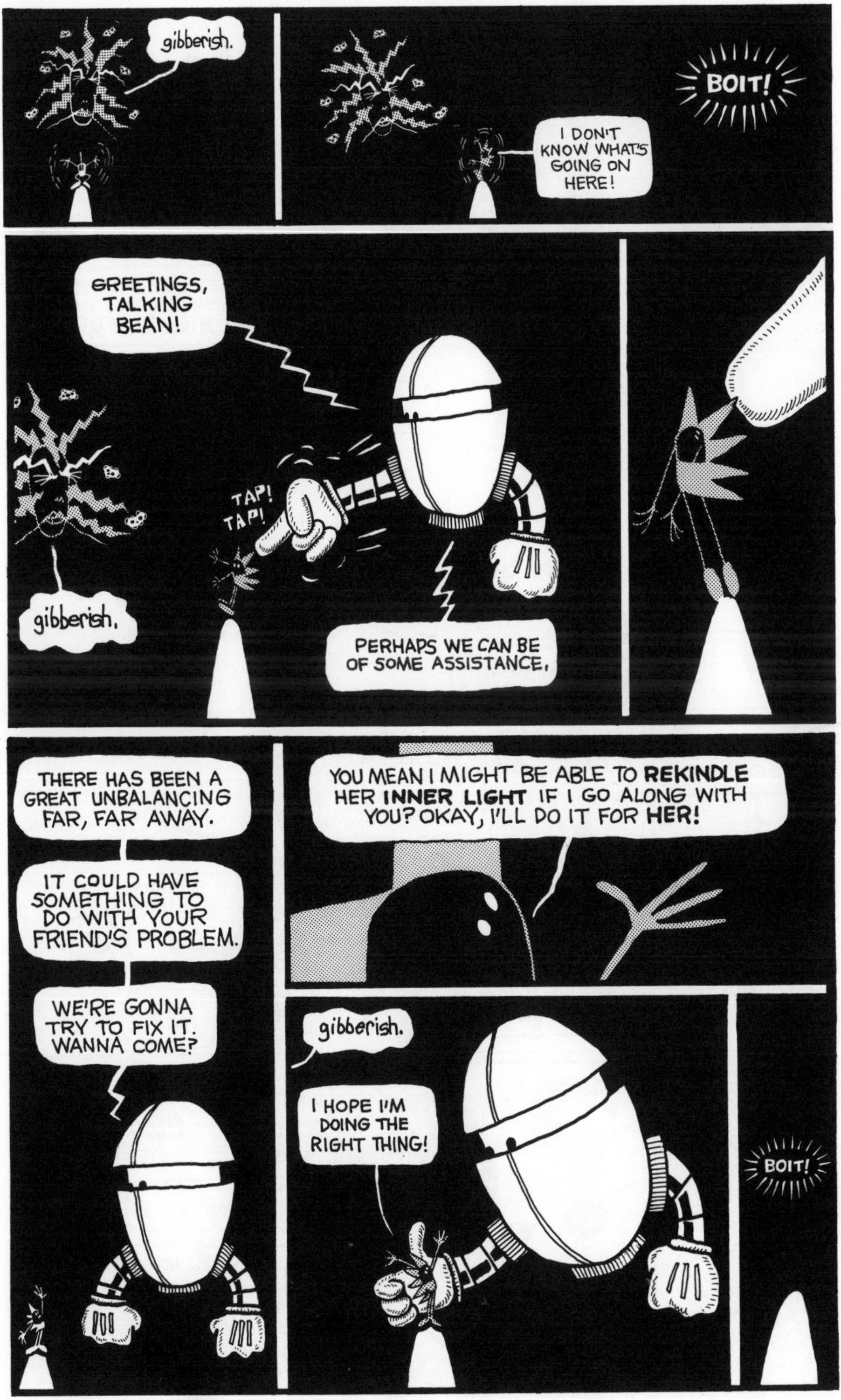
gibberish.
BOIT!
I DON'T KNOW WHAT'S GOING ON HERE!
GREETINGS, TALKING BEAN!
TAP! TAP!
gibberish.
PERHAPS WE CAN BE OF SOME ASSISTANCE.
THERE HAS BEEN A GREAT UNBALANCING FAR, FAR AWAY.
IT COULD HAVE SOMETHING TO DO WITH YOUR FRIEND'S PROBLEM.
WE'RE GONNA TRY TO FIX IT. WANNA COME?
YOU MEAN I MIGHT BE ABLE TO REKINDLE HER INNER LIGHT IF I GO ALONG WITH YOU? OKAY, I'LL DO IT FOR HER!
gibberish.
I HOPE I'M DOING THE RIGHT THING!
BOIT!

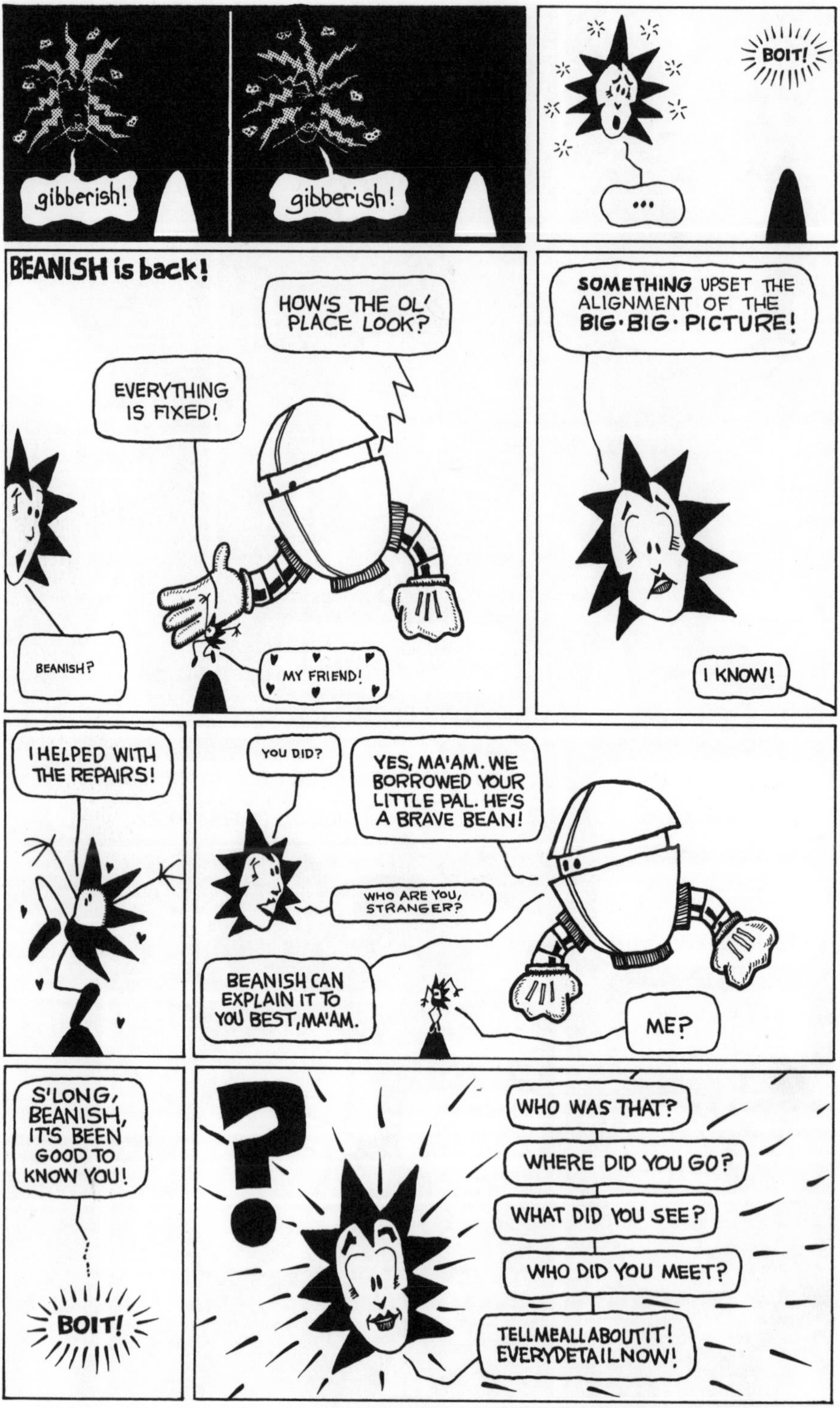
gibberish!
gibberish!
...
BOIT!
BEANISH is back!
HOW'S THE OL' PLACE LOOK?
EVERYTHING IS FIXED!
BEANISH?
MY FRIEND!
SOMETHING UPSET THE ALIGNMENT OF THE BIG·BIG·PICTURE!
I KNOW!
I HELPED WITH THE REPAIRS!
YOU DID?
YES, MA'AM. WE BORROWED YOUR LITTLE PAL. HE'S A BRAVE BEAN!
WHO ARE YOU, STRANGER?
BEANISH CAN EXPLAIN IT TO YOU BEST, MA'AM.
ME?
S'LONG, BEANISH, IT'S BEEN GOOD TO KNOW YOU!
BOIT!
?
WHO WAS THAT?
WHERE DID YOU GO?
WHAT DID YOU SEE?
WHO DID YOU MEET?
TELLMEALLABOUTIT! EVERYDETAILNOW!

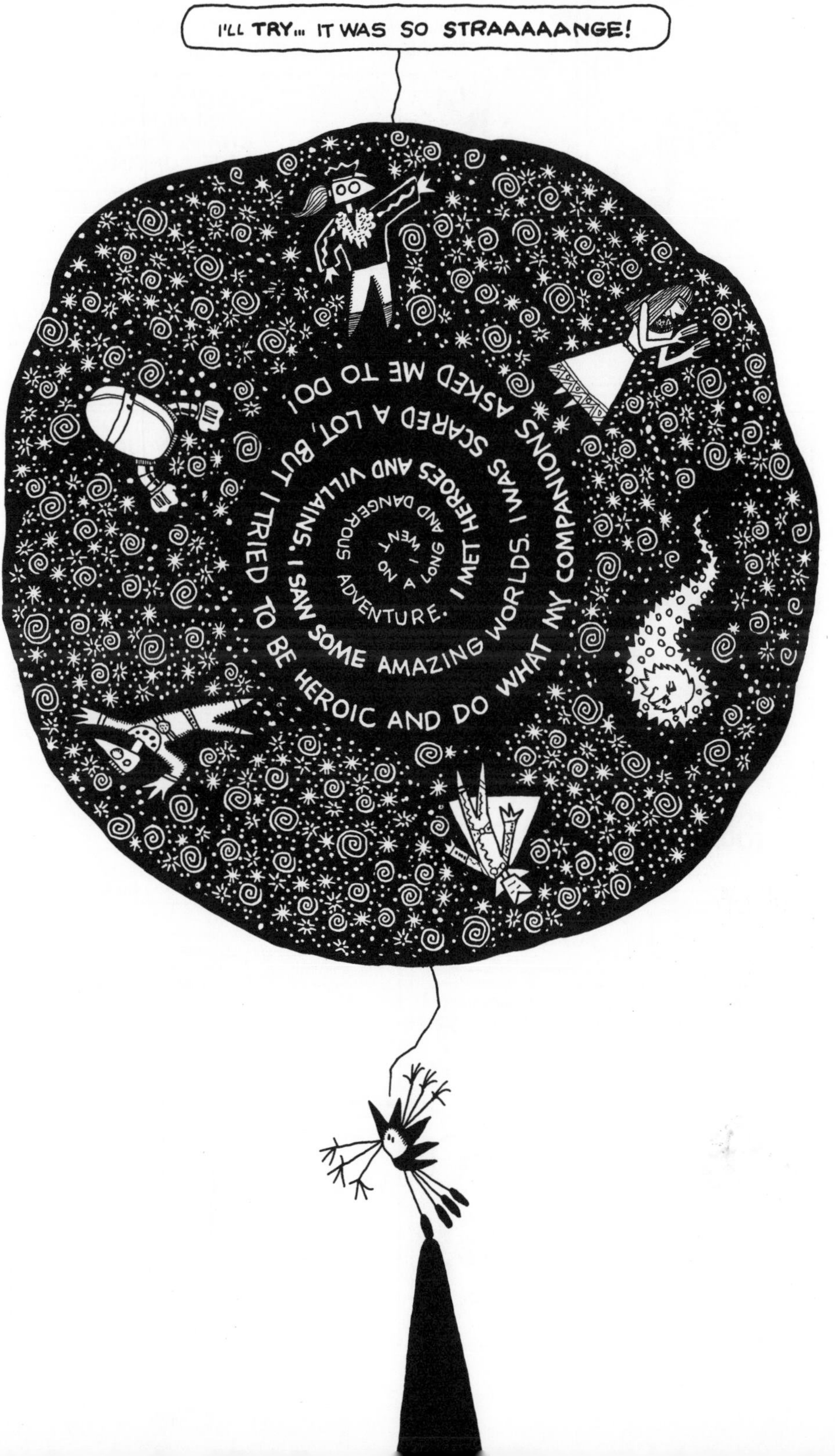
I'LL TRY... IT WAS SO STRAAAAAANGE!
I WENT ON A LONG AND DANGEROUS ADVENTURE. I MET HEROES AND VILLAINS. I SAW SOME AMAZING WORLDS. I WAS SCARED A LOT, BUT I TRIED TO BE HEROIC AND DO WHAT MY COMPANIONS ASKED ME TO DO!

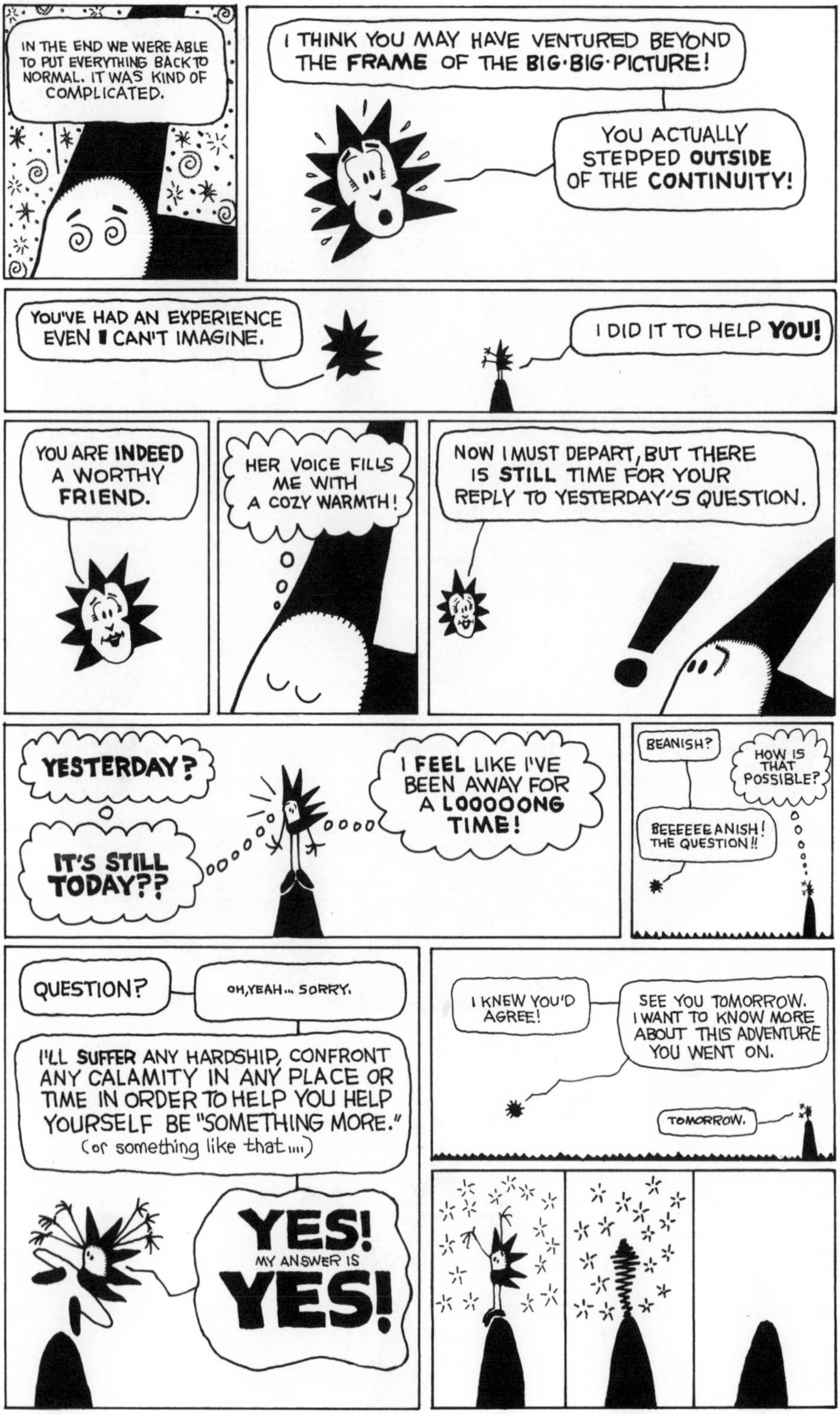
IN THE END WE WERE ABLE TO PUT EVERYTHING BACK TO NORMAL. IT WAS KIND OF COMPLICATED.
I THINK YOU MAY HAVE VENTURED BEYOND THE FRAME OF THE BIG·BIG·PICTURE!
YOU ACTUALLY STEPPED OUTSIDE OF THE CONTINUITY!
YOU'VE HAD AN EXPERIENCE EVEN I CAN'T IMAGINE.
I DID IT TO HELP YOU!
YOU ARE INDEED A WORTHY FRIEND.
HER VOICE FILLS ME WITH A COZY WARMTH!
NOW I MUST DEPART, BUT THERE IS STILL TIME FOR YOUR REPLY TO YESTERDAY'S QUESTION.
YESTERDAY?
IT'S STILL TODAY??
I FEEL LIKE I'VE BEEN AWAY FOR A LOOOOONG TIME!
BEANISH?
HOW IS THAT POSSIBLE?
BEEEEEEANISH! THE QUESTION!!
QUESTION?
OH, YEAH... SORRY.
I'LL SUFFER ANY HARDSHIP, CONFRONT ANY CALAMITY IN ANY PLACE OR TIME IN ORDER TO HELP YOU HELP YOURSELF BE "SOMETHING MORE." (or something like that....)
YES! MY ANSWER IS YES!
I KNEW YOU'D AGREE!
SEE YOU TOMORROW. I WANT TO KNOW MORE ABOUT THIS ADVENTURE YOU WENT ON.
TOMORROW.

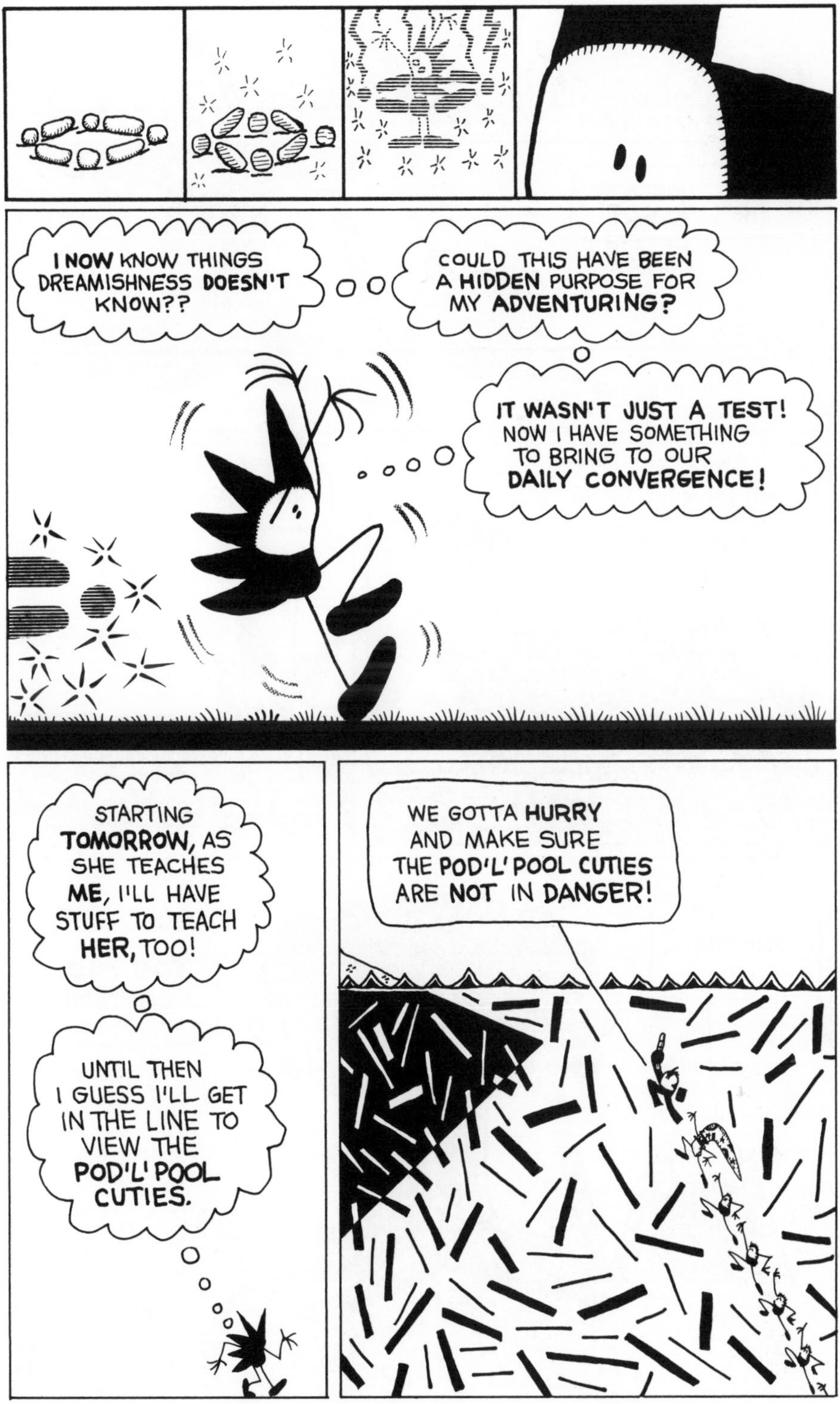
I NOW KNOW THINGS DREAMISHNESS DOESN'T KNOW??
COULD THIS HAVE BEEN A HIDDEN PURPOSE FOR MY ADVENTURING?
IT WASN'T JUST A TEST! NOW I HAVE SOMETHING TO BRING TO OUR DAILY CONVERGENCE!
STARTING TOMORROW, AS SHE TEACHES ME, I'LL HAVE STUFF TO TEACH HER, TOO!
UNTIL THEN I GUESS I'LL GET IN THE LINE TO VIEW THE POD'L'POOL CUTIES.
WE GOTTA HURRY AND MAKE SURE THE POD'L' POOL CUTIES ARE NOT IN DANGER!

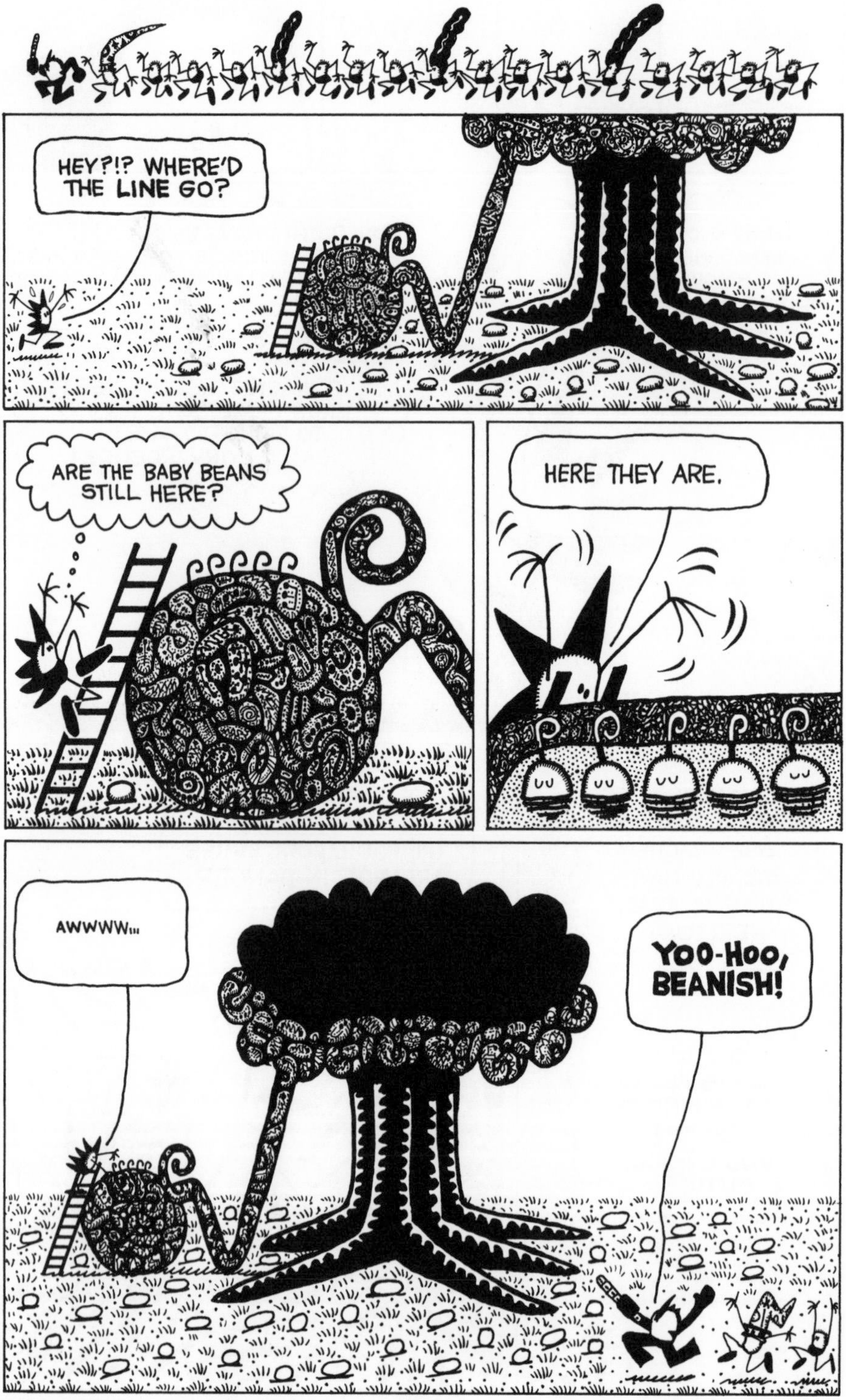
HEY?!? WHERE'D THE LINE GO?
ARE THE BABY BEANS STILL HERE?
HERE THEY ARE.
AWWWW...
YOO-HOO, BEANISH!

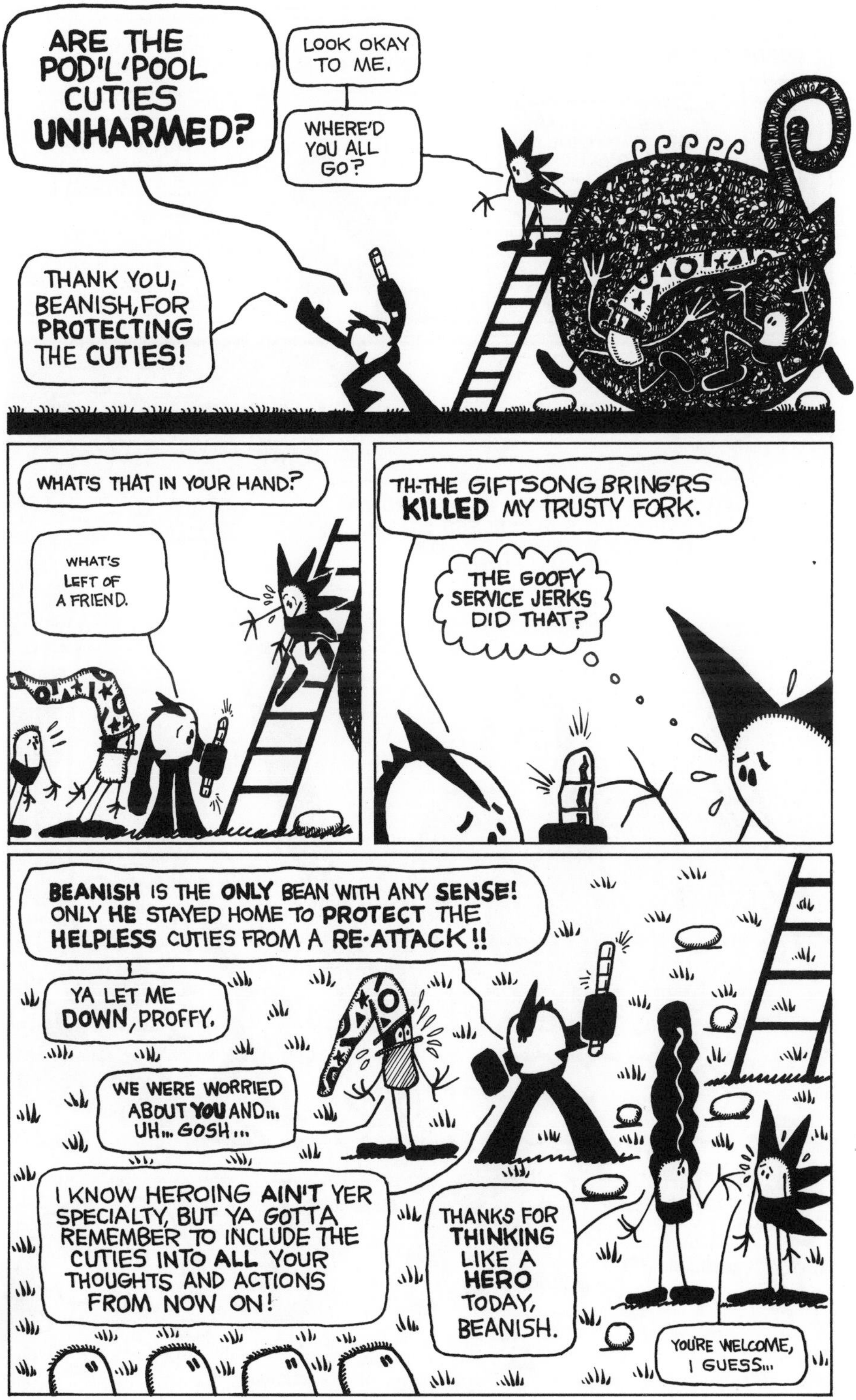

ARE THE POD'L'POOL CUTIES UNHARMED?
LOOK OKAY TO ME.
WHERE'D YOU ALL GO?
THANK YOU, BEANISH, FOR PROTECTING THE CUTIES!
WHAT'S THAT IN YOUR HAND?
WHAT'S LEFT OF A FRIEND.
TH-THE GIFTSONG BRING'RS KILLED MY TRUSTY FORK.
THE GOOFY SERVICE JERKS DID THAT?
BEANISH IS THE ONLY BEAN WITH ANY SENSE! ONLY HE STAYED HOME TO PROTECT THE HELPLESS CUTIES FROM A RE-ATTACK!!
YA LET ME DOWN, PROFFY.
WE WERE WORRIED ABOUT YOU AND... UH... GOSH...
I KNOW HEROING AIN'T YER SPECIALTY, BUT YA GOTTA REMEMBER TO INCLUDE THE CUTIES INTO ALL YOUR THOUGHTS AND ACTIONS FROM NOW ON!
THANKS FOR THINKING LIKE A HERO TODAY, BEANISH.
YOU'RE WELCOME, I GUESS...

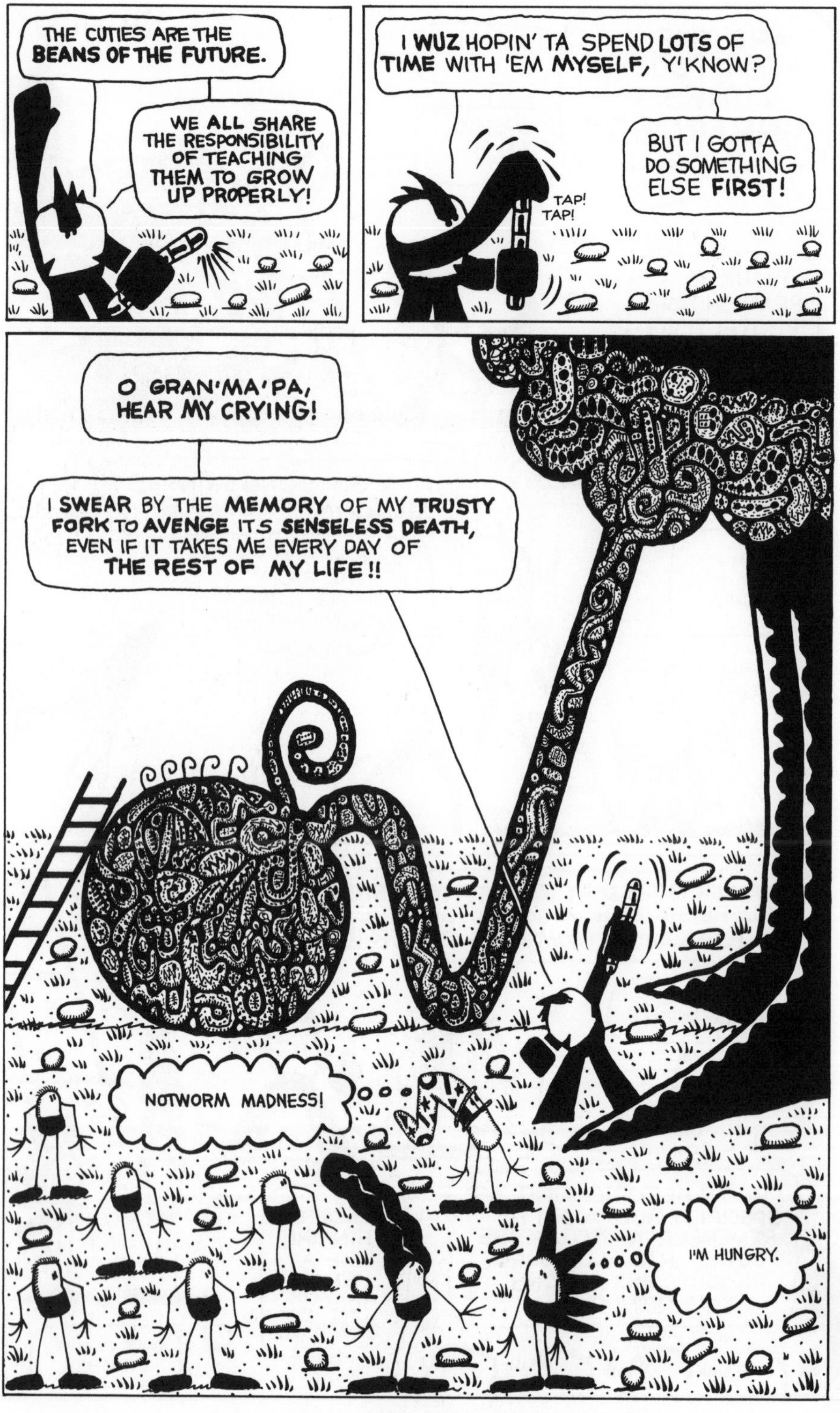
THE CUTIES ARE THE BEANS OF THE FUTURE.
WE ALL SHARE THE RESPONSIBILITY OF TEACHING THEM TO GROW UP PROPERLY!
I WUZ HOPIN' TA SPEND LOTS OF TIME WITH 'EM MYSELF, Y'KNOW?
BUT I GOTTA DO SOMETHING ELSE FIRST!
TAP! TAP!
O GRAN'MA'PA, HEAR MY CRYING!
I SWEAR BY THE MEMORY OF MY TRUSTY FORK TO AVENGE ITS SENSELESS DEATH, EVEN IF IT TAKES ME EVERY DAY OF THE REST OF MY LIFE!!
NOTWORM MADNESS!
I'M HUNGRY.

Something Growing. Something Slowing.

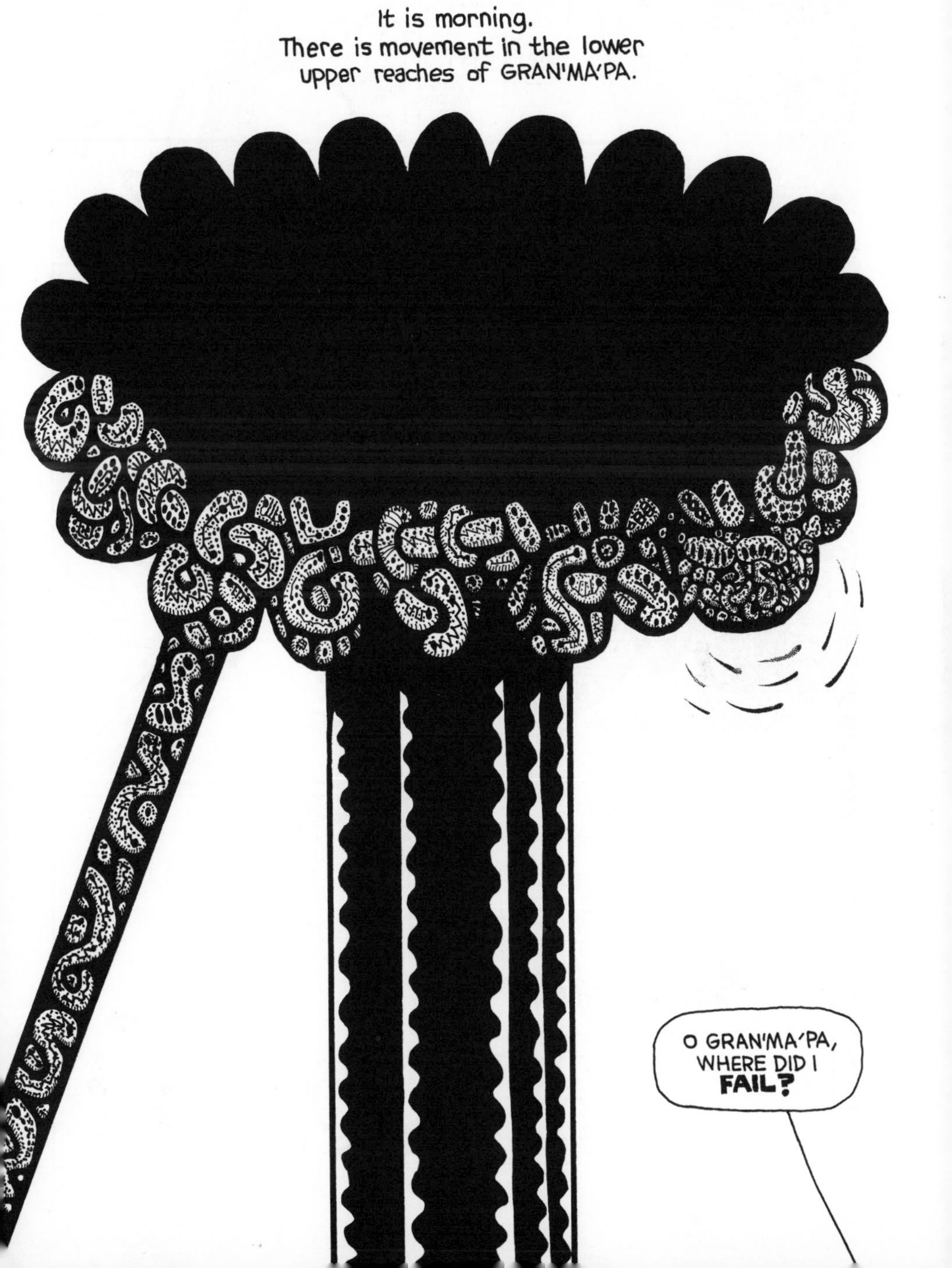
It is morning.
There is movement in the lower upper reaches of GRAN'MA'PA.
O GRAN'MA'PA, WHERE DID I **FAIL?**

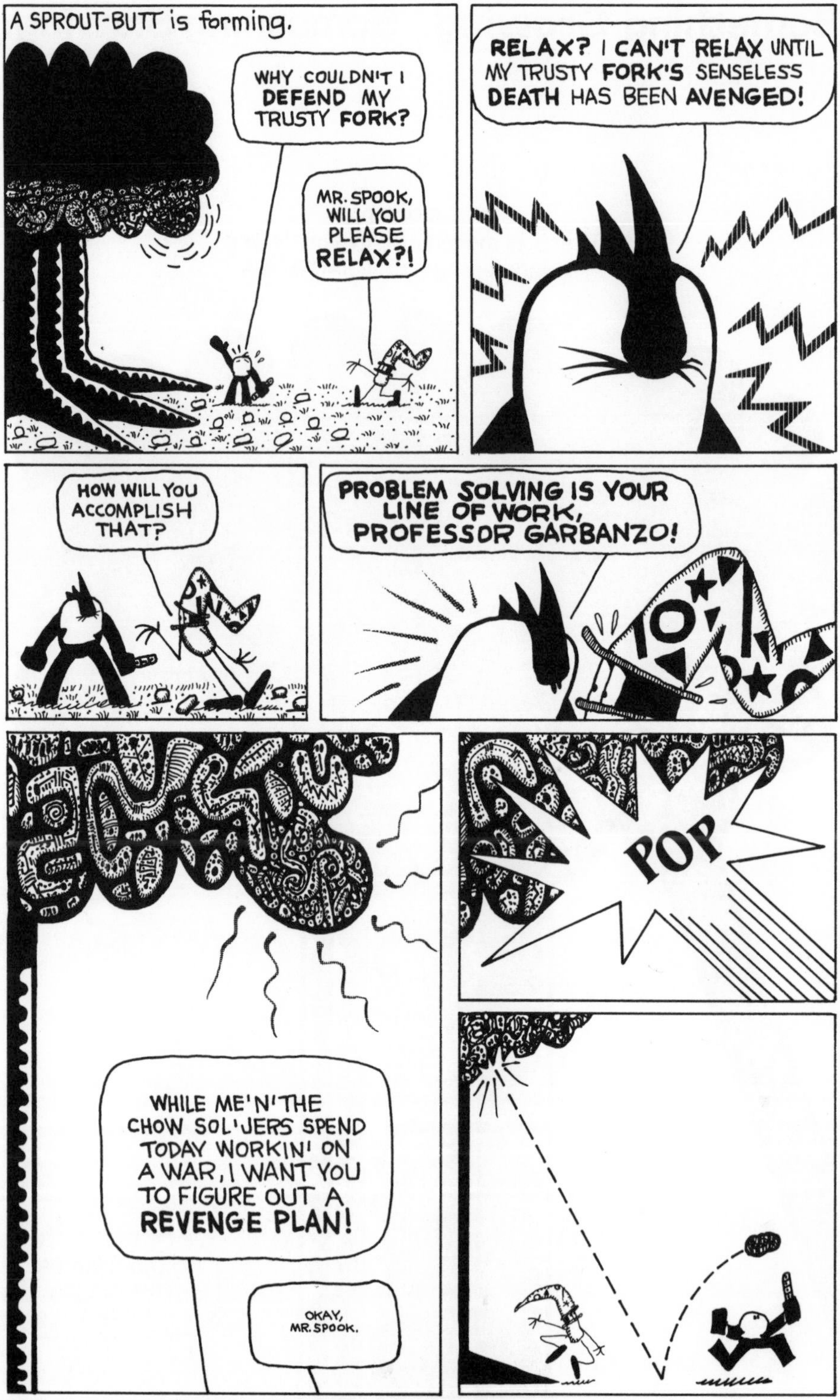
A SPROUT-BUTT is forming.
WHY COULDN'T I DEFEND MY TRUSTY FORK?
MR. SPOOK, WILL YOU PLEASE RELAX?!
RELAX? I CAN'T RELAX UNTIL MY TRUSTY FORK'S SENSELESS DEATH HAS BEEN AVENGED!
HOW WILL YOU ACCOMPLISH THAT?
PROBLEM SOLVING IS YOUR LINE OF WORK, PROFESSOR GARBANZO!
POP
WHILE ME'N'THE CHOW SOL'JERS SPEND TODAY WORKIN' ON A WAR, I WANT YOU TO FIGURE OUT A REVENGE PLAN!
OKAY, MR. SPOOK.

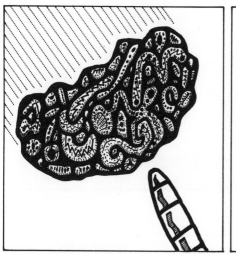

QUIT STANDIN' AROUND! LET'S GET JUMPIN'!

It's time for a CHOWRAID!

HURRY UP!

The CHOW SOL'JER ARMY assembles.

The SOL'JERS march! The SPROUT-BUTT sings! The BOOM'R BAND jams along!

MR. SPOOK leads them on their mission to steal CHOW.

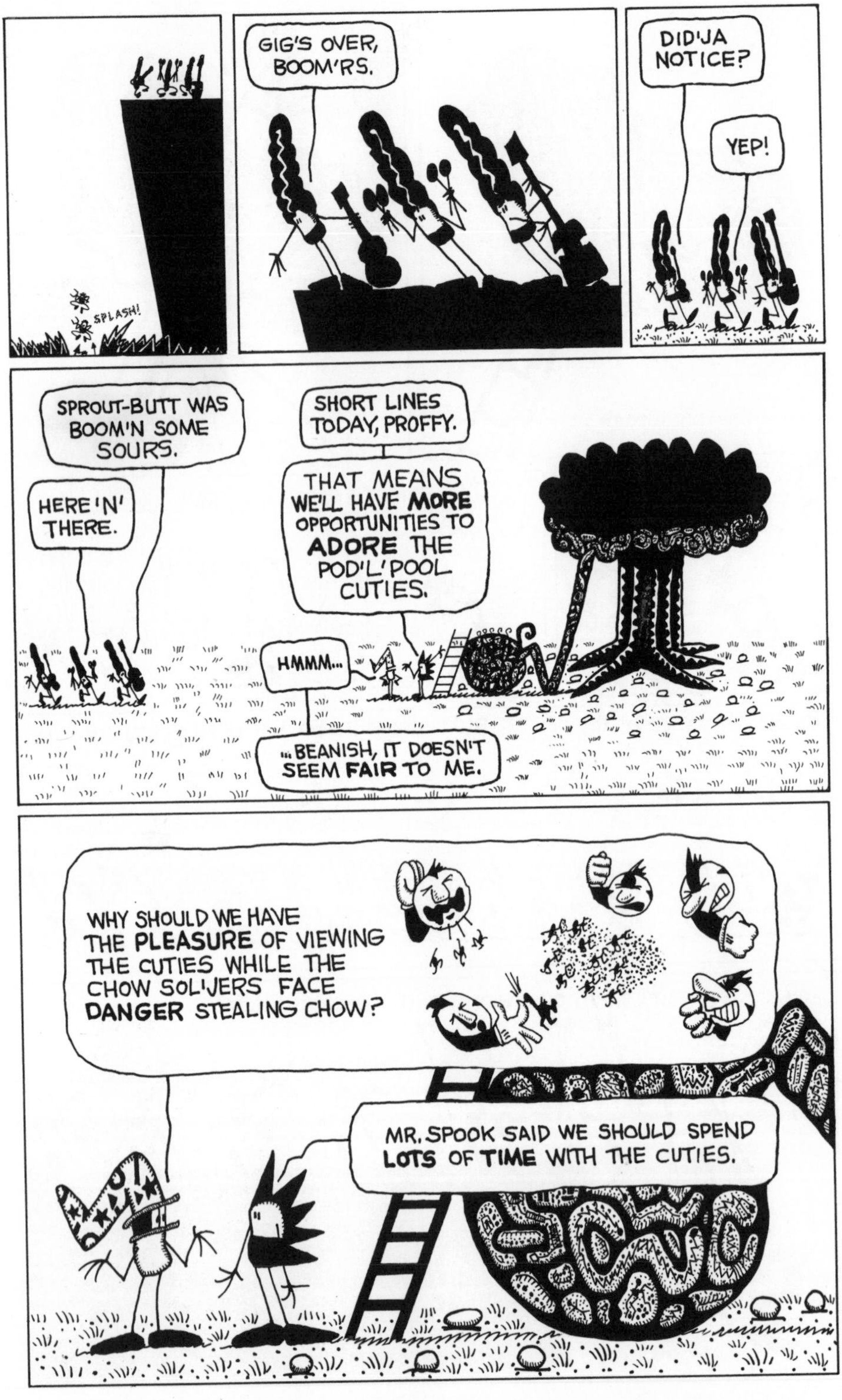
SPLASH!
GIG'S OVER, BOOM'RS.
DID'JA NOTICE?
YEP!
SPROUT-BUTT WAS BOOM'N SOME SOURS.
HERE 'N' THERE.
SHORT LINES TODAY, PROFFY.
THAT MEANS WE'LL HAVE MORE OPPORTUNITIES TO ADORE THE POD'L'POOL CUTIES.
HMMM...
...BEANISH, IT DOESN'T SEEM FAIR TO ME.
WHY SHOULD WE HAVE THE PLEASURE OF VIEWING THE CUTIES WHILE THE CHOW SOL'JERS FACE DANGER STEALING CHOW?
MR. SPOOK SAID WE SHOULD SPEND LOTS OF TIME WITH THE CUTIES.

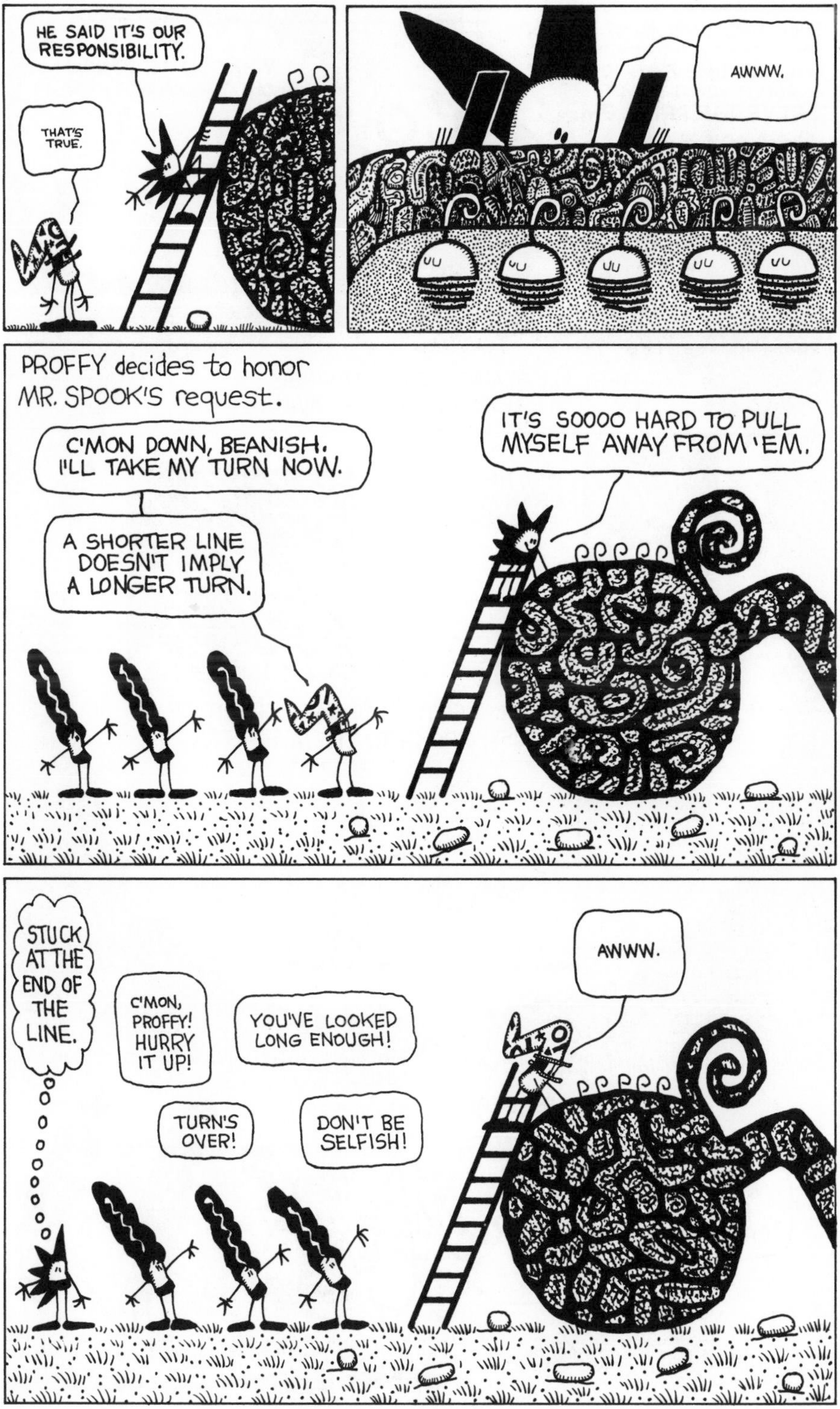
HE SAID IT'S OUR RESPONSIBILITY.
THAT'S TRUE.
AWWW.
PROFFY decides to honor MR. SPOOK'S request.
C'MON DOWN, BEANISH. I'LL TAKE MY TURN NOW.
A SHORTER LINE DOESN'T IMPLY A LONGER TURN.
IT'S SOOOO HARD TO PULL MYSELF AWAY FROM 'EM.
STUCK AT THE END OF THE LINE.
C'MON, PROFFY! HURRY IT UP!
YOU'VE LOOKED LONG ENOUGH!
TURN'S OVER!
DON'T BE SELFISH!
AWWW.

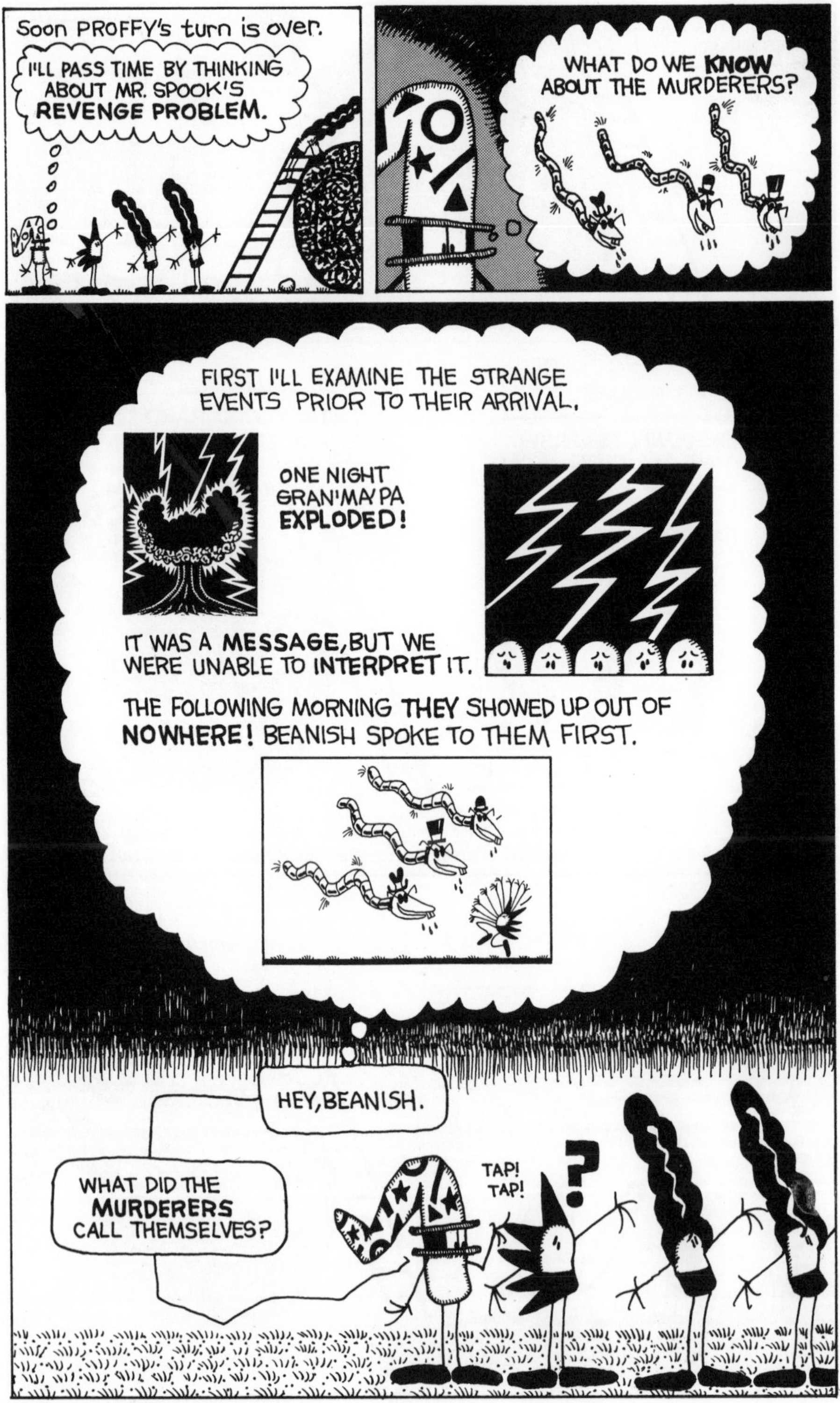
Soon PROFFY's turn is over.
I'LL PASS TIME BY THINKING ABOUT MR. SPOOK'S REVENGE PROBLEM.
WHAT DO WE KNOW ABOUT THE MURDERERS?
FIRST I'LL EXAMINE THE STRANGE EVENTS PRIOR TO THEIR ARRIVAL.
ONE NIGHT GRAN'MA'PA EXPLODED!
IT WAS A MESSAGE, BUT WE WERE UNABLE TO INTERPRET IT.
THE FOLLOWING MORNING THEY SHOWED UP OUT OF NOWHERE! BEANISH SPOKE TO THEM FIRST.
HEY, BEANISH.
WHAT DID THE MURDERERS CALL THEMSELVES?
TAP! TAP!
?

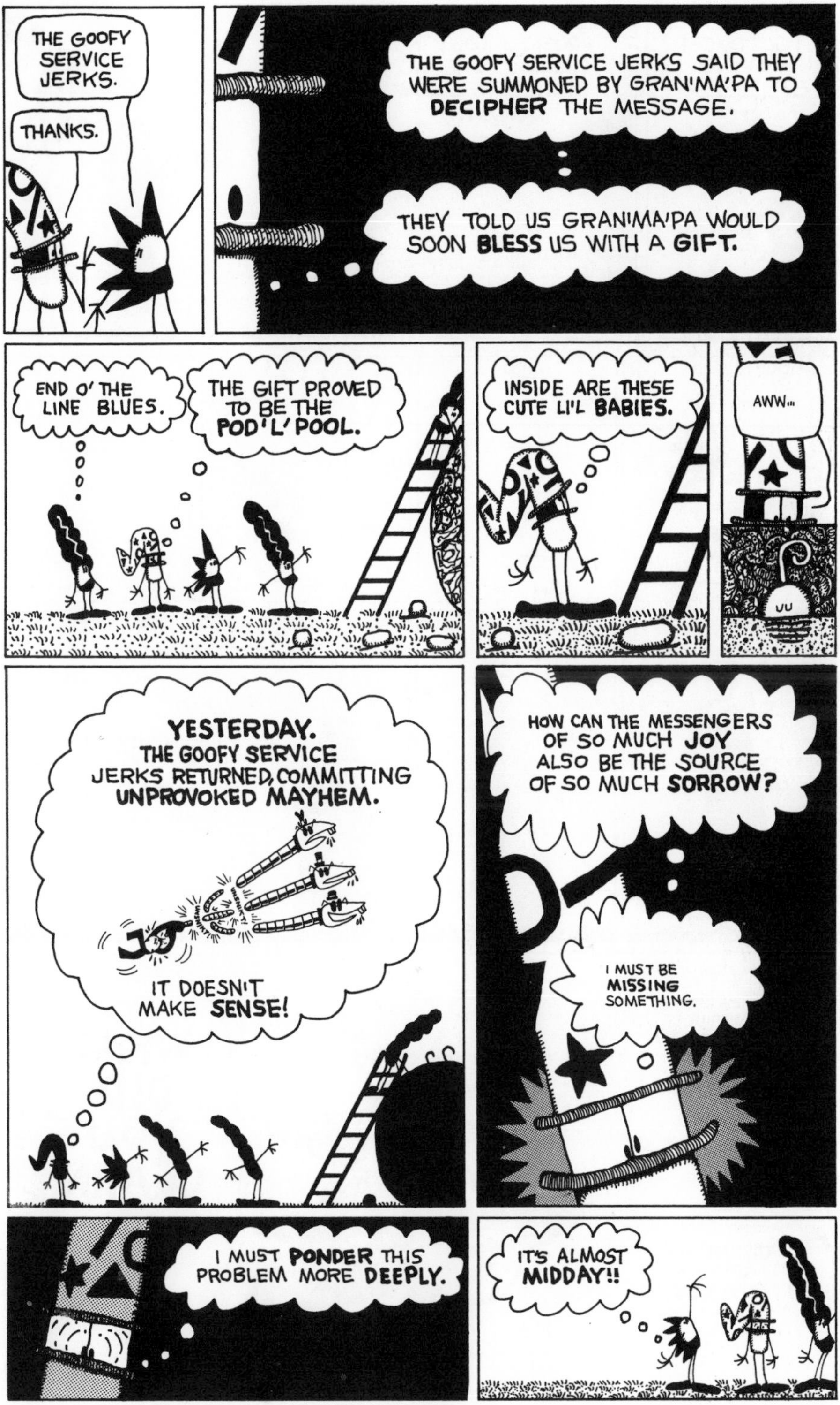
THE GOOFY SERVICE JERKS.
THANKS.
THE GOOFY SERVICE JERKS SAID THEY WERE SUMMONED BY GRAN'MA'PA TO DECIPHER THE MESSAGE.
THEY TOLD US GRAN'MA'PA WOULD SOON BLESS US WITH A GIFT.
END O' THE LINE BLUES.
THE GIFT PROVED TO BE THE POD'L'POOL.
INSIDE ARE THESE CUTE LI'L BABIES.
AWW...
YESTERDAY. THE GOOFY SERVICE JERKS RETURNED, COMMITTING UNPROVOKED MAYHEM.
IT DOESN'T MAKE SENSE!
HOW CAN THE MESSENGERS OF SO MUCH JOY ALSO BE THE SOURCE OF SO MUCH SORROW?
I MUST BE MISSING SOMETHING.
I MUST PONDER THIS PROBLEM MORE DEEPLY.
IT'S ALMOST MIDDAY!!

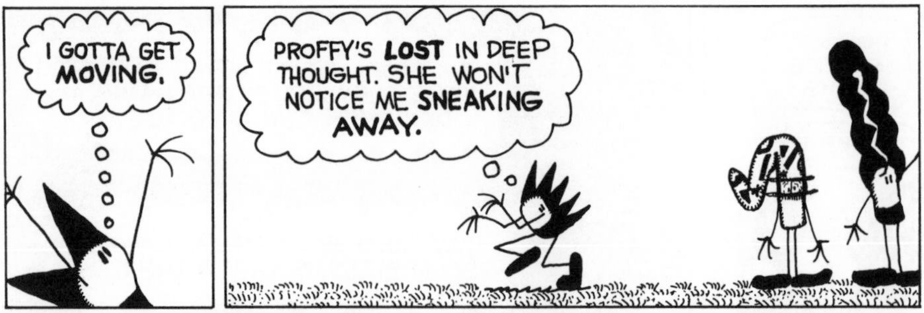
I GOTTA GET MOVING.
PROFFY'S LOST IN DEEP THOUGHT. SHE WON'T NOTICE ME SNEAKING AWAY.

Every day, at midday, **BEANISH** stands inside the "secret sketch" and travels to an unknown territory where he meets a secret friend.

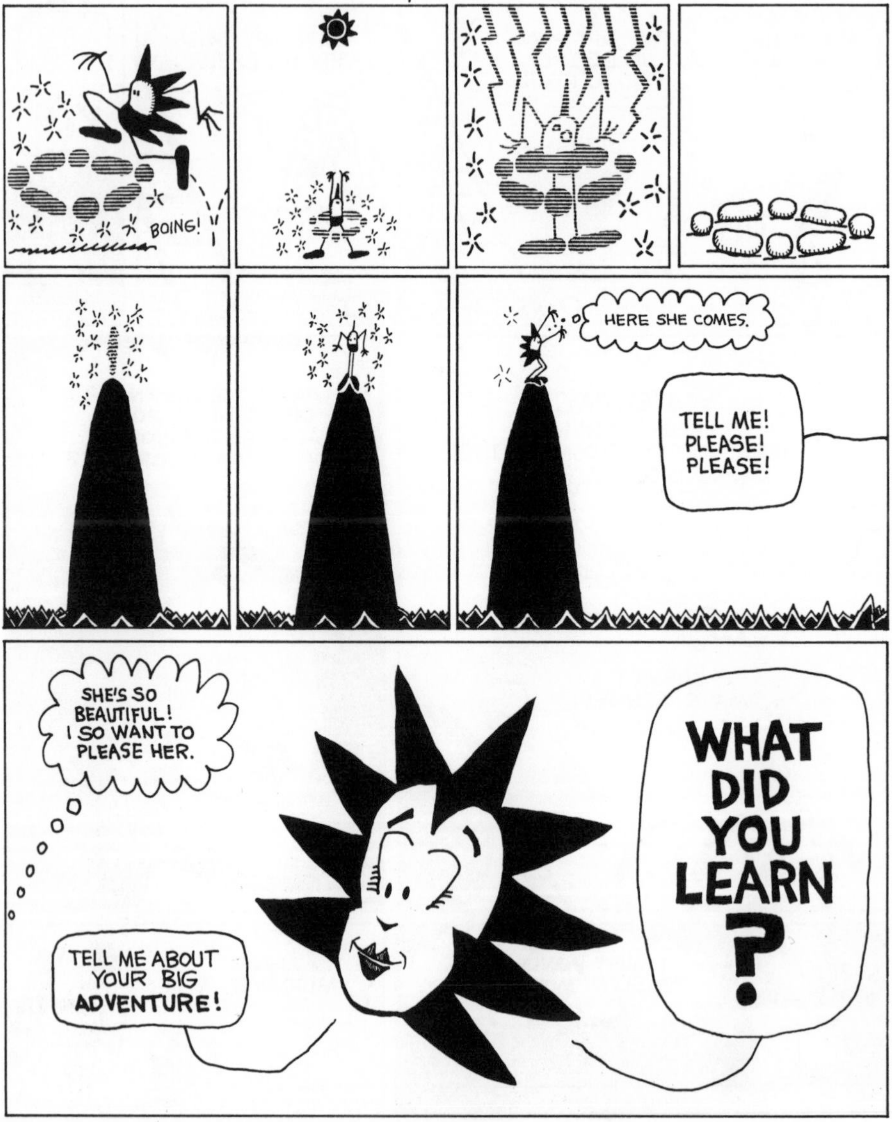
BOING!
HERE SHE COMES.
TELL ME! PLEASE! PLEASE!
SHE'S SO BEAUTIFUL! I SO WANT TO PLEASE HER.
TELL ME ABOUT YOUR BIG ADVENTURE!
WHAT DID YOU LEARN?

LEARN?

I DUNNO.

DON'T BE **SILLY!**

OF **COURSE** YOU DO!

THINK!

HOW CAN I THINK WHEN I'M BEING DAZZLED BY YOUR APPROACHING ILLUMINATION?

YOU'RE **SUPPOSED** TO HAVE LEARNED **SOMETHING!**

She's not coming or going.

CAN'T YOU THINK OF ANYTHING?

She's just **HERE!**

NOW!

NO.

GOTTA GO!

TRY TO THINK OF A LESSON BY TOMORROW.

The moment passes quickly; the heat cools rapidly.

He hurts when she leaves.

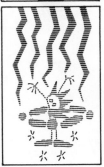

MAYBE I DIDN'T LEARN ANYTHING!

Meanwhile--- The CHOW SOL'JERS have smashed a HOI-POLLOI RING and plundered its wealth.

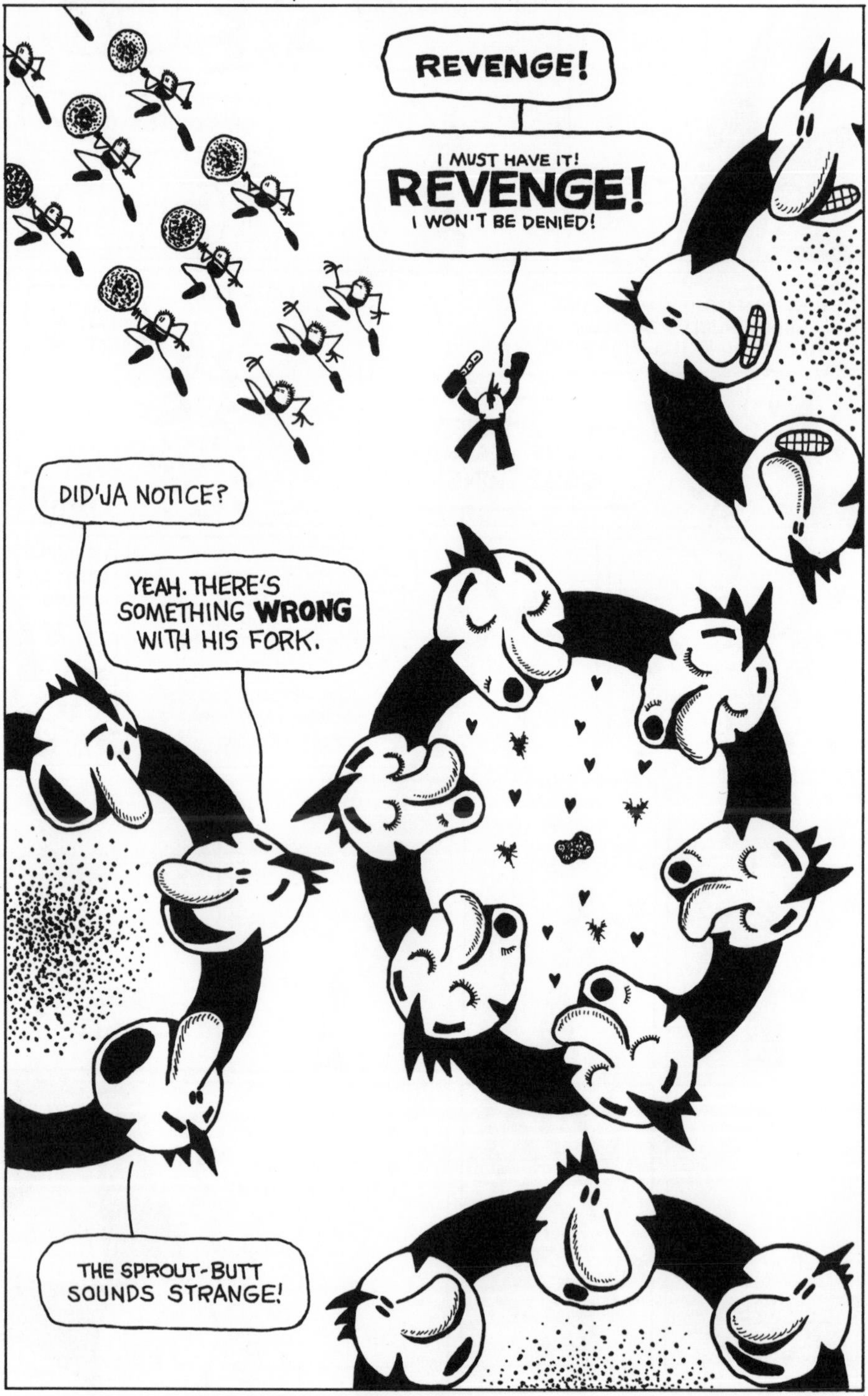
REVENGE!
I MUST HAVE IT! REVENGE! I WON'T BE DENIED!
DID'JA NOTICE?
YEAH. THERE'S SOMETHING **WRONG** WITH HIS FORK.
THE SPROUT-BUTT SOUNDS STRANGE!

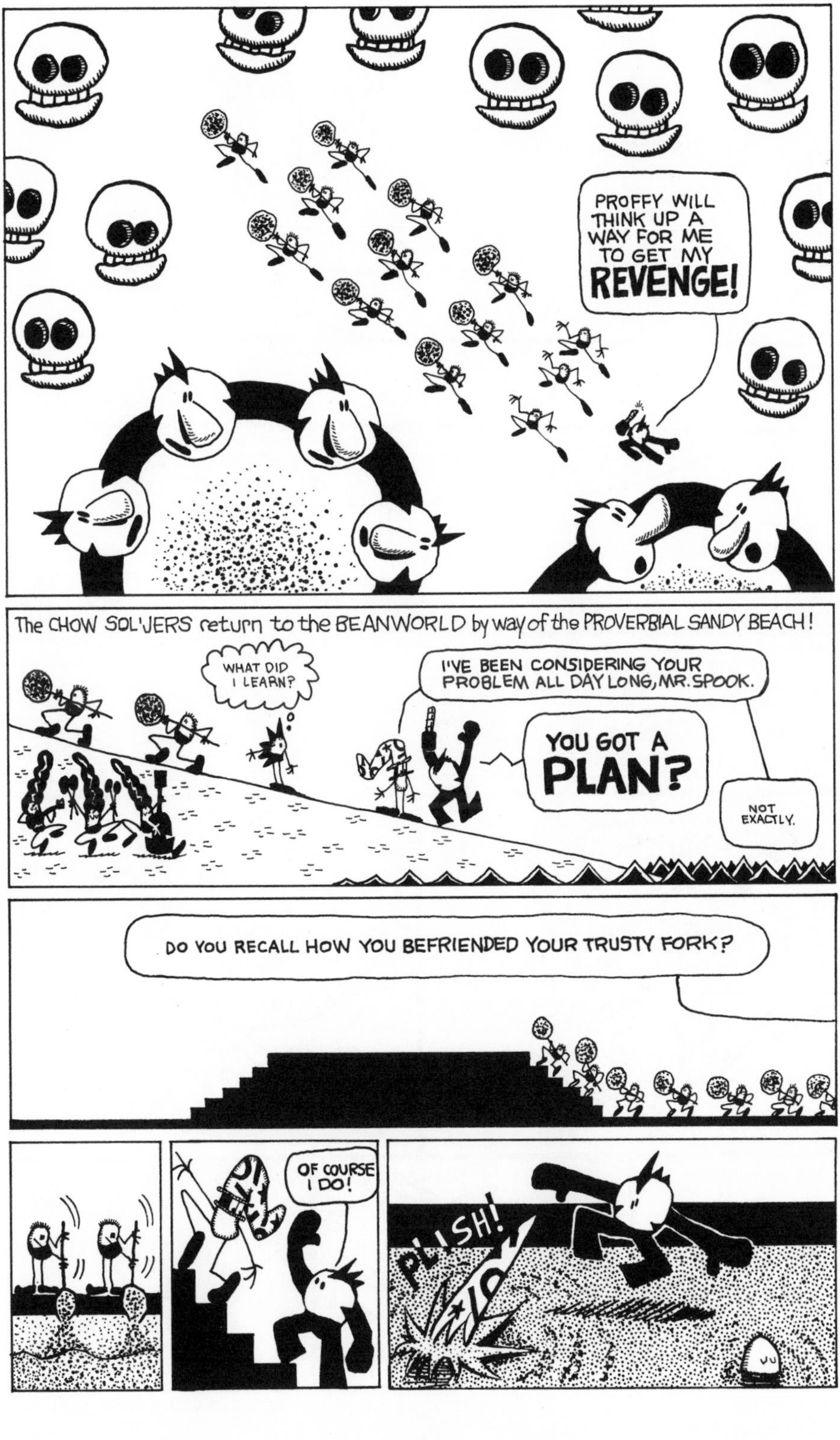
PROFFY WILL THINK UP A WAY FOR ME TO GET MY REVENGE!
The CHOW SOL'JERS return to the BEANWORLD by way of the PROVERBIAL SANDY BEACH!
WHAT DID I LEARN?
I'VE BEEN CONSIDERING YOUR PROBLEM ALL DAY LONG, MR. SPOOK.
YOU GOT A PLAN?
NOT EXACTLY.
DO YOU RECALL HOW YOU BEFRIENDED YOUR TRUSTY FORK?
OF COURSE I DO!
PLISH!

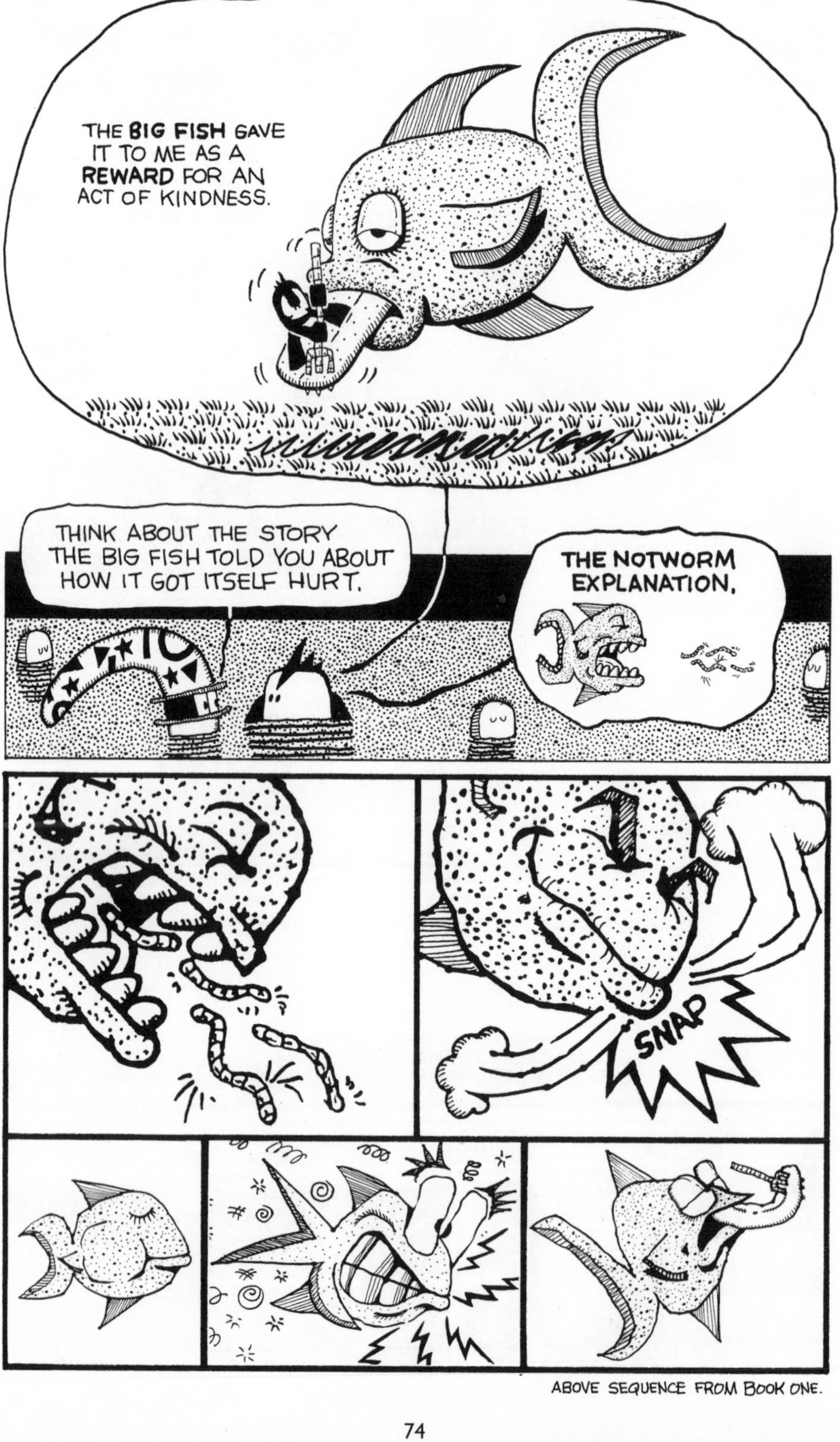
THE **BIG FISH** GAVE IT TO ME AS A **REWARD** FOR AN ACT OF KINDNESS.
THINK ABOUT THE STORY THE BIG FISH TOLD YOU ABOUT HOW IT GOT ITSELF HURT.
THE NOTWORM EXPLANATION.
SNAP

ABOVE SEQUENCE FROM BOOK ONE.

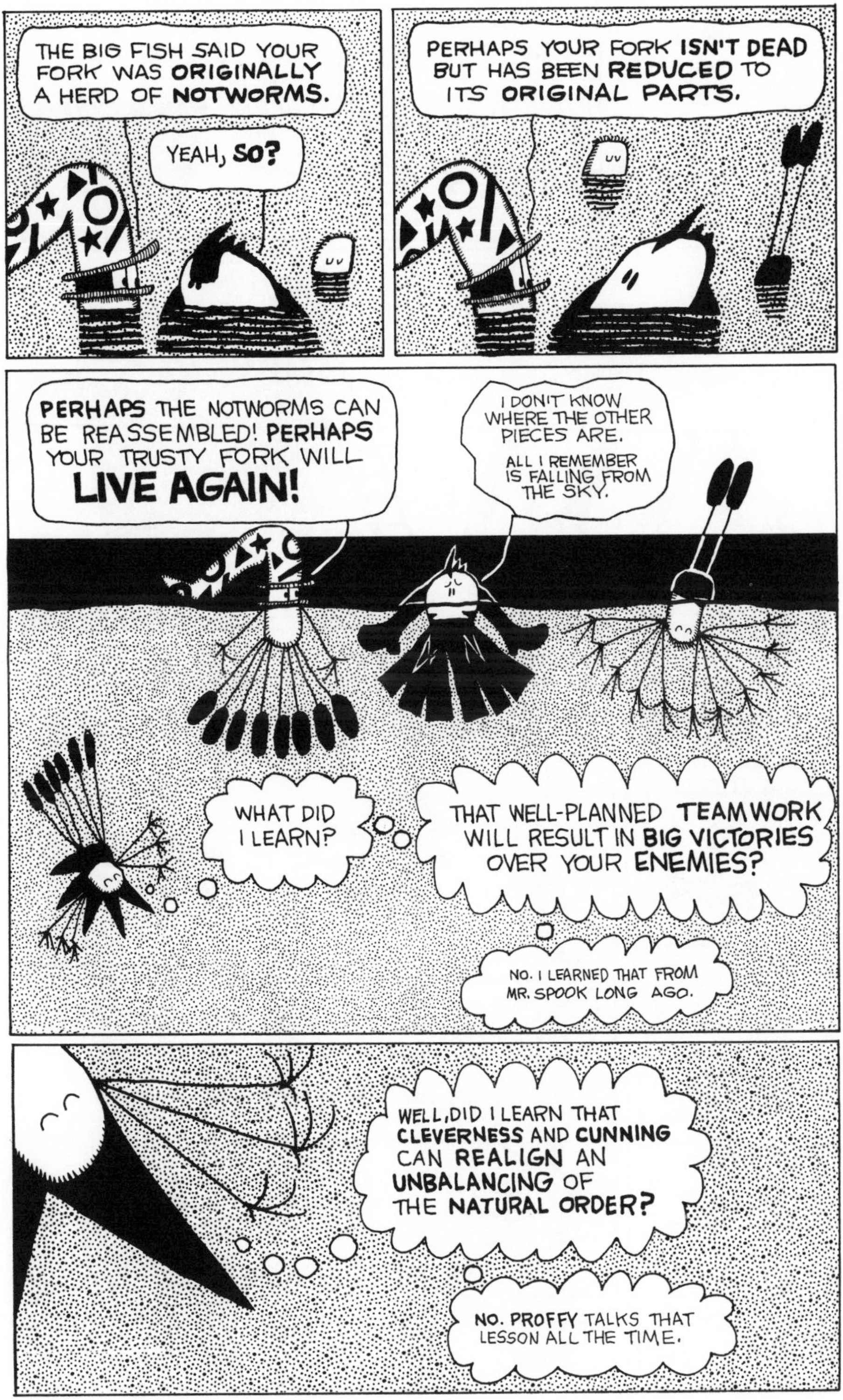
THE BIG FISH SAID YOUR FORK WAS ORIGINALLY A HERD OF NOTWORMS.
YEAH, SO?
PERHAPS YOUR FORK ISN'T DEAD BUT HAS BEEN REDUCED TO ITS ORIGINAL PARTS.
PERHAPS THE NOTWORMS CAN BE REASSEMBLED! PERHAPS YOUR TRUSTY FORK WILL LIVE AGAIN!
I DON'T KNOW WHERE THE OTHER PIECES ARE.
ALL I REMEMBER IS FALLING FROM THE SKY.
WHAT DID I LEARN?
THAT WELL-PLANNED TEAMWORK WILL RESULT IN BIG VICTORIES OVER YOUR ENEMIES?
NO. I LEARNED THAT FROM MR. SPOOK LONG AGO.
WELL, DID I LEARN THAT CLEVERNESS AND CUNNING CAN REALIGN AN UNBALANCING OF THE NATURAL ORDER?
NO. PROFFY TALKS THAT LESSON ALL THE TIME.

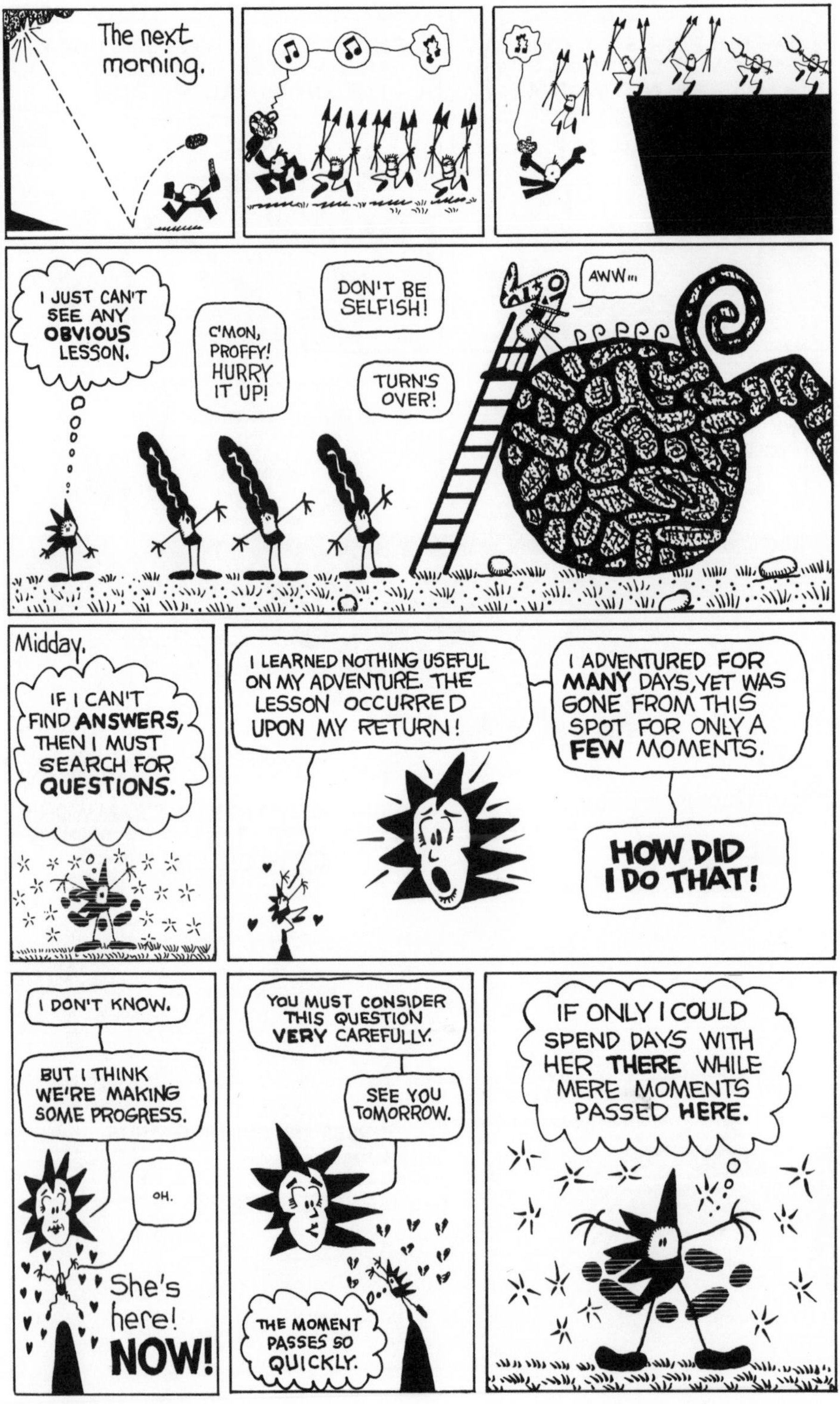
The next morning.
I JUST CAN'T SEE ANY OBVIOUS LESSON.
C'MON, PROFFY! HURRY IT UP!
DON'T BE SELFISH!
TURN'S OVER!
AWW...
Midday.
IF I CAN'T FIND ANSWERS, THEN I MUST SEARCH FOR QUESTIONS.
I LEARNED NOTHING USEFUL ON MY ADVENTURE. THE LESSON OCCURRED UPON MY RETURN!
I ADVENTURED FOR MANY DAYS, YET WAS GONE FROM THIS SPOT FOR ONLY A FEW MOMENTS.
HOW DID I DO THAT!
I DON'T KNOW.
BUT I THINK WE'RE MAKING SOME PROGRESS.
OH.
She's here! NOW!
YOU MUST CONSIDER THIS QUESTION VERY CAREFULLY.
SEE YOU TOMORROW.
THE MOMENT PASSES SO QUICKLY.
IF ONLY I COULD SPEND DAYS WITH HER THERE WHILE MERE MOMENTS PASSED HERE.

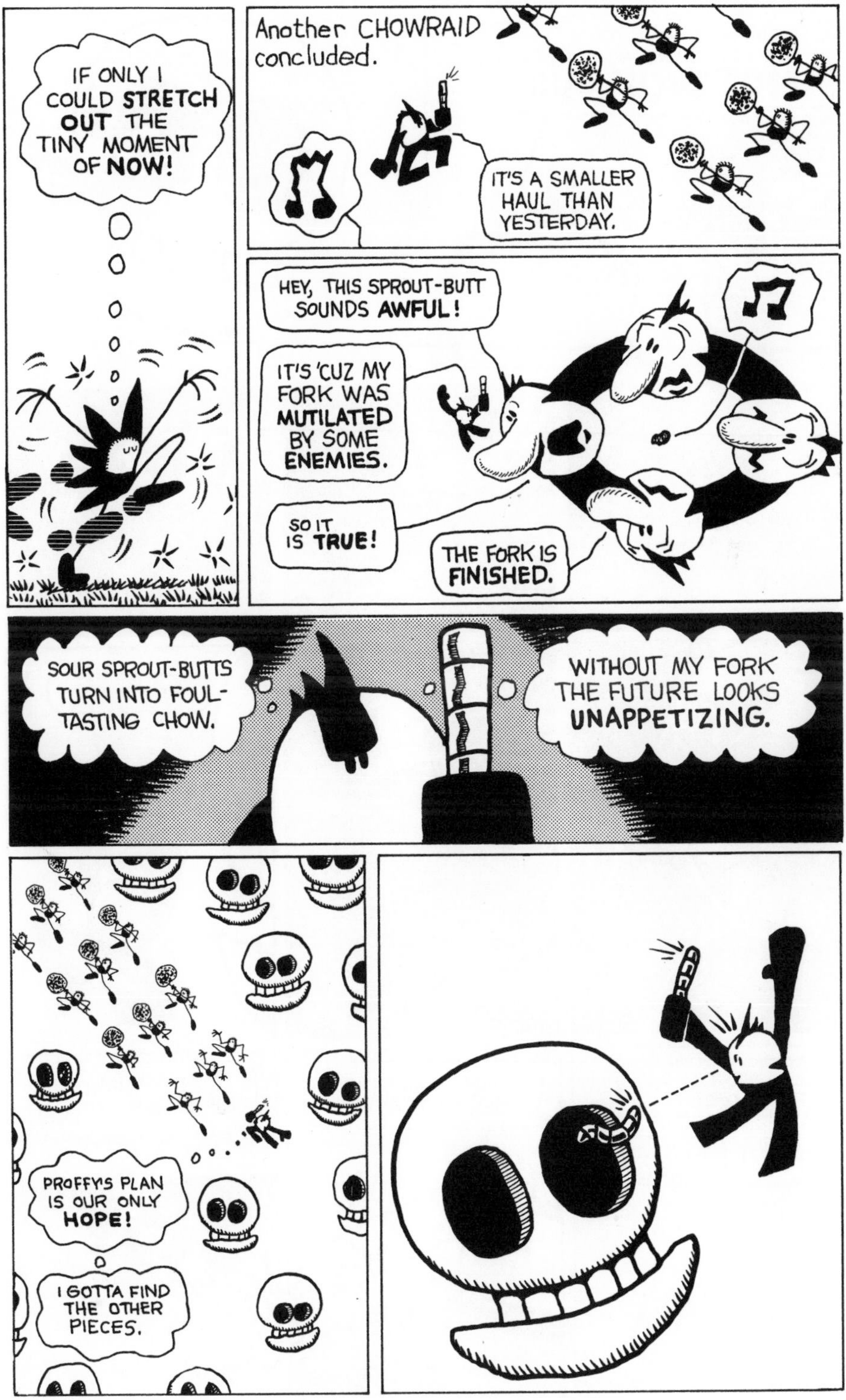
IF ONLY I COULD STRETCH OUT THE TINY MOMENT OF NOW!
Another CHOWRAID concluded.
IT'S A SMALLER HAUL THAN YESTERDAY.
HEY, THIS SPROUT-BUTT SOUNDS AWFUL!
IT'S 'CUZ MY FORK WAS MUTILATED BY SOME ENEMIES.
SO IT IS TRUE!
THE FORK IS FINISHED.
SOUR SPROUT-BUTTS TURN INTO FOUL-TASTING CHOW.
WITHOUT MY FORK THE FUTURE LOOKS UNAPPETIZING.
PROFFY'S PLAN IS OUR ONLY HOPE!
I GOTTA FIND THE OTHER PIECES.

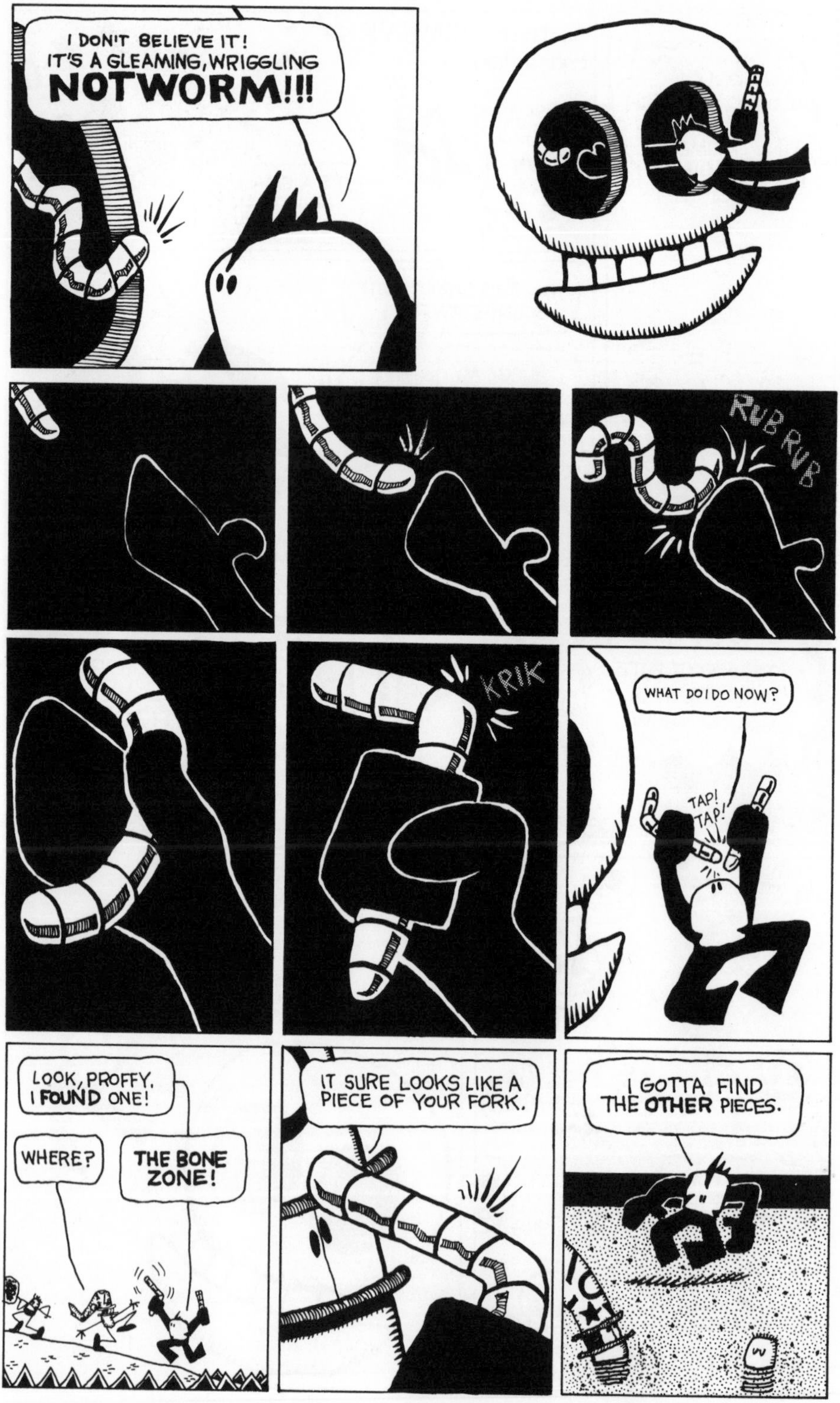
I DON'T BELIEVE IT! IT'S A GLEAMING, WRIGGLING NOTWORM!!!
RUB RUB
KRIK
WHAT DO I DO NOW?
TAP! TAP!
LOOK, PROFFY. I FOUND ONE!
WHERE?
THE BONE ZONE!
IT SURE LOOKS LIKE A PIECE OF YOUR FORK.
I GOTTA FIND THE OTHER PIECES.

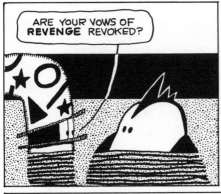

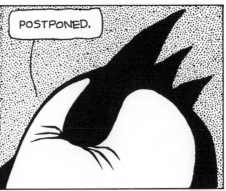

ARE YOUR VOWS OF REVENGE REVOKED?
POSTPONED.
The next morning. It's a GOOF-OFF DAY. The CHOW SOL'JERS line up to view.
TODAY MY FORKQUEST BEGINS.
WE'VE HAD MORE THAN OUR SHARE OF VIEWING TIME LATELY. WE'LL BE GLAD TO HELP YOU SEARCH.
The search party departs. The adoration continues.

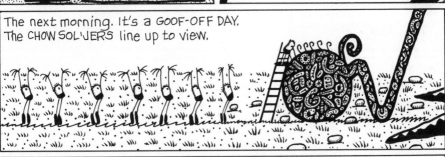

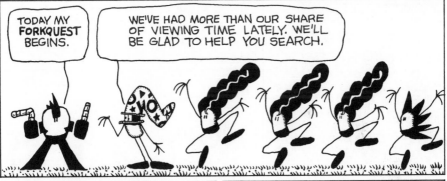

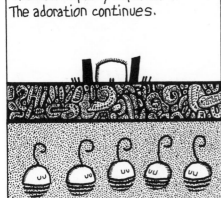

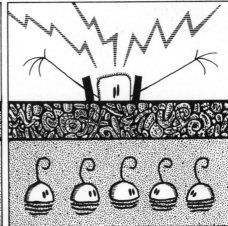

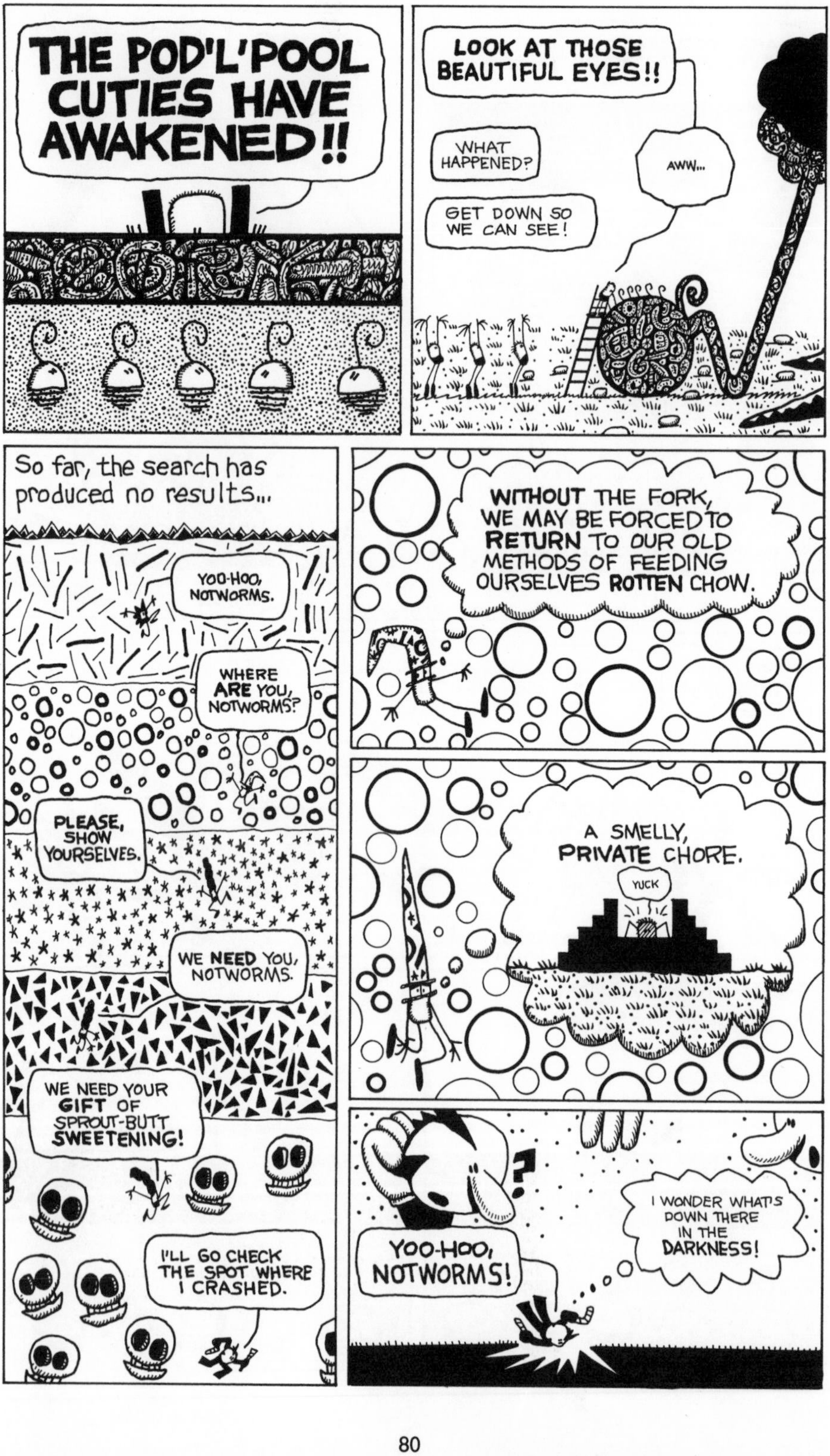
THE POD'L'POOL CUTIES HAVE AWAKENED!!
LOOK AT THOSE BEAUTIFUL EYES!!
WHAT HAPPENED?
AWW...
GET DOWN SO WE CAN SEE!
So far, the search has produced no results...
YOO-HOO, NOTWORMS.
WHERE ARE YOU, NOTWORMS?
PLEASE, SHOW YOURSELVES.
WE NEED YOU, NOTWORMS.
WE NEED YOUR GIFT OF SPROUT-BUTT SWEETENING!
I'LL GO CHECK THE SPOT WHERE I CRASHED.
WITHOUT THE FORK, WE MAY BE FORCED TO RETURN TO OUR OLD METHODS OF FEEDING OURSELVES ROTTEN CHOW.
A SMELLY, PRIVATE CHORE.
YUCK
?
YOO-HOO, NOTWORMS!
I WONDER WHAT'S DOWN THERE IN THE DARKNESS!

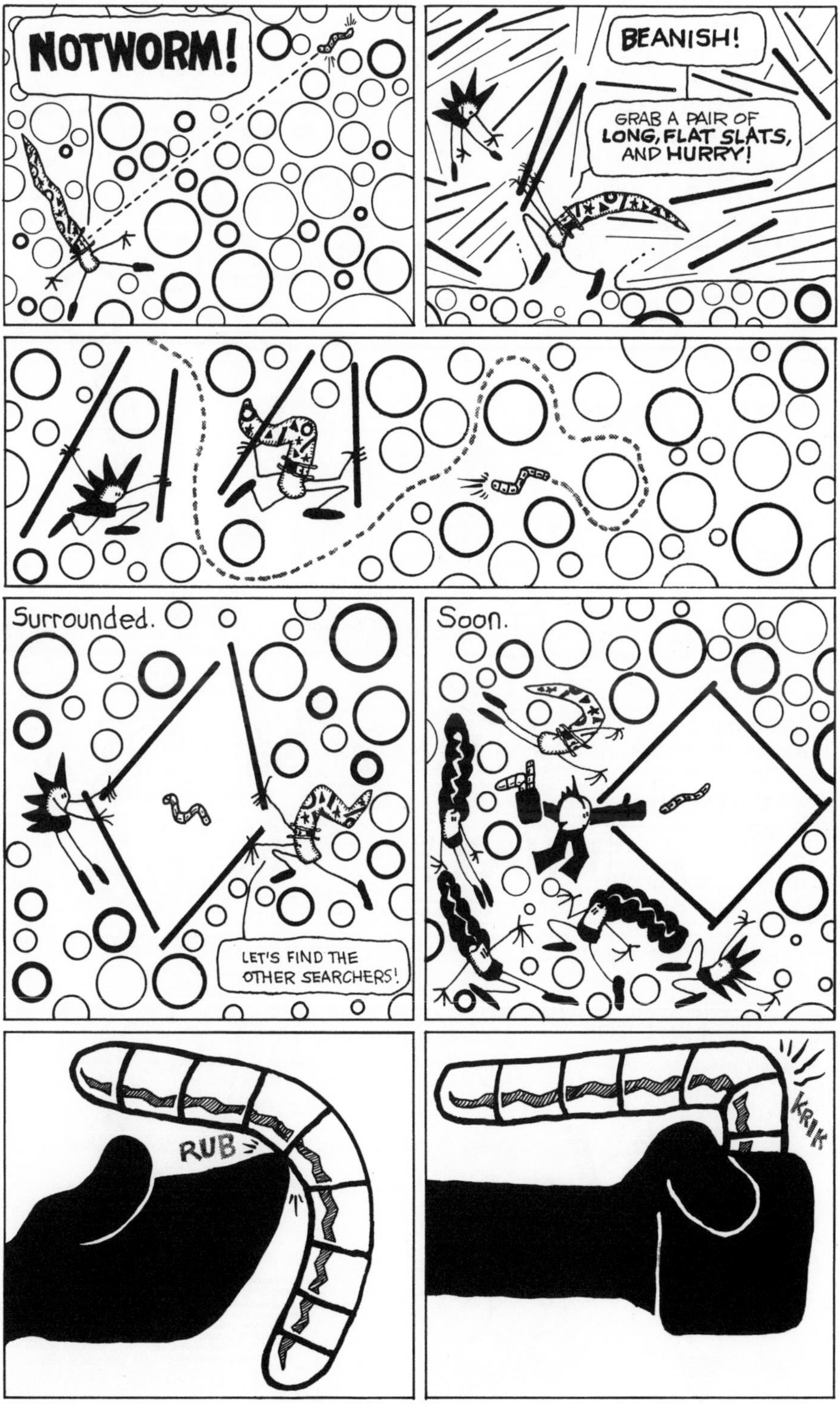
NOTWORM!
BEANISH!
GRAB A PAIR OF LONG, FLAT SLATS, AND HURRY!
Surrounded.
LET'S FIND THE OTHER SEARCHERS!
Soon.
RUB
KRIK

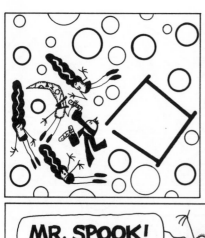

LET'S GO HOME AND **REASON** TOGETHER,

MR. SPOOK!

SOMETHING HAS HAPPENED TO THE POD'L' POOL CUTIES!!

WHAT?

THEY'RE MORE **CHARMING** THAN EVER!!

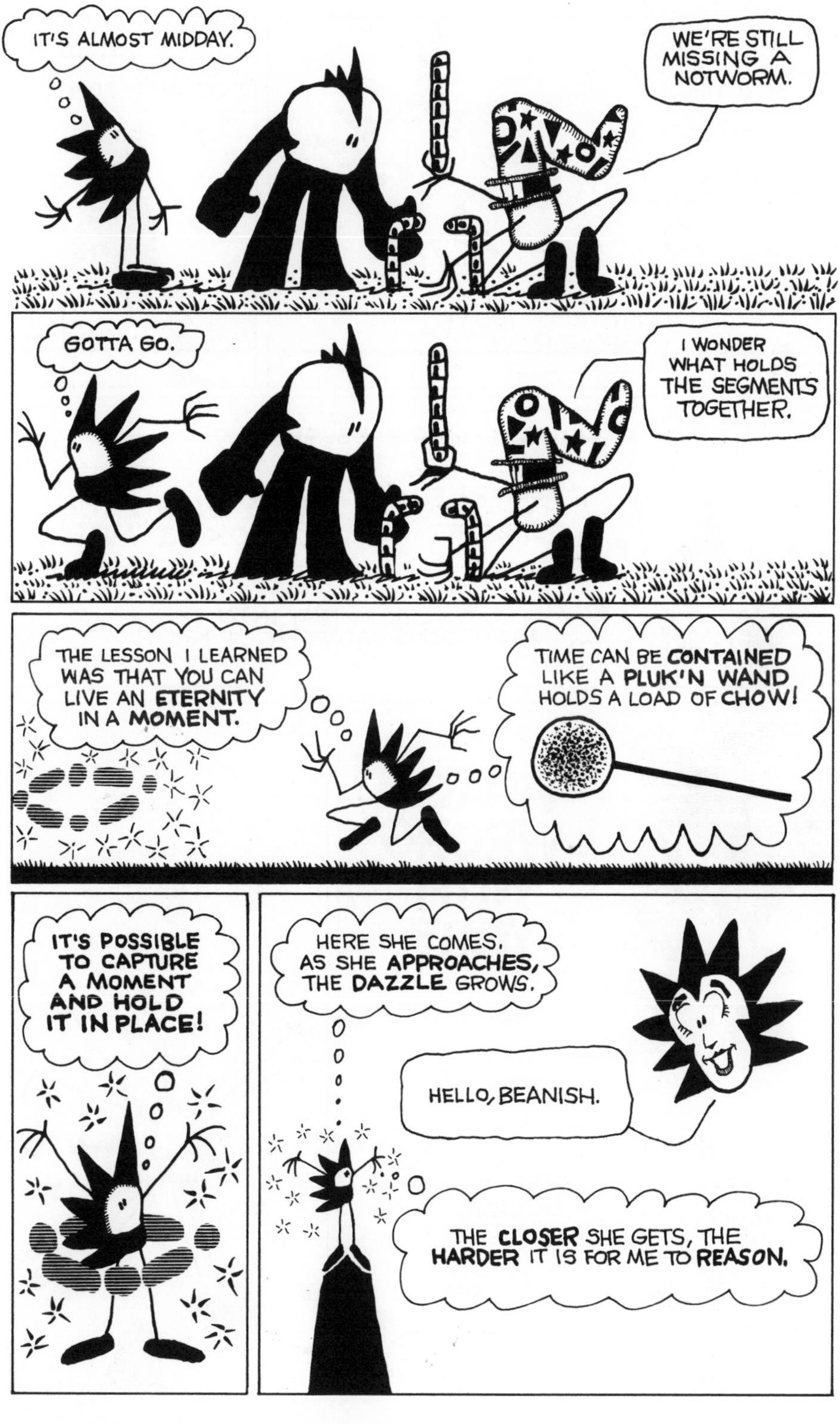
IT'S ALMOST MIDDAY.
WE'RE STILL MISSING A NOTWORM.
GOTTA GO.
I WONDER WHAT HOLDS THE SEGMENTS TOGETHER.
THE LESSON I LEARNED WAS THAT YOU CAN LIVE AN ETERNITY IN A MOMENT.
TIME CAN BE CONTAINED LIKE A PLUK'N WAND HOLDS A LOAD OF CHOW!
IT'S POSSIBLE TO CAPTURE A MOMENT AND HOLD IT IN PLACE!
HERE SHE COMES. AS SHE APPROACHES, THE DAZZLE GROWS.
HELLO, BEANISH.
THE CLOSER SHE GETS, THE HARDER IT IS FOR ME TO REASON.

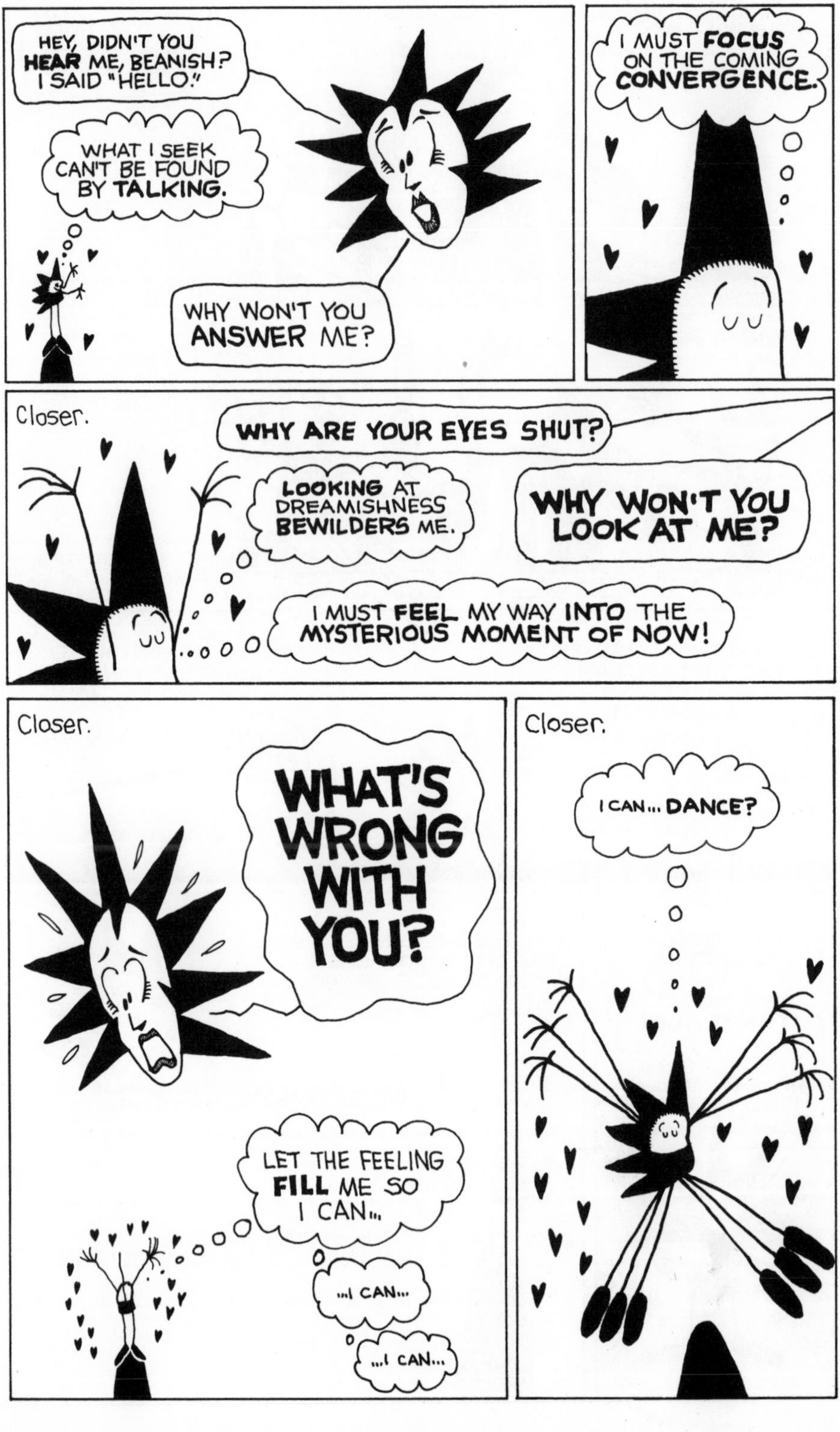
HEY, DIDN'T YOU HEAR ME, BEANISH? I SAID "HELLO."
WHAT I SEEK CAN'T BE FOUND BY TALKING.
WHY WON'T YOU ANSWER ME?
I MUST FOCUS ON THE COMING CONVERGENCE.
Closer.
WHY ARE YOUR EYES SHUT?
LOOKING AT DREAMISHNESS BEWILDERS ME.
WHY WON'T YOU LOOK AT ME?
I MUST FEEL MY WAY INTO THE MYSTERIOUS MOMENT OF NOW!
Closer.
WHAT'S WRONG WITH YOU?
LET THE FEELING FILL ME SO I CAN...
...I CAN...
...I CAN...
Closer.
I CAN... DANCE?

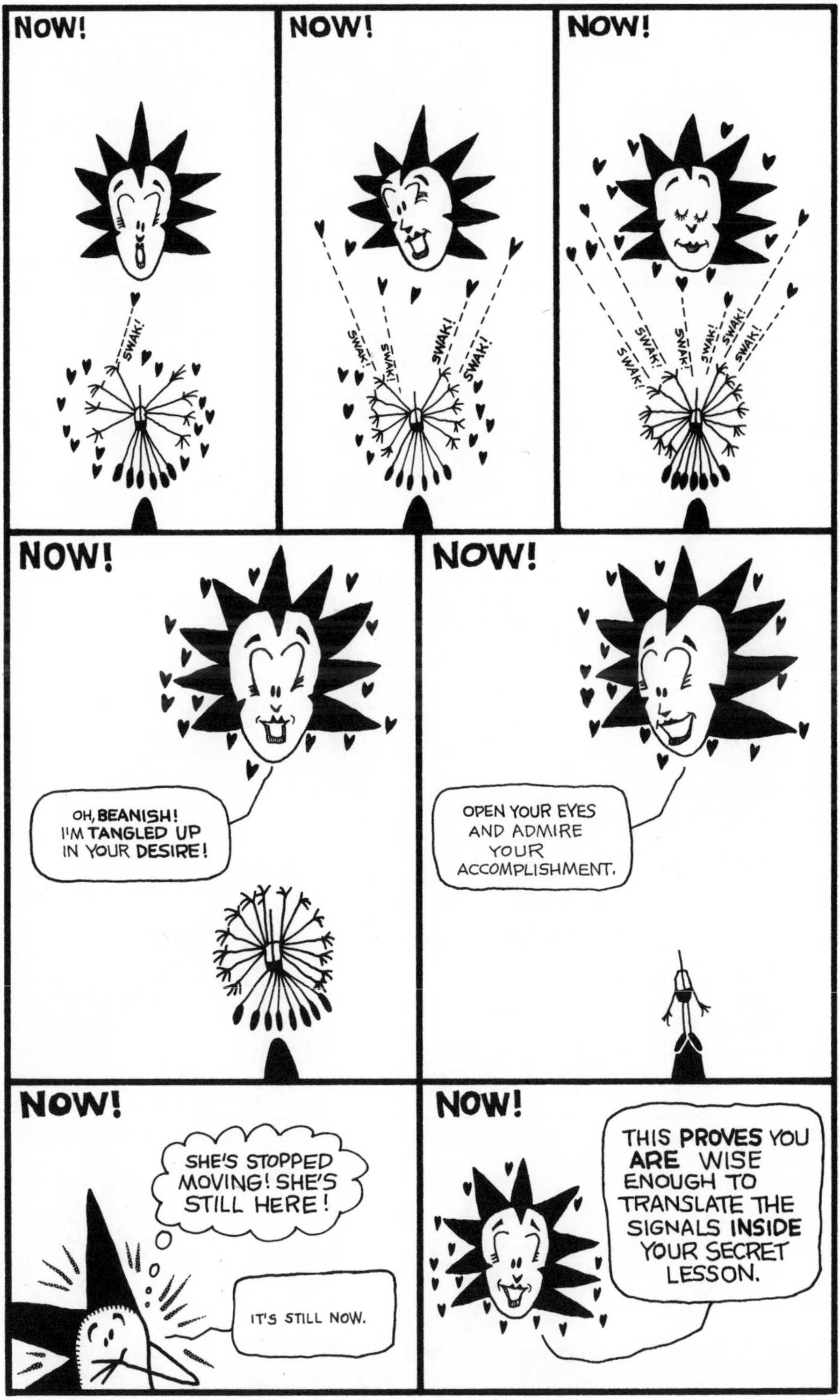
NOW!
SWAK!
NOW!
SWAK!
SWAK!
SWAK!
SWAK!
NOW!
SWAK!
SWAK!
SWAK!
SWAK!
SWAK!
SWAK!
NOW!
OH, BEANISH! I'M TANGLED UP IN YOUR DESIRE!
NOW!
OPEN YOUR EYES AND ADMIRE YOUR ACCOMPLISHMENT.
NOW!
SHE'S STOPPED MOVING! SHE'S STILL HERE!
IT'S STILL NOW.
NOW!
THIS PROVES YOU ARE WISE ENOUGH TO TRANSLATE THE SIGNALS INSIDE YOUR SECRET LESSON.

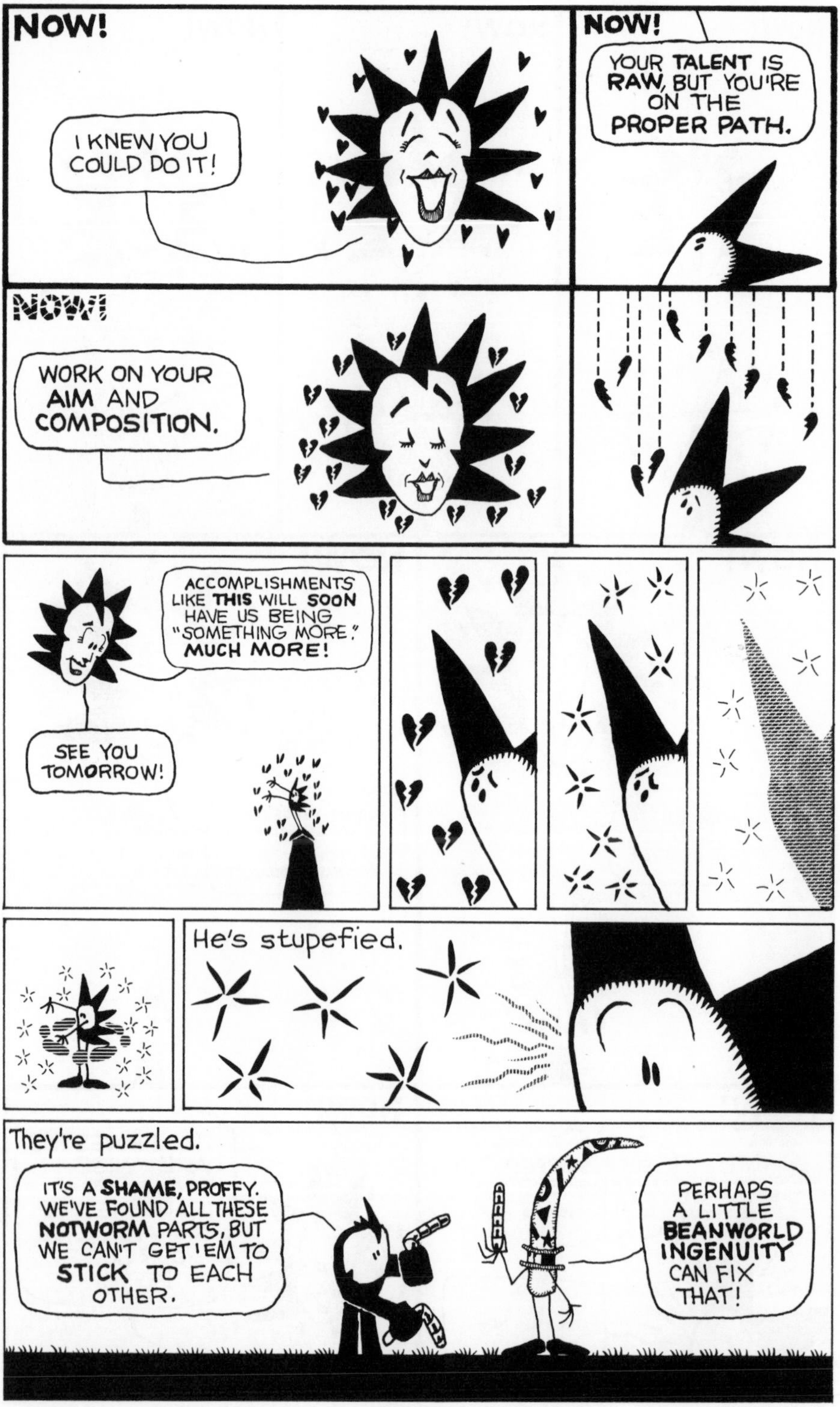
NOW!
I KNEW YOU COULD DO IT!
NOW!
YOUR TALENT IS RAW, BUT YOU'RE ON THE PROPER PATH.
NOW!
WORK ON YOUR AIM AND COMPOSITION.
ACCOMPLISHMENTS LIKE THIS WILL SOON HAVE US BEING "SOMETHING MORE." MUCH MORE!
SEE YOU TOMORROW!
He's stupefied.
They're puzzled.
IT'S A SHAME, PROFFY. WE'VE FOUND ALL THESE NOTWORM PARTS, BUT WE CAN'T GET 'EM TO STICK TO EACH OTHER.
PERHAPS A LITTLE BEANWORLD INGENUITY CAN FIX THAT!

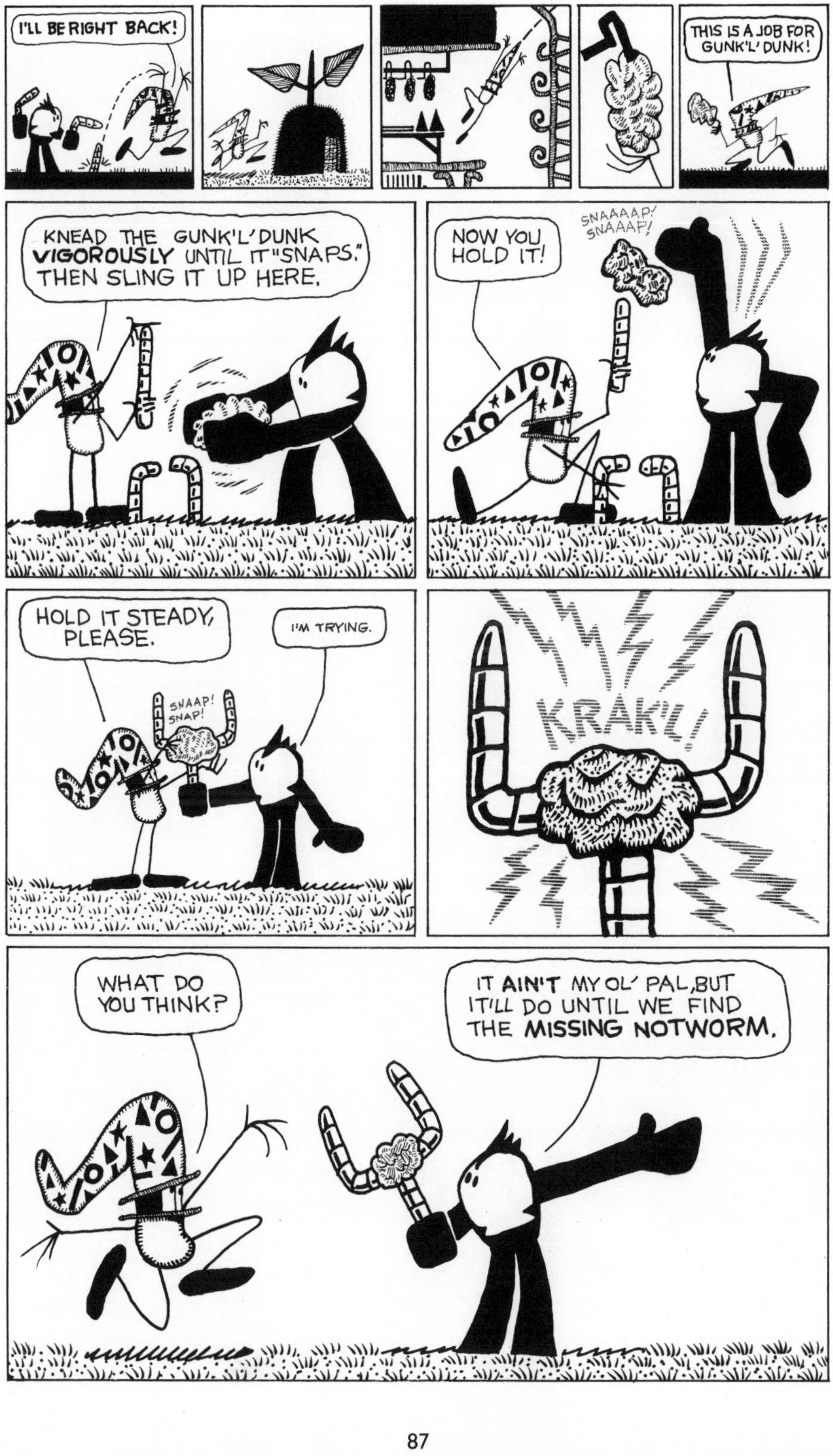
I'LL BE RIGHT BACK!
THIS IS A JOB FOR GUNK'L'DUNK!
KNEAD THE GUNK'L'DUNK **VIGOROUSLY** UNTIL IT "SNAPS." THEN SLING IT UP HERE.
NOW YOU HOLD IT!
SNAAAAP! SNAAAP!
HOLD IT STEADY, PLEASE.
I'M TRYING.
SNAAP! SNAP!
KRAK'L!
WHAT DO YOU THINK?
IT **AIN'T** MY OL' PAL, BUT IT'LL DO UNTIL WE FIND THE **MISSING NOTWORM.**

Night falls. The BEANS sleep. A visitor arrives.

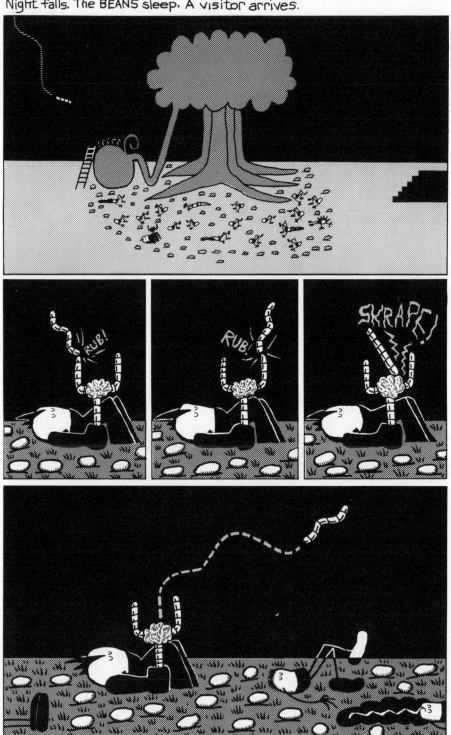

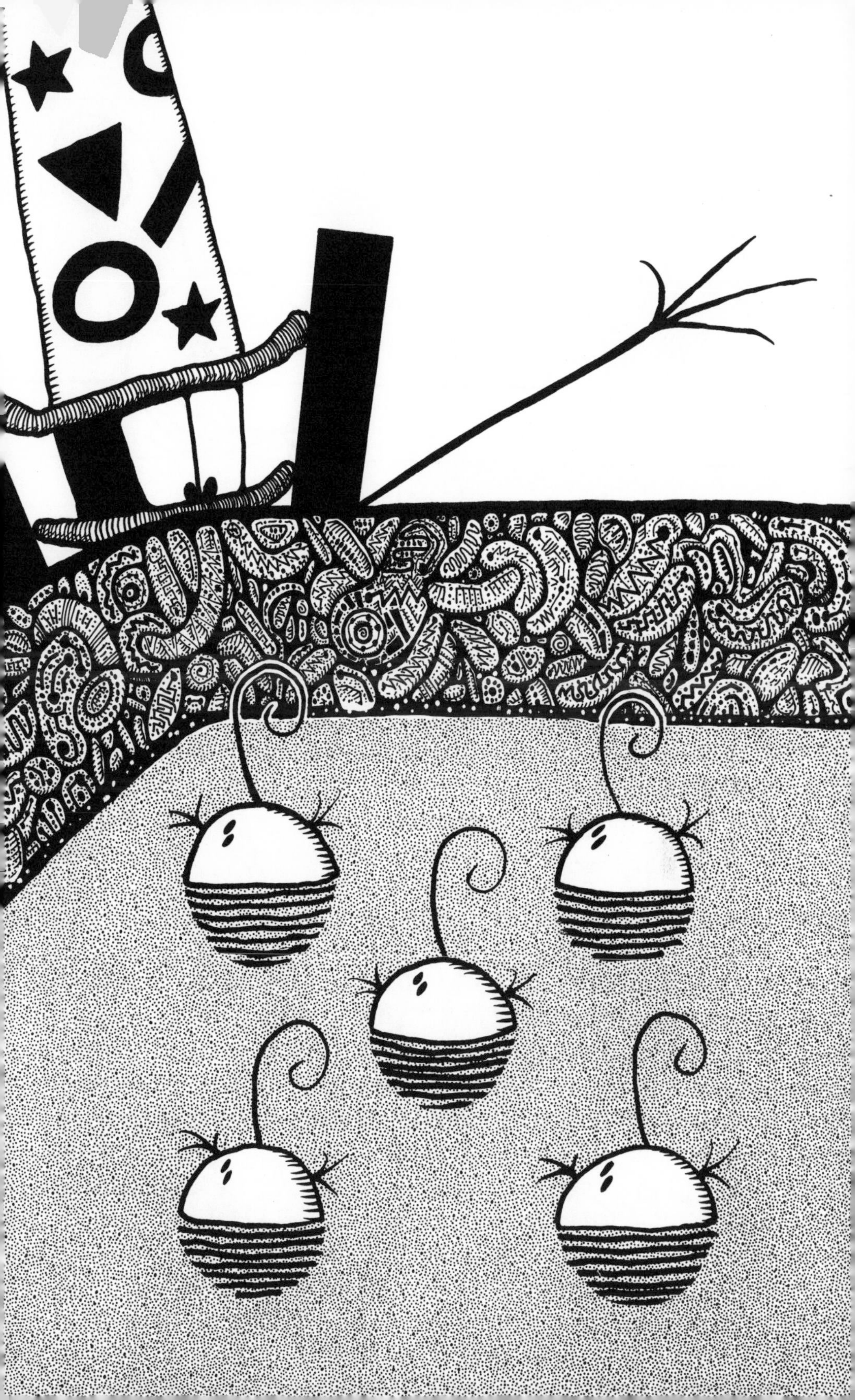

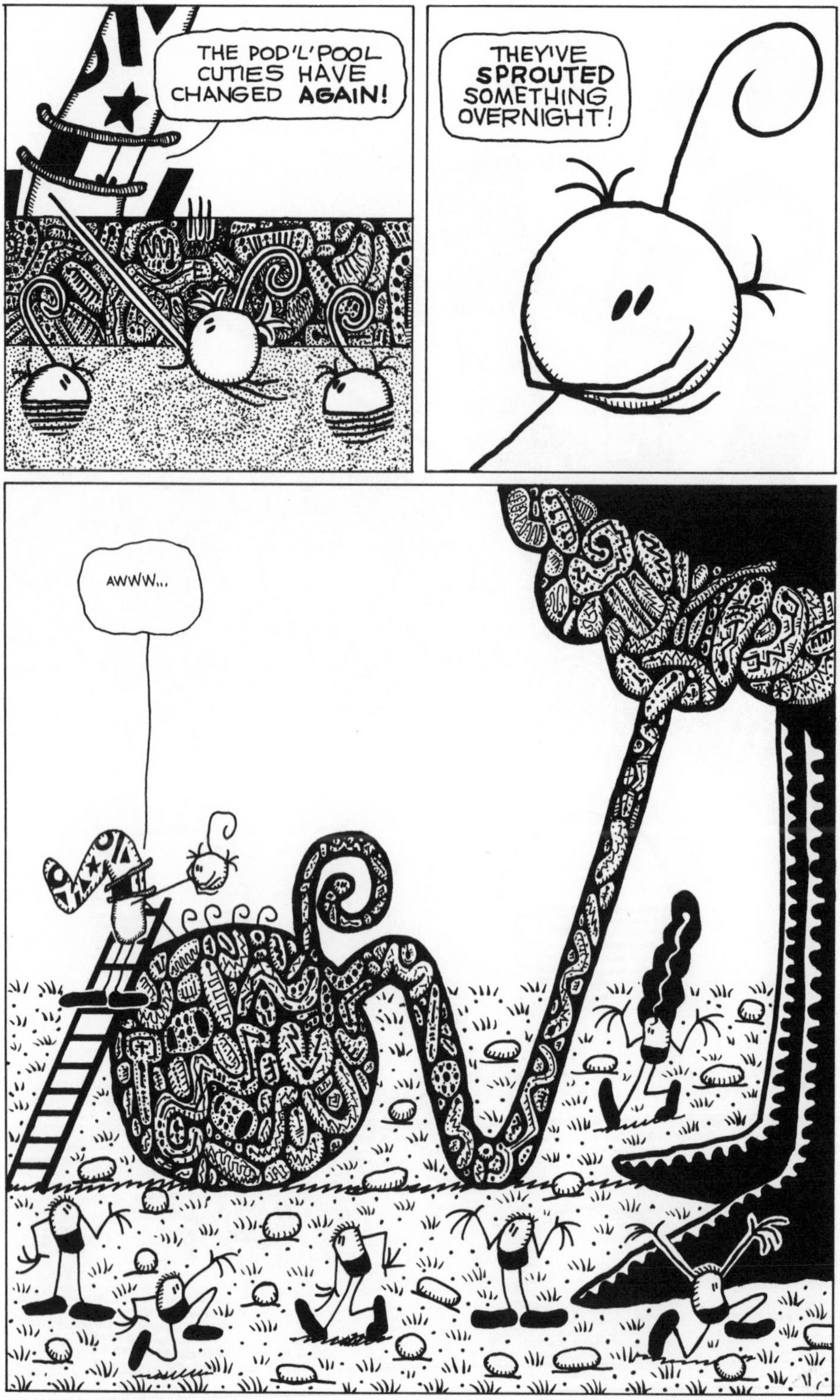
THE POD'L'POOL CUTIES HAVE CHANGED AGAIN!
THEY'VE SPROUTED SOMETHING OVERNIGHT!
AWWW...

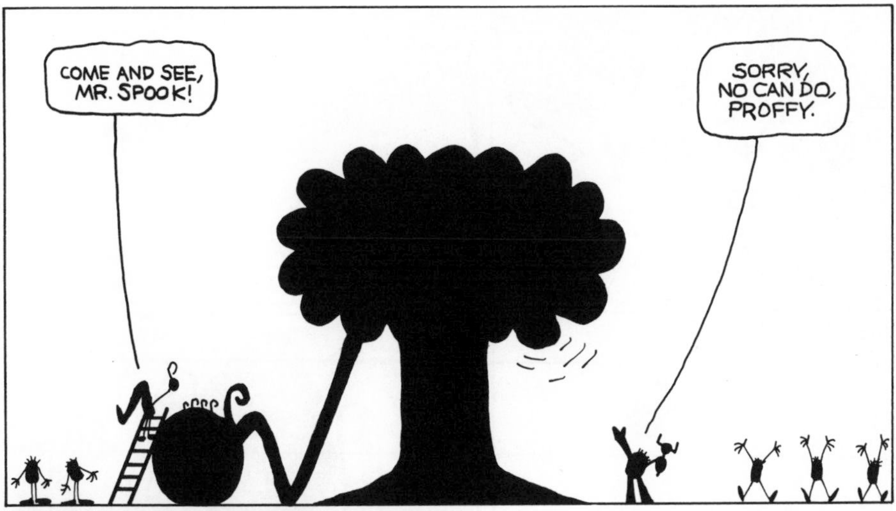
COME AND SEE, MR. SPOOK!
SORRY, NO CAN DO, PROFFY.

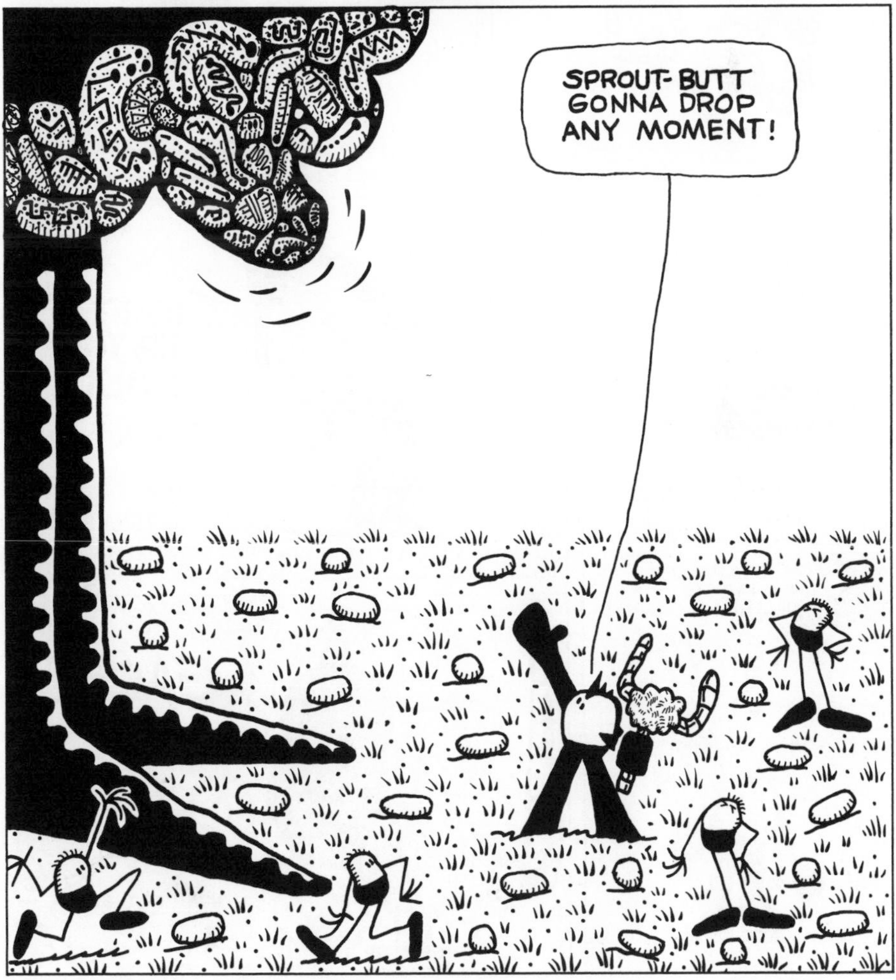
SPROUT-BUTT GONNA DROP ANY MOMENT!

POP
WHAT'S DIS?
I AIN'T SNAGGED!
I'M TRAPPED IN A PIECE OF JUNK!
I'LL TRY TO SNAG YOU BY HAND!
HURRY UP, YOU DOLT!
GACK!
NOW I'ZE DIZZY AND ITCHY!

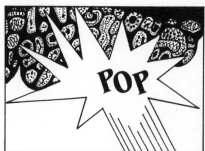

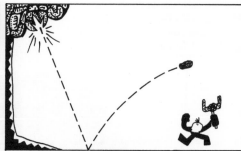

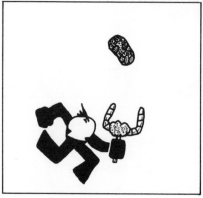

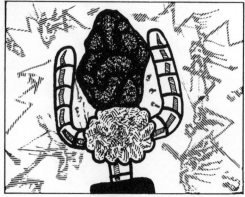

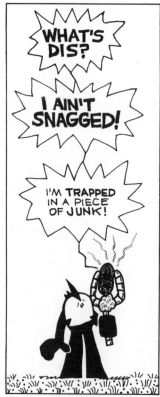

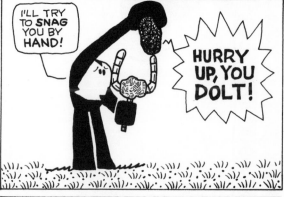

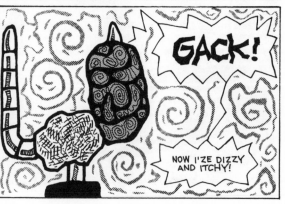

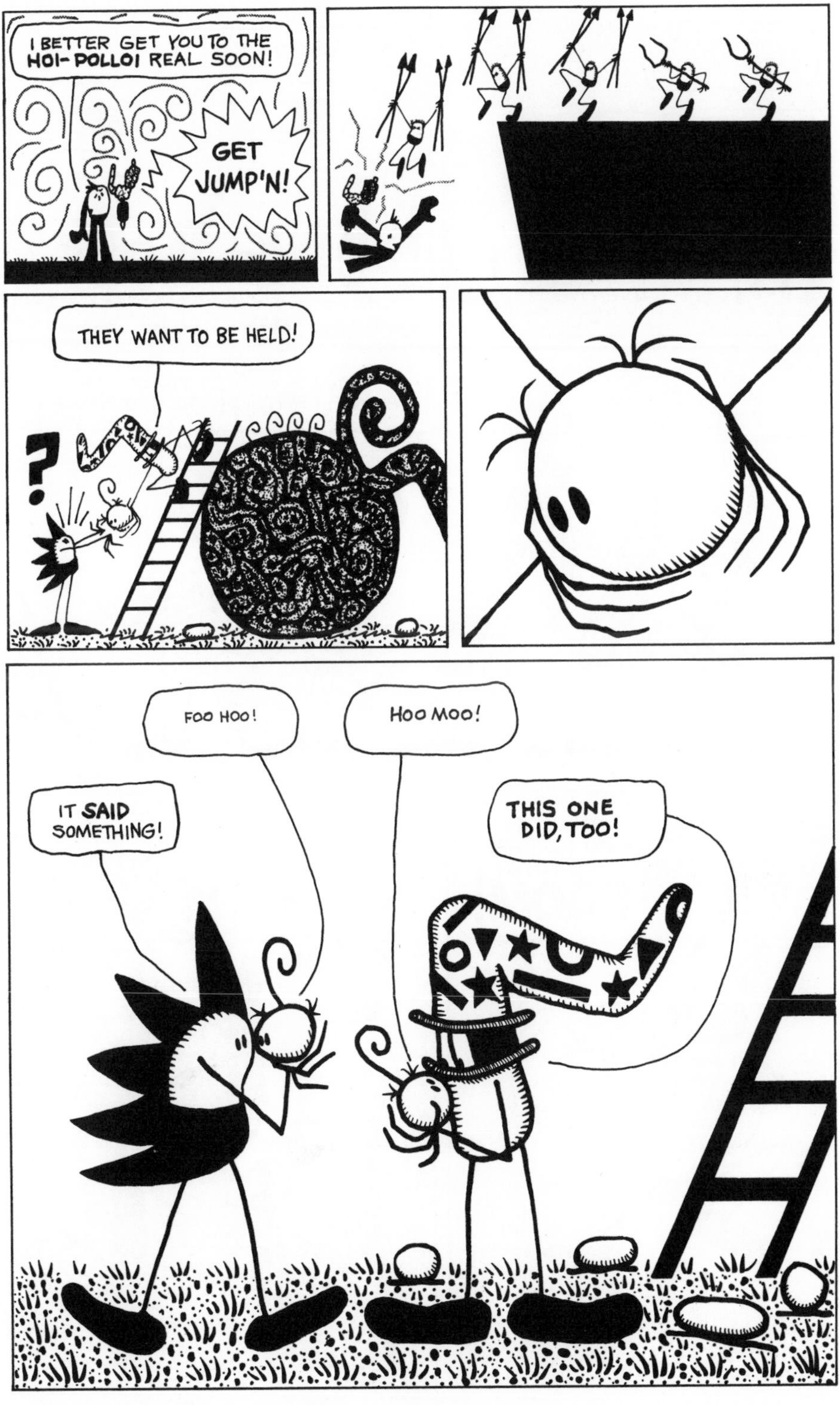
I BETTER GET YOU TO THE HOI-POLLOI REAL SOON!
GET JUMP'N!
THEY WANT TO BE HELD!
?
IT SAID SOMETHING!
FOO HOO!
HOO MOO!
THIS ONE DID, TOO!

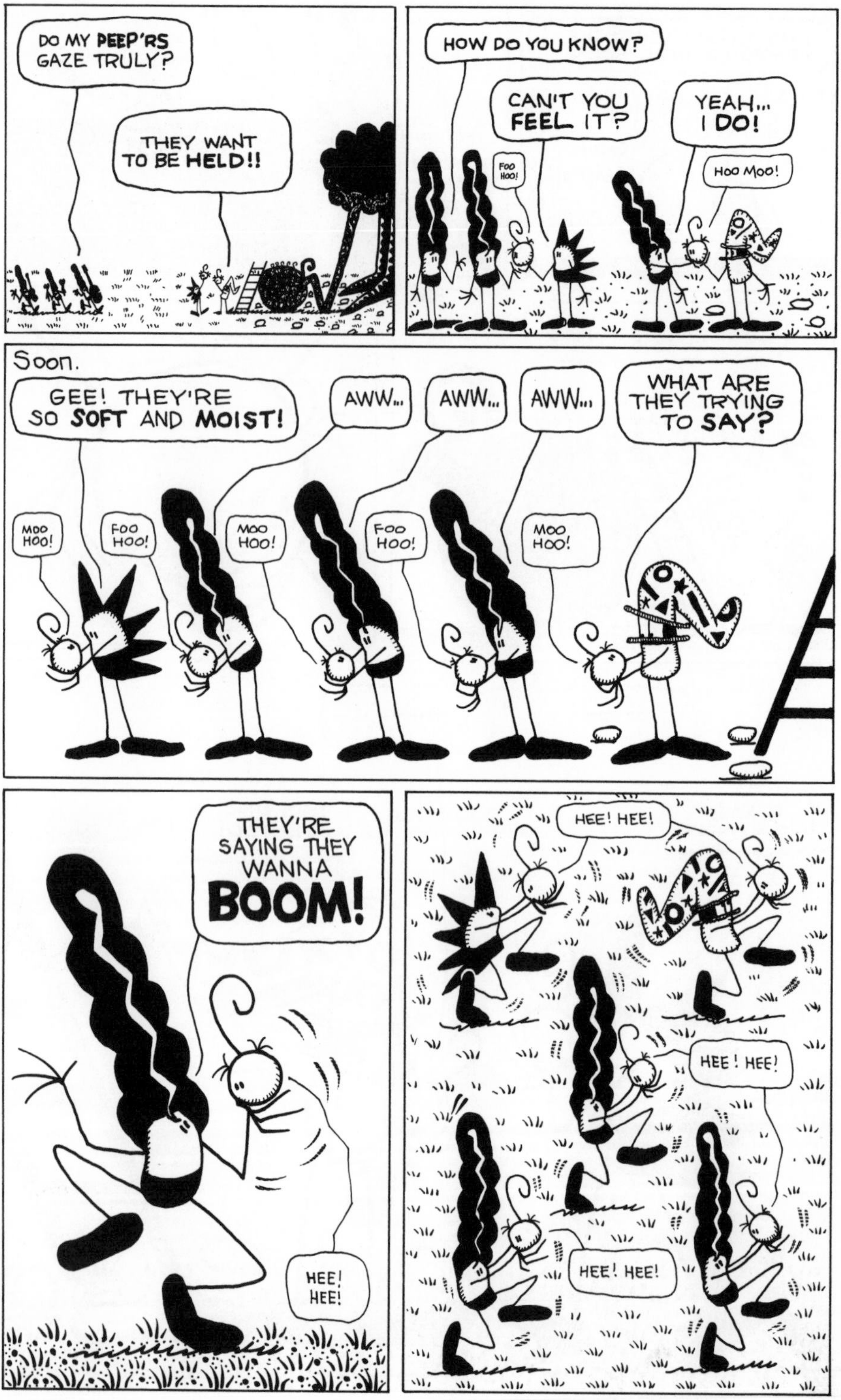
DO MY PEEP'RS GAZE TRULY?
THEY WANT TO BE HELD!!
HOW DO YOU KNOW?
CAN'T YOU FEEL IT?
FOO HOO!
YEAH... I DO!
HOO MOO!
Soon.
GEE! THEY'RE SO SOFT AND MOIST!
MOO HOO!
FOO HOO!
AWW...
MOO HOO!
AWW...
FOO HOO!
AWW...
MOO HOO!
WHAT ARE THEY TRYING TO SAY?
THEY'RE SAYING THEY WANNA BOOM!
HEE! HEE!
HEE! HEE!
HEE! HEE!
HEE! HEE!

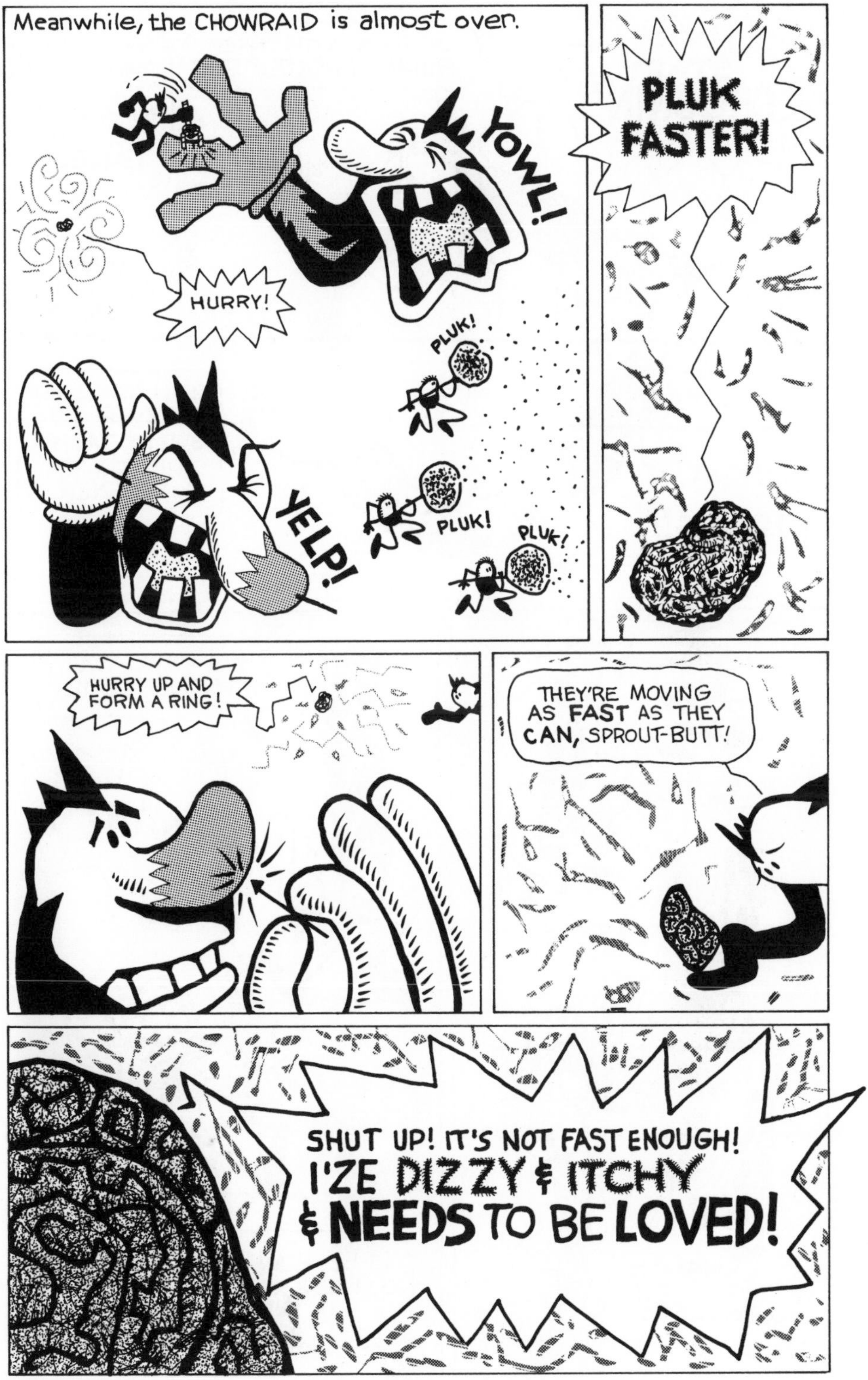
Meanwhile, the CHOWRAID is almost over.
YOWL!
HURRY!
PLUK!
YELP!
PLUK!
PLUK!
PLUK FASTER!
HURRY UP AND FORM A RING!
THEY'RE MOVING AS FAST AS THEY CAN, SPROUT-BUTT!
SHUT UP! IT'S NOT FAST ENOUGH! I'ZE DIZZY & ITCHY & NEEDS TO BE LOVED!

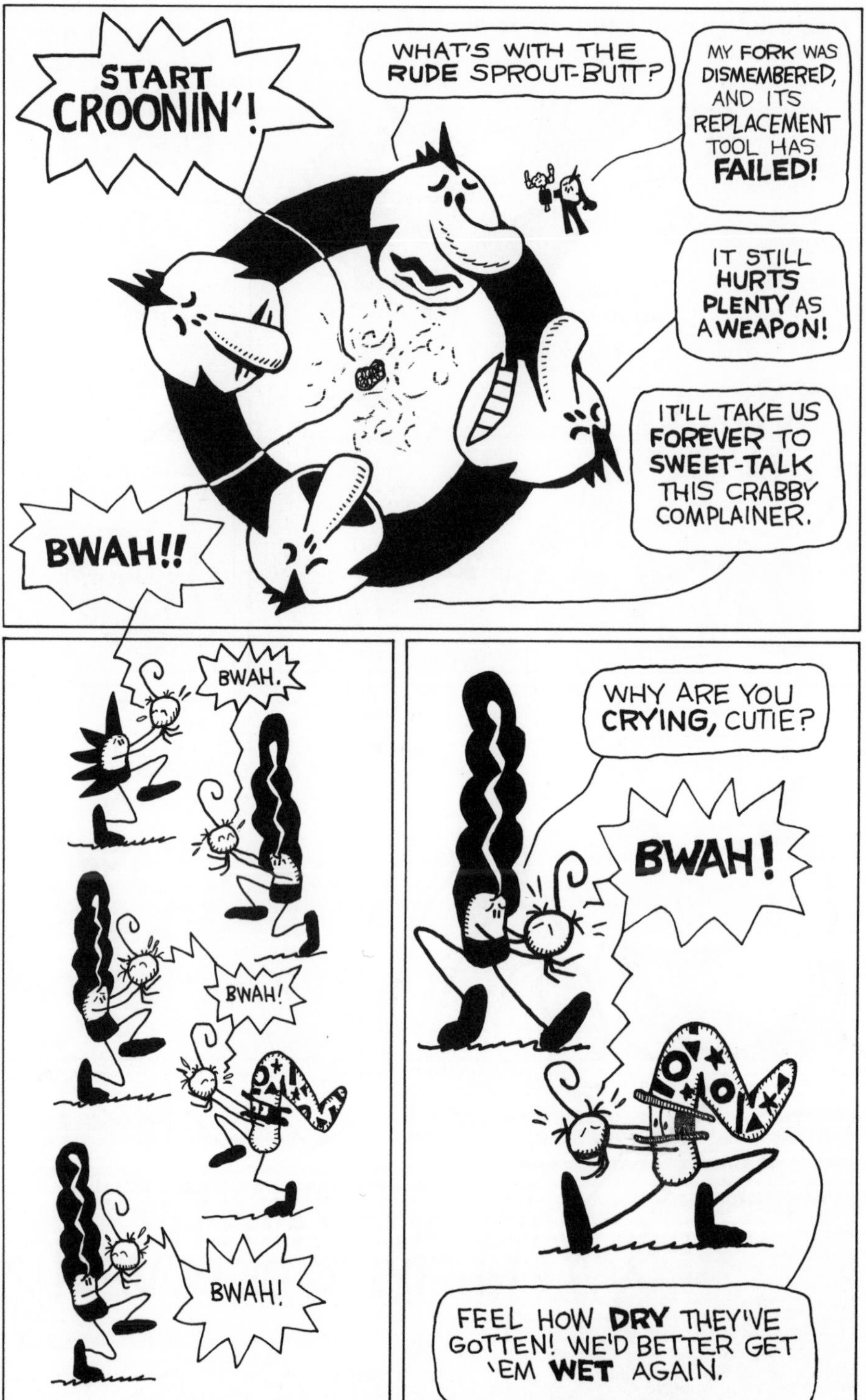
START CROONIN'!
WHAT'S WITH THE RUDE SPROUT-BUTT?
MY FORK WAS DISMEMBERED, AND ITS REPLACEMENT TOOL HAS FAILED!
IT STILL HURTS PLENTY AS A WEAPON!
IT'LL TAKE US FOREVER TO SWEET-TALK THIS CRABBY COMPLAINER.
BWAH!!
BWAH.
BWAH!
BWAH!
WHY ARE YOU CRYING, CUTIE?
BWAH!
FEEL HOW DRY THEY'VE GOTTEN! WE'D BETTER GET 'EM WET AGAIN.

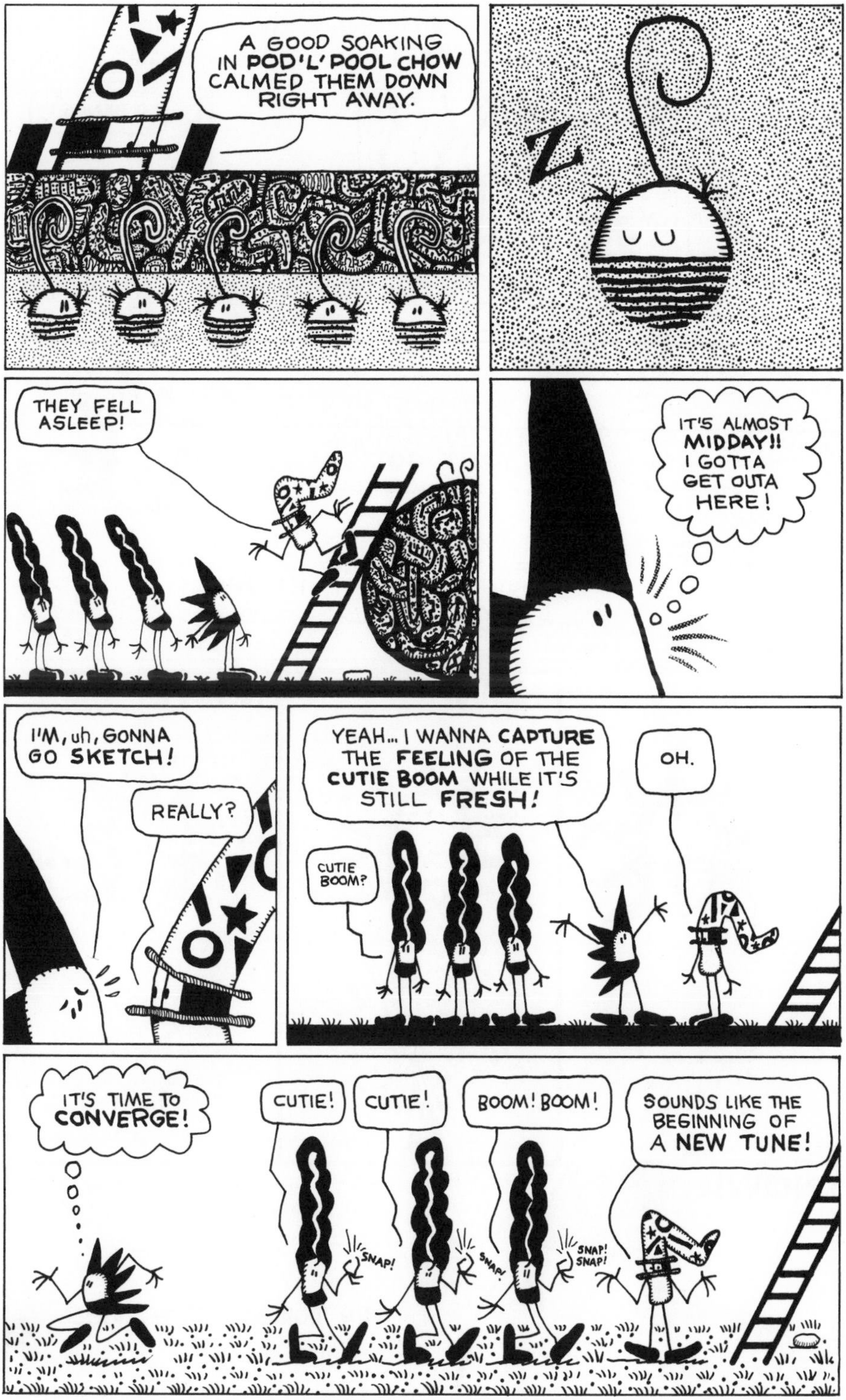
A GOOD SOAKING IN POD'L'POOL CHOW CALMED THEM DOWN RIGHT AWAY.
Z
THEY FELL ASLEEP!
IT'S ALMOST MIDDAY!! I GOTTA GET OUTA HERE!
I'M, uh, GONNA GO SKETCH!
REALLY?
YEAH... I WANNA CAPTURE THE FEELING OF THE CUTIE BOOM WHILE IT'S STILL FRESH!
OH.
CUTIE BOOM?
IT'S TIME TO CONVERGE!
CUTIE!
CUTIE!
BOOM! BOOM!
SOUNDS LIKE THE BEGINNING OF A NEW TUNE!
SNAP!
SNAP!
SNAP! SNAP!

Every day, at midday, **BEANISH** stands inside the "secret sketch" and travels to an unknown territory where he meets a secret friend.

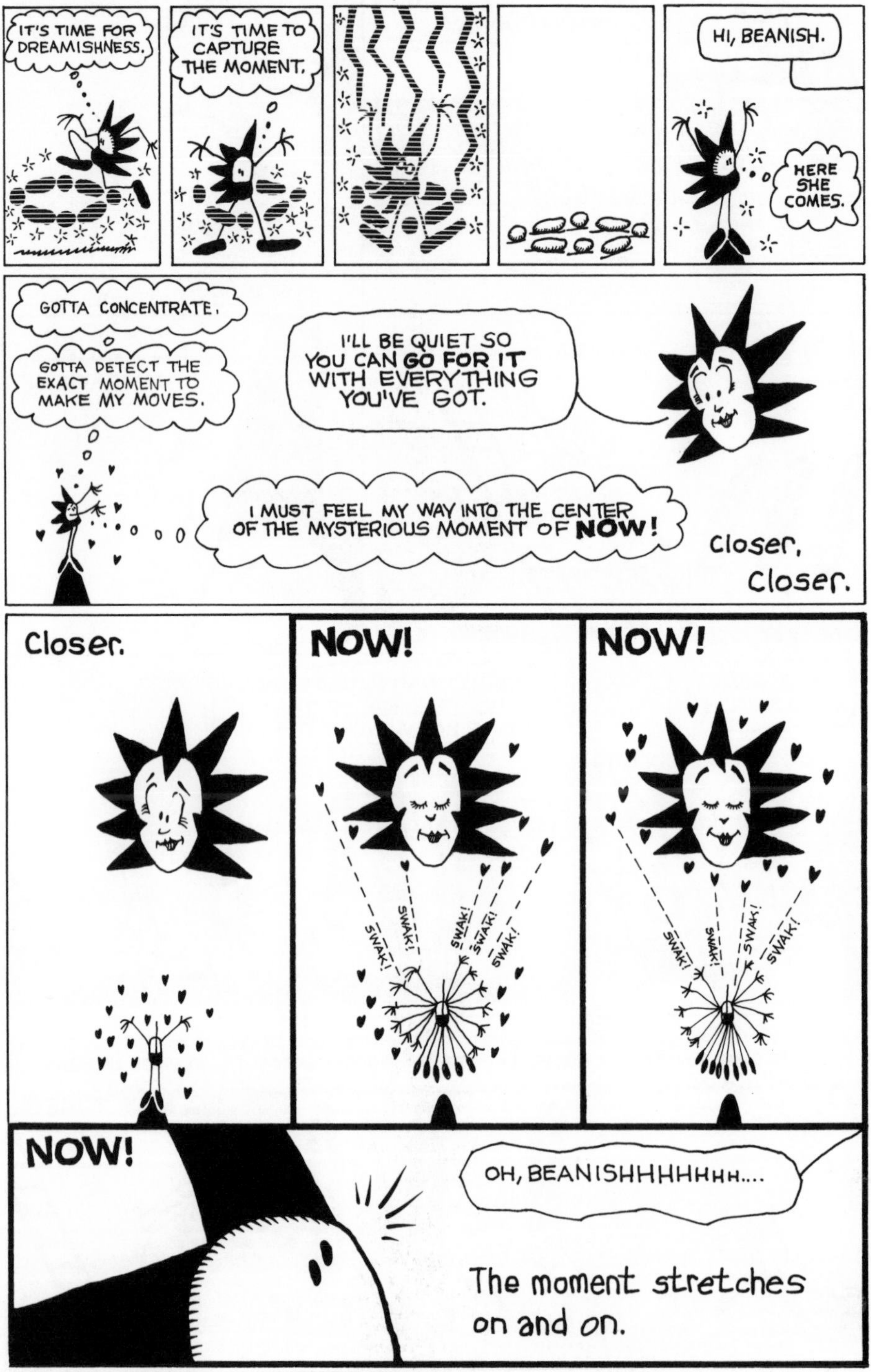
IT'S TIME FOR DREAMISHNESS.
IT'S TIME TO CAPTURE THE MOMENT.
HI, BEANISH.
HERE SHE COMES.
GOTTA CONCENTRATE.
GOTTA DETECT THE EXACT MOMENT TO MAKE MY MOVES.
I'LL BE QUIET SO YOU CAN GO FOR IT WITH EVERYTHING YOU'VE GOT.
I MUST FEEL MY WAY INTO THE CENTER OF THE MYSTERIOUS MOMENT OF NOW!
Closer, Closer.
Closer.
NOW!
SWAK! SWAK! SWAK! SWAK! SWAK!
NOW!
SWAK! SWAK! SWAK! SWAK!
NOW!
OH, BEANISHHHHHHHH....
The moment stretches on and on.

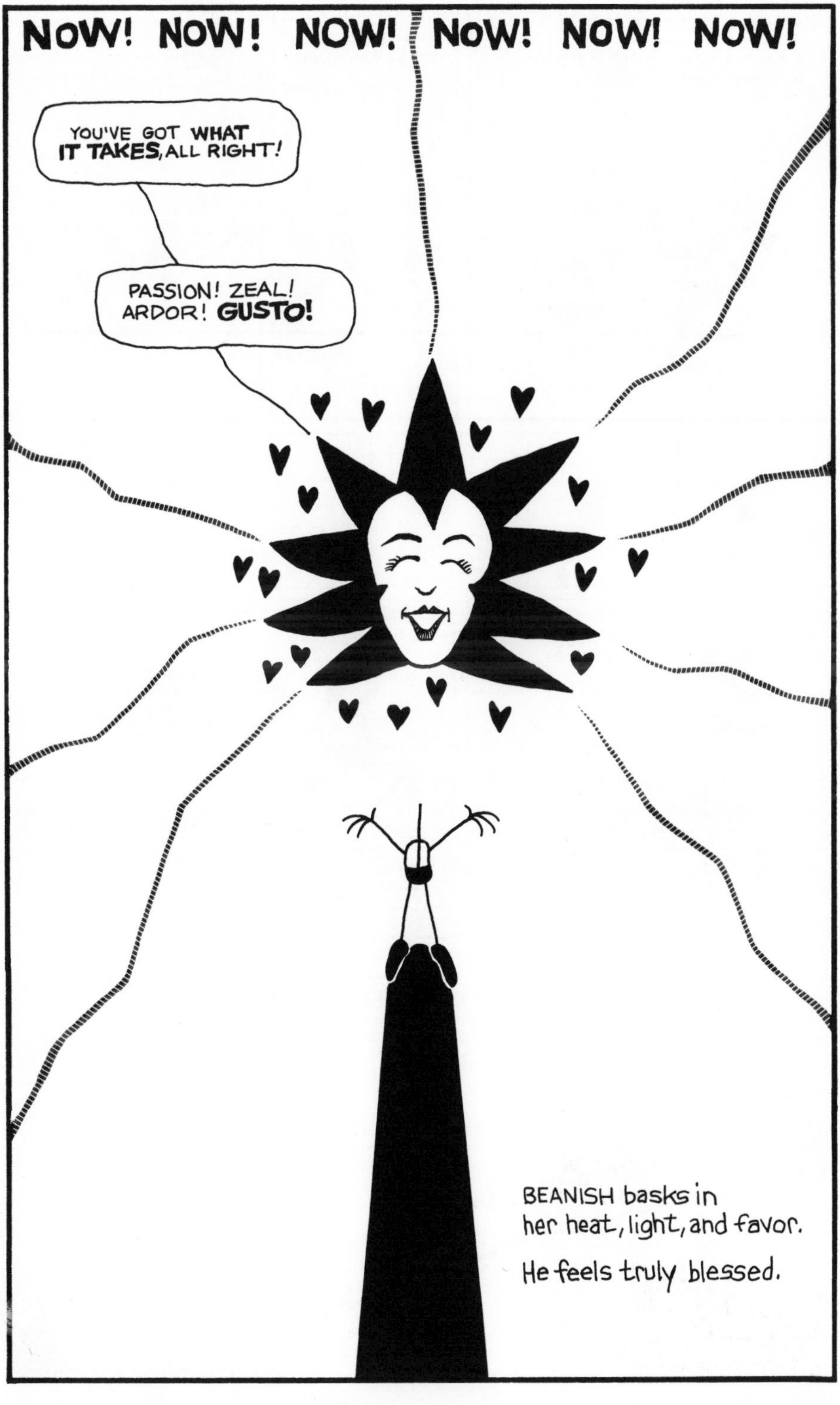
NOW! NOW! NOW! NOW! NOW! NOW!
YOU'VE GOT WHAT IT TAKES, ALL RIGHT!
PASSION! ZEAL! ARDOR! GUSTO!
BEANISH basks in her heat, light, and favor.
He feels truly blessed.

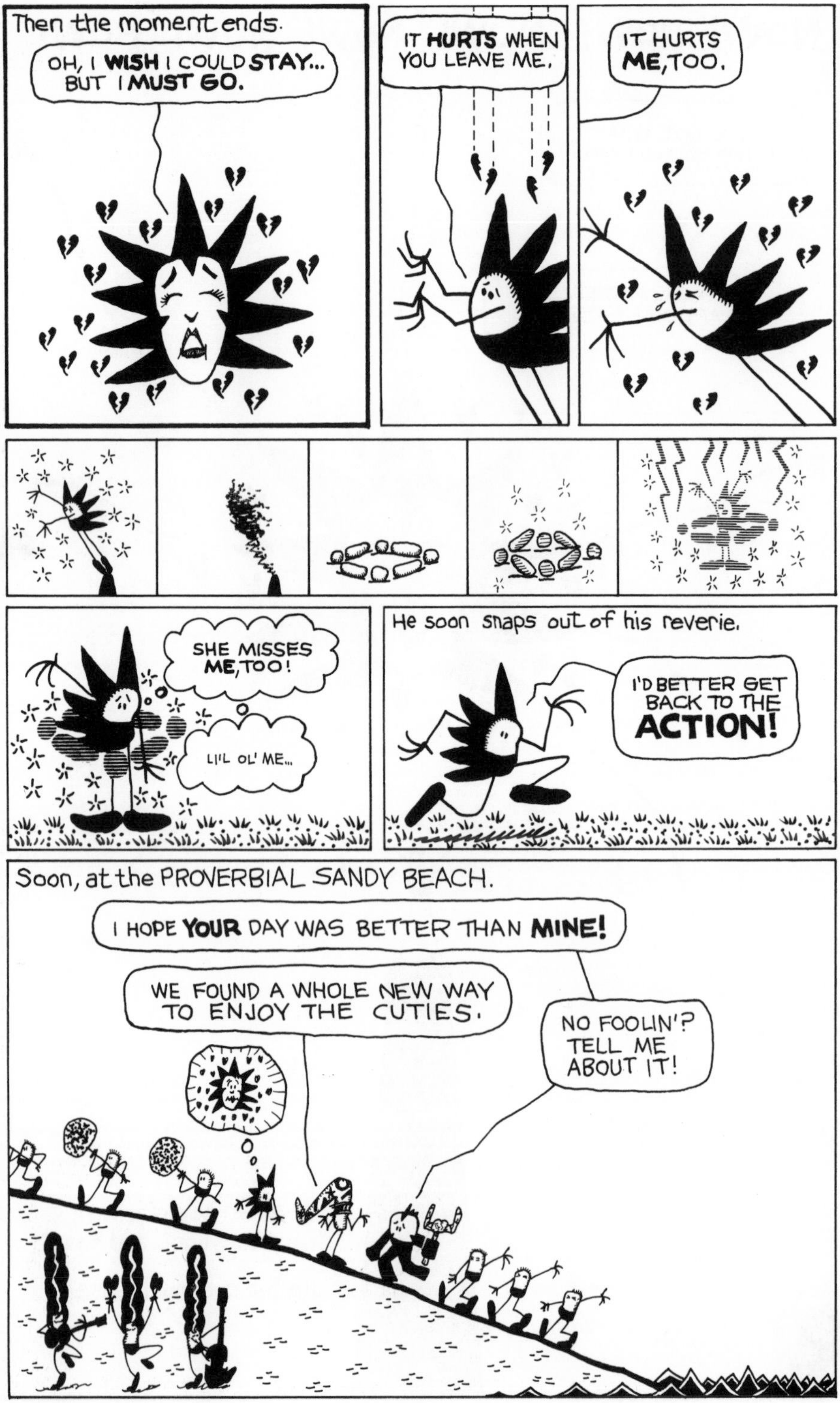
Then the moment ends.
OH, I WISH I COULD STAY... BUT I MUST GO.
IT HURTS WHEN YOU LEAVE ME.
IT HURTS ME, TOO.
SHE MISSES ME, TOO!
LI'L OL' ME...
He soon snaps out of his reverie.
I'D BETTER GET BACK TO THE ACTION!
Soon, at the PROVERBIAL SANDY BEACH.
I HOPE YOUR DAY WAS BETTER THAN MINE!
WE FOUND A WHOLE NEW WAY TO ENJOY THE CUTIES.
NO FOOLIN'? TELL ME ABOUT IT!

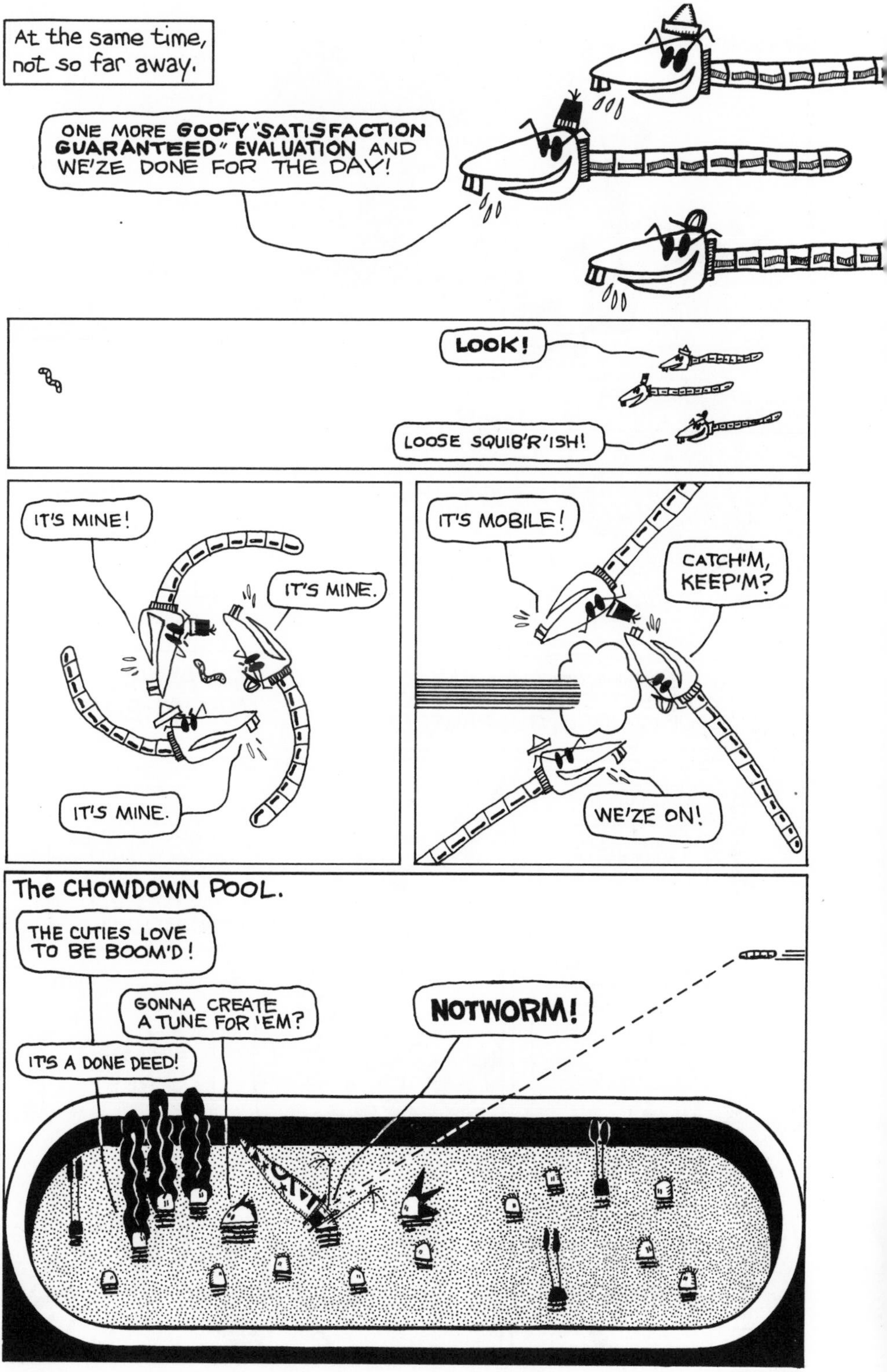
At the same time, not so far away.
ONE MORE GOOFY "SATISFACTION GUARANTEED" EVALUATION AND WE'ZE DONE FOR THE DAY!
LOOK!
LOOSE SQUIB'R'ISH!
IT'S MINE!
IT'S MINE.
IT'S MINE.
IT'S MOBILE!
CATCH'M, KEEP'M?
WE'ZE ON!
The CHOWDOWN POOL.
THE CUTIES LOVE TO BE BOOM'D!
GONNA CREATE A TUNE FOR 'EM?
IT'S A DONE DEED!
NOTWORM!

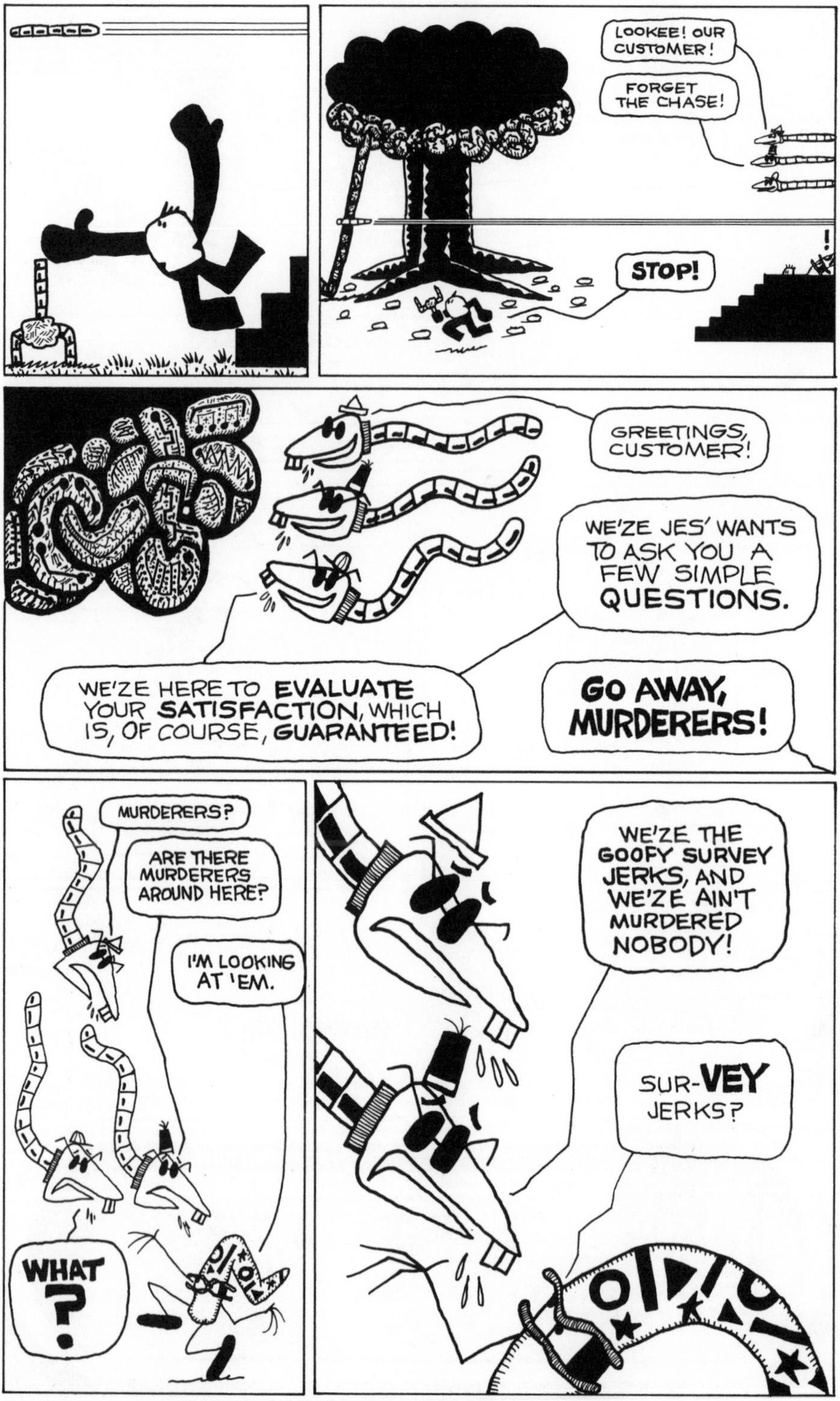
LOOKEE! OUR CUSTOMER!
FORGET THE CHASE!
!
STOP!
GREETINGS, CUSTOMER!
WE'ZE JES' WANTS TO ASK YOU A FEW SIMPLE QUESTIONS.
WE'ZE HERE TO EVALUATE YOUR SATISFACTION, WHICH IS, OF COURSE, GUARANTEED!
GO AWAY, MURDERERS!
MURDERERS?
ARE THERE MURDERERS AROUND HERE?
I'M LOOKING AT 'EM.
WHAT?
WE'ZE THE GOOFY SURVEY JERKS, AND WE'ZE AIN'T MURDERED NOBODY!
SUR-VEY JERKS?

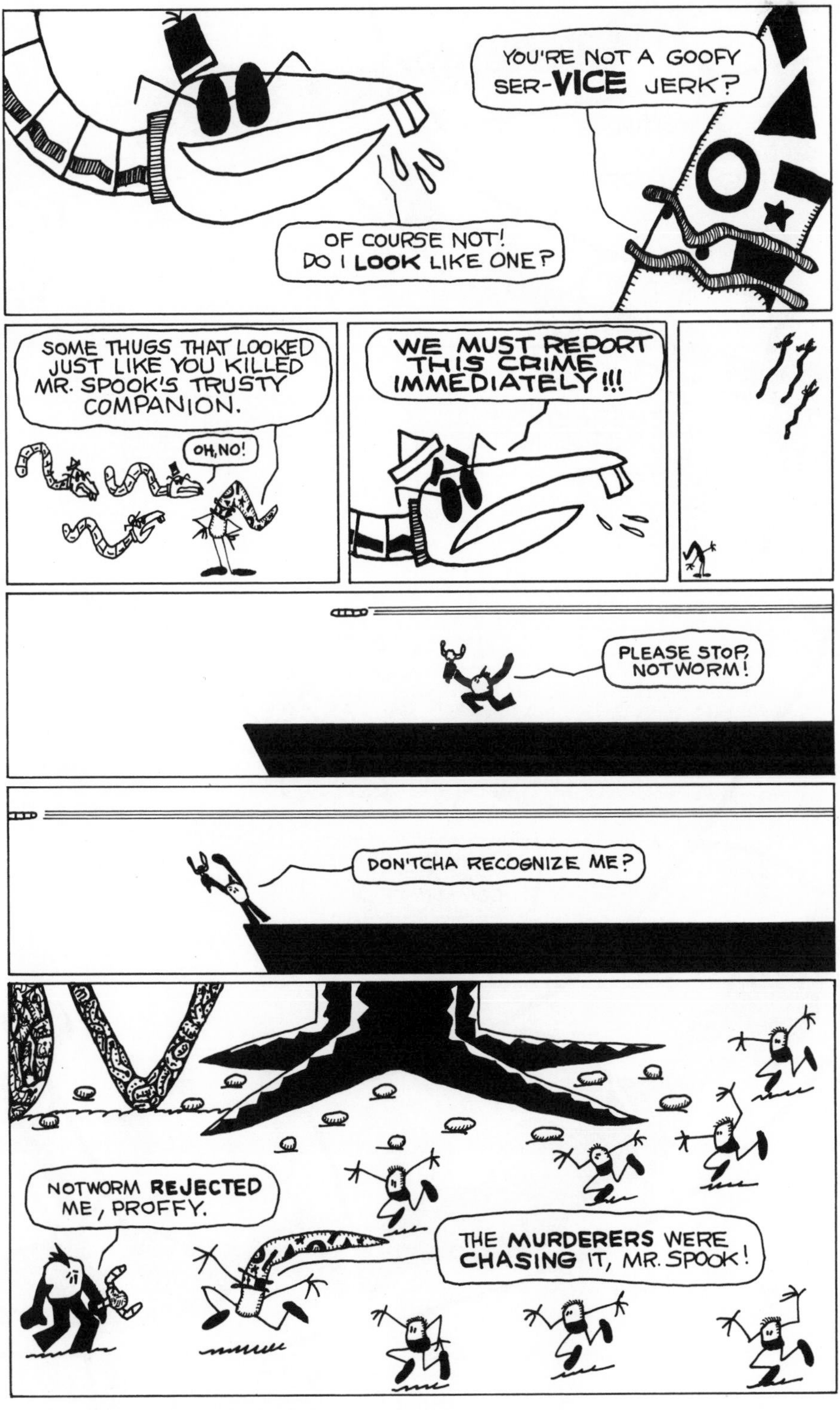
YOU'RE NOT A GOOFY SER-VICE JERK?
OF COURSE NOT! DO I LOOK LIKE ONE?
SOME THUGS THAT LOOKED JUST LIKE YOU KILLED MR. SPOOK'S TRUSTY COMPANION.
OH, NO!
WE MUST REPORT THIS CRIME IMMEDIATELY!!!
PLEASE STOP, NOTWORM!
DON'TCHA RECOGNIZE ME?
NOTWORM REJECTED ME, PROFFY.
THE MURDERERS WERE CHASING IT, MR. SPOOK!

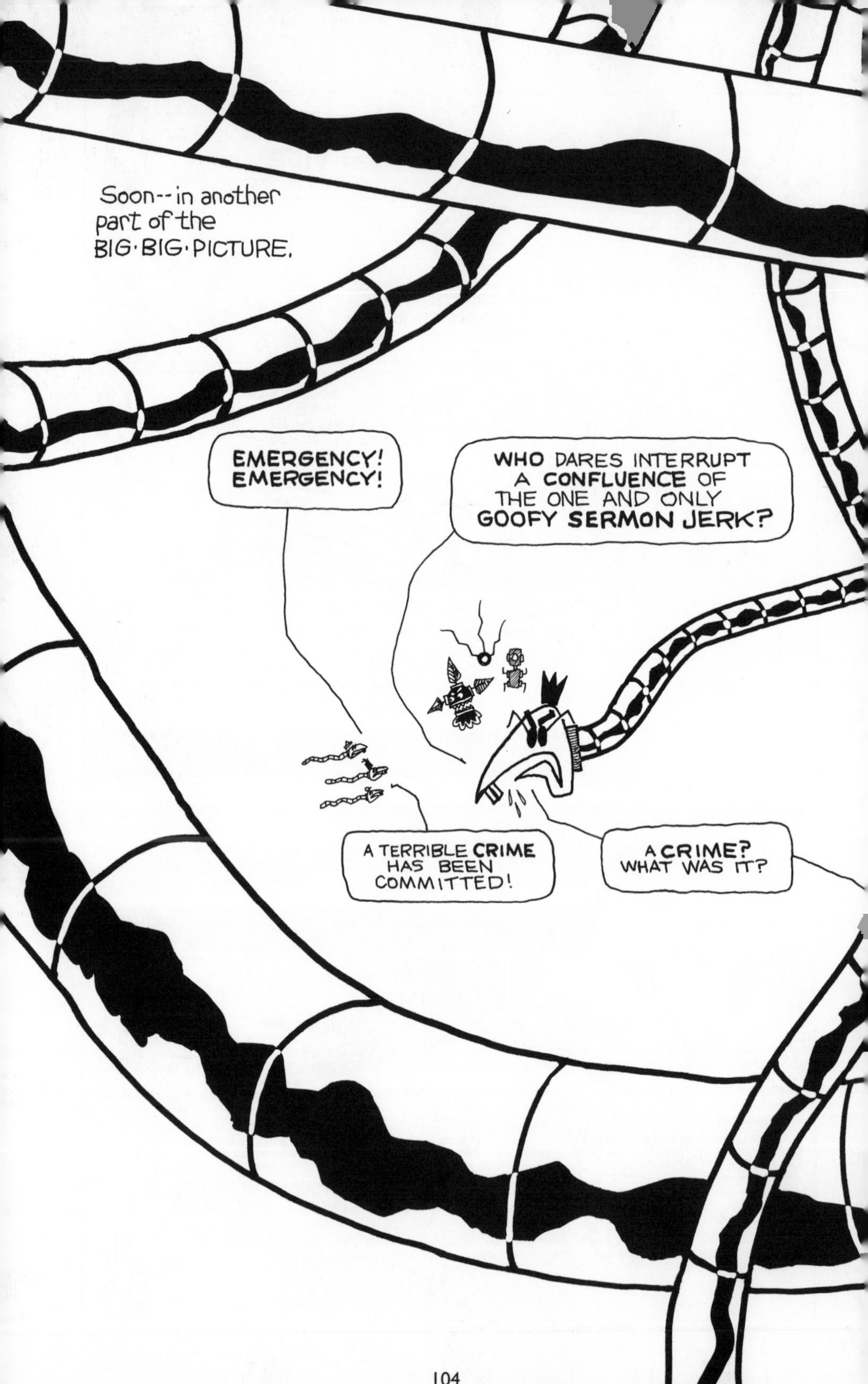

Soon--in another part of the BIG·BIG·PICTURE.
EMERGENCY! EMERGENCY!
WHO DARES INTERRUPT A CONFLUENCE OF THE ONE AND ONLY GOOFY SERMON JERK?
A TERRIBLE CRIME HAS BEEN COMMITTED!
A CRIME? WHAT WAS IT?

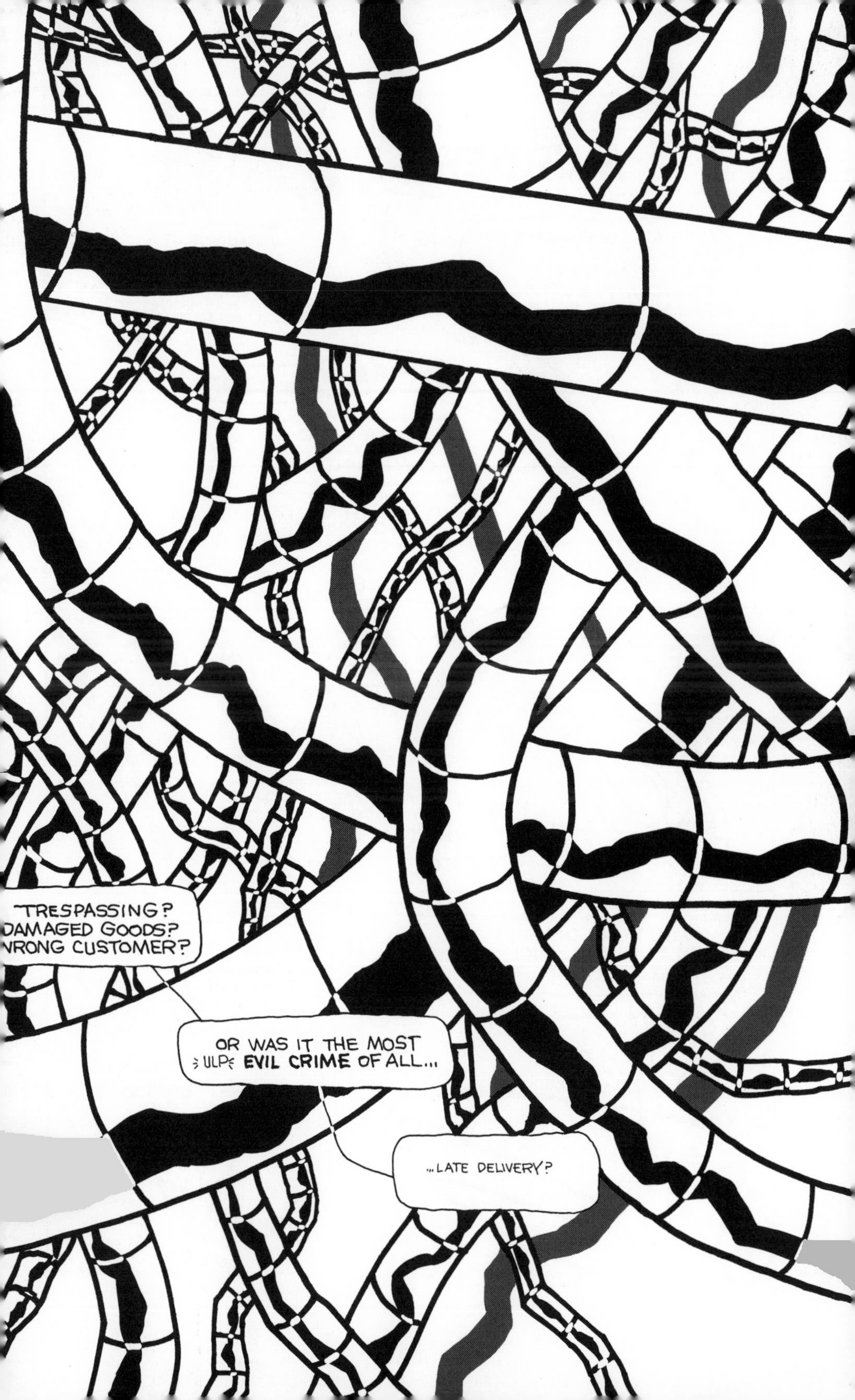
TRESPASSING?
DAMAGED GOODS?
WRONG CUSTOMER?
OR WAS IT THE MOST
ULP EVIL CRIME OF ALL...
...LATE DELIVERY?

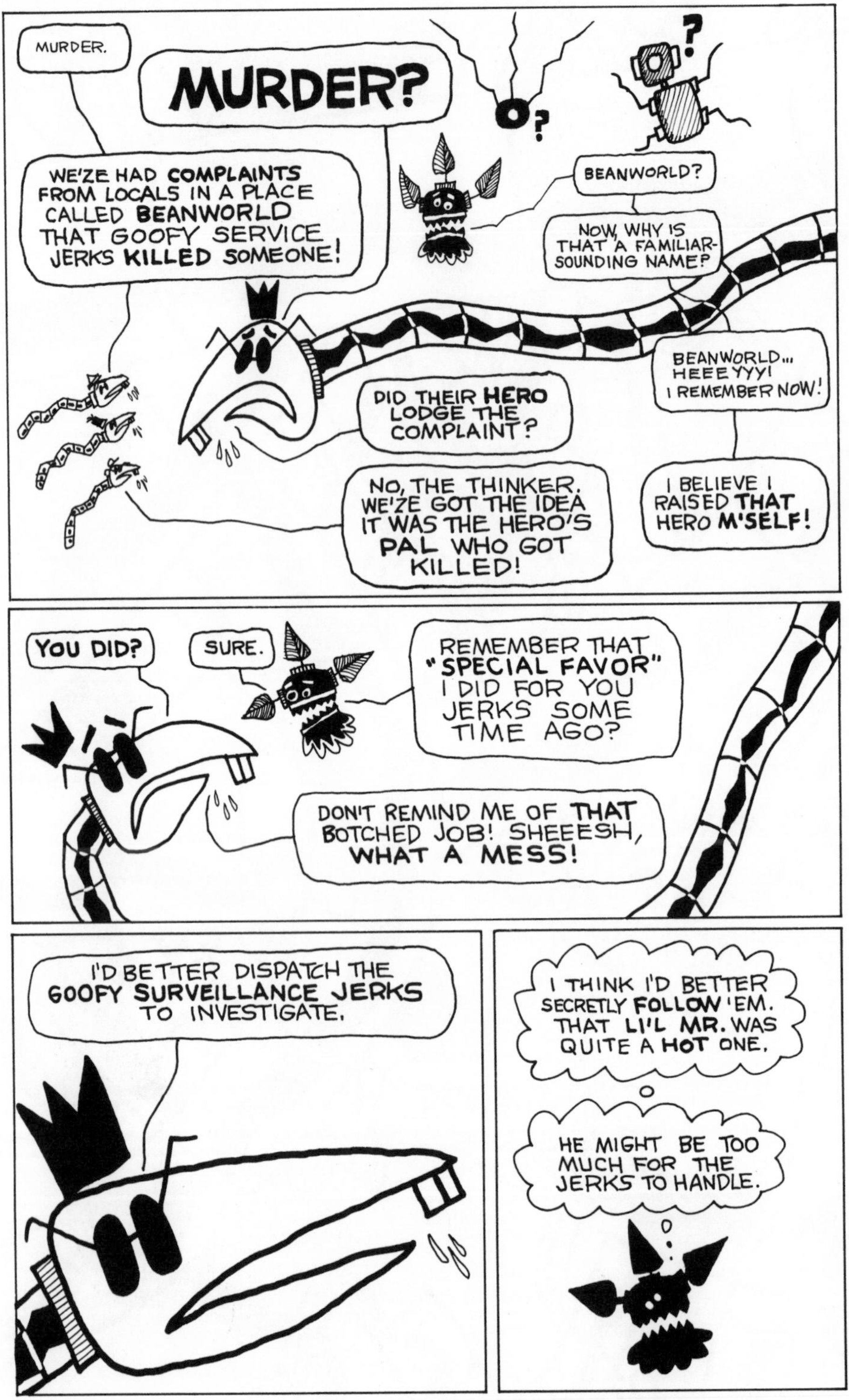
MURDER.
MURDER?
WE'ZE HAD COMPLAINTS FROM LOCALS IN A PLACE CALLED BEANWORLD THAT GOOFY SERVICE JERKS KILLED SOMEONE!
BEANWORLD?
NOW, WHY IS THAT A FAMILIAR-SOUNDING NAME?
BEANWORLD... HEEEYYY! I REMEMBER NOW!
DID THEIR HERO LODGE THE COMPLAINT?
NO, THE THINKER. WE'ZE GOT THE IDEA IT WAS THE HERO'S PAL WHO GOT KILLED!
I BELIEVE I RAISED THAT HERO M'SELF!
YOU DID?
SURE.
REMEMBER THAT "SPECIAL FAVOR" I DID FOR YOU JERKS SOME TIME AGO?
DON'T REMIND ME OF THAT BOTCHED JOB! SHEEESH, WHAT A MESS!
I'D BETTER DISPATCH THE GOOFY SURVEILLANCE JERKS TO INVESTIGATE.
I THINK I'D BETTER SECRETLY FOLLOW 'EM. THAT LI'L MR. WAS QUITE A HOT ONE.
HE MIGHT BE TOO MUCH FOR THE JERKS TO HANDLE.

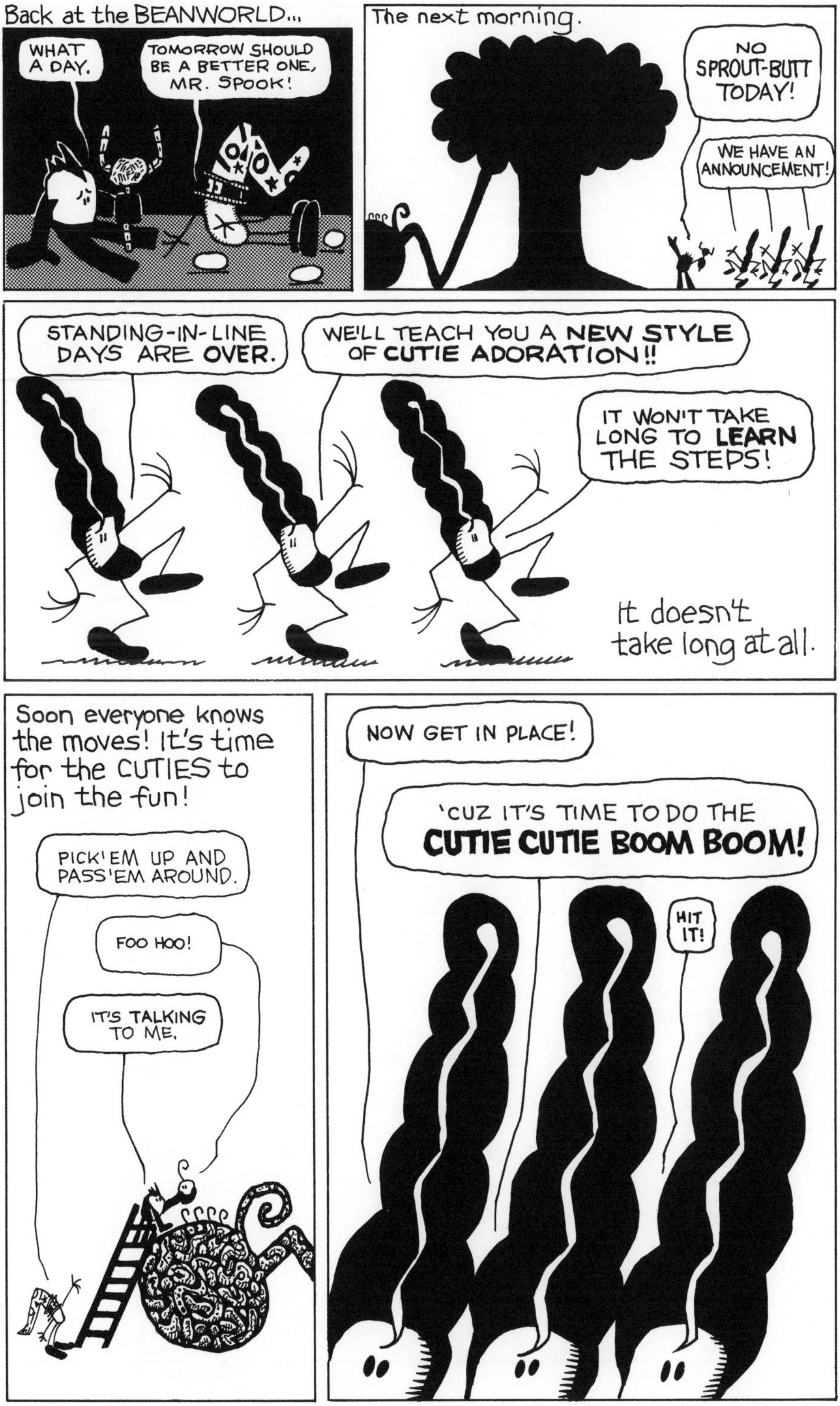
Back at the BEANWORLD...
WHAT A DAY.
TOMORROW SHOULD BE A BETTER ONE, MR. SPOOK!
The next morning.
NO SPROUT-BUTT TODAY!
WE HAVE AN ANNOUNCEMENT!
STANDING-IN-LINE DAYS ARE OVER.
WE'LL TEACH YOU A NEW STYLE OF CUTIE ADORATION!!
IT WON'T TAKE LONG TO LEARN THE STEPS!
It doesn't take long at all.
Soon everyone knows the moves! It's time for the CUTIES to join the fun!
PICK'EM UP AND PASS'EM AROUND.
FOO HOO!
IT'S TALKING TO ME.
NOW GET IN PLACE!
'CUZ IT'S TIME TO DO THE CUTIE CUTIE BOOM BOOM!
HIT IT!

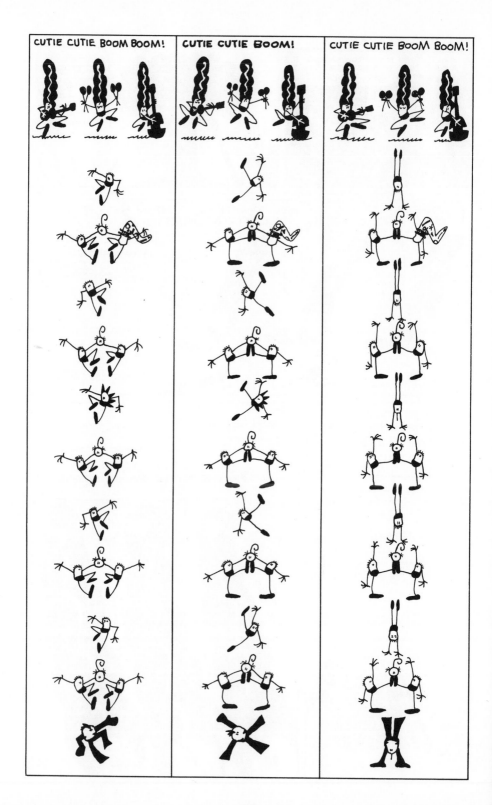

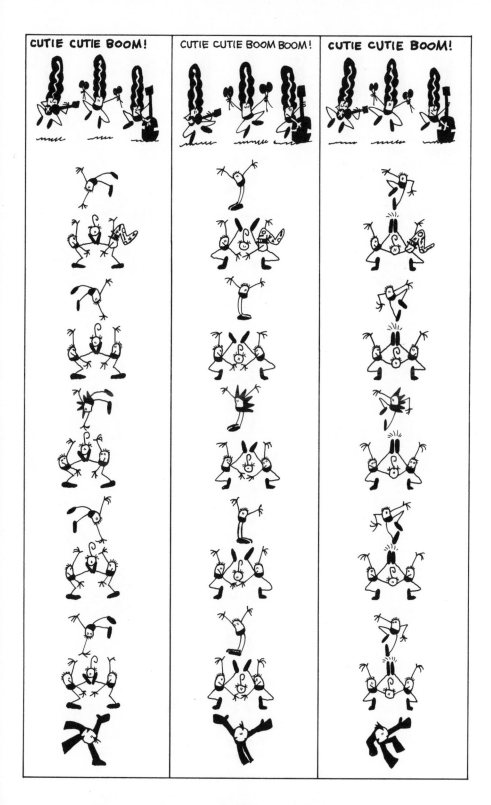

CUTIE CUTIE BOOM! CUTIE CUTIE BOOM BOOM! CUTIE CUTIE BOOM!

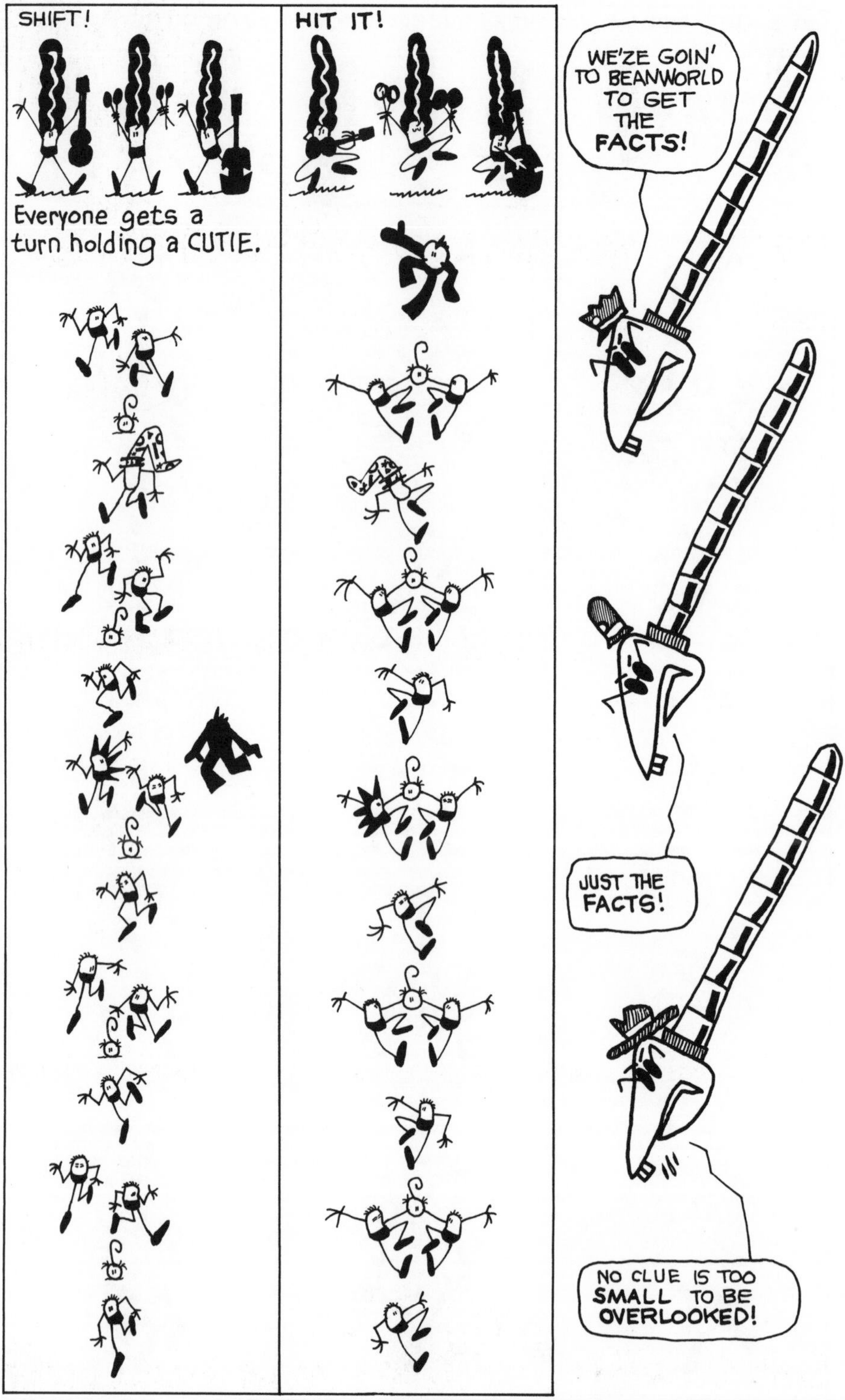
SHIFT!
Everyone gets a turn holding a CUTIE.
HIT IT!
WE'ZE GOIN' TO BEANWORLD TO GET THE FACTS!
JUST THE FACTS!
NO CLUE IS TOO SMALL TO BE OVERLOOKED!

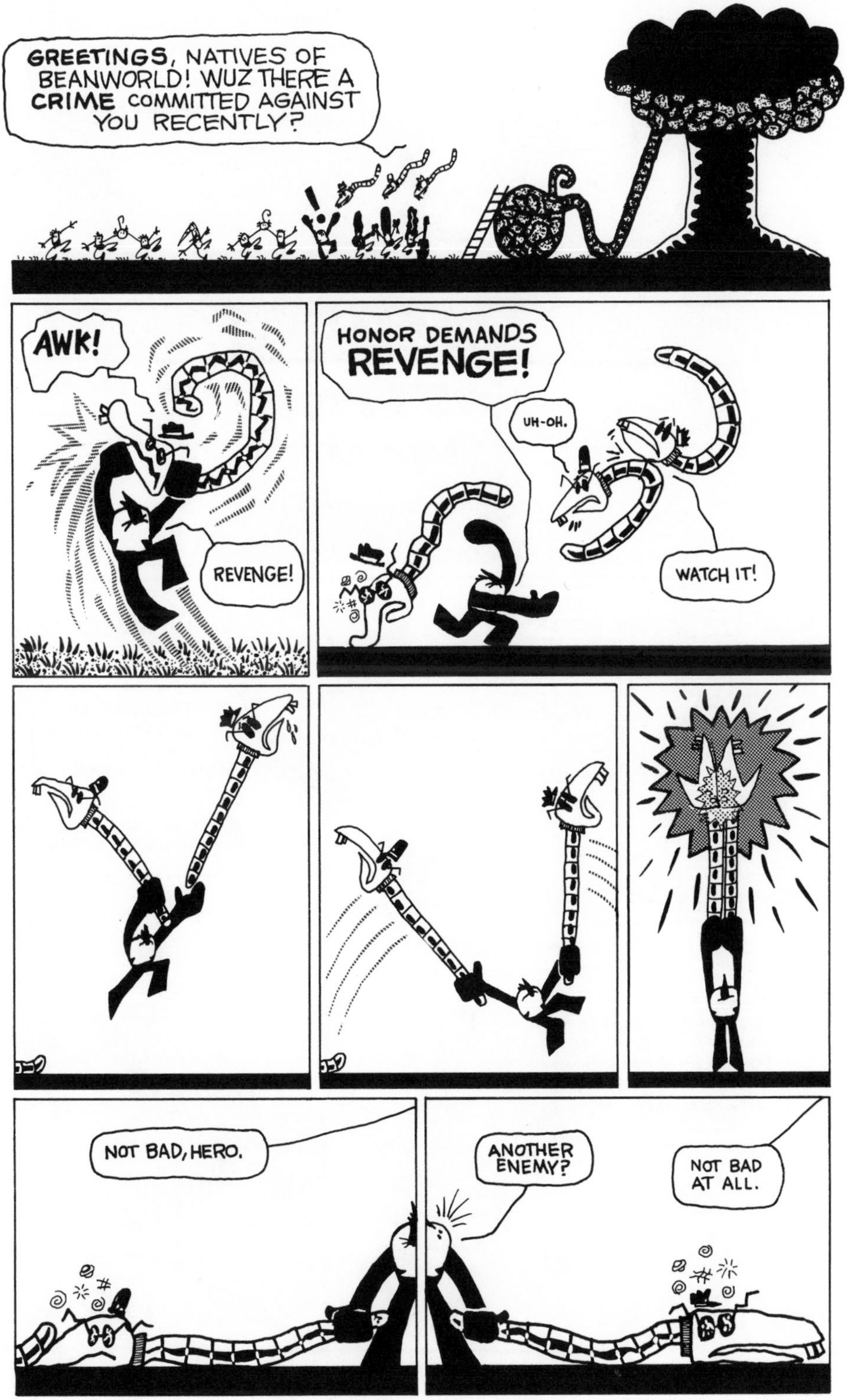
GREETINGS, NATIVES OF BEANWORLD! WUZ THERE A CRIME COMMITTED AGAINST YOU RECENTLY?
AWK!
REVENGE!
HONOR DEMANDS REVENGE!
UH-OH.
WATCH IT!
NOT BAD, HERO.
ANOTHER ENEMY?
NOT BAD AT ALL.

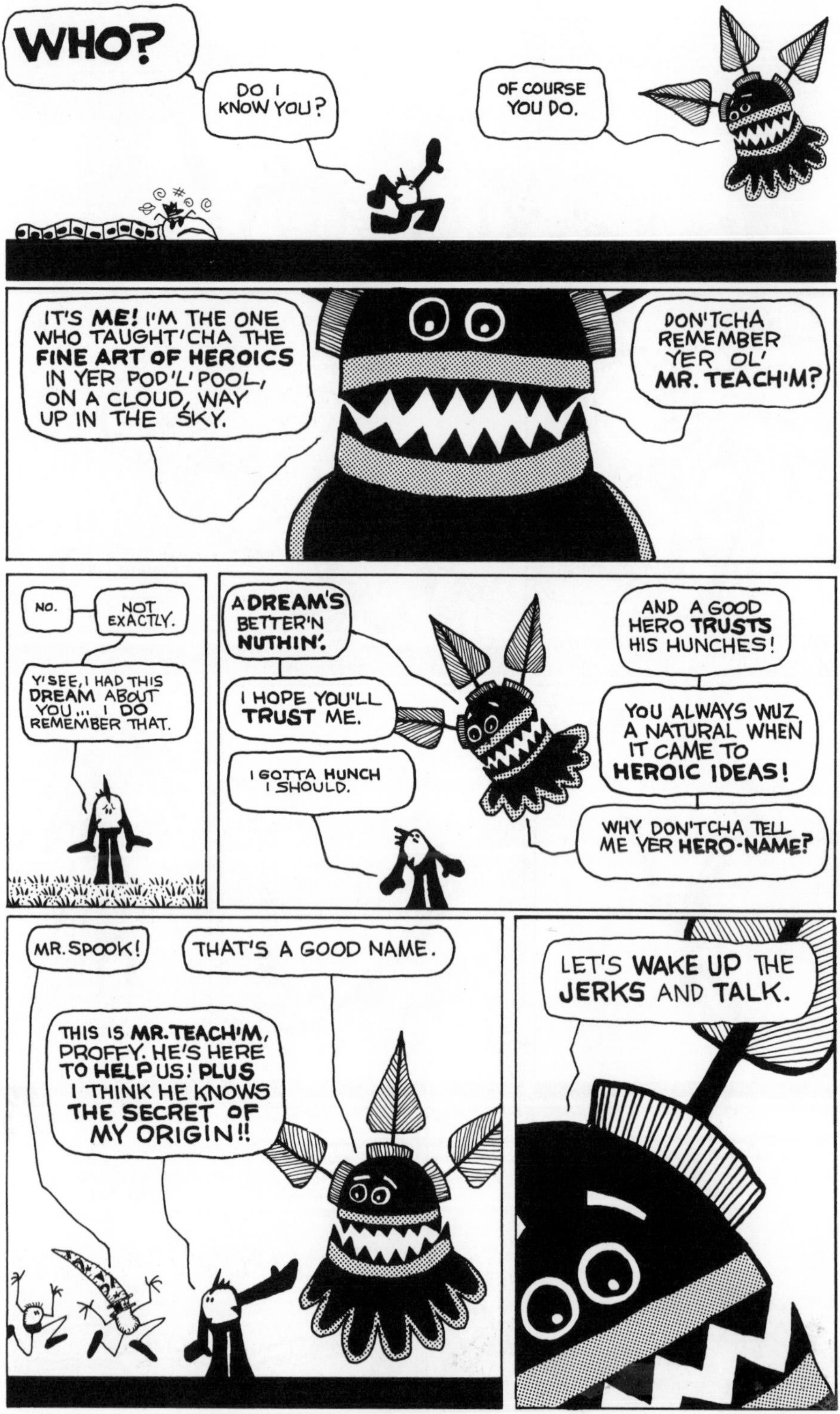
WHO?
DO I KNOW YOU?
OF COURSE YOU DO.
IT'S ME! I'M THE ONE WHO TAUGHT'CHA THE FINE ART OF HEROICS IN YER POD'L'POOL, ON A CLOUD, WAY UP IN THE SKY.
DON'TCHA REMEMBER YER OL' MR. TEACH'M?
NO.
NOT EXACTLY.
Y'SEE, I HAD THIS DREAM ABOUT YOU... I DO REMEMBER THAT.
A DREAM'S BETTER'N NUTHIN'.
I HOPE YOU'LL TRUST ME.
I GOTTA HUNCH I SHOULD.
AND A GOOD HERO TRUSTS HIS HUNCHES!
YOU ALWAYS WUZ A NATURAL WHEN IT CAME TO HEROIC IDEAS!
WHY DON'TCHA TELL ME YER HERO-NAME?
MR. SPOOK!
THAT'S A GOOD NAME.
THIS IS MR. TEACH'M, PROFFY. HE'S HERE TO HELP US! PLUS I THINK HE KNOWS THE SECRET OF MY ORIGIN!!
LET'S WAKE UP THE JERKS AND TALK.

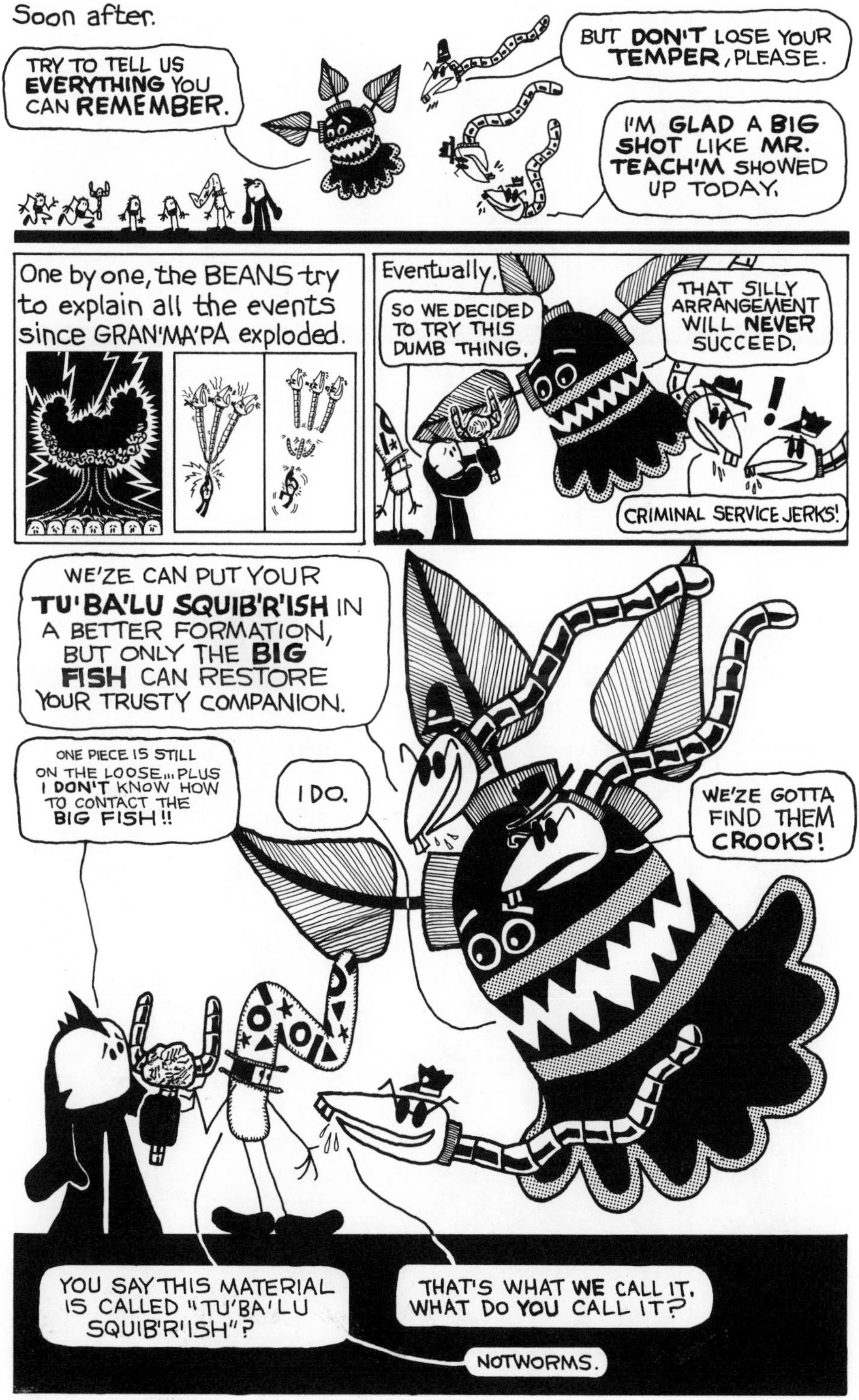

Soon after.
TRY TO TELL US EVERYTHING YOU CAN REMEMBER.
BUT DON'T LOSE YOUR TEMPER, PLEASE.
I'M GLAD A BIG SHOT LIKE MR. TEACH'M SHOWED UP TODAY.
One by one, the BEANS try to explain all the events since GRAN'MA'PA exploded.
Eventually.
SO WE DECIDED TO TRY THIS DUMB THING.
THAT SILLY ARRANGEMENT WILL NEVER SUCCEED.
!
CRIMINAL SERVICE JERKS!
WE'ZE CAN PUT YOUR TU'BA'LU SQUIB'R'ISH IN A BETTER FORMATION, BUT ONLY THE BIG FISH CAN RESTORE YOUR TRUSTY COMPANION.
ONE PIECE IS STILL ON THE LOOSE... PLUS I DON'T KNOW HOW TO CONTACT THE BIG FISH!!
I DO.
WE'ZE GOTTA FIND THEM CROOKS!
YOU SAY THIS MATERIAL IS CALLED "TU'BA'LU SQUIB'R'ISH"?
THAT'S WHAT WE CALL IT. WHAT DO YOU CALL IT?
NOTWORMS.

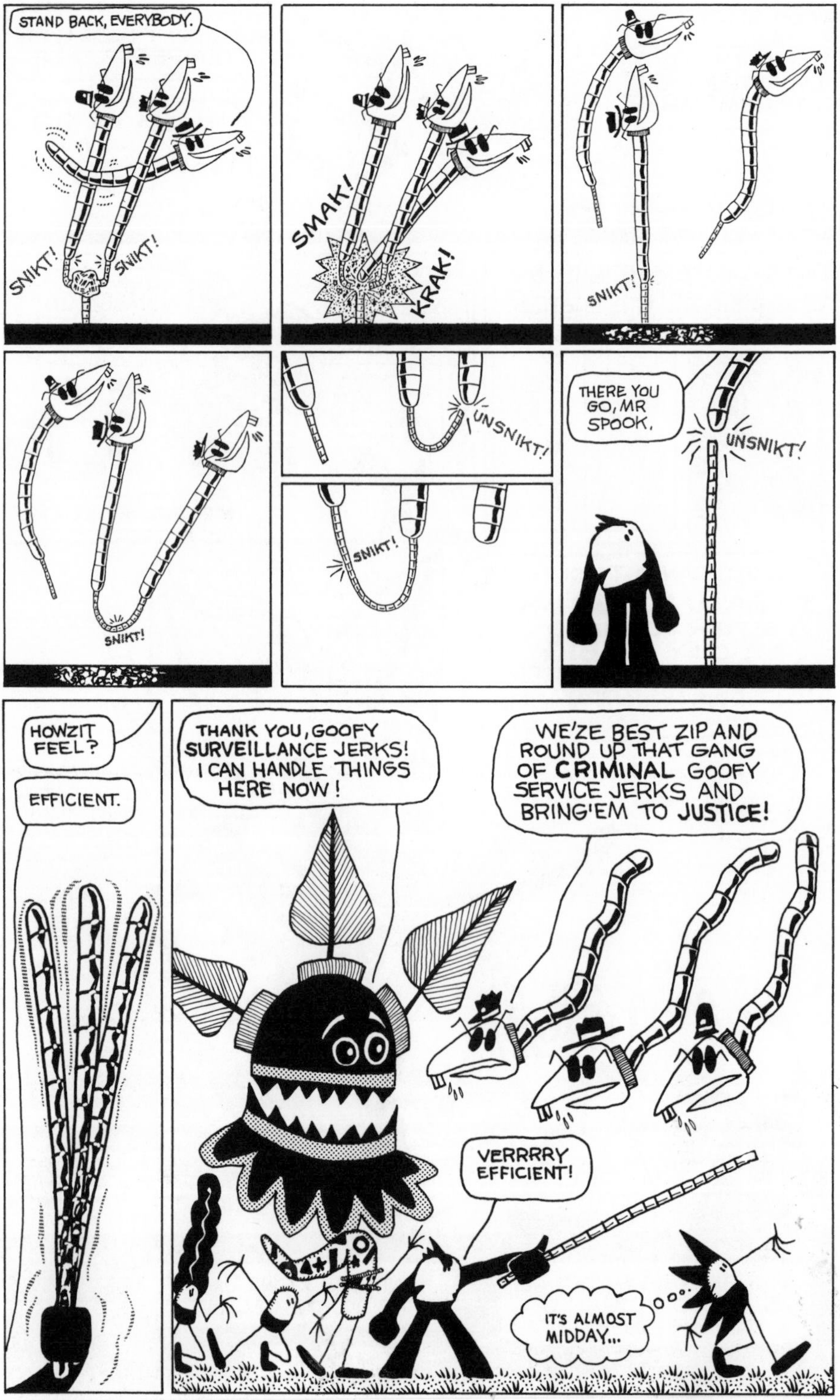
STAND BACK, EVERYBODY.
SNIKT!
SNIKT!
SMAK!
KRAK!
SNIKT!
SNIKT!
UNSNIKT!
SNIKT!
THERE YOU GO, MR SPOOK.
UNSNIKT!
HOWZIT FEEL?
EFFICIENT.
THANK YOU, GOOFY SURVEILLANCE JERKS! I CAN HANDLE THINGS HERE NOW!
WE'ZE BEST ZIP AND ROUND UP THAT GANG OF CRIMINAL GOOFY SERVICE JERKS AND BRING'EM TO JUSTICE!
VERRRRY EFFICIENT!
IT'S ALMOST MIDDAY...
ooo.

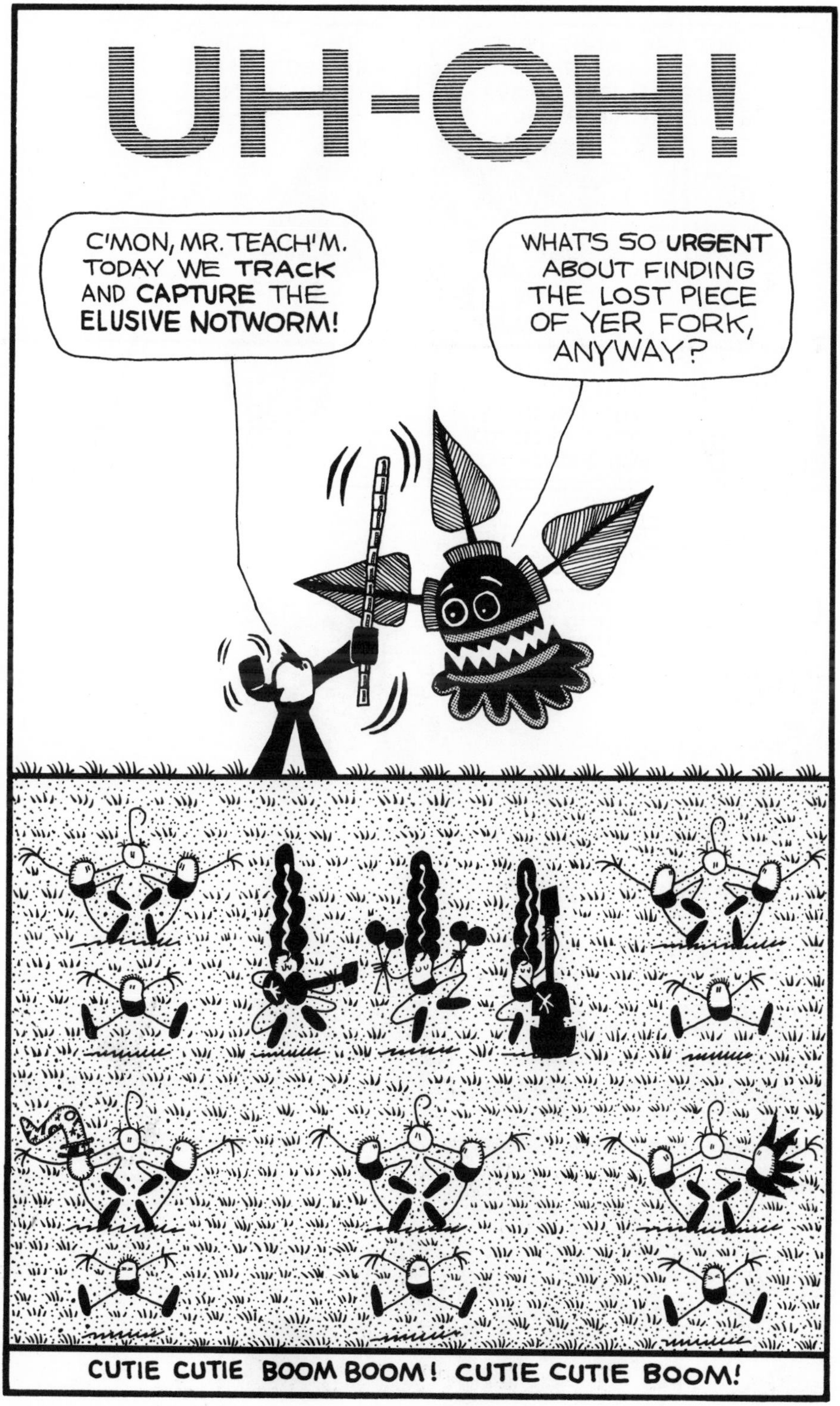
UH-OH!
C'MON, MR. TEACH'M. TODAY WE TRACK AND CAPTURE THE ELUSIVE NOTWORM!
WHAT'S SO URGENT ABOUT FINDING THE LOST PIECE OF YER FORK, ANYWAY?
CUTIE CUTIE BOOM BOOM! CUTIE CUTIE BOOM!

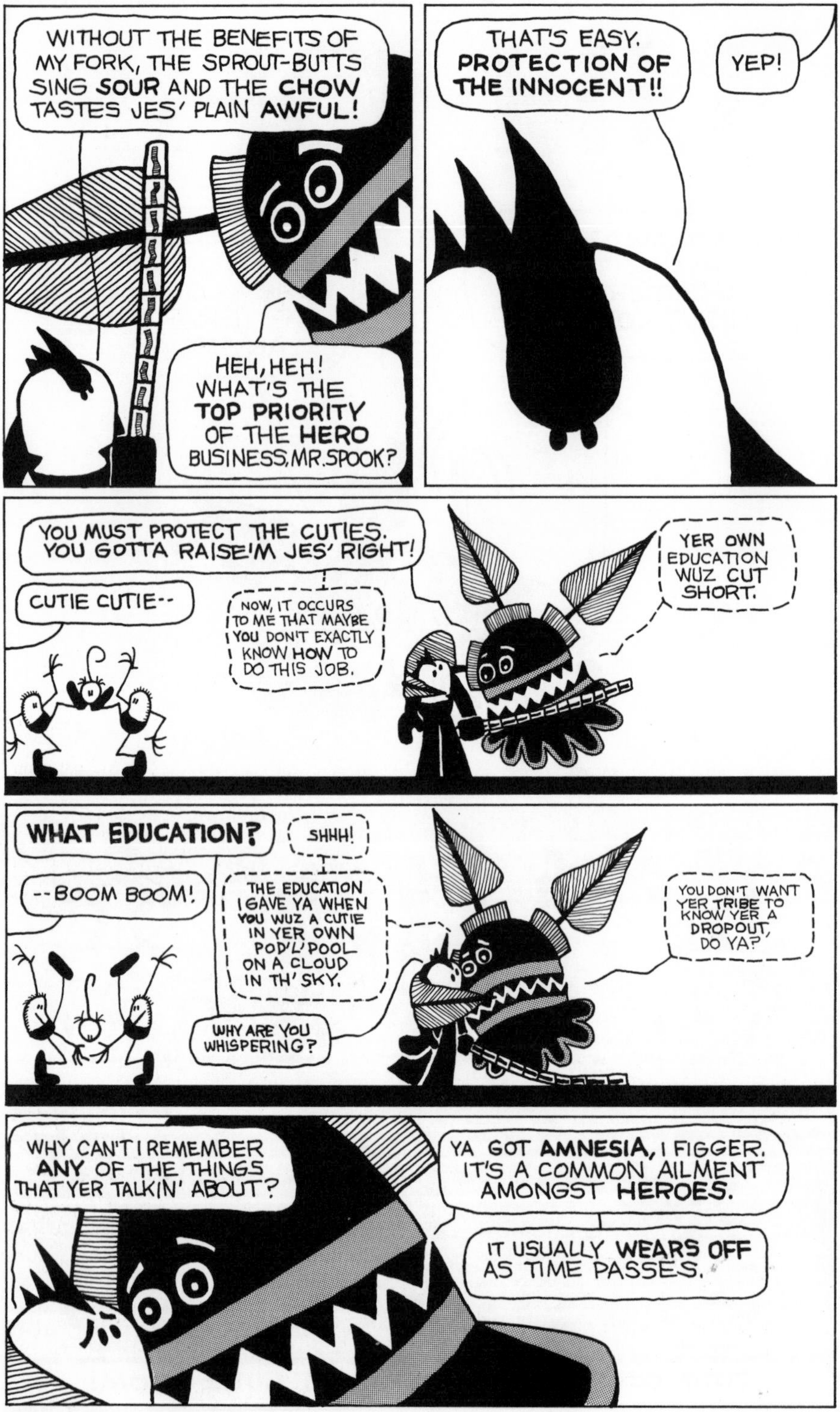

WITHOUT THE BENEFITS OF MY FORK, THE SPROUT-BUTTS SING SOUR AND THE CHOW TASTES JES' PLAIN AWFUL!
HEH, HEH! WHAT'S THE TOP PRIORITY OF THE HERO BUSINESS, MR. SPOOK?
THAT'S EASY. PROTECTION OF THE INNOCENT!!
YEP!
YOU MUST PROTECT THE CUTIES. YOU GOTTA RAISE'M JES' RIGHT!
CUTIE CUTIE--
NOW, IT OCCURS TO ME THAT MAYBE YOU DON'T EXACTLY KNOW HOW TO DO THIS JOB.
YER OWN EDUCATION WUZ CUT SHORT.
WHAT EDUCATION?
SHHH!
--BOOM BOOM!
THE EDUCATION I GAVE YA WHEN YOU WUZ A CUTIE IN YER OWN POD'L'POOL ON A CLOUD IN TH' SKY.
WHY ARE YOU WHISPERING?
YOU DON'T WANT YER TRIBE TO KNOW YER A DROPOUT, DO YA?
WHY CAN'T I REMEMBER ANY OF THE THINGS THAT YER TALKIN' ABOUT?
YA GOT AMNESIA, I FIGGER. IT'S A COMMON AILMENT AMONGST HEROES.
IT USUALLY WEARS OFF AS TIME PASSES.

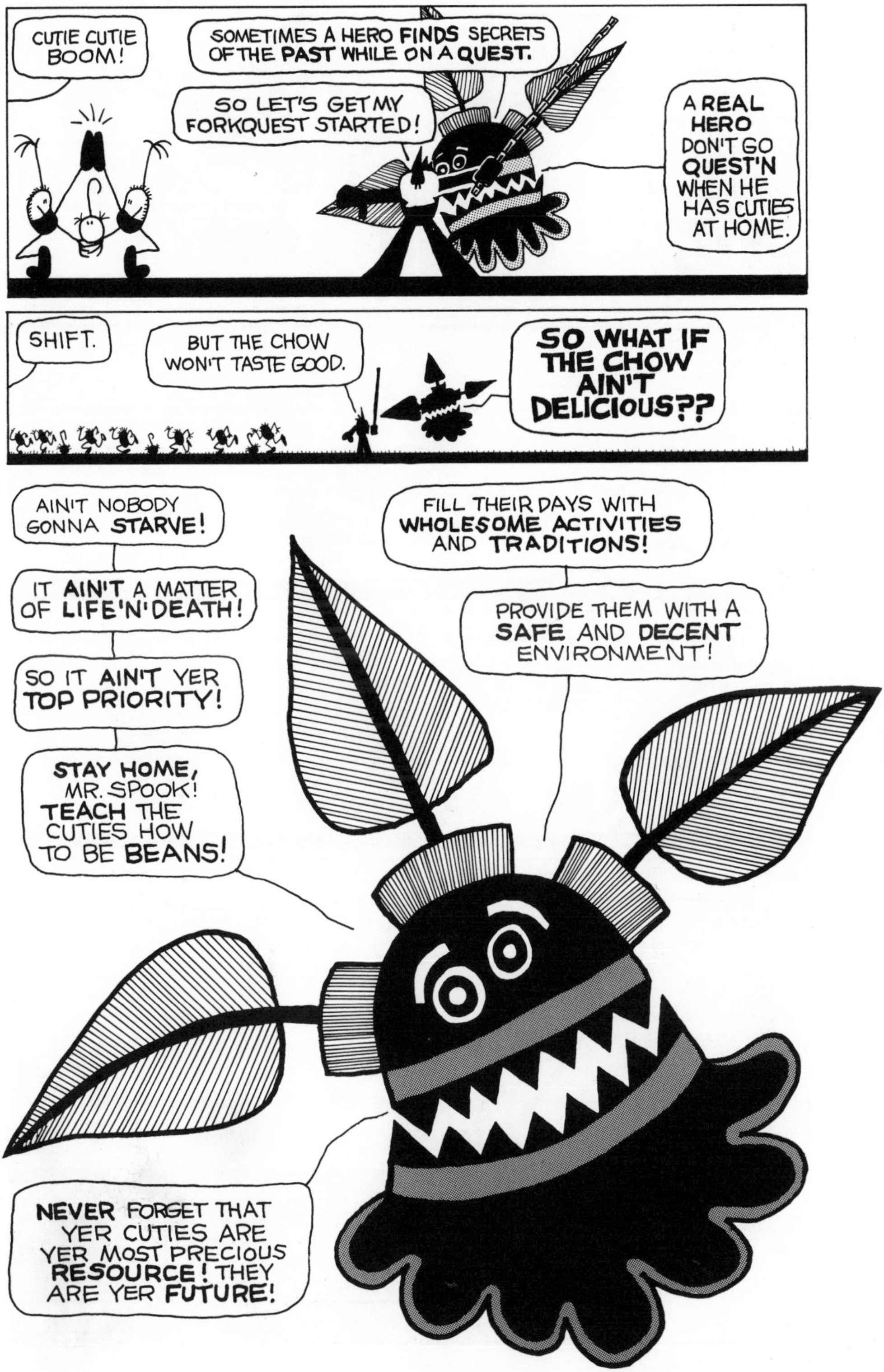
CUTIE CUTIE BOOM!
SOMETIMES A HERO FINDS SECRETS OF THE PAST WHILE ON A QUEST.
SO LET'S GET MY FORKQUEST STARTED!
A REAL HERO DON'T GO QUEST'N WHEN HE HAS CUTIES AT HOME.
SHIFT.
BUT THE CHOW WON'T TASTE GOOD.
SO WHAT IF THE CHOW AIN'T DELICIOUS??
AIN'T NOBODY GONNA STARVE!
IT AIN'T A MATTER OF LIFE'N'DEATH!
SO IT AIN'T YER TOP PRIORITY!
STAY HOME, MR. SPOOK! TEACH THE CUTIES HOW TO BE BEANS!
FILL THEIR DAYS WITH WHOLESOME ACTIVITIES AND TRADITIONS!
PROVIDE THEM WITH A SAFE AND DECENT ENVIRONMENT!
NEVER FORGET THAT YER CUTIES ARE YER MOST PRECIOUS RESOURCE! THEY ARE YER FUTURE!

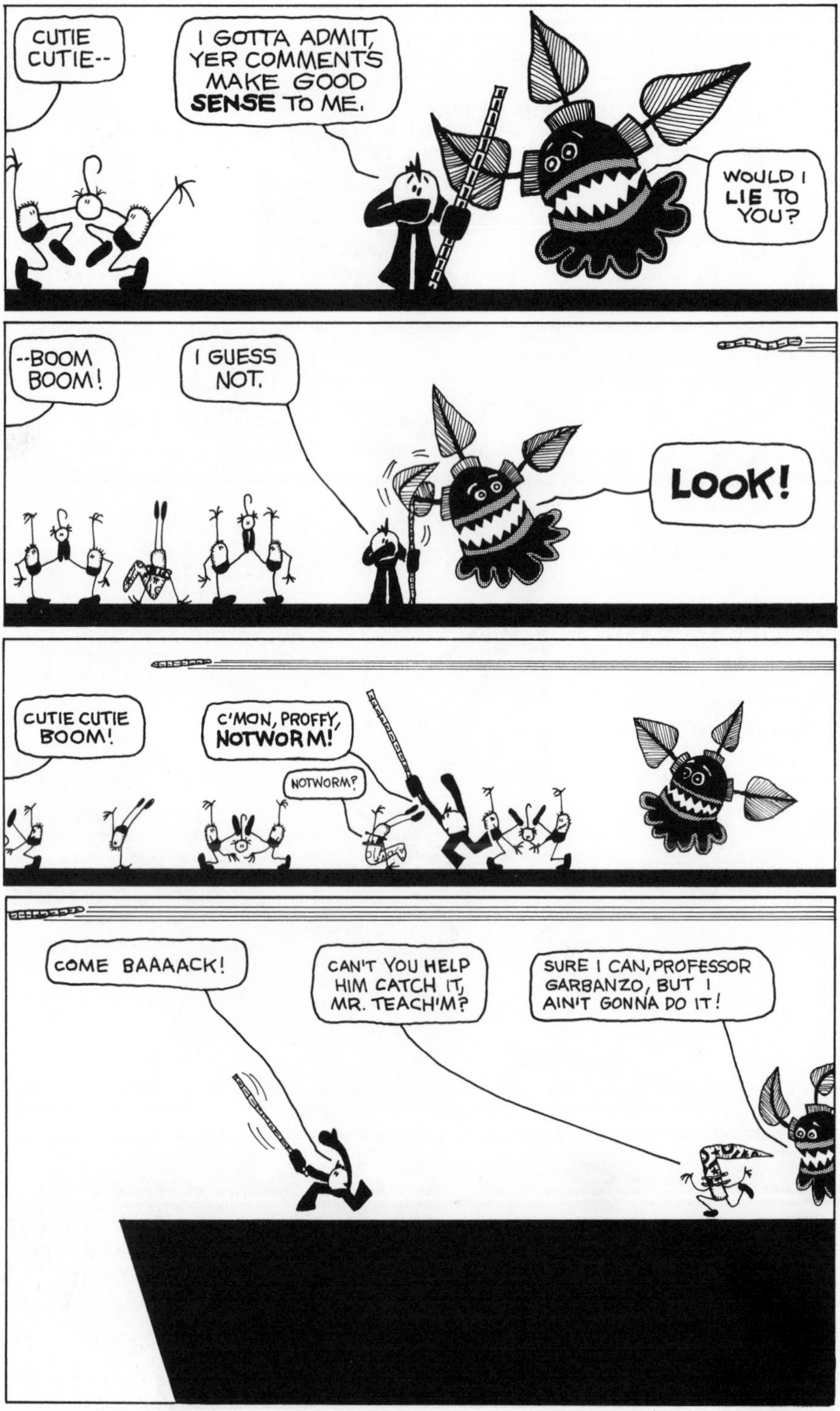
CUTIE CUTIE--
I GOTTA ADMIT, YER COMMENTS MAKE GOOD SENSE TO ME.
WOULD I LIE TO YOU?
--BOOM BOOM!
I GUESS NOT.
LOOK!
CUTIE CUTIE BOOM!
C'MON, PROFFY, NOTWORM!
NOTWORM?
COME BAAAACK!
CAN'T YOU HELP HIM CATCH IT, MR. TEACH'M?
SURE I CAN, PROFESSOR GARBANZO, BUT I AIN'T GONNA DO IT!

IT'S GONE.

THE NOTWORM DIDN'T **REMEMBER** ME LIKE THE **OTHER** PIECES DID.

I GUESS **IT** HAS AMNESIA TOO.

I'M DOIN' YOU BEANS A **FAVOR** BY **NOT** CATCH'N IT FOR YA.

A FAVOR?

YEP.

SLAM!

OOF!

THERE ARE RULES AND REGULATIONS REGARDING OWNERSHIP OF TU'BA'LU SQUIB'R'ISH!

YOW!

HEY!

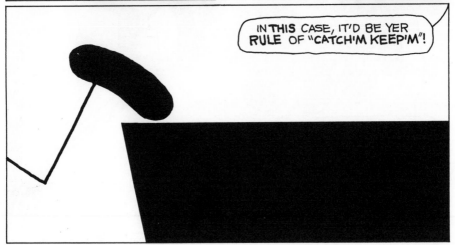

IN **THIS** CASE, IT'D BE YER **RULE** OF "CATCH'M KEEP'M"!

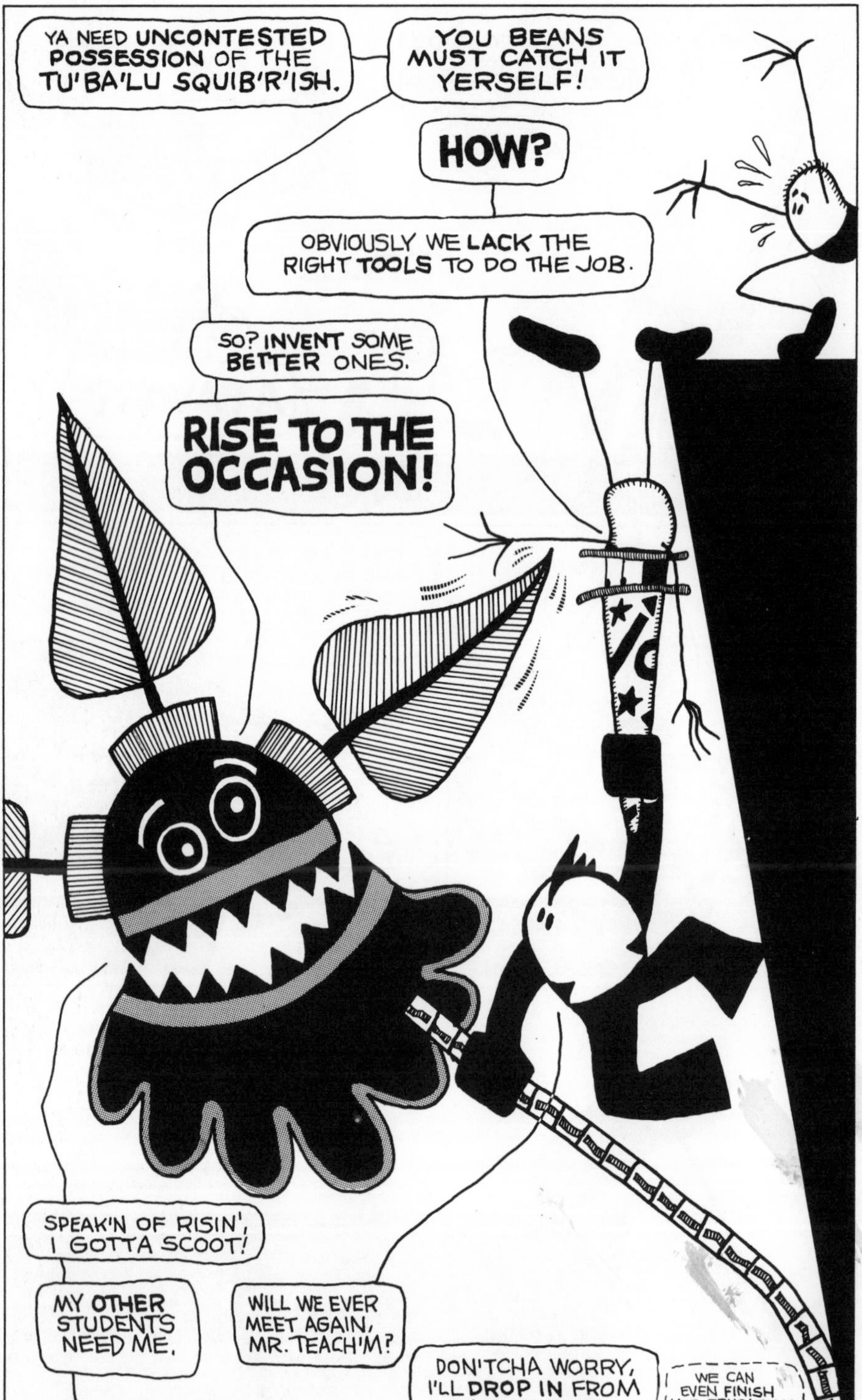
YA NEED UNCONTESTED POSSESSION OF THE TU'BA'LU SQUIB'R'ISH.
YOU BEANS MUST CATCH IT YERSELF!
HOW?
OBVIOUSLY WE LACK THE RIGHT TOOLS TO DO THE JOB.
SO? INVENT SOME BETTER ONES.
RISE TO THE OCCASION!
SPEAK'N OF RISIN', I GOTTA SCOOT!
MY OTHER STUDENTS NEED ME.
WILL WE EVER MEET AGAIN, MR. TEACH'M?
DON'TCHA WORRY, I'LL DROP IN FROM TIME TO TIME.
WE CAN EVEN FINISH YER EDUCATION IF YA WANT TO!

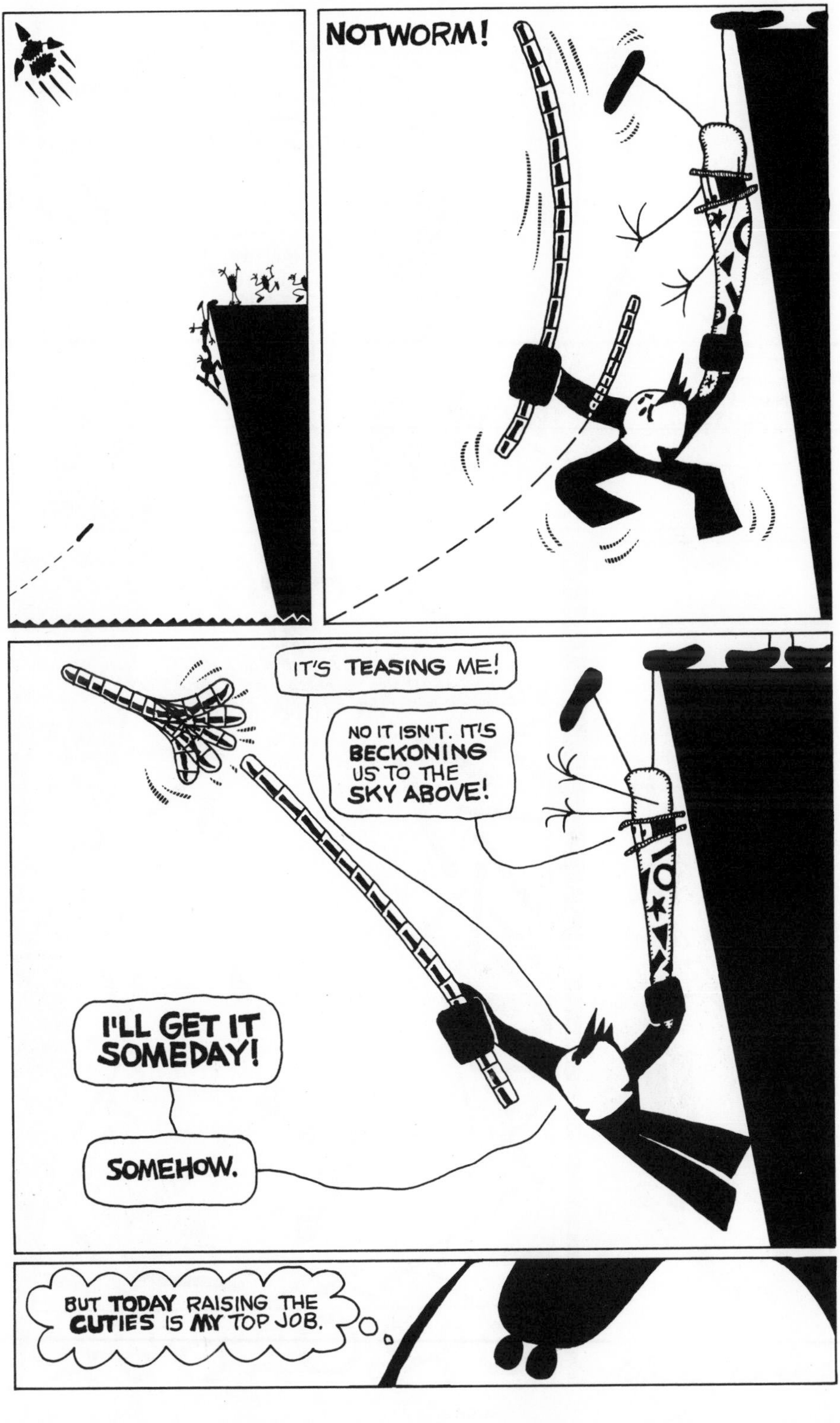
NOTWORM!
IT'S TEASING ME!
NO IT ISN'T. IT'S BECKONING US TO THE SKY ABOVE!
I'LL GET IT SOMEDAY!
SOMEHOW.
BUT TODAY RAISING THE CUTIES IS MY TOP JOB.

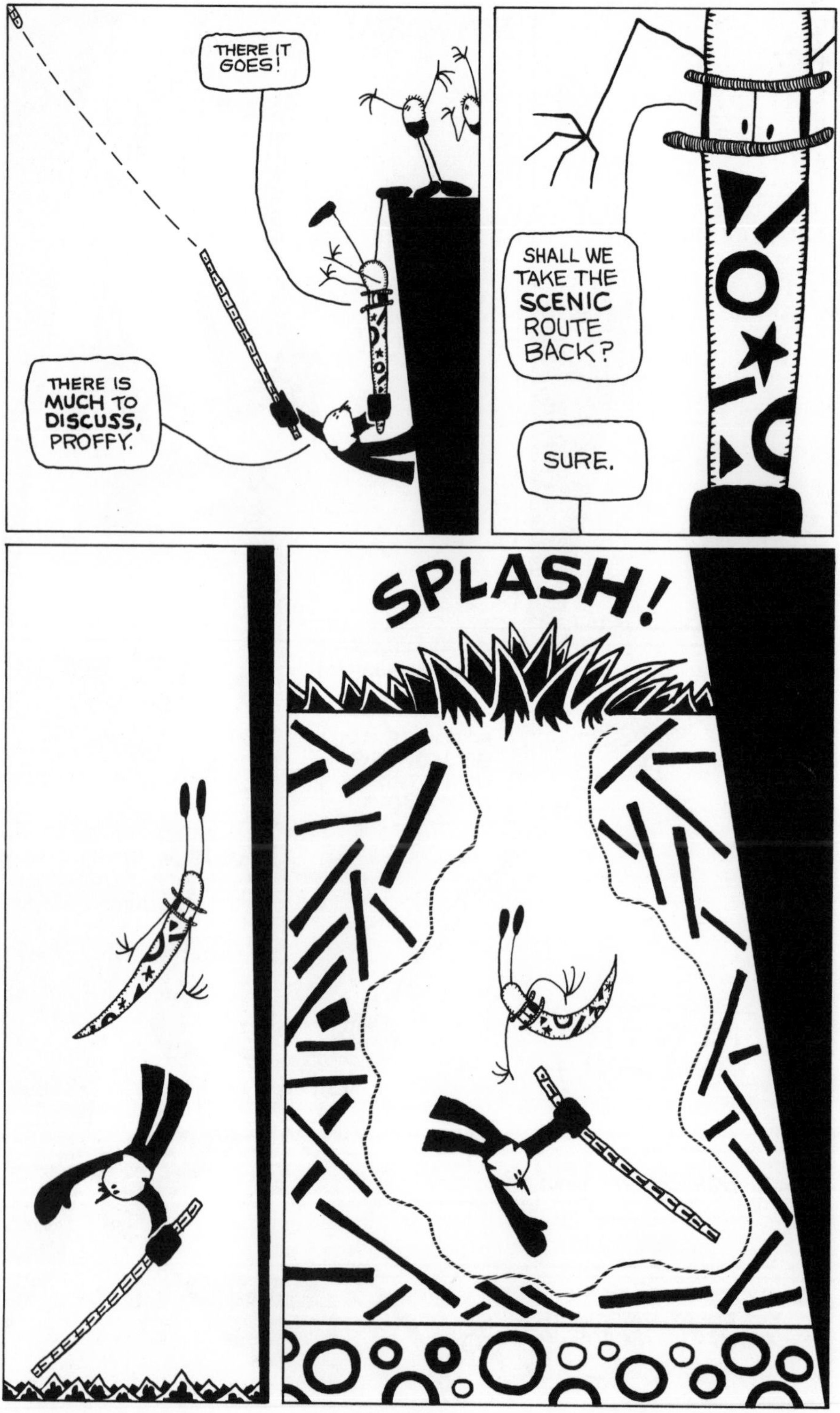
THERE IT GOES!
THERE IS MUCH TO DISCUSS, PROFFY.
SHALL WE TAKE THE SCENIC ROUTE BACK?
SURE.
SPLASH!

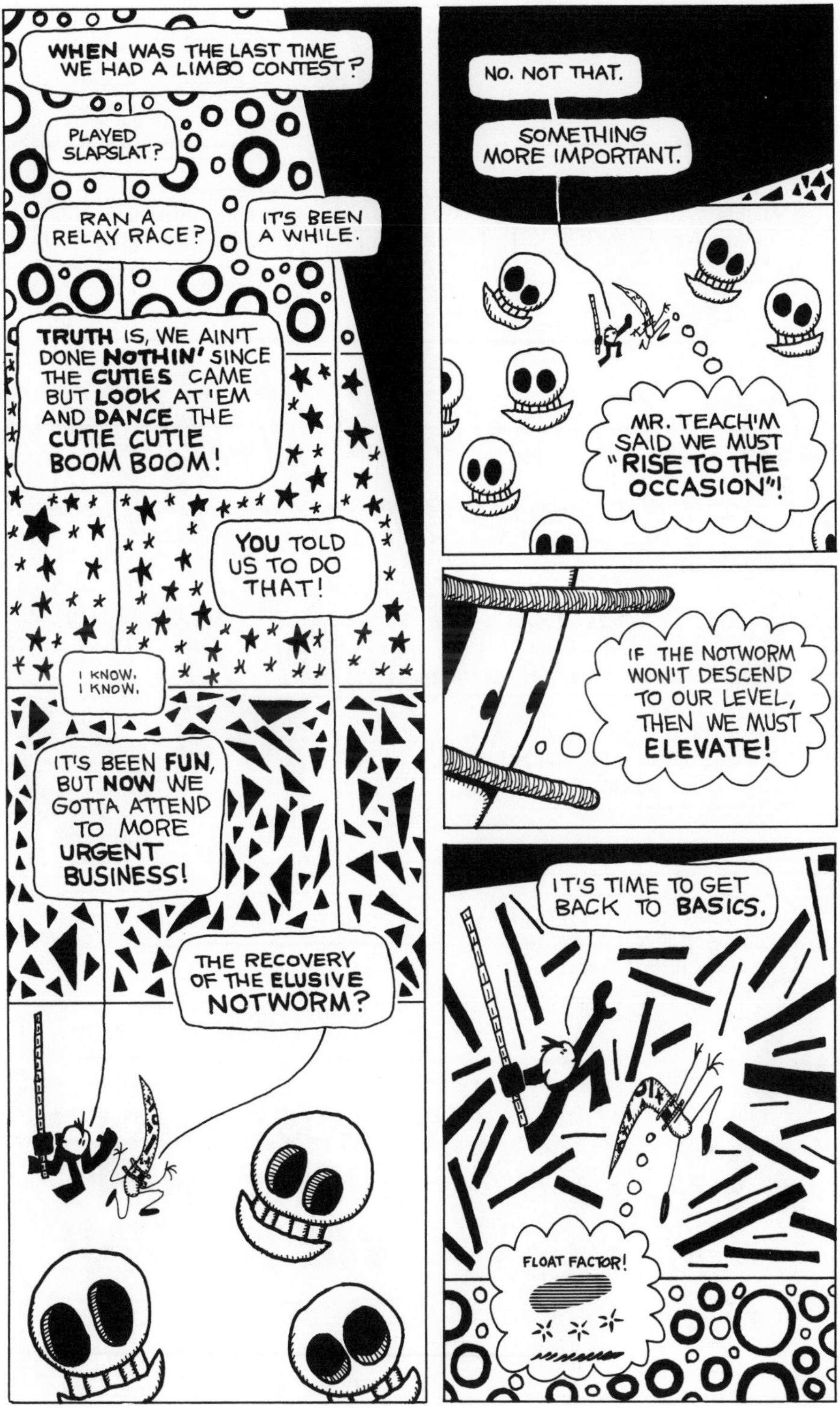

WHEN WAS THE LAST TIME WE HAD A LIMBO CONTEST?
PLAYED SLAPSLAT?
RAN A RELAY RACE?
IT'S BEEN A WHILE.
TRUTH IS, WE AIN'T DONE NOTHIN' SINCE THE CUTIES CAME BUT LOOK AT 'EM AND DANCE THE CUTIE CUTIE BOOM BOOM!
YOU TOLD US TO DO THAT!
I KNOW. I KNOW.
IT'S BEEN FUN, BUT NOW WE GOTTA ATTEND TO MORE URGENT BUSINESS!
THE RECOVERY OF THE ELUSIVE NOTWORM?
NO. NOT THAT.
SOMETHING MORE IMPORTANT.
MR. TEACH'M SAID WE MUST "RISE TO THE OCCASION"!
IF THE NOTWORM WON'T DESCEND TO OUR LEVEL, THEN WE MUST ELEVATE!
IT'S TIME TO GET BACK TO BASICS.
FLOAT FACTOR!

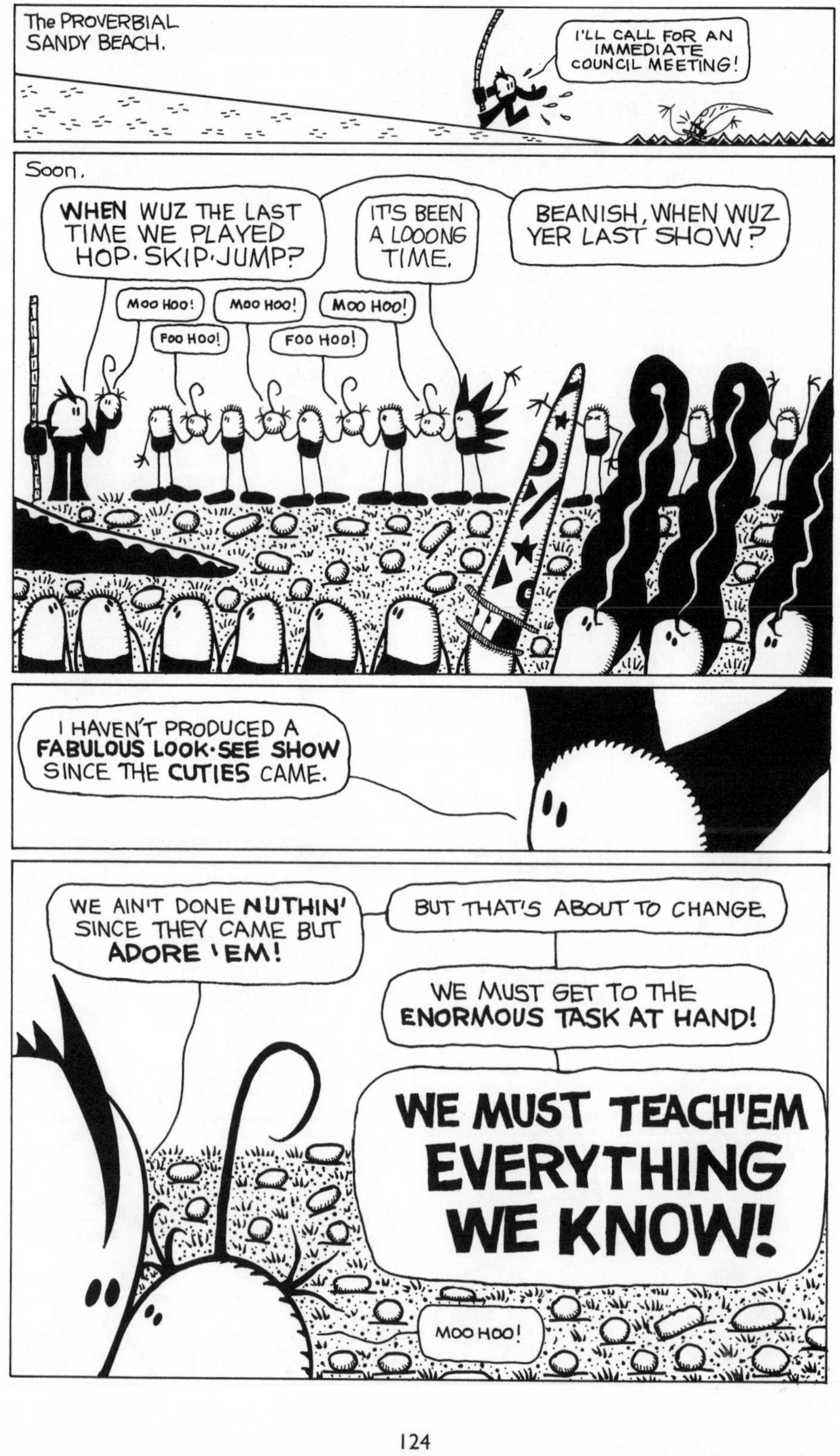
The PROVERBIAL SANDY BEACH.
I'LL CALL FOR AN IMMEDIATE COUNCIL MEETING!
Soon.
WHEN WUZ THE LAST TIME WE PLAYED HOP·SKIP·JUMP?
IT'S BEEN A LOOONG TIME.
BEANISH, WHEN WUZ YER LAST SHOW?
MOO HOO!
MOO HOO!
MOO HOO!
FOO HOO!
FOO HOO!
I HAVEN'T PRODUCED A FABULOUS LOOK·SEE SHOW SINCE THE CUTIES CAME.
WE AIN'T DONE NUTHIN' SINCE THEY CAME BUT ADORE 'EM!
BUT THAT'S ABOUT TO CHANGE.
WE MUST GET TO THE ENORMOUS TASK AT HAND!
WE MUST TEACH'EM EVERYTHING WE KNOW!
MOO HOO!

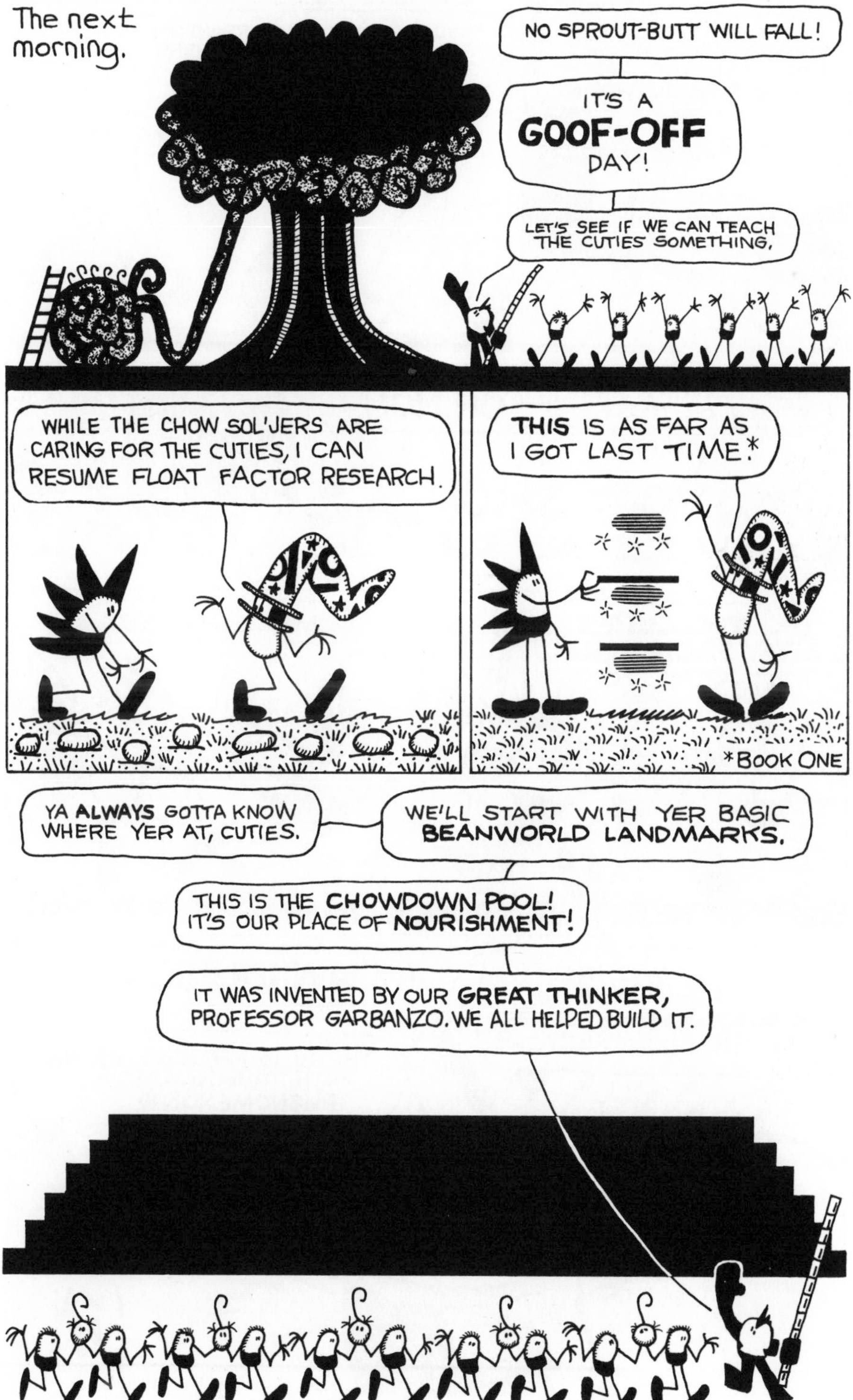
The next morning.
NO SPROUT-BUTT WILL FALL!
IT'S A GOOF-OFF DAY!
LET'S SEE IF WE CAN TEACH THE CUTIES SOMETHING.
WHILE THE CHOW SOL'JERS ARE CARING FOR THE CUTIES, I CAN RESUME FLOAT FACTOR RESEARCH.
THIS IS AS FAR AS I GOT LAST TIME.*
*BOOK ONE
YA ALWAYS GOTTA KNOW WHERE YER AT, CUTIES.
WE'LL START WITH YER BASIC BEANWORLD LANDMARKS.
THIS IS THE CHOWDOWN POOL! IT'S OUR PLACE OF NOURISHMENT!
IT WAS INVENTED BY OUR GREAT THINKER, PROFESSOR GARBANZO. WE ALL HELPED BUILD IT.

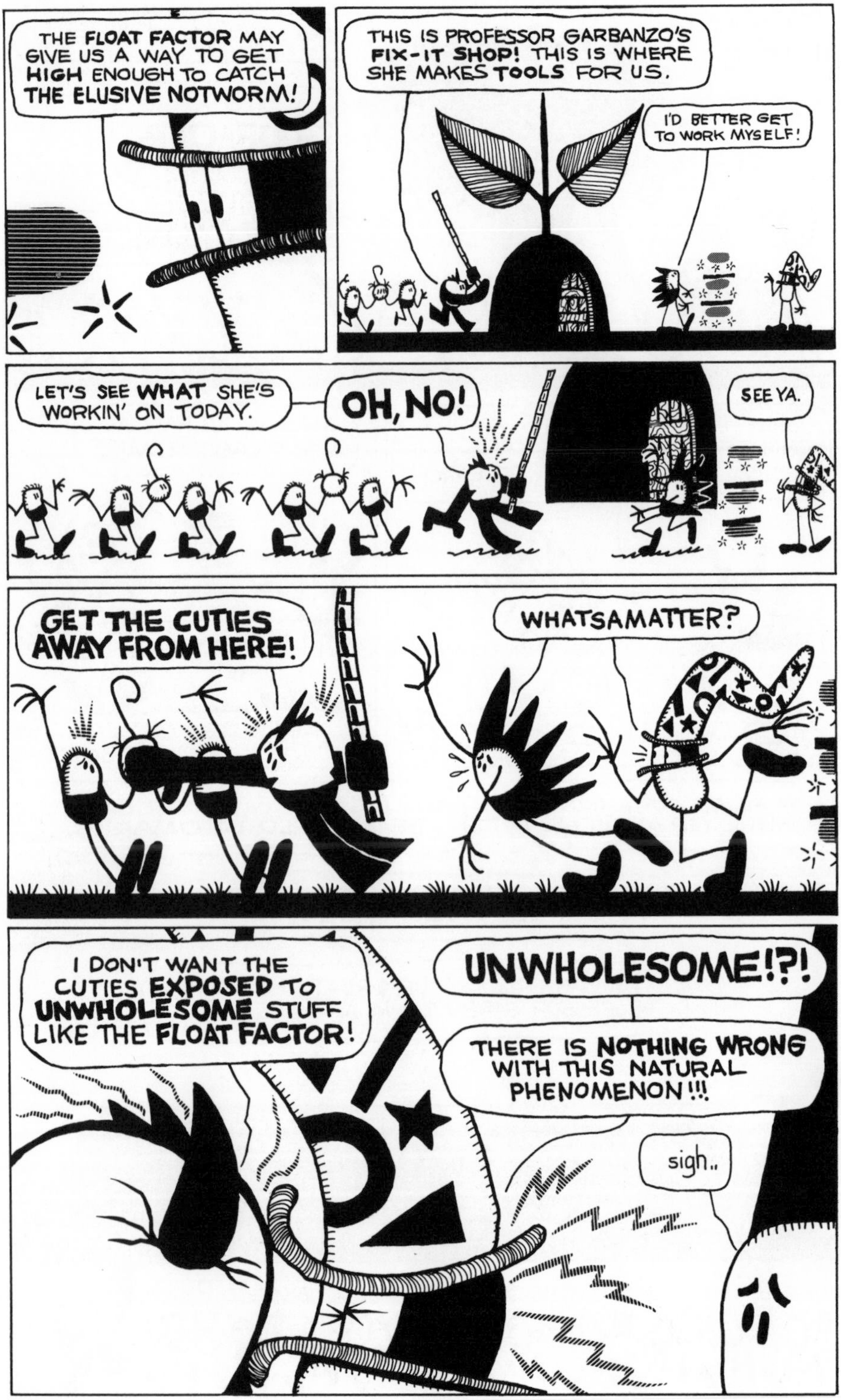

THE FLOAT FACTOR MAY GIVE US A WAY TO GET HIGH ENOUGH TO CATCH THE ELUSIVE NOTWORM!
THIS IS PROFESSOR GARBANZO'S FIX-IT SHOP! THIS IS WHERE SHE MAKES TOOLS FOR US.
I'D BETTER GET TO WORK MYSELF!
LET'S SEE WHAT SHE'S WORKIN' ON TODAY.
OH, NO!
SEE YA.
GET THE CUTIES AWAY FROM HERE!
WHATSAMATTER?
I DON'T WANT THE CUTIES EXPOSED TO UNWHOLESOME STUFF LIKE THE FLOAT FACTOR!
UNWHOLESOME!?!
THERE IS NOTHING WRONG WITH THIS NATURAL PHENOMENON!!!
sigh..

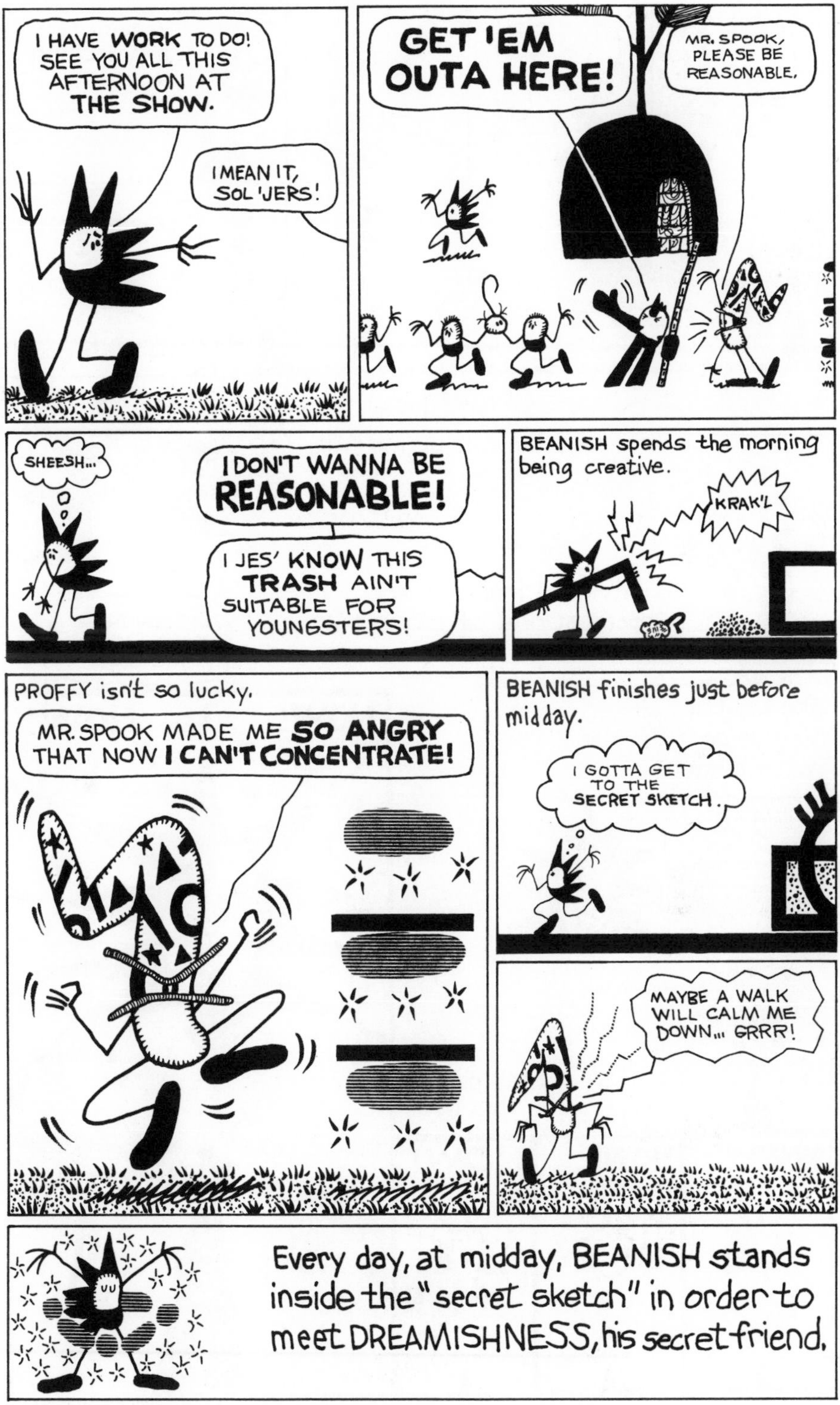
I HAVE WORK TO DO! SEE YOU ALL THIS AFTERNOON AT THE SHOW.
I MEAN IT, SOL'JERS!
GET 'EM OUTA HERE!
MR. SPOOK, PLEASE BE REASONABLE.
SHEESH...
I DON'T WANNA BE REASONABLE!
I JES' KNOW THIS TRASH AIN'T SUITABLE FOR YOUNGSTERS!
BEANISH spends the morning being creative.
KRAK'L
PROFFY isn't so lucky.
MR. SPOOK MADE ME SO ANGRY THAT NOW I CAN'T CONCENTRATE!
BEANISH finishes just before midday.
I GOTTA GET TO THE SECRET SKETCH.
MAYBE A WALK WILL CALM ME DOWN... GRRR!
Every day, at midday, BEANISH stands inside the "secret sketch" in order to meet DREAMISHNESS, his secret friend.

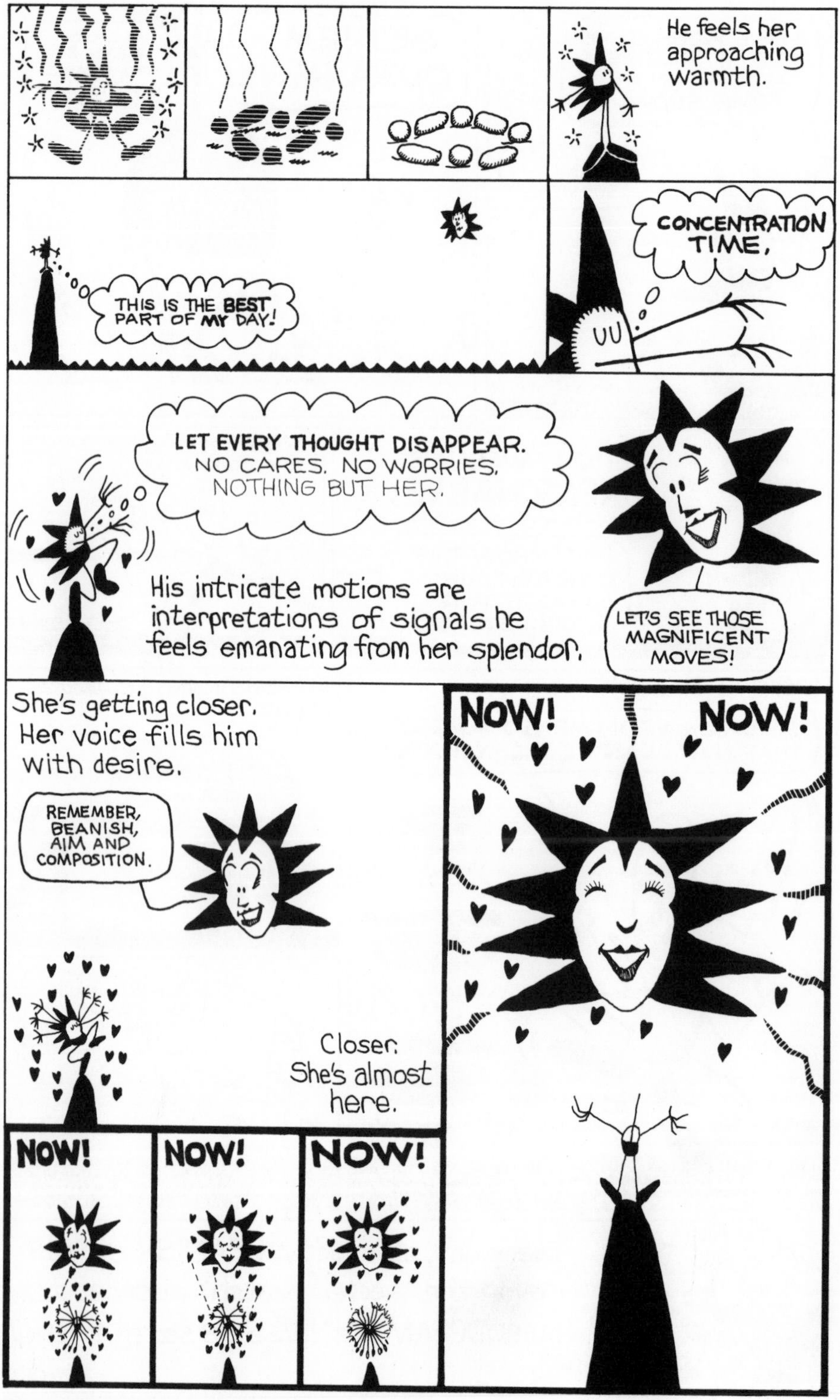
He feels her approaching warmth.
THIS IS THE BEST PART OF MY DAY!
CONCENTRATION TIME,
LET EVERY THOUGHT DISAPPEAR. NO CARES. NO WORRIES. NOTHING BUT HER.
His intricate motions are interpretations of signals he feels emanating from her splendor.
LET'S SEE THOSE MAGNIFICENT MOVES!
She's getting closer. Her voice fills him with desire.
REMEMBER, BEANISH, AIM AND COMPOSITION.
Closer. She's almost here.
NOW!
NOW!
NOW!
NOW!
NOW!

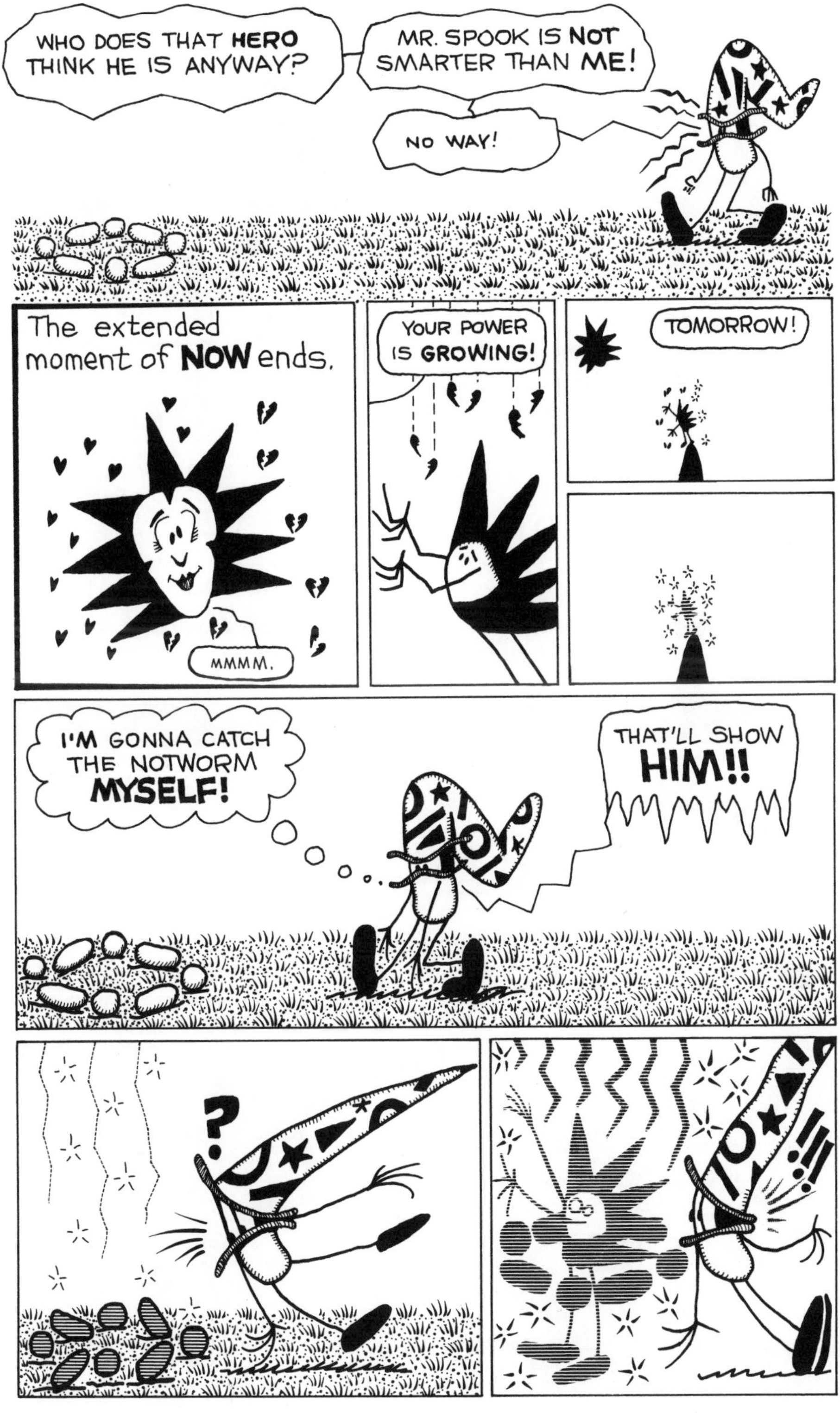
WHO DOES THAT HERO THINK HE IS ANYWAY?
MR. SPOOK IS NOT SMARTER THAN ME!
NO WAY!
The extended moment of NOW ends.
MMMM.
YOUR POWER IS GROWING!
TOMORROW!
I'M GONNA CATCH THE NOTWORM MYSELF!
THAT'LL SHOW HIM!!
?

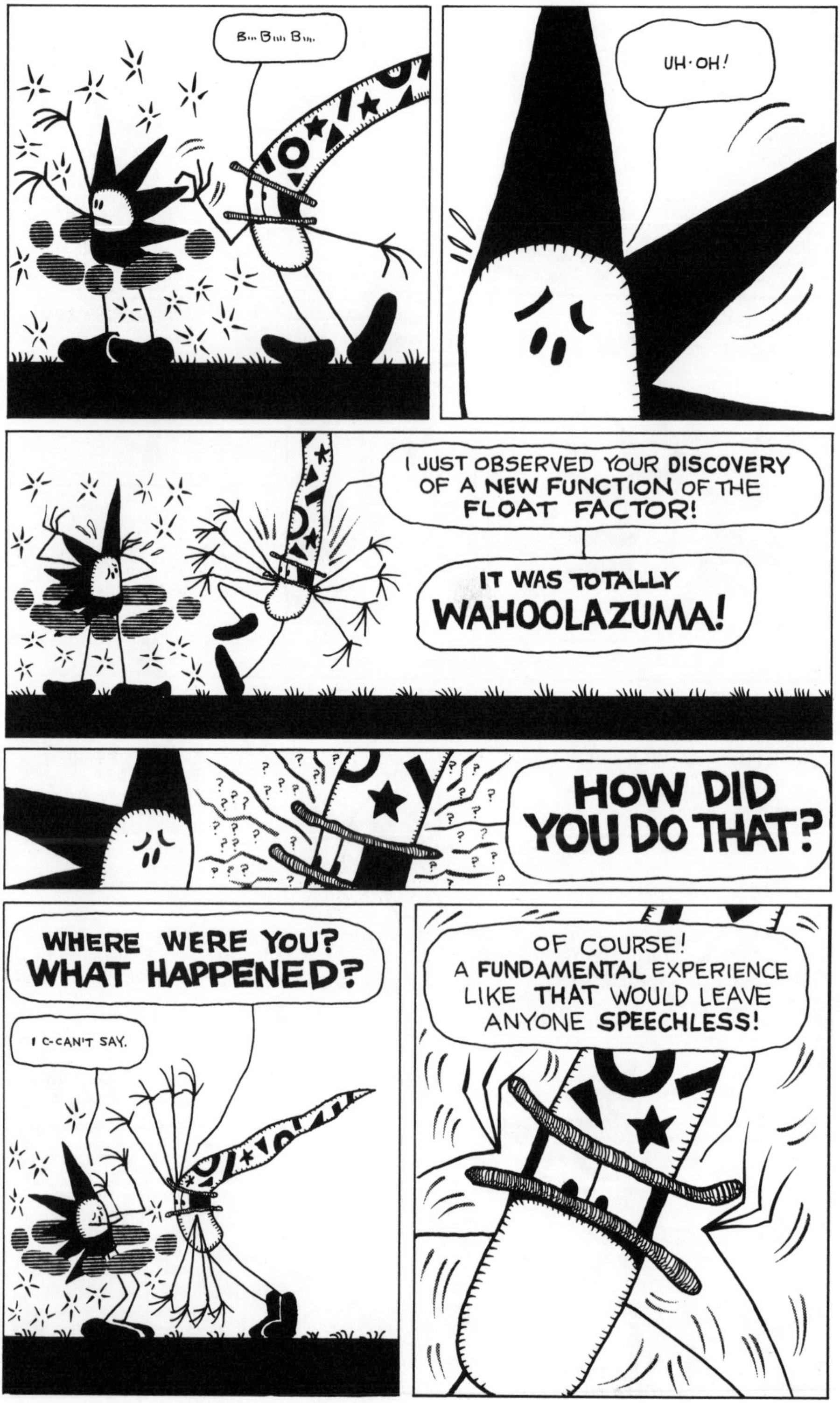
B... B... B...
UH-OH!
I JUST OBSERVED YOUR DISCOVERY OF A NEW FUNCTION OF THE FLOAT FACTOR!
IT WAS TOTALLY WAHOOLAZUMA!
HOW DID YOU DO THAT?
WHERE WERE YOU? WHAT HAPPENED?
I C-CAN'T SAY.
OF COURSE! A FUNDAMENTAL EXPERIENCE LIKE THAT WOULD LEAVE ANYONE SPEECHLESS!

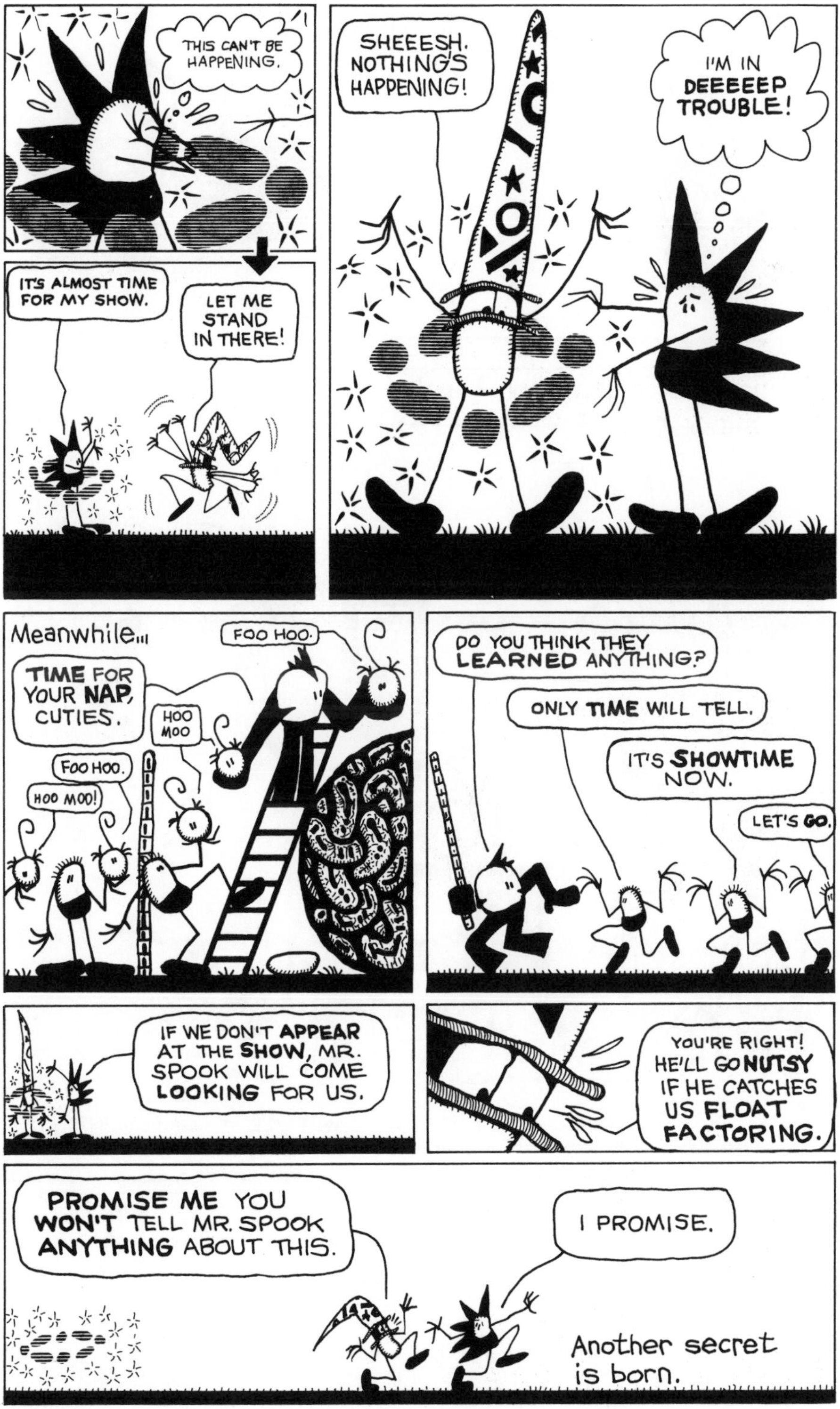
THIS CAN'T BE HAPPENING.
SHEEESH. NOTHING'S HAPPENING!
I'M IN DEEEEEP TROUBLE!
IT'S ALMOST TIME FOR MY SHOW.
LET ME STAND IN THERE!
Meanwhile...
TIME FOR YOUR NAP, CUTIES.
FOO HOO.
HOO MOO
FOO HOO.
HOO MOO!
DO YOU THINK THEY LEARNED ANYTHING?
ONLY TIME WILL TELL.
IT'S SHOWTIME NOW.
LET'S GO.
IF WE DON'T APPEAR AT THE SHOW, MR. SPOOK WILL COME LOOKING FOR US.
YOU'RE RIGHT! HE'LL GO NUTSY IF HE CATCHES US FLOAT FACTORING.
PROMISE ME YOU WON'T TELL MR. SPOOK ANYTHING ABOUT THIS.
I PROMISE.
Another secret is born.

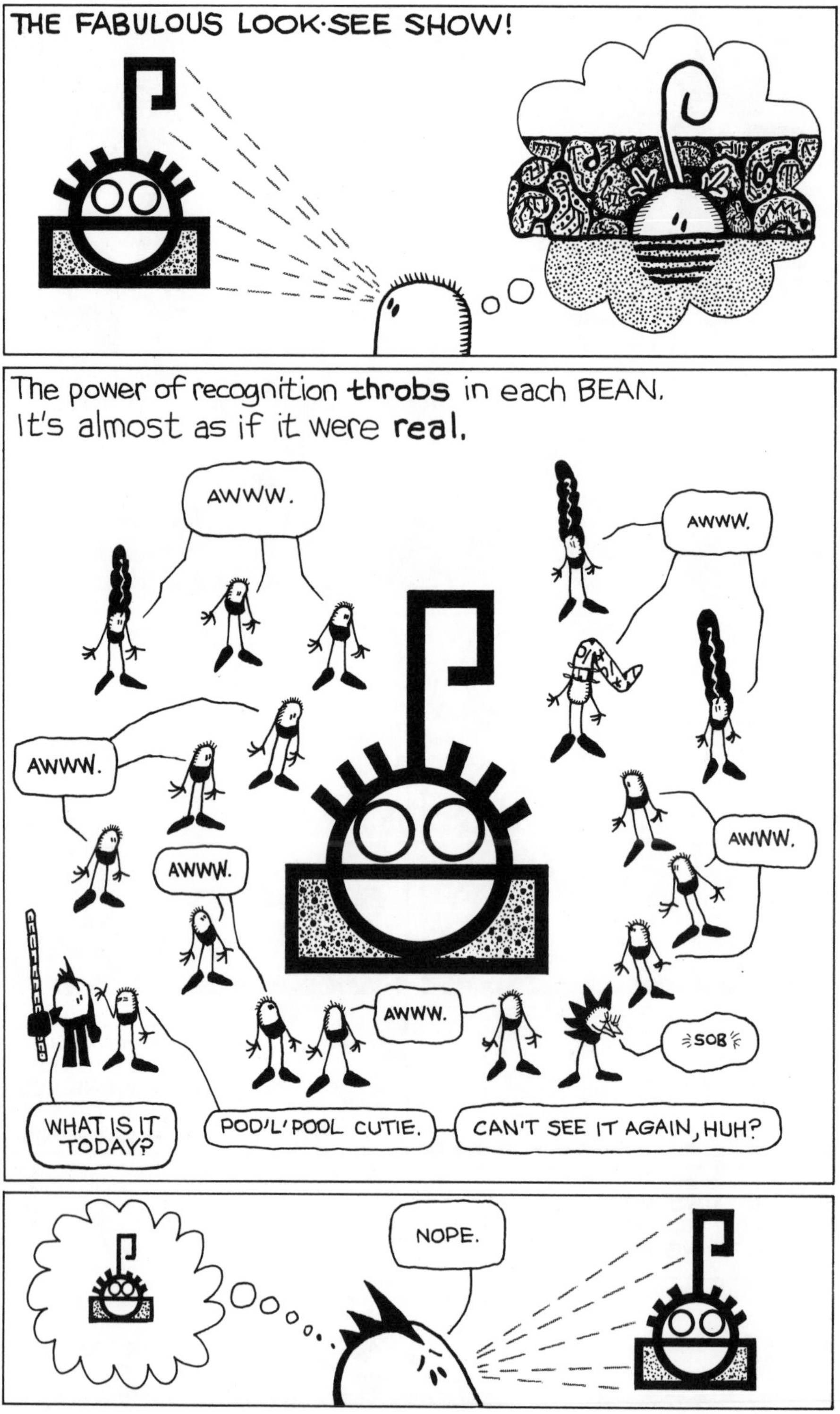
THE FABULOUS LOOK·SEE SHOW!
The power of recognition throbs in each BEAN. It's almost as if it were real.
AWWW.
AWWW.
AWWW.
AWWW.
AWWW.
AWWW.
SOB
WHAT IS IT TODAY?
POD'L'POOL CUTIE.
CAN'T SEE IT AGAIN, HUH?
NOPE.

The next day. A SPROUT-BUTT falls.

WOO!!

POP!

GOTTA SNAG IT ON TH' FIRST BOUNCE!

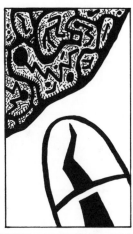

SKIIIIIID!

WHAT'S WIT' TH' **LOW RIDE?**

IT'S TH' BEST I CAN DO RIGHT NOW.

IT'S **NO GOOD!**

ANOTHER UNHAPPY SPROUT-BUTT.

The CHOW SOL'JERS assemble and go to steal CHOW from their enemies, the HOI-POLLOI.

I DIDN'T SLEEP A WINK LAST NIGHT.

BEANISH AND I HAVE VERY IMPORTANT WORK TO DO, SO YOU MIND THE CUTIES TODAY, OKAY?

OKAY.

I'M SOOOO EXCITED, BEANISH!

THIS IS NOT GOOD.

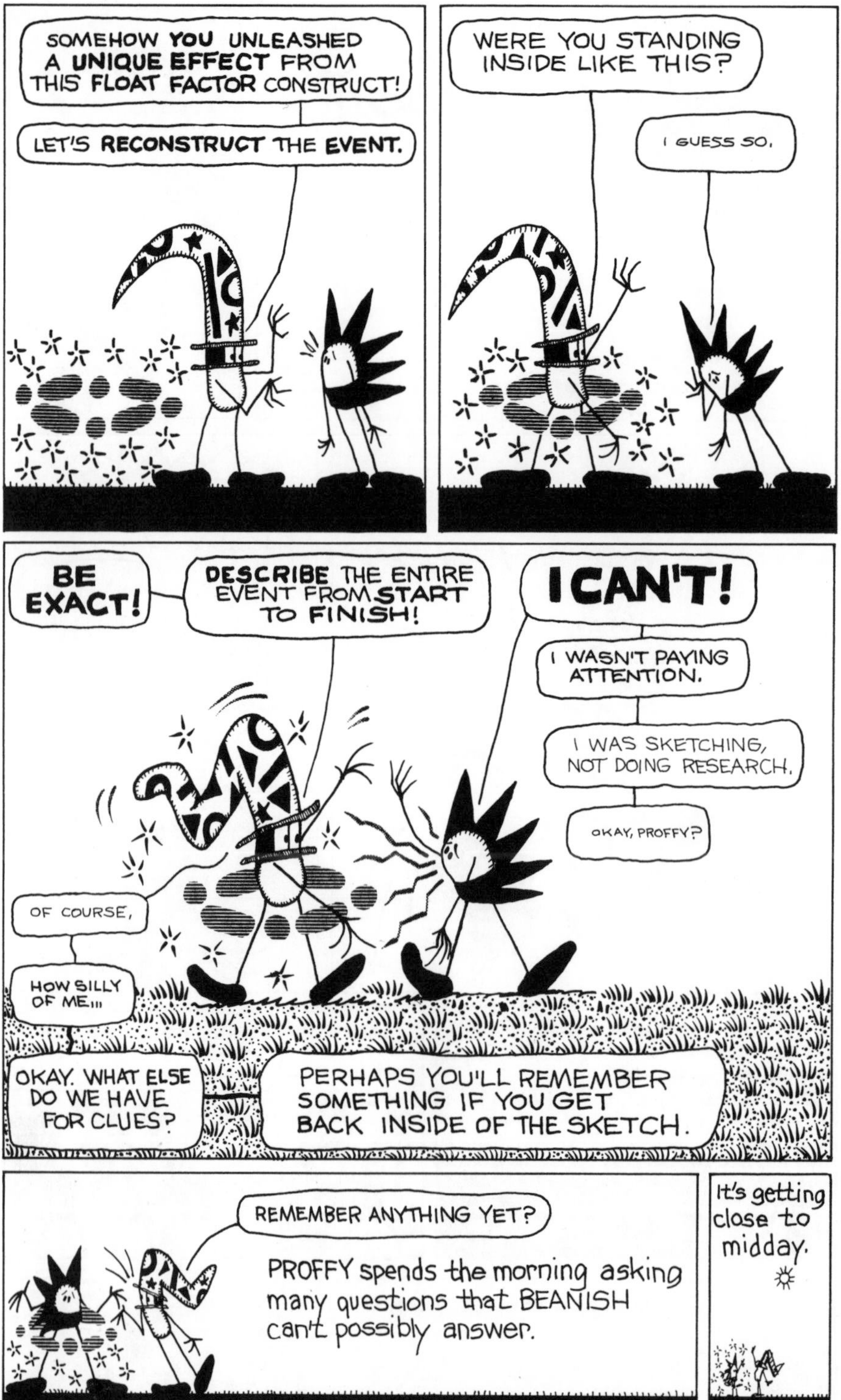

SOMEHOW YOU UNLEASHED A UNIQUE EFFECT FROM THIS FLOAT FACTOR CONSTRUCT!
LET'S RECONSTRUCT THE EVENT.
WERE YOU STANDING INSIDE LIKE THIS?
I GUESS SO.
BE EXACT!
DESCRIBE THE ENTIRE EVENT FROM START TO FINISH!
I CAN'T!
I WASN'T PAYING ATTENTION.
I WAS SKETCHING, NOT DOING RESEARCH.
OKAY, PROFFY?
OF COURSE,
HOW SILLY OF ME...
OKAY. WHAT ELSE DO WE HAVE FOR CLUES?
PERHAPS YOU'LL REMEMBER SOMETHING IF YOU GET BACK INSIDE OF THE SKETCH.
REMEMBER ANYTHING YET?
PROFFY spends the morning asking many questions that BEANISH can't possibly answer.
It's getting close to midday.

Closer.

MAYBE BODY POSITION IS A FACTOR.

YOU WERE POSED THIS WAY.

Almost.

LIKE THIS?

ARMS A BIT HIGHER.

Midday.

THAT'S IT!

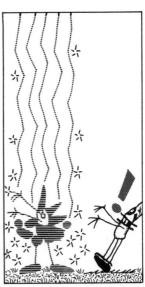

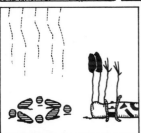

BEANISH IS **GONE** AND SO ARE THE TWINKS.

HEY, SILLY, I'M OVER **HERE!**

A DISASTER HAS OCCURRED, MY FRIEND!

WHAT?

He explains as well as he can.

SO?

YOUR **PRIVATE** SECRET IS NOW A **PUBLIC** SECRET.

BUT IT IS STILL A **SECRET!**

RELAX.

LET'S ENJOY OUR FEW MOMENTS TOGETHER.

SUMMON YOUR POWER.

OKAY.

He concentrates on the feel of her fabulous heat.

Closer.
Closer.
Closer.

135

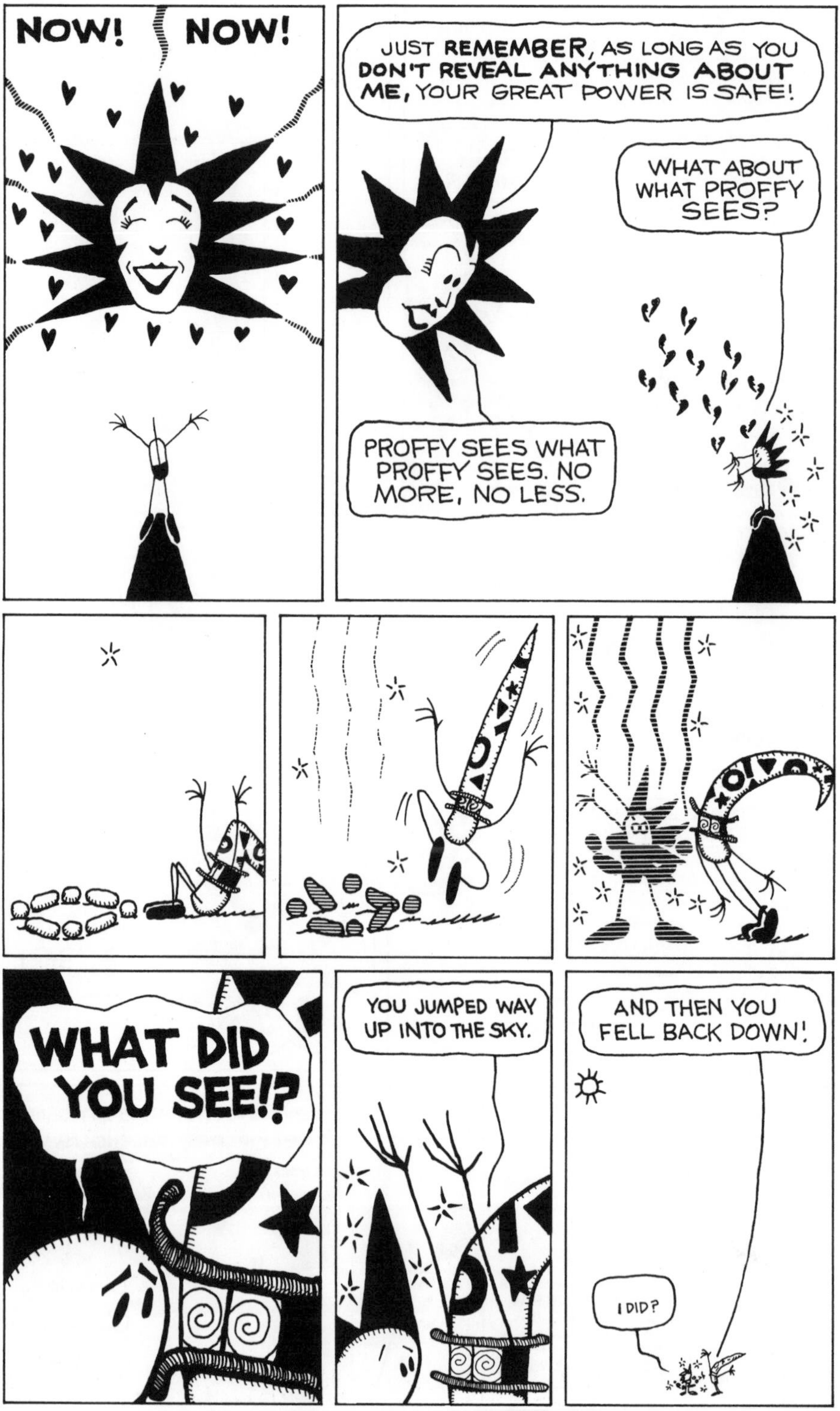
NOW! NOW!
JUST REMEMBER, AS LONG AS YOU DON'T REVEAL ANYTHING ABOUT ME, YOUR GREAT POWER IS SAFE!
WHAT ABOUT WHAT PROFFY SEES?
PROFFY SEES WHAT PROFFY SEES. NO MORE, NO LESS.
WHAT DID YOU SEE!?
YOU JUMPED WAY UP INTO THE SKY.
AND THEN YOU FELL BACK DOWN!
I DID?

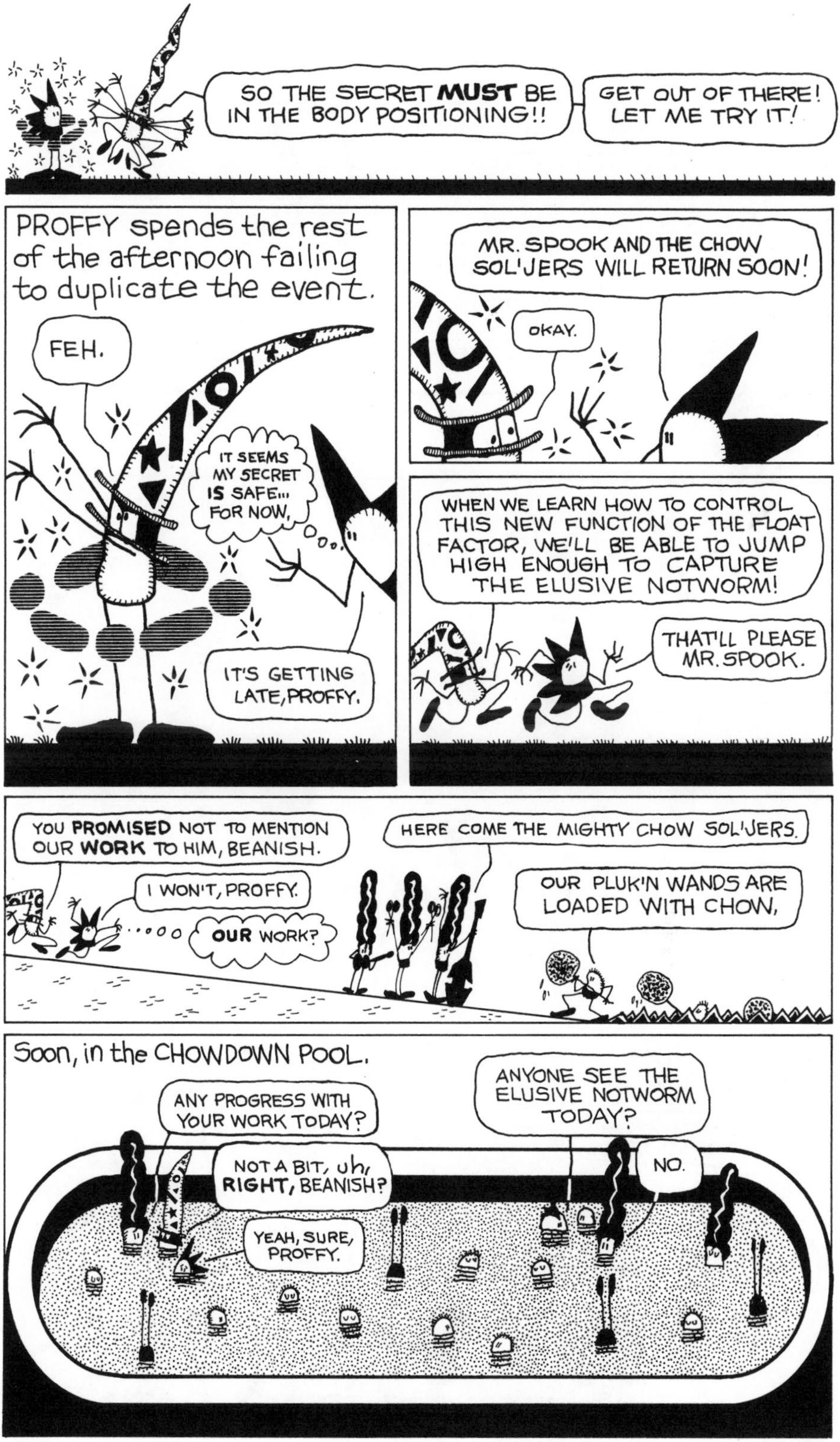

SO THE SECRET **MUST** BE IN THE BODY POSITIONING!!
GET OUT OF THERE! LET ME TRY IT!
PROFFY spends the rest of the afternoon failing to duplicate the event.
FEH.
IT SEEMS MY SECRET **IS** SAFE... FOR NOW,
IT'S GETTING LATE, PROFFY.
MR. SPOOK AND THE CHOW SOL'JERS WILL RETURN SOON!
OKAY.
WHEN WE LEARN HOW TO CONTROL THIS NEW FUNCTION OF THE FLOAT FACTOR, WE'LL BE ABLE TO JUMP HIGH ENOUGH TO CAPTURE THE ELUSIVE NOTWORM!
THAT'LL PLEASE MR. SPOOK.
YOU **PROMISED** NOT TO MENTION OUR **WORK** TO HIM, BEANISH.
I WON'T, PROFFY.
OUR WORK?
HERE COME THE MIGHTY CHOW SOL'JERS.
OUR PLUK'N WANDS ARE LOADED WITH CHOW,
Soon, in the CHOWDOWN POOL.
ANY PROGRESS WITH YOUR WORK TODAY?
NOT A BIT, uh, **RIGHT**, BEANISH?
YEAH, SURE, PROFFY.
ANYONE SEE THE ELUSIVE NOTWORM TODAY?
NO.

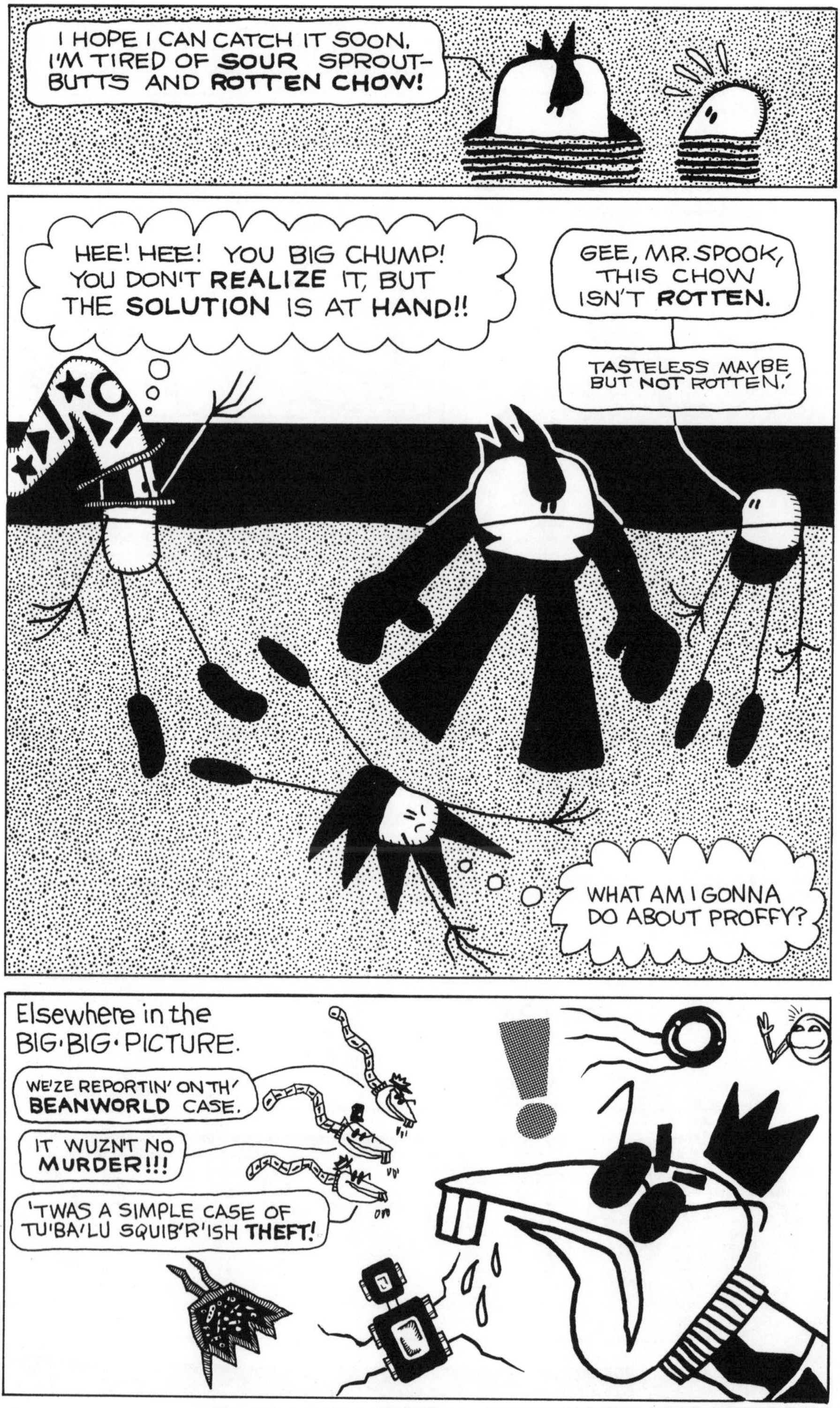
I HOPE I CAN CATCH IT SOON. I'M TIRED OF SOUR SPROUT-BUTTS AND ROTTEN CHOW!
HEE! HEE! YOU BIG CHUMP! YOU DON'T REALIZE IT, BUT THE SOLUTION IS AT HAND!!
GEE, MR. SPOOK, THIS CHOW ISN'T ROTTEN.
TASTELESS MAYBE BUT NOT ROTTEN.
WHAT AM I GONNA DO ABOUT PROFFY?
Elsewhere in the BIG·BIG·PICTURE.
WE'ZE REPORTIN' ON TH' BEANWORLD CASE.
IT WUZN'T NO MURDER!!!
'TWAS A SIMPLE CASE OF TU'BA'LU SQUIB'R'ISH THEFT!

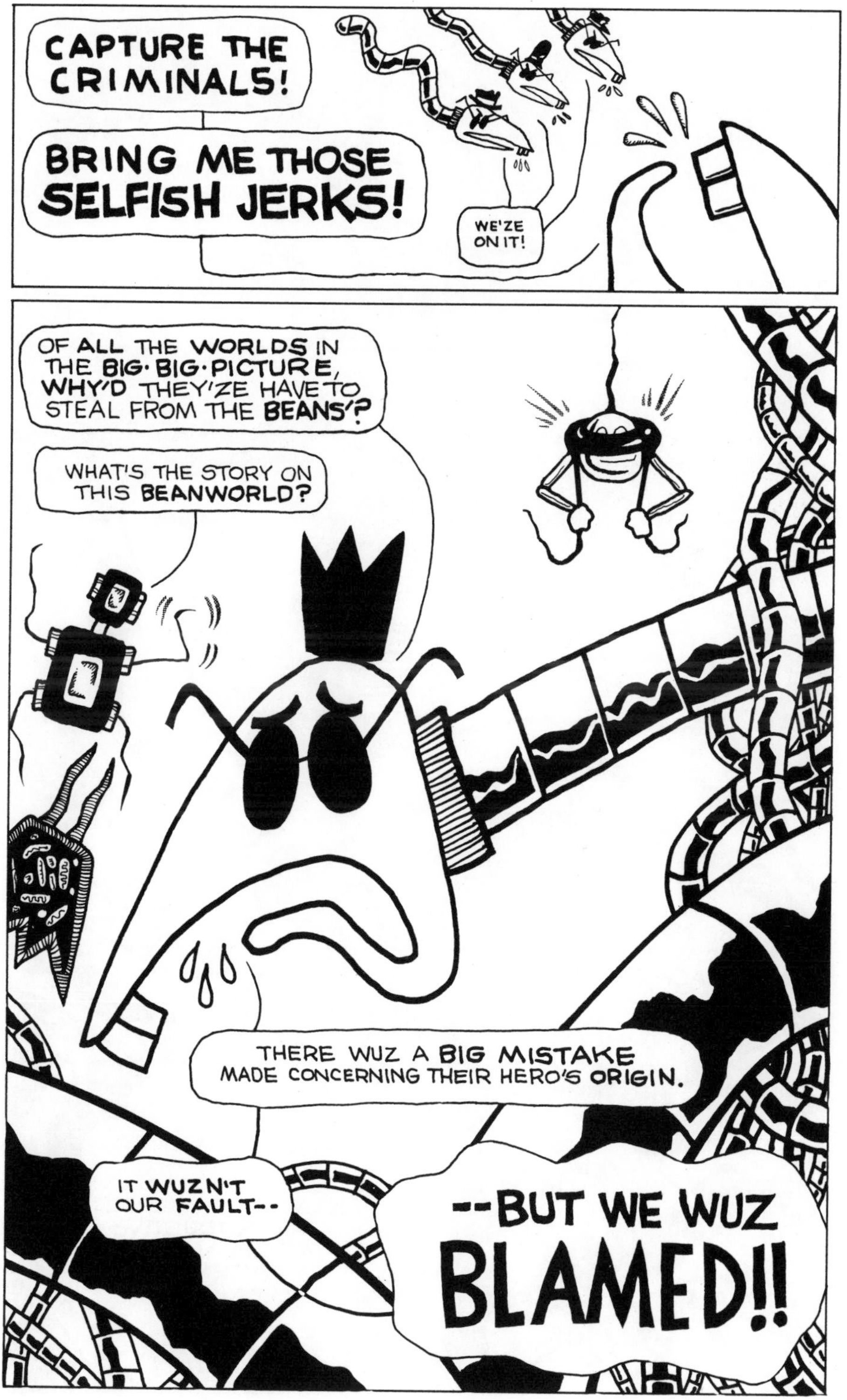
CAPTURE THE CRIMINALS!
BRING ME THOSE SELFISH JERKS!
WE'ZE ON IT!
OF ALL THE WORLDS IN THE BIG·BIG·PICTURE, WHY'D THEY'ZE HAVE TO STEAL FROM THE BEANS'?
WHAT'S THE STORY ON THIS BEANWORLD?
THERE WUZ A BIG MISTAKE MADE CONCERNING THEIR HERO'S ORIGIN.
IT WUZN'T OUR FAULT--
--BUT WE WUZ BLAMED!!

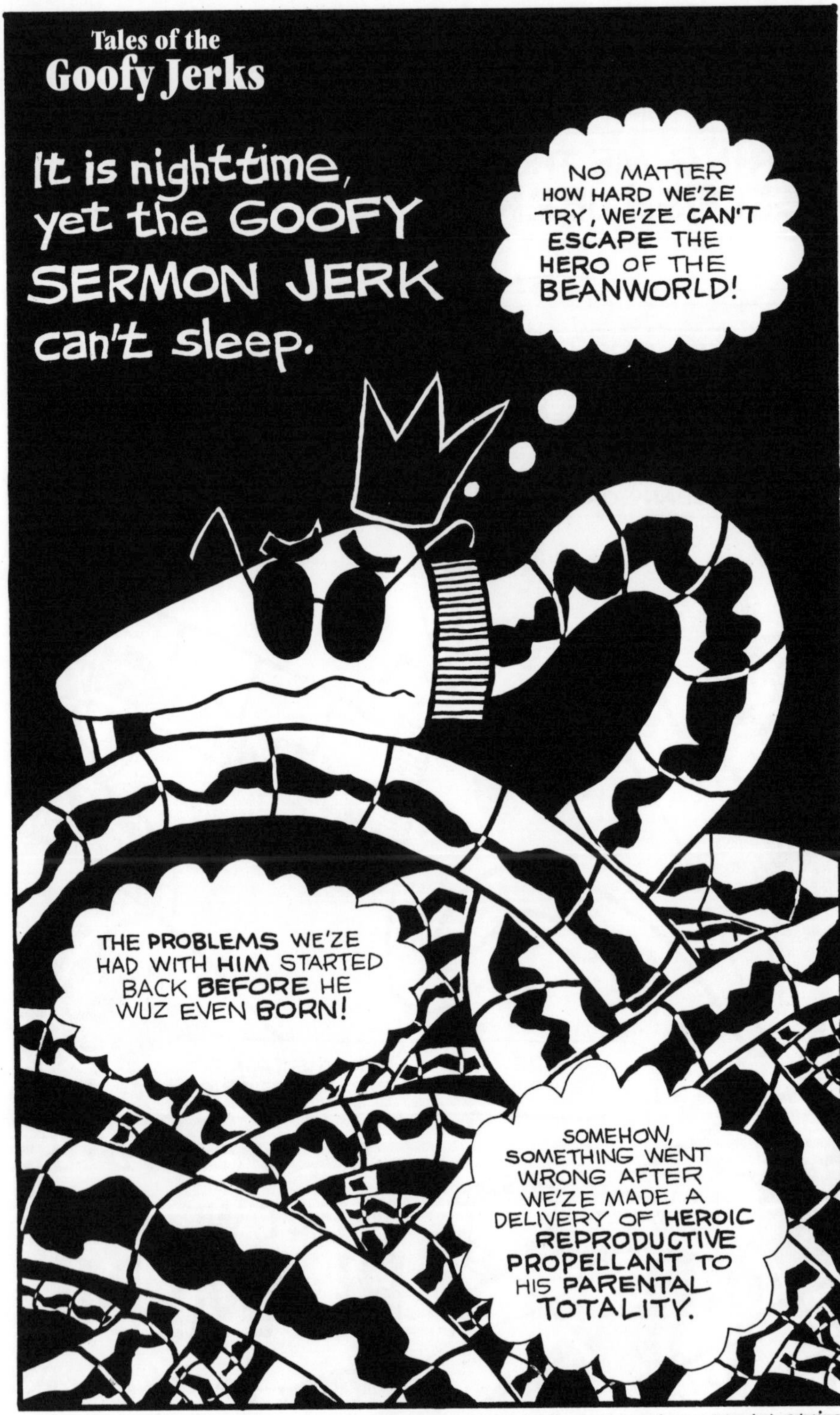
Tales of the
Goofy Jerks
It is nighttime, yet the GOOFY SERMON JERK can't sleep.
NO MATTER HOW HARD WE'ZE TRY, WE'ZE CAN'T ESCAPE THE HERO OF THE BEANWORLD!
THE PROBLEMS WE'ZE HAD WITH HIM STARTED BACK BEFORE HE WUZ EVEN BORN!
SOMEHOW, SOMETHING WENT WRONG AFTER WE'ZE MADE A DELIVERY OF HEROIC REPRODUCTIVE PROPELLANT TO HIS PARENTAL TOTALITY.

An extra special "Thanks" to cat for her editorial advice.

A ROUTINE GOOFY SURVEY INSPECTION HAD REVEALED A VERY SERIOUS **HEALTHINESS DEFICIENCY!** THE GOOFY SURGICAL JERKS WERE SENT TO MAKE A DIAGNOSIS!

WHAT **AILS** YOU, CUSTOMER?

ODD VISUAL PATTERNS ON THE DEVELOPMENTAL POD'L' POOL BULBING!

THIS AIN'T LIKE NO **SICKLINESS** WE'ZE SEEN BEFORE.

SAY SOMETHING, CUSTOMER!

HMM... INABILITY TO SPEAK IS A BAD SYMPTOM!

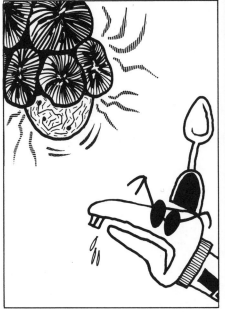

SLIP!

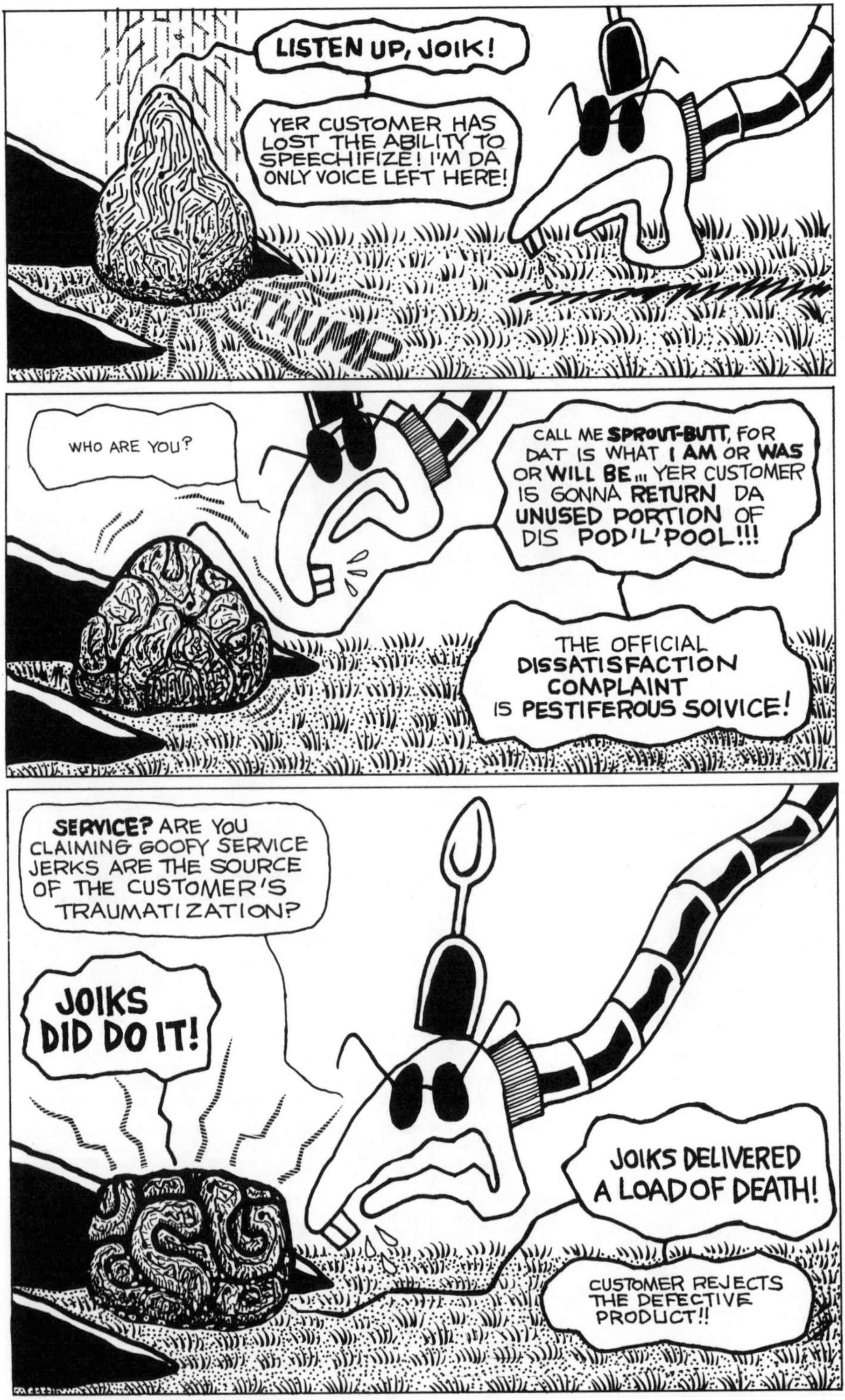
LISTEN UP, JOIK!
YER CUSTOMER HAS LOST THE ABILITY TO SPEECHIFIZE! I'M DA ONLY VOICE LEFT HERE!
THUMP
WHO ARE YOU?
CALL ME SPROUT-BUTT, FOR DAT IS WHAT I AM OR WAS OR WILL BE... YER CUSTOMER IS GONNA RETURN DA UNUSED PORTION OF DIS POD'L'POOL!!!
THE OFFICIAL DISSATISFACTION COMPLAINT IS PESTIFEROUS SOIVICE!
SERVICE? ARE YOU CLAIMING GOOFY SERVICE JERKS ARE THE SOURCE OF THE CUSTOMER'S TRAUMATIZATION?
JOIKS DID DO IT!
JOIKS DELIVERED A LOAD OF DEATH!
CUSTOMER REJECTS THE DEFECTIVE PRODUCT!!

THE UMBILICAL LINKAGE IS BLOATING!
FEH!
BLOOP!
BOING
TAKE IT BACK!
JOIKS BRUNG DA TOXIC WASTES!
NO WAY!
AIN'T NO GOOFY JERKS HAULIN' A SURFIETY SURPLUS OF GARBAGE!
POD'L'POOL'S DETACHED, YET THE VISUAL PATTERNS INDICATE LIFE INSIDE.
IT'S ALIVE!
DAT AIN'T LIFE, DAT'S DEATH BY TOXIFEROUS TAINT! TAKE IT AWAY... TAKE IT AWAY....
WHAT'LL WE'ZE DO WITH A DETACHED POD'L'POOL?

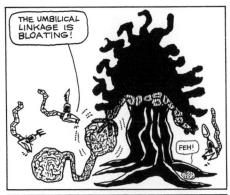

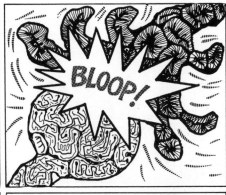

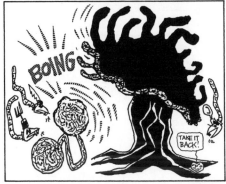

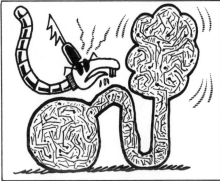

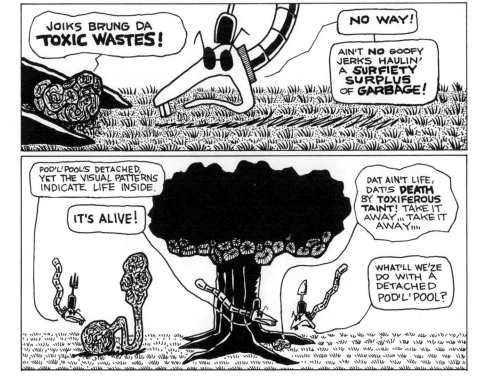

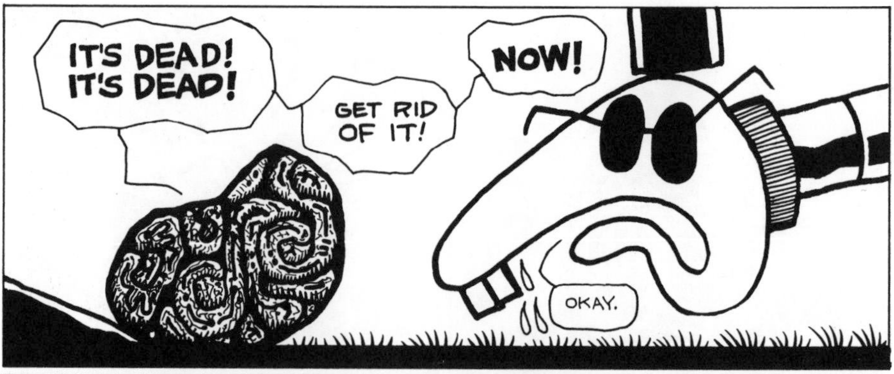
IT'S DEAD! IT'S DEAD!
GET RID OF IT!
NOW!
OKAY.

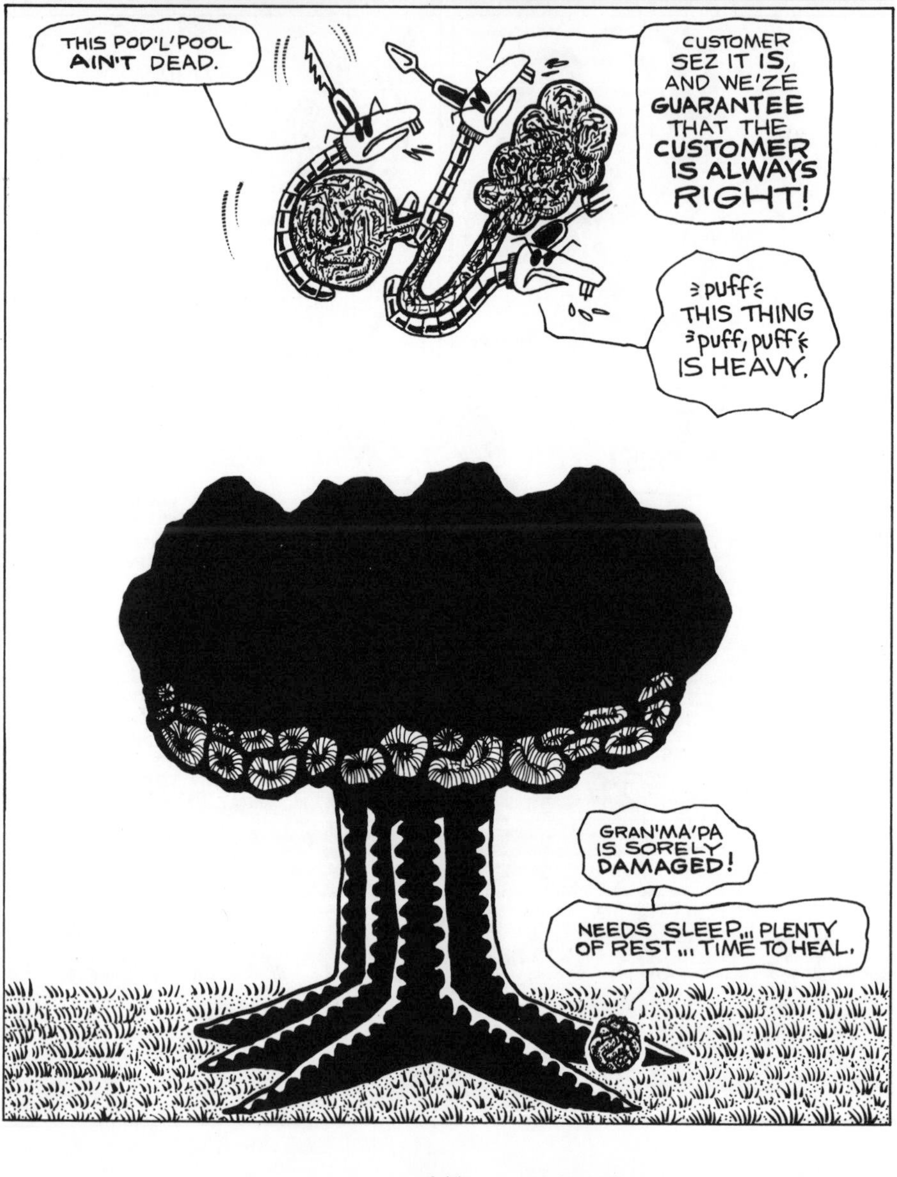
THIS POD'L'POOL AIN'T DEAD.
CUSTOMER SEZ IT IS, AND WE'ZE GUARANTEE THAT THE CUSTOMER IS ALWAYS RIGHT!
puff THIS THING puff, puff IS HEAVY.
GRAN'MA'PA IS SORELY DAMAGED!
NEEDS SLEEP... PLENTY OF REST... TIME TO HEAL.

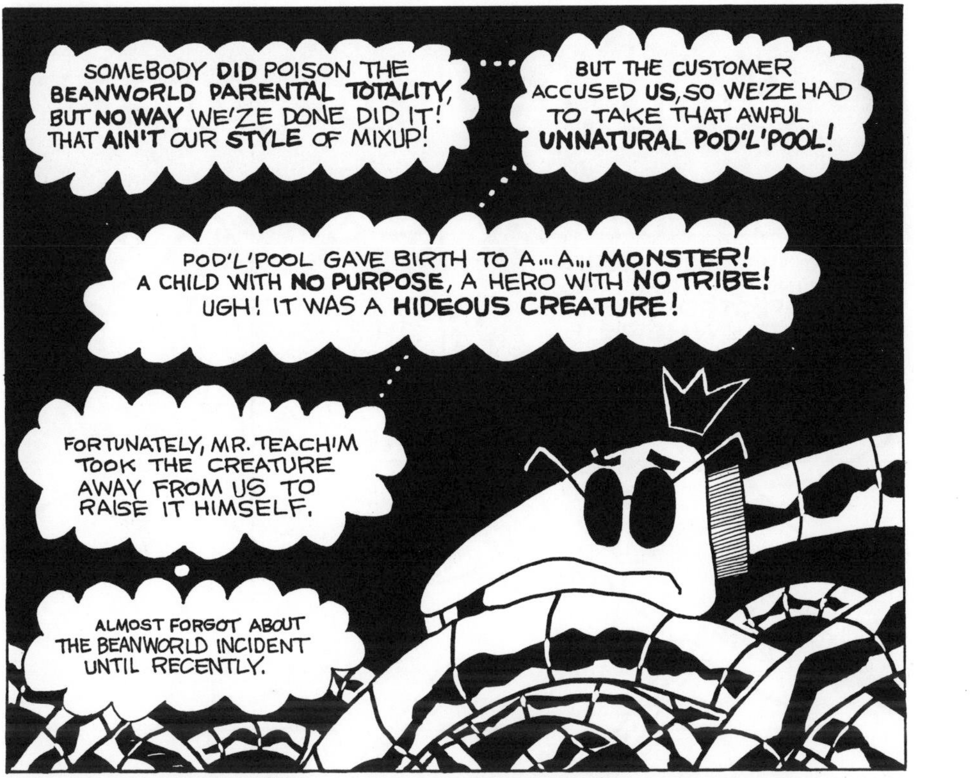
SOMEBODY DID POISON THE BEANWORLD PARENTAL TOTALITY, BUT NO WAY WE'ZE DONE DID IT! THAT AIN'T OUR STYLE OF MIXUP!
BUT THE CUSTOMER ACCUSED US, SO WE'ZE HAD TO TAKE THAT AWFUL UNNATURAL POD'L'POOL!
POD'L'POOL GAVE BIRTH TO A... A... MONSTER! A CHILD WITH NO PURPOSE, A HERO WITH NO TRIBE! UGH! IT WAS A HIDEOUS CREATURE!
FORTUNATELY, MR. TEACH'IM TOOK THE CREATURE AWAY FROM US TO RAISE IT HIMSELF.
ALMOST FORGOT ABOUT THE BEANWORLD INCIDENT UNTIL RECENTLY.

Later, the GOOFY SERMON JERK has a nightmare about the orphan, LI'L MR. SPOOK!

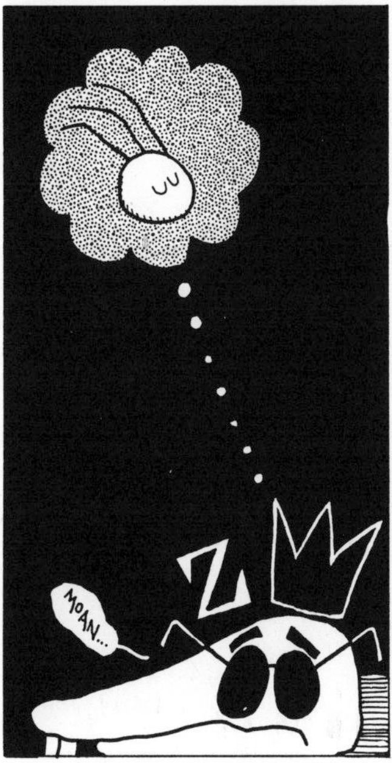
Z
MOAN...

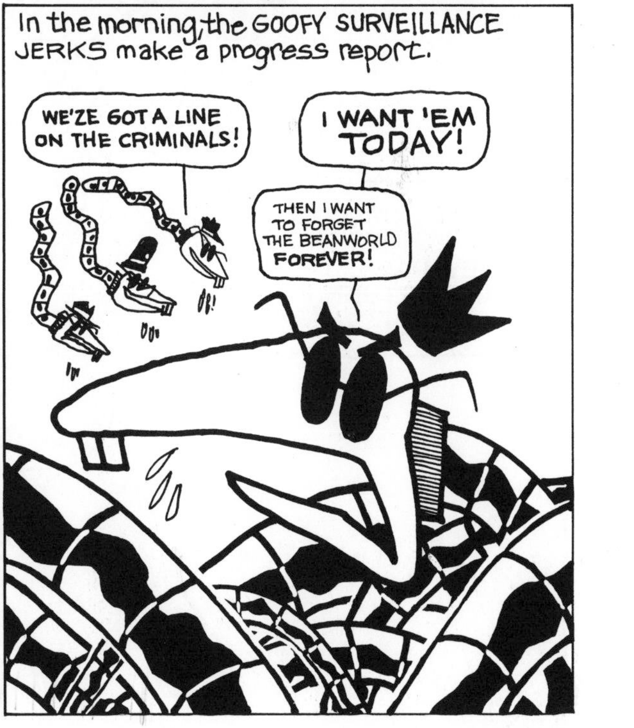
In the morning, the GOOFY SURVEILLANCE JERKS make a progress report.
WE'ZE GOT A LINE ON THE CRIMINALS!
I WANT 'EM TODAY!
THEN I WANT TO FORGET THE BEANWORLD FOREVER!

Goofy Jerk Dragnet

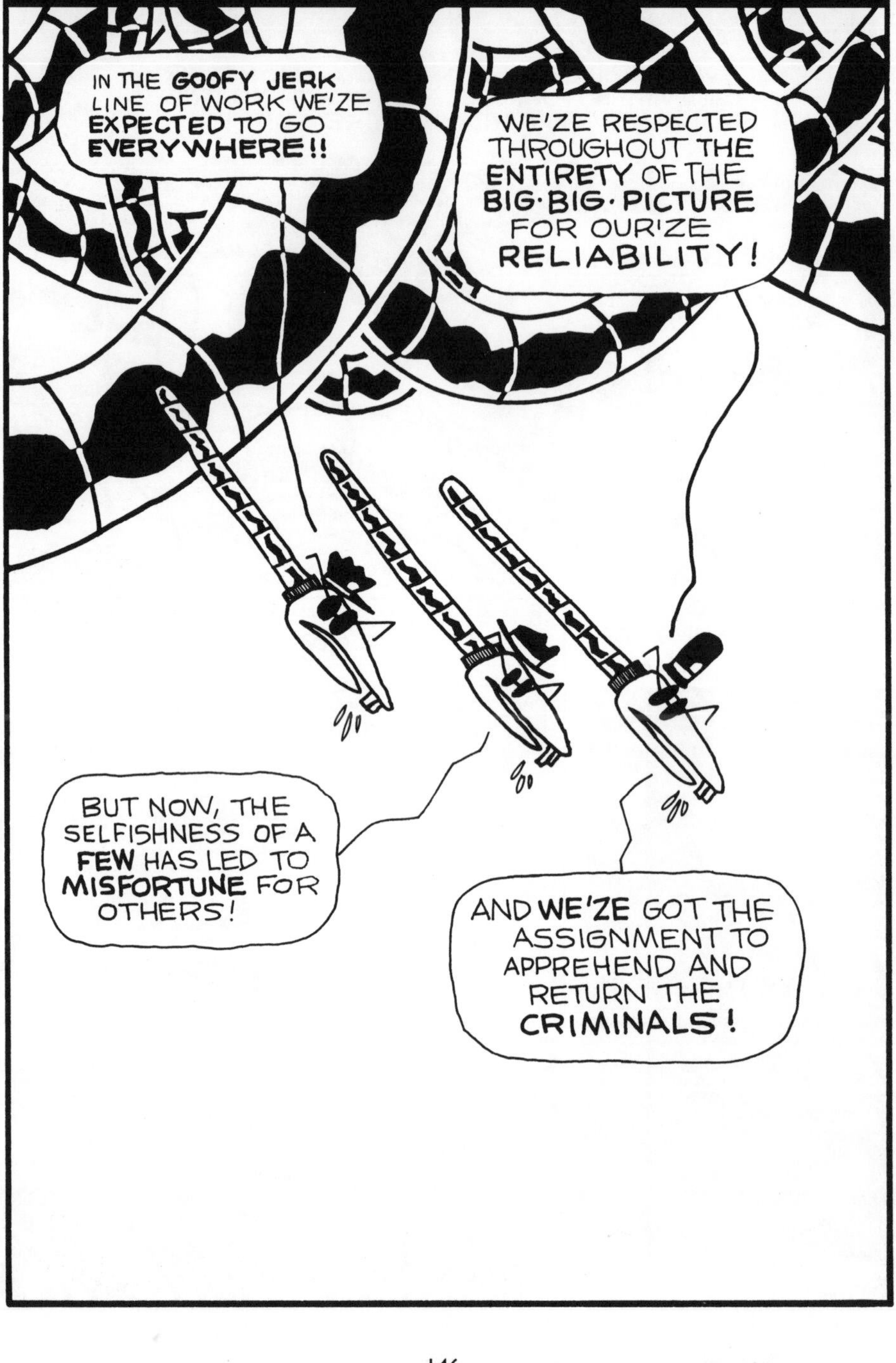
IN THE GOOFY JERK LINE OF WORK WE'ZE EXPECTED TO GO EVERYWHERE!!
WE'ZE RESPECTED THROUGHOUT THE ENTIRETY OF THE BIG·BIG·PICTURE FOR OUR'ZE RELIABILITY!
BUT NOW, THE SELFISHNESS OF A FEW HAS LED TO MISFORTUNE FOR OTHERS!
AND WE'ZE GOT THE ASSIGNMENT TO APPREHEND AND RETURN THE CRIMINALS!

THE BEANS SAID THE THIEVES WERE THE **SAME** TEAM THAT HAD PREVIOUSLY BROUGHT **GRAN'MA'PA** A LOAD OF REPRODUCTIVE PROPELLANT.

ALL **GOOFY SERVICE JERKS** ARE **INDENTURED** TO A SPECIFIC **SERVICE STATION.**

THAT'S WHAT WE'ZE **KNOW** ABOUT THE **THIEVES.** NOW, WHAT DO WE'ZE KNOW ABOUT THE **CUSTOMER?**

GRAN'MA'PA IS A **POD'L'POOL** TYPE OF **PARENTAL TOTALITY.**

WE'ZE KNOW WHAT **STYLE** OF LOCAL YOKEL **GRAN'MA'PA'S POD'L'POOL** YIELDS-- **BEANS!**

SO, WE'ZE GOTTA FIND **SERVICE STATIONS** OF **POD'L'POOL PERSUASION.**

FIND THE STATION WITH A BEAN-SHAPED **INFLUENCE** INSIDE, AND WE'ZE APPREHENDED **THE FUGITIVES!**

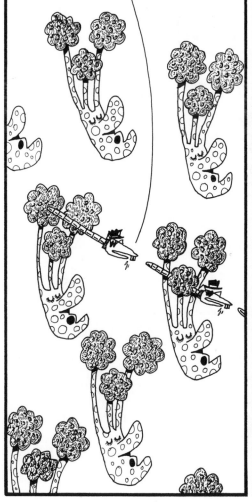
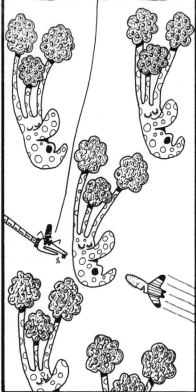

147

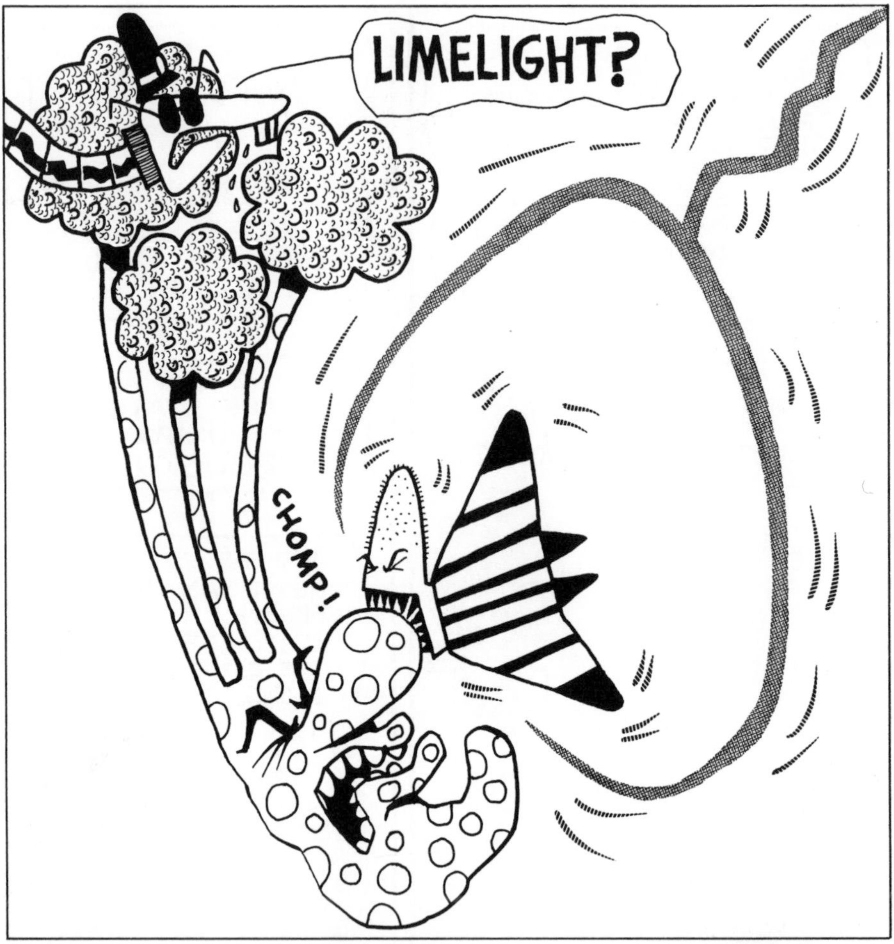
LIMELIGHT?
CHOMP!

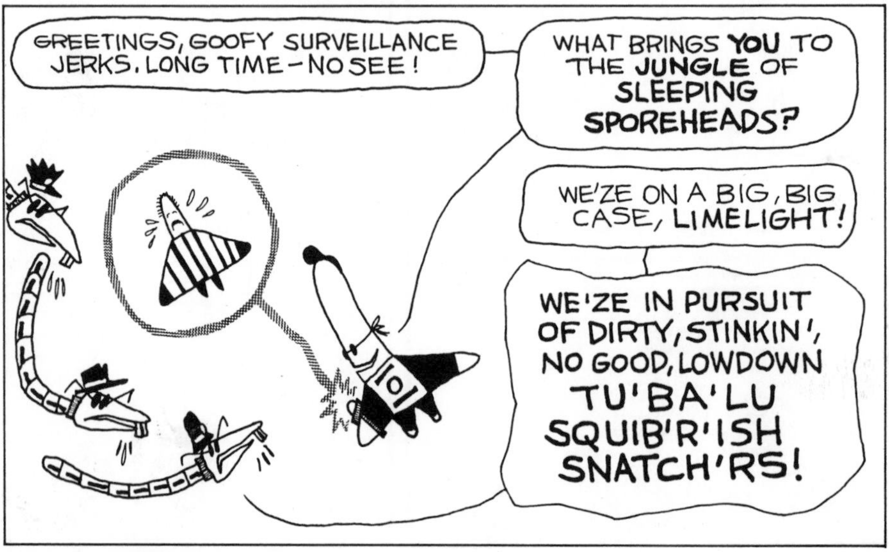
GREETINGS, GOOFY SURVEILLANCE JERKS. LONG TIME–NO SEE!
WHAT BRINGS YOU TO THE JUNGLE OF SLEEPING SPOREHEADS?
WE'ZE ON A BIG, BIG CASE, LIMELIGHT!
WE'ZE IN PURSUIT OF DIRTY, STINKIN', NO GOOD, LOWDOWN TU'BA'LU SQUIB'R'ISH SNATCH'RS!

WHO'ZE THE PUNK?
THE BITESTER! WHAT A LOSER!
THE FOOL ESCAPED INCARCERATION. HE ALWAYS COMES HERE TO RAMPAGE!
NOW I MUST RETURN THIS CROOK TO THE JUG. GOOD LUCK IN YOUR DUTY, FELLOW CRIME FIGHTERS!
BE'ZE SEEIN' YA, LIMELIGHT!
Soon, in a nearby cluster of SERVICE CENTERS...
WE'ZE MUST INSPECT EVERY FACTORY THAT PRODUCES POD'L'POOL PROPELLANT.

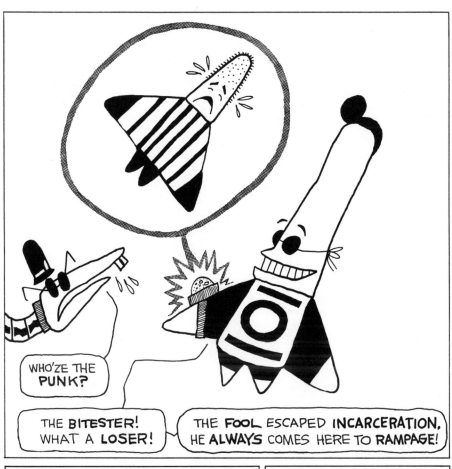

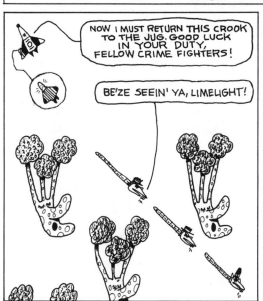

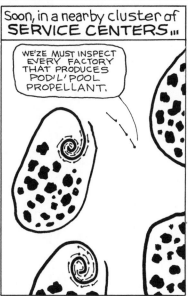

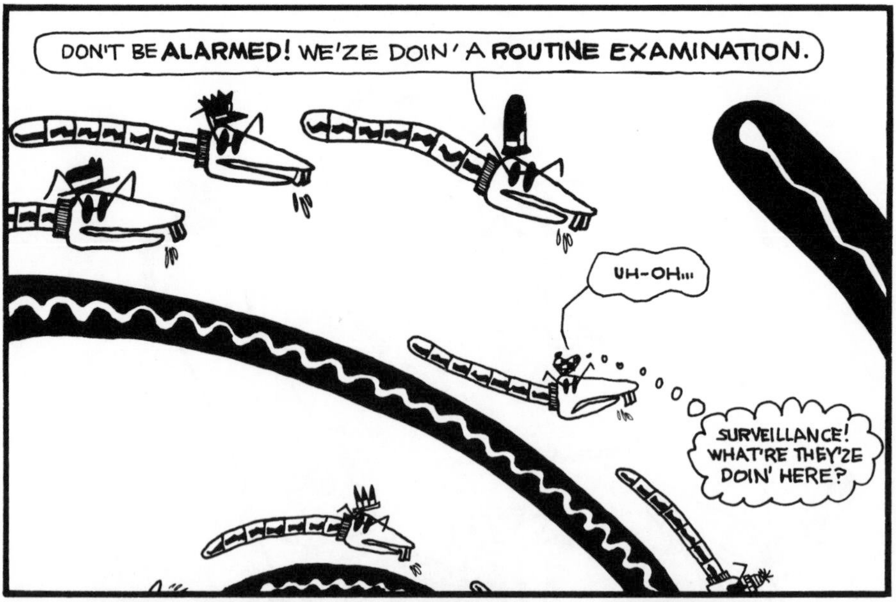
DON'T BE ALARMED! WE'ZE DOIN' A ROUTINE EXAMINATION.
UH-OH...
SURVEILLANCE! WHAT'RE THEY'ZE DOIN' HERE?

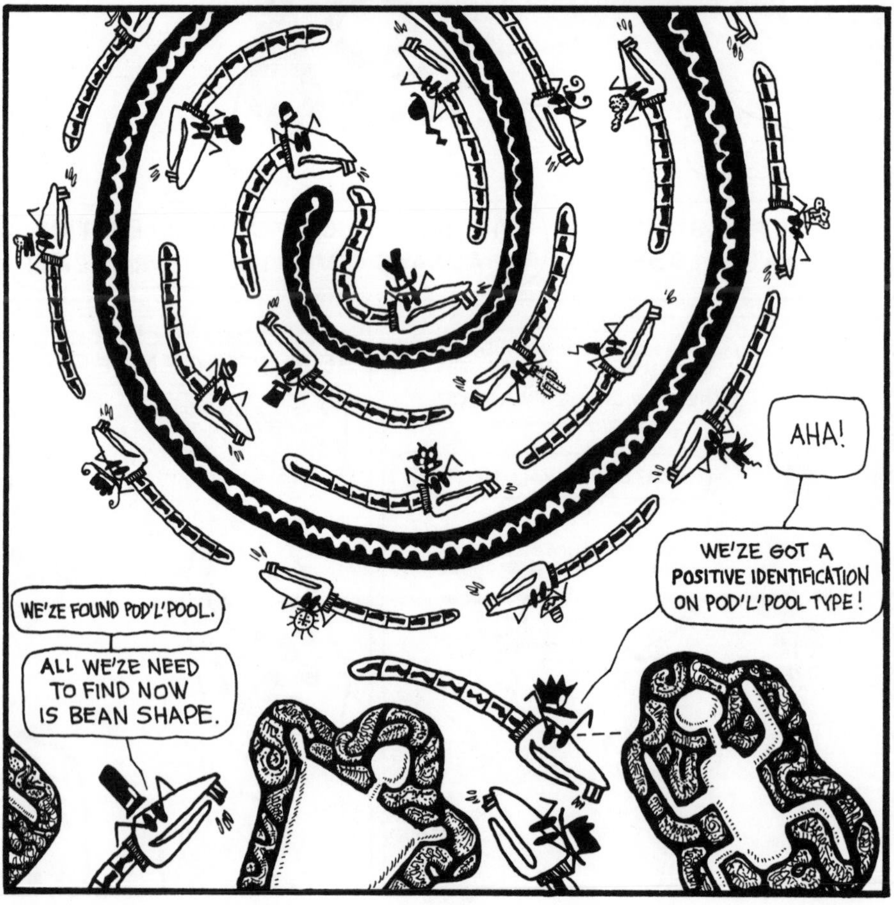
AHA!
WE'ZE GOT A POSITIVE IDENTIFICATION ON POD'L'POOL TYPE!
WE'ZE FOUND POD'L'POOL.
ALL WE'ZE NEED TO FIND NOW IS BEAN SHAPE.

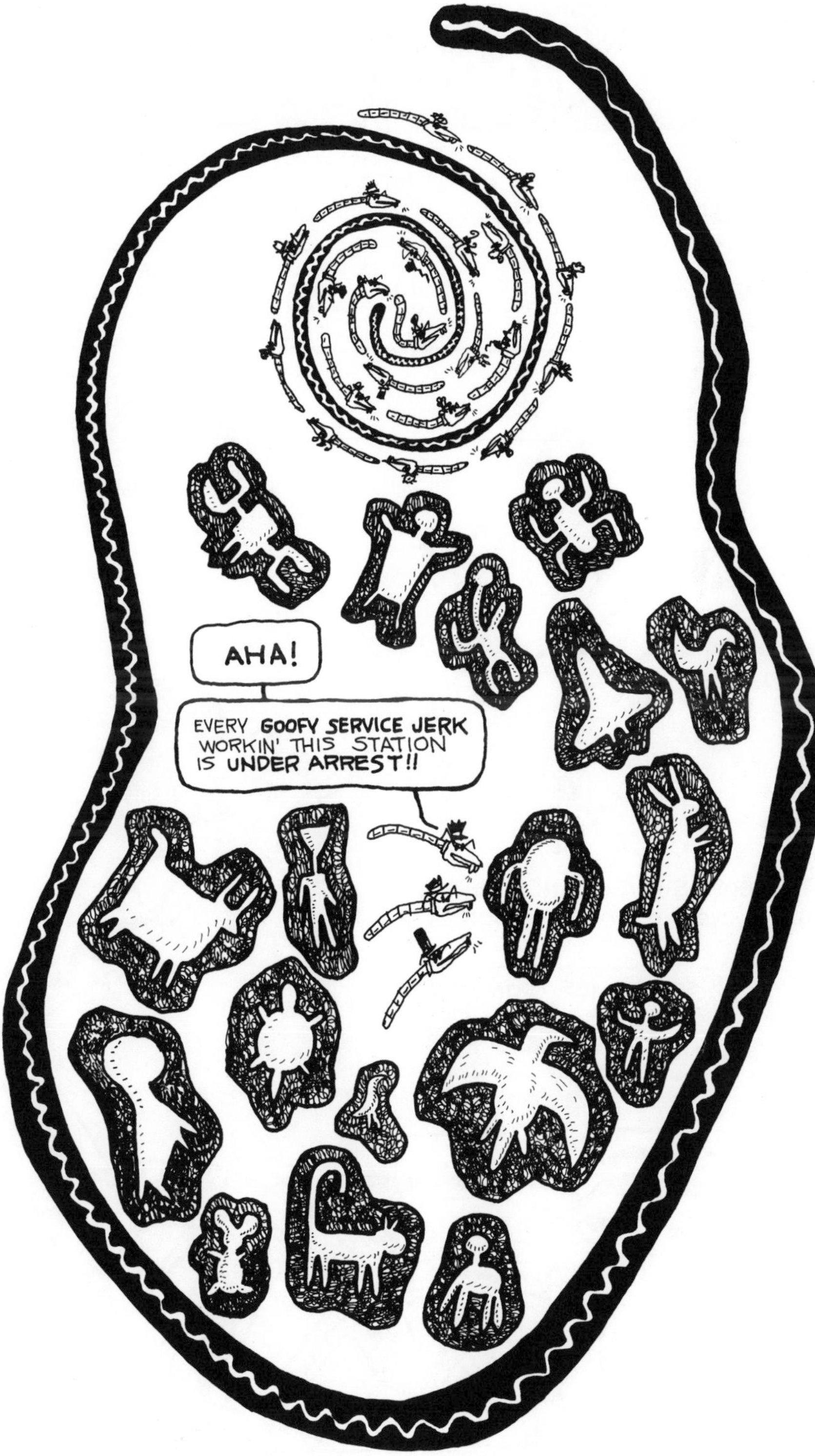
AHA!
EVERY GOOFY SERVICE JERK WORKIN' THIS STATION IS UNDER ARREST!!

The Goofy Sermon

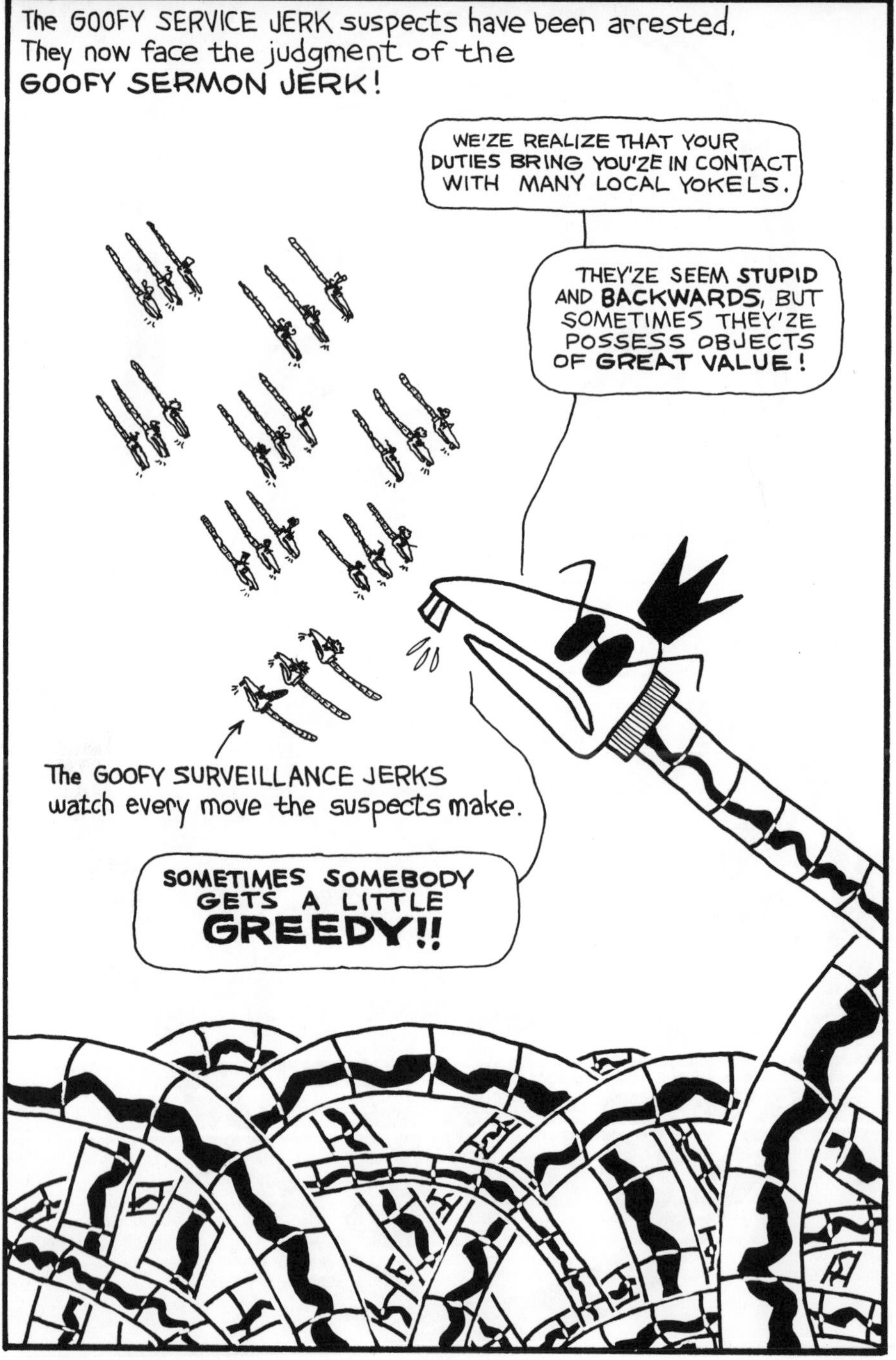

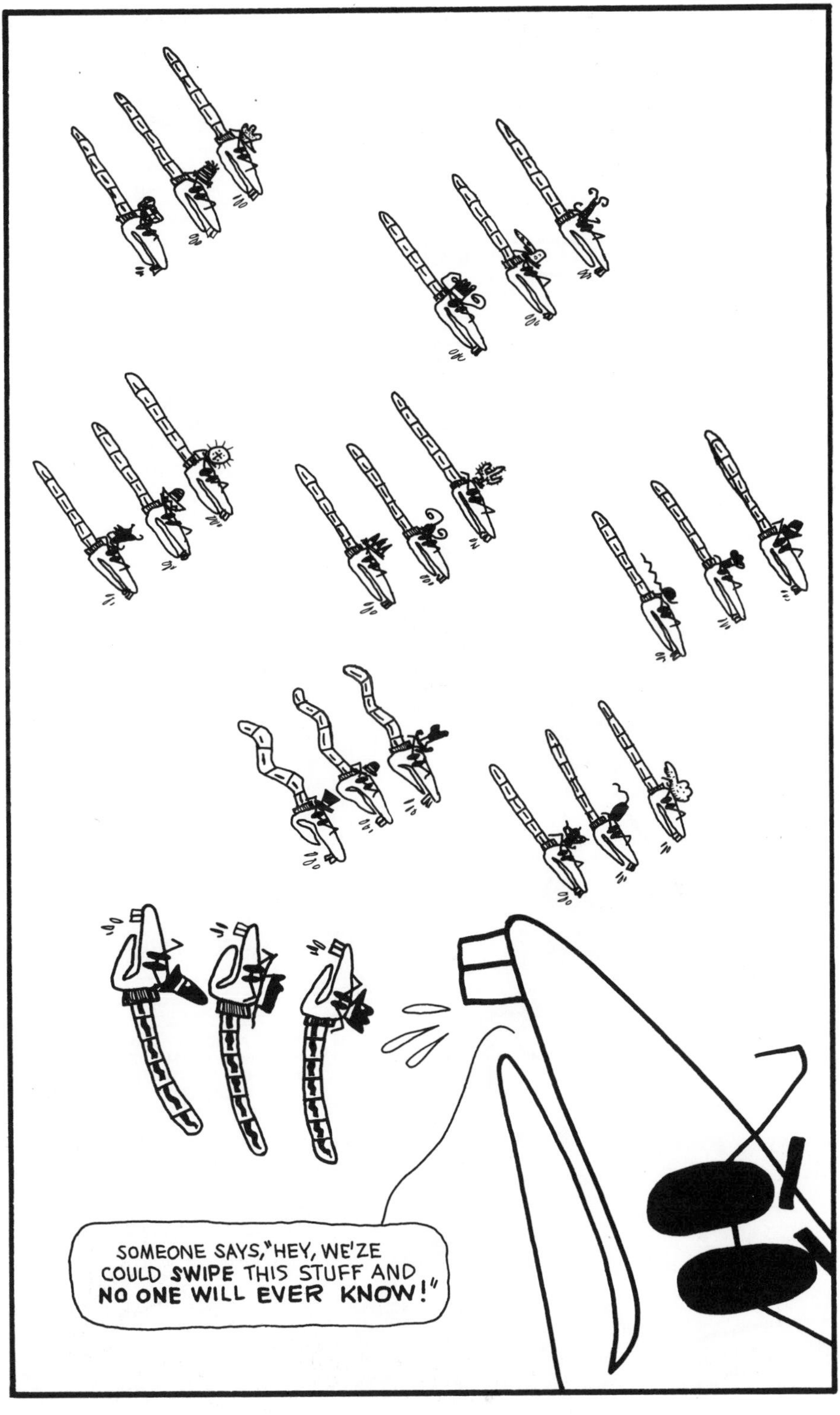
SOMEONE SAYS, "HEY, WE'ZE COULD SWIPE THIS STUFF AND NO ONE WILL EVER KNOW!"

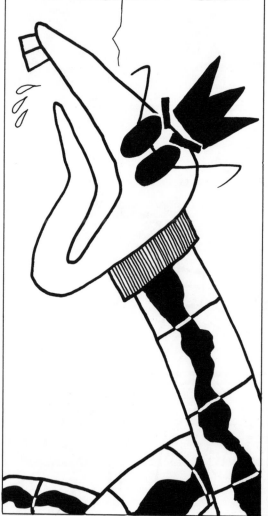

" WE'ZE CAN USE THIS STUFF TO INCREASE OUR WEALTH AND ESTEEM.... MAYBE WE'ZE'LL QUALIFY FOR BIGGER 'N' BETTER SERVICE STATION JOBS!"

"ALL WE GOTTA DO IS STEAL THIS FORK FROM THE BEANWORLD!"

FORK?

BEANWORLD?

UH-OH.

THIS TRIO IS LOOKIN' SUSPICIOUS!

THEY'ZE A CODE OF CONDUCT FOR DEALIN'S WITH CUSTOMERS AND THEY'ZE TRIBES AND CORPORATE STATES.

VERY SUSPICIOUS!

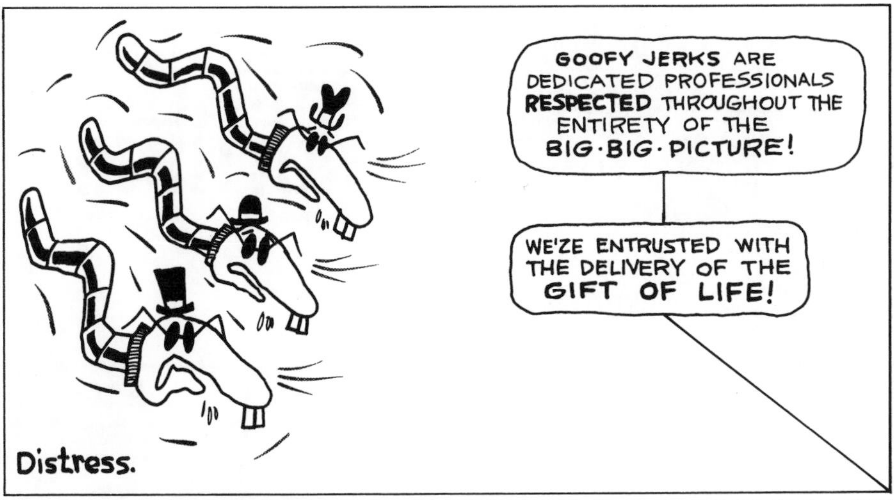
GOOFY JERKS ARE DEDICATED PROFESSIONALS RESPECTED THROUGHOUT THE ENTIRETY OF THE BIG·BIG·PICTURE!
WE'ZE ENTRUSTED WITH THE DELIVERY OF THE GIFT OF LIFE!
Distress.

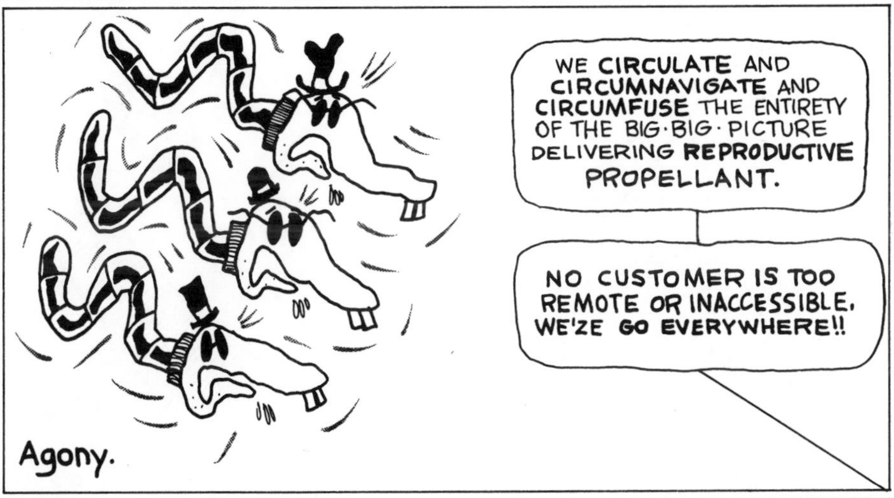
WE CIRCULATE AND CIRCUMNAVIGATE AND CIRCUMFUSE THE ENTIRETY OF THE BIG·BIG·PICTURE DELIVERING REPRODUCTIVE PROPELLANT.
NO CUSTOMER IS TOO REMOTE OR INACCESSIBLE. WE'ZE GO EVERYWHERE!!
Agony.

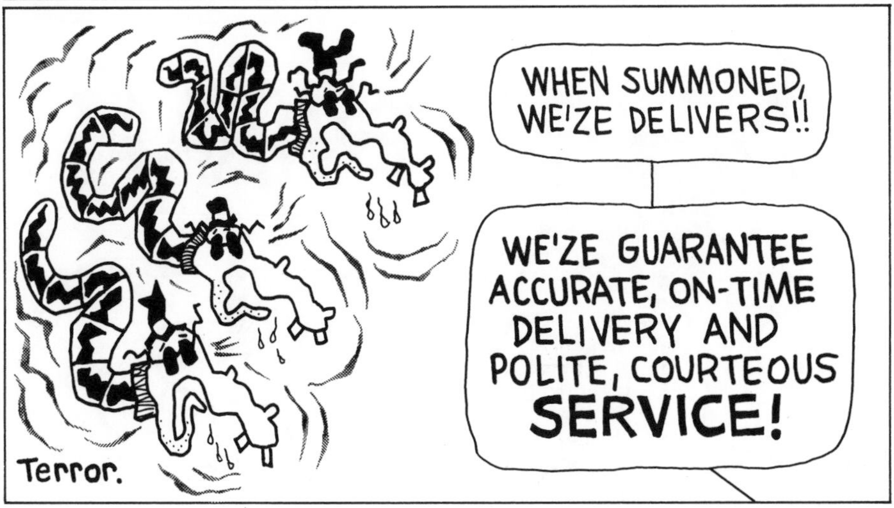
WHEN SUMMONED, WE'ZE DELIVERS!!
WE'ZE GUARANTEE ACCURATE, ON-TIME DELIVERY AND POLITE, COURTEOUS SERVICE!
Terror.

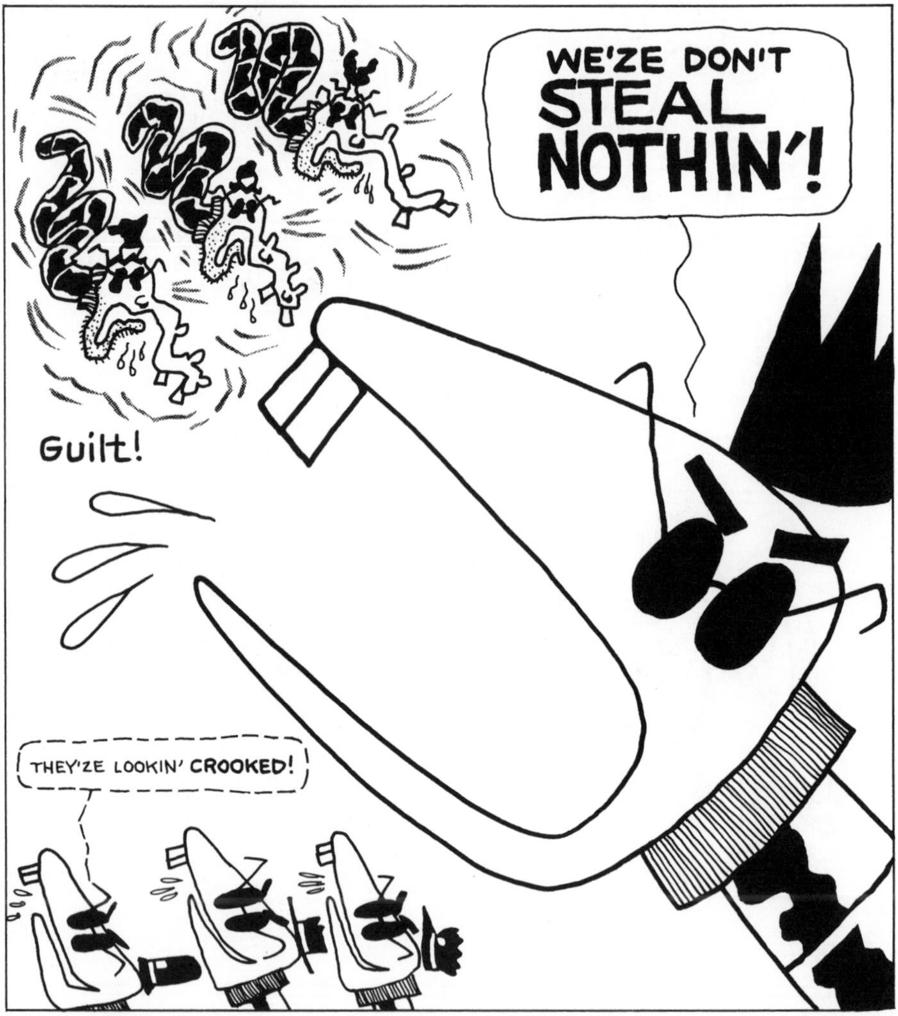

WE'ZE DON'T STEAL NOTHIN'!
Guilt!
THEY'ZE LOOKIN' CROOKED!

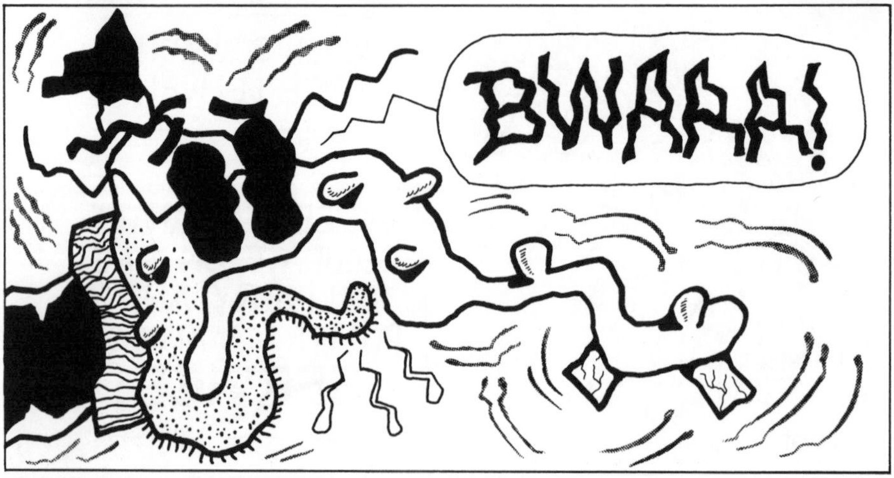

BWAAA!

No Goofy Excuses!

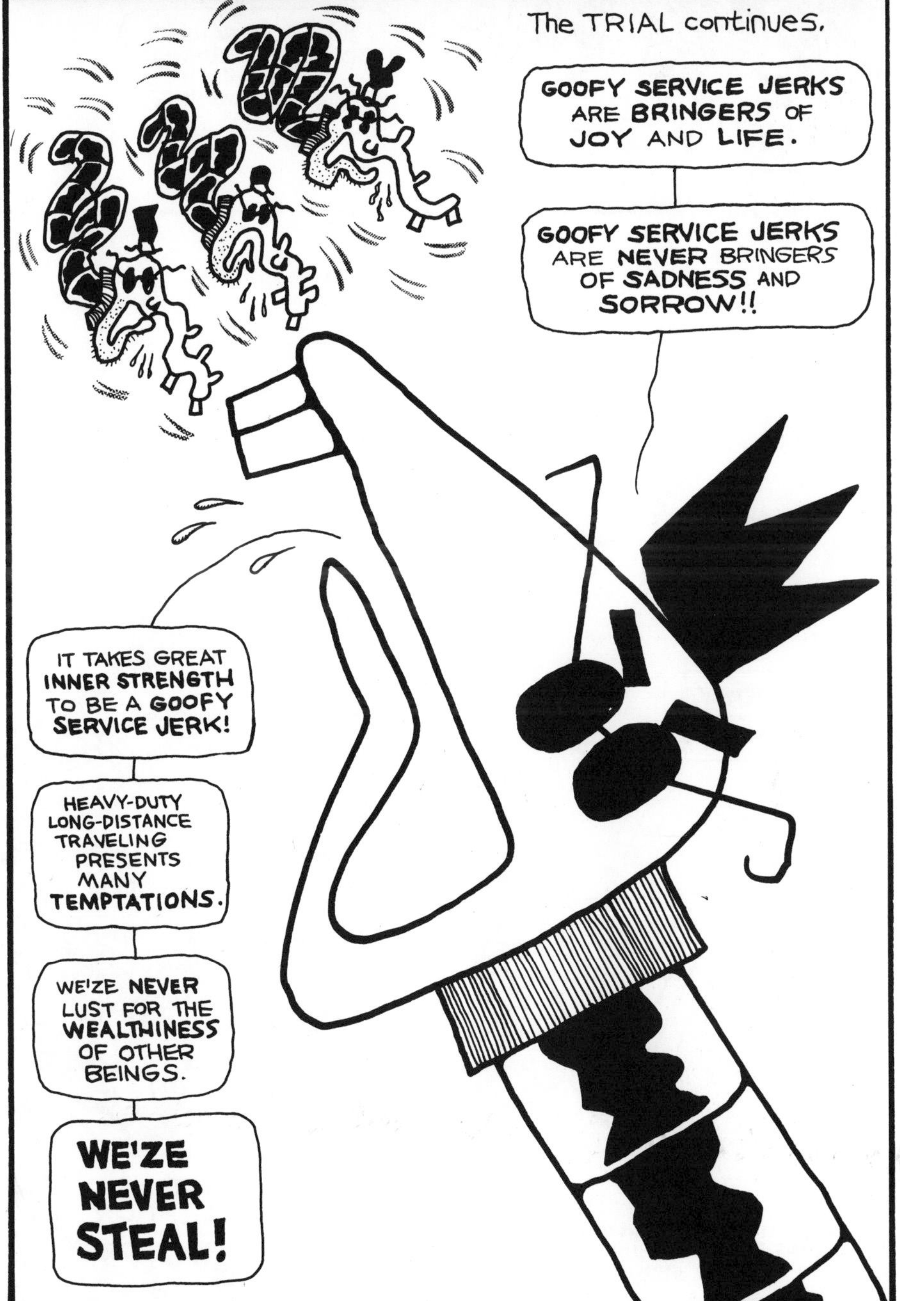

The TRIAL continues.
GOOFY SERVICE JERKS ARE BRINGERS OF JOY AND LIFE.
GOOFY SERVICE JERKS ARE NEVER BRINGERS OF SADNESS AND SORROW!!
IT TAKES GREAT INNER STRENGTH TO BE A GOOFY SERVICE JERK!
HEAVY-DUTY LONG-DISTANCE TRAVELING PRESENTS MANY TEMPTATIONS.
WE'ZE NEVER LUST FOR THE WEALTHINESS OF OTHER BEINGS.
WE'ZE NEVER STEAL!

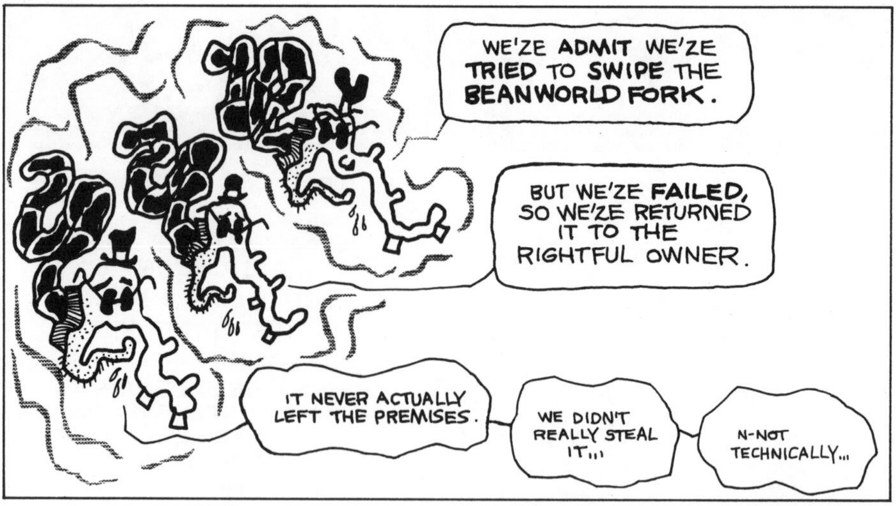
WE'ZE ADMIT WE'ZE TRIED TO SWIPE THE BEANWORLD FORK.
BUT WE'ZE FAILED, SO WE'ZE RETURNED IT TO THE RIGHTFUL OWNER.
IT NEVER ACTUALLY LEFT THE PREMISES.
WE DIDN'T REALLY STEAL IT...
N-NOT TECHNICALLY...

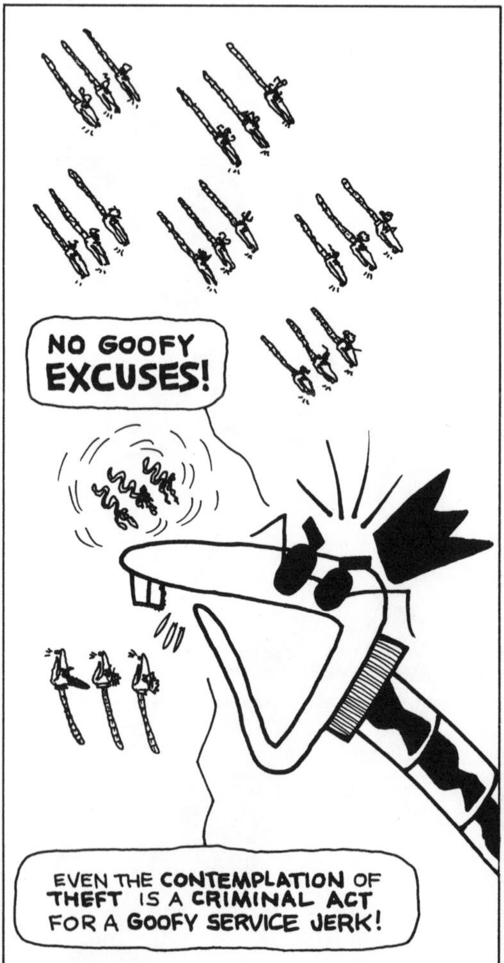
NO GOOFY EXCUSES!
EVEN THE CONTEMPLATION OF THEFT IS A CRIMINAL ACT FOR A GOOFY SERVICE JERK!

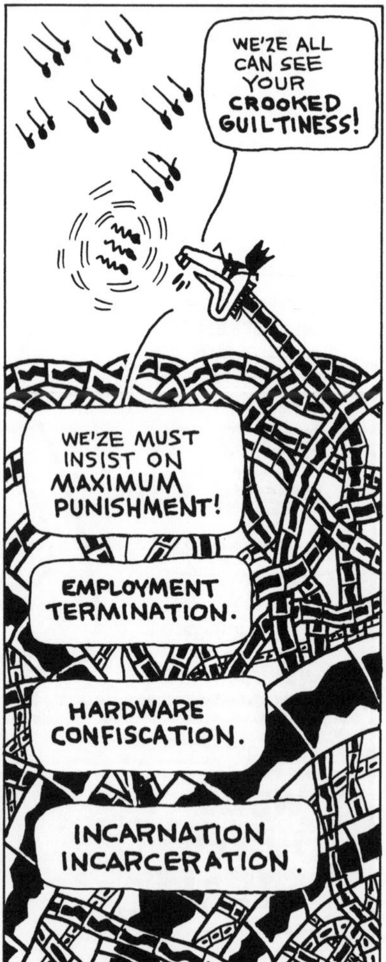
WE'ZE ALL CAN SEE YOUR CROOKED GUILTINESS!
WE'ZE MUST INSIST ON MAXIMUM PUNISHMENT!
EMPLOYMENT TERMINATION.
HARDWARE CONFISCATION.
INCARNATION INCARCERATION.

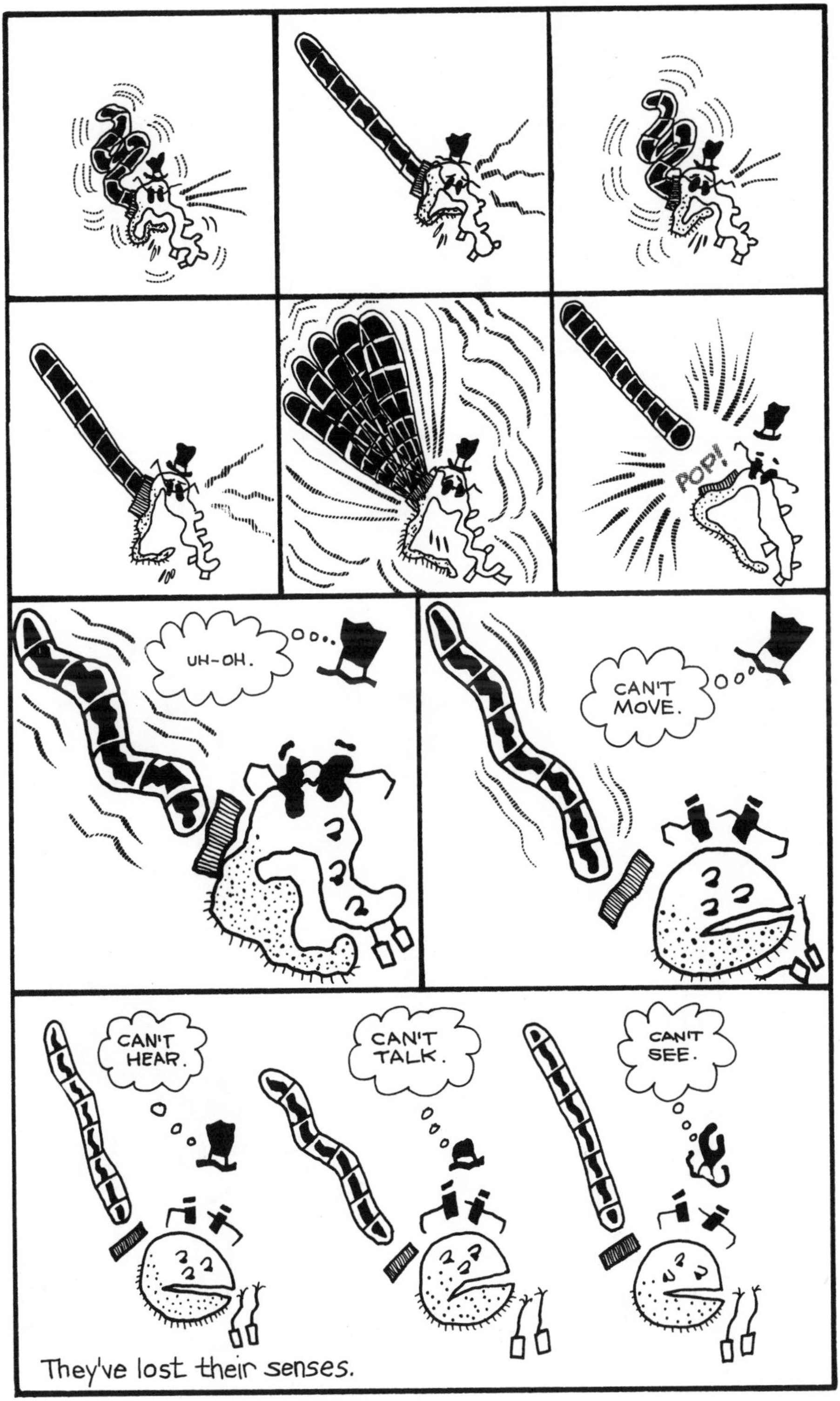
POP!
UH-OH.
CAN'T MOVE.
CAN'T HEAR.
CAN'T TALK.
CAN'T SEE.
They've lost their senses.

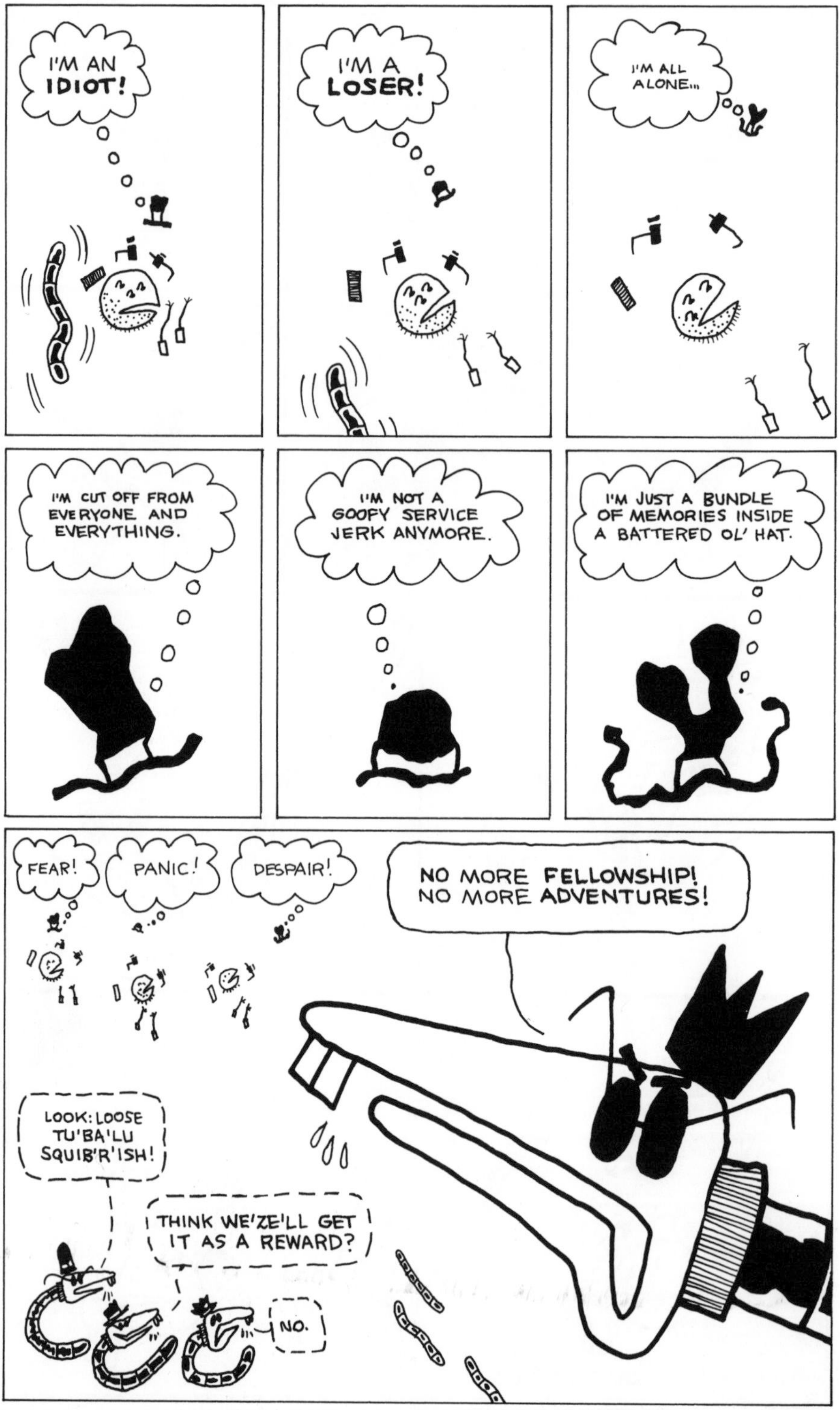
I'M AN IDIOT!
I'M A LOSER!
I'M ALL ALONE...
I'M CUT OFF FROM EVERYONE AND EVERYTHING.
I'M NOT A GOOFY SERVICE JERK ANYMORE.
I'M JUST A BUNDLE OF MEMORIES INSIDE A BATTERED OL' HAT.
FEAR!
PANIC!
DESPAIR!
NO MORE FELLOWSHIP! NO MORE ADVENTURES!
LOOK: LOOSE TU'BA'LU SQUIB'R'ISH!
THINK WE'ZE'LL GET IT AS A REWARD?
NO.

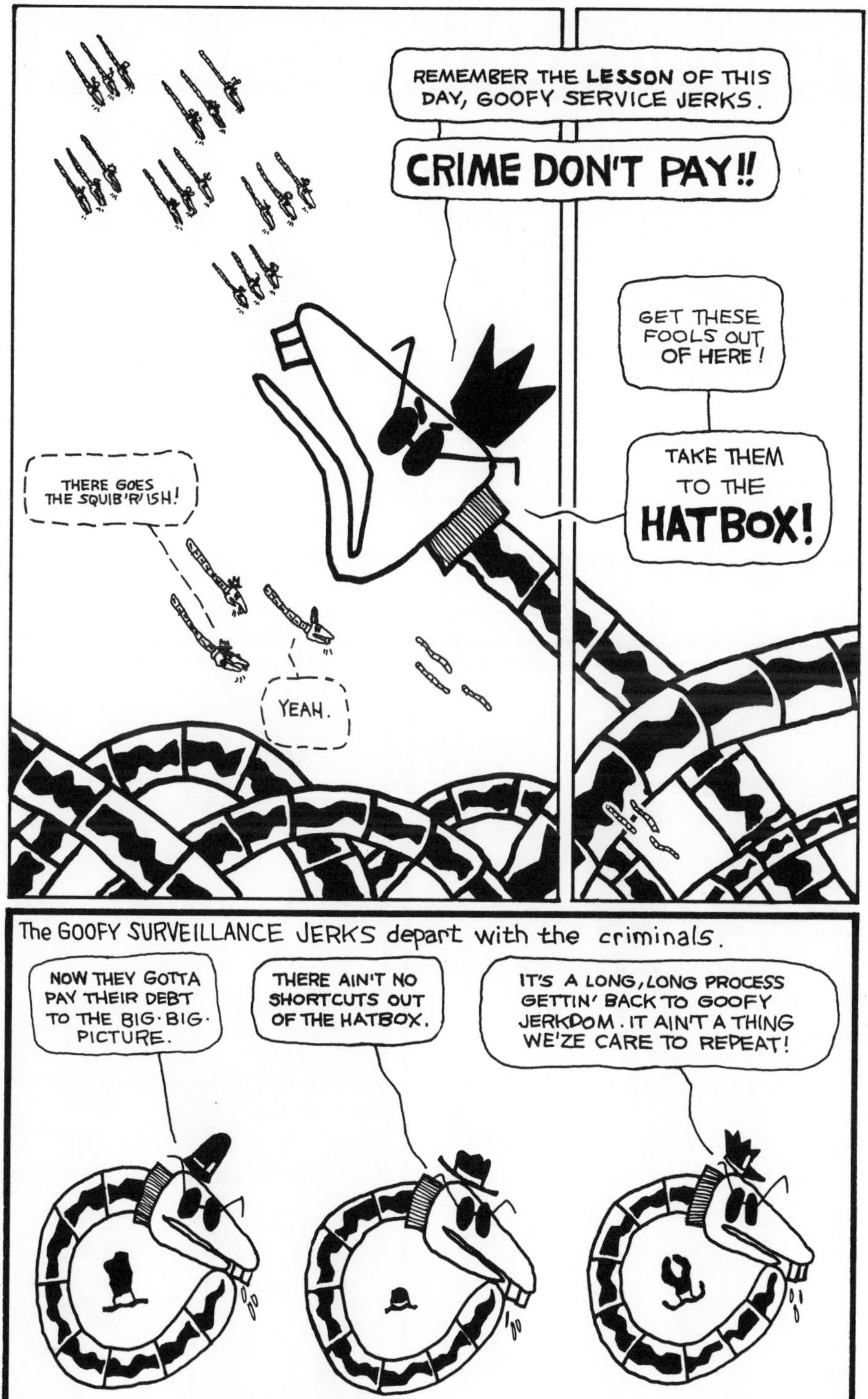

REMEMBER THE LESSON OF THIS DAY, GOOFY SERVICE JERKS.
CRIME DON'T PAY!!
THERE GOES THE SQUIB'R'ISH!
YEAH.
GET THESE FOOLS OUT OF HERE!
TAKE THEM TO THE HATBOX!
The GOOFY SURVEILLANCE JERKS depart with the criminals.
NOW THEY GOTTA PAY THEIR DEBT TO THE BIG·BIG· PICTURE.
THERE AIN'T NO SHORTCUTS OUT OF THE HATBOX.
IT'S A LONG, LONG PROCESS GETTIN' BACK TO GOOFY JERKDOM. IT AIN'T A THING WE'ZE CARE TO REPEAT!

The Horror of the Hatbox!

The **Goofy Surveillance Jerks** are transporting the **criminals**.

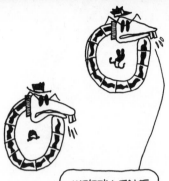

WE'ZE HATE **THIS** PART OF OUR CAREER.

YEP. WE'ZE'RE **TREKKIN'** TO **THE HATBOX**!

WE'ZE'LL TAKE A **DROP** UP YONDER.

THAT'S TH' END OF THE **NICE** SCENERY.

YEP.

HERE COME **THE CRUDE PARTS.**

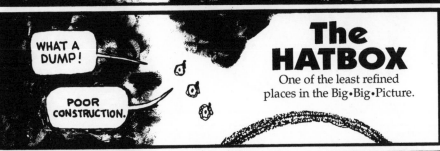

IT'S SO UGLY IN THIS AREA.
WHAT A DUMP!
POOR CONSTRUCTION.
The HATBOX
One of the least refined places in the Big•Big•Picture.
SLOPPY ARCHITECTURE.
TO THINK WE'ZE ALL STARTED IN THIS PLACE!
HURRY!

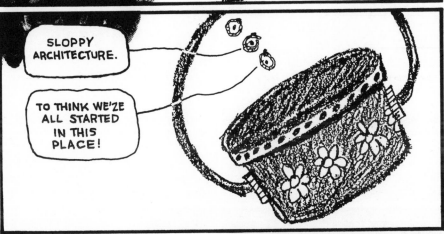

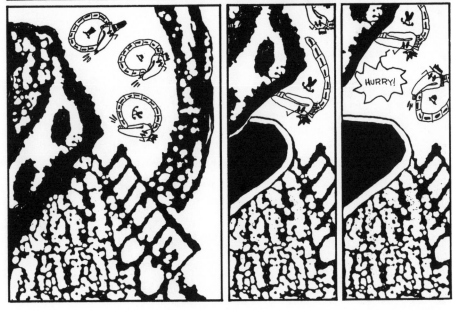

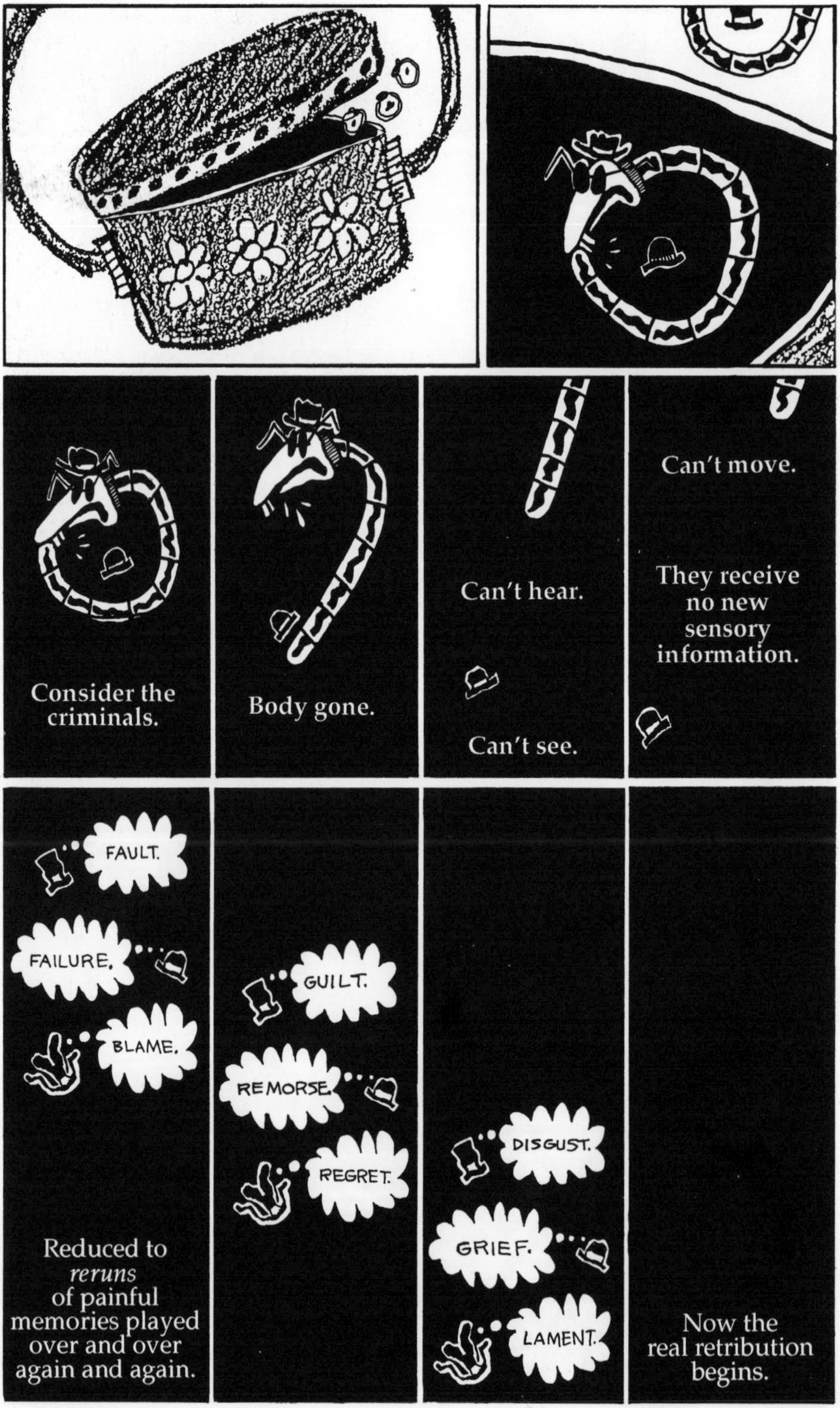
Consider the criminals.
Body gone.
Can't hear.
Can't see.
Can't move.
They receive no new sensory information.
FAULT.
FAILURE.
BLAME.
Reduced to *reruns* of painful memories played over and over again and again.
GUILT.
REMORSE.
REGRET.
DISGUST.
GRIEF.
LAMENT.
Now the real retribution begins.

As our crooks are about to learn.

MOURN.

DEPLORE.

RUE RUE RUE

GLUM GLUM GLUM

This is the horror of the Hatbox!
The endless collisions deny even the privilege of wallowing in self-pity.
It's awful!

The Goofy Surveillance Jerks close the lid of the Hatbox and flee as fast as they can!

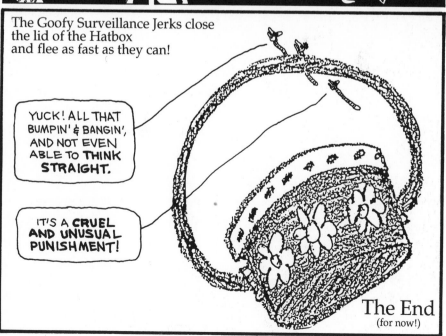

YUCK! ALL THAT BUMPIN' & BANGIN', AND NOT EVEN ABLE TO **THINK STRAIGHT.**

IT'S A **CRUEL AND UNUSUAL** PUNISHMENT!

The End
(for now!)

165

Jump'n Beanish!

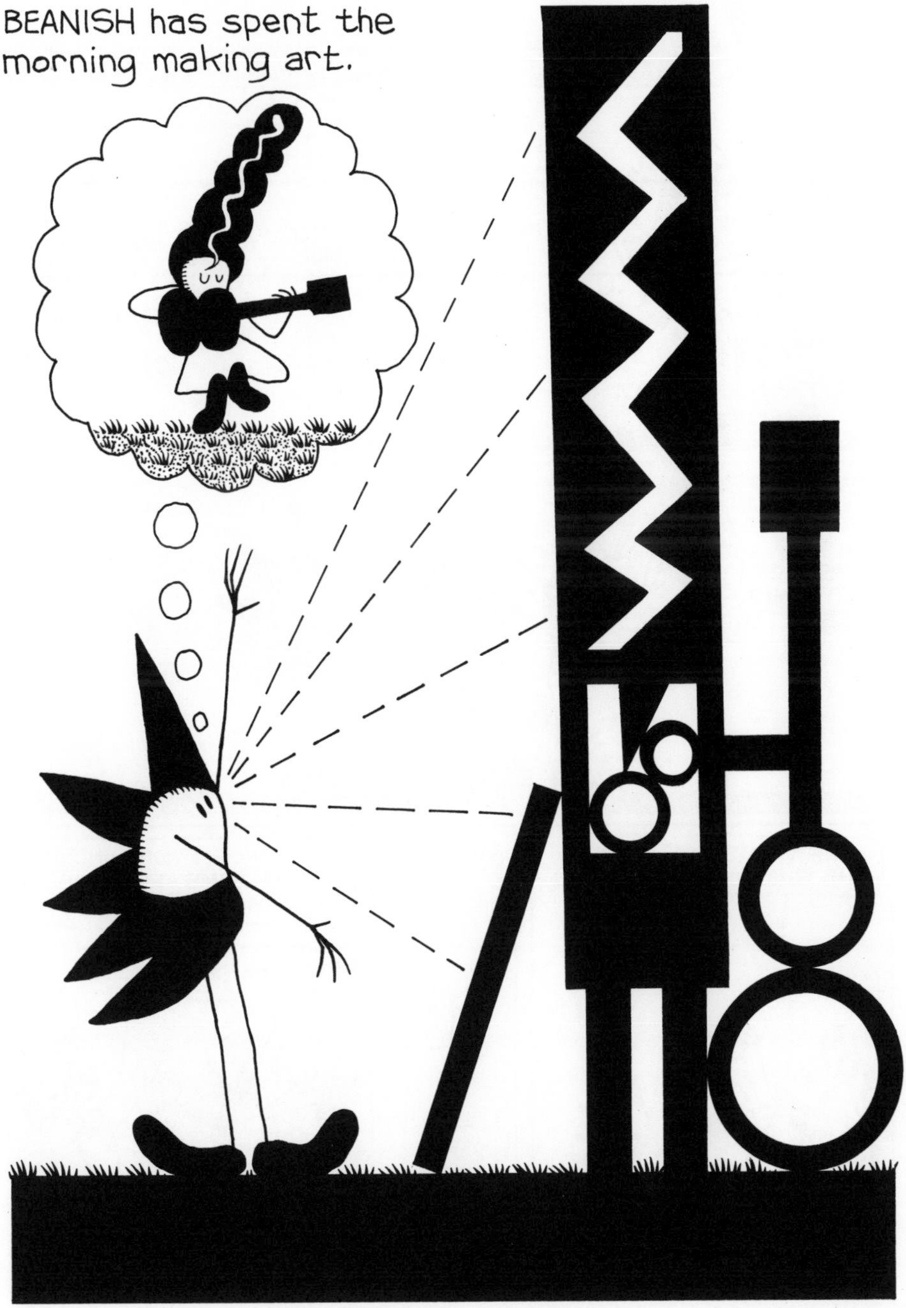

BEANISH has spent the morning making art.

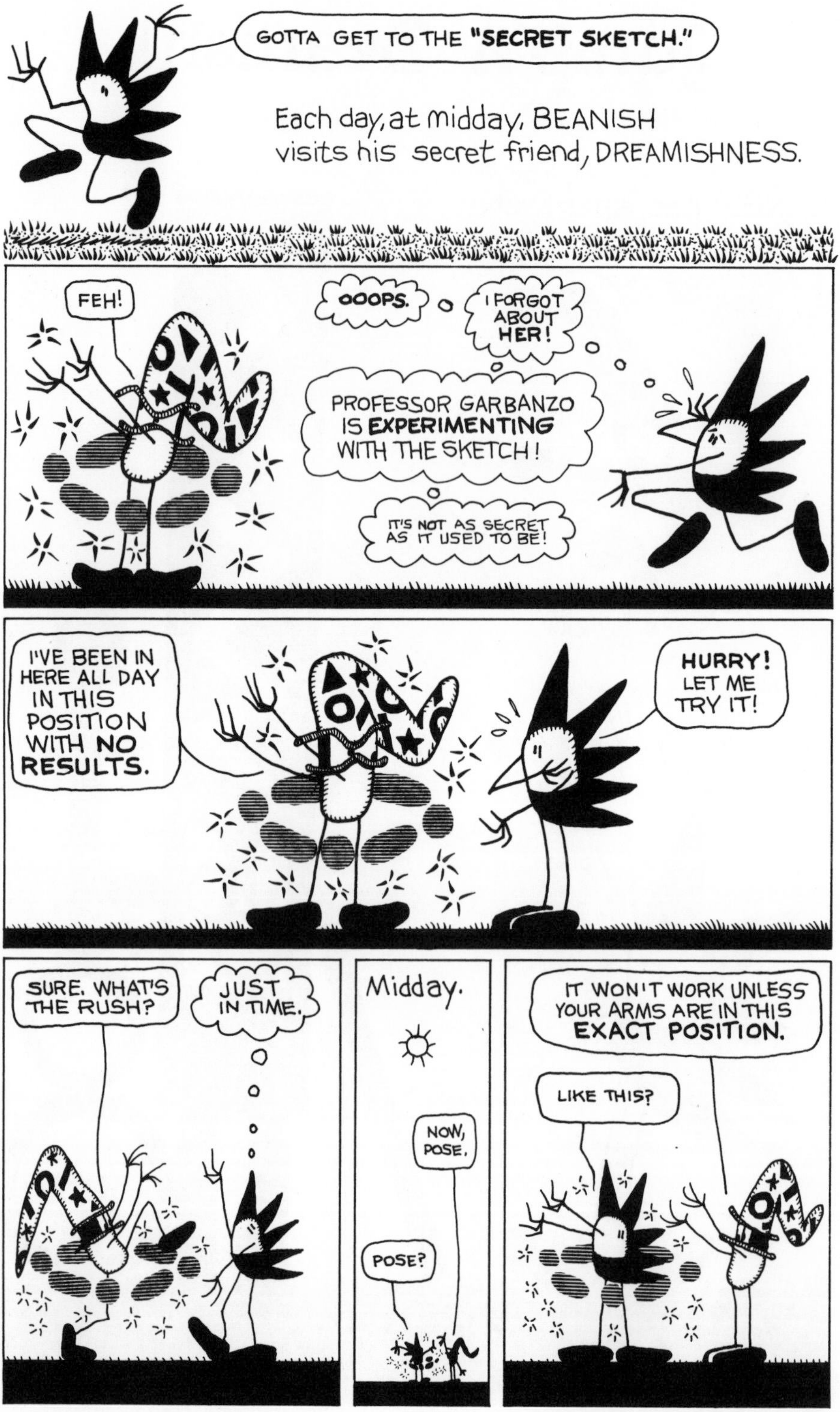
GOTTA GET TO THE "SECRET SKETCH."
Each day, at midday, BEANISH visits his secret friend, DREAMISHNESS.
FEH!
OOOPS.
I FORGOT ABOUT HER!
PROFESSOR GARBANZO IS EXPERIMENTING WITH THE SKETCH!
IT'S NOT AS SECRET AS IT USED TO BE!
I'VE BEEN IN HERE ALL DAY IN THIS POSITION WITH NO RESULTS.
HURRY! LET ME TRY IT!
SURE. WHAT'S THE RUSH?
JUST IN TIME.
Midday.
NOW, POSE.
POSE?
IT WON'T WORK UNLESS YOUR ARMS ARE IN THIS EXACT POSITION.
LIKE THIS?

THAT'S IT.
JUMP'N BEANISH.

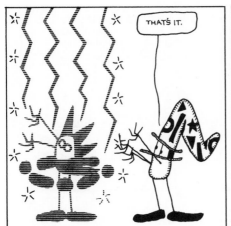

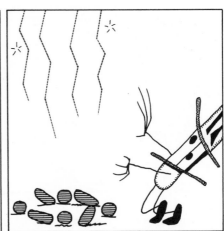

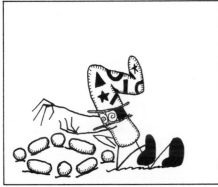

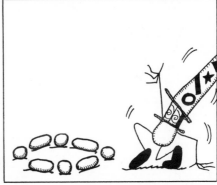

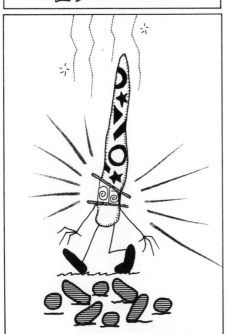

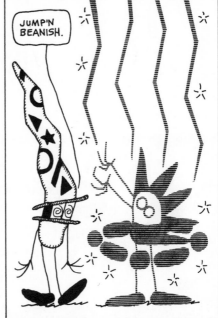

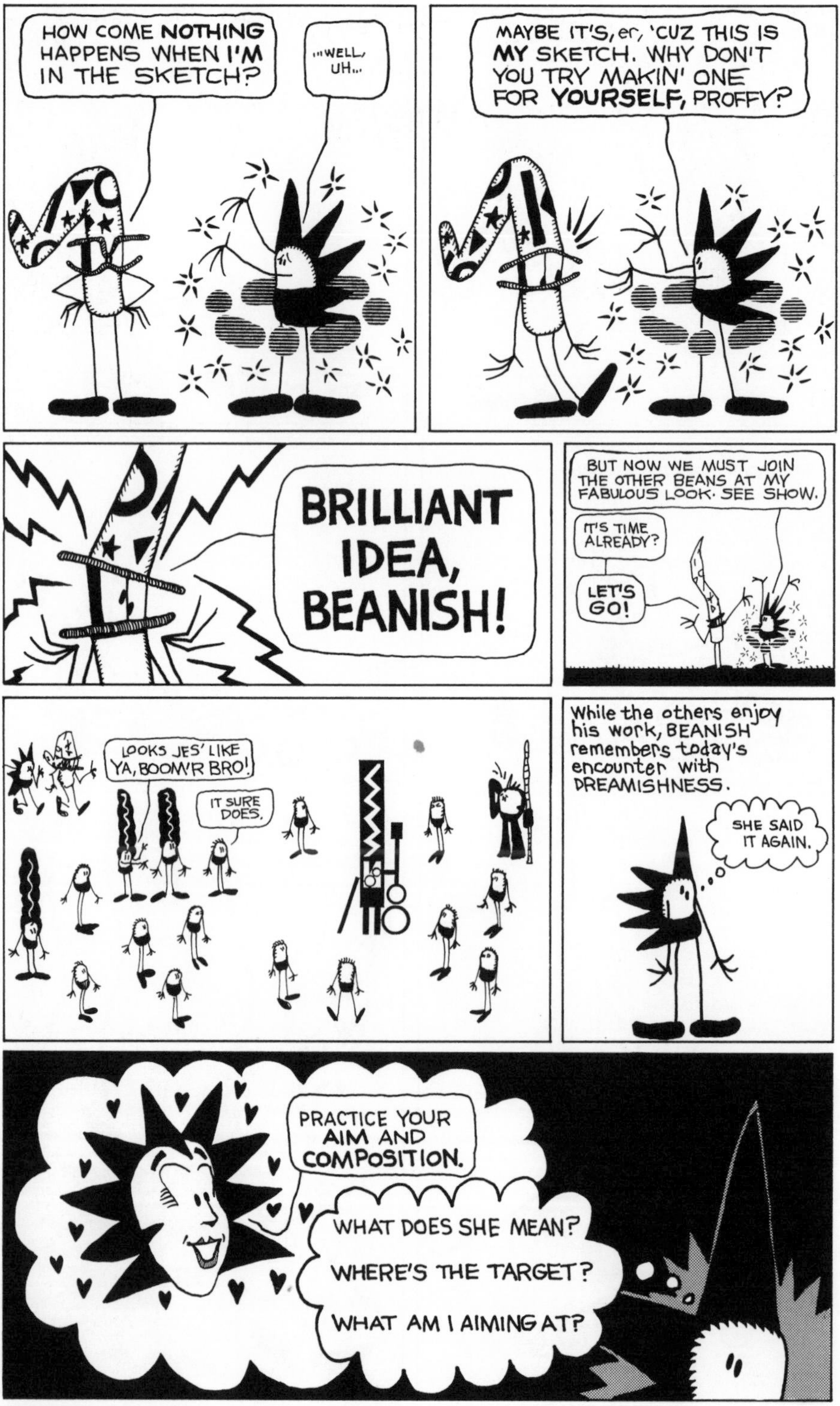
HOW COME **NOTHING** HAPPENS WHEN **I'M** IN THE SKETCH?
...WELL, UH...
MAYBE IT'S, er, 'CUZ THIS IS **MY** SKETCH. WHY DON'T YOU TRY MAKIN' ONE FOR **YOURSELF**, PROFFY?
BRILLIANT IDEA, BEANISH!
BUT NOW WE MUST JOIN THE OTHER BEANS AT MY FABULOUS LOOK. SEE SHOW.
IT'S TIME ALREADY?
LET'S GO!
LOOKS JES' LIKE YA, BOOM'R BRO!
IT SURE DOES.
While the others enjoy his work, BEANISH remembers today's encounter with DREAMISHNESS.
SHE SAID IT AGAIN.
PRACTICE YOUR AIM AND COMPOSITION.
WHAT DOES SHE MEAN?
WHERE'S THE TARGET?
WHAT AM I AIMING AT?

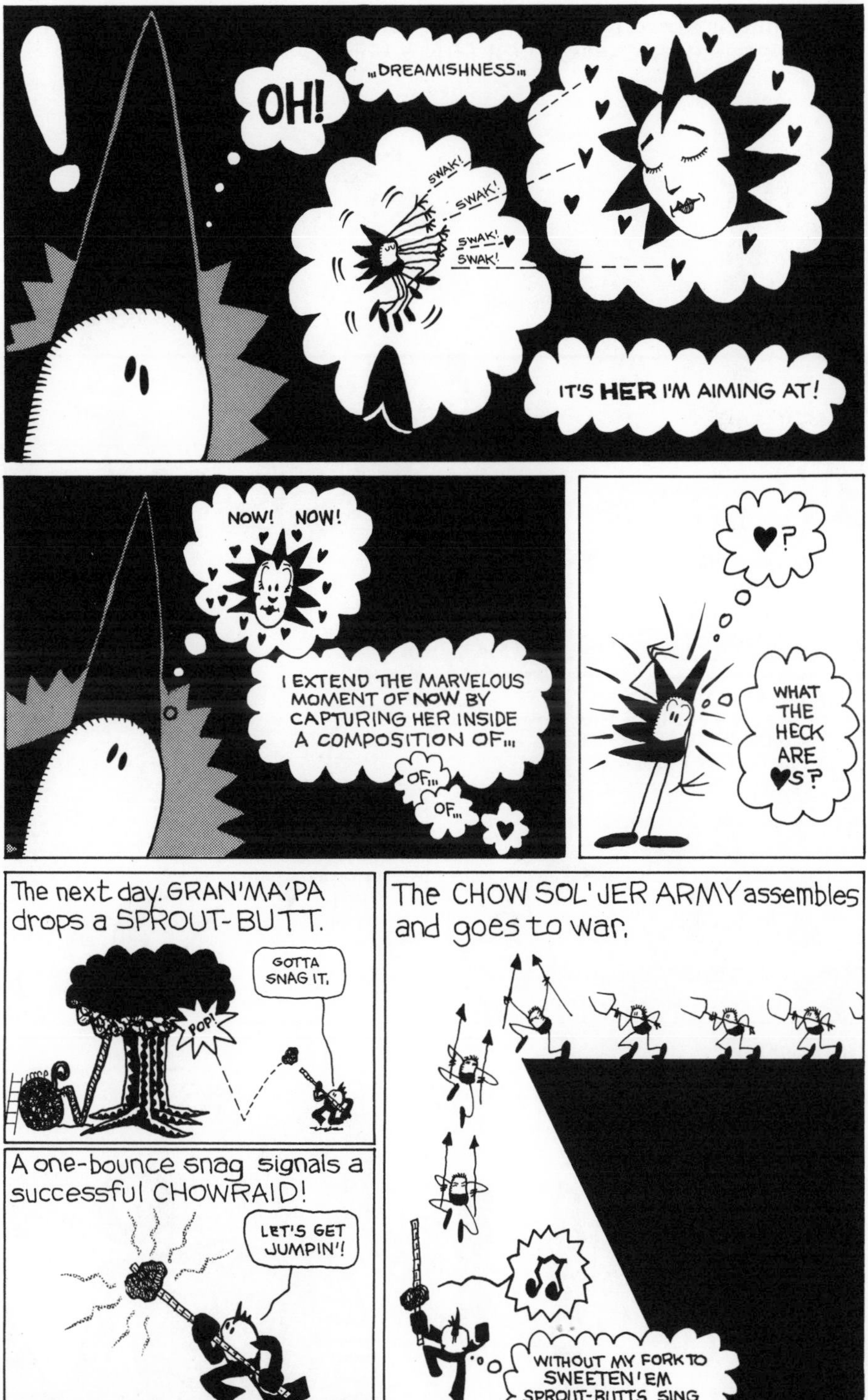

OH!
...DREAMISHNESS...
SWAK!
SWAK!
SWAK!
SWAK!
IT'S HER I'M AIMING AT!
NOW! NOW!
I EXTEND THE MARVELOUS MOMENT OF NOW BY CAPTURING HER INSIDE A COMPOSITION OF...
OF...
OF...
♥?
WHAT THE HECK ARE ♥S?
The next day, GRAN'MA'PA drops a SPROUT-BUTT.
POP!
GOTTA SNAG IT.
A one-bounce snag signals a successful CHOWRAID!
LET'S GET JUMPIN'!
The CHOW SOL'JER ARMY assembles and goes to war.
WITHOUT MY FORK TO SWEETEN 'EM SPROUT-BUTTS SING SO SOUR.

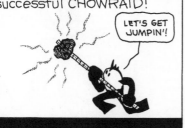

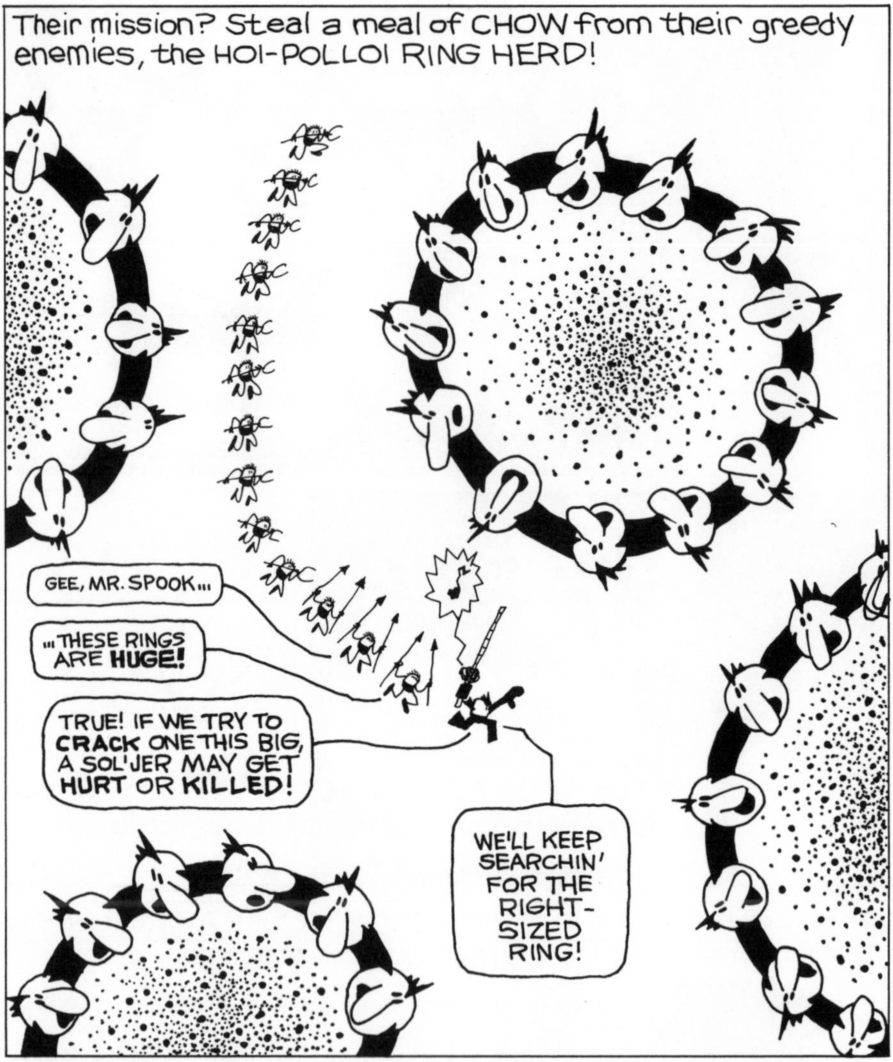
Their mission? Steal a meal of CHOW from their greedy enemies, the HOI-POLLOI RING HERD!
GEE, MR. SPOOK...
...THESE RINGS ARE HUGE!
TRUE! IF WE TRY TO CRACK ONE THIS BIG, A SOL'JER MAY GET HURT OR KILLED!
WE'LL KEEP SEARCHIN' FOR THE RIGHT-SIZED RING!

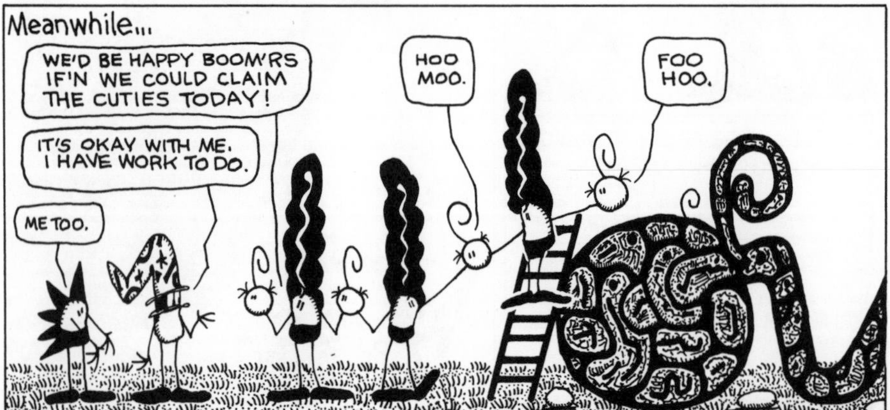
Meanwhile...
WE'D BE HAPPY BOOM'RS IF'N WE COULD CLAIM THE CUTIES TODAY!
IT'S OKAY WITH ME. I HAVE WORK TO DO.
ME TOO.
HOO MOO.
FOO HOO.

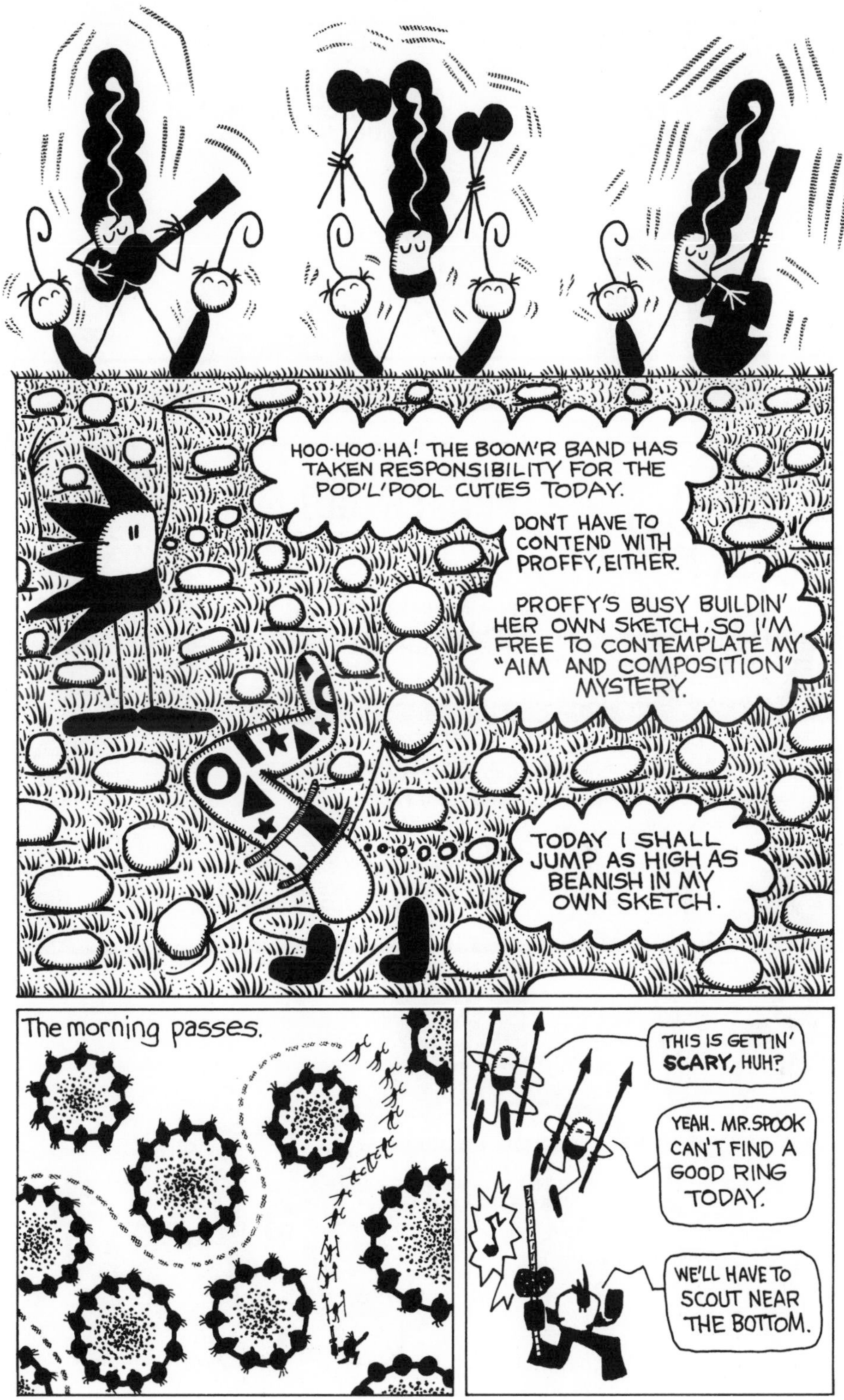
HOO·HOO·HA! THE BOOM'R BAND HAS TAKEN RESPONSIBILITY FOR THE POD'L'POOL CUTIES TODAY.
DON'T HAVE TO CONTEND WITH PROFFY, EITHER.
PROFFY'S BUSY BUILDIN' HER OWN SKETCH, SO I'M FREE TO CONTEMPLATE MY "AIM AND COMPOSITION" MYSTERY.
TODAY I SHALL JUMP AS HIGH AS BEANISH IN MY OWN SKETCH.
The morning passes.
THIS IS GETTIN' SCARY, HUH?
YEAH. MR.SPOOK CAN'T FIND A GOOD RING TODAY.
WE'LL HAVE TO SCOUT NEAR THE BOTTOM.

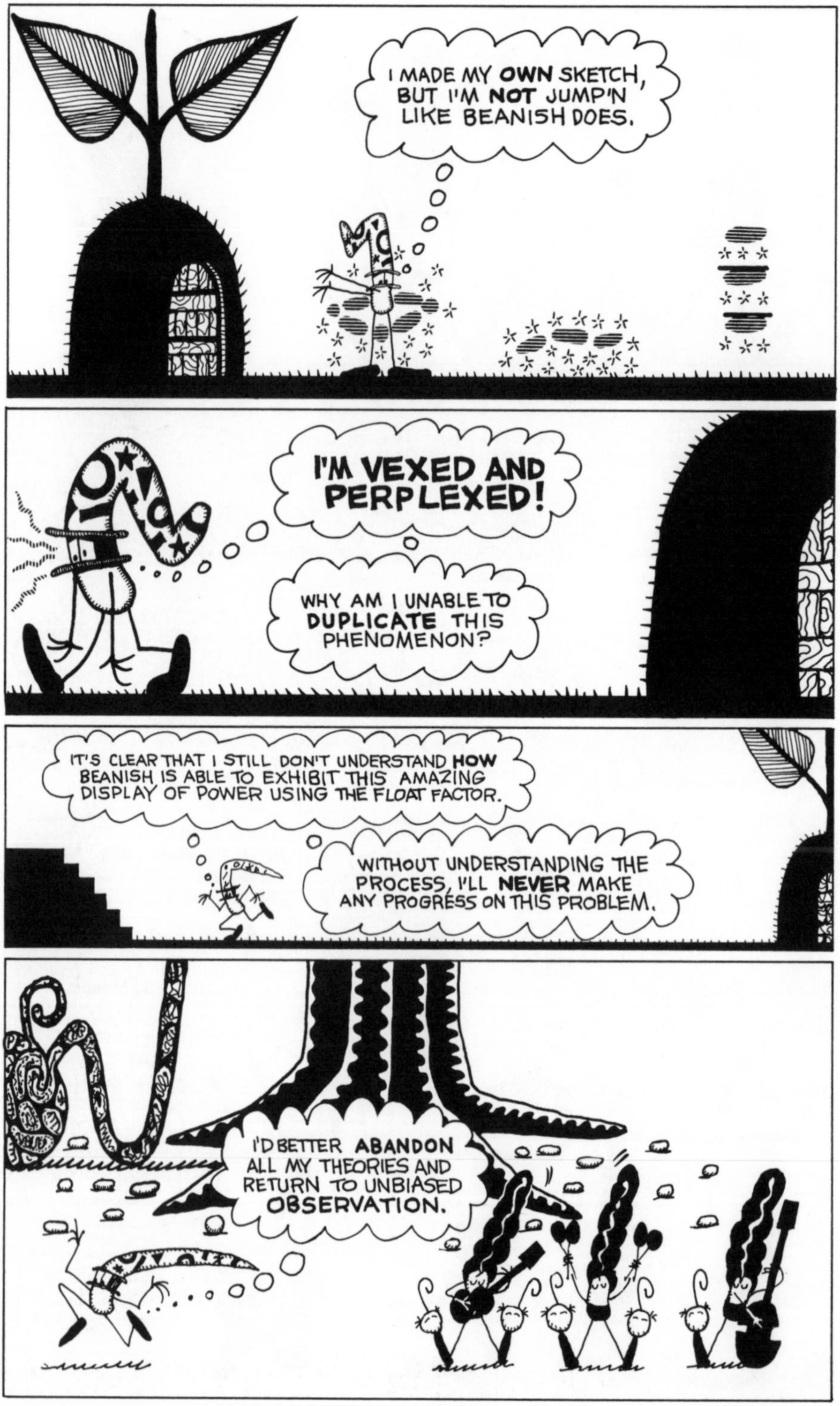
I MADE MY OWN SKETCH, BUT I'M NOT JUMP'N LIKE BEANISH DOES.
I'M VEXED AND PERPLEXED!
WHY AM I UNABLE TO DUPLICATE THIS PHENOMENON?
IT'S CLEAR THAT I STILL DON'T UNDERSTAND HOW BEANISH IS ABLE TO EXHIBIT THIS AMAZING DISPLAY OF POWER USING THE FLOAT FACTOR.
WITHOUT UNDERSTANDING THE PROCESS, I'LL NEVER MAKE ANY PROGRESS ON THIS PROBLEM.
I'D BETTER ABANDON ALL MY THEORIES AND RETURN TO UNBIASED OBSERVATION.

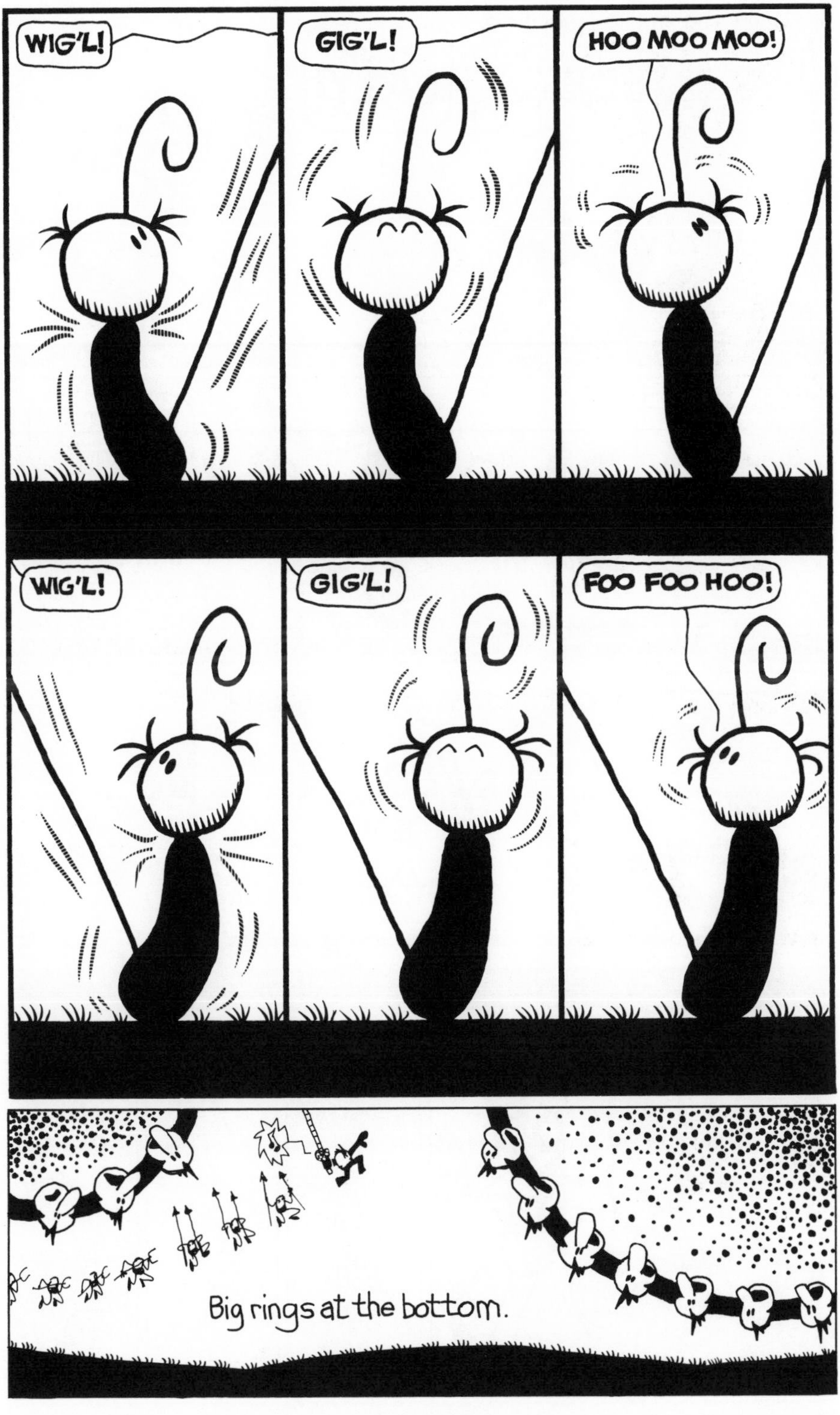
WIG'L!
GIG'L!
HOO MOO MOO!
WIG'L!
GIG'L!
FOO FOO HOO!
Big rings at the bottom.

Towards the end of morning.

WHATEVER ♥'s ARE THEY'RE **VERY** POWERFUL.

GET UP, **LAZY!**

TAP! TAP!

I W-WASN'T JES' LYIN' AROUND, PROFFY. I WAS TH-THINKIN',...

MY SKETCH **FAILED!**

LET'S GO BACK TO EXPERIMENTING WITH YOURS.

I WILL OBSERVE YOU **VERY** CAREFULLY.

IT'S ALMOST MIDDAY.

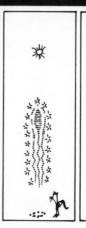

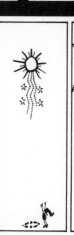

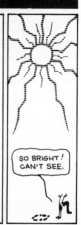

SO BRIGHT! CAN'T SEE.

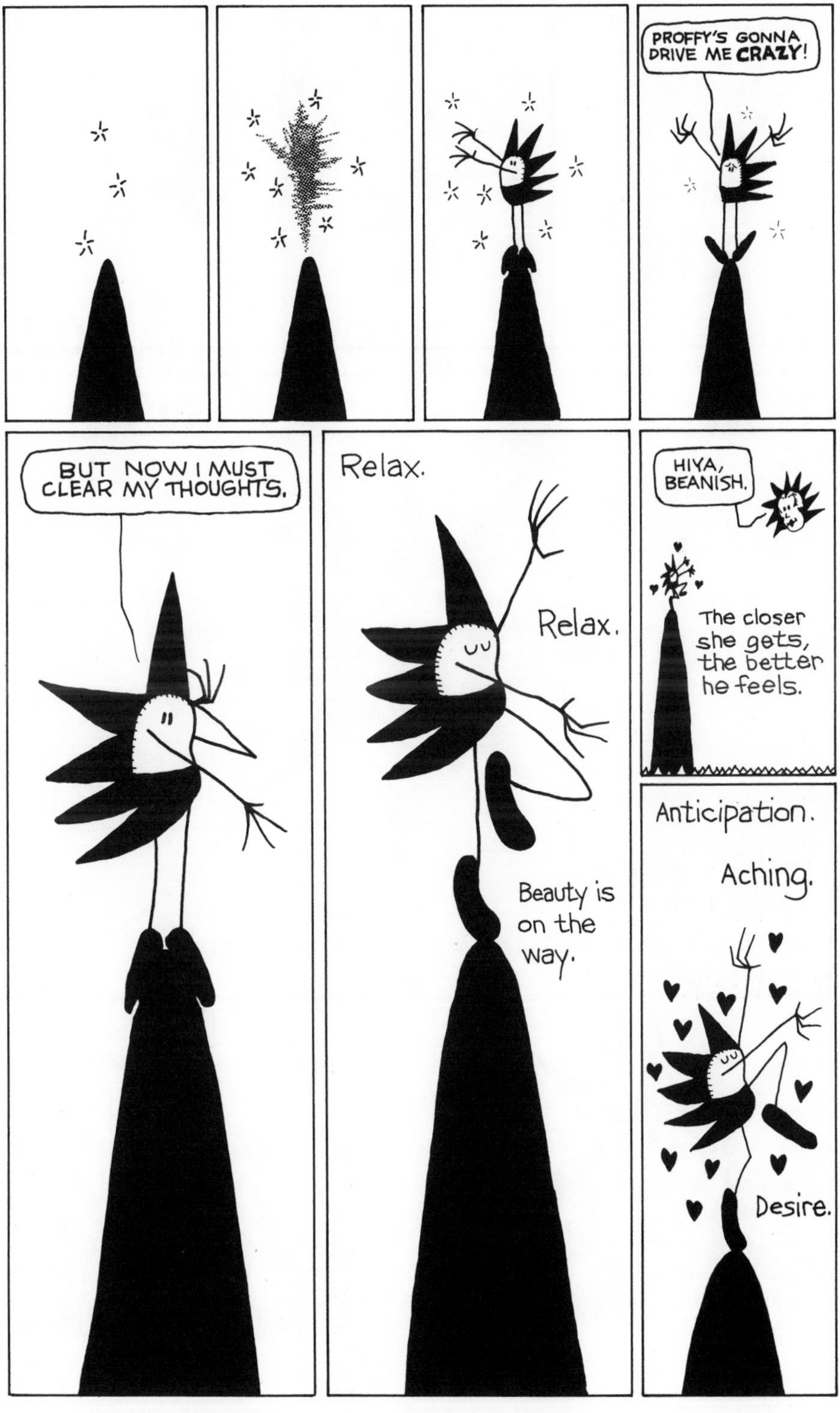
PROFFY'S GONNA DRIVE ME CRAZY!
BUT NOW I MUST CLEAR MY THOUGHTS.
Relax.
Relax.
Beauty is on the way.
HIYA, BEANISH.
The closer she gets, the better he feels.
Anticipation.
Aching.
Desire.

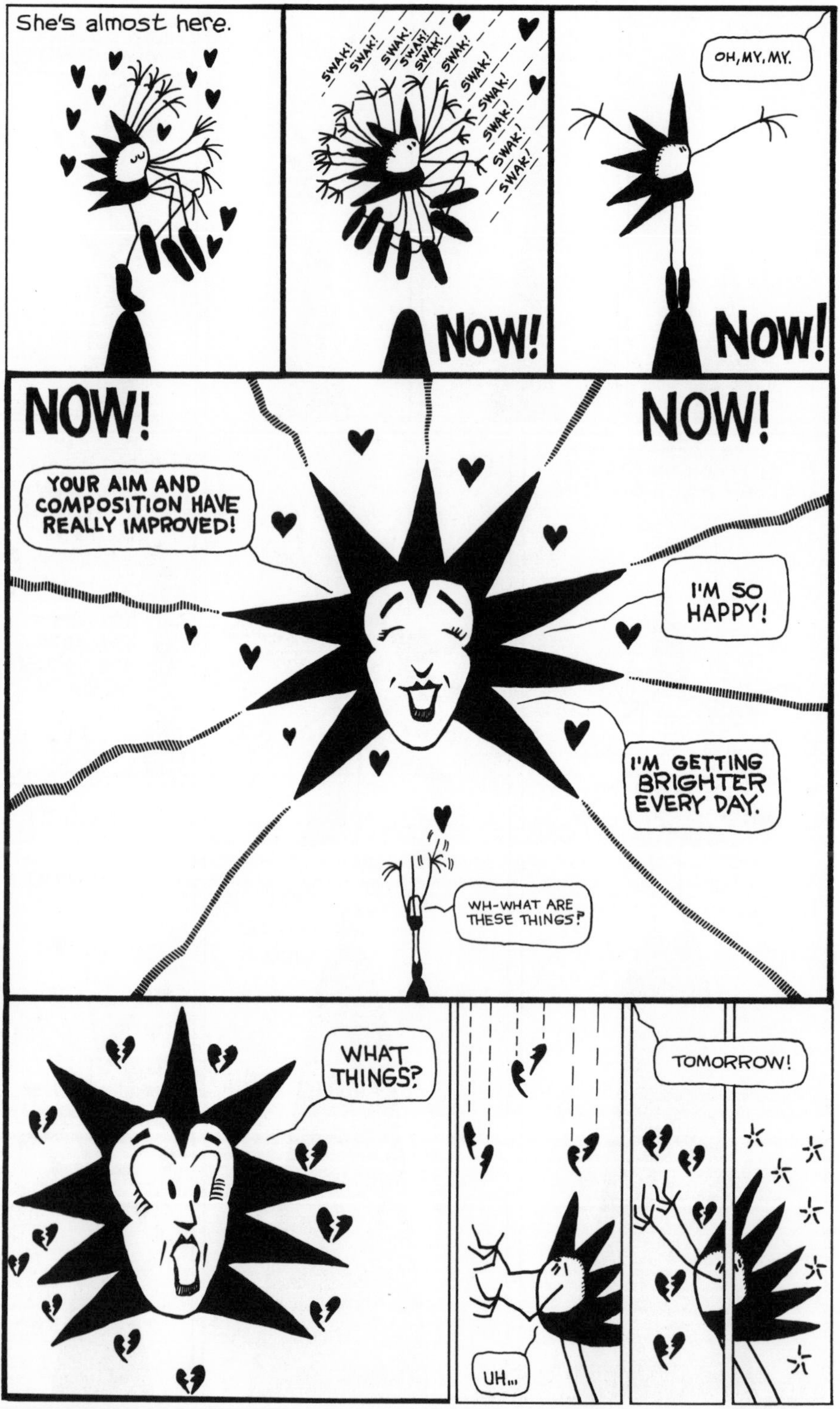
She's almost here.
SWAK! SWAK! SWAK! SWAK! SWAK! SWAK! SWAK! SWAK! SWAK! SWAK! SWAK!
NOW!
OH, MY, MY.
NOW!
NOW!
NOW!
YOUR AIM AND COMPOSITION HAVE REALLY IMPROVED!
I'M SO HAPPY!
I'M GETTING BRIGHTER EVERY DAY.
WH-WHAT ARE THESE THINGS?
WHAT THINGS?
UH...
TOMORROW!

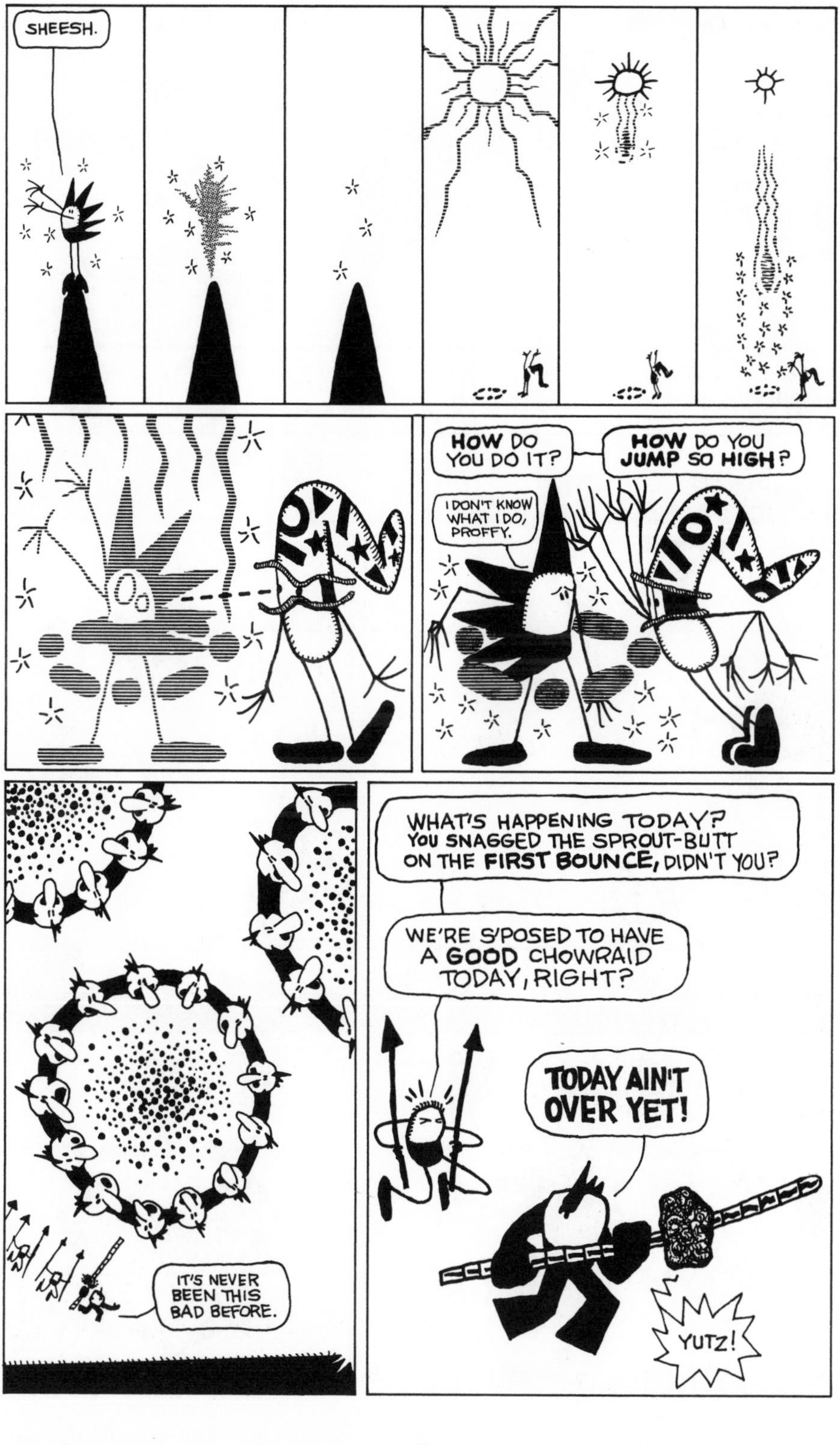

SHEESH.
HOW DO YOU DO IT?
HOW DO YOU JUMP SO HIGH?
I DON'T KNOW WHAT I DO, PROFFY.
IT'S NEVER BEEN THIS BAD BEFORE.
WHAT'S HAPPENING TODAY? YOU SNAGGED THE SPROUT-BUTT ON THE FIRST BOUNCE, DIDN'T YOU?
WE'RE S'POSED TO HAVE A GOOD CHOWRAID TODAY, RIGHT?
TODAY AIN'T OVER YET!
YUTZ!

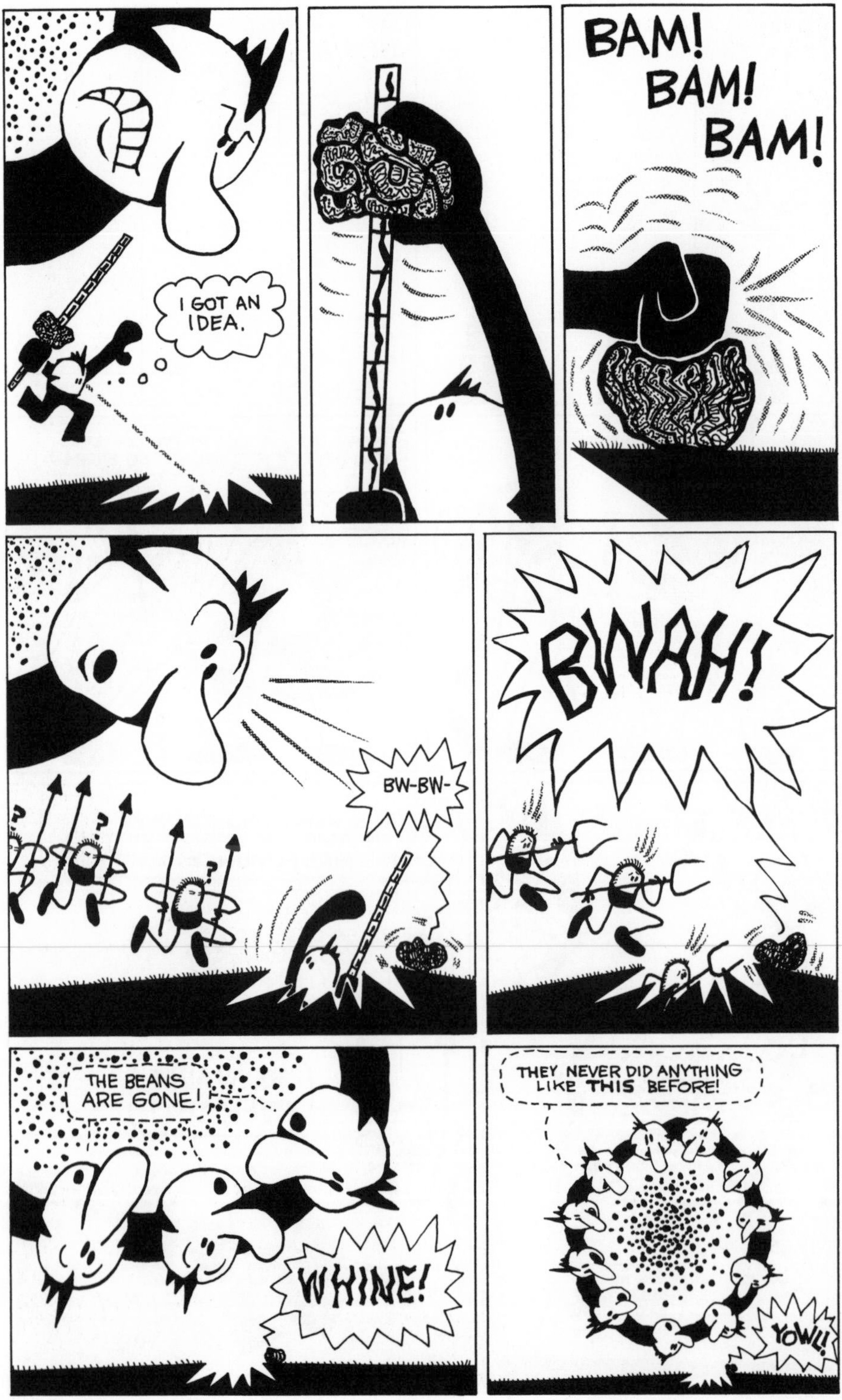
I GOT AN IDEA.
BAM! BAM! BAM!
BW-BW-
BWAH!
THE BEANS ARE GONE!
WHINE!
THEY NEVER DID ANYTHING LIKE THIS BEFORE!
YOWL!

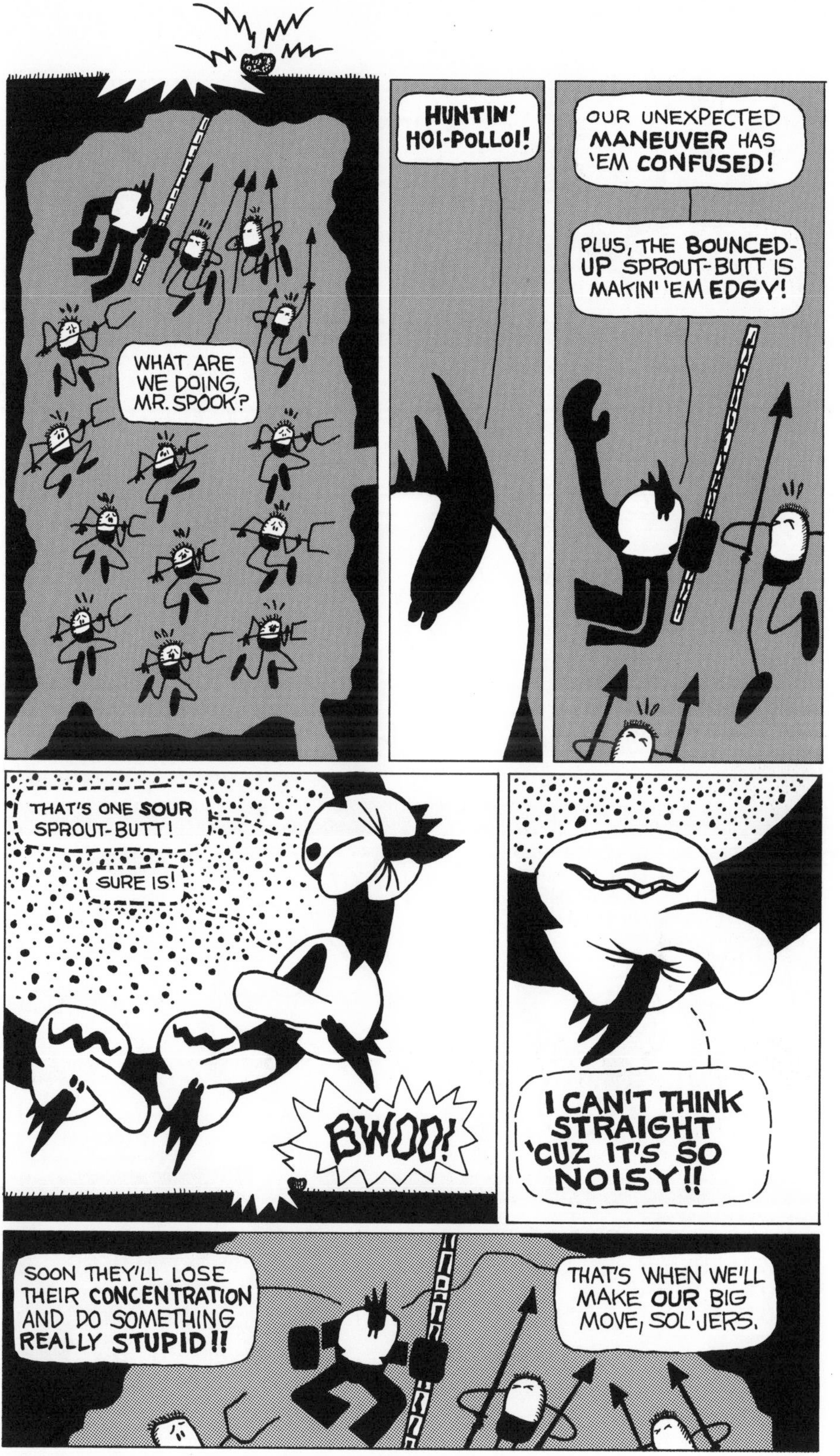

WHAT ARE WE DOING, MR. SPOOK?
HUNTIN' HOI-POLLOI!
OUR UNEXPECTED MANEUVER HAS 'EM CONFUSED!
PLUS, THE BOUNCED-UP SPROUT-BUTT IS MAKIN' 'EM EDGY!
THAT'S ONE SOUR SPROUT-BUTT!
SURE IS!
BWOO!
I CAN'T THINK STRAIGHT 'CUZ IT'S SO NOISY!!
SOON THEY'LL LOSE THEIR CONCENTRATION AND DO SOMETHING REALLY STUPID!!
THAT'S WHEN WE'LL MAKE OUR BIG MOVE, SOL'JERS.

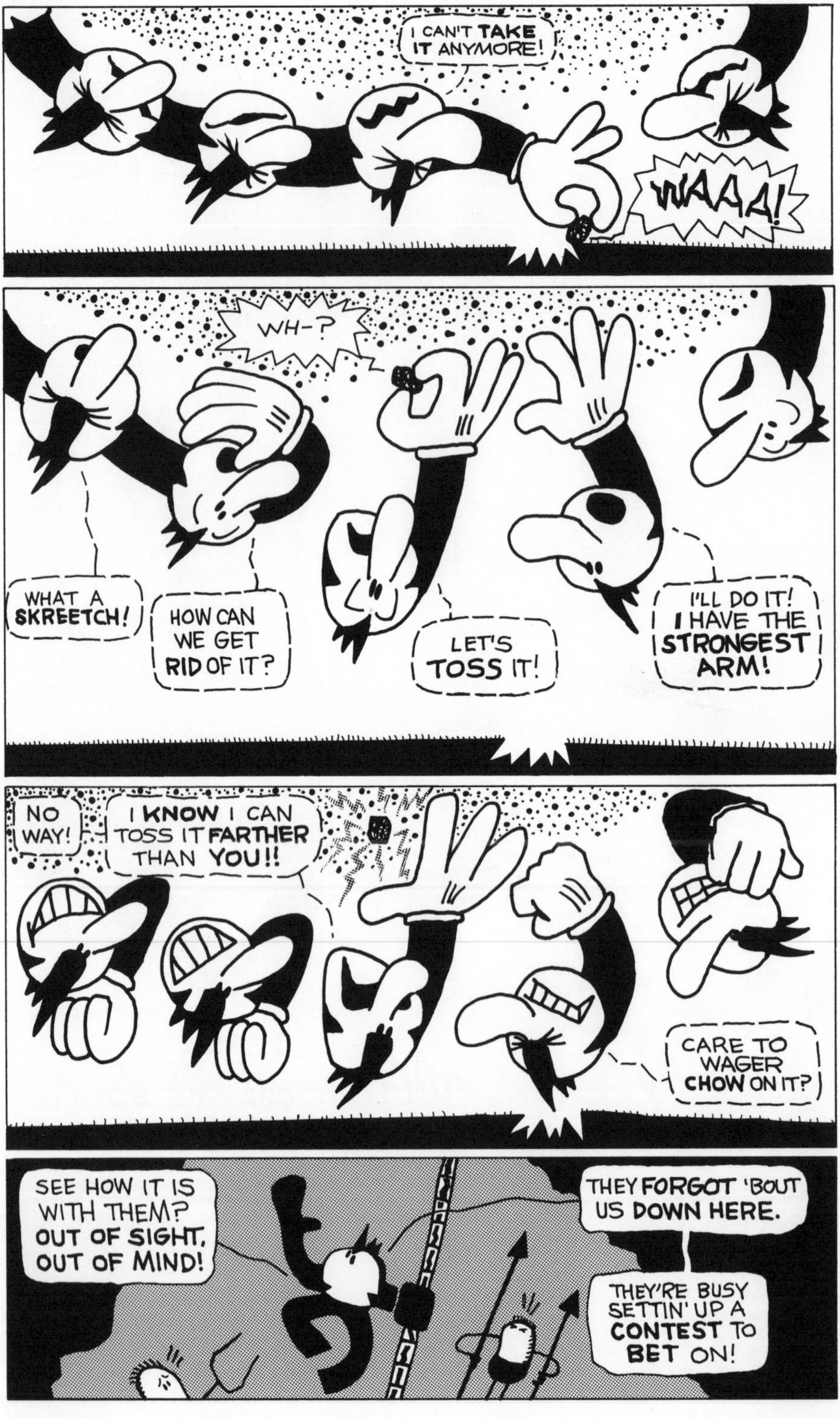
I CAN'T TAKE IT ANYMORE!
WAAAA!
WH-?
WHAT A SKREETCH!
HOW CAN WE GET RID OF IT?
LET'S TOSS IT!
I'LL DO IT! I HAVE THE STRONGEST ARM!
NO WAY!
I KNOW I CAN TOSS IT FARTHER THAN YOU!!
CARE TO WAGER CHOW ON IT?
SEE HOW IT IS WITH THEM? OUT OF SIGHT, OUT OF MIND!
THEY FORGOT 'BOUT US DOWN HERE.
THEY'RE BUSY SETTIN' UP A CONTEST TO BET ON!

It's true.

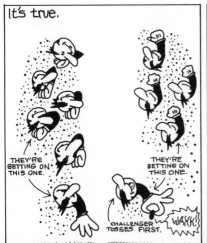

THEY'RE BETTING ON THIS ONE.

THEY'RE BETTING ON THIS ONE.

CHALLENGER TOSSES FIRST.

WAKK!

Suddenly...

HOO-HOO-**HA!**

HOKA-HOKA-**HEY!**

BWOOO!

WE'RE UNDER ATTACK! **FORM RINGS!**

C'MON UP, SOL'JERS!

UH-OH...

ZOT!

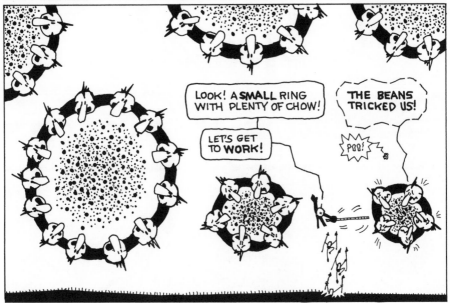

LOOK! A **SMALL** RING WITH PLENTY OF CHOW!

LET'S GET TO **WORK!**

THE BEANS TRICKED US!

POO!

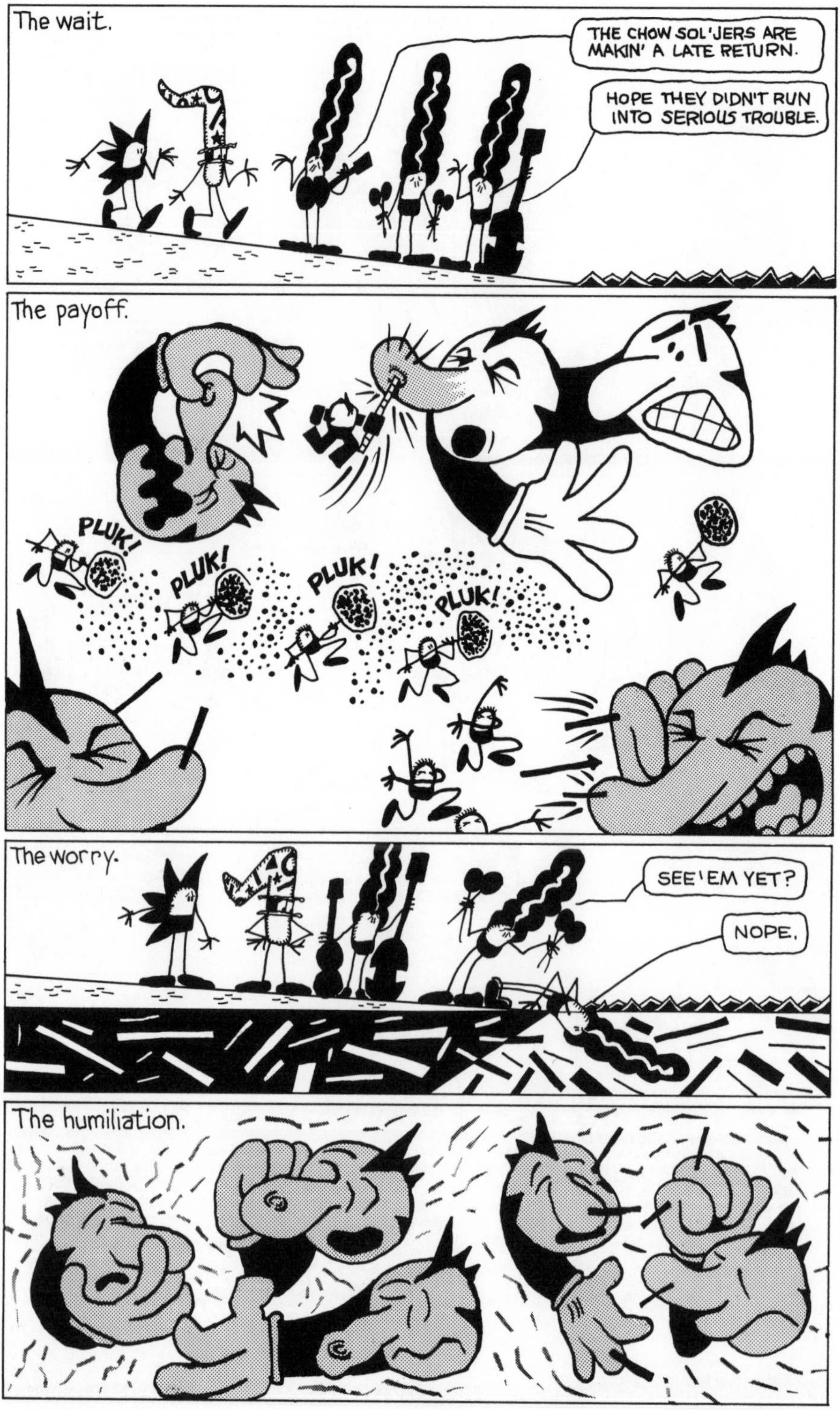
The wait.
THE CHOW SOL'JERS ARE MAKIN' A LATE RETURN.
HOPE THEY DIDN'T RUN INTO SERIOUS TROUBLE.
The payoff.
PLUK!
PLUK!
PLUK!
PLUK!
The worry.
SEE'EM YET?
NOPE.
The humiliation.

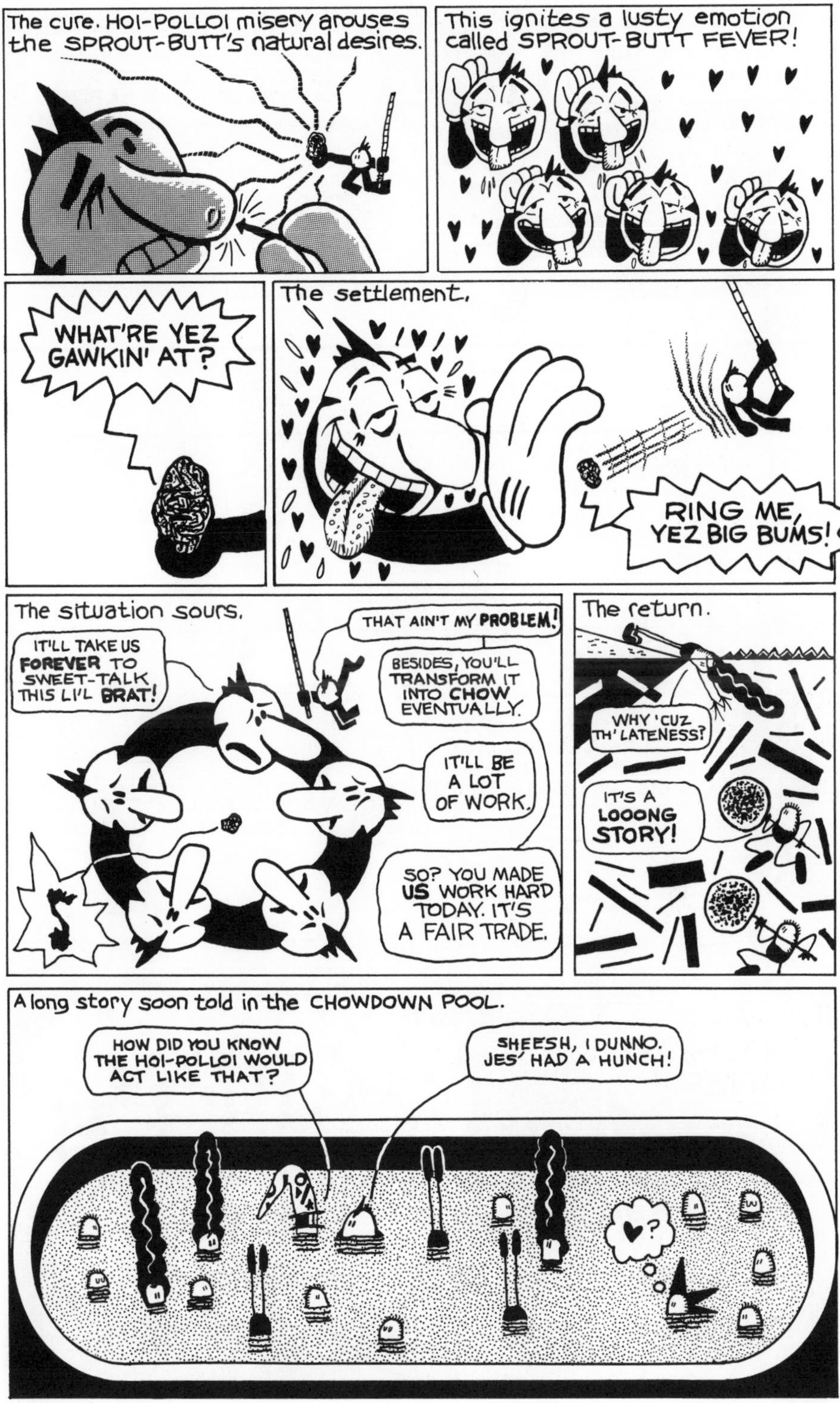
The cure. HOI-POLLOI misery arouses the SPROUT-BUTT's natural desires.
This ignites a lusty emotion called SPROUT-BUTT FEVER!
WHAT'RE YEZ GAWKIN' AT?
The settlement.
RING ME, YEZ BIG BUMS!
The situation sours.
IT'LL TAKE US FOREVER TO SWEET-TALK THIS LI'L BRAT!
THAT AIN'T MY PROBLEM!
BESIDES, YOU'LL TRANSFORM IT INTO CHOW EVENTUALLY.
IT'LL BE A LOT OF WORK.
SO? YOU MADE US WORK HARD TODAY. IT'S A FAIR TRADE.
The return.
WHY 'CUZ TH' LATENESS?
IT'S A LOOONG STORY!
A long story soon told in the CHOWDOWN POOL.
HOW DID YOU KNOW THE HOI-POLLOI WOULD ACT LIKE THAT?
SHEESH, I DUNNO. JES' HAD A HUNCH!

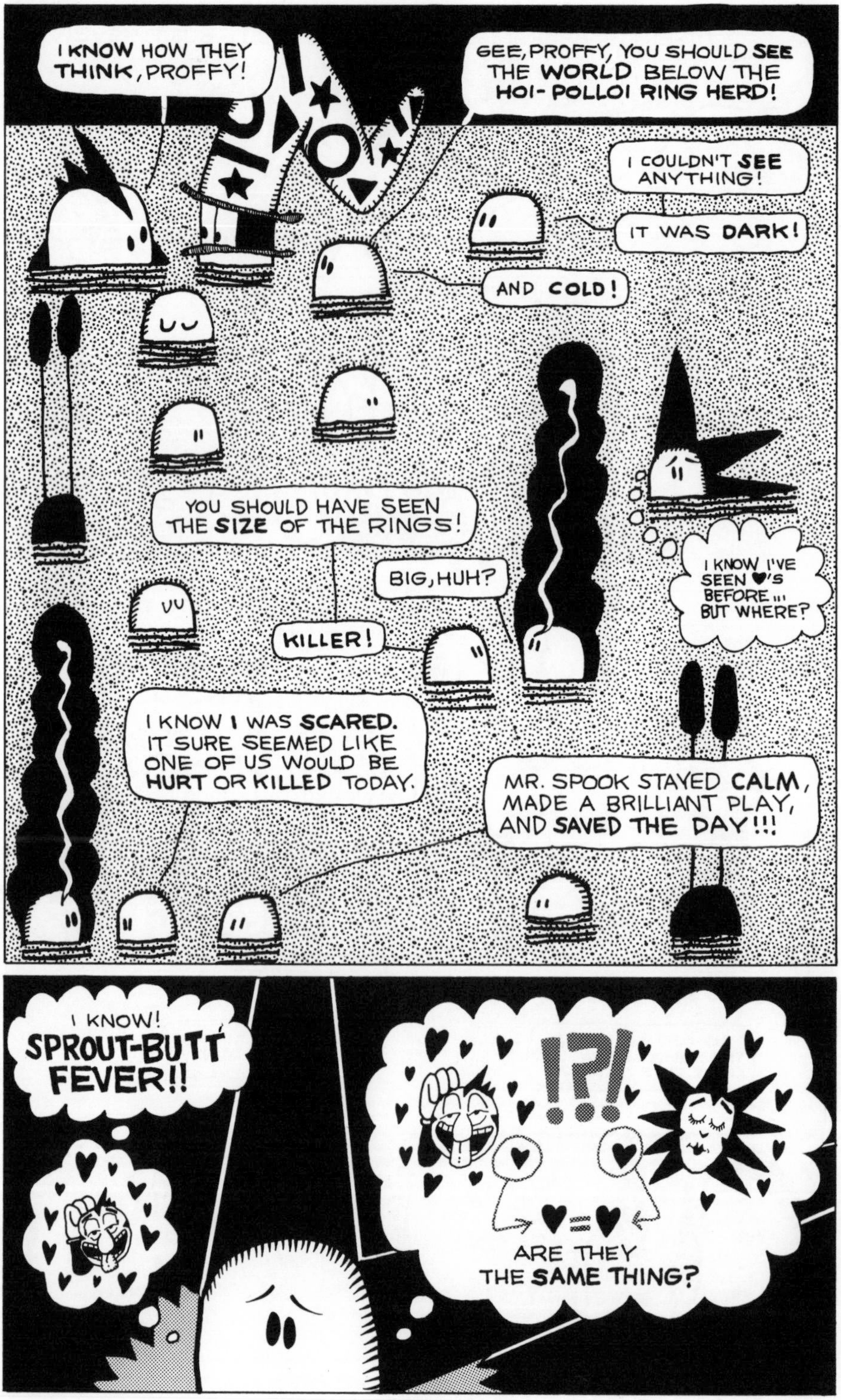
I KNOW HOW THEY THINK, PROFFY!
GEE, PROFFY, YOU SHOULD SEE THE WORLD BELOW THE HOI-POLLOI RING HERD!
I COULDN'T SEE ANYTHING!
IT WAS DARK!
AND COLD!
YOU SHOULD HAVE SEEN THE SIZE OF THE RINGS!
BIG, HUH?
KILLER!
I KNOW I'VE SEEN ♥'S BEFORE... BUT WHERE?
I KNOW I WAS SCARED. IT SURE SEEMED LIKE ONE OF US WOULD BE HURT OR KILLED TODAY.
MR. SPOOK STAYED CALM, MADE A BRILLIANT PLAY, AND SAVED THE DAY!!!
I KNOW! SPROUT-BUTT FEVER!!
!?!
♥=♥
ARE THEY THE SAME THING?

LOVE & SPROUT-BUTTS

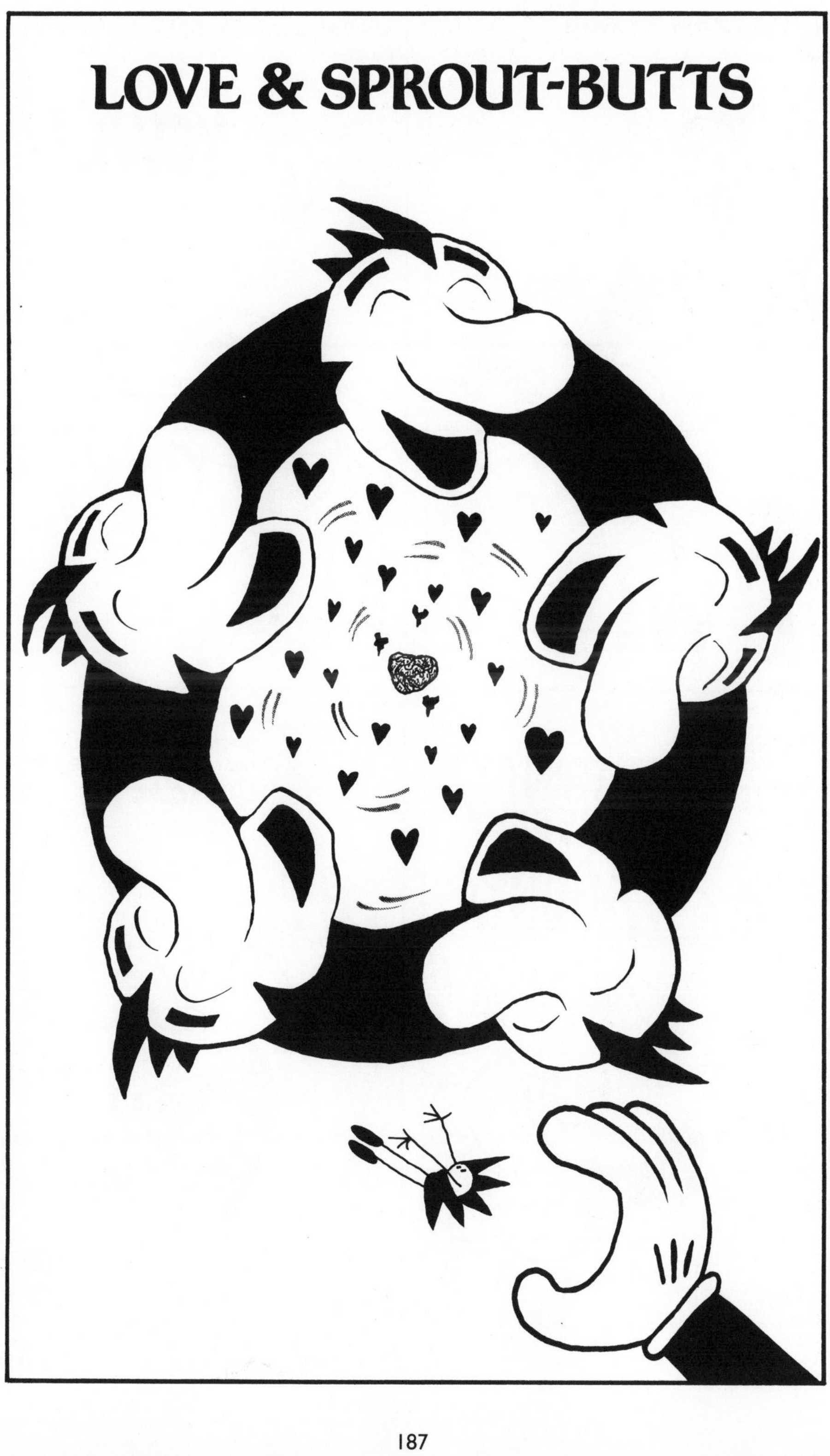

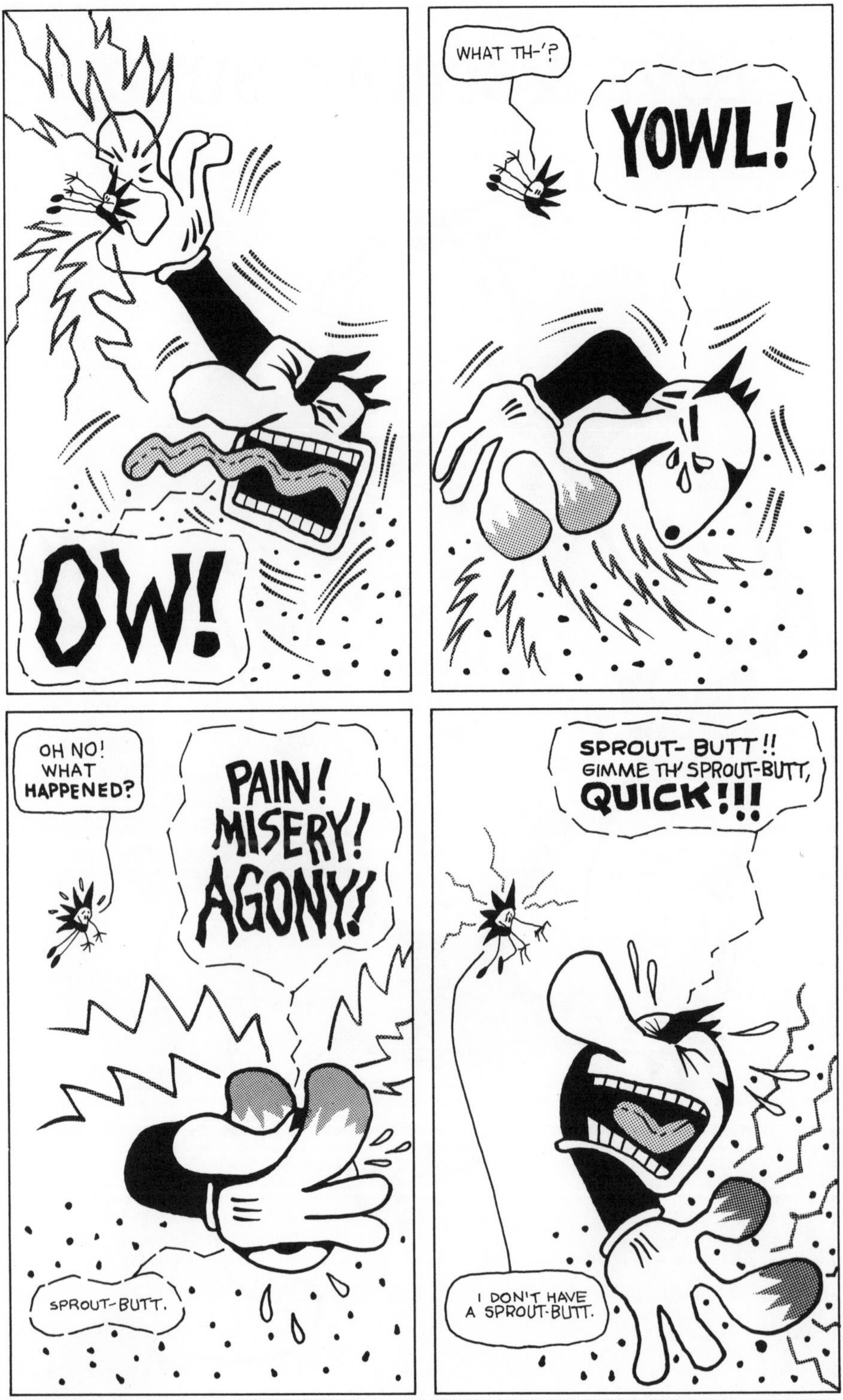
OW!
WHAT TH-'?
YOWL!
OH NO! WHAT HAPPENED?
PAIN! MISERY! AGONY!
SPROUT-BUTT.
SPROUT- BUTT!! GIMME TH' SPROUT-BUTT, QUICK!!!
I DON'T HAVE A SPROUT-BUTT.

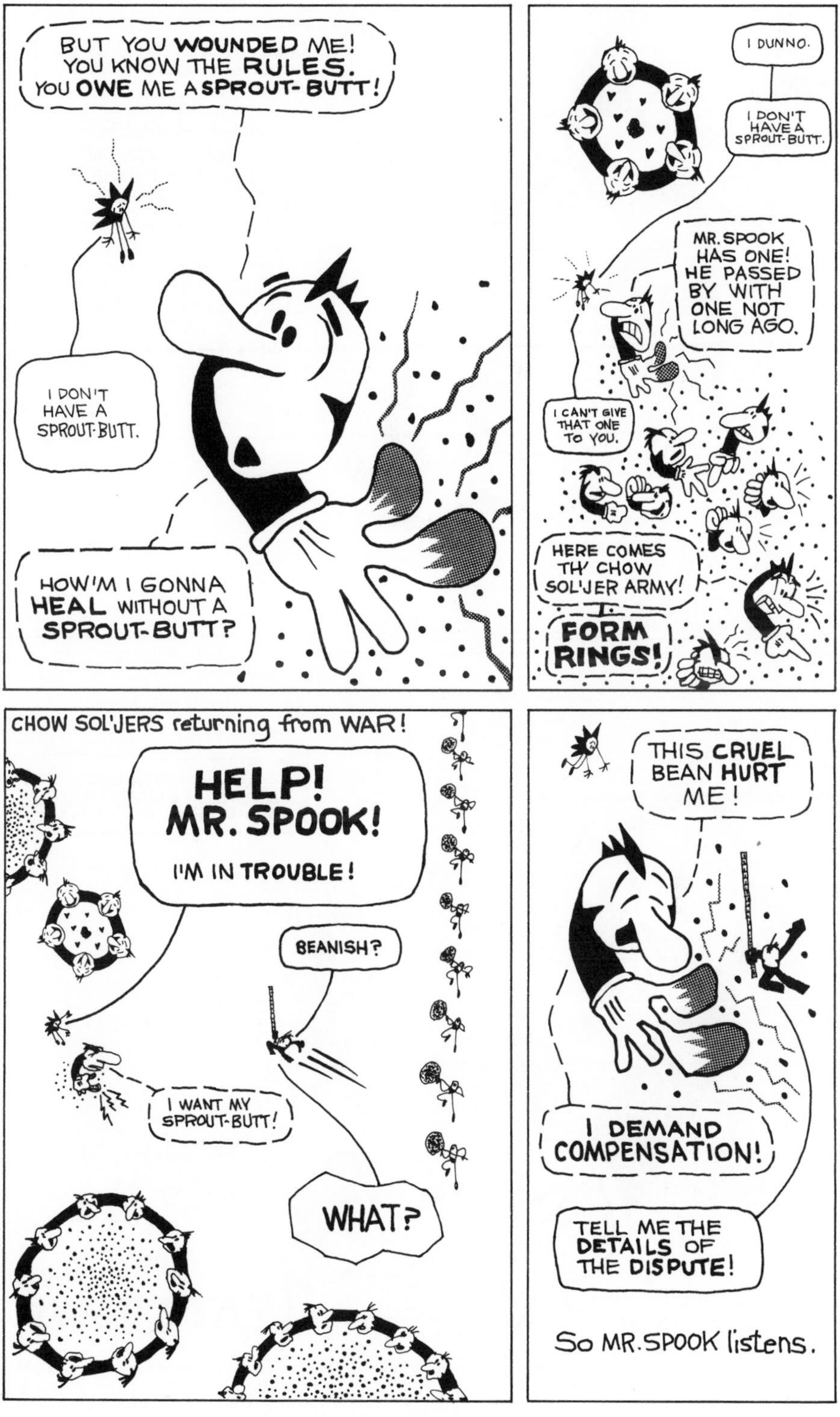
BUT YOU WOUNDED ME! YOU KNOW THE RULES. YOU OWE ME A SPROUT-BUTT!
I DON'T HAVE A SPROUT-BUTT.
HOW'M I GONNA HEAL WITHOUT A SPROUT-BUTT?
I DUNNO.
I DON'T HAVE A SPROUT-BUTT.
MR. SPOOK HAS ONE! HE PASSED BY WITH ONE NOT LONG AGO.
I CAN'T GIVE THAT ONE TO YOU.
HERE COMES TH' CHOW SOL'JER ARMY!
FORM RINGS!
CHOW SOL'JERS returning from WAR!
HELP! MR. SPOOK! I'M IN TROUBLE!
BEANISH?
I WANT MY SPROUT-BUTT!
WHAT?
THIS CRUEL BEAN HURT ME!
I DEMAND COMPENSATION!
TELL ME THE DETAILS OF THE DISPUTE!
So MR. SPOOK listens.

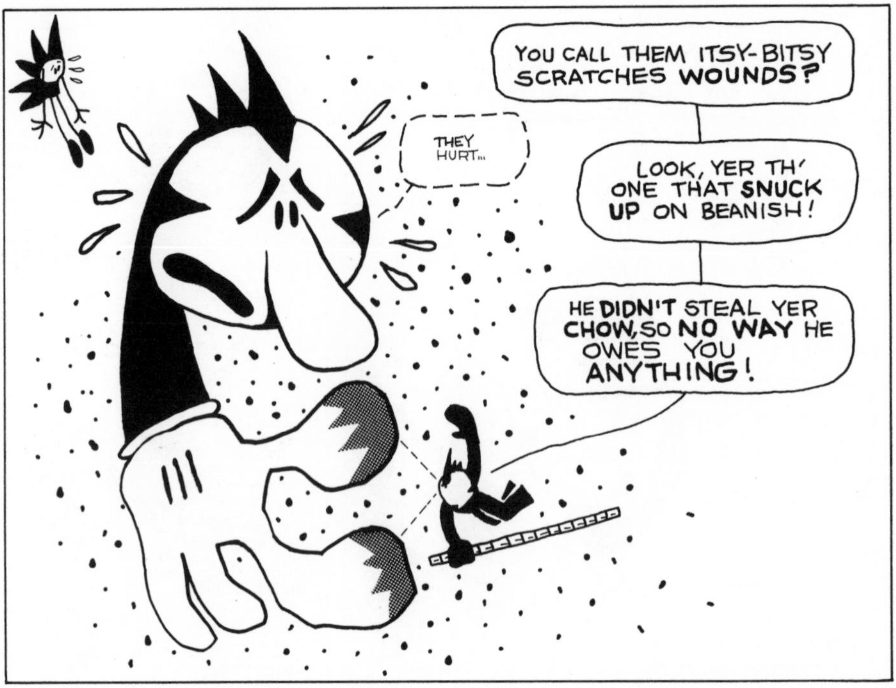
YOU CALL THEM ITSY-BITSY SCRATCHES WOUNDS?
THEY HURT...
LOOK, YER TH' ONE THAT SNUCK UP ON BEANISH!
HE DIDN'T STEAL YER CHOW, SO NO WAY HE OWES YOU ANYTHING!

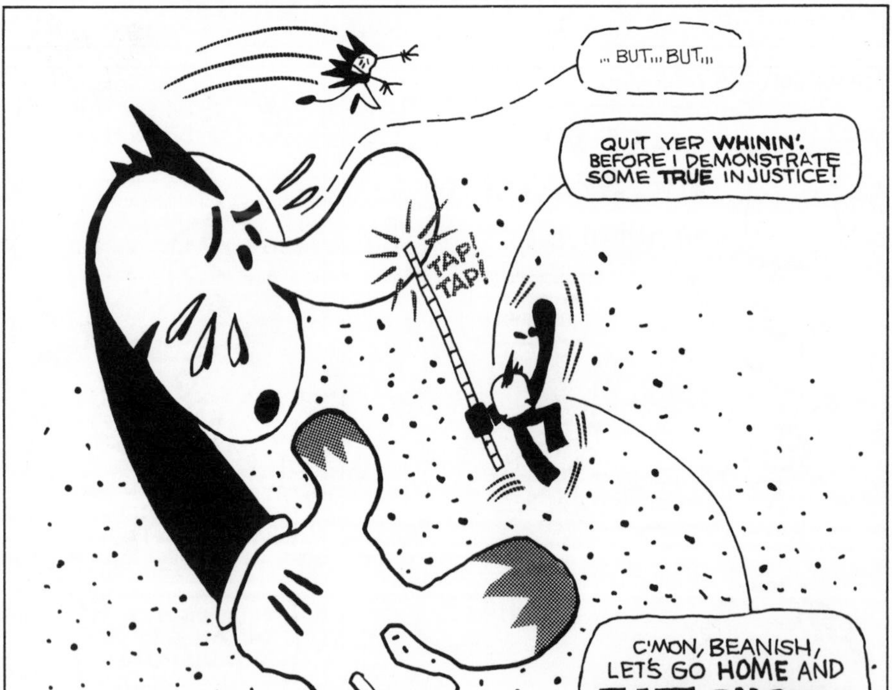
... BUT... BUT...
QUIT YER WHININ'. BEFORE I DEMONSTRATE SOME TRUE INJUSTICE!
TAP! TAP!
C'MON, BEANISH, LET'S GO HOME AND EAT CHOW!

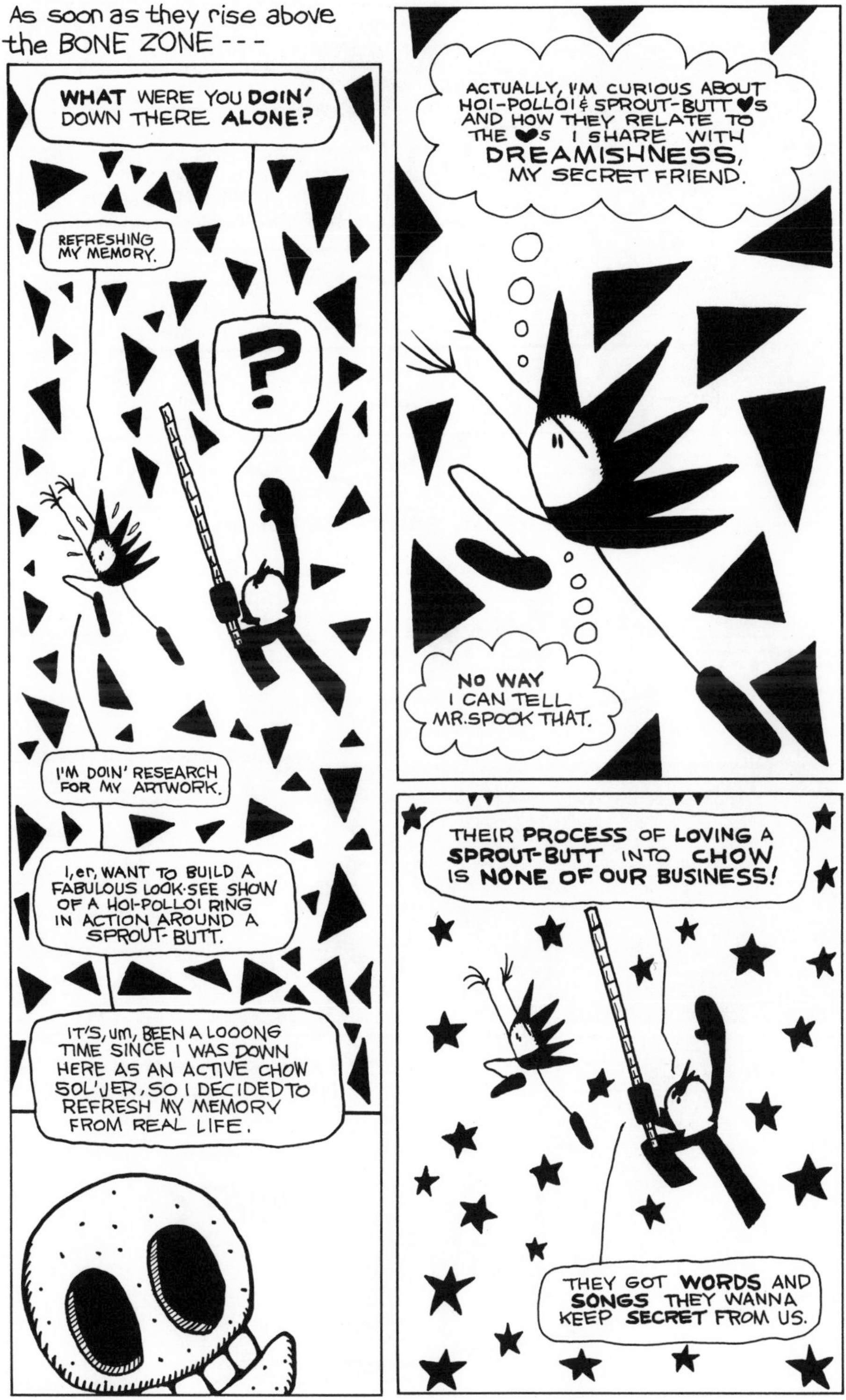
As soon as they rise above the BONE ZONE---
WHAT WERE YOU DOIN' DOWN THERE ALONE?
REFRESHING MY MEMORY.
?
I'M DOIN' RESEARCH FOR MY ARTWORK.
I, er, WANT TO BUILD A FABULOUS LOOK-SEE SHOW OF A HOI-POLLOI RING IN ACTION AROUND A SPROUT-BUTT.
IT'S, um, BEEN A LOOONG TIME SINCE I WAS DOWN HERE AS AN ACTIVE CHOW SOL'JER, SO I DECIDED TO REFRESH MY MEMORY FROM REAL LIFE.
ACTUALLY, I'M CURIOUS ABOUT HOI-POLLOI & SPROUT-BUTT ♥S AND HOW THEY RELATE TO THE ♥S I SHARE WITH DREAMISHNESS, MY SECRET FRIEND.
NO WAY I CAN TELL MR. SPOOK THAT.
THEIR PROCESS OF LOVING A SPROUT-BUTT INTO CHOW IS NONE OF OUR BUSINESS!
THEY GOT WORDS AND SONGS THEY WANNA KEEP SECRET FROM US.

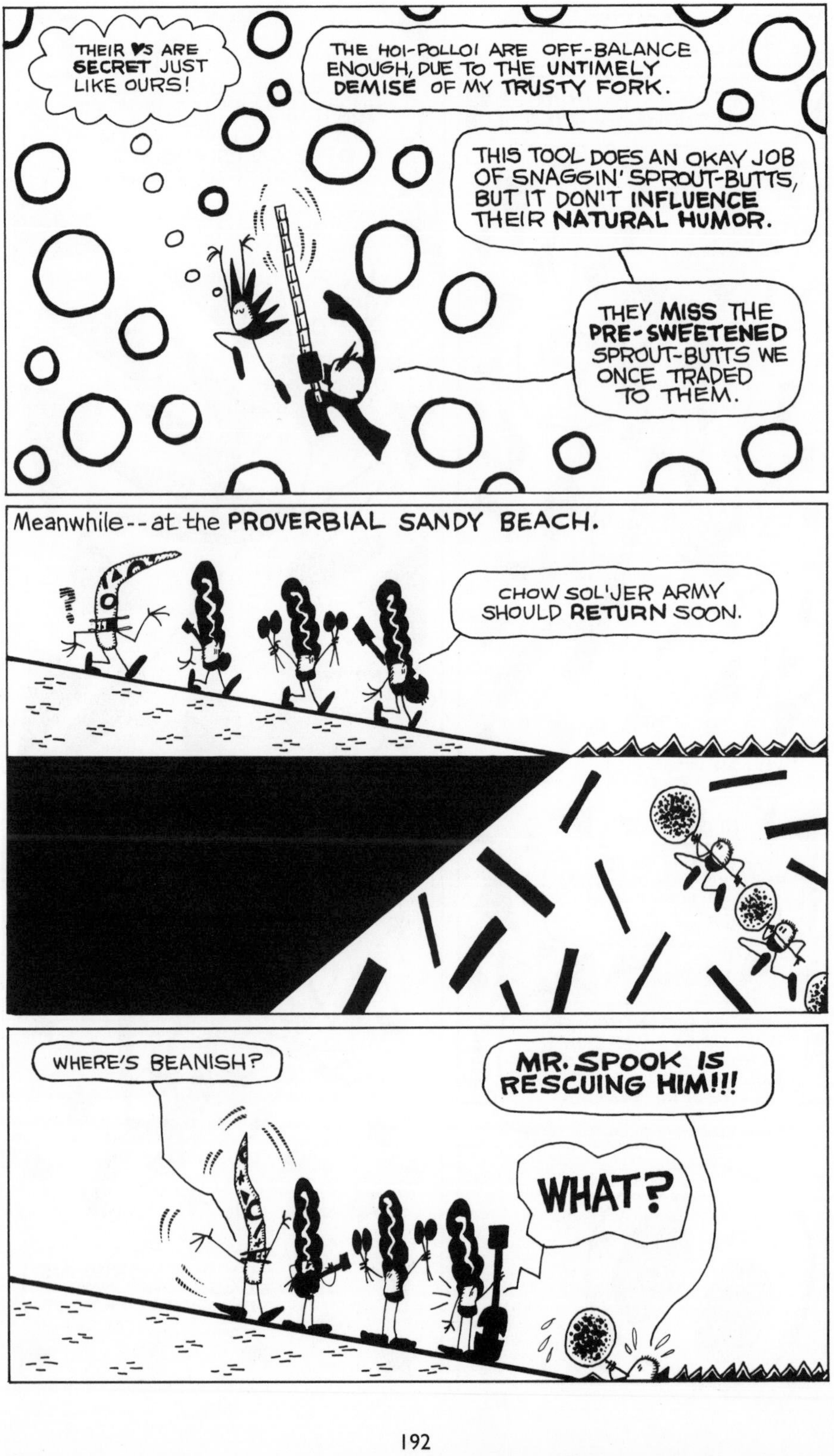
THEIR ♥S ARE SECRET JUST LIKE OURS!
THE HOI-POLLOI ARE OFF-BALANCE ENOUGH, DUE TO THE UNTIMELY DEMISE OF MY TRUSTY FORK.
THIS TOOL DOES AN OKAY JOB OF SNAGGIN' SPROUT-BUTTS, BUT IT DON'T INFLUENCE THEIR NATURAL HUMOR.
THEY MISS THE PRE-SWEETENED SPROUT-BUTTS WE ONCE TRADED TO THEM.
Meanwhile--at the PROVERBIAL SANDY BEACH.
CHOW SOL'JER ARMY SHOULD RETURN SOON.
WHERE'S BEANISH?
MR. SPOOK IS RESCUING HIM!!!
WHAT?

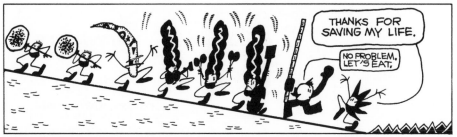

THANKS FOR SAVING MY LIFE.
NO PROBLEM. LET'S EAT.
They march to the CHOWDOWN POOL.
Shake the CHOW into the POOL.
The burbling begins.
A close-up of dissolving CHOW cooking itself.
IT'S CHOWDOWN TIME!
JUMP IN!
Soak, soak, soak.
SPLASH!
SPLASH!
The BEANS bathe in the life-giving soup.
TRACE MINERALS soaked thru the feet.
VITAMINS & NUTRIENTS absorbed thru the head.

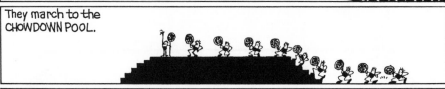

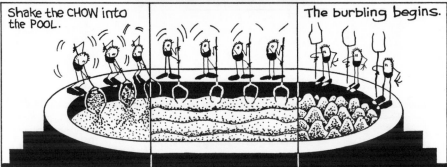

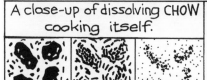

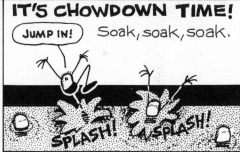

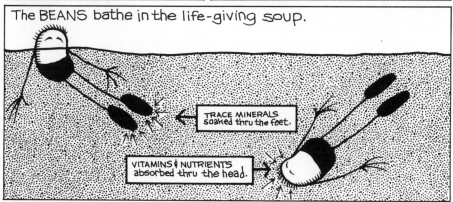

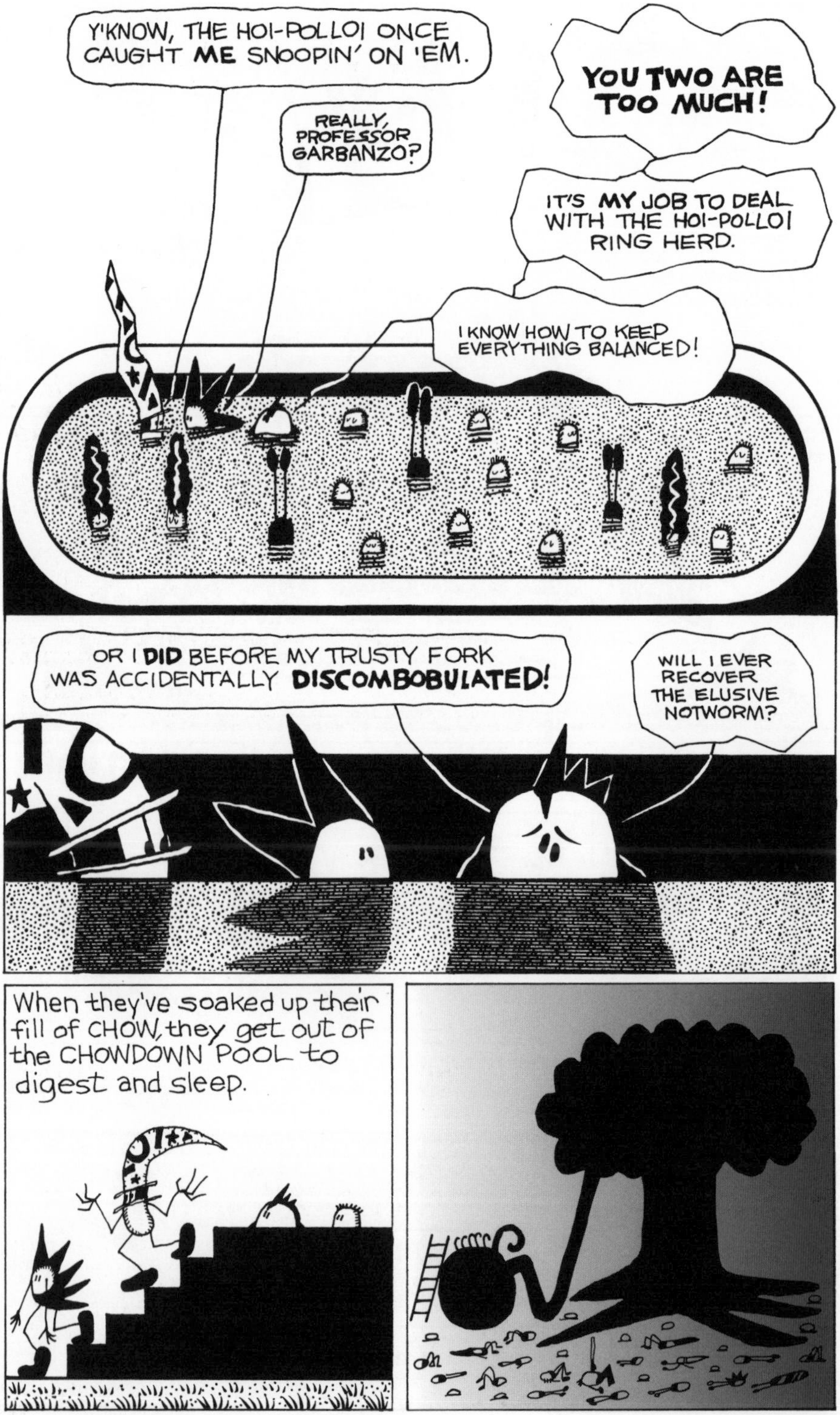

Y'KNOW, THE HOI-POLLOI ONCE CAUGHT **ME** SNOOPIN' ON 'EM.
REALLY, PROFESSOR GARBANZO?
YOU TWO ARE TOO MUCH!
IT'S **MY** JOB TO DEAL WITH THE HOI-POLLOI RING HERD.
I KNOW HOW TO KEEP EVERYTHING BALANCED!
OR I **DID** BEFORE MY TRUSTY FORK WAS ACCIDENTALLY **DISCOMBOBULATED!**
WILL I EVER RECOVER THE ELUSIVE NOTWORM?
When they've soaked up their fill of CHOW, they get out of the CHOWDOWN POOL to digest and sleep.

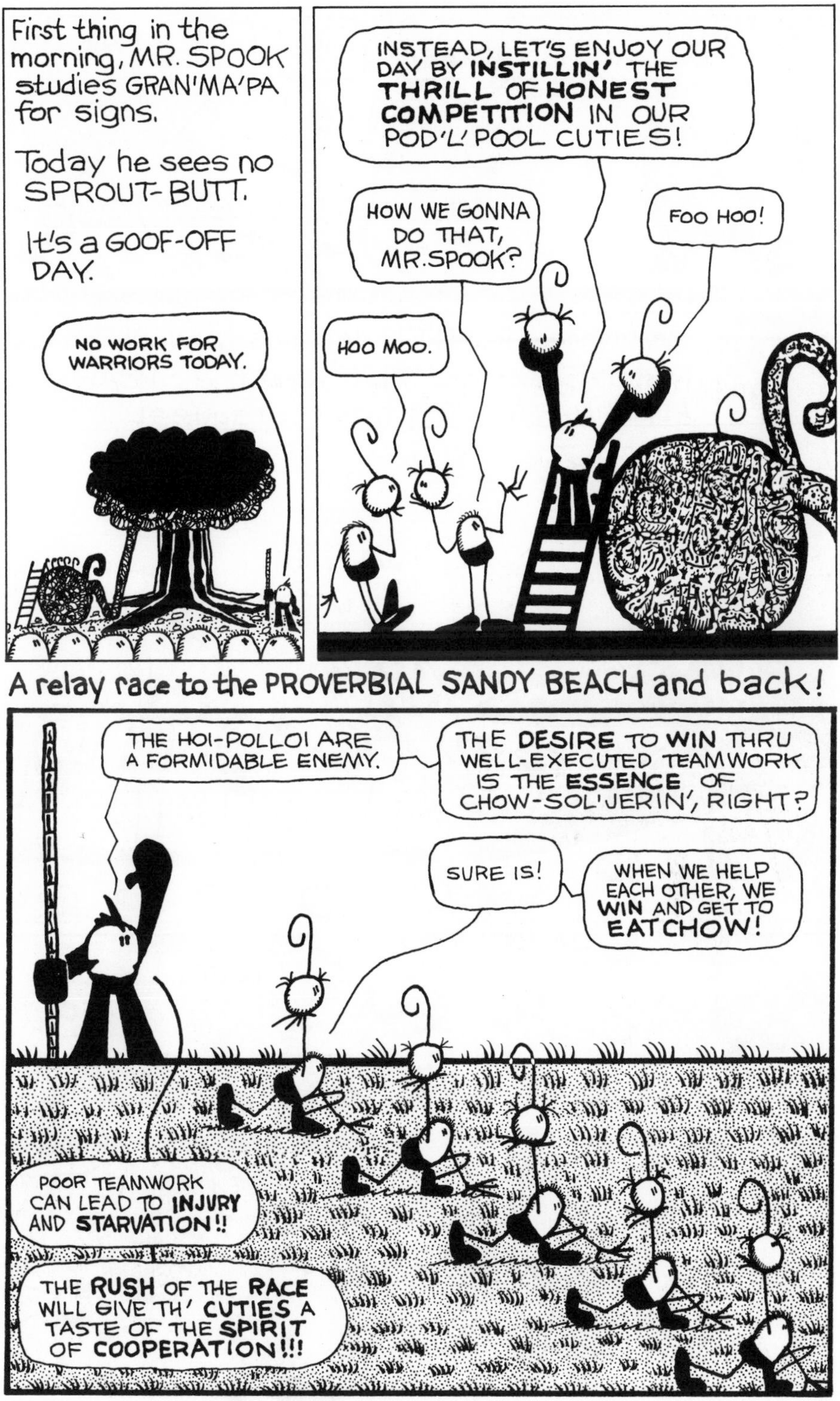
First thing in the morning, MR. SPOOK studies GRAN'MA'PA for signs.
Today he sees no SPROUT-BUTT.
It's a GOOF-OFF DAY.
NO WORK FOR WARRIORS TODAY.
INSTEAD, LET'S ENJOY OUR DAY BY INSTILLIN' THE THRILL OF HONEST COMPETITION IN OUR POD'L' POOL CUTIES!
HOW WE GONNA DO THAT, MR. SPOOK?
FOO HOO!
HOO MOO.
A relay race to the PROVERBIAL SANDY BEACH and back!
THE HOI-POLLOI ARE A FORMIDABLE ENEMY.
THE DESIRE TO WIN THRU WELL-EXECUTED TEAMWORK IS THE ESSENCE OF CHOW-SOL'JERIN', RIGHT?
SURE IS!
WHEN WE HELP EACH OTHER, WE WIN AND GET TO EATCHOW!
POOR TEAMWORK CAN LEAD TO INJURY AND STARVATION!!
THE RUSH OF THE RACE WILL GIVE TH' CUTIES A TASTE OF THE SPIRIT OF COOPERATION!!!

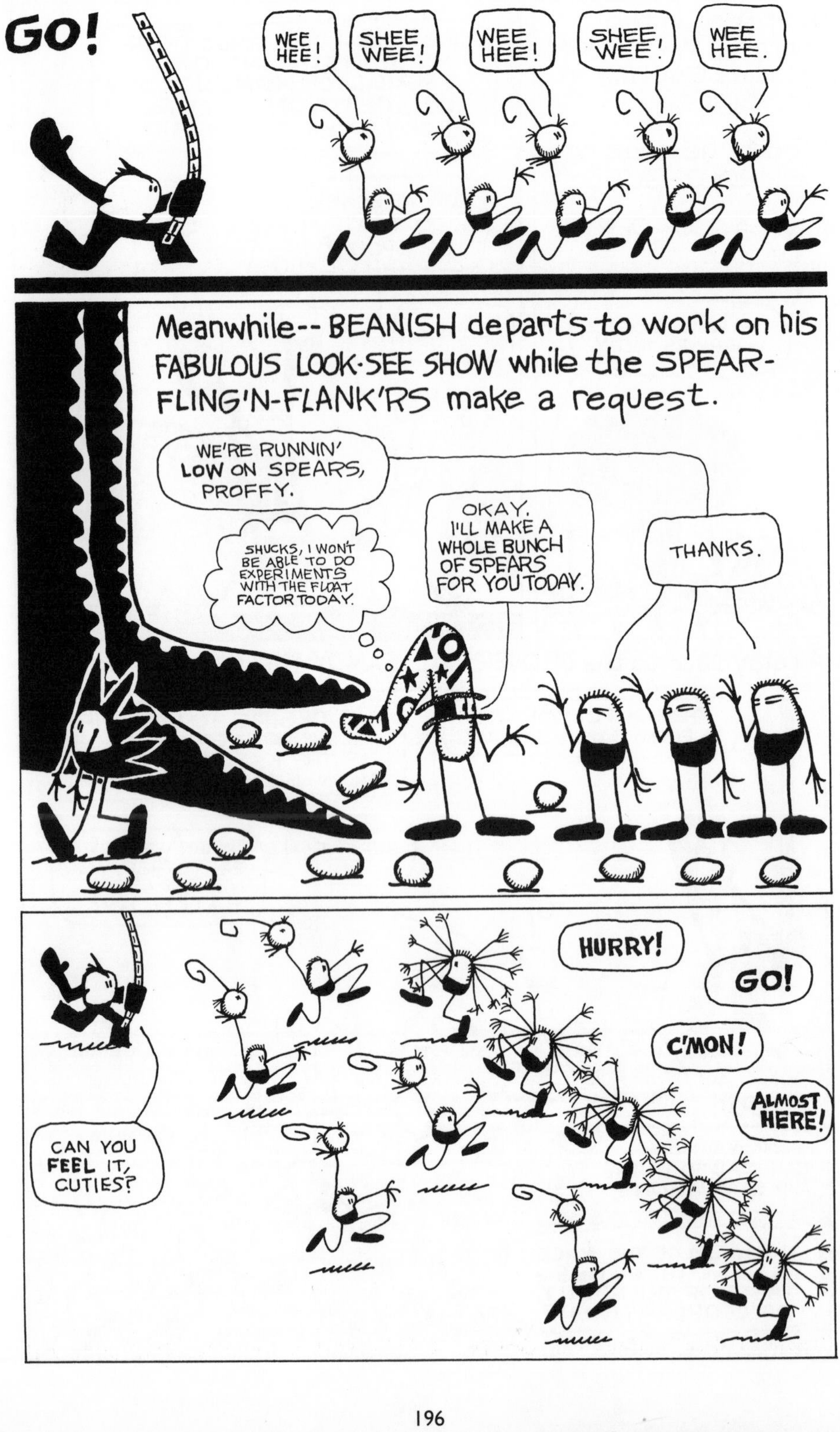
GO!
WEE HEE!
SHEE WEE!
WEE HEE!
SHEE WEE!
WEE HEE.
Meanwhile-- BEANISH departs to work on his FABULOUS LOOK-SEE SHOW while the SPEAR-FLING'N-FLANK'RS make a request.
WE'RE RUNNIN' LOW ON SPEARS, PROFFY.
SHUCKS, I WON'T BE ABLE TO DO EXPERIMENTS WITH THE FLOAT FACTOR TODAY.
OKAY. I'LL MAKE A WHOLE BUNCH OF SPEARS FOR YOU TODAY.
THANKS.
CAN YOU FEEL IT, CUTIES?
HURRY!
GO!
C'MON!
ALMOST HERE!

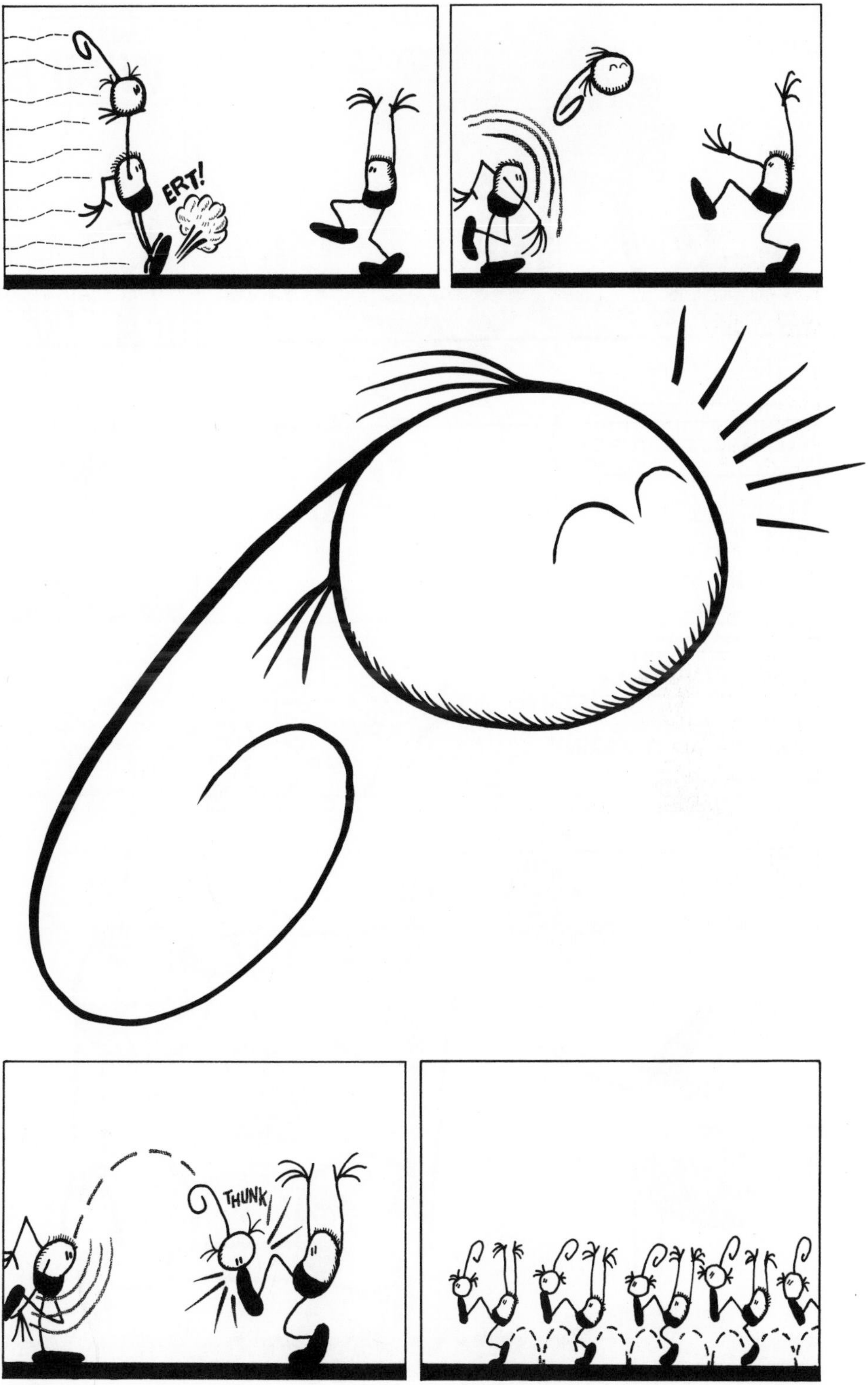
ERT!
THUNK

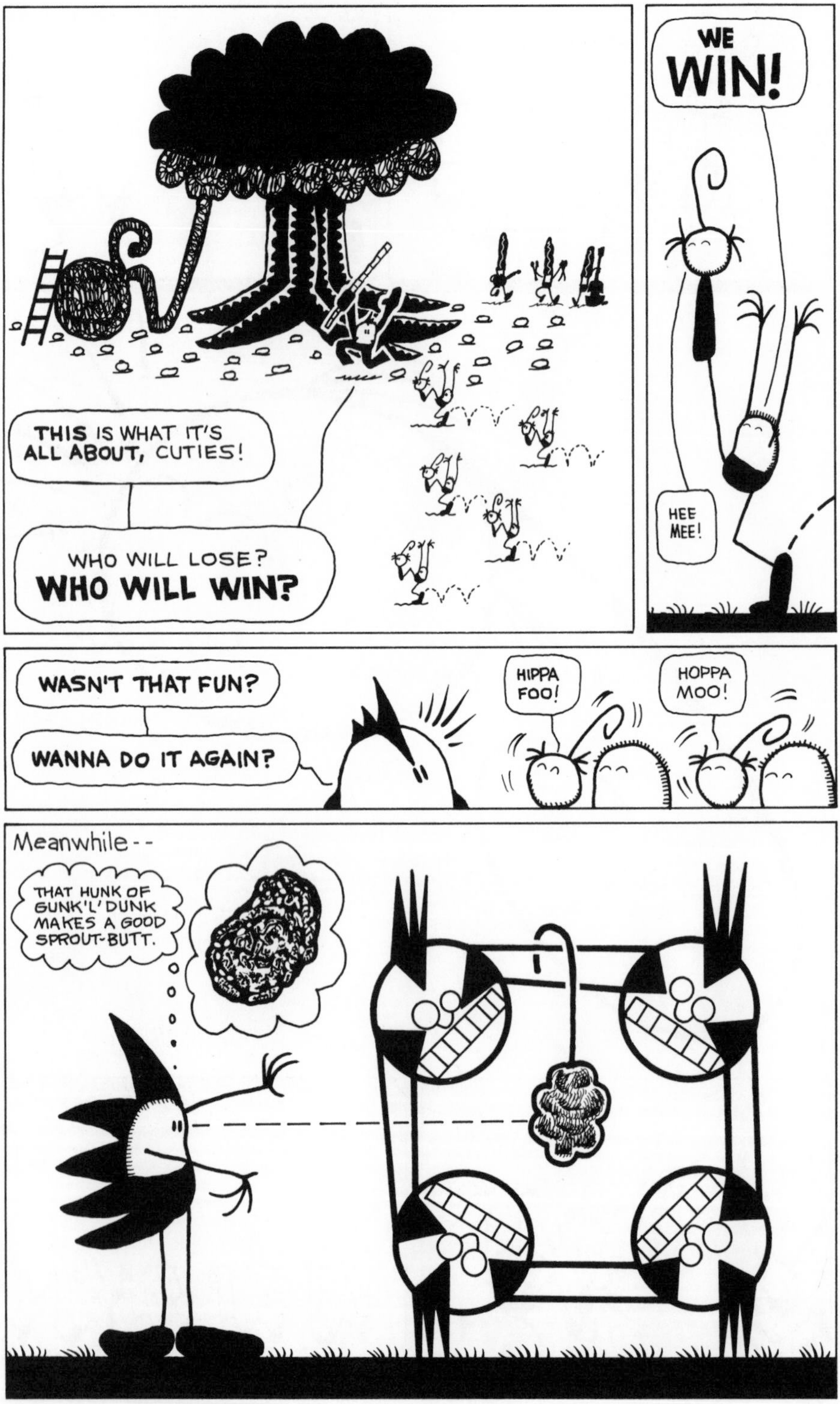
THIS IS WHAT IT'S ALL ABOUT, CUTIES!
WHO WILL LOSE? WHO WILL WIN?
WE WIN!
HEE MEE!
WASN'T THAT FUN?
WANNA DO IT AGAIN?
HIPPA FOO!
HOPPA MOO!
Meanwhile--
THAT HUNK OF GUNK'L'DUNK MAKES A GOOD SPROUT-BUTT.

His labor on the FABULOUS LOOK·SEE SHOW is finished. It's almost midday -- time for his daily rendezvous with DREAMISHNESS, his secret friend. Recently, BEANISH has learned how to delay her movement in a tangle of ♥s.

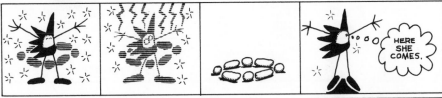

HERE SHE COMES.

HELLO, MY LI'L BEANISH!

I'M HERS.

Anticipation.
Aching.
Desire. She's almost here.

NOW!

NOW!

NOW!

NOW!

OH, BEANISH!

BATHE ME IN BLISS!

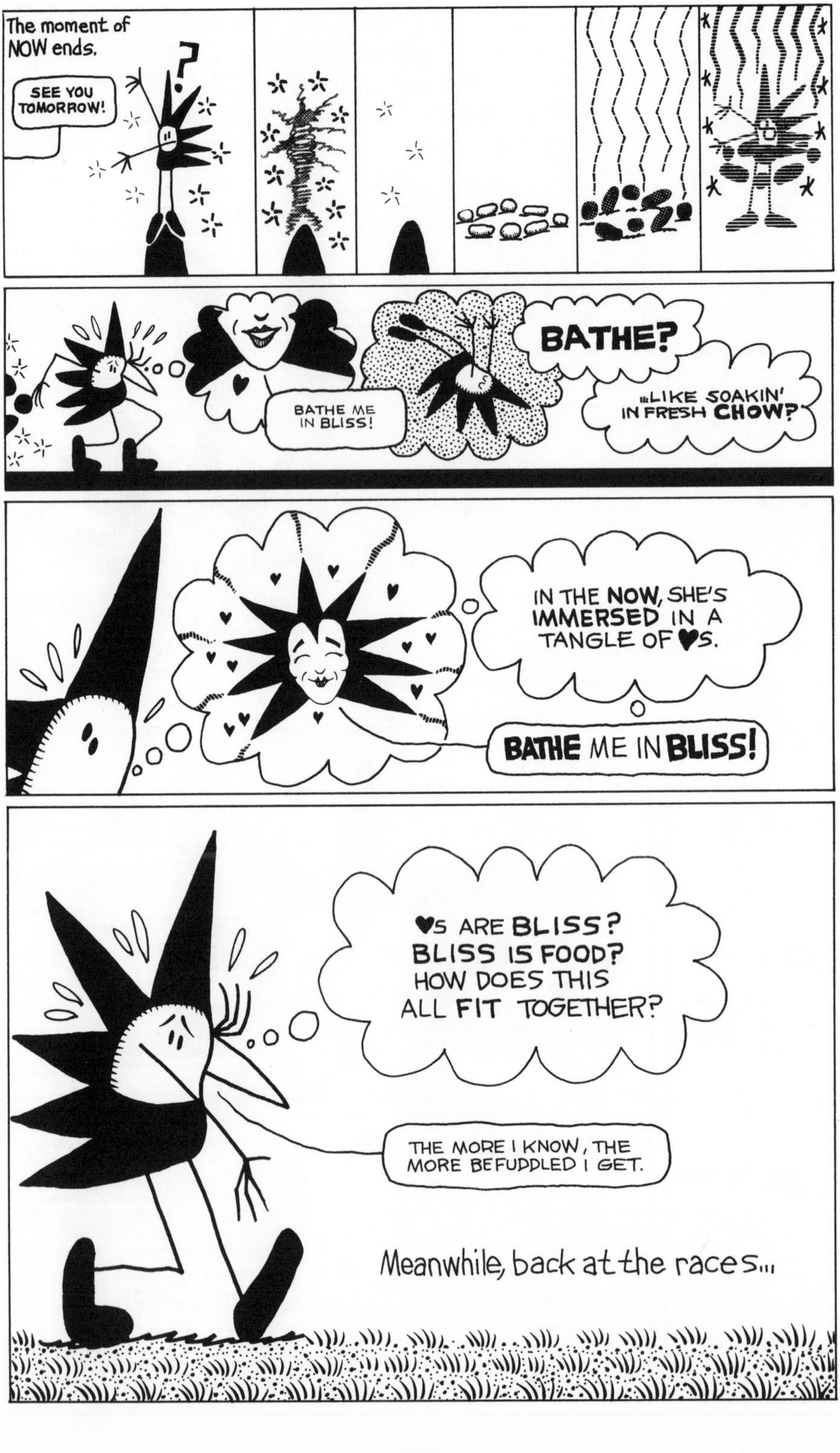
The moment of NOW ends.
SEE YOU TOMORROW!
?
BATHE ME IN BLISS!
BATHE?
...LIKE SOAKIN' IN FRESH CHOW?
IN THE NOW, SHE'S IMMERSED IN A TANGLE OF ♥S.
BATHE ME IN BLISS!
♥S ARE BLISS? BLISS IS FOOD? HOW DOES THIS ALL FIT TOGETHER?
THE MORE I KNOW, THE MORE BEFUDDLED I GET.
Meanwhile, back at the races...

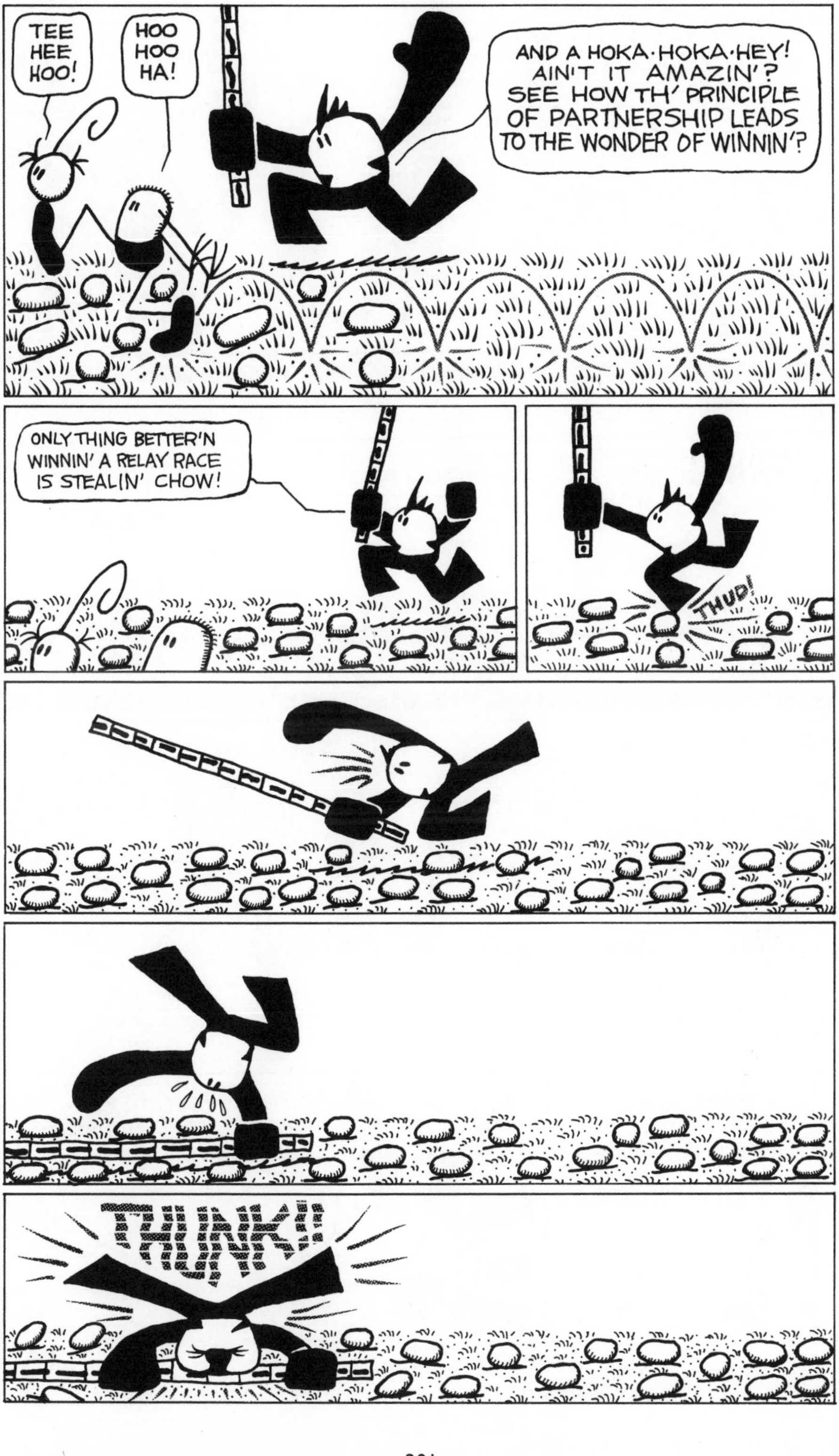
TEE HEE HOO!
HOO HOO HA!
AND A HOKA·HOKA·HEY! AIN'T IT AMAZIN'? SEE HOW TH' PRINCIPLE OF PARTNERSHIP LEADS TO THE WONDER OF WINNIN'?
ONLY THING BETTER'N WINNIN' A RELAY RACE IS STEALIN' CHOW!
THUD!
THUNK!!

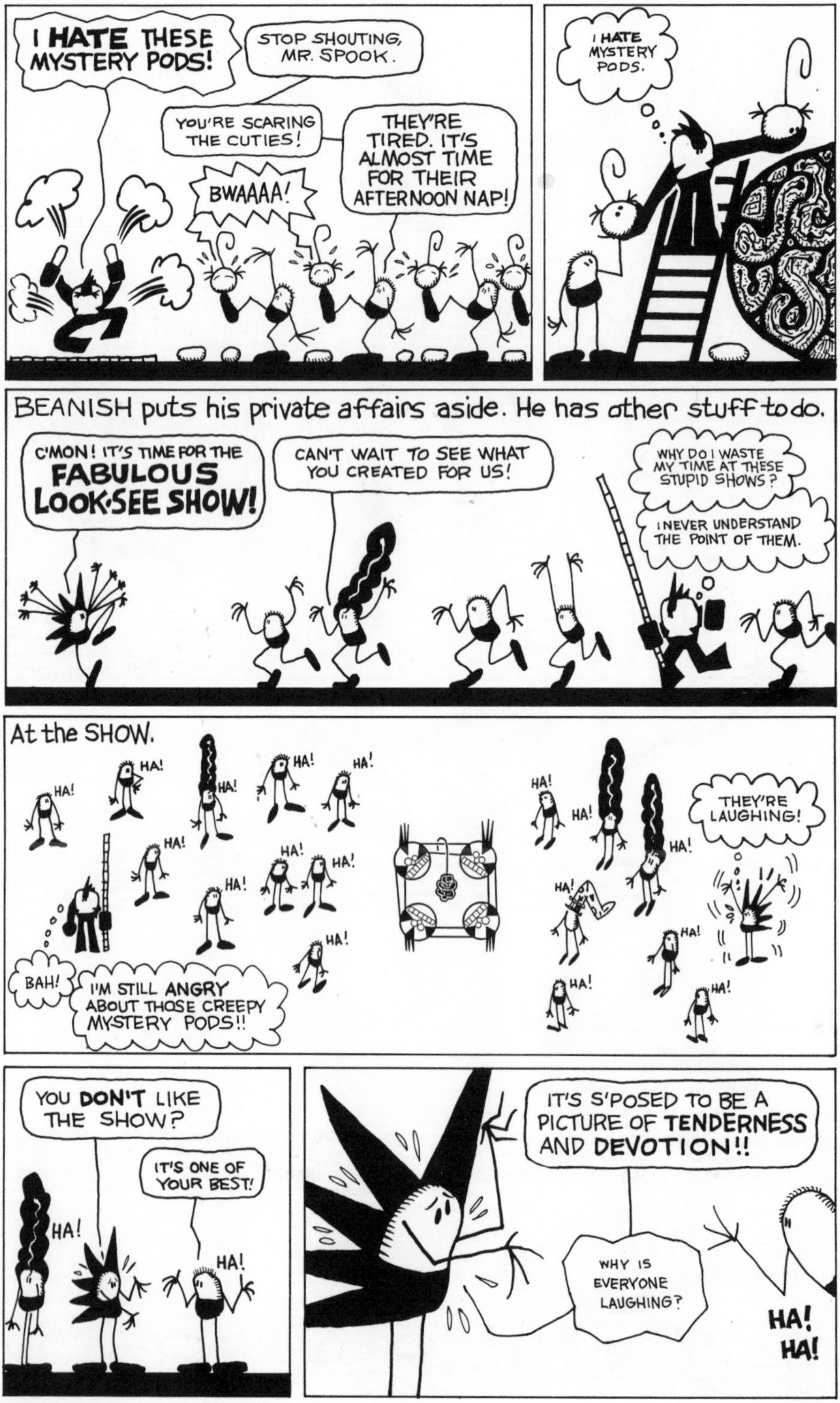
I HATE THESE MYSTERY PODS!
STOP SHOUTING, MR. SPOOK.
YOU'RE SCARING THE CUTIES!
THEY'RE TIRED. IT'S ALMOST TIME FOR THEIR AFTERNOON NAP!
BWAAAA!
I HATE MYSTERY PODS.
BEANISH puts his private affairs aside. He has other stuff to do.
C'MON! IT'S TIME FOR THE FABULOUS LOOK-SEE SHOW!
CAN'T WAIT TO SEE WHAT YOU CREATED FOR US!
WHY DO I WASTE MY TIME AT THESE STUPID SHOWS?
I NEVER UNDERSTAND THE POINT OF THEM.
At the SHOW.
HA!
THEY'RE LAUGHING!
BAH!
I'M STILL ANGRY ABOUT THOSE CREEPY MYSTERY PODS!!
YOU DON'T LIKE THE SHOW?
IT'S ONE OF YOUR BEST!
HA!
IT'S S'POSED TO BE A PICTURE OF TENDERNESS AND DEVOTION!!
WHY IS EVERYONE LAUGHING?
HA! HA!

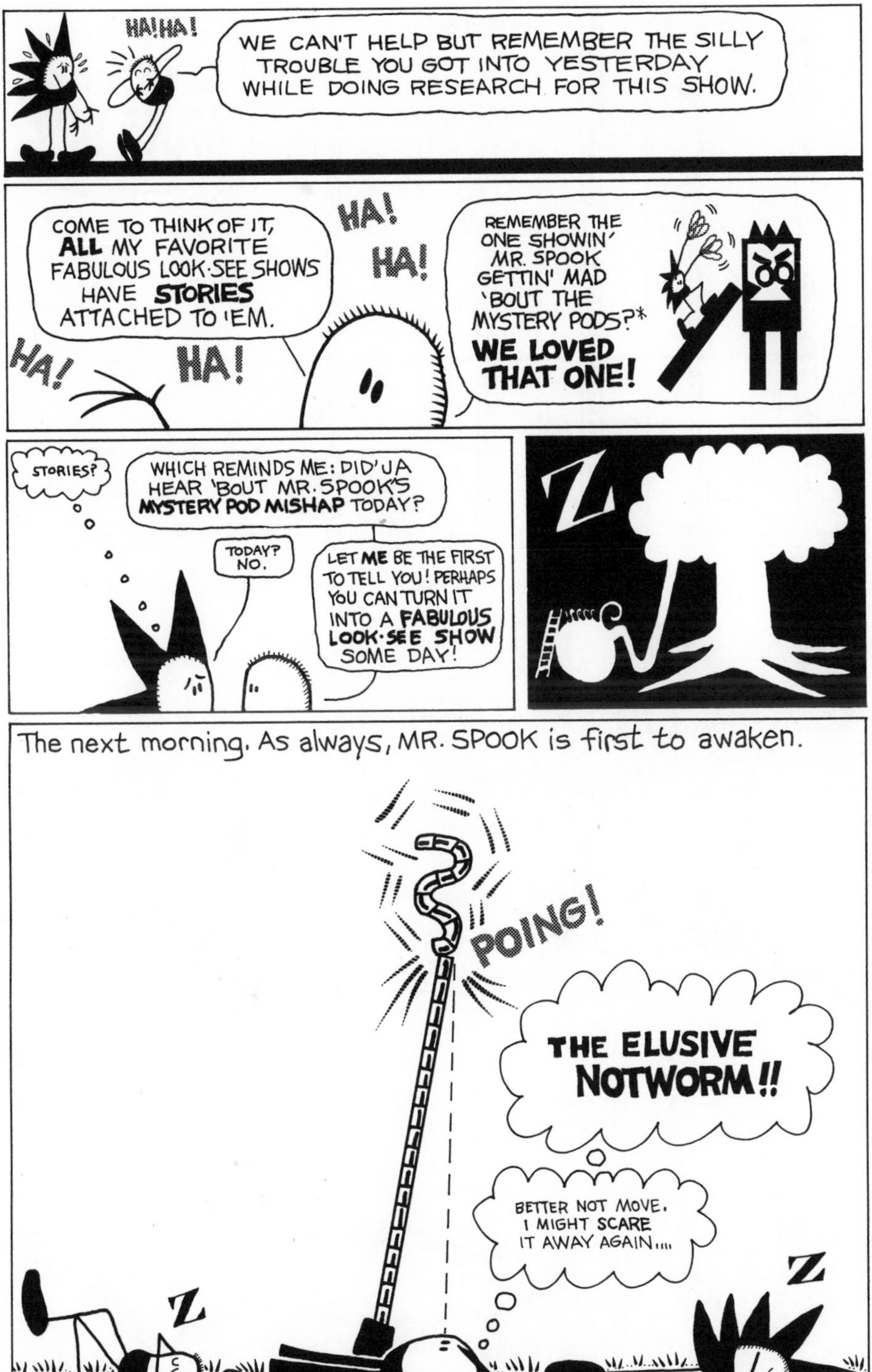
HA! HA!
WE CAN'T HELP BUT REMEMBER THE SILLY TROUBLE YOU GOT INTO YESTERDAY WHILE DOING RESEARCH FOR THIS SHOW.
COME TO THINK OF IT, ALL MY FAVORITE FABULOUS LOOK·SEE SHOWS HAVE STORIES ATTACHED TO 'EM.
HA! HA! HA! HA!
REMEMBER THE ONE SHOWIN' MR. SPOOK GETTIN' MAD 'BOUT THE MYSTERY PODS?* WE LOVED THAT ONE!
STORIES?
WHICH REMINDS ME: DID'JA HEAR 'BOUT MR. SPOOK'S MYSTERY POD MISHAP TODAY?
TODAY? NO.
LET ME BE THE FIRST TO TELL YOU! PERHAPS YOU CAN TURN IT INTO A FABULOUS LOOK·SEE SHOW SOME DAY!
Z
The next morning. As always, MR. SPOOK is first to awaken.
POING!
THE ELUSIVE NOTWORM!!
BETTER NOT MOVE. I MIGHT SCARE IT AWAY AGAIN....
Z
Z

*BOOK ONE

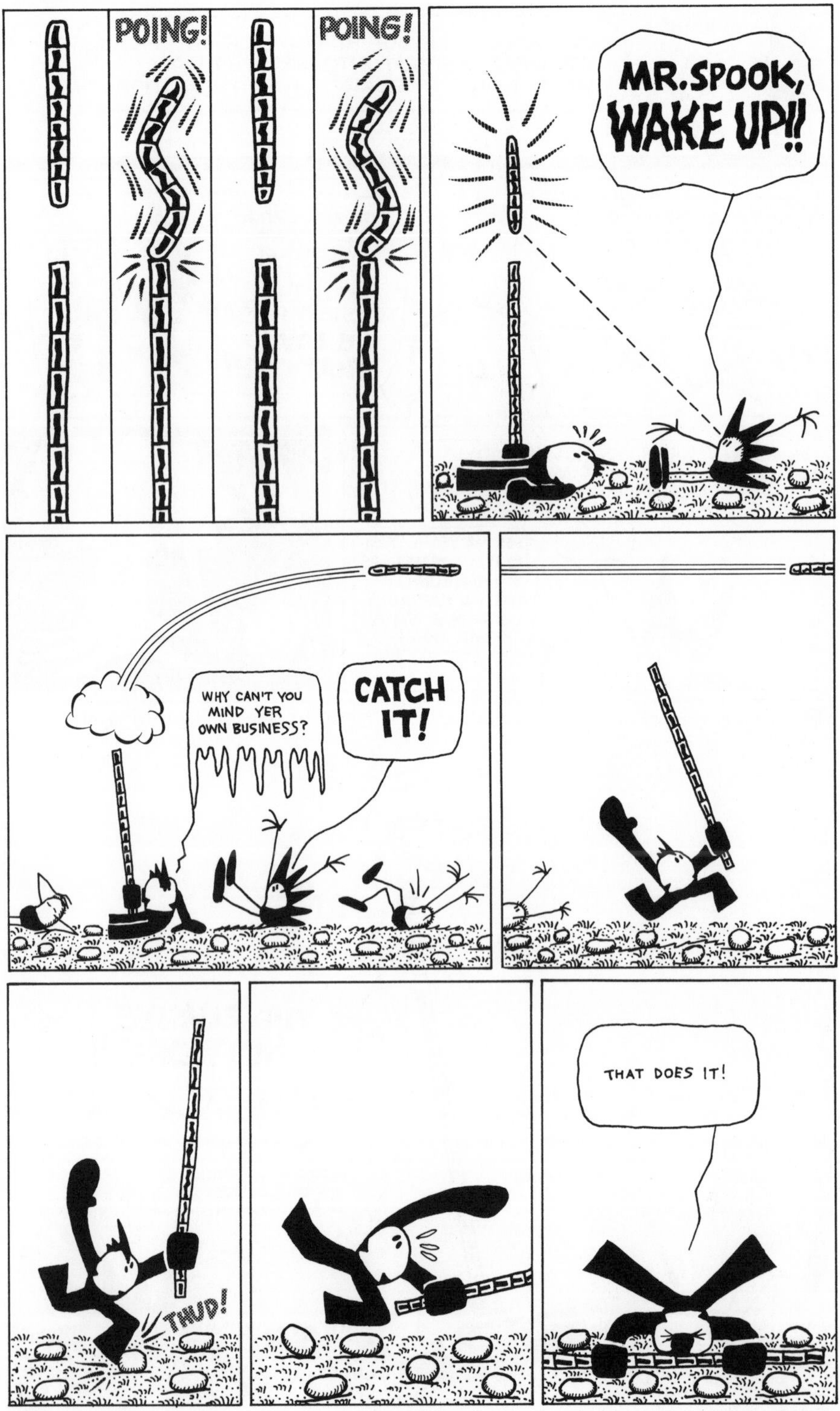
POING!
POING!
MR. SPOOK, WAKE UP!!
WHY CAN'T YOU MIND YER OWN BUSINESS?
CATCH IT!
THUD!
THAT DOES IT!

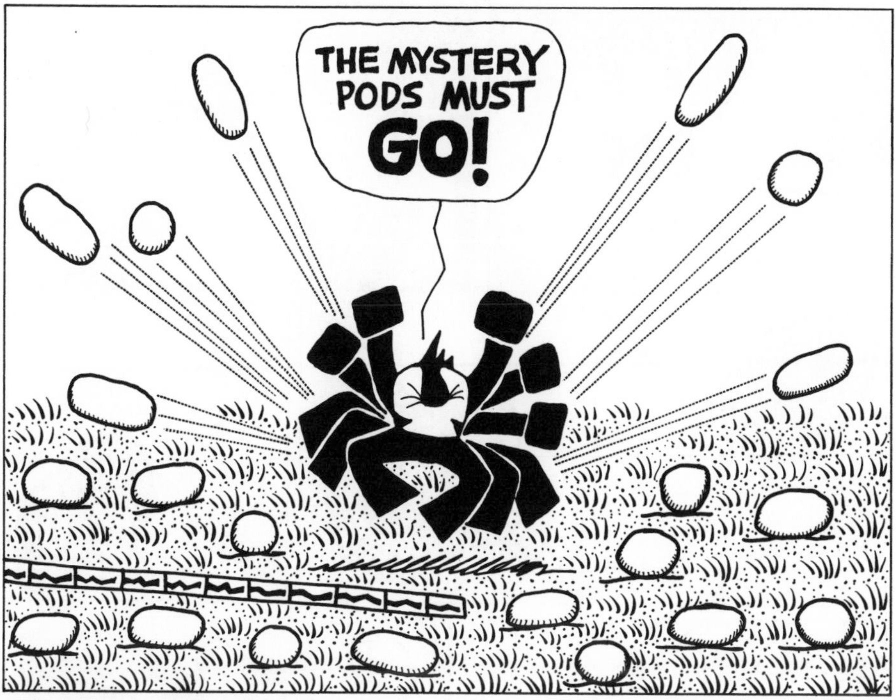
THE MYSTERY PODS MUST GO!

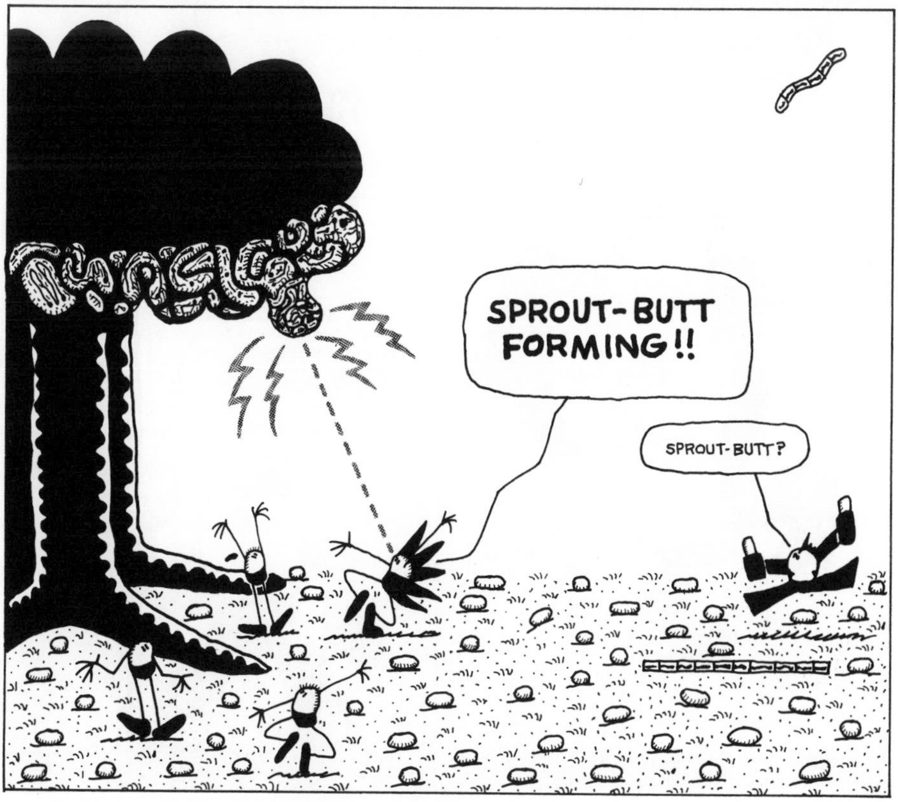
SPROUT-BUTT FORMING!!
SPROUT-BUTT?

POP
WOO!
SQUISH!
WHO WUZ DAT HEAVENLY INTERLOPER?
THE ELUSIVE NOTWORM.
DIS NOTWOIM KNOWS HOW TO **DANCE!**
I'M A HAPPY HAPPY SPROUT-BUTT!
POING!
POING!
WELL, AIN'T THIS AN INTERESTING TWIST OF EVENTS?

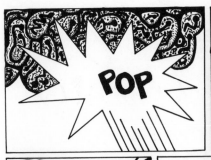

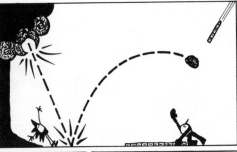

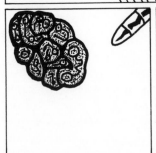

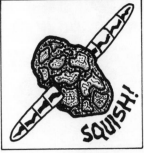

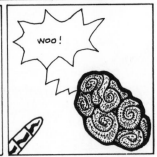

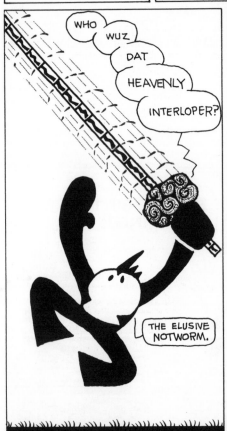

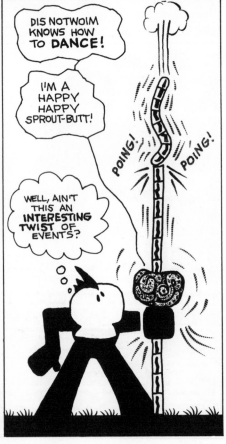

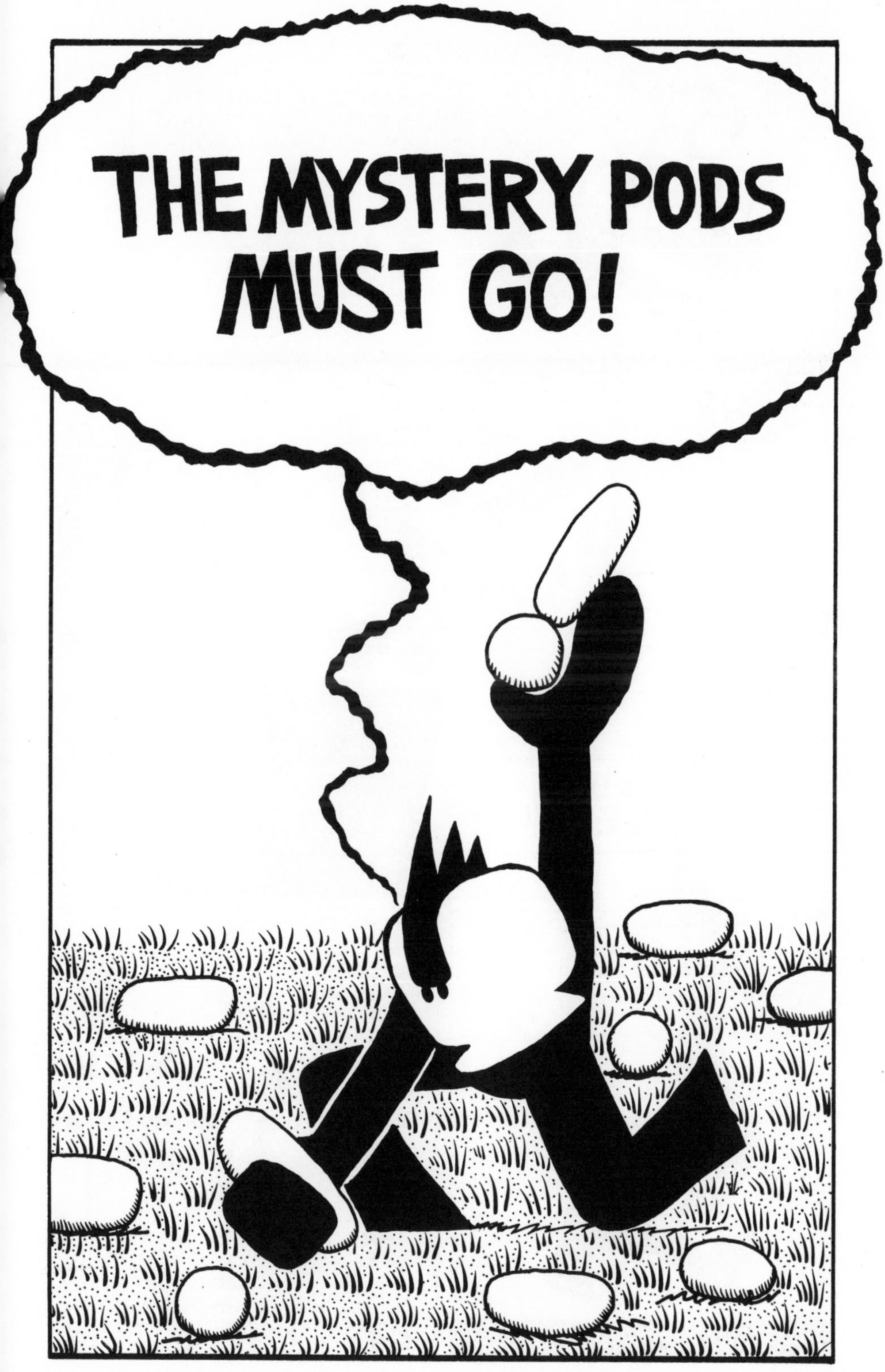
THE MYSTERY PODS MUST GO!

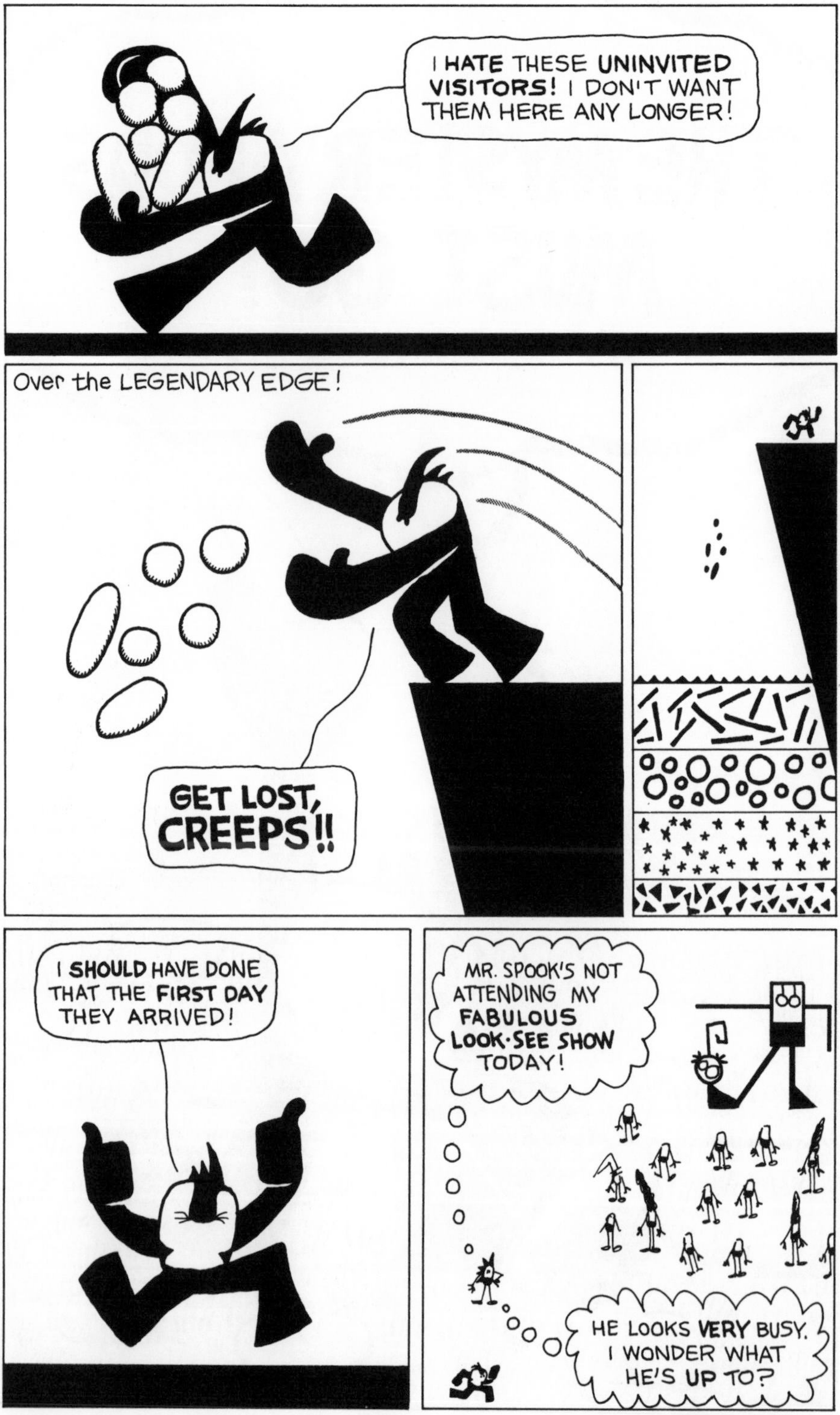
I HATE THESE UNINVITED VISITORS! I DON'T WANT THEM HERE ANY LONGER!
Over the LEGENDARY EDGE!
GET LOST, CREEPS!!
I SHOULD HAVE DONE THAT THE FIRST DAY THEY ARRIVED!
MR. SPOOK'S NOT ATTENDING MY FABULOUS LOOK·SEE SHOW TODAY!
HE LOOKS VERY BUSY. I WONDER WHAT HE'S UP TO?

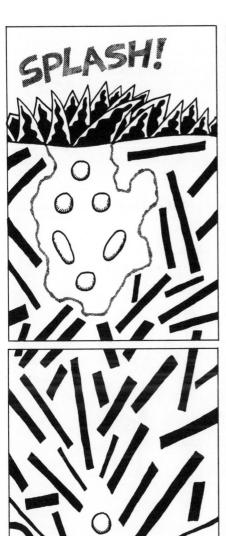

SPLASH!

WHATCHA **DOIN'**, MR. SPOOK?

GETTIN' **RID** OF THE MYSTERY PODS, BEANISH!

THIS HASN'T BEEN **DECIDED** IN A **COUNCIL MEETING!**

I'M **TIRED** OF WASTING TIME IN COUNCIL MEETINGS!

I **KNOW** I'M **RIGHT**. I'M GOIN' ON WITH MY **PLAN!!**

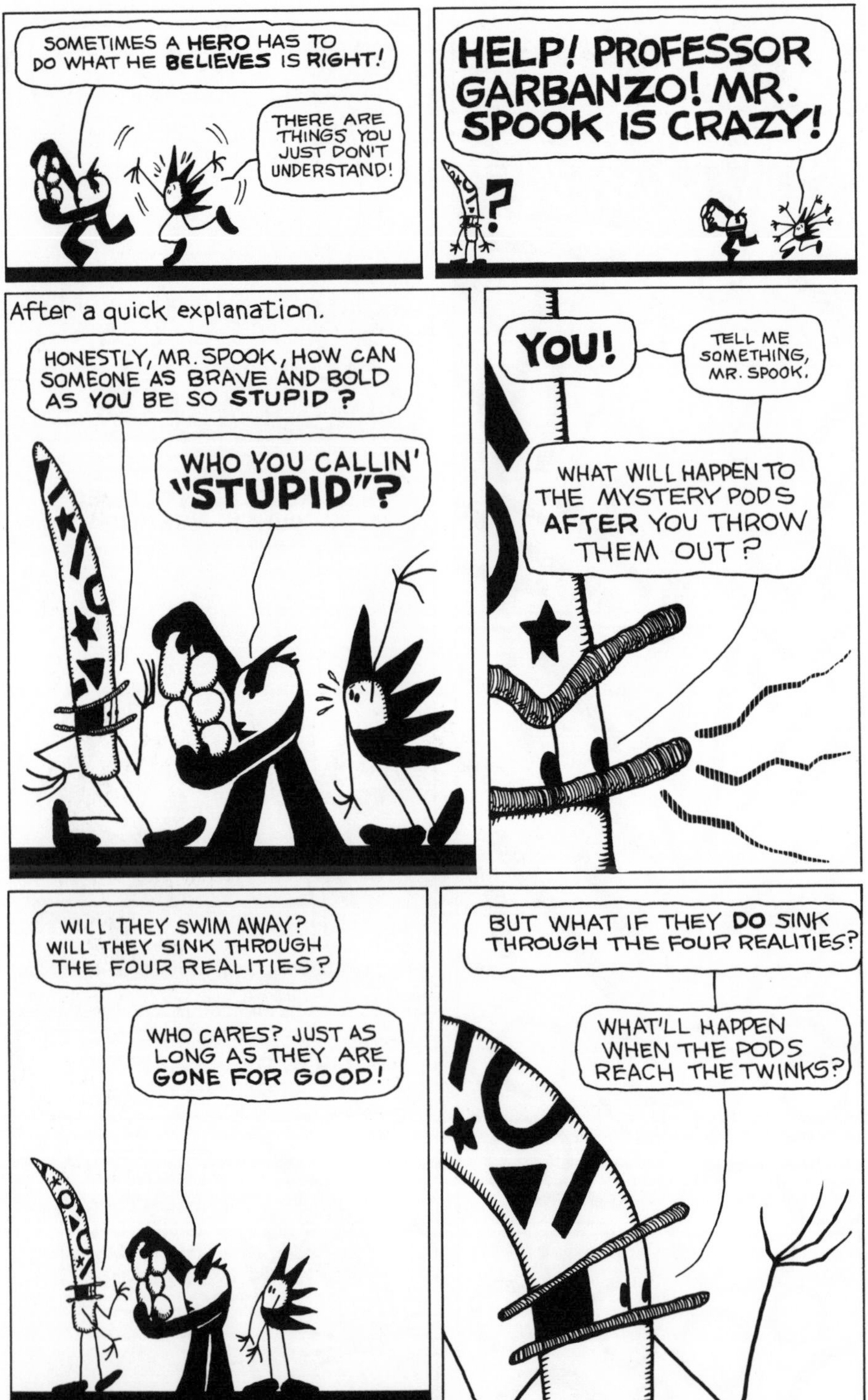
SOMETIMES A HERO HAS TO DO WHAT HE BELIEVES IS RIGHT!
THERE ARE THINGS YOU JUST DON'T UNDERSTAND!
HELP! PROFESSOR GARBANZO! MR. SPOOK IS CRAZY!
?
After a quick explanation.
HONESTLY, MR. SPOOK, HOW CAN SOMEONE AS BRAVE AND BOLD AS YOU BE SO STUPID?
WHO YOU CALLIN' "STUPID"?
YOU!
TELL ME SOMETHING, MR. SPOOK.
WHAT WILL HAPPEN TO THE MYSTERY PODS AFTER YOU THROW THEM OUT?
WILL THEY SWIM AWAY? WILL THEY SINK THROUGH THE FOUR REALITIES?
WHO CARES? JUST AS LONG AS THEY ARE GONE FOR GOOD!
BUT WHAT IF THEY DO SINK THROUGH THE FOUR REALITIES?
WHAT'LL HAPPEN WHEN THE PODS REACH THE TWINKS?

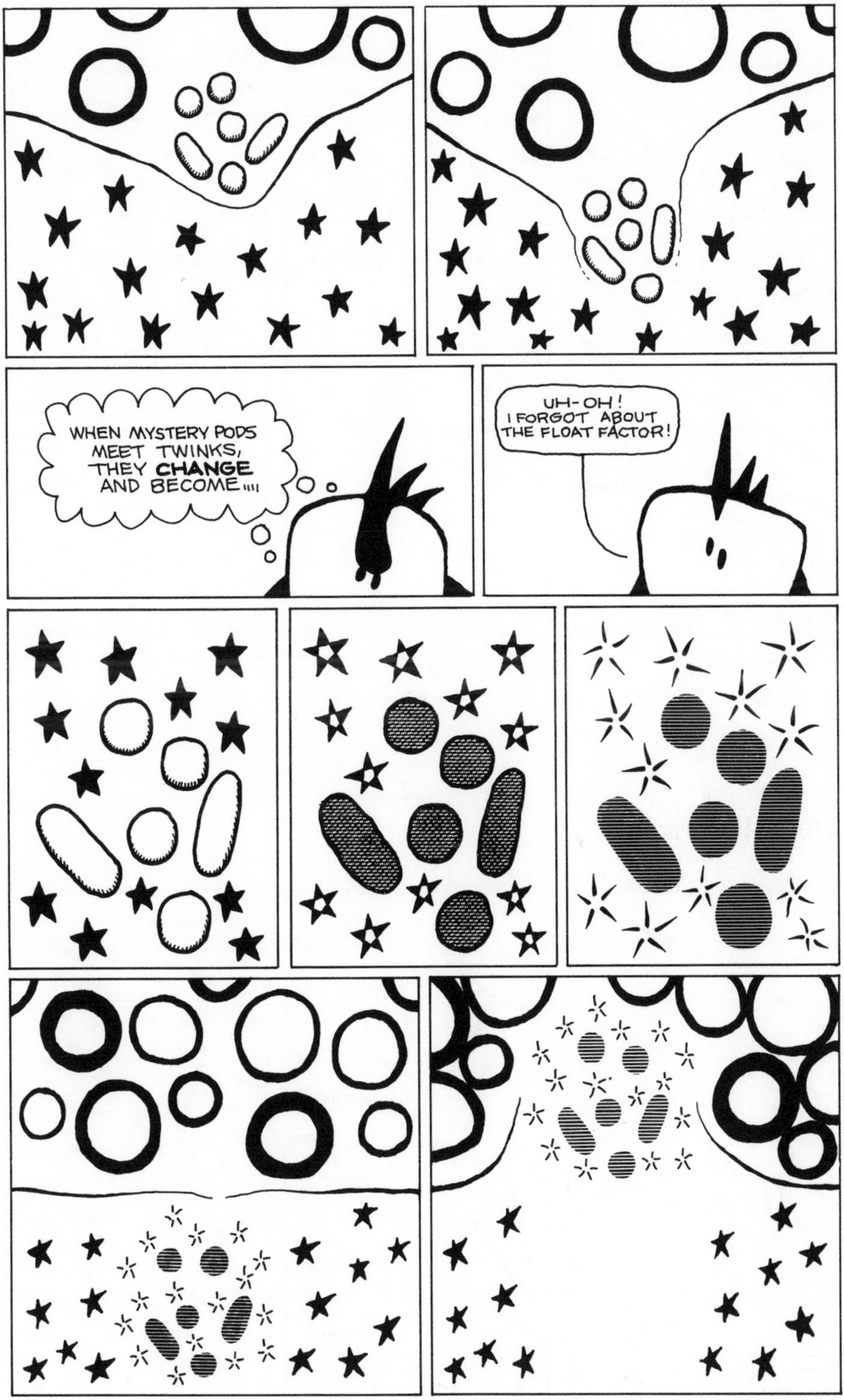
WHEN MYSTERY PODS MEET TWINKS, THEY **CHANGE** AND BECOME....
UH-OH! I FORGOT ABOUT THE FLOAT FACTOR!

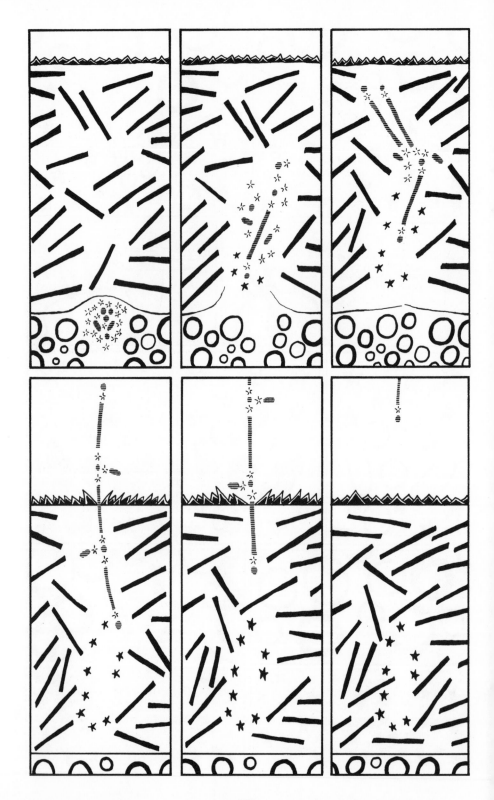

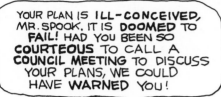

I HATE THAT FLOAT FACTOR STUFF **MORE** THAN JUS' THE MYSTERY PODS BY THEMSELVES!!

YOUR PLAN IS **ILL-CONCEIVED**, MR. SPOOK, IT IS **DOOMED** TO **FAIL!** HAD YOU BEEN SO **COURTEOUS** TO CALL A **COUNCIL MEETING** TO DISCUSS YOUR PLANS, WE COULD HAVE **WARNED** YOU!

LUCKY FOR YOU WE SQUELCHED YOUR PLOT **BEFORE** YOU MADE A **FOOL** OF YOURSELF!

TAP! TAP! TAP!

I ALREADY TOSSED A LOAD OVER THE LEGENDARY EDGE.

WHAT HAPPENED?

I DUNNO, PROFFY. I FORGOT TO LOOK.

They hurry to the LEGENDARY EDGE to see what kind of effect MR. SPOOK'S reckless action caused.

UH-OH.

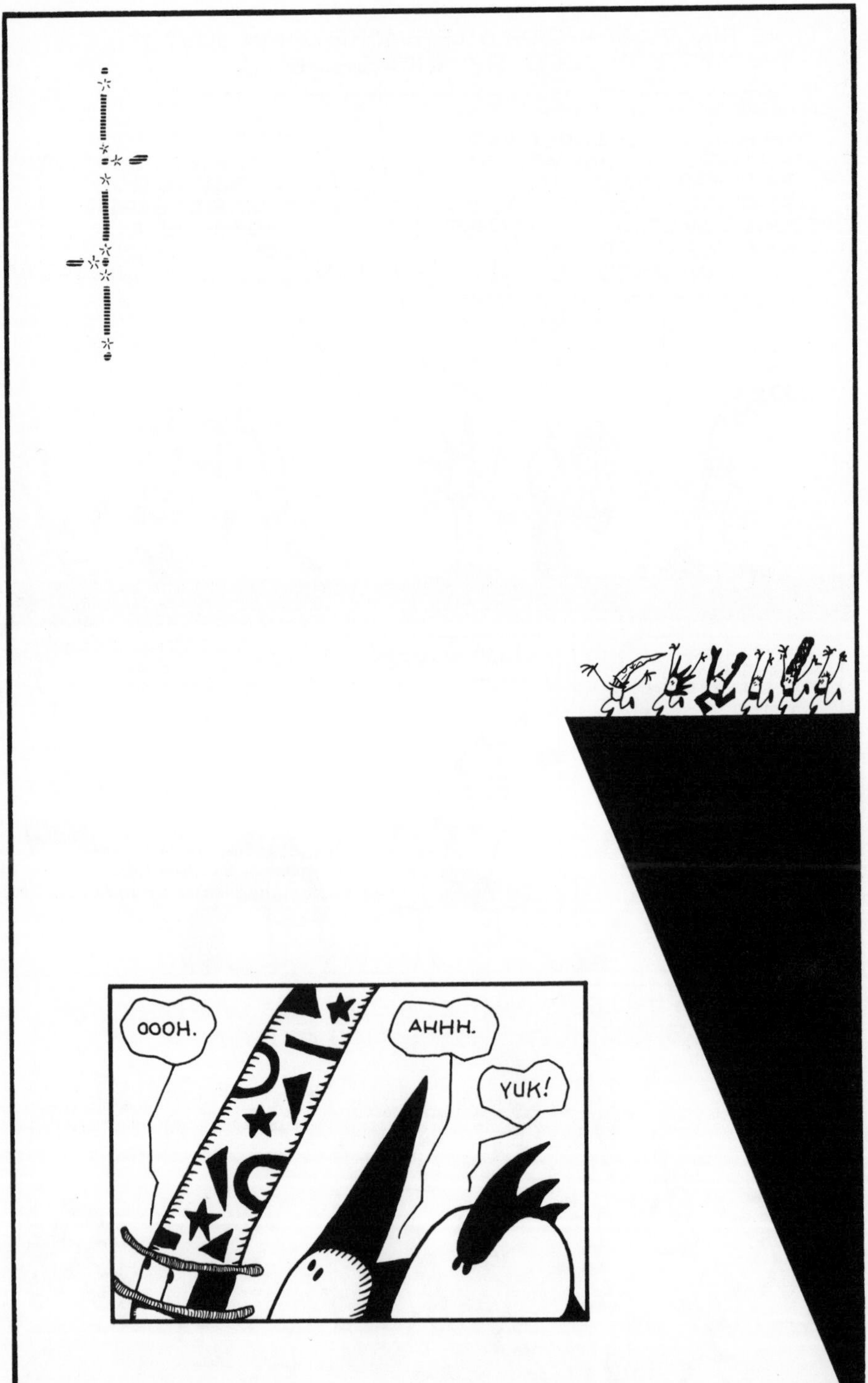
OOOH.
AHHH.
YUK!

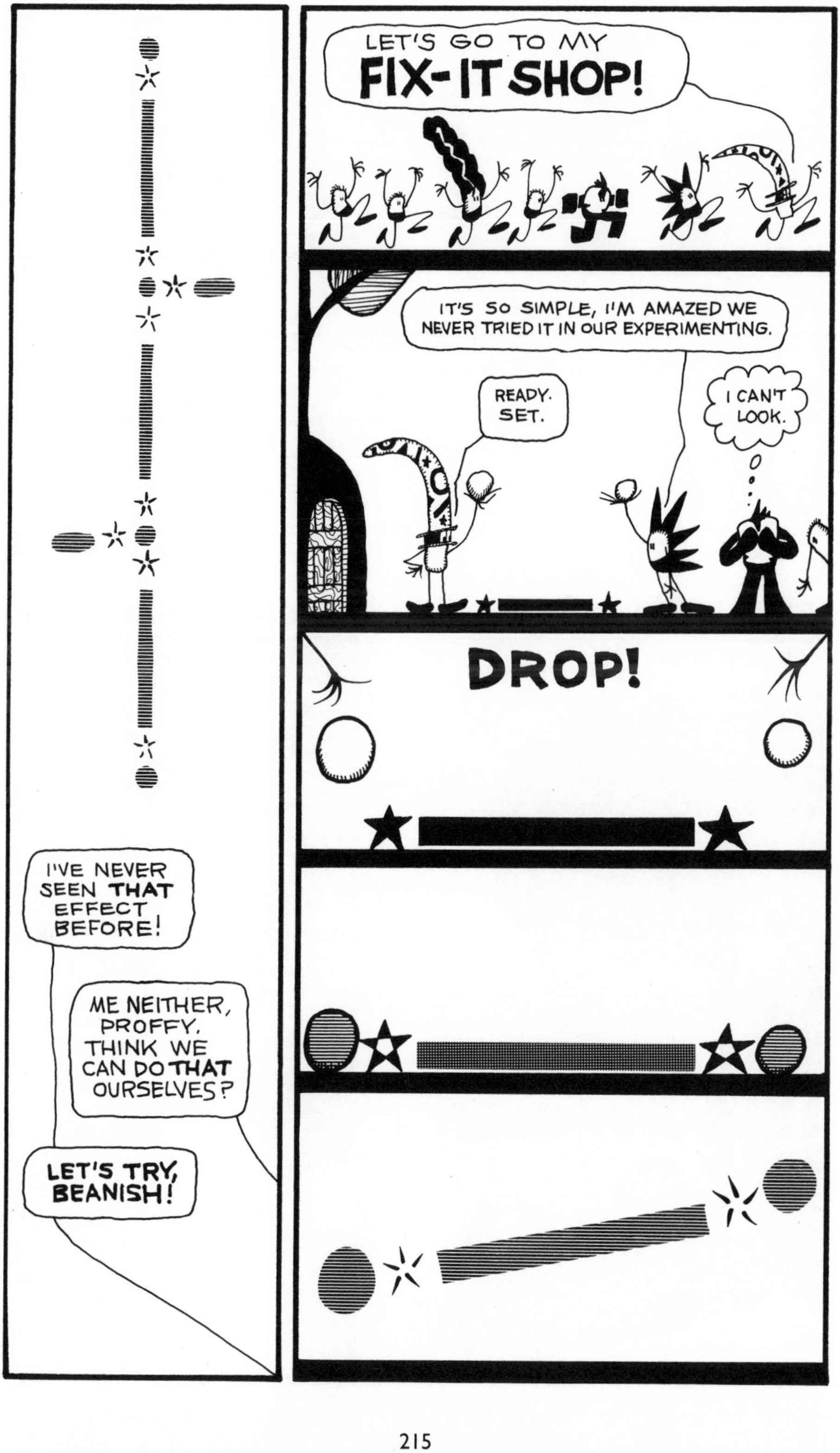
LET'S GO TO MY FIX-IT SHOP!
IT'S SO SIMPLE, I'M AMAZED WE NEVER TRIED IT IN OUR EXPERIMENTING.
READY. SET.
I CAN'T LOOK.
DROP!
I'VE NEVER SEEN THAT EFFECT BEFORE!
ME NEITHER, PROFFY. THINK WE CAN DO THAT OURSELVES?
LET'S TRY, BEANISH!

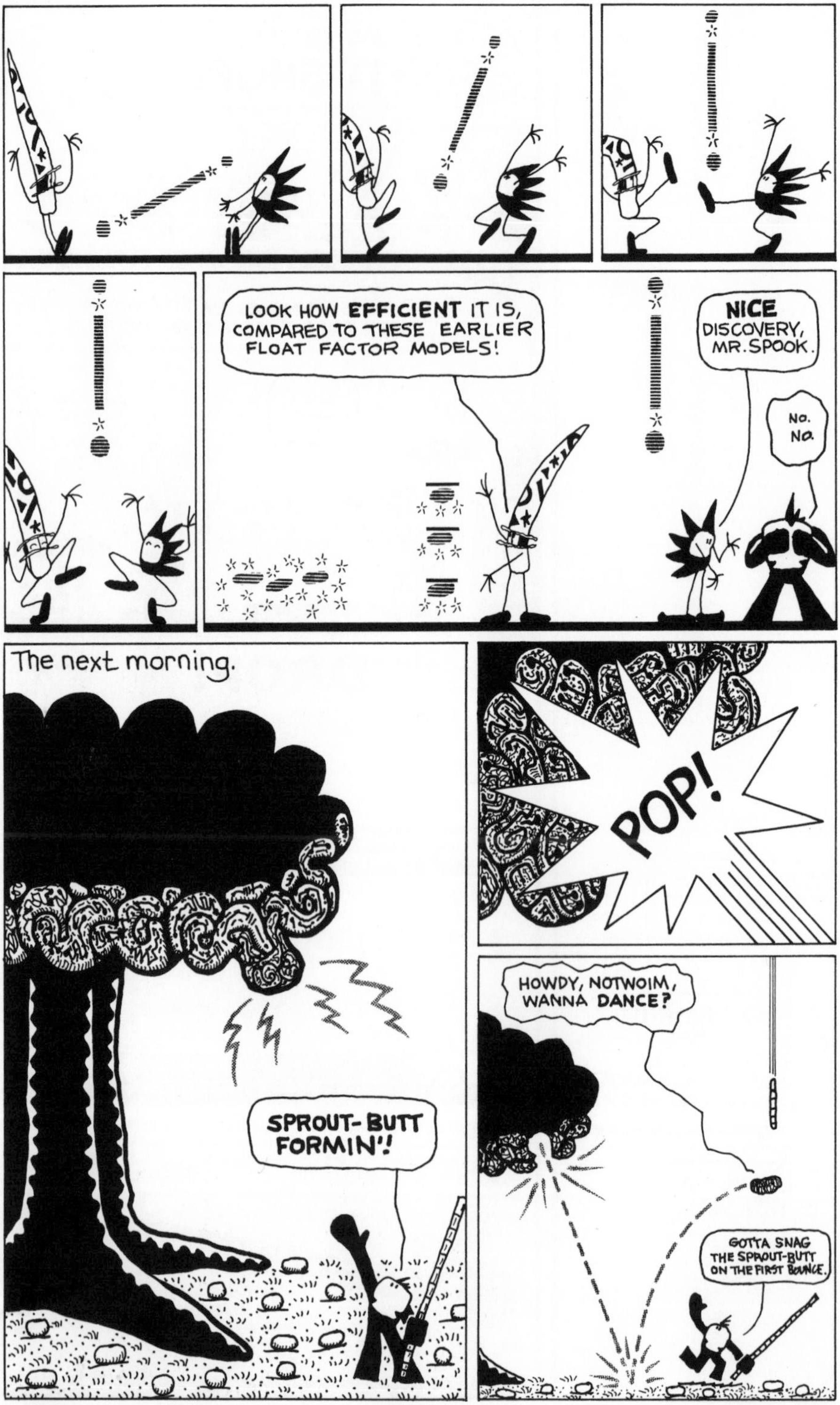
LOOK HOW EFFICIENT IT IS, COMPARED TO THESE EARLIER FLOAT FACTOR MODELS!
NICE DISCOVERY, MR. SPOOK.
No. No.
The next morning.
SPROUT-BUTT FORMIN'!
POP!
HOWDY, NOTWOIM, WANNA DANCE?
GOTTA SNAG THE SPROUT-BUTT ON THE FIRST BOUNCE.

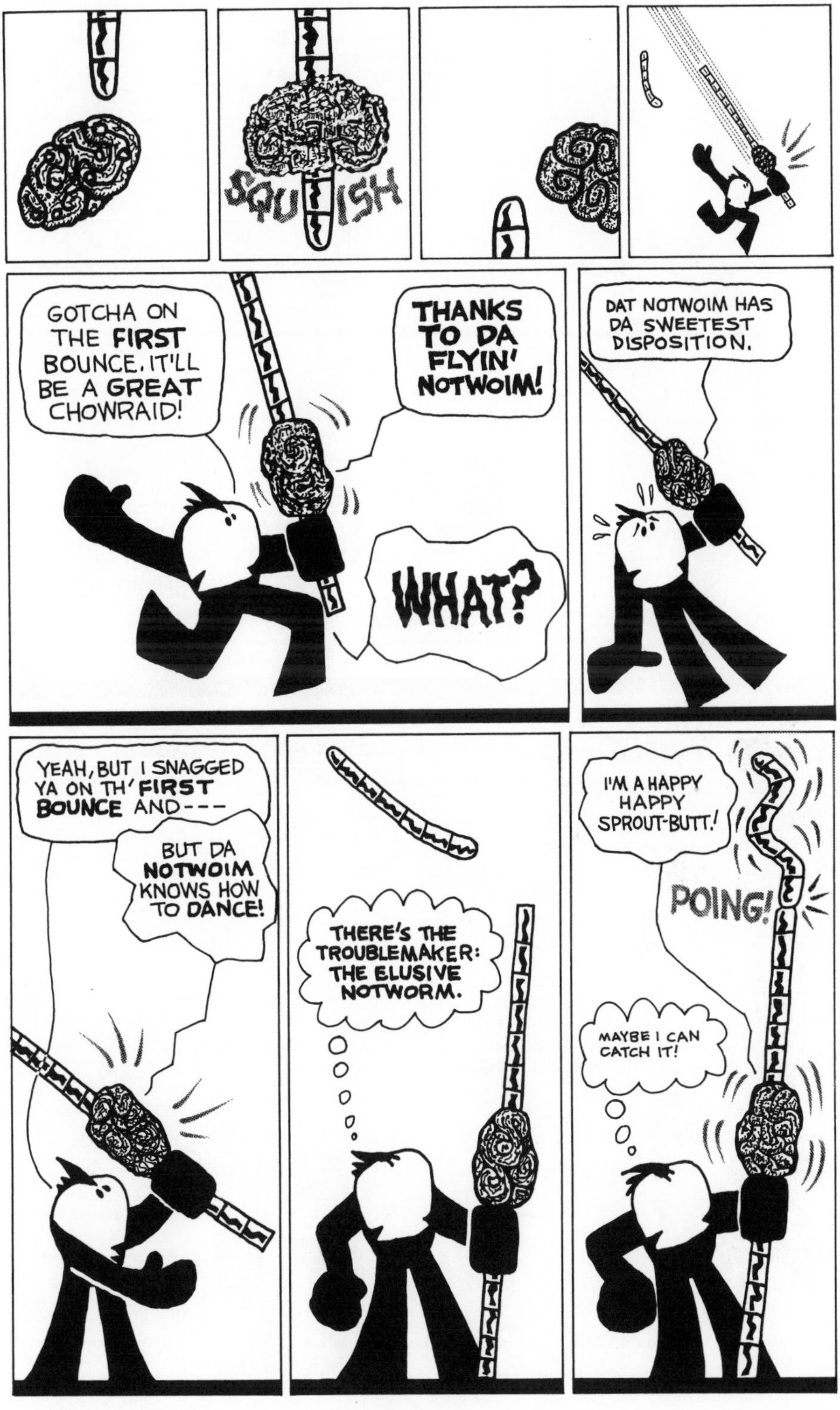
SQUISH
GOTCHA ON THE FIRST BOUNCE. IT'LL BE A GREAT CHOWRAID!
THANKS TO DA FLYIN' NOTWOIM!
WHAT?
DAT NOTWOIM HAS DA SWEETEST DISPOSITION.
YEAH, BUT I SNAGGED YA ON TH' FIRST BOUNCE AND---
BUT DA NOTWOIM KNOWS HOW TO DANCE!
THERE'S THE TROUBLEMAKER: THE ELUSIVE NOTWORM.
I'M A HAPPY HAPPY SPROUT-BUTT!
POING!
MAYBE I CAN CATCH IT!

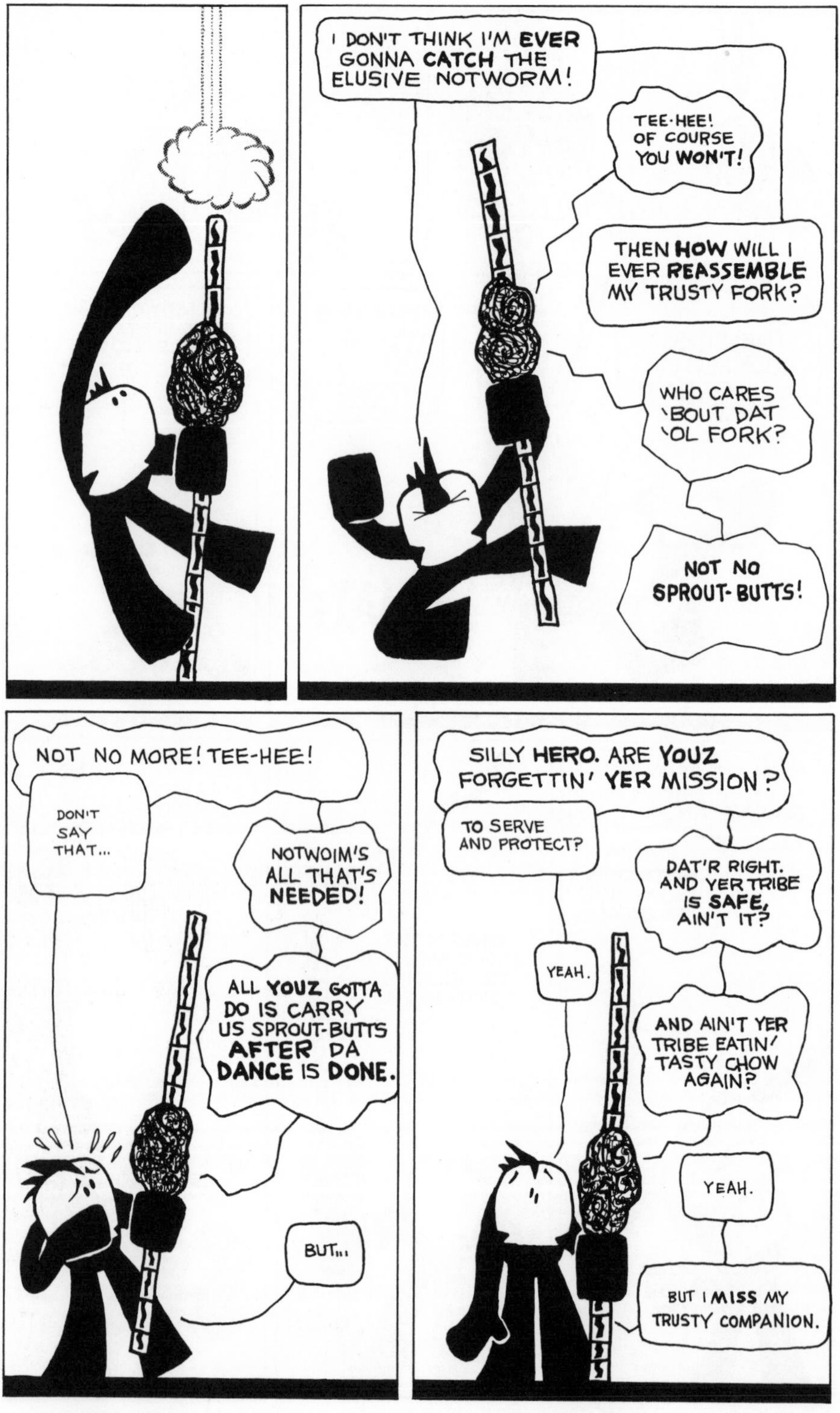
I DON'T THINK I'M EVER GONNA CATCH THE ELUSIVE NOTWORM!
TEE-HEE! OF COURSE YOU WON'T!
THEN HOW WILL I EVER REASSEMBLE MY TRUSTY FORK?
WHO CARES 'BOUT DAT 'OL FORK?
NOT NO SPROUT-BUTTS!
NOT NO MORE! TEE-HEE!
DON'T SAY THAT...
NOTWOIM'S ALL THAT'S NEEDED!
ALL YOUZ GOTTA DO IS CARRY US SPROUT-BUTTS AFTER DA DANCE IS DONE.
BUT...
SILLY HERO. ARE YOUZ FORGETTIN' YER MISSION?
TO SERVE AND PROTECT?
DAT'R RIGHT. AND YER TRIBE IS SAFE, AIN'T IT?
YEAH.
AND AIN'T YER TRIBE EATIN' TASTY CHOW AGAIN?
YEAH.
BUT I MISS MY TRUSTY COMPANION.

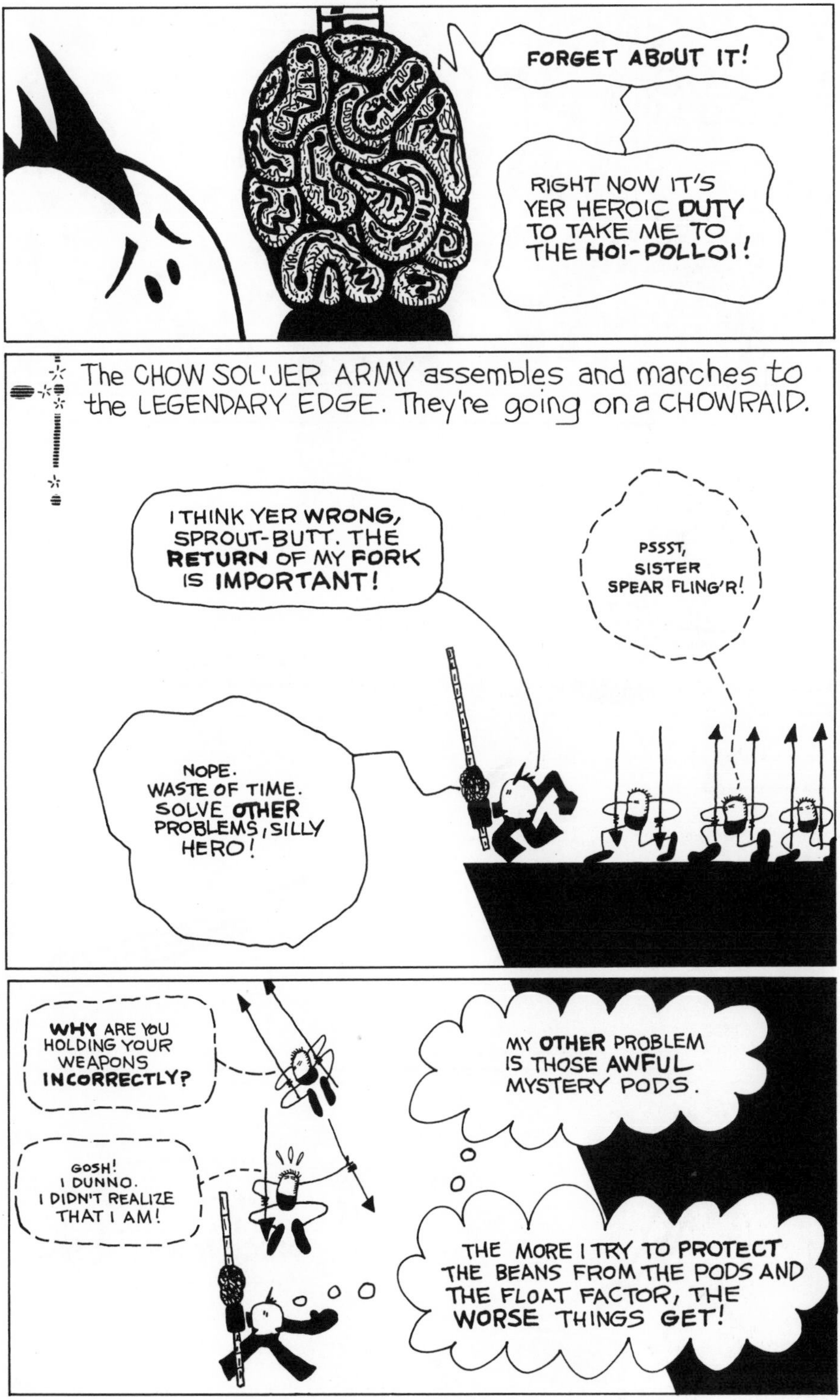
FORGET ABOUT IT!
RIGHT NOW IT'S YER HEROIC DUTY TO TAKE ME TO THE HOI-POLLOI!
The CHOW SOL'JER ARMY assembles and marches to the LEGENDARY EDGE. They're going on a CHOWRAID.
I THINK YER WRONG, SPROUT-BUTT. THE RETURN OF MY FORK IS IMPORTANT!
PSSST, SISTER SPEAR FLING'R!
NOPE. WASTE OF TIME. SOLVE OTHER PROBLEMS, SILLY HERO!
WHY ARE YOU HOLDING YOUR WEAPONS INCORRECTLY?
MY OTHER PROBLEM IS THOSE AWFUL MYSTERY PODS.
GOSH! I DUNNO. I DIDN'T REALIZE THAT I AM!
THE MORE I TRY TO PROTECT THE BEANS FROM THE PODS AND THE FLOAT FACTOR, THE WORSE THINGS GET!

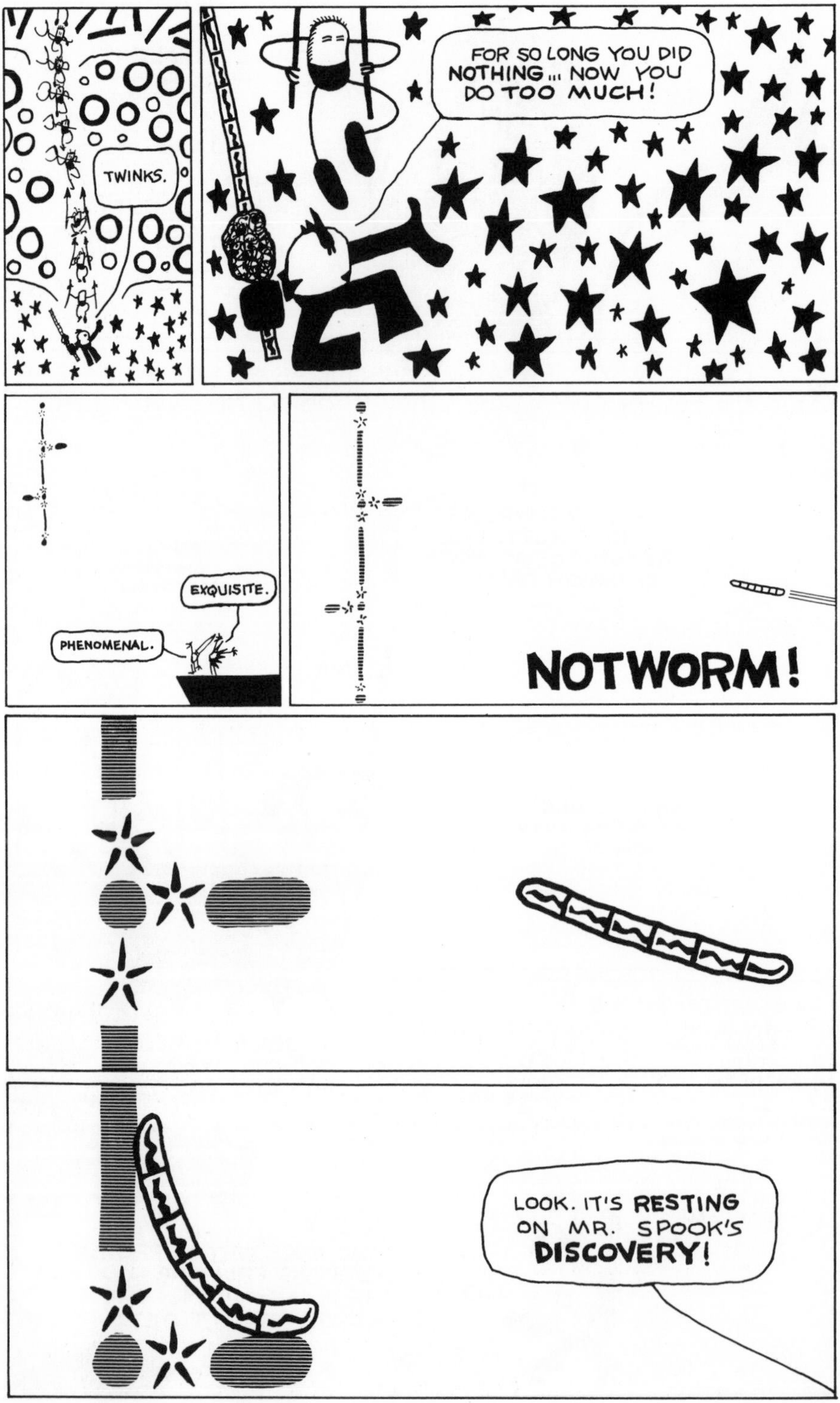
TWINKS.
FOR SO LONG YOU DID NOTHING... NOW YOU DO TOO MUCH!
EXQUISITE.
PHENOMENAL.
NOTWORM!
LOOK. IT'S RESTING ON MR. SPOOK'S DISCOVERY!

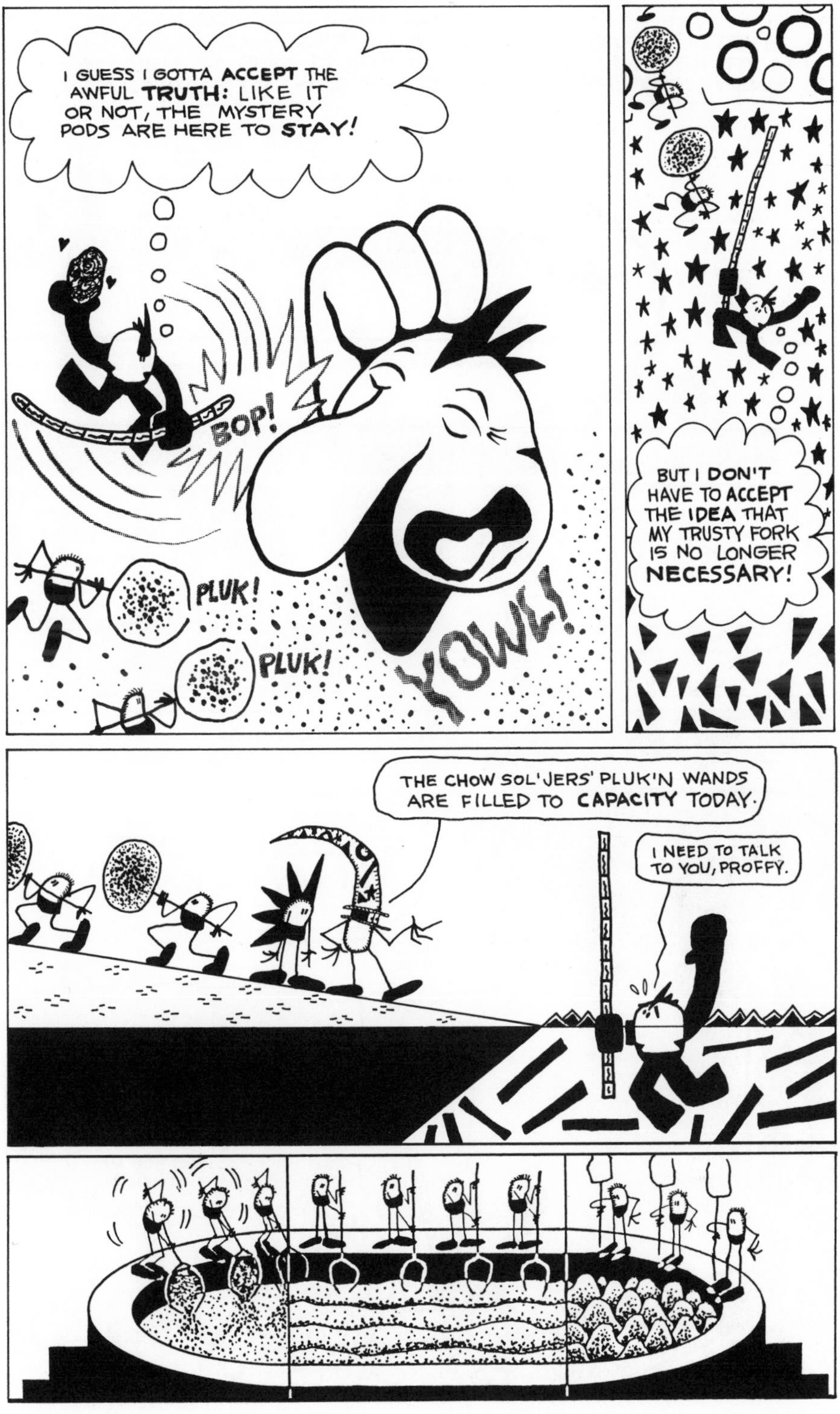
I GUESS I GOTTA ACCEPT THE AWFUL TRUTH: LIKE IT OR NOT, THE MYSTERY PODS ARE HERE TO STAY!
BOP!
PLUK!
PLUK!
YOWL!
BUT I DON'T HAVE TO ACCEPT THE IDEA THAT MY TRUSTY FORK IS NO LONGER NECESSARY!
THE CHOW SOL'JERS' PLUK'N WANDS ARE FILLED TO CAPACITY TODAY.
I NEED TO TALK TO YOU, PROFFY.

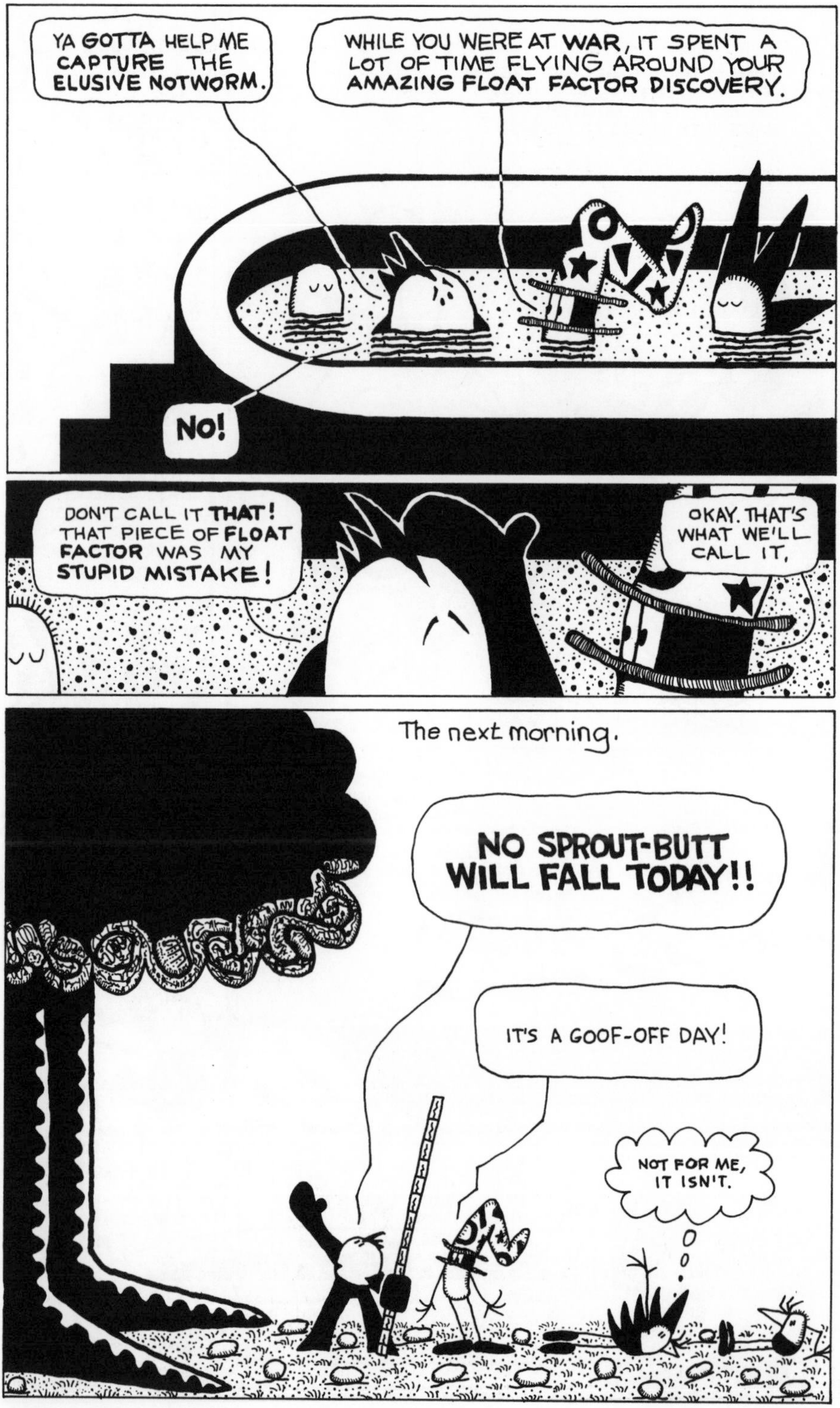
YA GOTTA HELP ME CAPTURE THE ELUSIVE NOTWORM.
WHILE YOU WERE AT WAR, IT SPENT A LOT OF TIME FLYING AROUND YOUR AMAZING FLOAT FACTOR DISCOVERY.
NO!
DON'T CALL IT THAT! THAT PIECE OF FLOAT FACTOR WAS MY STUPID MISTAKE!
OKAY. THAT'S WHAT WE'LL CALL IT.
The next morning.
NO SPROUT-BUTT WILL FALL TODAY!!
IT'S A GOOF-OFF DAY!
NOT FOR ME, IT ISN'T.

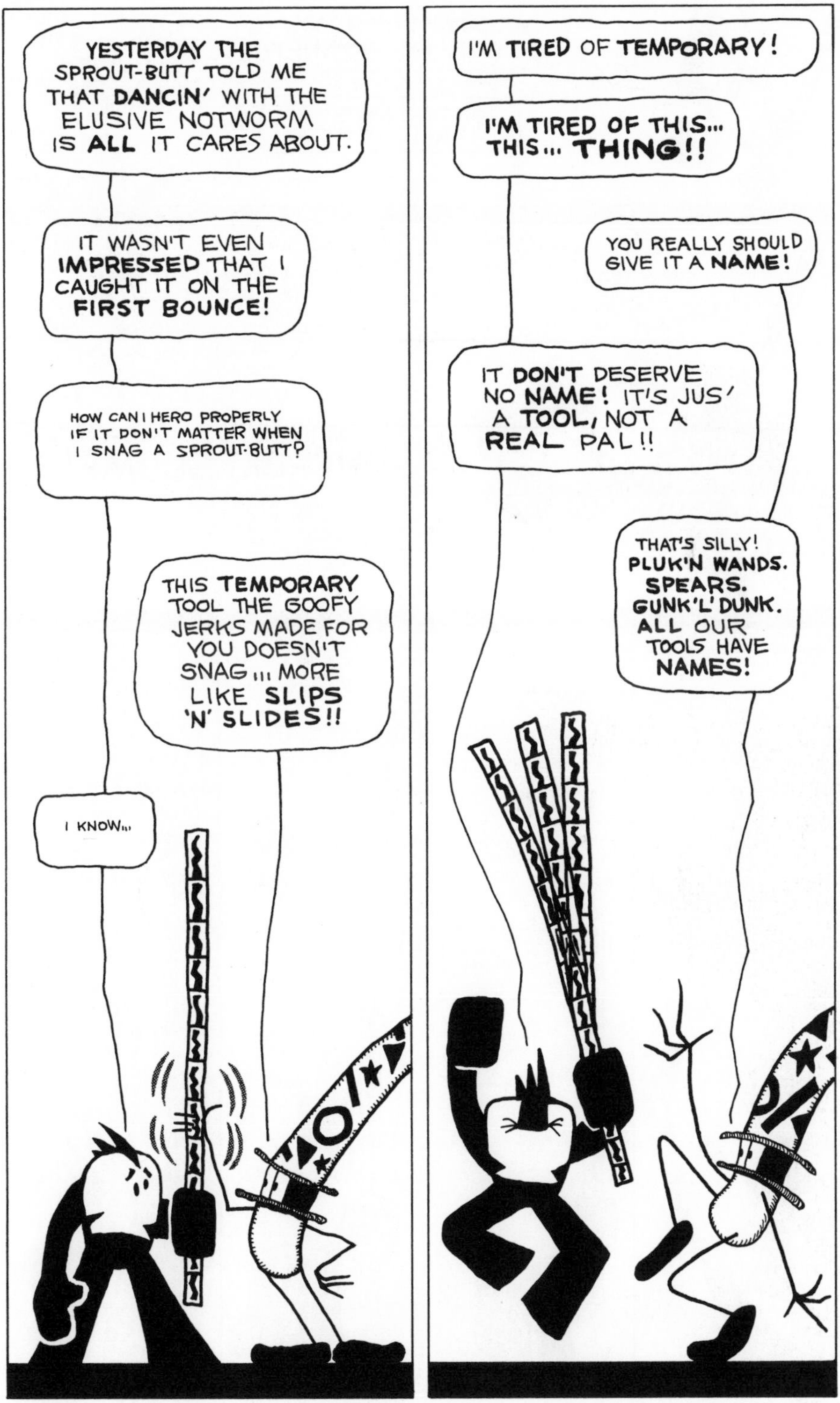
YESTERDAY THE SPROUT-BUTT TOLD ME THAT DANCIN' WITH THE ELUSIVE NOTWORM IS ALL IT CARES ABOUT.
IT WASN'T EVEN IMPRESSED THAT I CAUGHT IT ON THE FIRST BOUNCE!
HOW CAN I HERO PROPERLY IF IT DON'T MATTER WHEN I SNAG A SPROUT-BUTT?
THIS TEMPORARY TOOL THE GOOFY JERKS MADE FOR YOU DOESN'T SNAG... MORE LIKE SLIPS 'N' SLIDES!!
I KNOW...
I'M TIRED OF TEMPORARY!
I'M TIRED OF THIS... THIS... THING!!
YOU REALLY SHOULD GIVE IT A NAME!
IT DON'T DESERVE NO NAME! IT'S JUS' A TOOL, NOT A REAL PAL!!
THAT'S SILLY! PLUK'N WANDS. SPEARS. GUNK'L'DUNK. ALL OUR TOOLS HAVE NAMES!

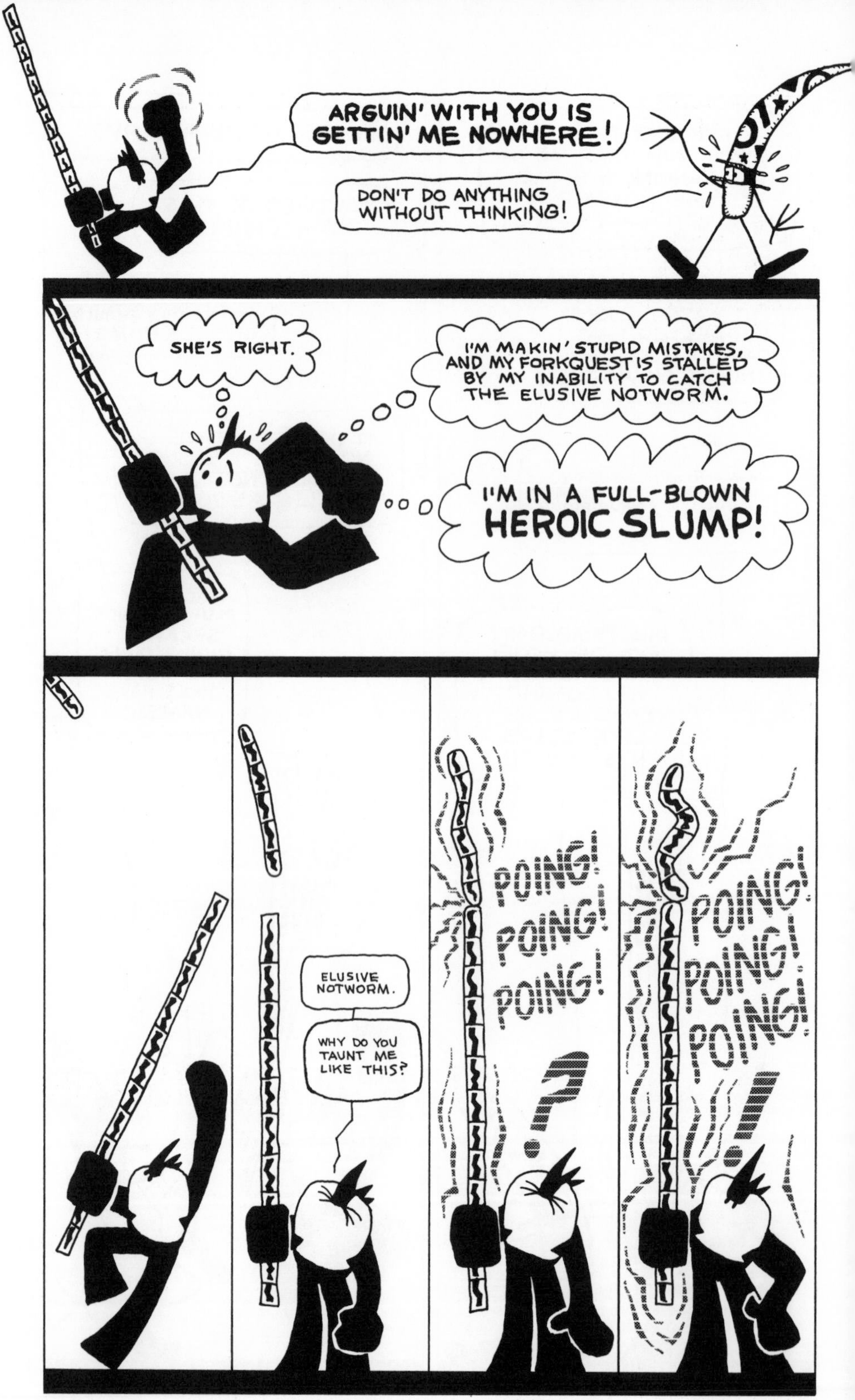
ARGUIN' WITH YOU IS GETTIN' ME NOWHERE!
DON'T DO ANYTHING WITHOUT THINKING!
SHE'S RIGHT.
I'M MAKIN' STUPID MISTAKES, AND MY FORKQUEST IS STALLED BY MY INABILITY TO CATCH THE ELUSIVE NOTWORM.
I'M IN A FULL-BLOWN HEROIC SLUMP!
ELUSIVE NOTWORM.
WHY DO YOU TAUNT ME LIKE THIS?
POING! POING! POING!
?
POING! POING! POING!
!

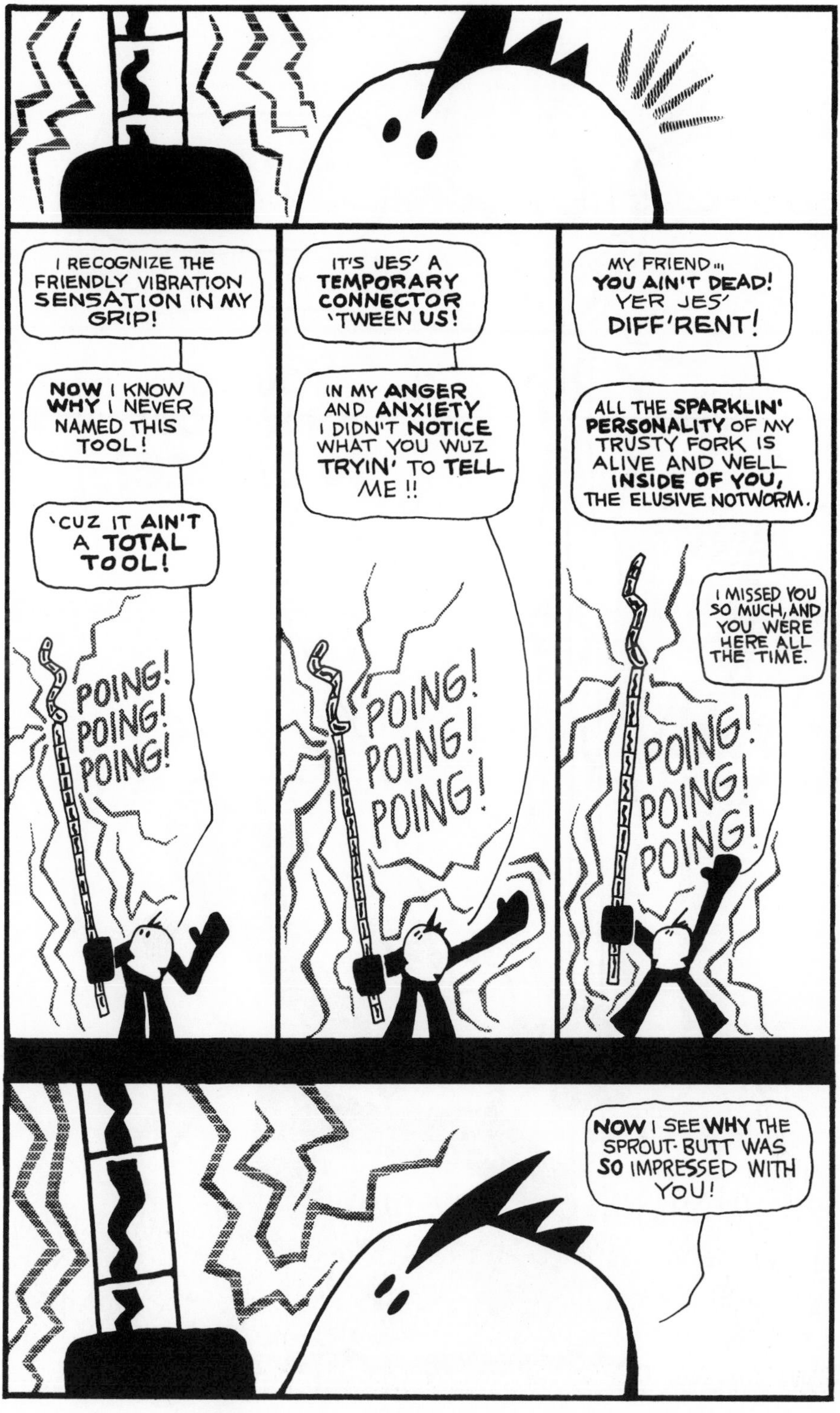
I RECOGNIZE THE FRIENDLY VIBRATION SENSATION IN MY GRIP!
NOW I KNOW WHY I NEVER NAMED THIS TOOL!
'CUZ IT AIN'T A TOTAL TOOL!
POING! POING! POING!
IT'S JES' A TEMPORARY CONNECTOR 'TWEEN US!
IN MY ANGER AND ANXIETY I DIDN'T NOTICE WHAT YOU WUZ TRYIN' TO TELL ME !!
POING! POING! POING!
MY FRIEND... YOU AIN'T DEAD! YER JES' DIFF'RENT!
ALL THE SPARKLIN' PERSONALITY OF MY TRUSTY FORK IS ALIVE AND WELL INSIDE OF YOU, THE ELUSIVE NOTWORM.
I MISSED YOU SO MUCH, AND YOU WERE HERE ALL THE TIME.
POING! POING! POING!
NOW I SEE WHY THE SPROUT-BUTT WAS SO IMPRESSED WITH YOU!

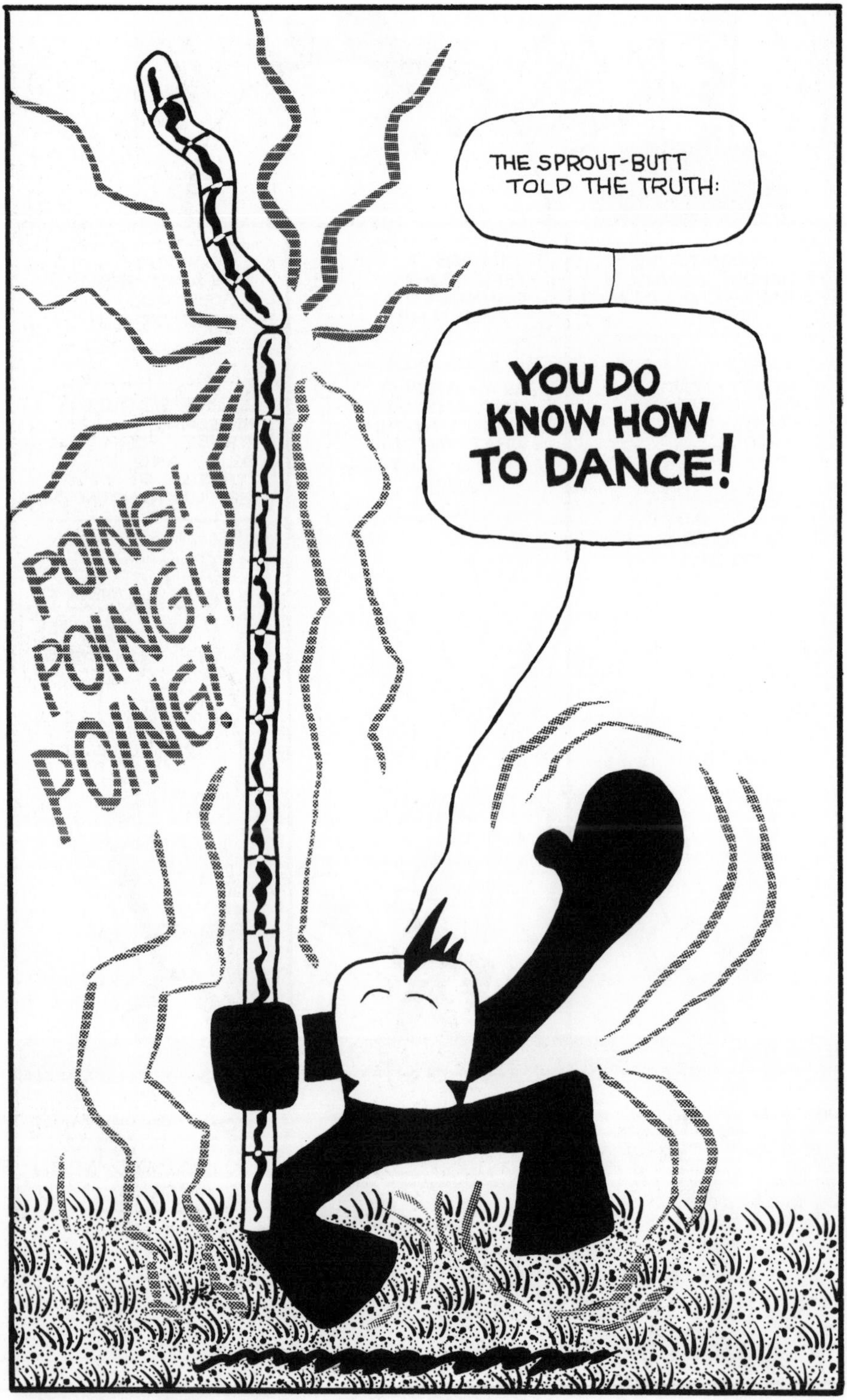
THE SPROUT-BUTT TOLD THE TRUTH:
YOU DO KNOW HOW TO DANCE!
POING! POING! POING!

Many days have passed. It's almost morning.

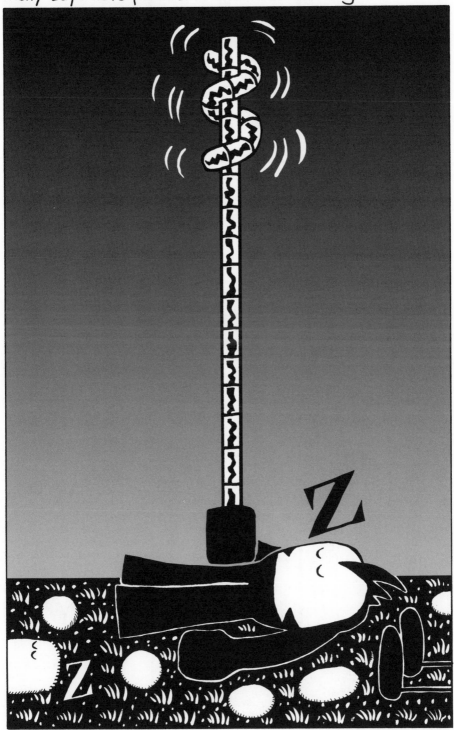

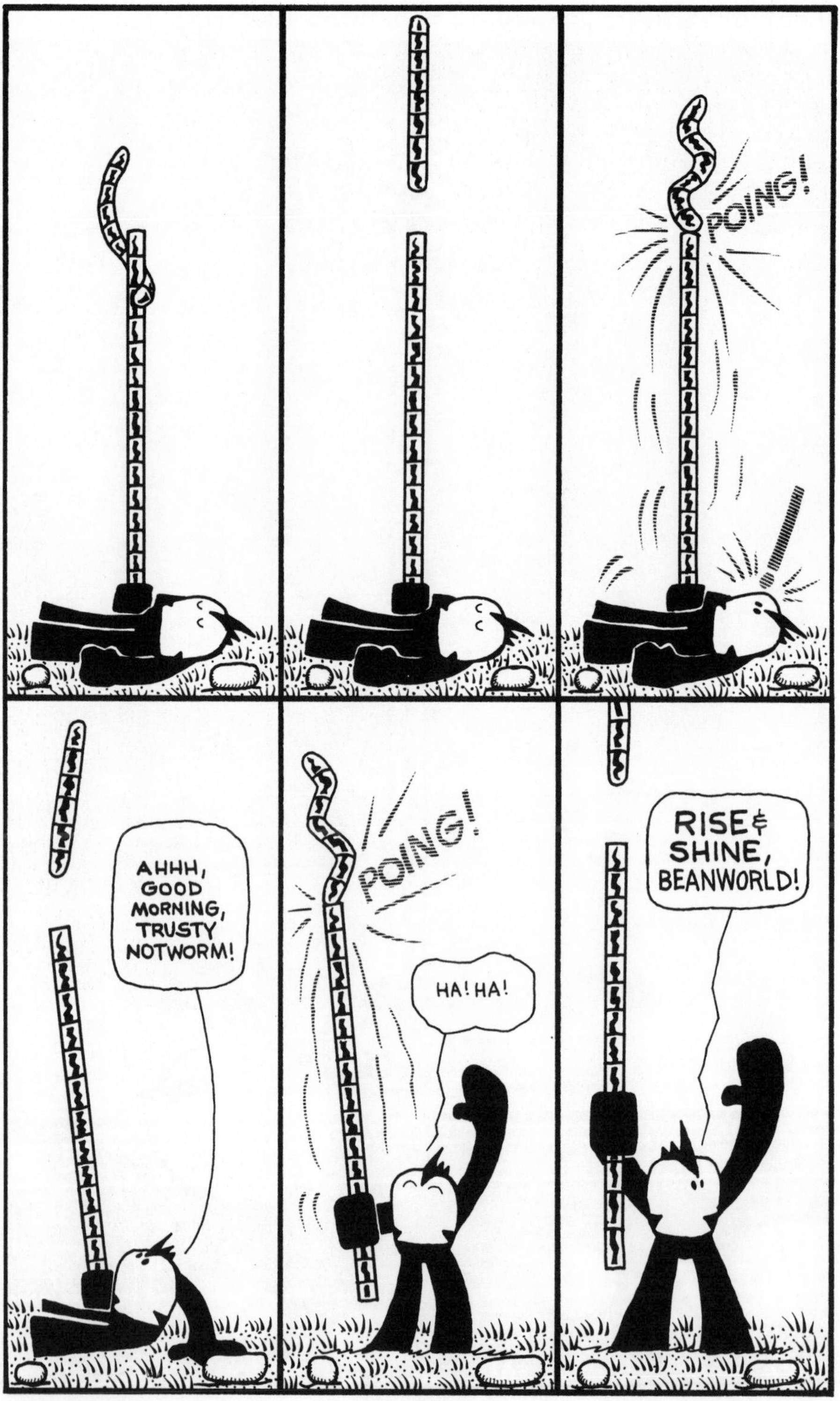
POING!
AHHH, GOOD MORNING, TRUSTY NOTWORM!
POING!
HA! HA!
RISE & SHINE, BEANWORLD!

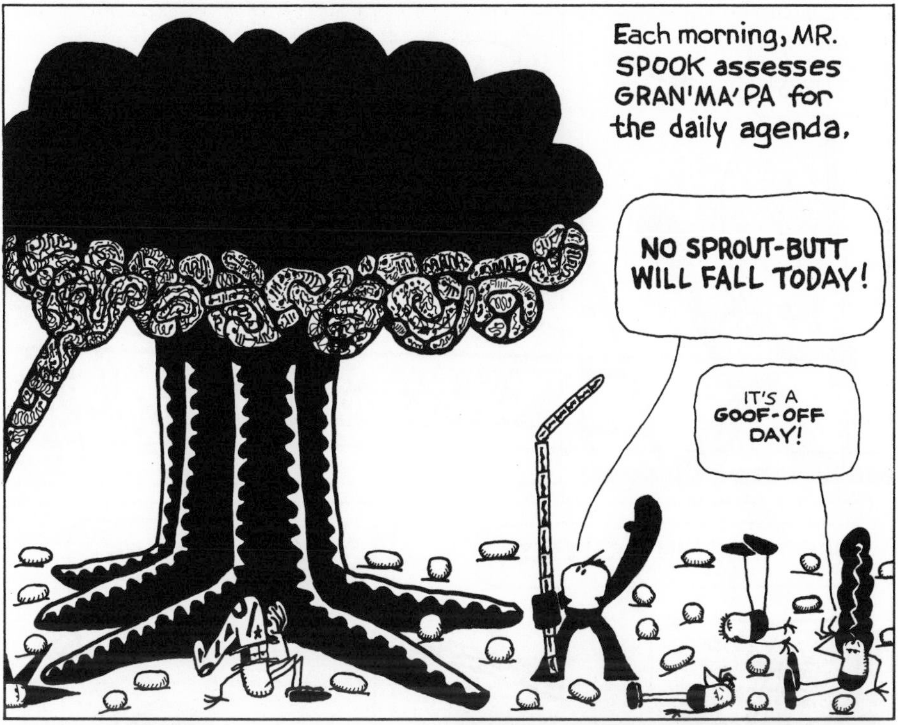
Each morning, MR. SPOOK assesses GRAN'MA'PA for the daily agenda,
NO SPROUT-BUTT WILL FALL TODAY!
IT'S A GOOF-OFF DAY!

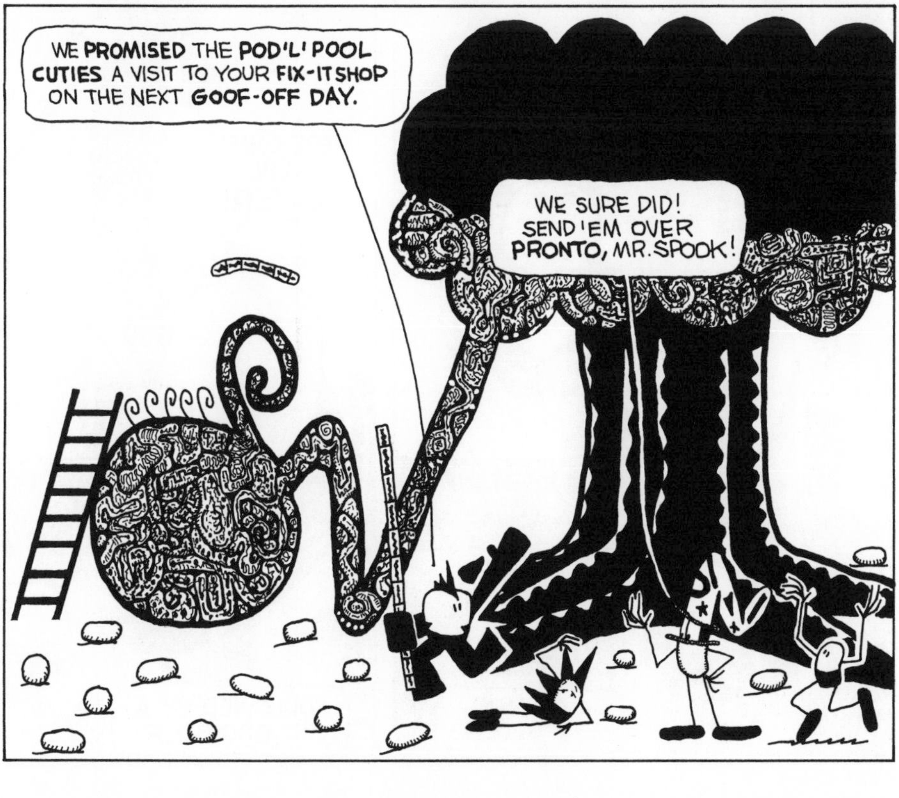
WE PROMISED THE POD'L'POOL CUTIES A VISIT TO YOUR FIX-IT SHOP ON THE NEXT GOOF-OFF DAY.
WE SURE DID! SEND'EM OVER PRONTO, MR. SPOOK!

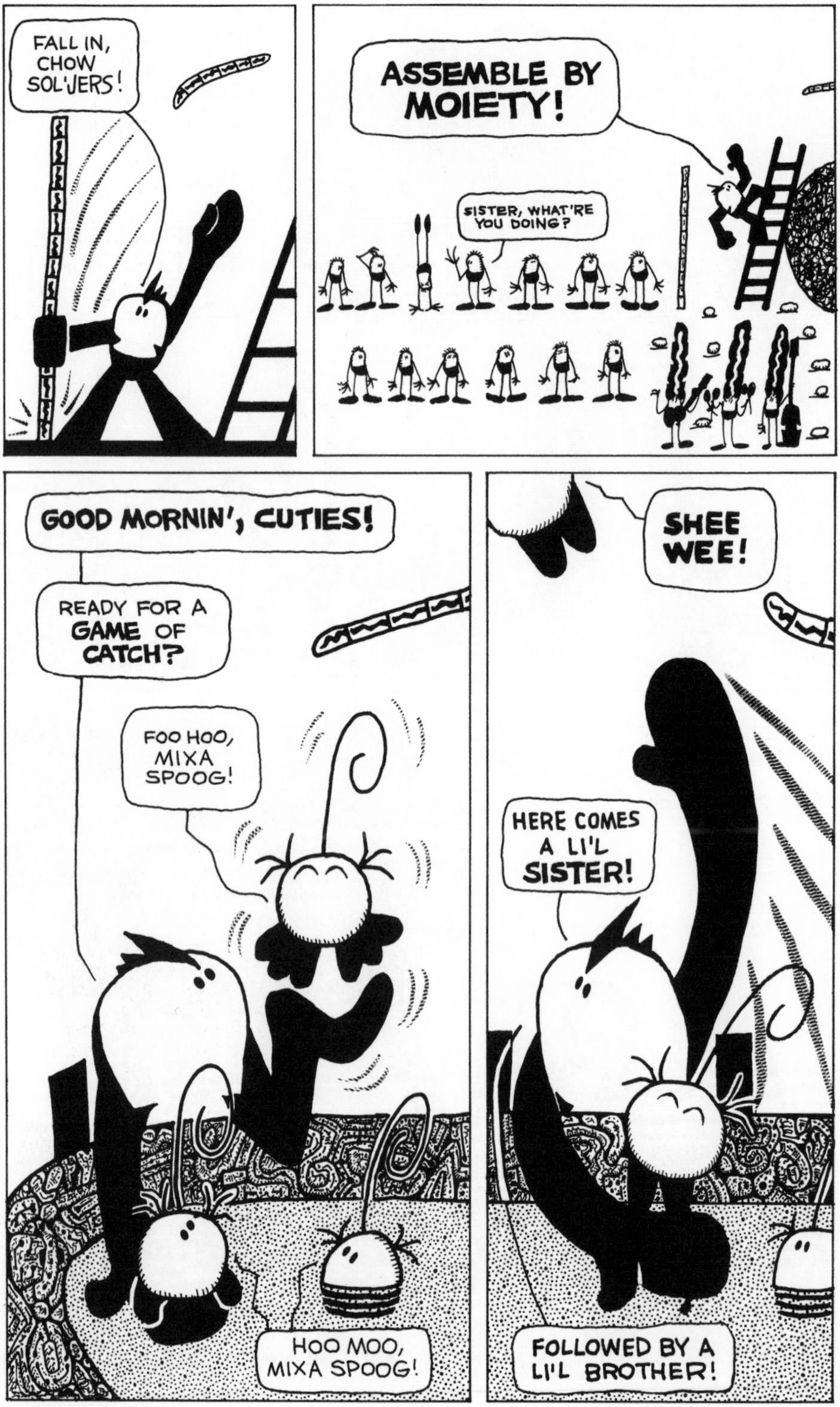
FALL IN, CHOW SOL'JERS!
ASSEMBLE BY MOIETY!
SISTER, WHAT'RE YOU DOING?
GOOD MORNIN', CUTIES!
READY FOR A GAME OF CATCH?
FOO HOO, MIXA SPOOG!
HOO MOO, MIXA SPOOG!
SHEE WEE!
HERE COMES A LI'L SISTER!
FOLLOWED BY A LI'L BROTHER!

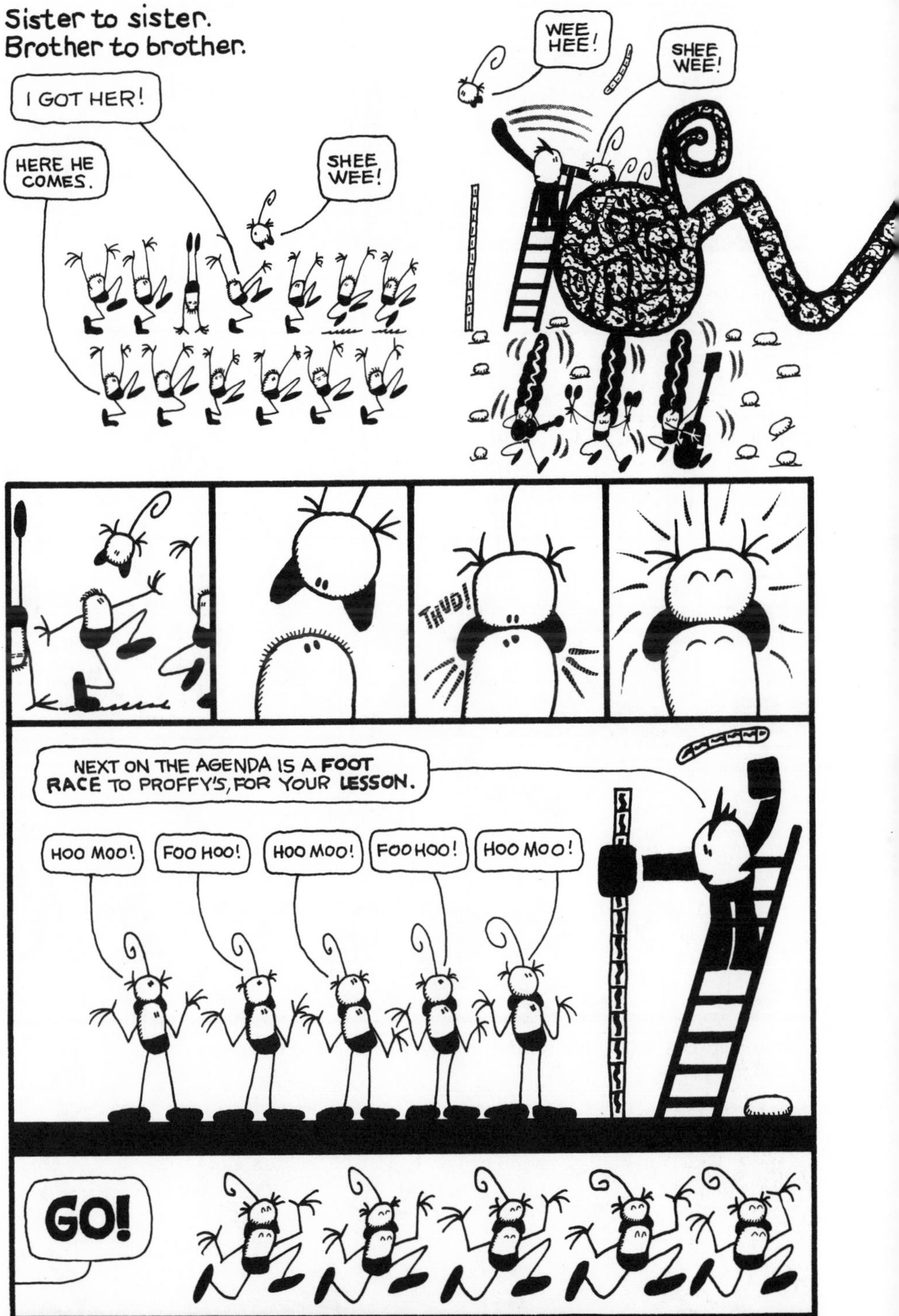

Sister to sister.
Brother to brother.
I GOT HER!
HERE HE COMES.
SHEE WEE!
WEE HEE!
SHEE WEE!
THUD!
NEXT ON THE AGENDA IS A FOOT RACE TO PROFFY'S, FOR YOUR LESSON.
HOO MOO!
FOO HOO!
HOO MOO!
FOO HOO!
HOO MOO!
GO!

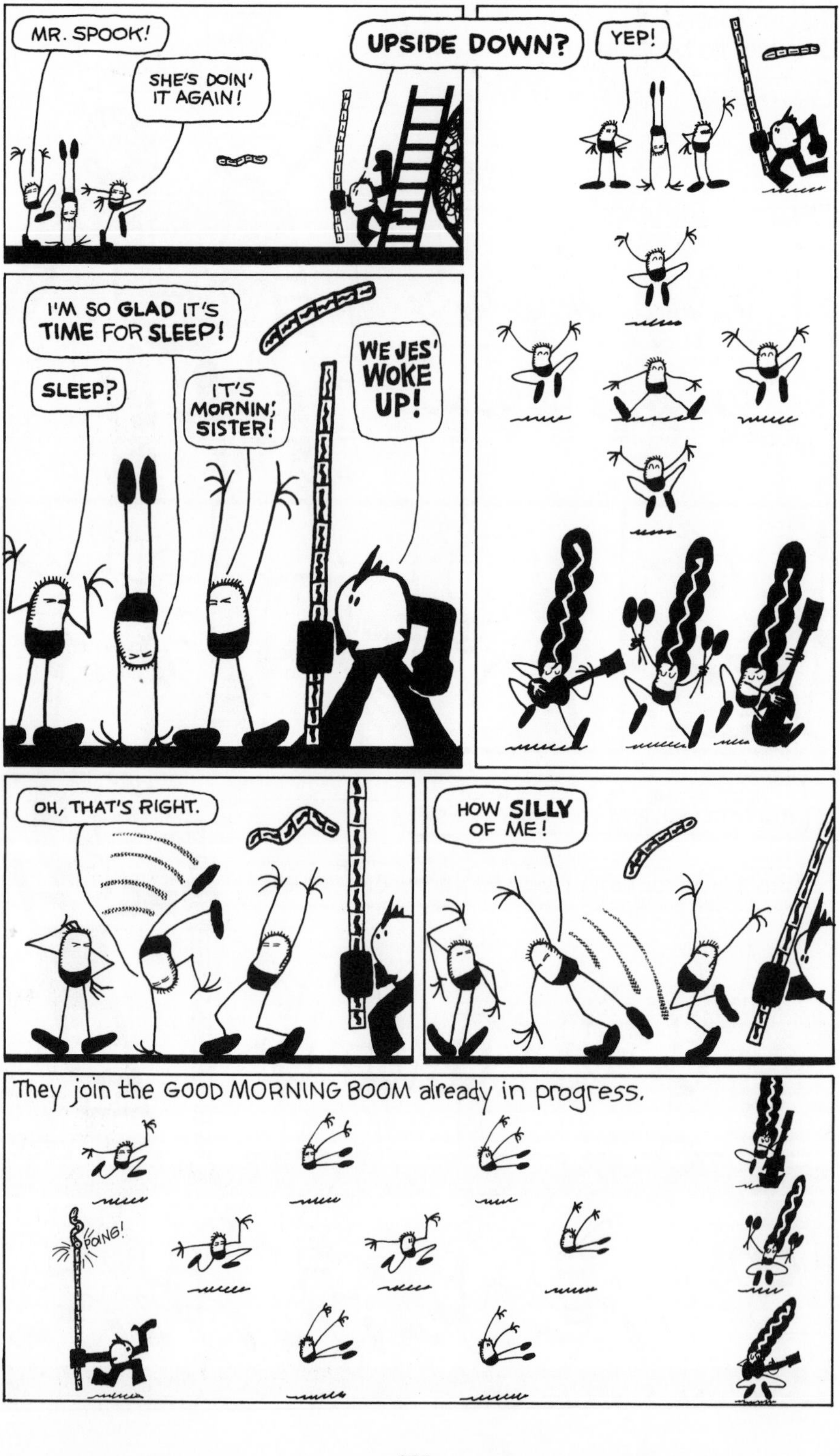
MR. SPOOK!
SHE'S DOIN' IT AGAIN!
UPSIDE DOWN?
YEP!
I'M SO GLAD IT'S TIME FOR SLEEP!
SLEEP?
IT'S MORNIN', SISTER!
WE JES' WOKE UP!
OH, THAT'S RIGHT.
HOW SILLY OF ME!
They join the GOOD MORNING BOOM already in progress.
POING!

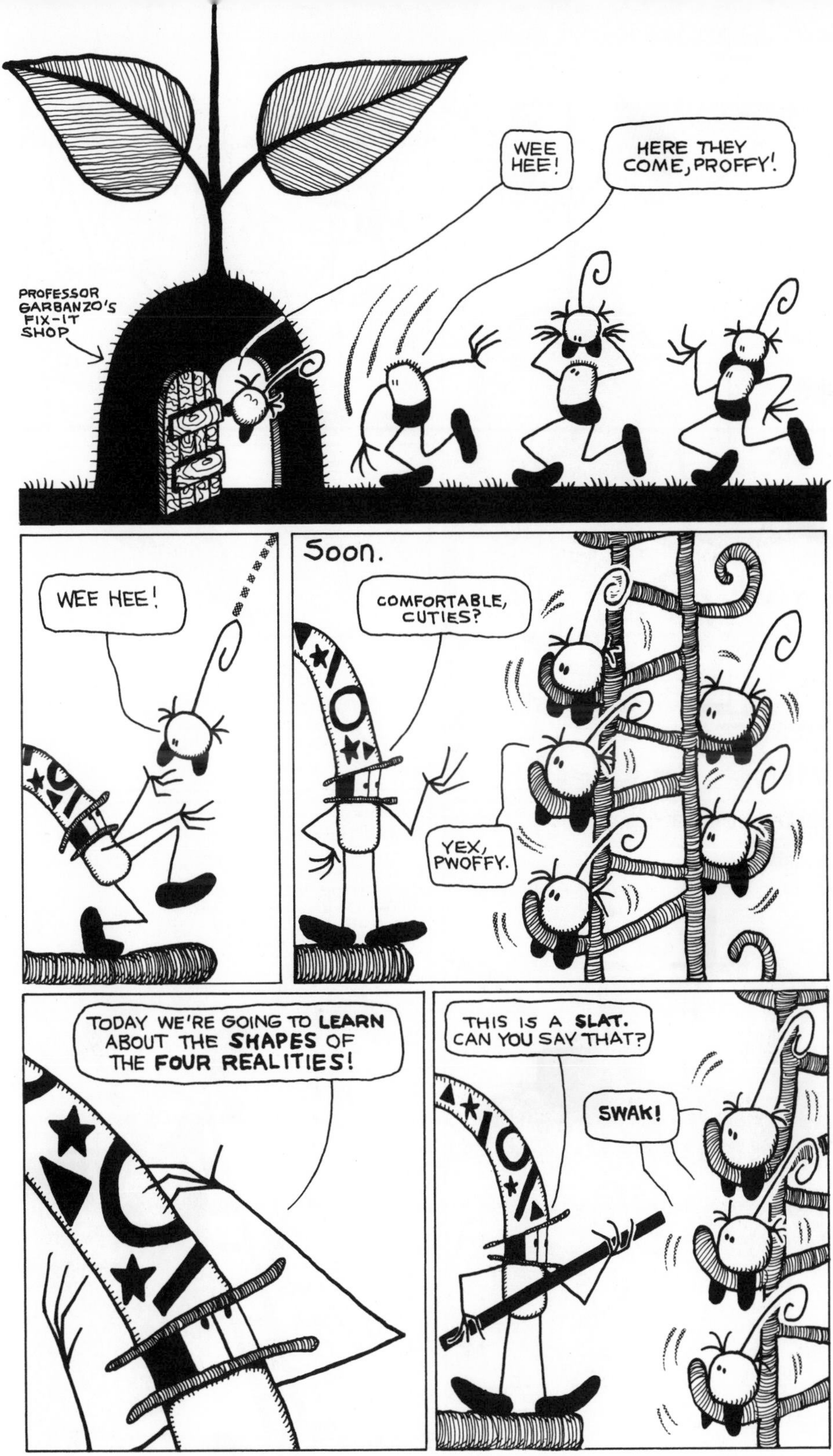
PROFESSOR GARBANZO'S FIX-IT SHOP
WEE HEE!
HERE THEY COME, PROFFY!
WEE HEE!
Soon.
COMFORTABLE, CUTIES?
YEX, PWOFFY.
TODAY WE'RE GOING TO LEARN ABOUT THE SHAPES OF THE FOUR REALITIES!
THIS IS A SLAT. CAN YOU SAY THAT?
SWAK!

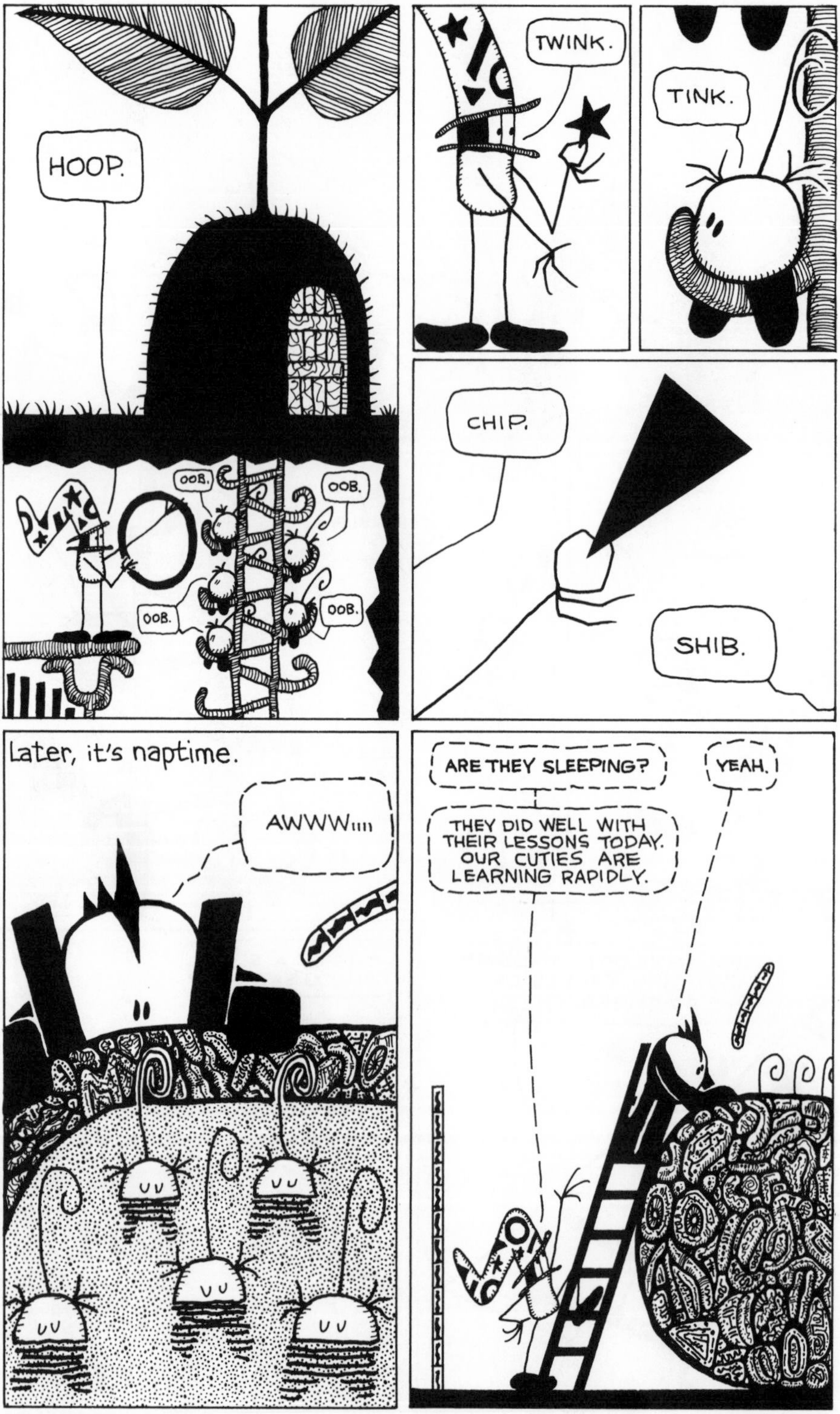
HOOP.
OOB.
OOB.
OOB.
OOB.
TWINK.
TINK.
CHIP.
SHIB.
Later, it's naptime.
AWWW
ARE THEY SLEEPING?
THEY DID WELL WITH THEIR LESSONS TODAY. OUR CUTIES ARE LEARNING RAPIDLY.
YEAH.

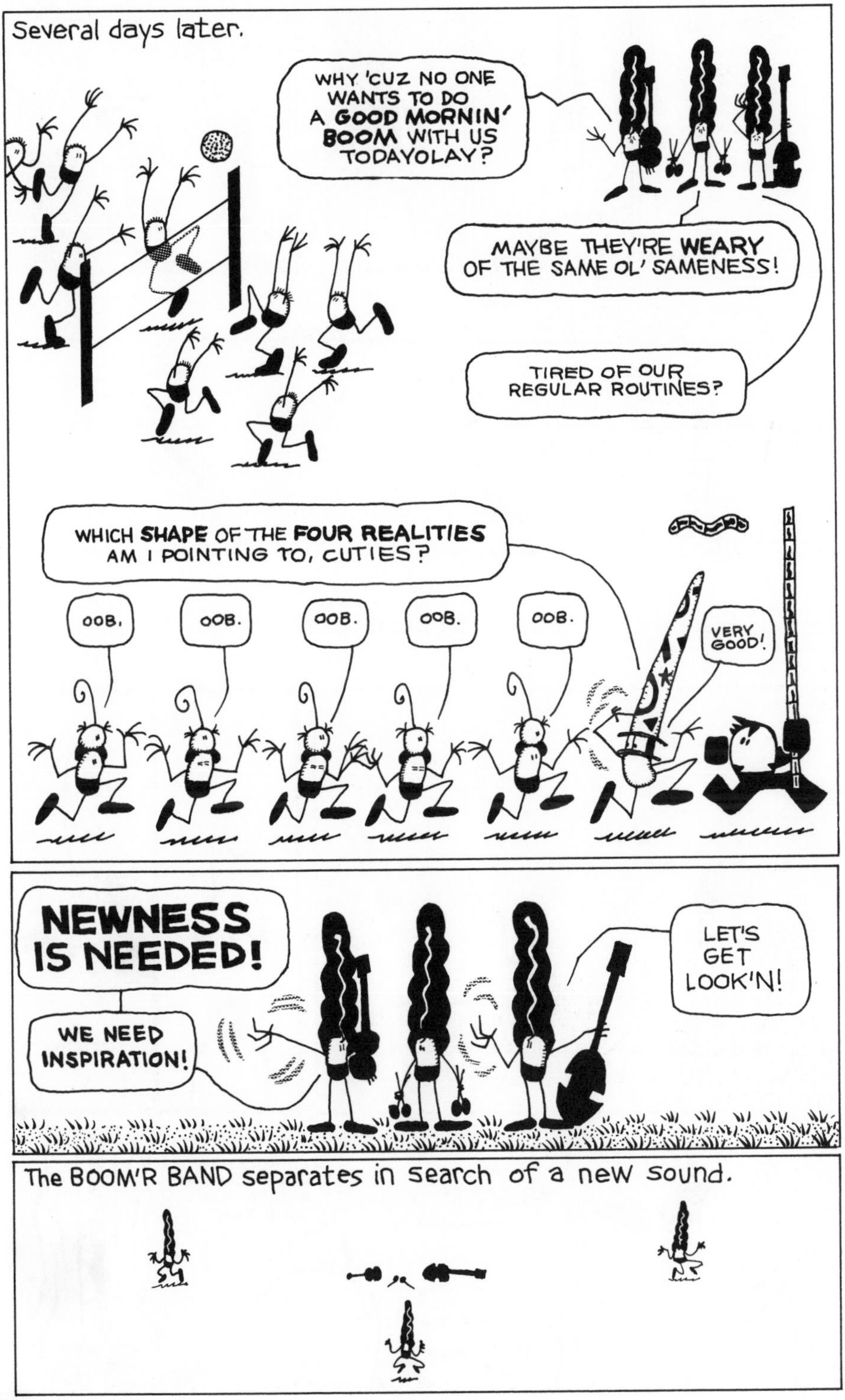
Several days later.
WHY 'CUZ NO ONE WANTS TO DO A GOOD MORNIN' BOOM WITH US TODAYOLAY?
MAYBE THEY'RE WEARY OF THE SAME OL' SAMENESS!
TIRED OF OUR REGULAR ROUTINES?
WHICH SHAPE OF THE FOUR REALITIES AM I POINTING TO, CUTIES?
OOB.
OOB.
OOB.
OOB.
OOB.
VERY GOOD!
NEWNESS IS NEEDED!
WE NEED INSPIRATION!
LET'S GET LOOK'N!
The BOOM'R BAND separates in search of a new sound.

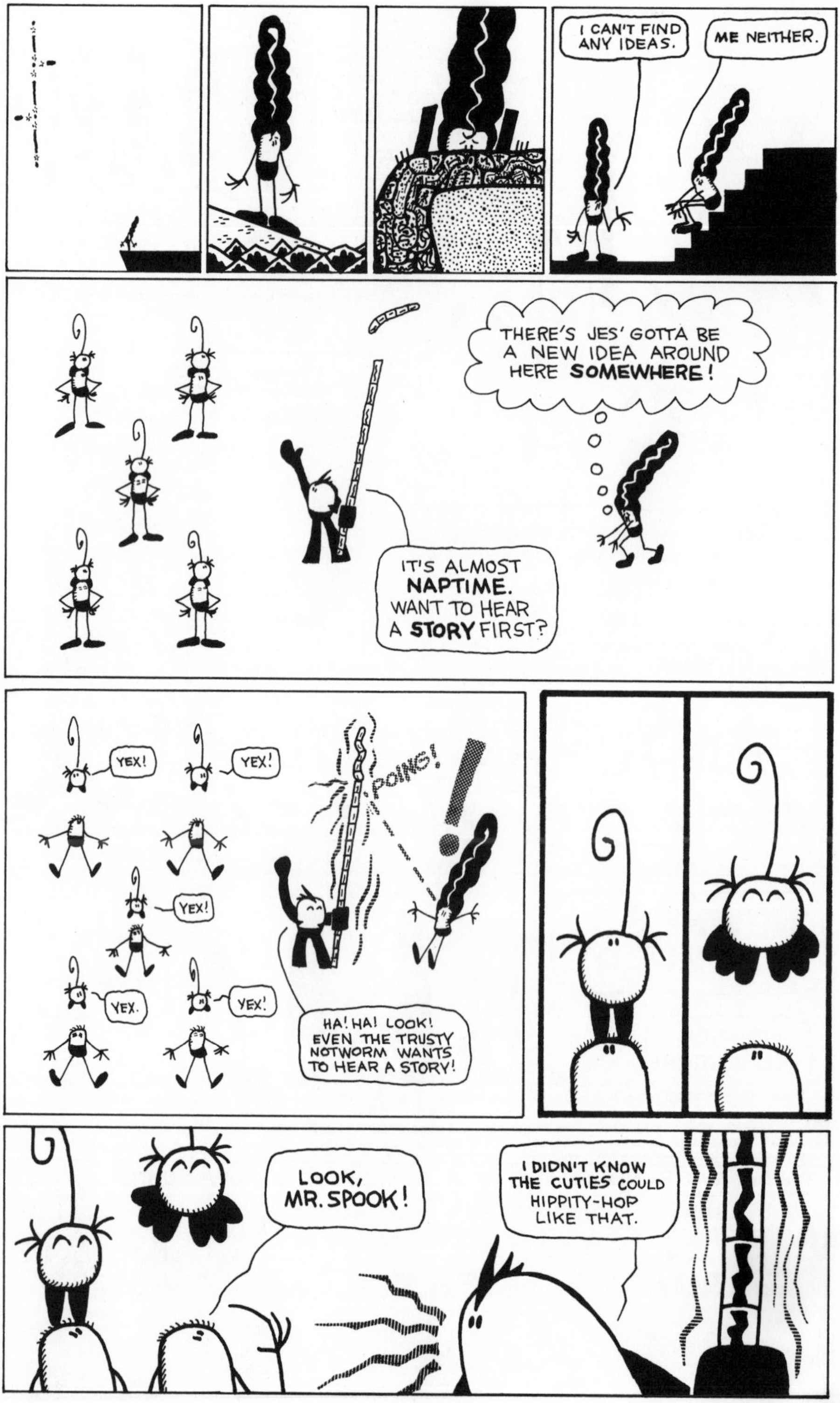
I CAN'T FIND ANY IDEAS.
ME NEITHER.
THERE'S JES' GOTTA BE A NEW IDEA AROUND HERE SOMEWHERE!
IT'S ALMOST NAPTIME. WANT TO HEAR A STORY FIRST?
YEX!
YEX!
YEX!
YEX.
YEX!
POING!
HA! HA! LOOK! EVEN THE TRUSTY NOTWORM WANTS TO HEAR A STORY!
LOOK, MR. SPOOK!
I DIDN'T KNOW THE CUTIES COULD HIPPITY-HOP LIKE THAT.

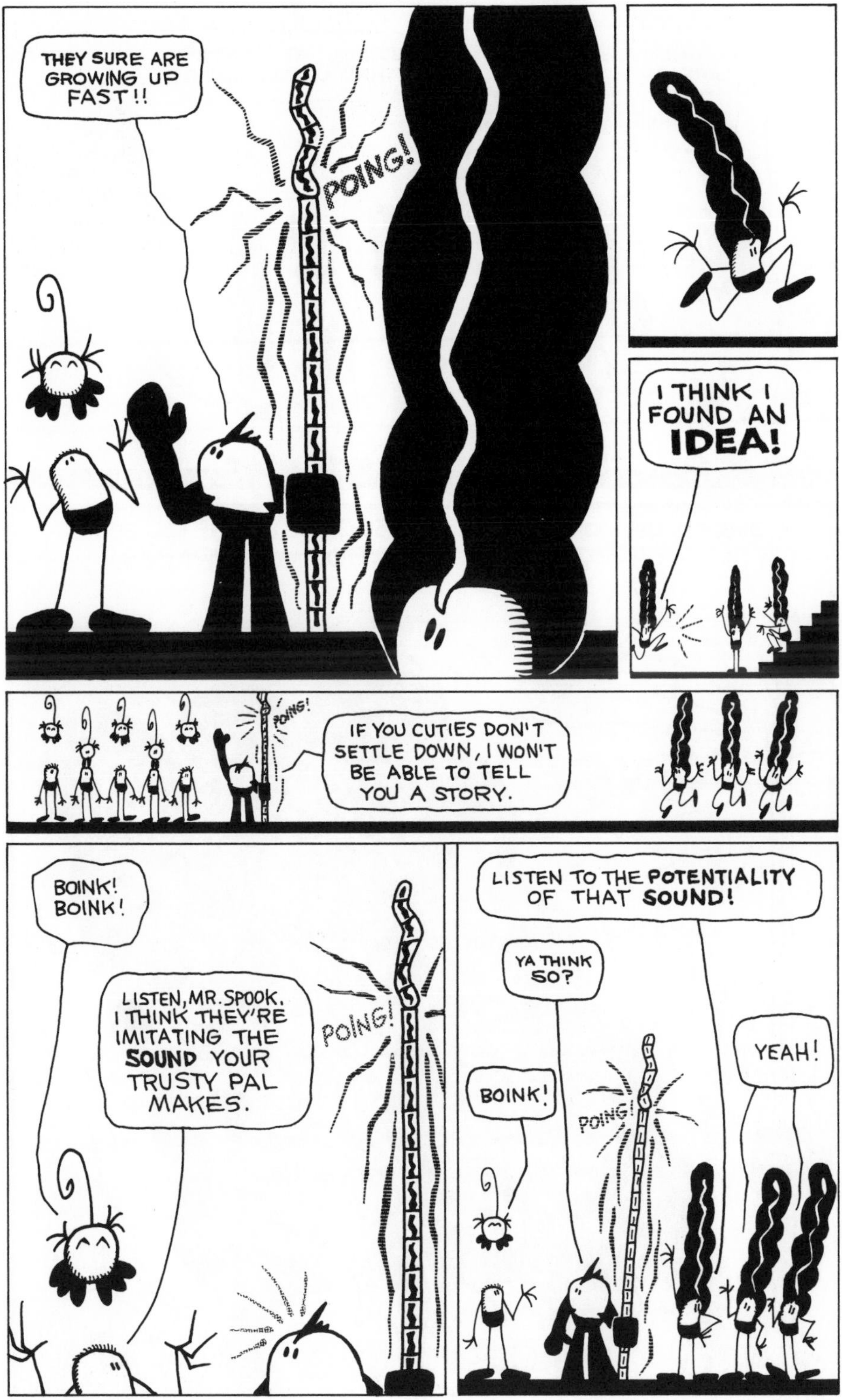
THEY SURE ARE GROWING UP FAST!!
POING!
I THINK I FOUND AN IDEA!
POING!
IF YOU CUTIES DON'T SETTLE DOWN, I WON'T BE ABLE TO TELL YOU A STORY.
BOINK! BOINK!
LISTEN, MR. SPOOK. I THINK THEY'RE IMITATING THE SOUND YOUR TRUSTY PAL MAKES.
POING!
LISTEN TO THE POTENTIALITY OF THAT SOUND!
YA THINK SO?
BOINK!
POING!
YEAH!

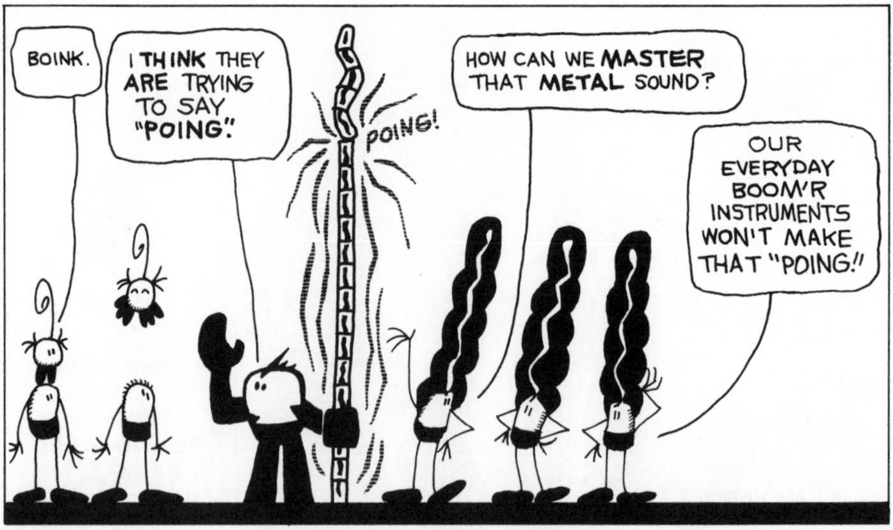
BOINK.
I THINK THEY ARE TRYING TO SAY "POING."
POING!
HOW CAN WE MASTER THAT METAL SOUND?
OUR EVERYDAY BOOM'R INSTRUMENTS WON'T MAKE THAT "POING."

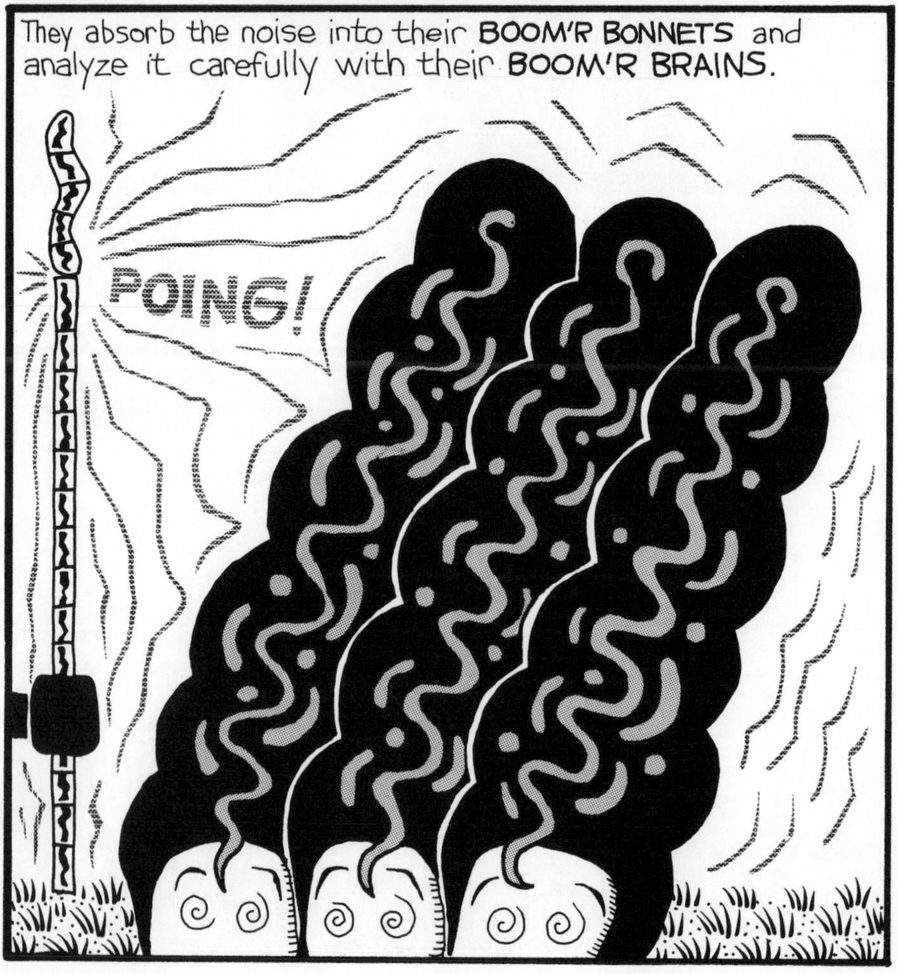
They absorb the noise into their BOOM'R BONNETS and analyze it carefully with their BOOM'R BRAINS.
POING!

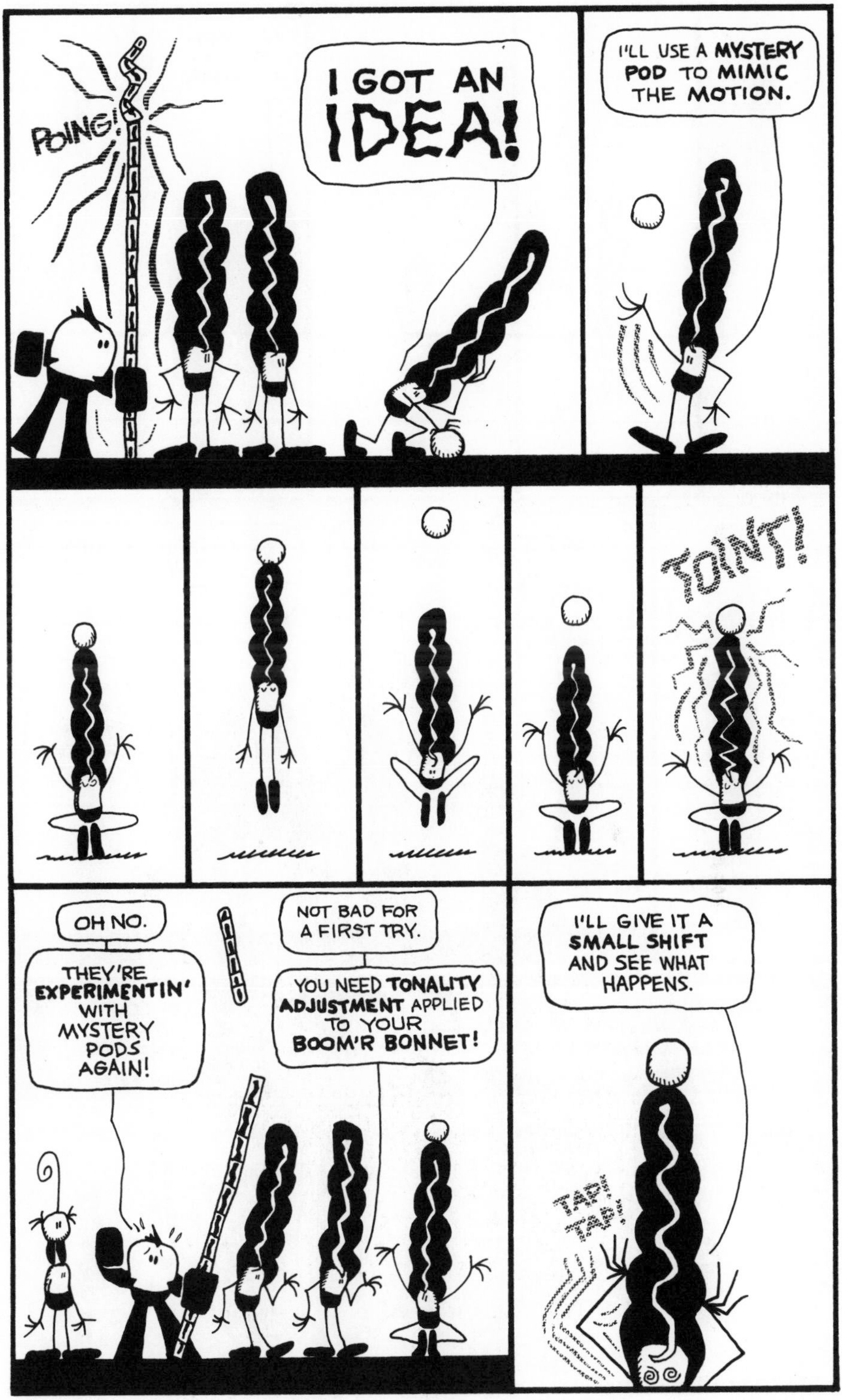

POING!
I GOT AN IDEA!
I'LL USE A MYSTERY POD TO MIMIC THE MOTION.
TOINT!
OH NO.
THEY'RE EXPERIMENTIN' WITH MYSTERY PODS AGAIN!
NOT BAD FOR A FIRST TRY.
YOU NEED TONALITY ADJUSTMENT APPLIED TO YOUR BOOM'R BONNET!
I'LL GIVE IT A SMALL SHIFT AND SEE WHAT HAPPENS.
TAP TAP

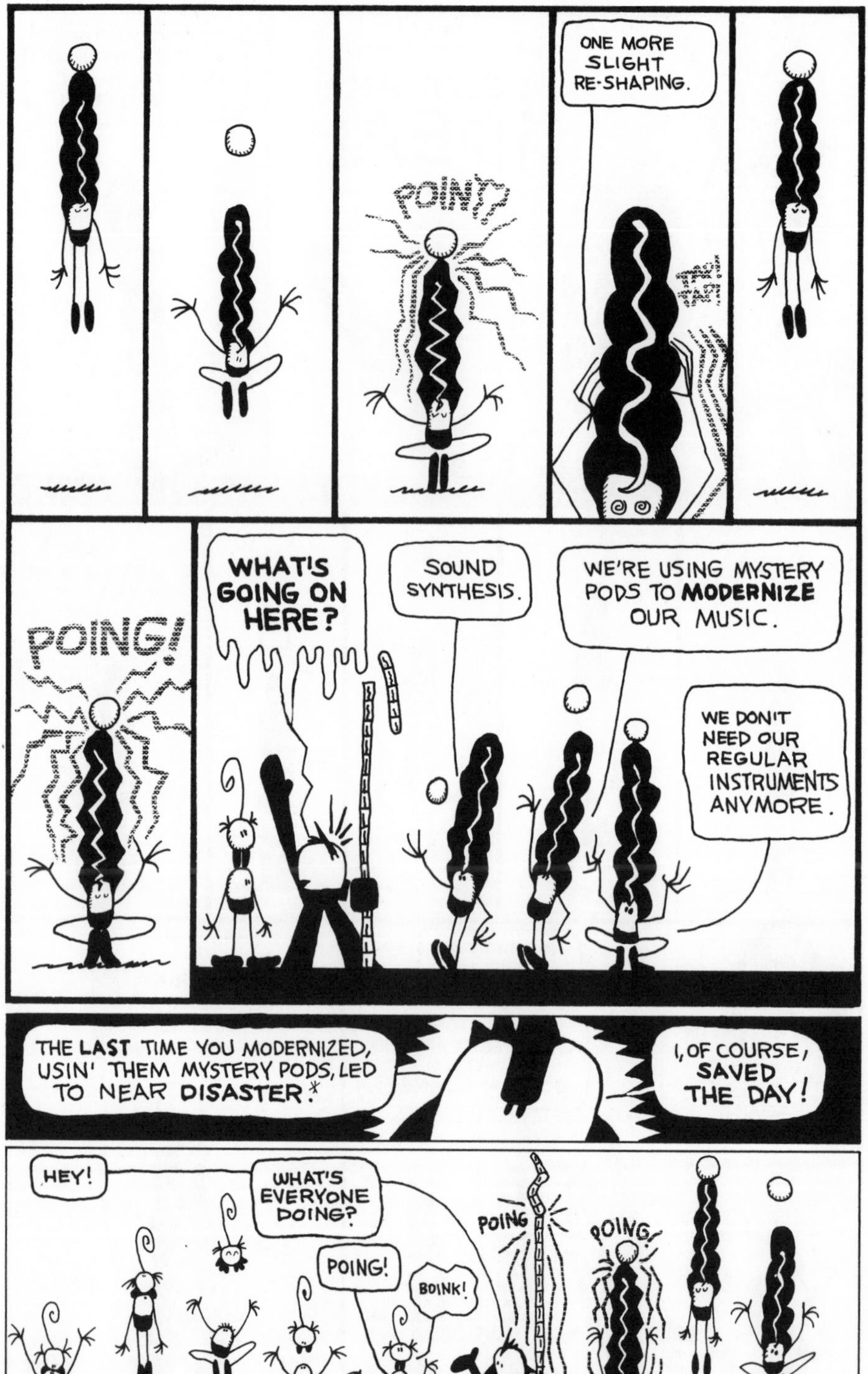
ONE MORE SLIGHT RE-SHAPING.
POING!?
POING!
WHAT'S GOING ON HERE?
SOUND SYNTHESIS.
WE'RE USING MYSTERY PODS TO MODERNIZE OUR MUSIC.
WE DON'T NEED OUR REGULAR INSTRUMENTS ANYMORE.
THE LAST TIME YOU MODERNIZED, USIN' THEM MYSTERY PODS, LED TO NEAR DISASTER.*
I, OF COURSE, SAVED THE DAY!
HEY!
WHAT'S EVERYONE DOING?
POING!
BOINK!
POING
POING!

*BOOK ONE – "Yeah! Yeah! The Clang Twang!"

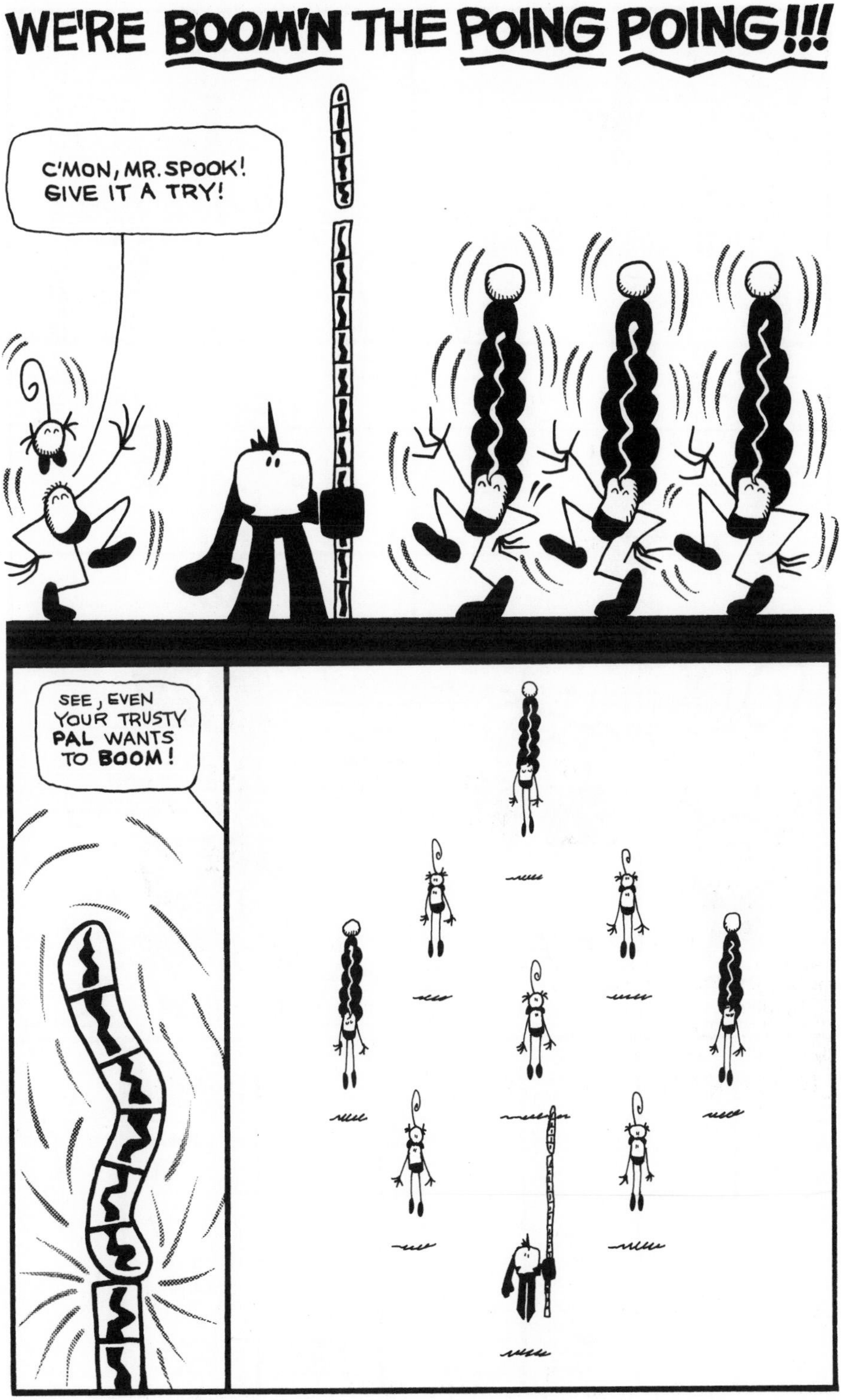
WE'RE BOOM'N THE POING POING!!!
C'MON, MR. SPOOK! GIVE IT A TRY!
SEE, EVEN YOUR TRUSTY PAL WANTS TO BOOM!

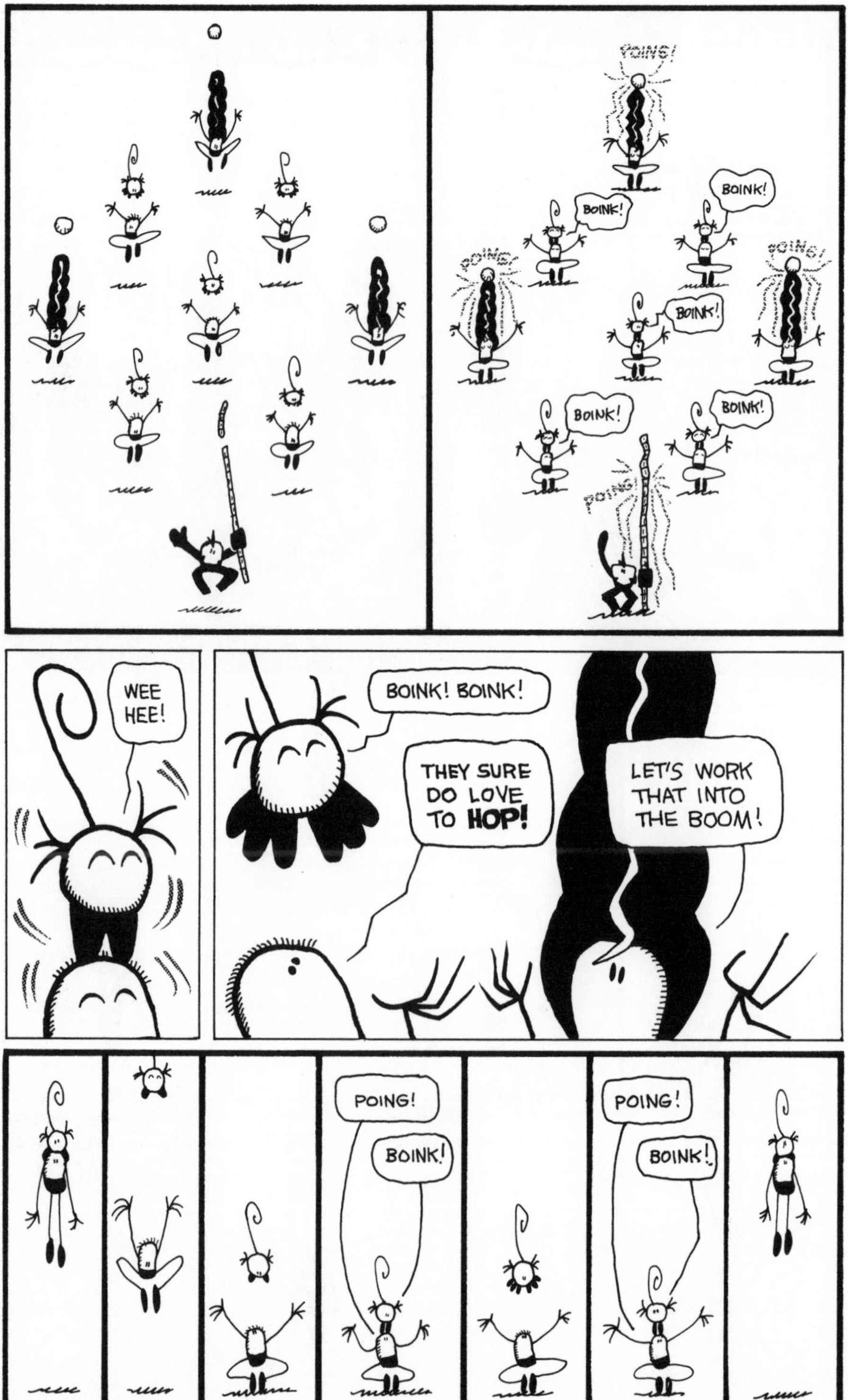
POING!
BOINK!
BOINK!
POING!
POING!
BOINK!
BOINK!
BOINK!
POING!
WEE HEE!
BOINK! BOINK!
THEY SURE DO LOVE TO **HOP!**
LET'S WORK THAT INTO THE BOOM!
POING!
BOINK!
POING!
BOINK!

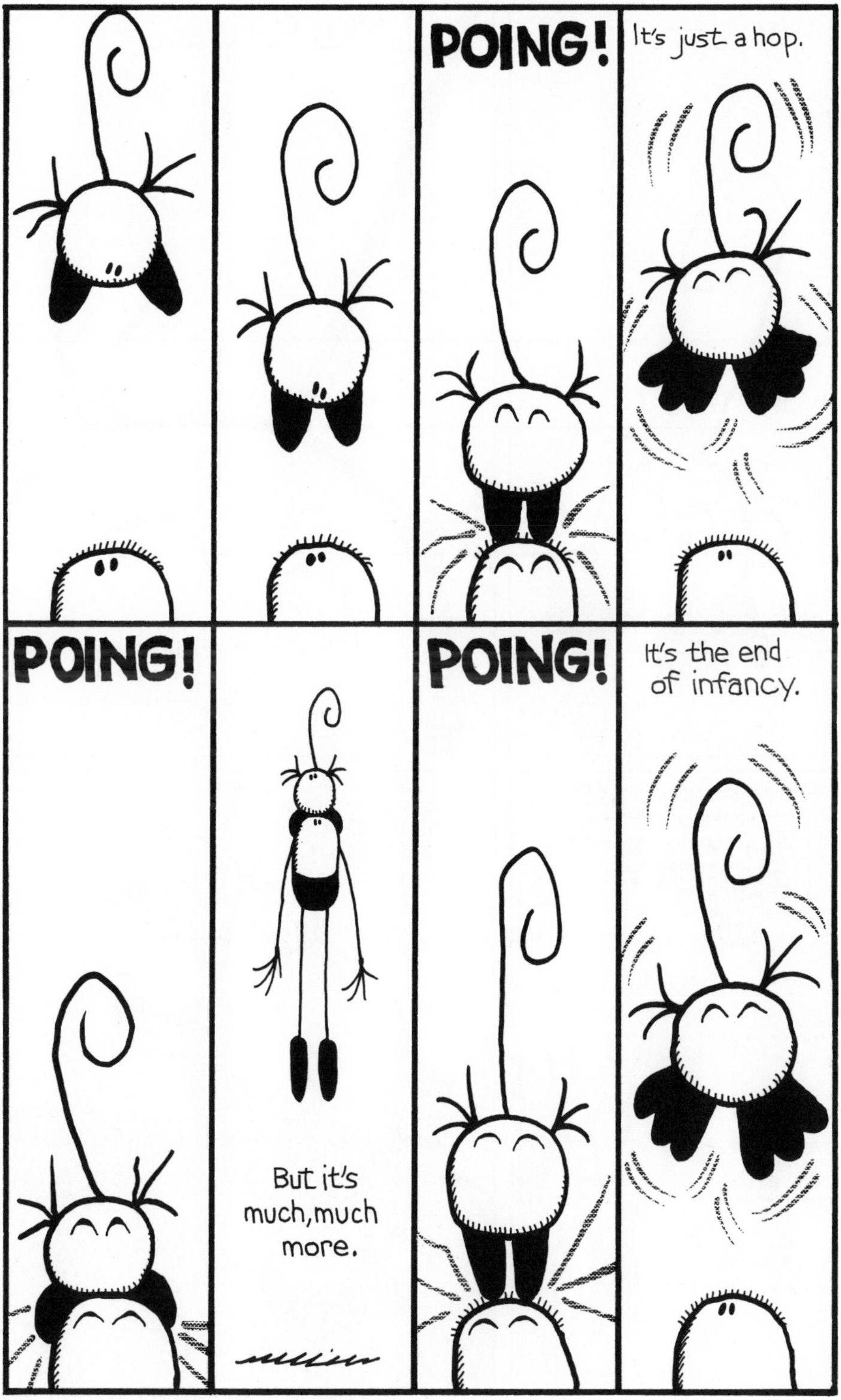
POING!
It's just a hop.
POING!
But it's much, much more.
POING!
It's the end of infancy.

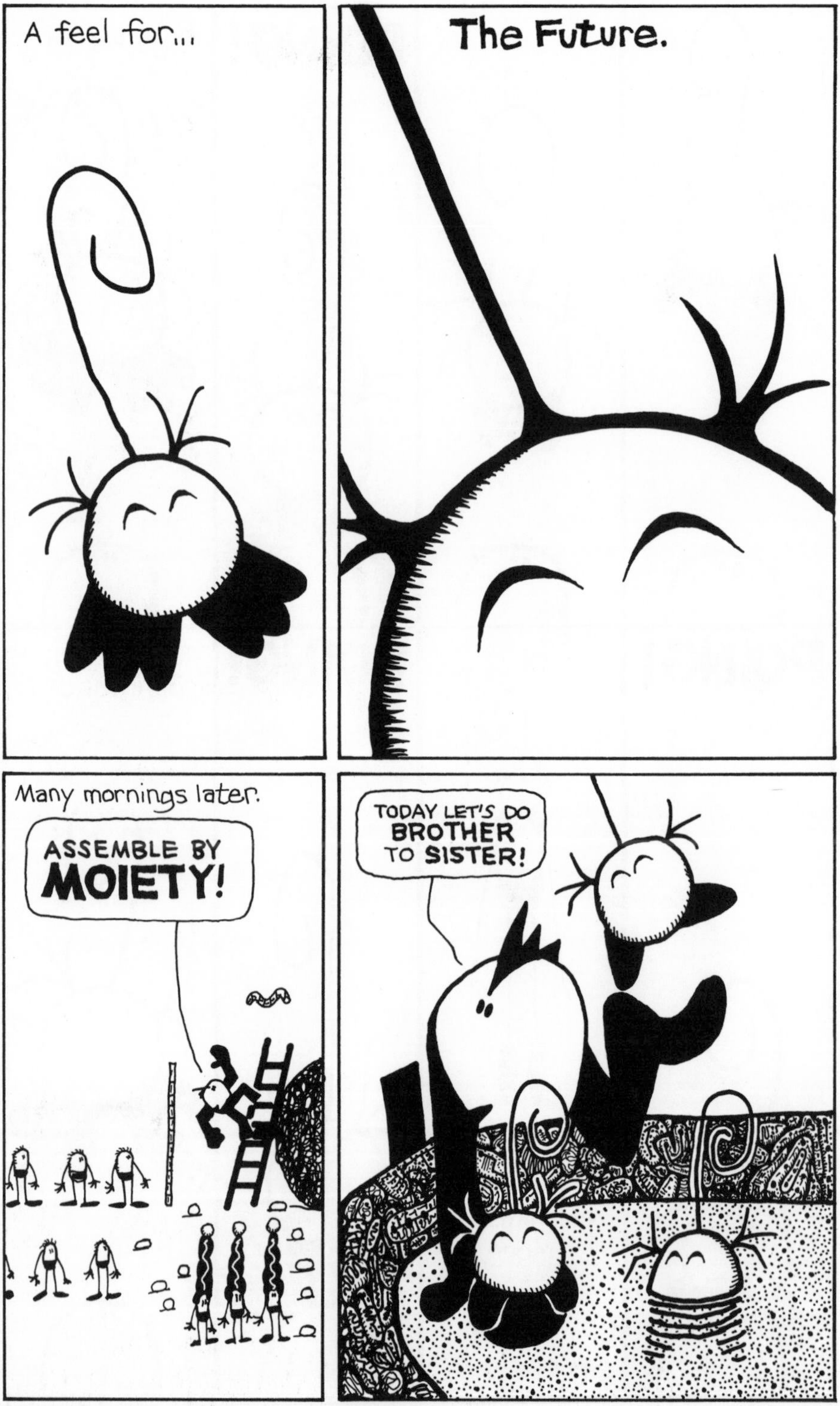
A feel for...
The Future.
Many mornings later.
ASSEMBLE BY MOIETY!
TODAY LET'S DO BROTHER TO SISTER!

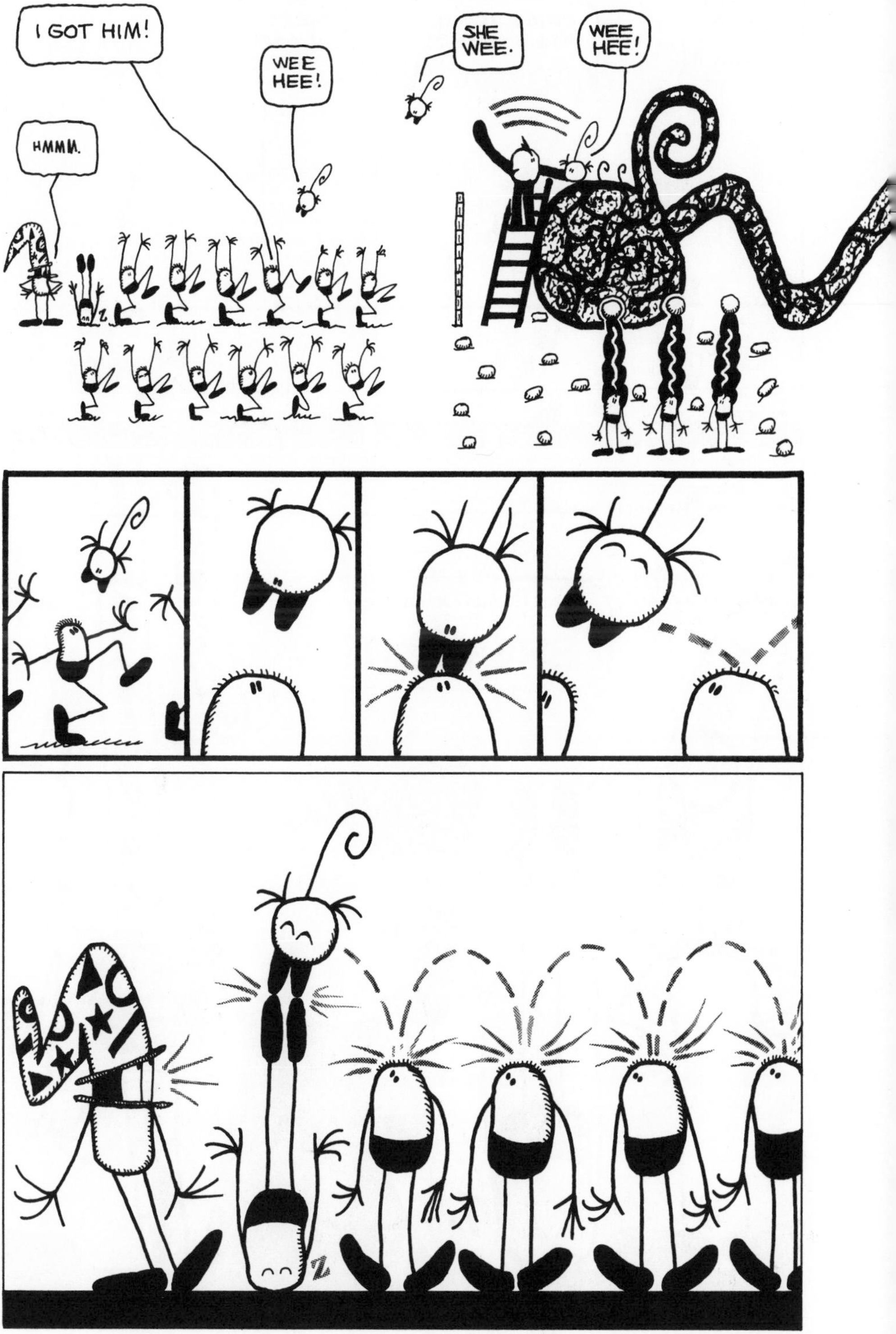
HMMM.
I GOT HIM!
WEE HEE!
SHE WEE.
WEE HEE!

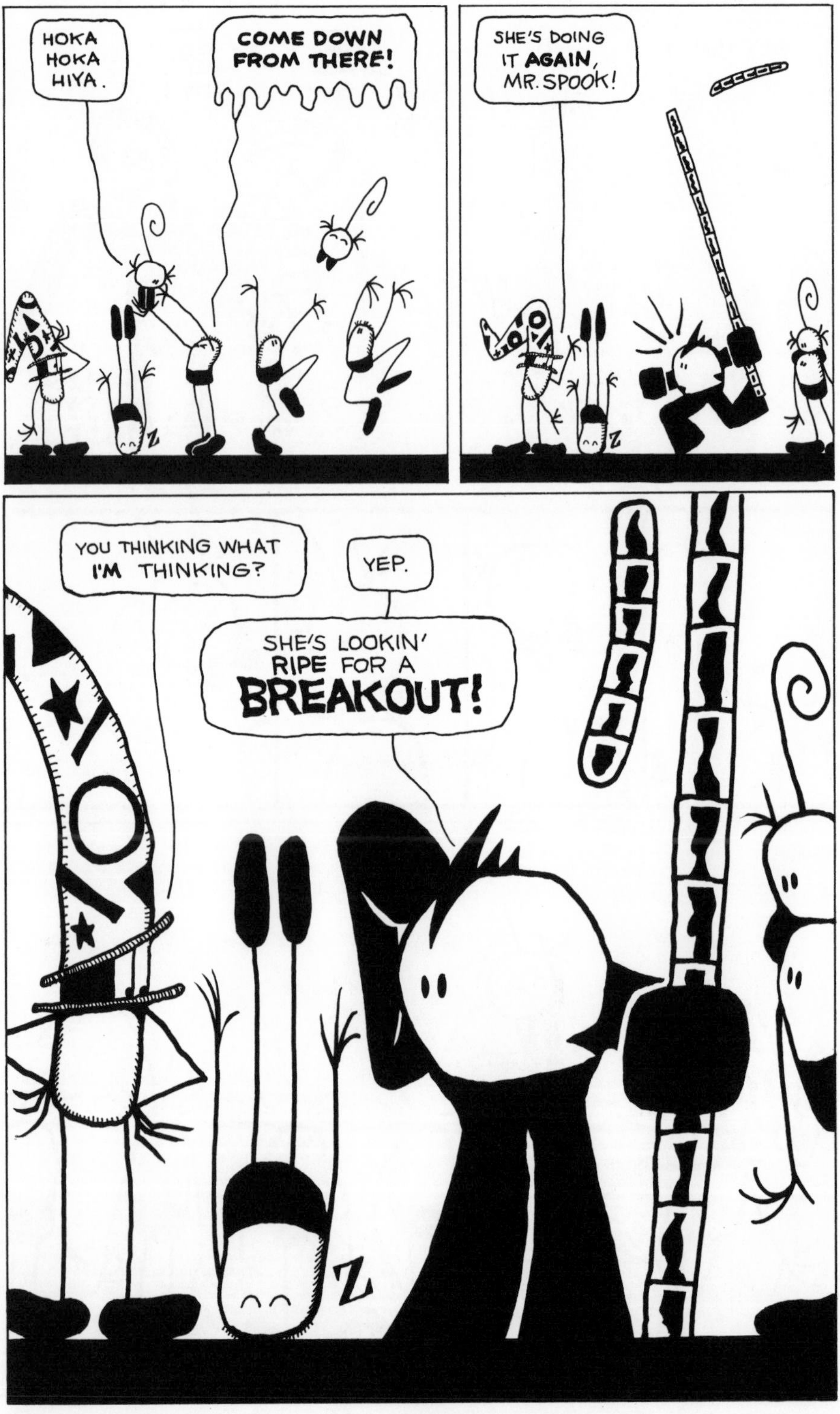
HOKA HOKA HIYA.
COME DOWN FROM THERE!
SHE'S DOING IT AGAIN, MR. SPOOK!
YOU THINKING WHAT I'M THINKING?
YEP.
SHE'S LOOKIN' RIPE FOR A BREAKOUT!

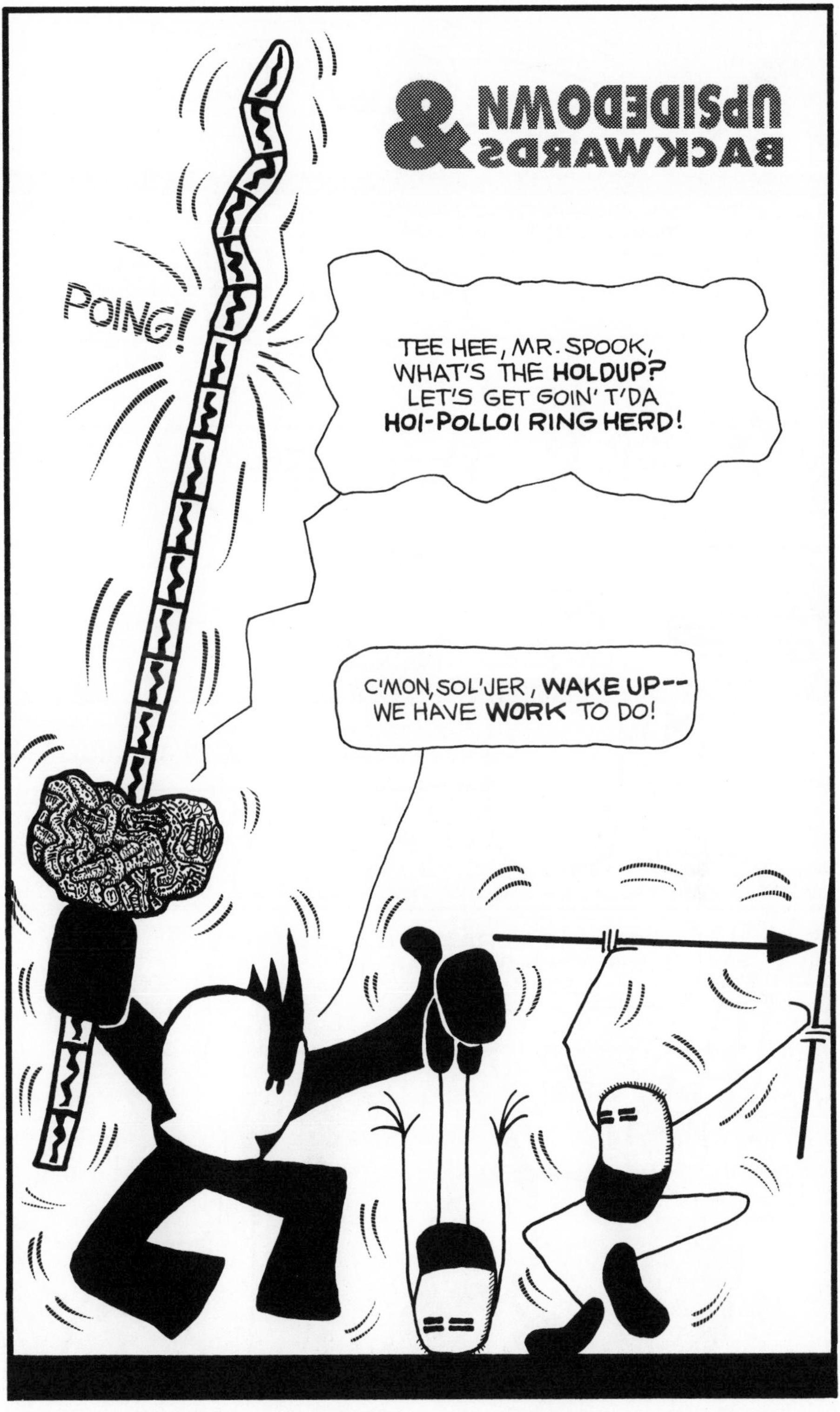

UPSIDEDOWN & BACKWARDS
POING!
TEE HEE, MR. SPOOK, WHAT'S THE HOLDUP? LET'S GET GOIN' T'DA HOI-POLLOI RING HERD!
C'MON, SOL'JER, WAKE UP-- WE HAVE WORK TO DO!

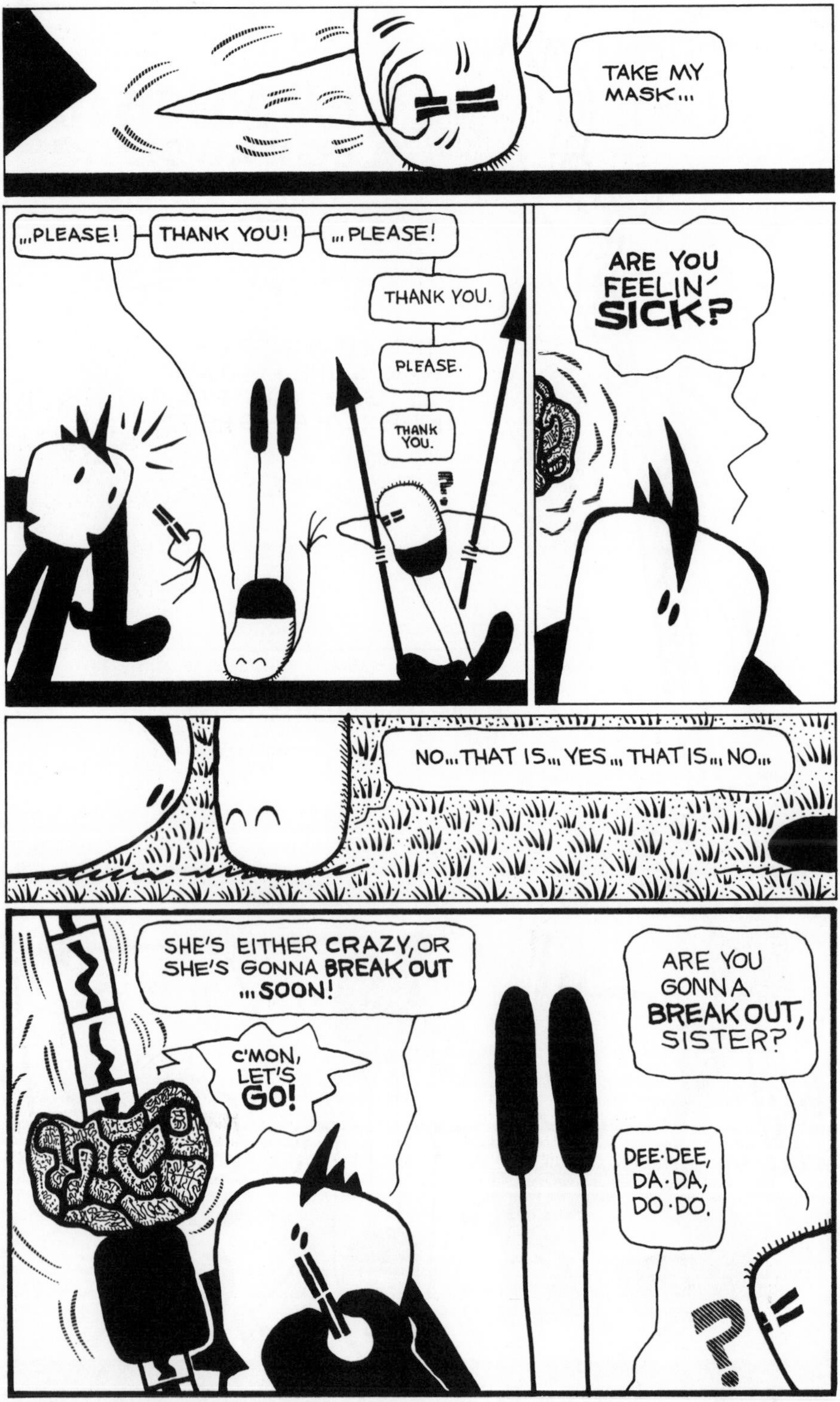
TAKE MY MASK...
...PLEASE!
THANK YOU!
...PLEASE!
THANK YOU.
PLEASE.
THANK YOU.
ARE YOU FEELIN' SICK?
NO... THAT IS... YES... THAT IS... NO...
SHE'S EITHER CRAZY, OR SHE'S GONNA BREAK OUT ...SOON!
C'MON, LET'S GO!
ARE YOU GONNA BREAK OUT, SISTER?
DEE·DEE, DA·DA, DO·DO.

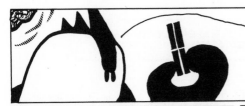

C'MON, LET'S GO, FLANK'RS, WE **GOTTA** GET US A **NEW SISTER** TO FILL THIS **MASK**!!

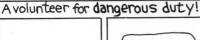

A volunteer for **dangerous duty!**

MAY YOUR AIM BE TRUE!

A smaller CHOW SOL'JER ARMY departs to swipe CHOW from the HOI-POLLOI RING HERD!

Meanwhile, BEANISH and PROFESSOR GARBANZO ponder:

MAYBE SHE **IS** SICK. PERHAPS SHE HAS AN **EATING DISORDER** AND IS STARVING TO DEATH!

MAYBE... I THINK SHE **IS** ABOUT TO **BREAK OUT.**

SHE'S JUST GOING ABOUT IT **TOTALLY BACKWARDS.**

WHICH IN A **WEIRD WAY** MAKES A LOT OF **SENSE...**

...BECAUSE SHE'S DOING **EVERYTHING** UPSIDEDOWN OR BACKWARDS!

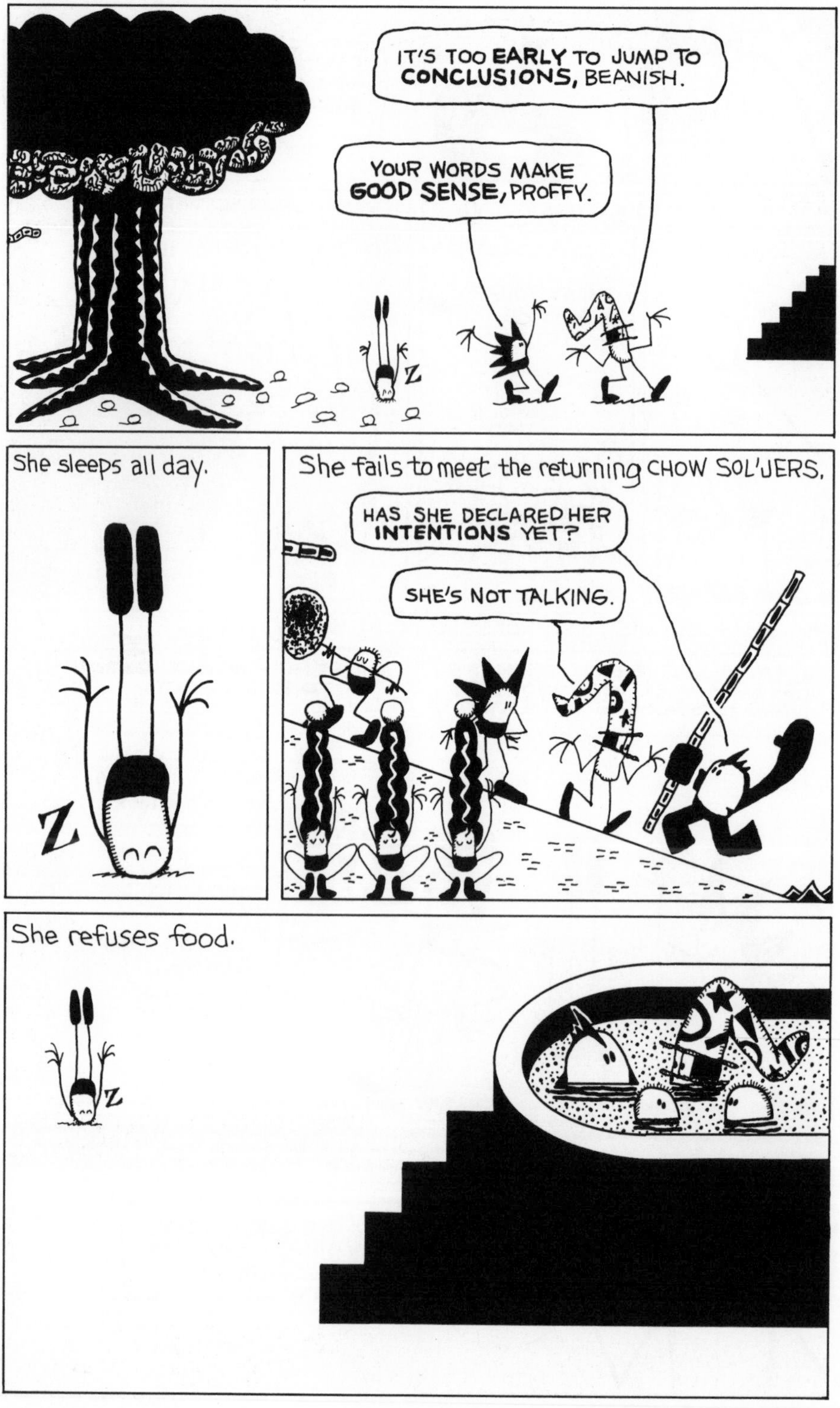

IT'S TOO EARLY TO JUMP TO CONCLUSIONS, BEANISH.
YOUR WORDS MAKE GOOD SENSE, PROFFY.
Z
She sleeps all day.
Z
She fails to meet the returning CHOW SOL'JERS.
HAS SHE DECLARED HER INTENTIONS YET?
SHE'S NOT TALKING.
She refuses food.
Z

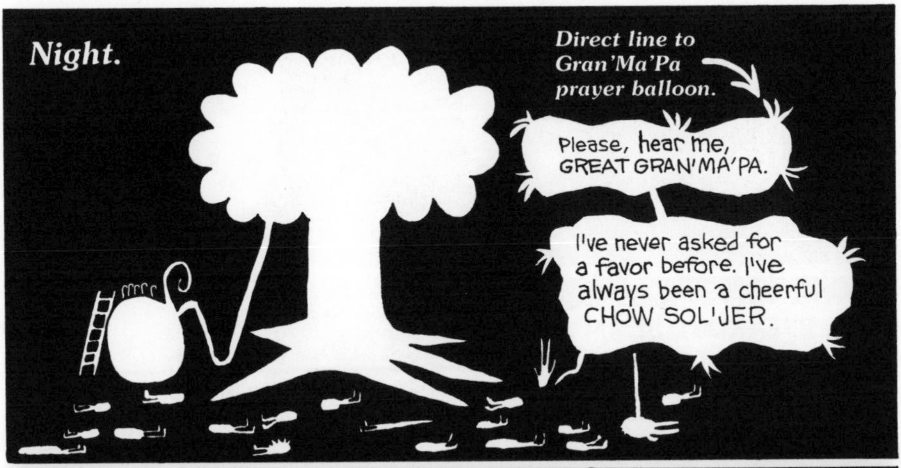
Night.
Direct line to Gran'Ma'Pa prayer balloon.
Please, hear me, GREAT GRAN'MA'PA.
I've never asked for a favor before. I've always been a cheerful CHOW SOL'JER.

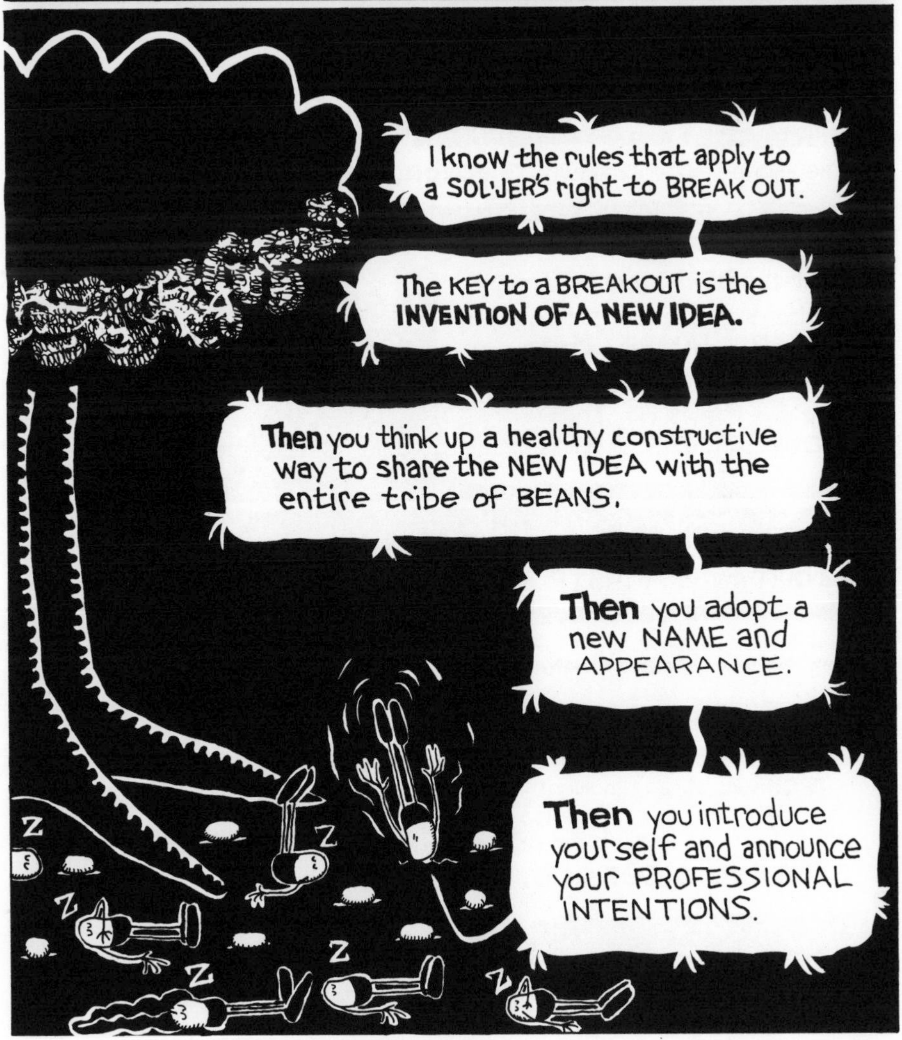
I know the rules that apply to a SOL'JER'S right to BREAK OUT.
The KEY to a BREAKOUT is the INVENTION OF A NEW IDEA.
Then you think up a healthy constructive way to share the NEW IDEA with the entire tribe of BEANS.
Then you adopt a new NAME and APPEARANCE.
Then you introduce yourself and announce your PROFESSIONAL INTENTIONS.
Z
Z
Z
Z
Z
Z

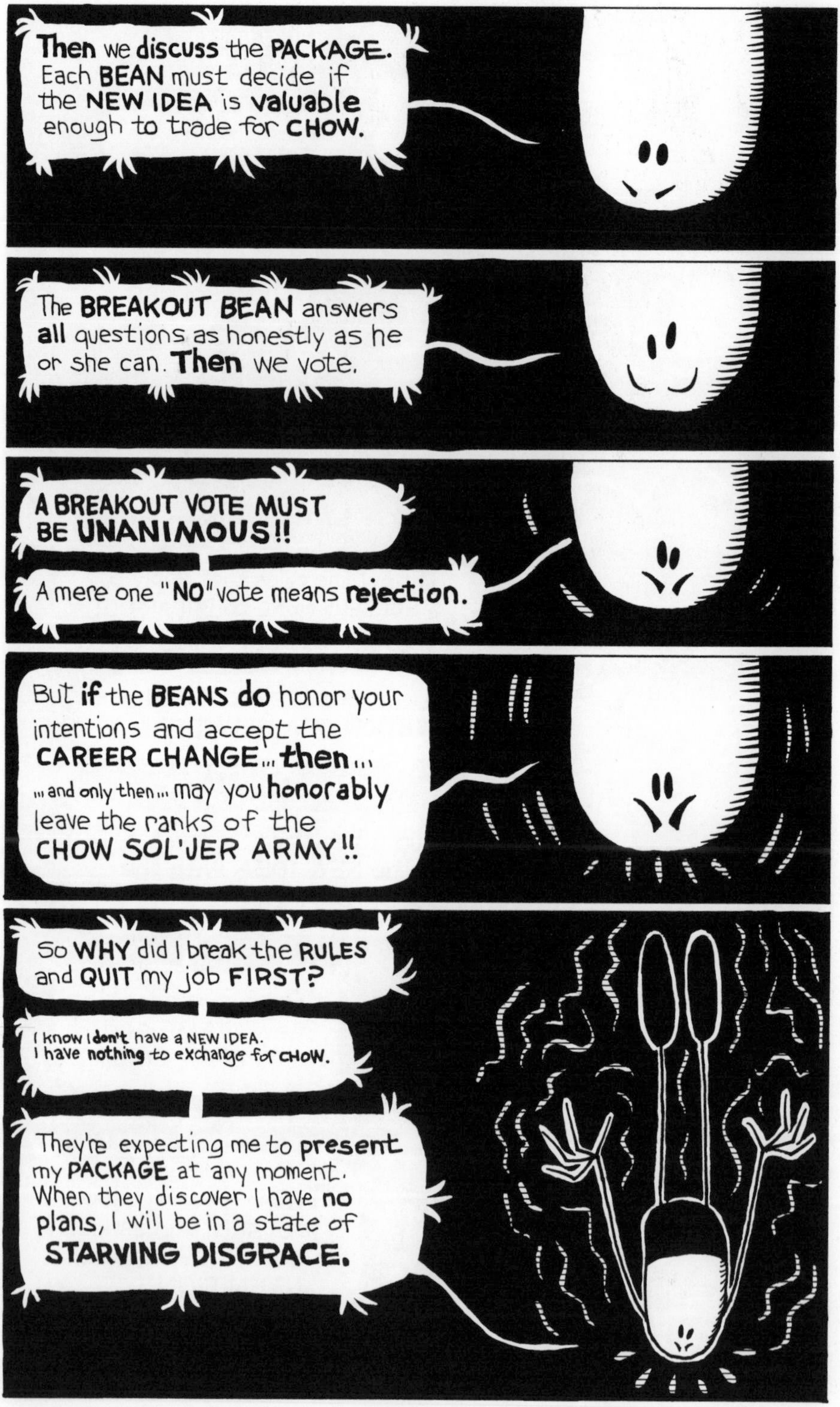
Then we discuss the PACKAGE. Each BEAN must decide if the NEW IDEA is valuable enough to trade for CHOW.
The BREAKOUT BEAN answers all questions as honestly as he or she can. Then we vote.
A BREAKOUT VOTE MUST BE UNANIMOUS!!
A mere one "NO" vote means rejection.
But if the BEANS do honor your intentions and accept the CAREER CHANGE... then... ...and only then... may you honorably leave the ranks of the CHOW SOL'JER ARMY!!
So WHY did I break the RULES and QUIT my job FIRST?
I know I don't have a NEW IDEA. I have nothing to exchange for CHOW.
They're expecting me to present my PACKAGE at any moment. When they discover I have no plans, I will be in a state of STARVING DISGRACE.

Am I sick? Crazy?

Please help me, GRAN'MA'PA!

RISE & SHINE, BEANWORLD!

Every morning MR. SPOOK assesses GRAN'MA'PA for the daily agenda.

GRAN'MA'PA SHAKES! LOOKS LIKE WE'RE **WORKIN'** TODAY!

SLEEPING AGAIN? MAYBE SHE **IS** SICK!!

POING!

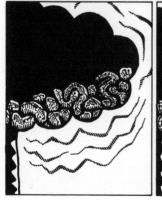

FIZ!

HEY! THAT'S NOT A SPROUT-BUTT!

It's the answer to an anguished prayer.

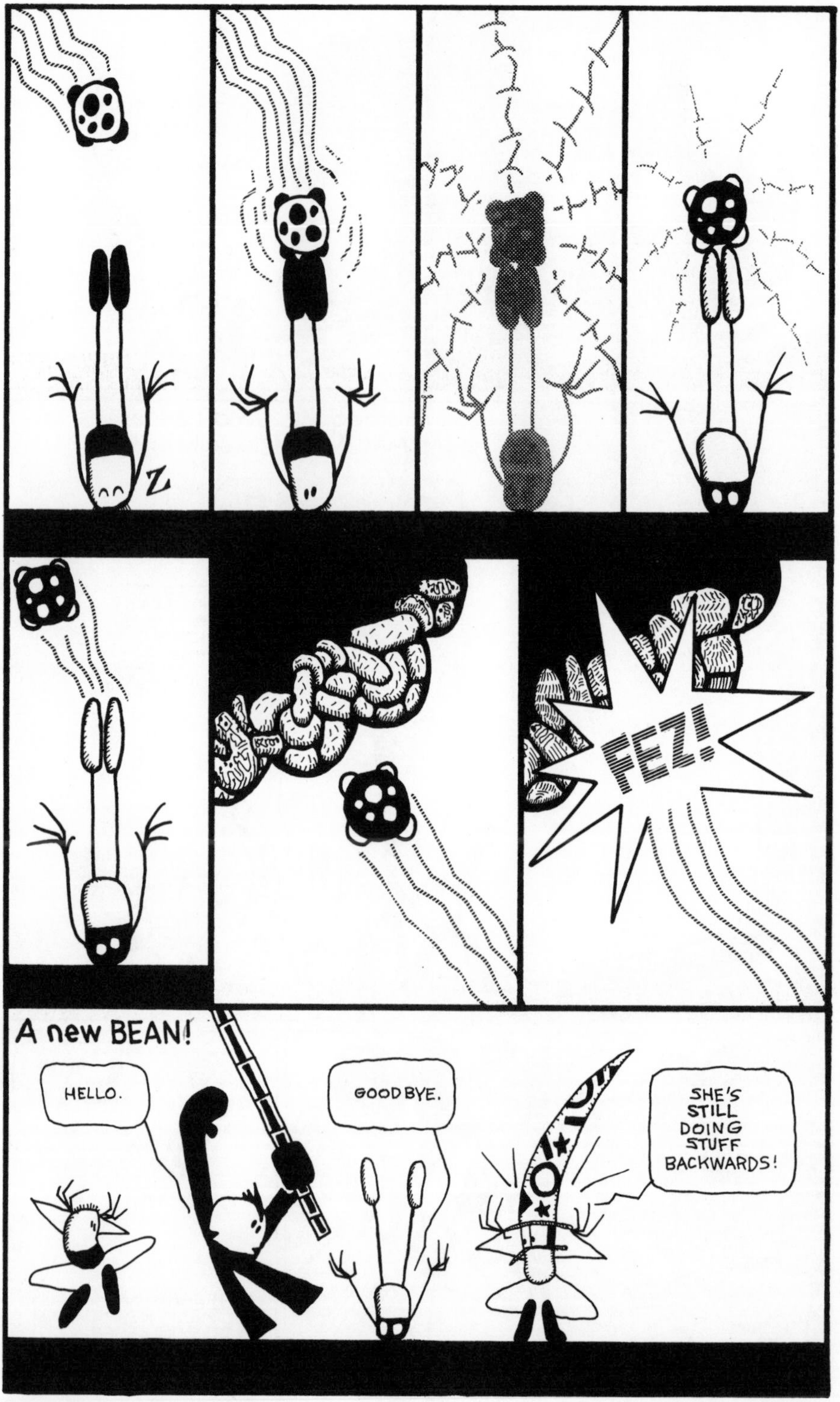
FEZ!
A new BEAN!
HELLO.
GOODBYE.
SHE'S STILL DOING STUFF BACKWARDS!

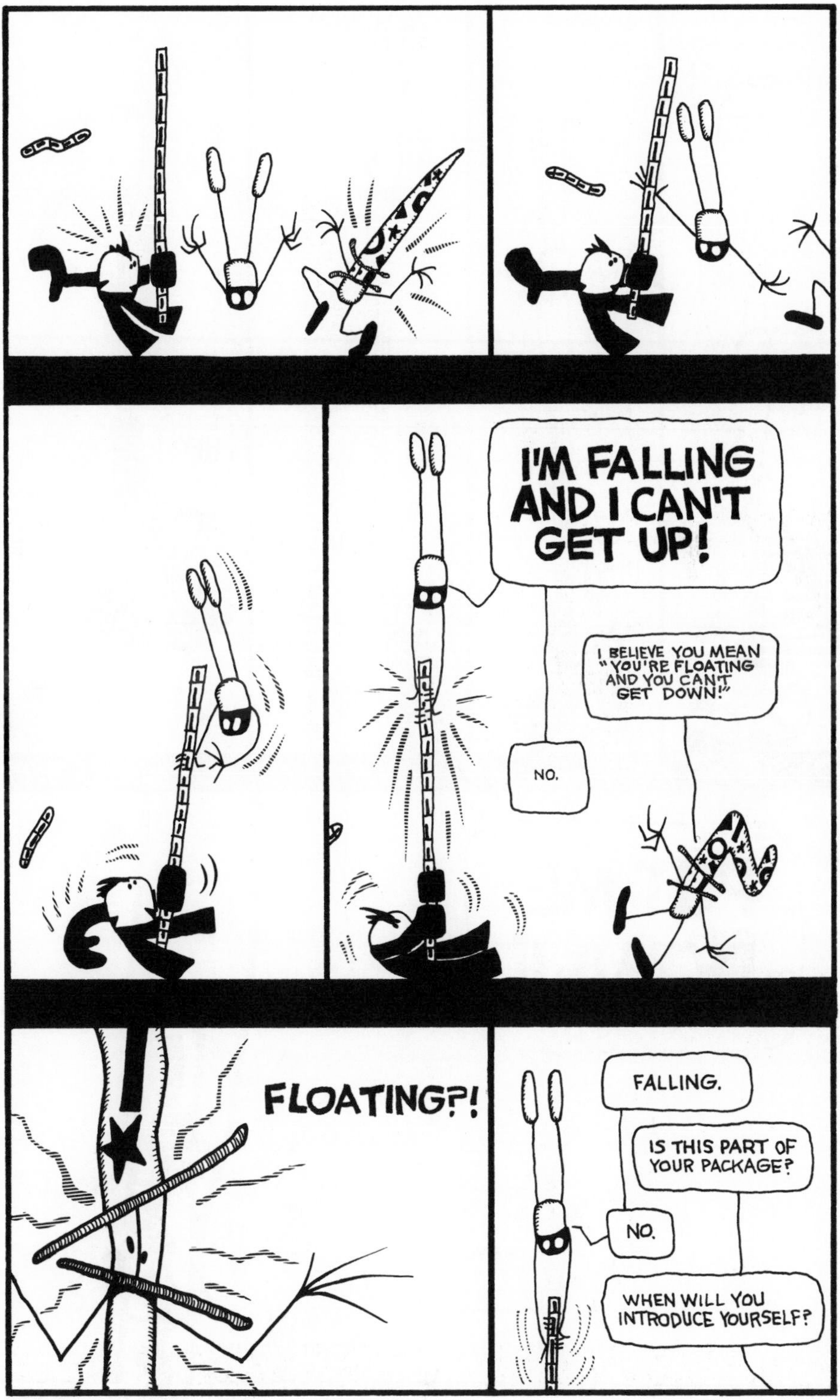
I'M FALLING AND I CAN'T GET UP!
I BELIEVE YOU MEAN "YOU'RE FLOATING AND YOU CAN'T GET DOWN!"
NO.
FLOATING?!
FALLING.
IS THIS PART OF YOUR PACKAGE?
NO.
WHEN WILL YOU INTRODUCE YOURSELF?

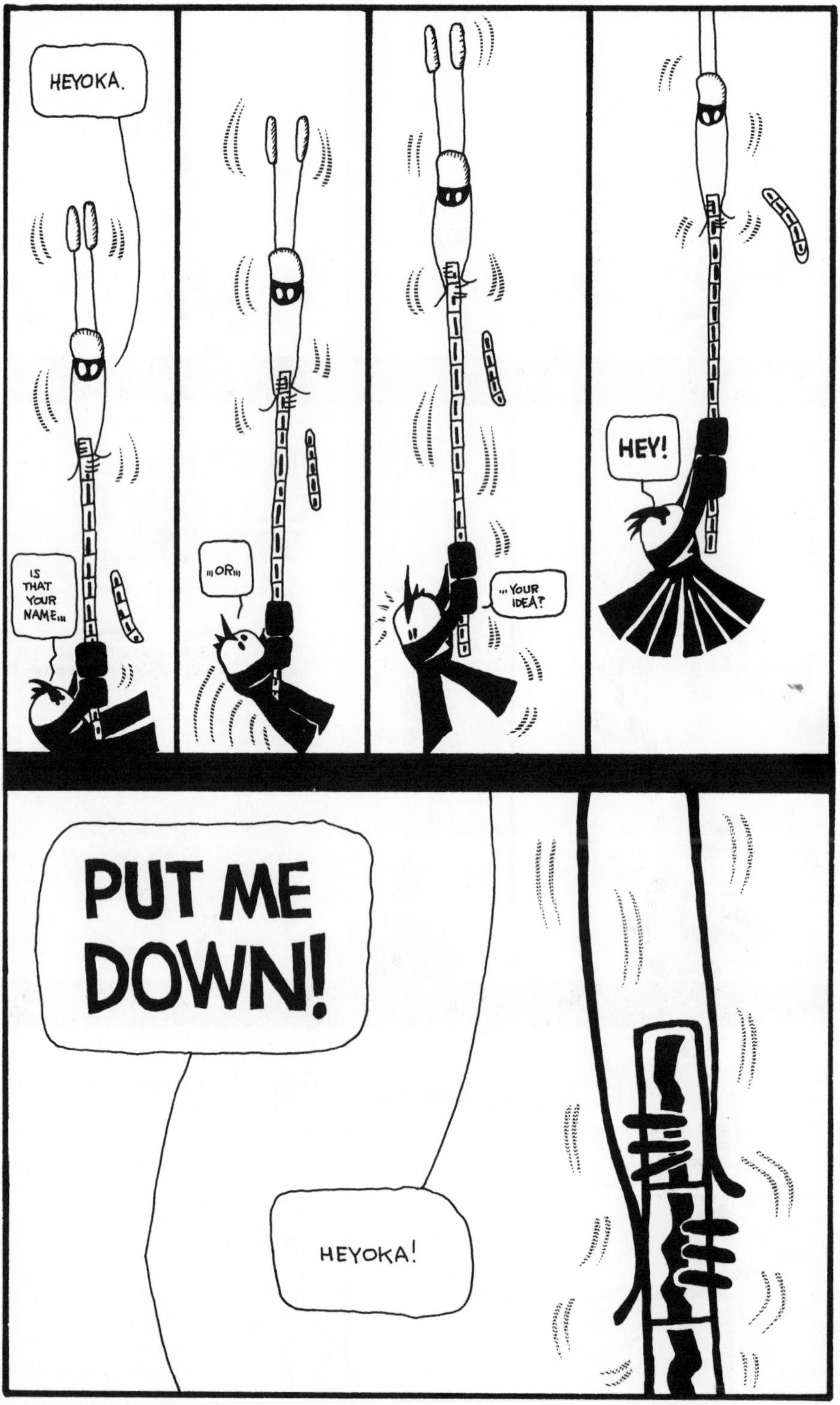
HEYOKA.
IS THAT YOUR NAME...
...OR...
...YOUR IDEA?
HEY!
PUT ME DOWN!
HEYOKA!

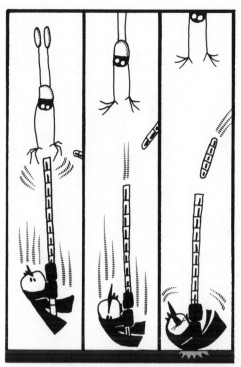

HELLO.

LOOK AT HER **GO**, PROFFY!

I WONDER IF SHE'LL COME RIGHT DOWN LIKE BEANISH DOES?

BEANISH?

BEANISH KNOWS HOW TO **FLY**?

NOT EXACTLY, MR. SPOOK.

TELL ME EXACTLY WHAT BEANISH **DOES**!

BEANISH JUMPS.

er, uh, REAL H-HIGH...

And thus HEYOKA, the UPSIDEDOWN and BACKWARDS BEAN, leaves home!

HOW LONG HAS THIS **JUMPIN' STUFF** BEEN GOIN' ON?

"er,"

UNGUNK'L'DUNKED from everything she has ever known.

She's not afraid. She's not sad. She's

HEYOKA.

Yeah.

Tales of Heyoka

Still falling up, **Heyoka** runs into the **Inspiration Constellation!**

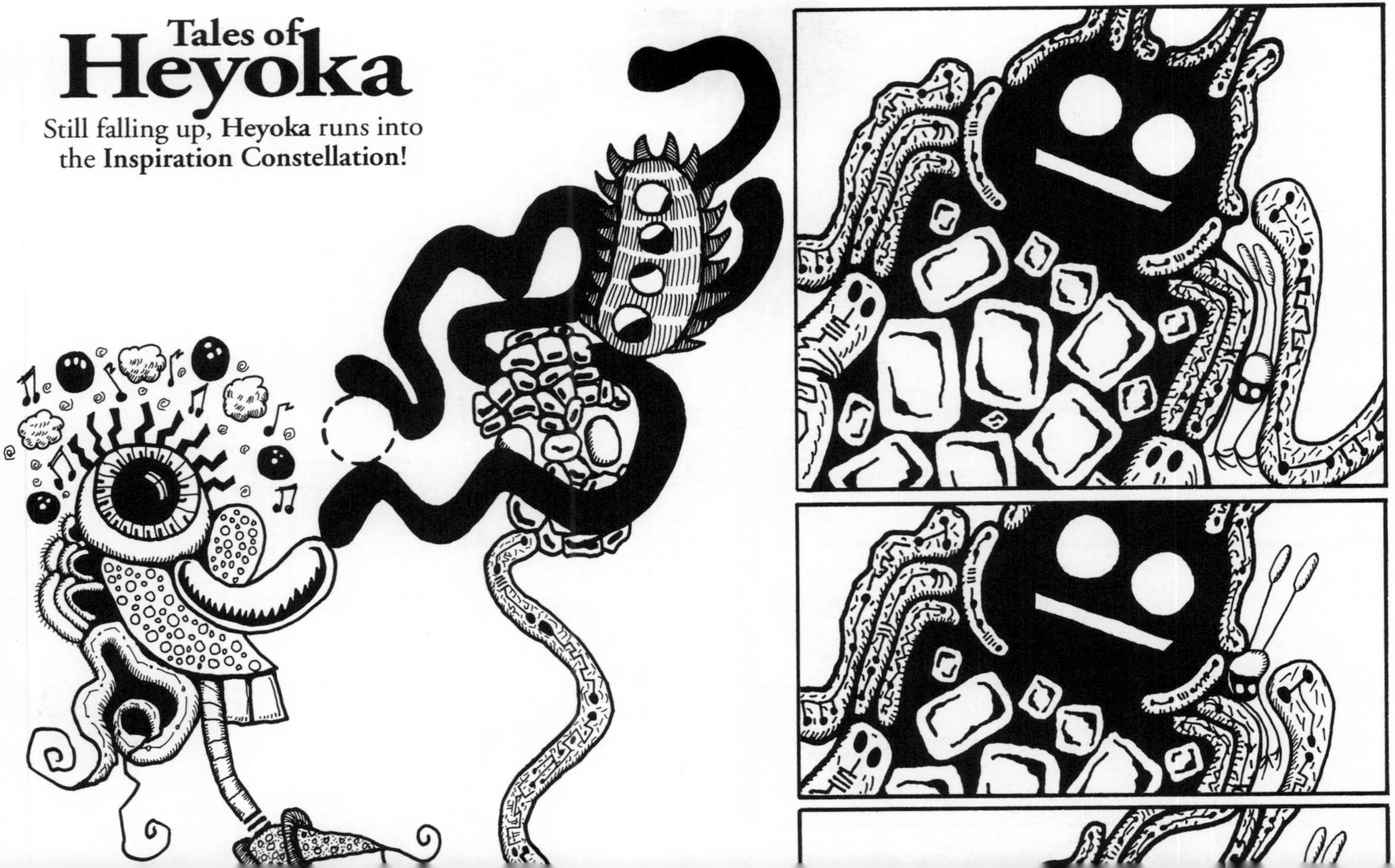

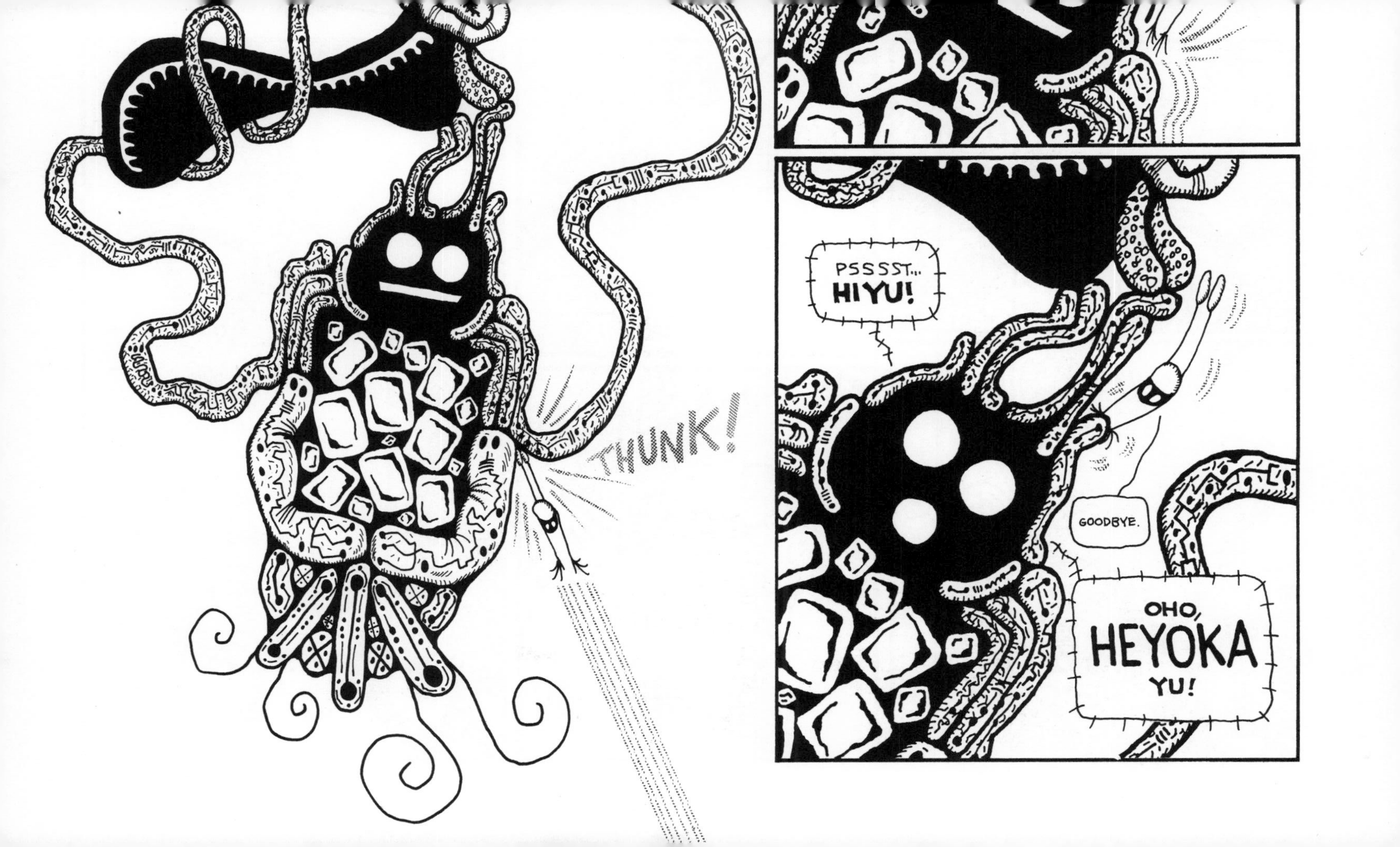
THUNK!
PSSSST... HIYU!
GOODBYE.
OHO, HEYOKA YU!

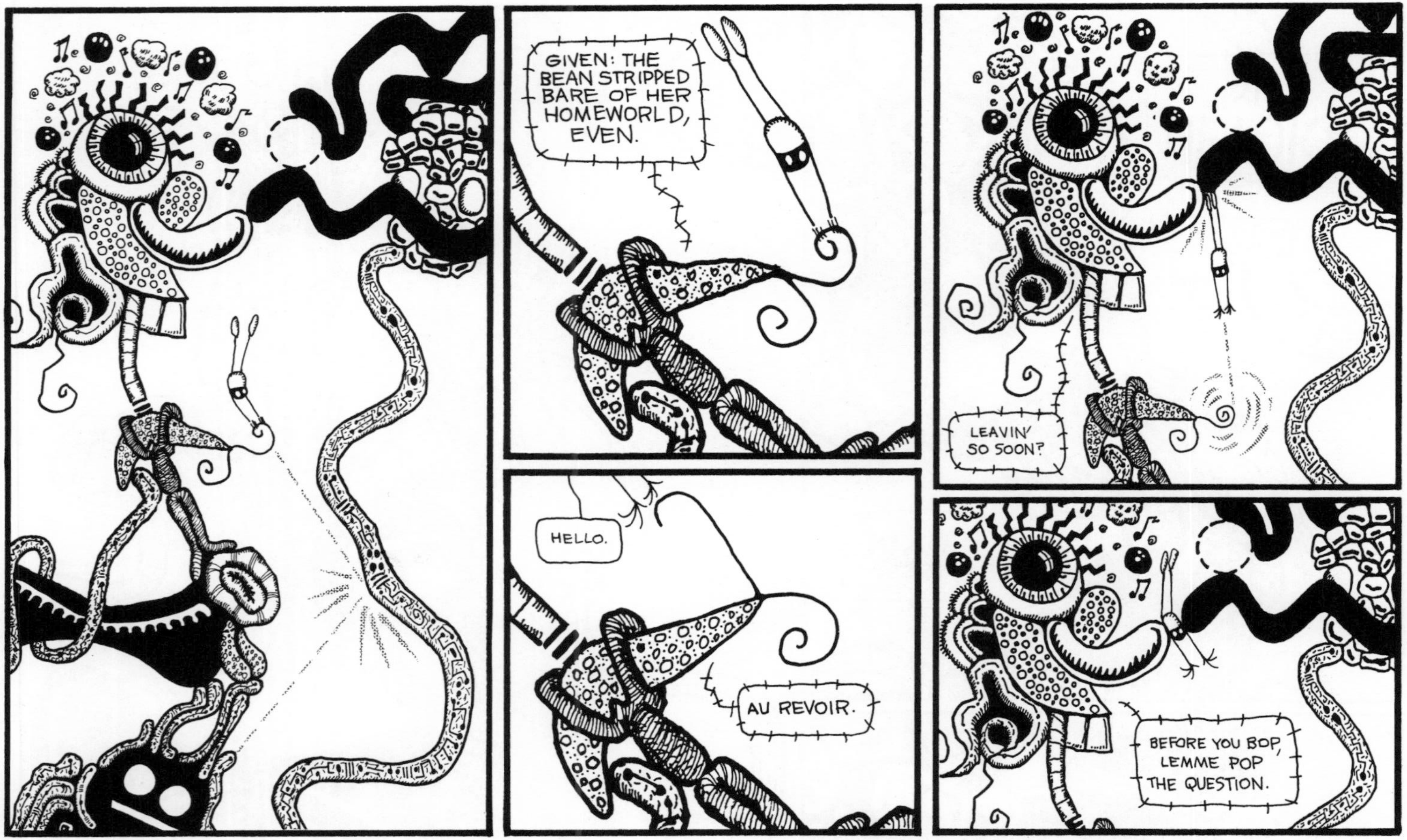
GIVEN: THE BEAN STRIPPED BARE OF HER HOMEWORLD, EVEN.
HELLO.
AU REVOIR.
LEAVIN' SO SOON?
BEFORE YOU BOP, LEMME POP THE QUESTION.

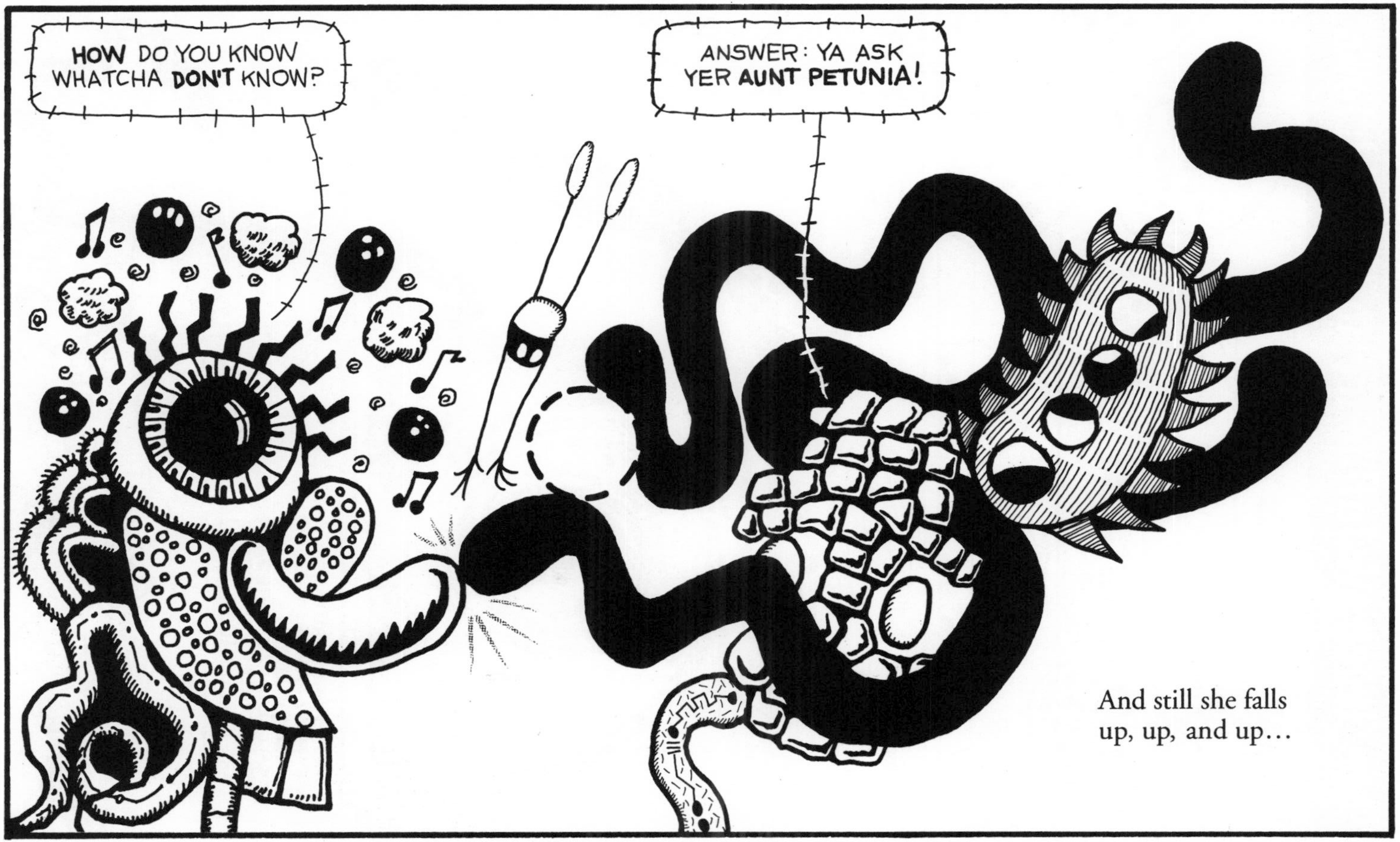
HOW DO YOU KNOW WHATCHA DON'T KNOW?
ANSWER: YA ASK YER AUNT PETUNIA!
And still she falls up, up, and up…

Mr. Teach'm's Influence and World Tour.

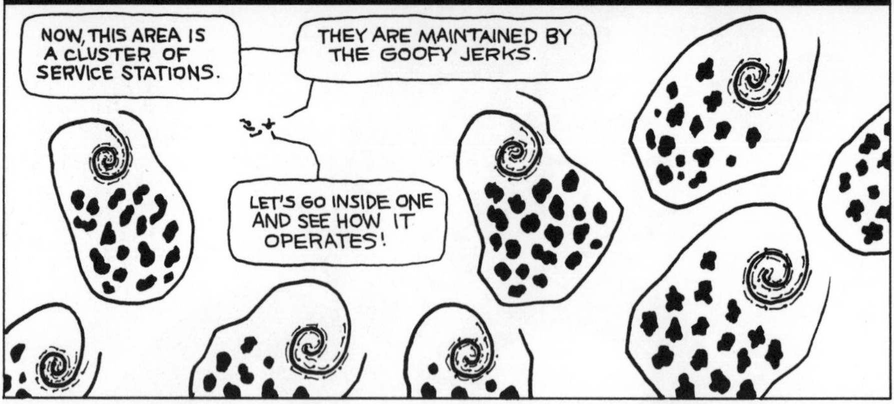
NOW, THIS AREA IS A CLUSTER OF SERVICE STATIONS.
THEY ARE MAINTAINED BY THE GOOFY JERKS.
LET'S GO INSIDE ONE AND SEE HOW IT OPERATES!

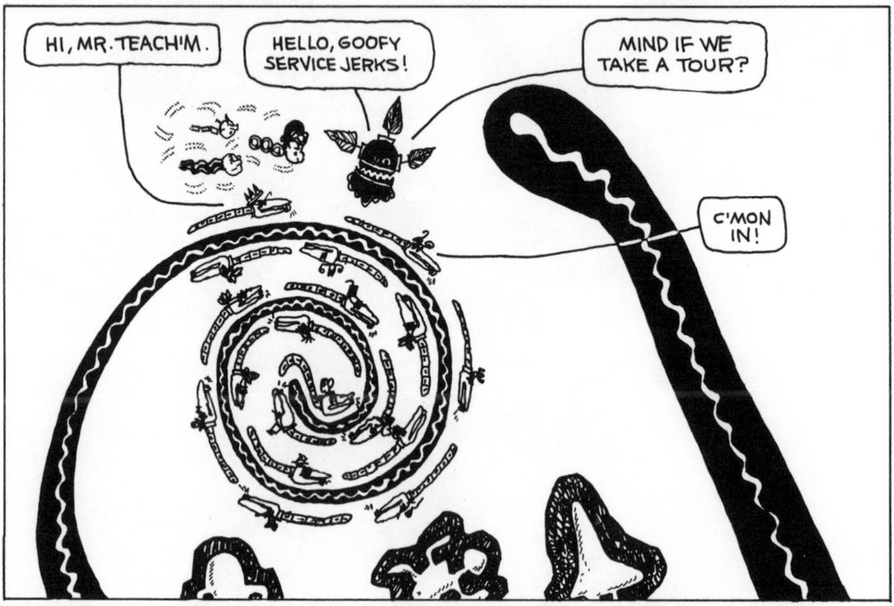
HI, MR. TEACH'M.
HELLO, GOOFY SERVICE JERKS!
MIND IF WE TAKE A TOUR?
C'MON IN!

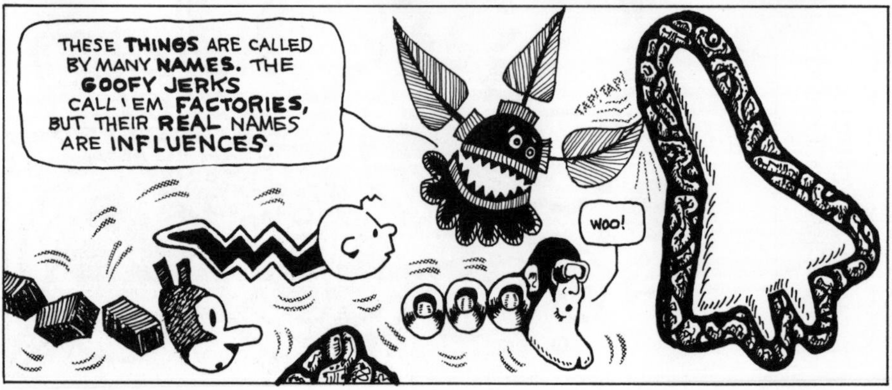
THESE THINGS ARE CALLED BY MANY NAMES. THE GOOFY JERKS CALL 'EM FACTORIES, BUT THEIR REAL NAMES ARE INFLUENCES.
TAP! TAP!
WOO!

EVERY **WORLD** HAS ITS OWN **INFLUENCE**.

EVERY **INFLUENCE** HAS ITS OWN **WORLD**!

IT'S SAID, BY SOME, THAT ONCE UPON A TIME, ALL THE **WORLDS** AND **INFLUENCES** LIVED TOGETHER IN **PERFECT HARMONY**.

WELL, IT AIN'T LIKE THAT NOW! THE **WORLDS** AND **INFLUENCES** ARE **SCATTERED** ALL OVER THE **BIG·BIG·PICTURE**.

WHEN A **WORLD** ITCHES TO **EXPAND** BY INCREASING ITS **POPULATION**, IT MUST RECEIVE THE **BLESSING** OF ITS **DISTANT INFLUENCE**.

THE GOOFY JERKS CALL THE **BLESSING STUFF** BY ANOTHER NAME: **REPRODUCTIVE PROPELLANT**!

FIRST, AT **DEEPEST, DARKEST MIDNIGHT**, THE **WORLD** BROADCASTS ITS **HUNGER**.

WHEN THE CODED MESSAGE REACHES THE PROPER SERVICE STATION...

... IT BEATS ON THE **BOOMRAIL**.

THE CODED MESSAGE EXCITES THE DESIRED **INFLUENCE**, CAUSING IT TO FLIP OVER.

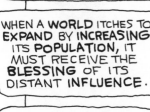

263

...AND THE REPRO FLOWS!

THE GOOFY SERVICE JERKS LOAD UP!

THE LOAD KNOWS THE WAY!

DIRECTIONS ARE ENCODED IN THE CUSTOMER'S REQUEST.

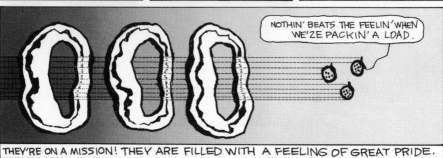

NOTHIN' BEATS THE FEELIN' WHEN WE'ZE PACKIN' A LOAD.

THEY'RE ON A MISSION! THEY ARE FILLED WITH A FEELING OF GREAT PRIDE.

BUT AFTER THE DELIVERY IS DOWNLOADED, THE FEELING EVAPORATES!

THEY FIND THEMSELVES MAKIN' IDLE CHITCHAT WITH THE LOCAL NATIVES!

SO WHAT'S THE WEATHER LIKE IN THE O-RINGS?

PLEASANT.

THAT'S NICE.

THEY ARE FATIGUED AND DISORIENTED FROM THEIR HASTY JOURNEY. OFTEN THEY AREN'T REALLY SURE OF THE BEST ROUTE HOME.

UH-OH.   WE'ZE LOSTED.

AGAIN!

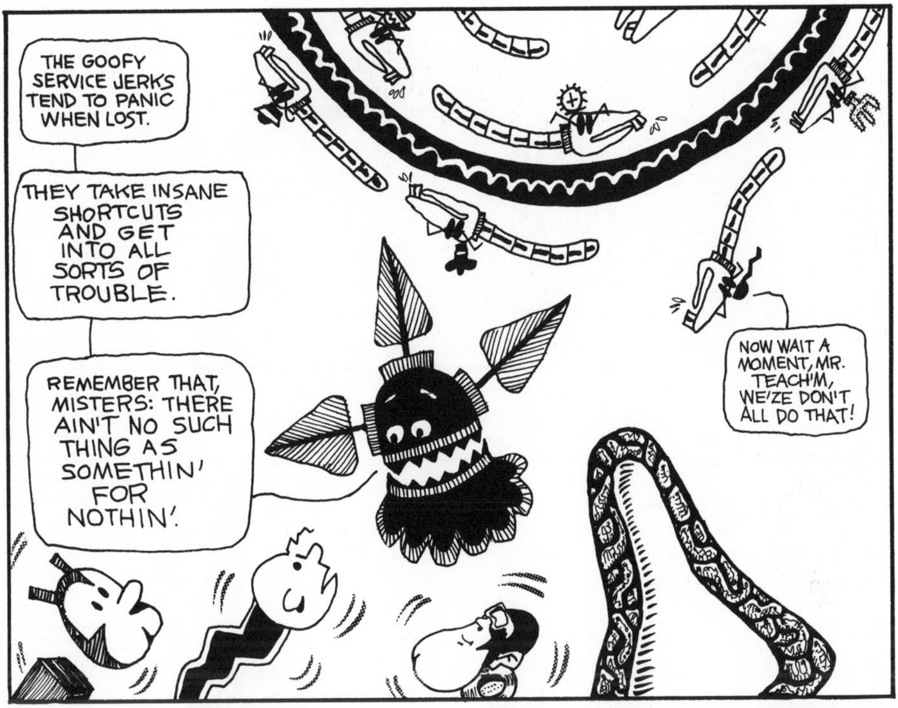
THE GOOFY SERVICE JERKS TEND TO PANIC WHEN LOST.
THEY TAKE INSANE SHORTCUTS AND GET INTO ALL SORTS OF TROUBLE.
REMEMBER THAT, MISTERS: THERE AIN'T NO SUCH THING AS SOMETHIN' FOR NOTHIN'.
NOW WAIT A MOMENT, MR. TEACH'M, WE'ZE DON'T ALL DO THAT!

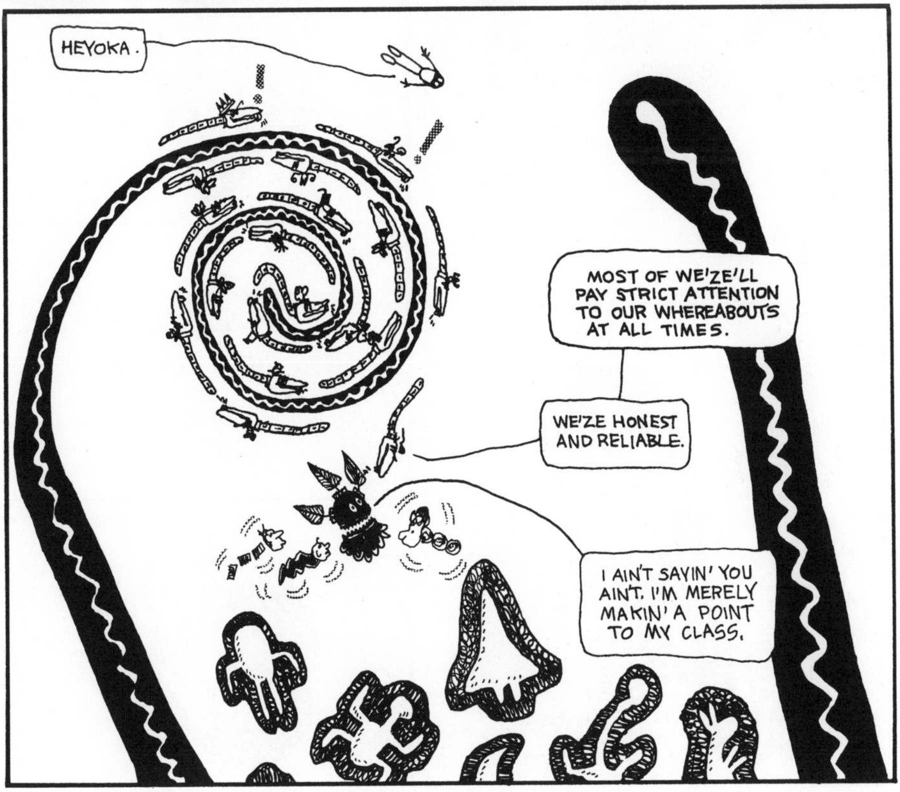
HEYOKA.
MOST OF WE'ZE'LL PAY STRICT ATTENTION TO OUR WHEREABOUTS AT ALL TIMES.
WE'ZE HONEST AND RELIABLE.
I AIN'T SAYIN' YOU AIN'T. I'M MERELY MAKIN' A POINT TO MY CLASS.

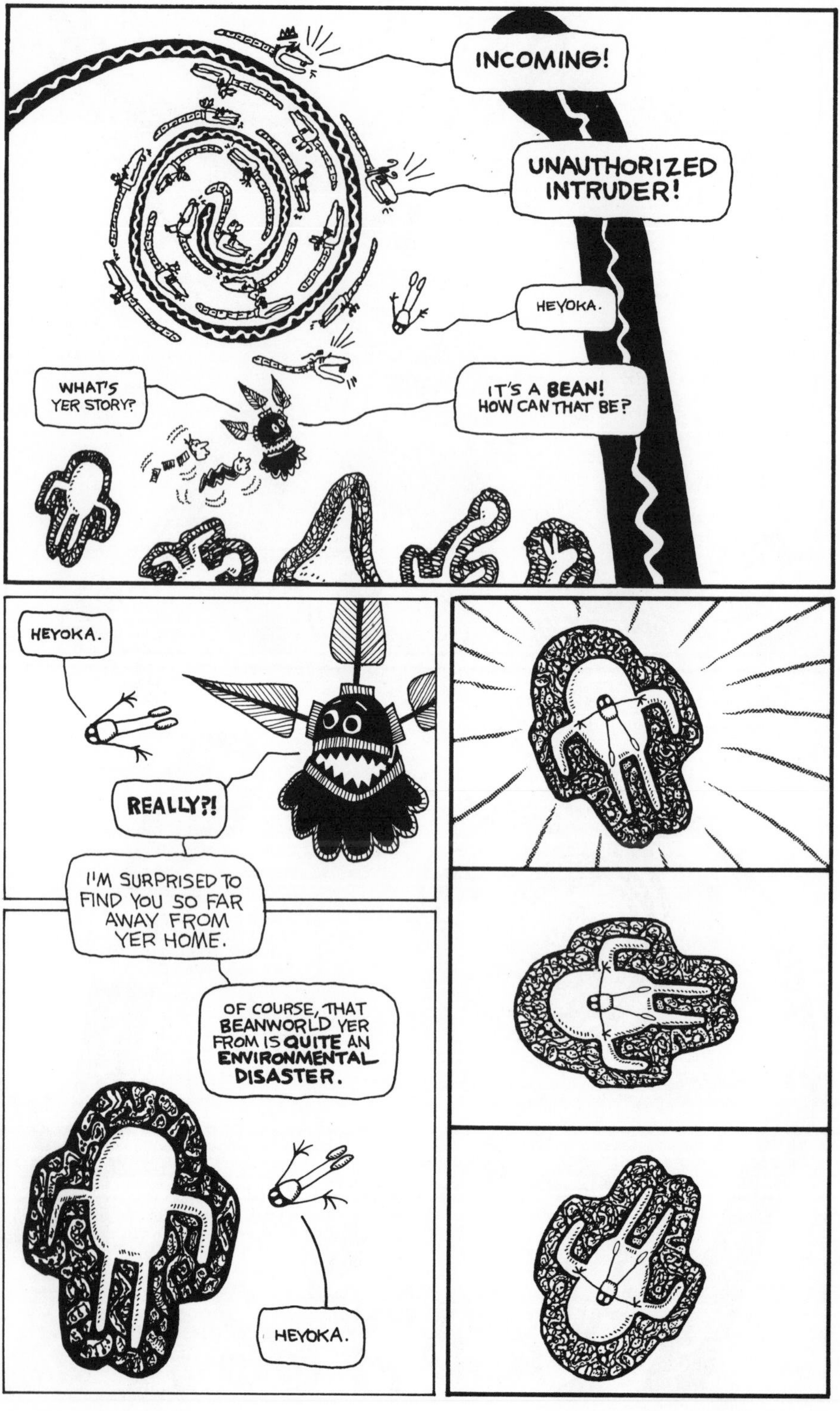
INCOMING!
UNAUTHORIZED INTRUDER!
HEYOKA.
WHAT'S YER STORY?
IT'S A BEAN! HOW CAN THAT BE?
HEYOKA.
REALLY?!
I'M SURPRISED TO FIND YOU SO FAR AWAY FROM YER HOME.
OF COURSE, THAT BEANWORLD YER FROM IS QUITE AN ENVIRONMENTAL DISASTER.
HEYOKA.

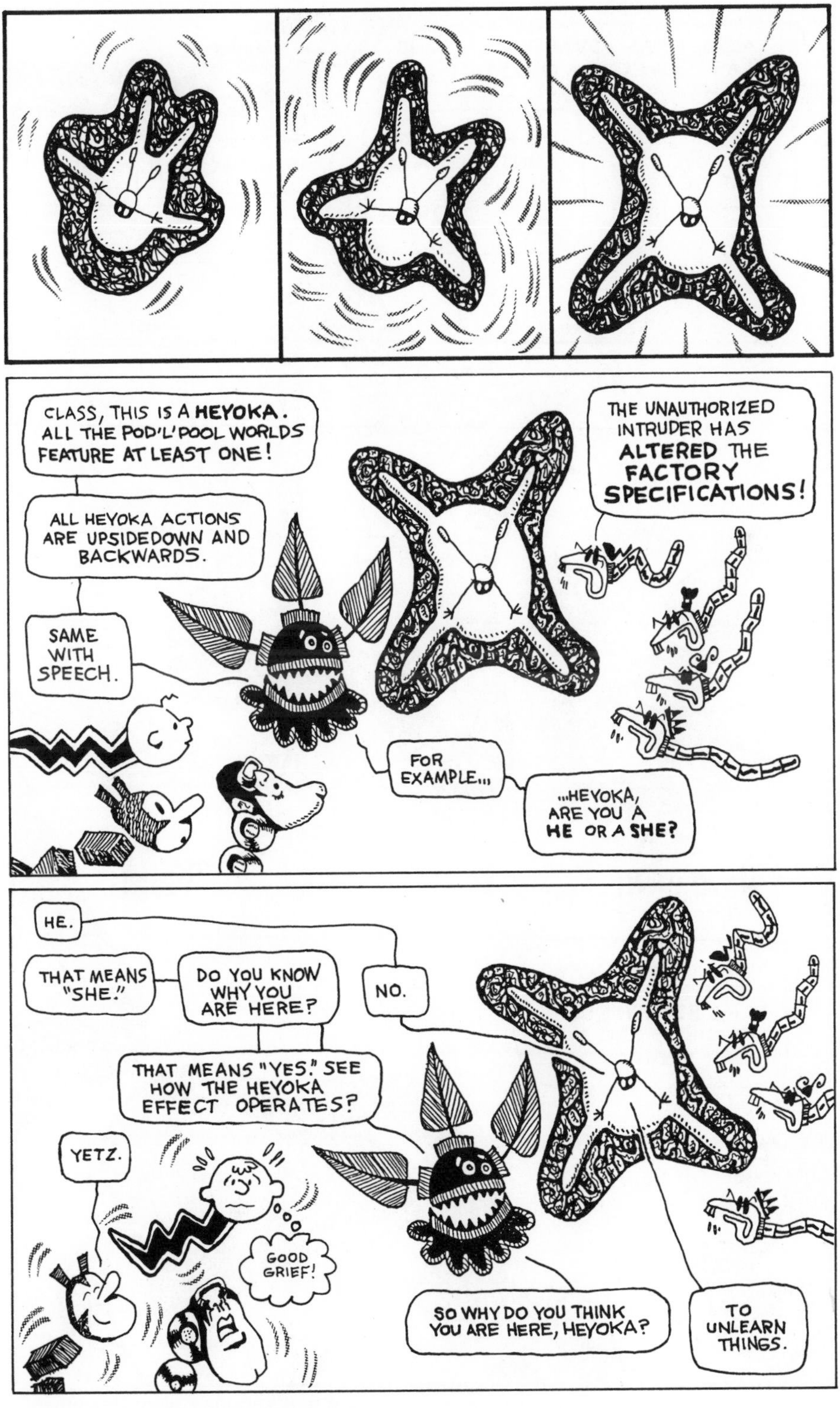
CLASS, THIS IS A HEYOKA. ALL THE POD'L'POOL WORLDS FEATURE AT LEAST ONE!
ALL HEYOKA ACTIONS ARE UPSIDEDOWN AND BACKWARDS.
SAME WITH SPEECH.
THE UNAUTHORIZED INTRUDER HAS ALTERED THE FACTORY SPECIFICATIONS!
FOR EXAMPLE...
...HEYOKA, ARE YOU A HE OR A SHE?
HE.
THAT MEANS "SHE."
DO YOU KNOW WHY YOU ARE HERE?
NO.
THAT MEANS "YES." SEE HOW THE HEYOKA EFFECT OPERATES?
YETZ.
GOOD GRIEF!
SO WHY DO YOU THINK YOU ARE HERE, HEYOKA?
TO UNLEARN THINGS.

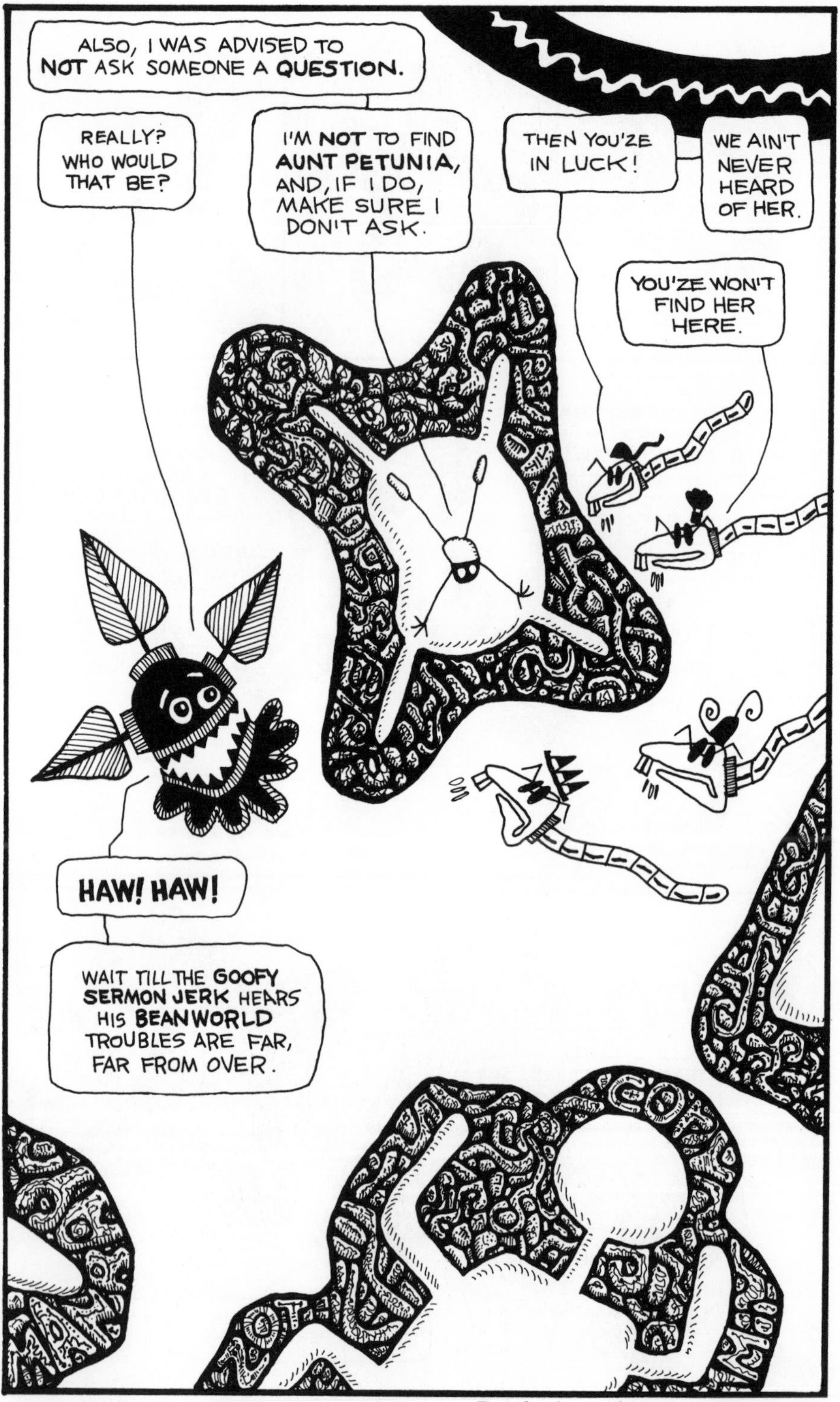
ALSO, I WAS ADVISED TO NOT ASK SOMEONE A QUESTION.
REALLY? WHO WOULD THAT BE?
I'M NOT TO FIND AUNT PETUNIA, AND, IF I DO, MAKE SURE I DON'T ASK.
THEN YOU'ZE IN LUCK!
WE AIN'T NEVER HEARD OF HER.
YOU'ZE WON'T FIND HER HERE.
HAW! HAW!
WAIT TILL THE GOOFY SERMON JERK HEARS HIS BEANWORLD TROUBLES ARE FAR, FAR FROM OVER.

But that's another story altogether...

Beanworld

Zero

This story starts
immediately after
THE GOOFY JERKS
remove the
poisoned
POD'L'POOL
rejected by
GRAN'MA'PA.

GRAN'MA'PA is sorely damaged
and needs plenty of rest.

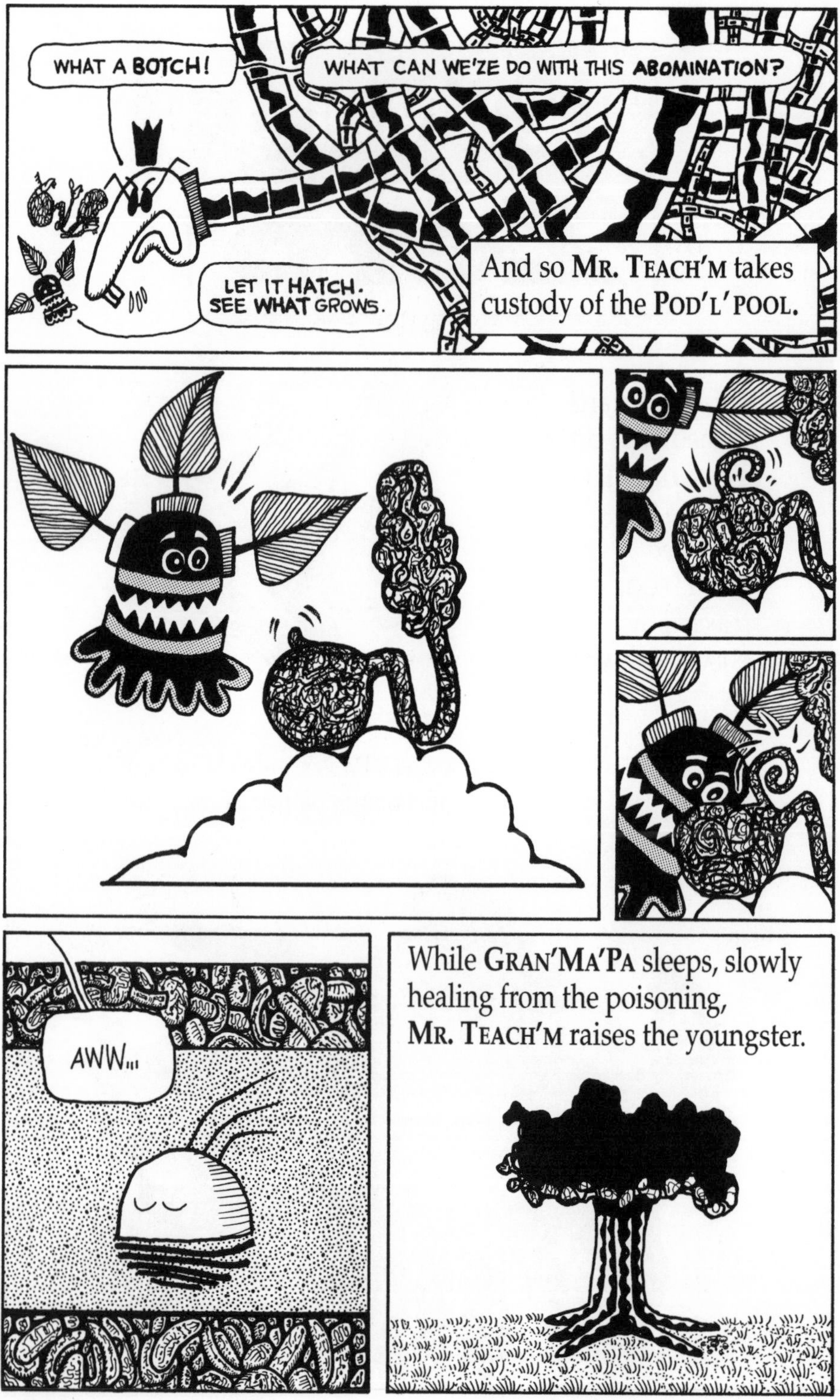
WHAT A BOTCH!
WHAT CAN WE'ZE DO WITH THIS ABOMINATION?
LET IT HATCH. SEE WHAT GROWS.
And so MR. TEACH'M takes custody of the POD'L'POOL.
AWW...
While GRAN'MA'PA sleeps, slowly healing from the poisoning, MR. TEACH'M raises the youngster.

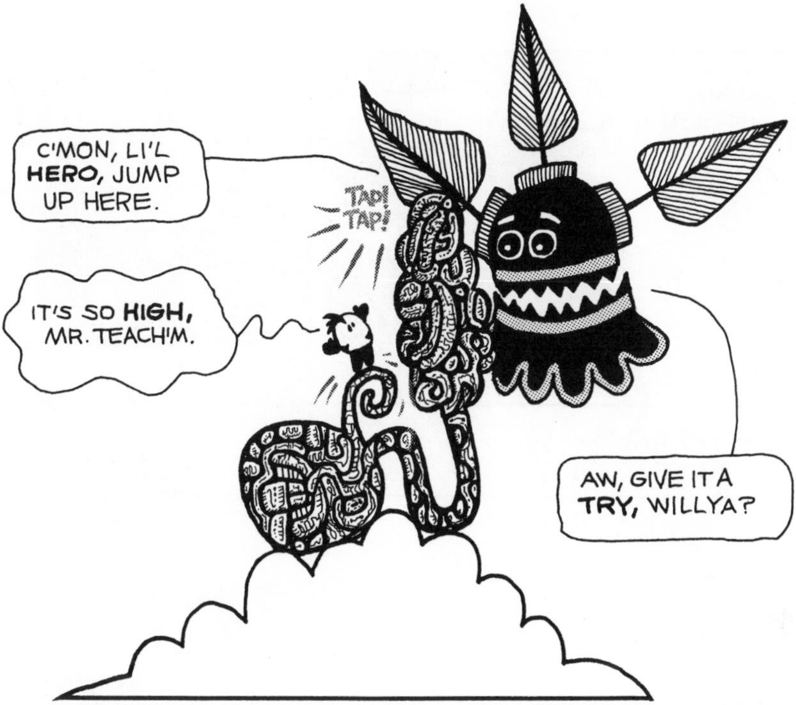
C'MON, LI'L **HERO,** JUMP UP HERE.
TAP! TAP!
IT'S SO **HIGH,** MR. TEACH'M.
AW, GIVE IT A **TRY,** WILLYA?

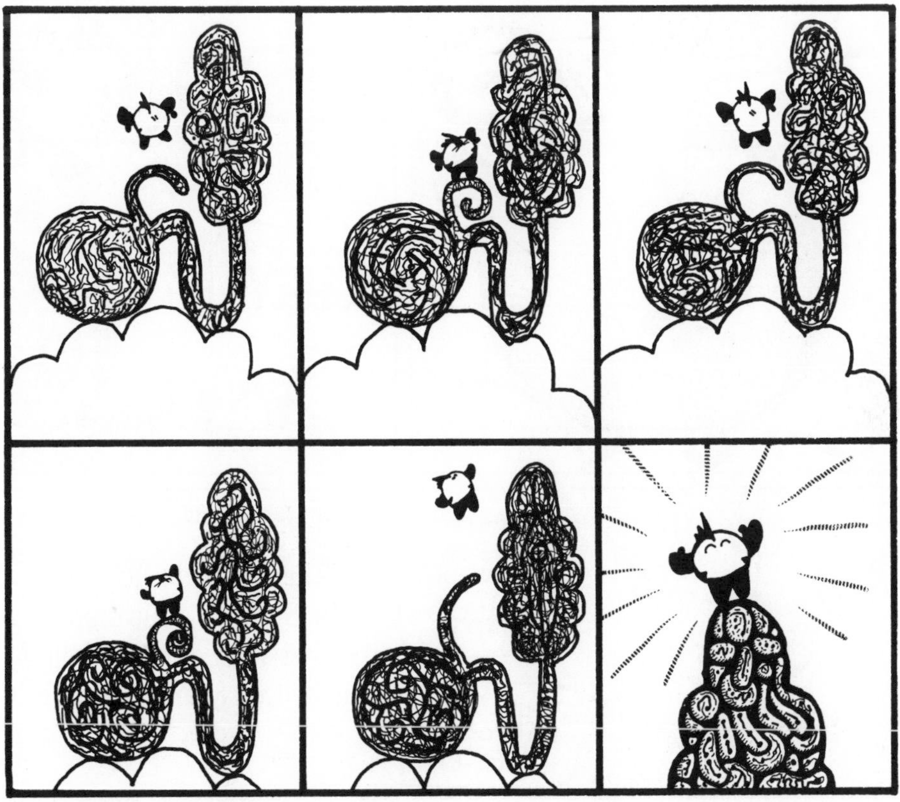

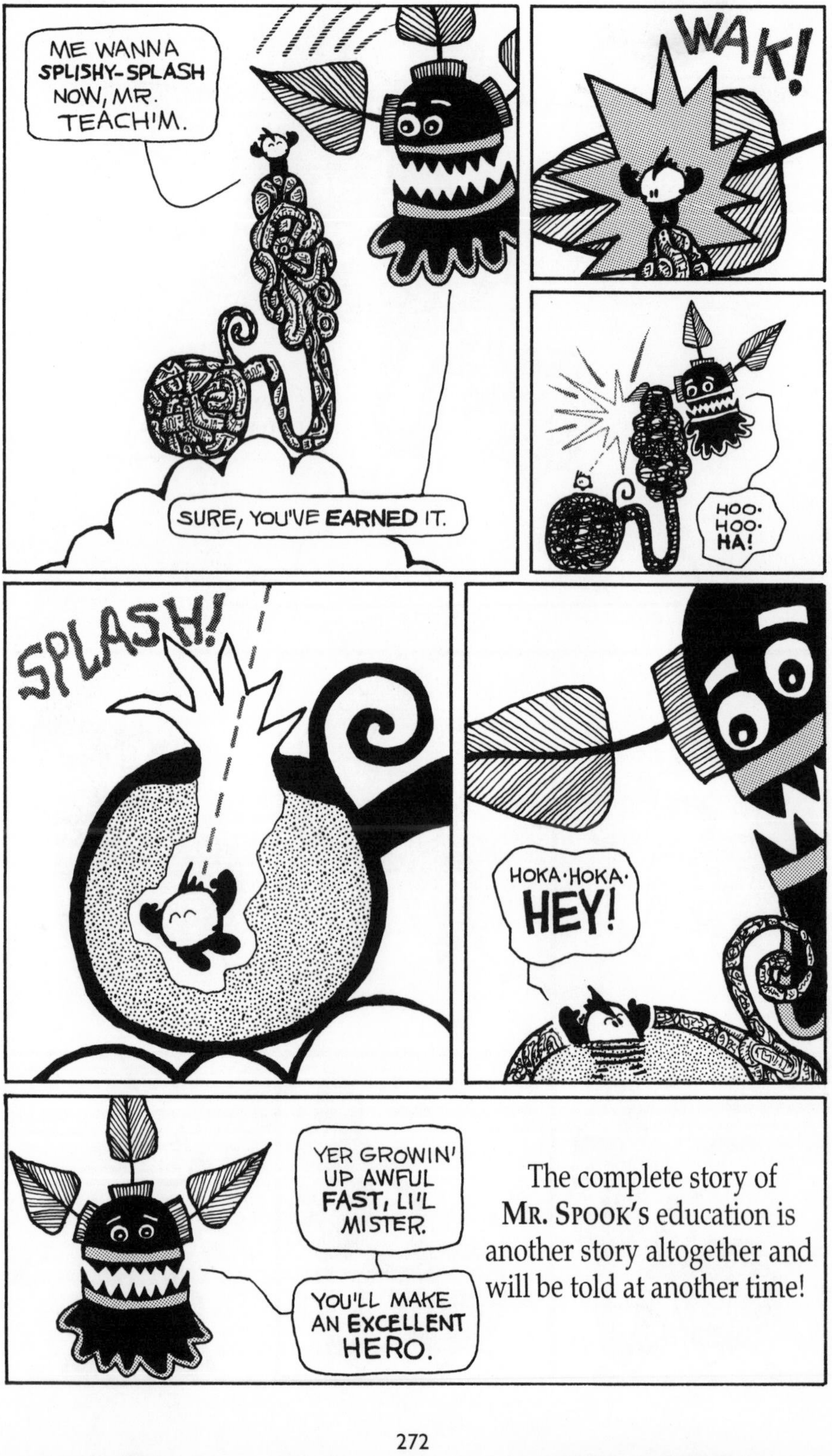
ME WANNA SPLISHY-SPLASH NOW, MR. TEACH'M.
SURE, YOU'VE EARNED IT.
WAK!
HOO·HOO·HA!
SPLASH!
HOKA·HOKA·HEY!
YER GROWIN' UP AWFUL FAST, LI'L MISTER.
YOU'LL MAKE AN EXCELLENT HERO.
The complete story of Mr. Spook's education is another story altogether and will be told at another time!

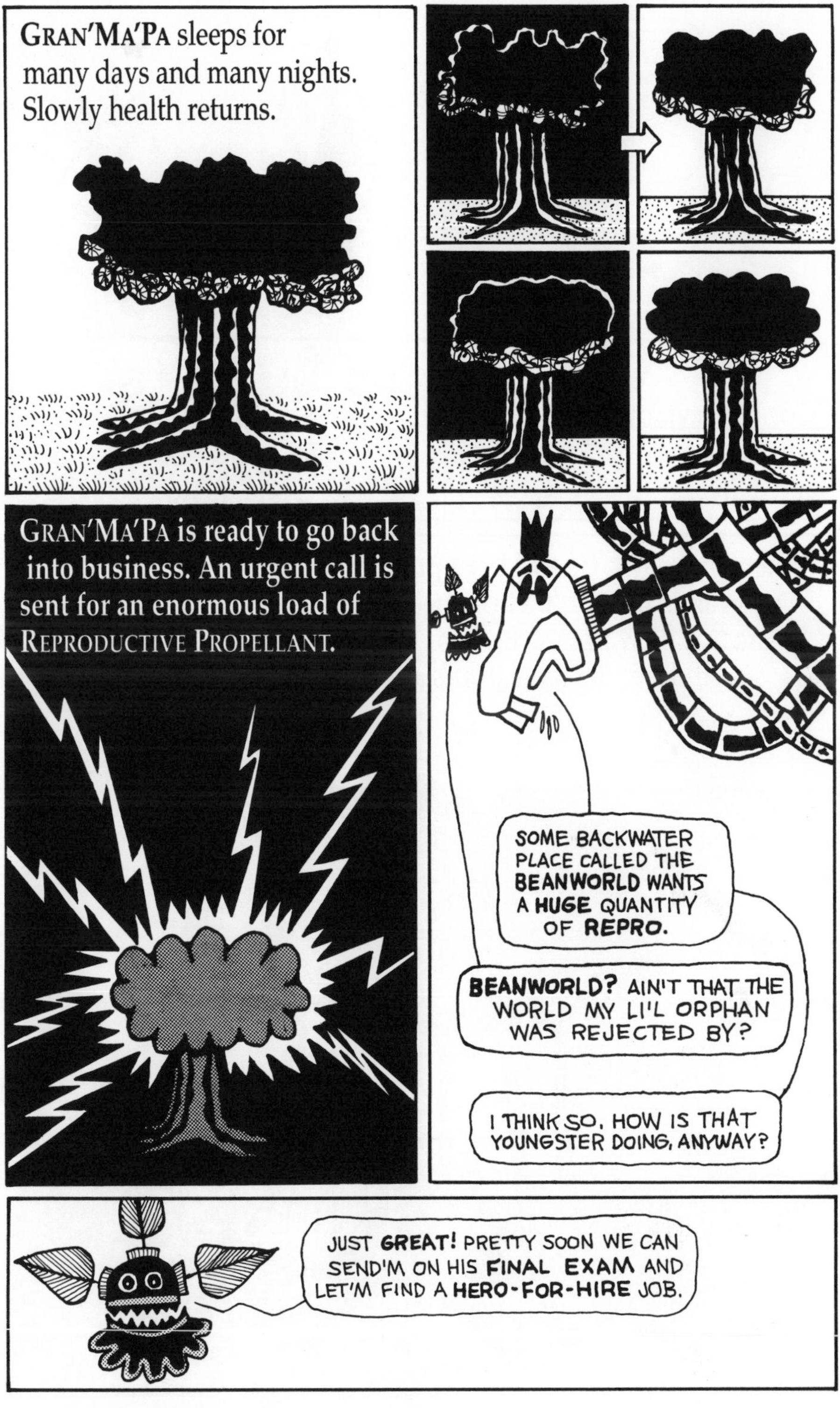
GRAN'MA'PA sleeps for many days and many nights. Slowly health returns.
GRAN'MA'PA is ready to go back into business. An urgent call is sent for an enormous load of REPRODUCTIVE PROPELLANT.
SOME BACKWATER PLACE CALLED THE BEANWORLD WANTS A HUGE QUANTITY OF REPRO.
BEANWORLD? AIN'T THAT THE WORLD MY LI'L ORPHAN WAS REJECTED BY?
I THINK SO. HOW IS THAT YOUNGSTER DOING, ANYWAY?
JUST GREAT! PRETTY SOON WE CAN SEND'M ON HIS FINAL EXAM AND LET'M FIND A HERO-FOR-HIRE JOB.

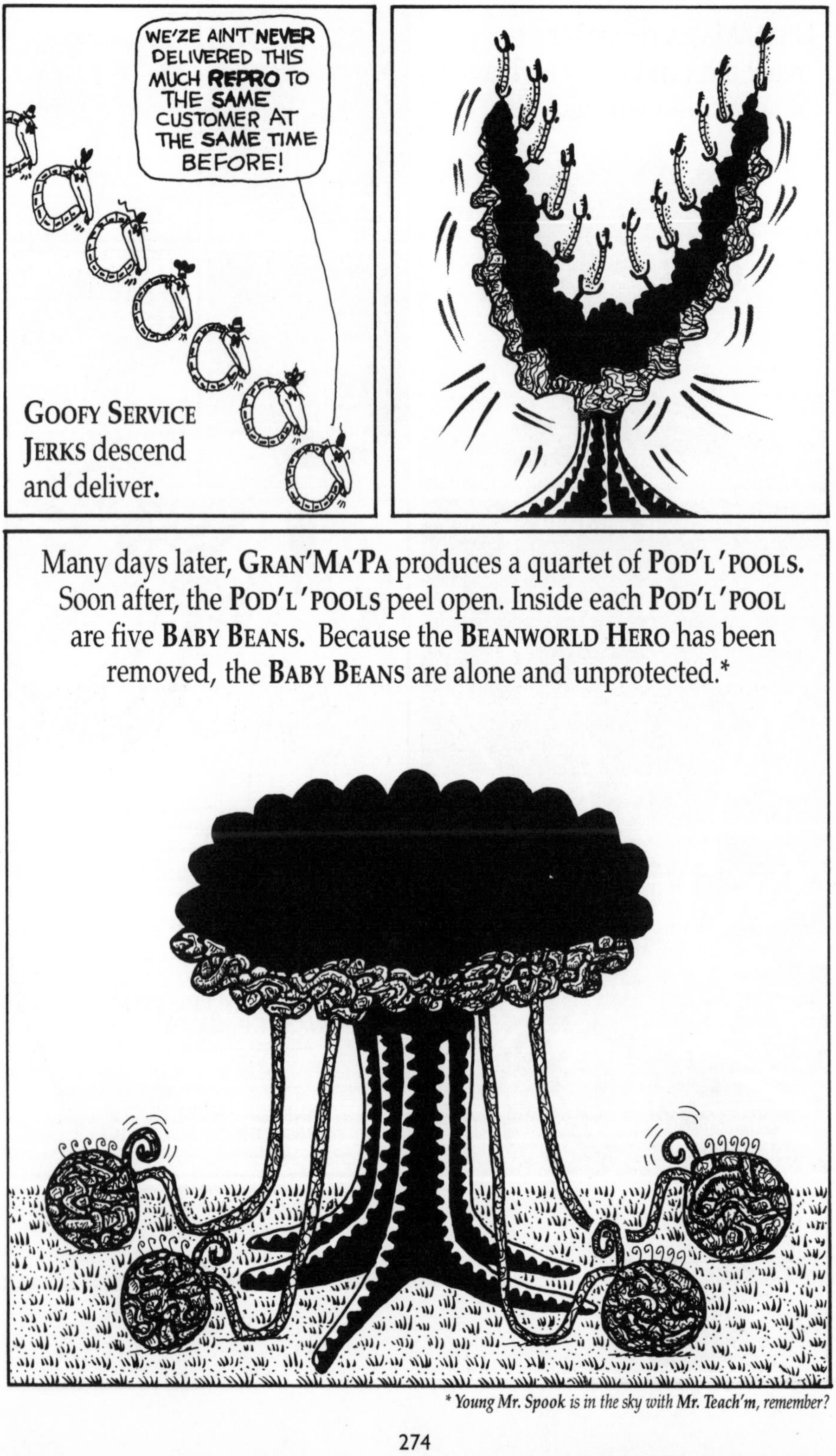
WE'ZE AIN'T NEVER DELIVERED THIS MUCH REPRO TO THE SAME CUSTOMER AT THE SAME TIME BEFORE!
GOOFY SERVICE JERKS descend and deliver.
Many days later, GRAN'MA'PA produces a quartet of POD'L'POOLS. Soon after, the POD'L'POOLS peel open. Inside each POD'L'POOL are five BABY BEANS. Because the BEANWORLD HERO has been removed, the BABY BEANS are alone and unprotected.*

** Young Mr. Spook is in the sky with Mr. Teach'm, remember?*

No one teaches the **Baby Beans** the things they need to know.

Quietly they float in their **Pod'l'pools** soaking up **Chow**. They don't know how to talk.

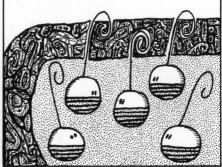

Many days and many nights pass.

They grow in absolute silence.

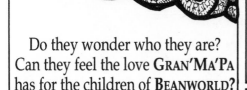

Do they wonder who they are? Can they feel the love **Gran'Ma'Pa** has for the children of **Beanworld**?

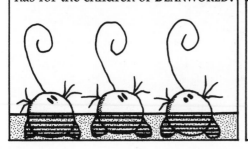

They live in food, but they eat too much.

Chow dwindles. **Pod'l'pools** sag.

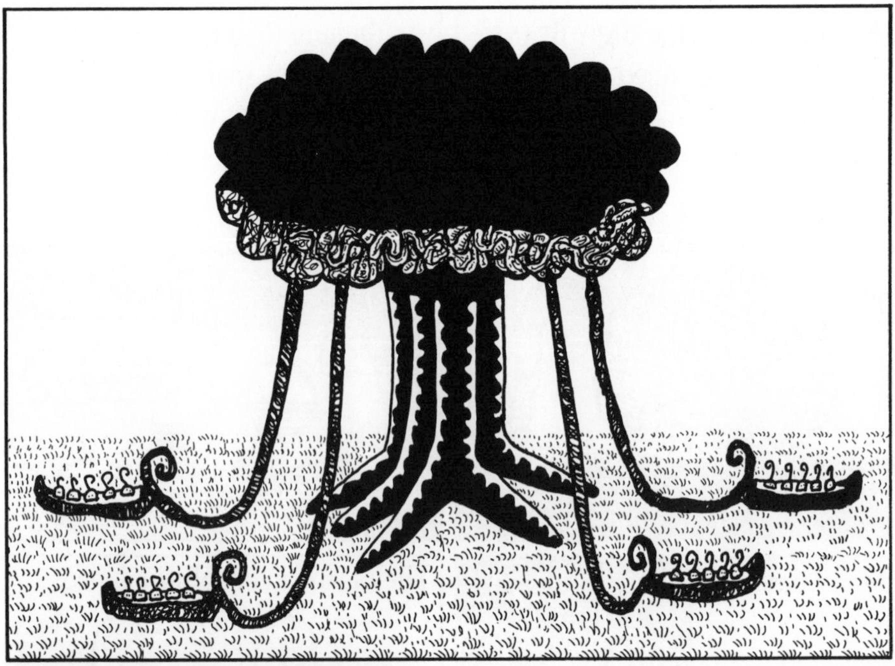

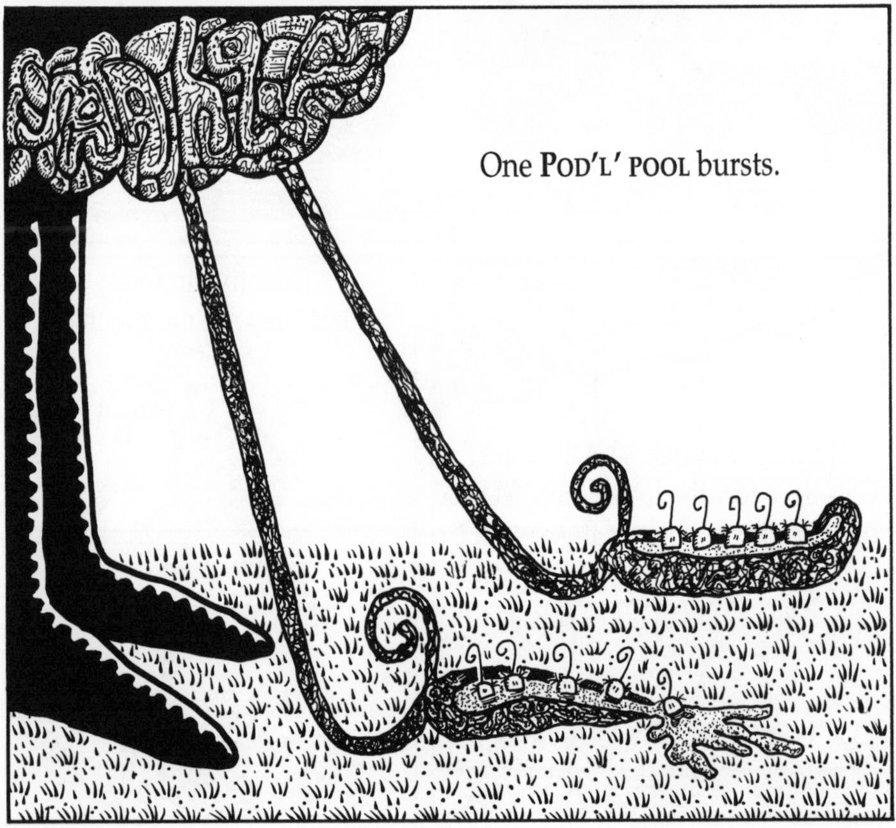
One POD'L' POOL bursts.

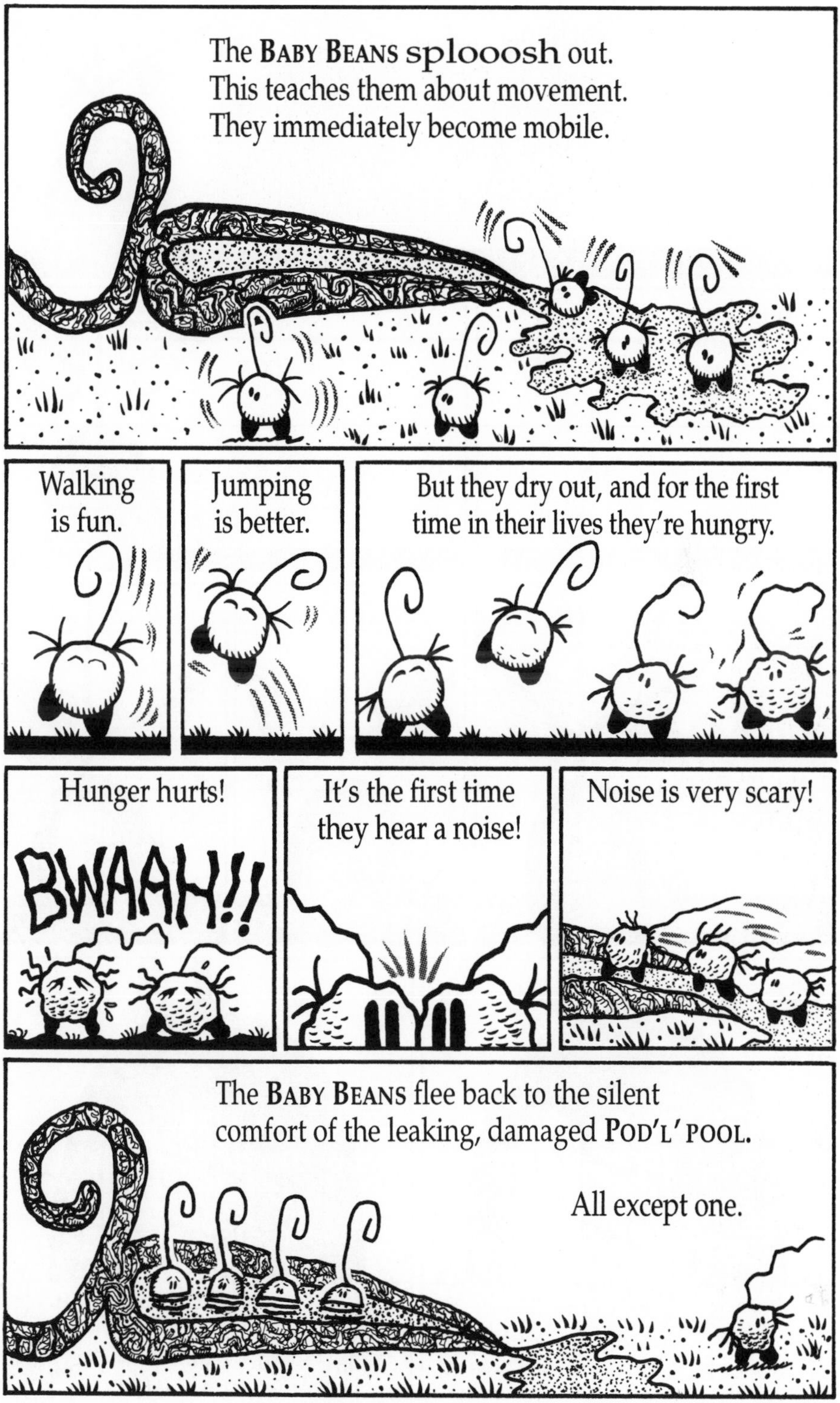

The BABY BEANS splooosh out.
This teaches them about movement.
They immediately become mobile.
Walking is fun.
Jumping is better.
But they dry out, and for the first time in their lives they're hungry.
Hunger hurts!
BWAAH!!
It's the first time they hear a noise!
Noise is very scary!
The BABY BEANS flee back to the silent comfort of the leaking, damaged POD'L'POOL.
All except one.

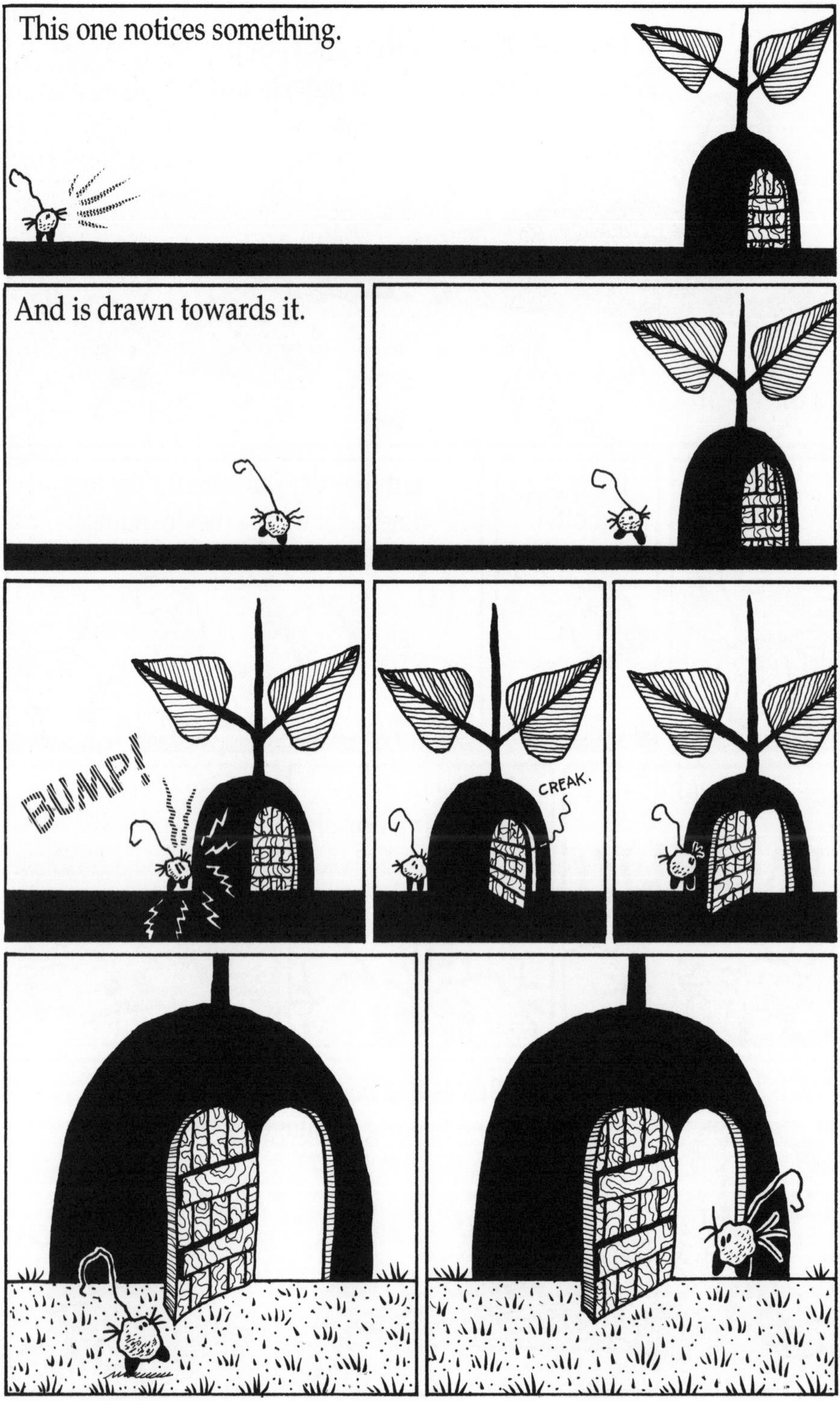
This one notices something.
And is drawn towards it.
BUMP!
CREAK.

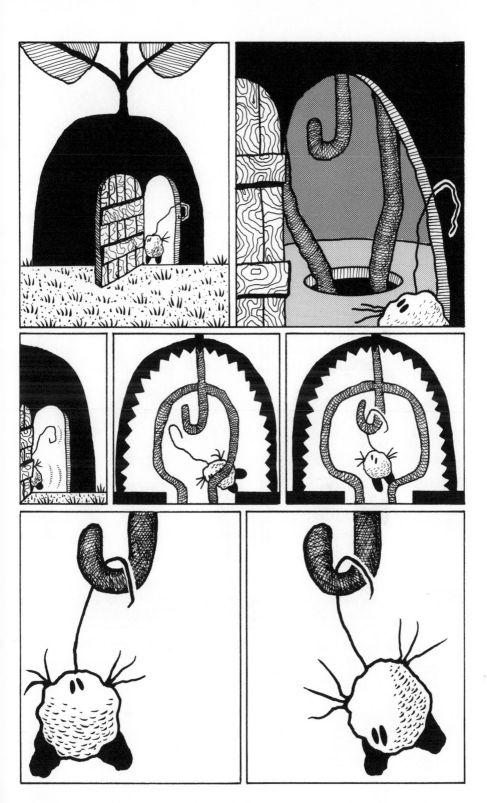

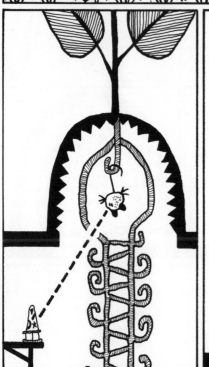 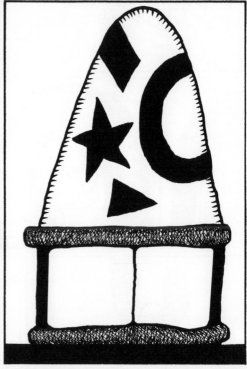

One brief glance fills the young BEAN with a burning desire to possess the object.

The young **BEAN**'s bewildering desire leads to a sudden growth spurt!

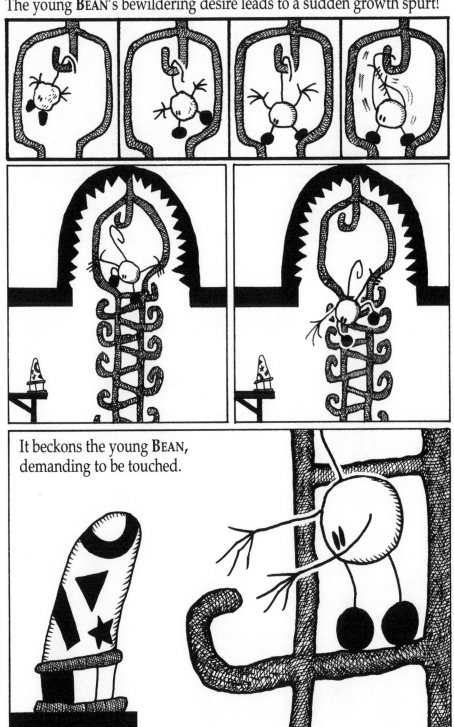

It beckons the young **BEAN**, demanding to be touched.

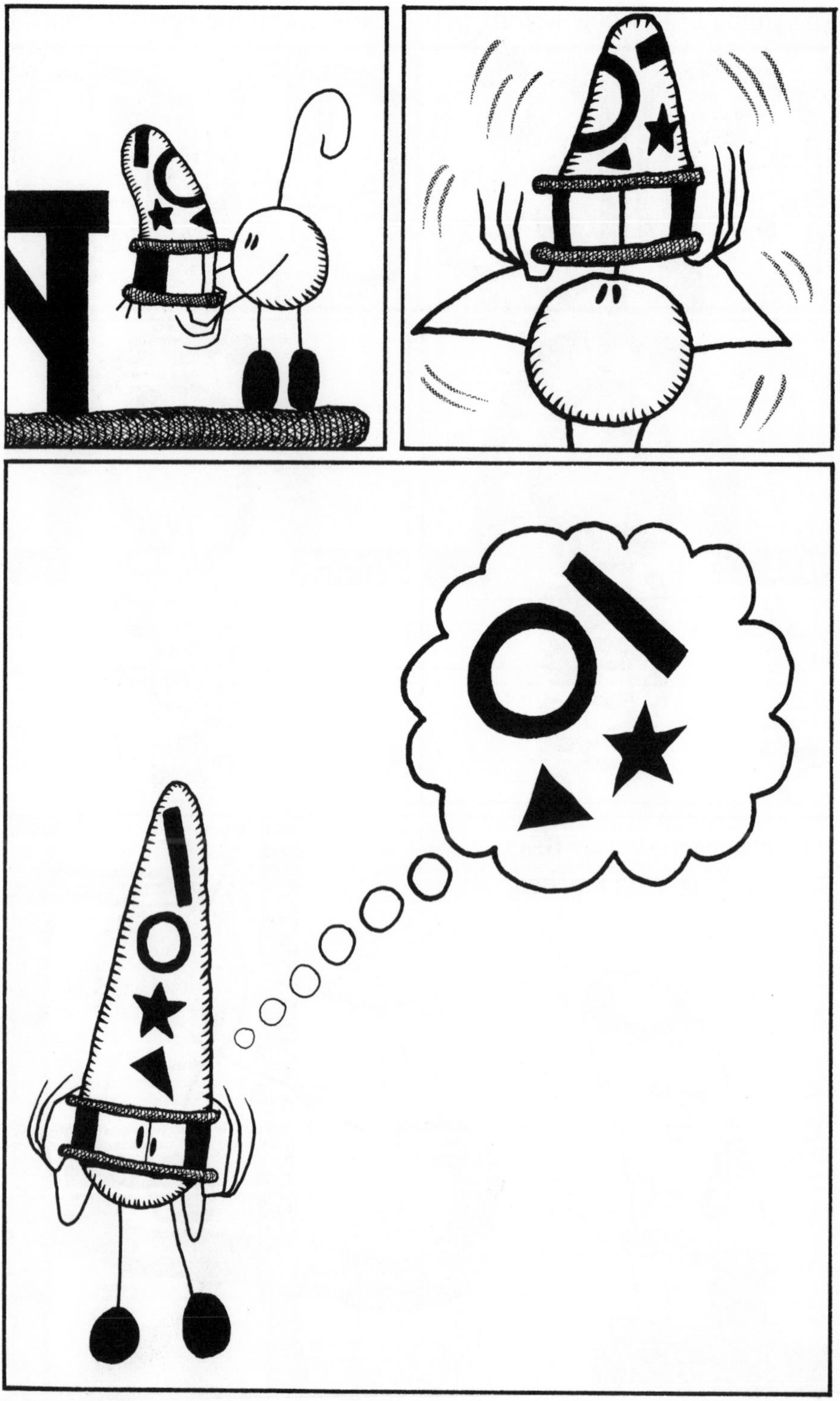

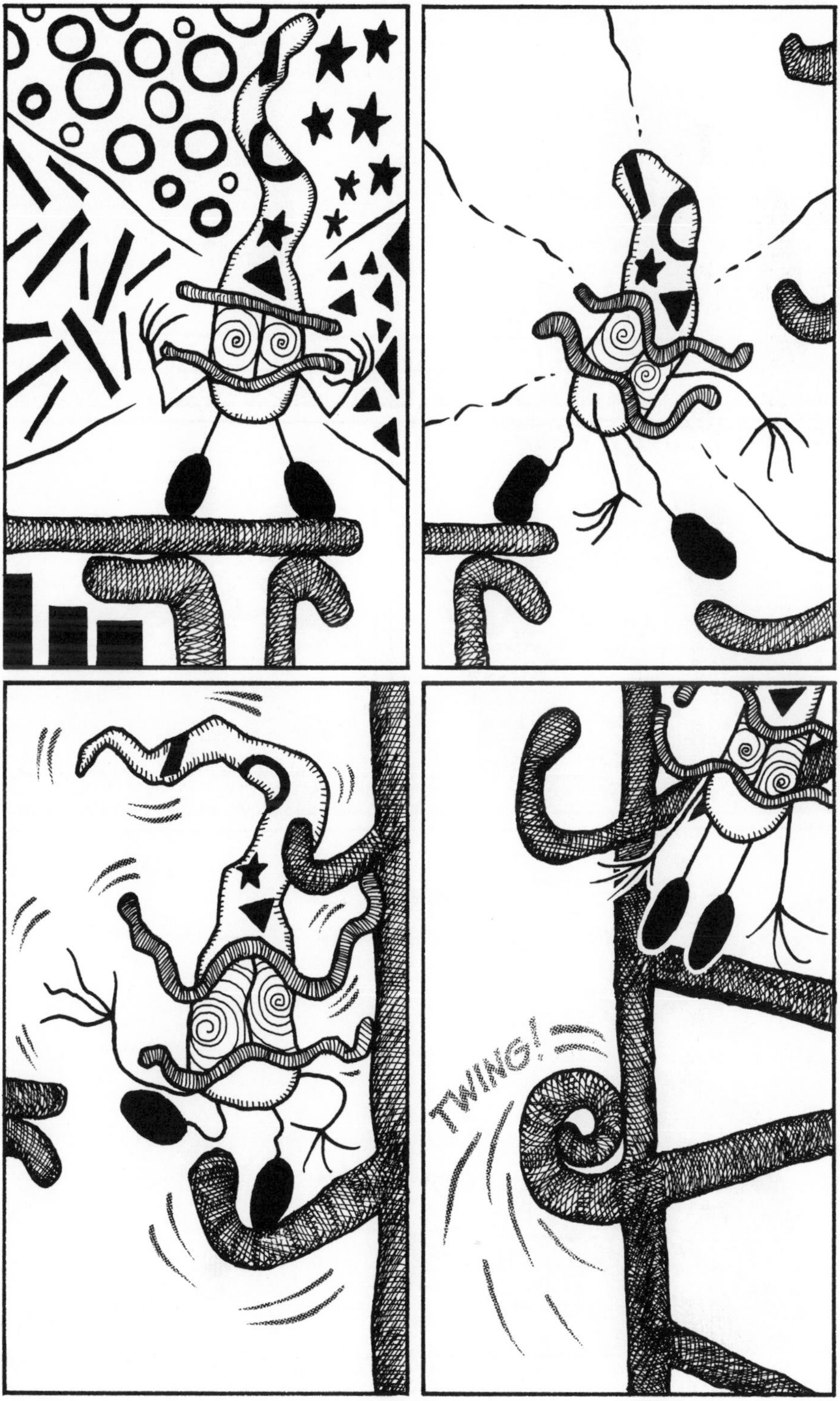
TWING!

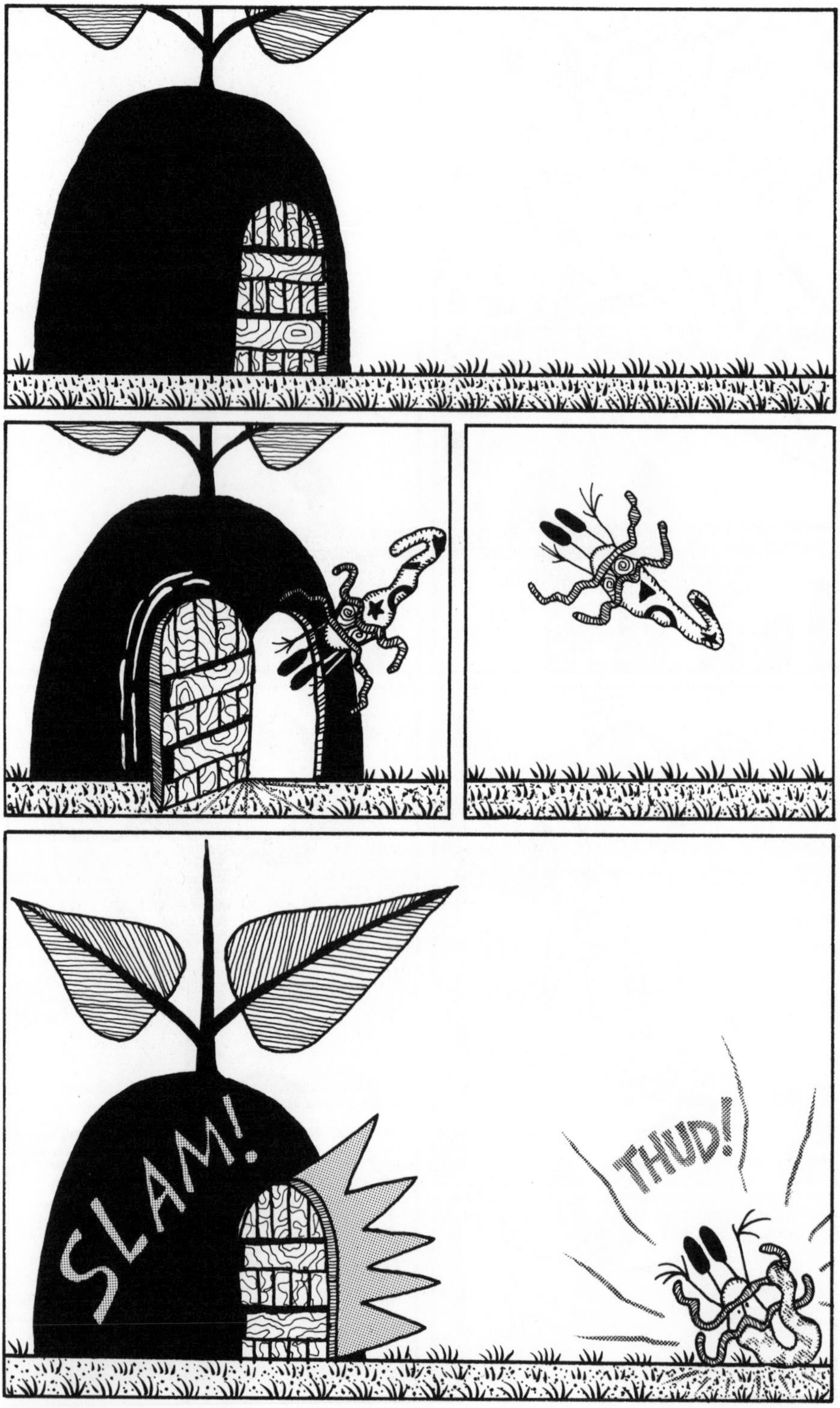
SLAM!
THUD!

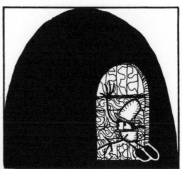

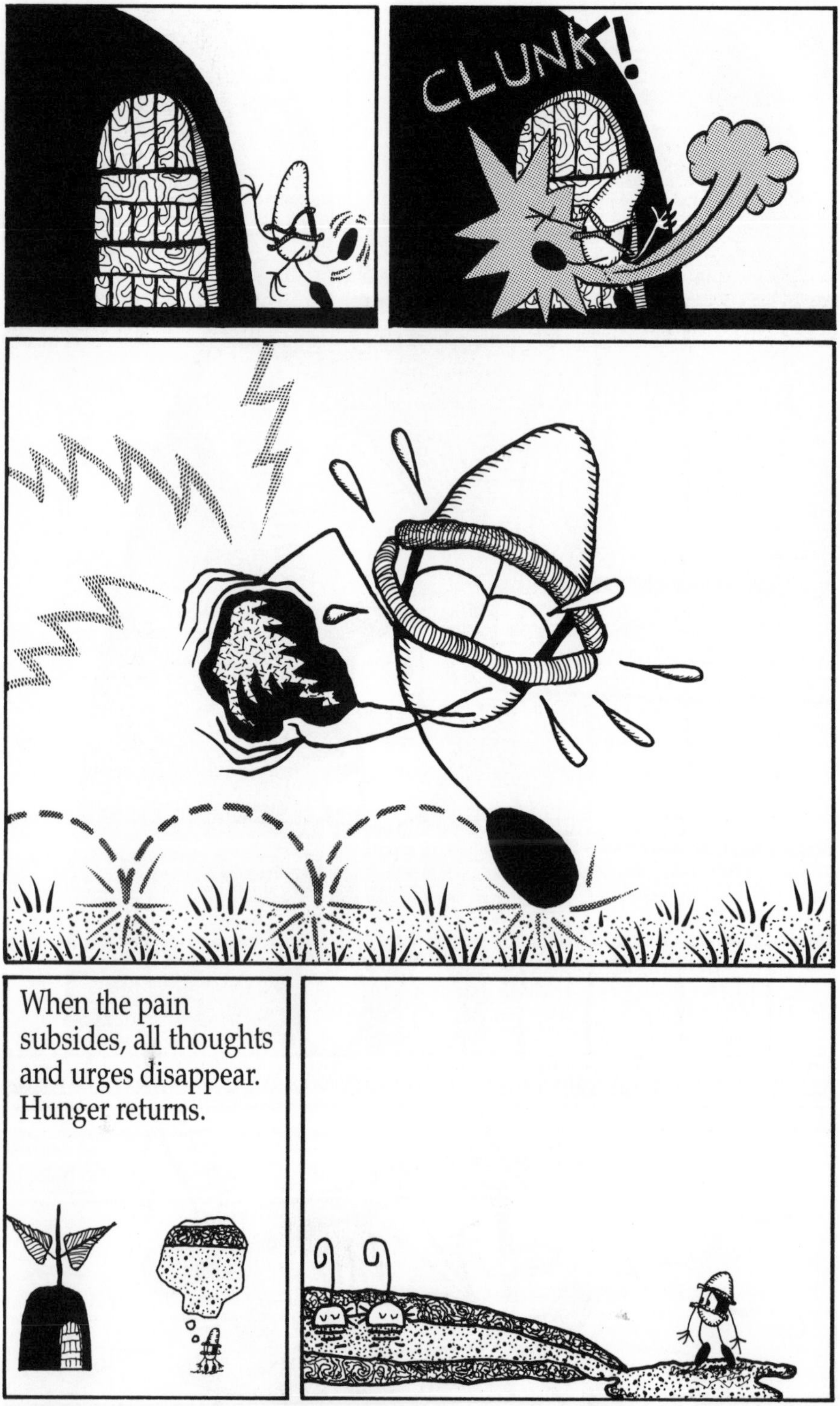
CLUNK!
When the pain subsides, all thoughts and urges disappear. Hunger returns.

More time passes.

Many, many days and nights.

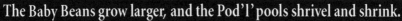

The Baby Beans grow larger, and the Pod'l' pools shrivel and shrink.

Soon the "**POOL**" disappears. The Beans rest against the remains of the semi-moist "**POD**" in order to soak up whatever nutrients remain.

There aren't many.

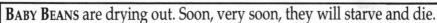

BABY BEANS are drying out. Soon, very soon, they will starve and die.

Meanwhile, the orphan's POD' L' POOL is shrinking, too.

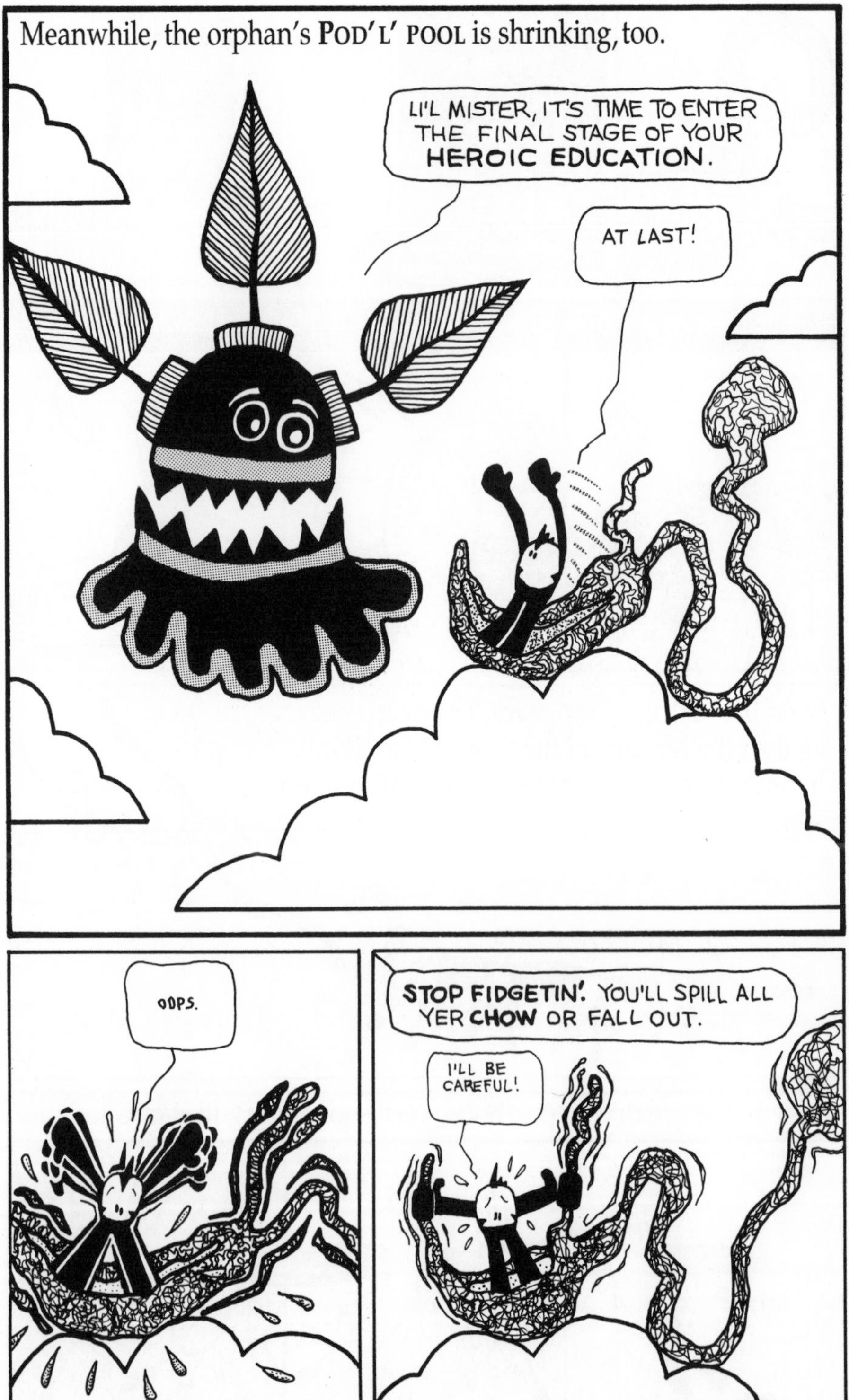
LI'L MISTER, IT'S TIME TO ENTER THE FINAL STAGE OF YOUR HEROIC EDUCATION.
AT LAST!
OOPS.
STOP FIDGETIN'. YOU'LL SPILL ALL YER CHOW OR FALL OUT.
I'LL BE CAREFUL!

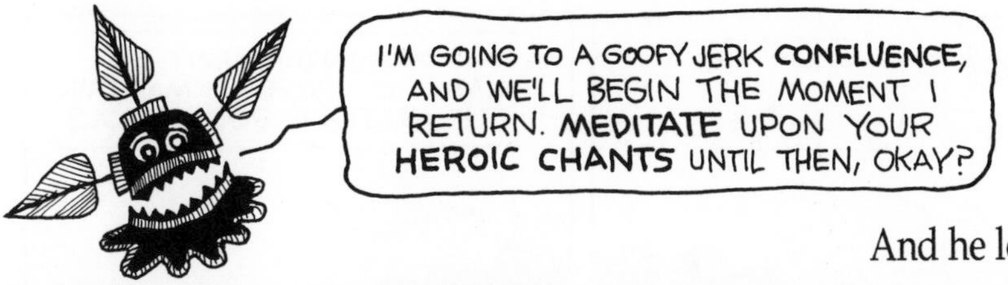
I'M GOING TO A GOOFY JERK CONFLUENCE, AND WE'LL BEGIN THE MOMENT I RETURN. MEDITATE UPON YOUR HEROIC CHANTS UNTIL THEN, OKAY?

And he leaves.

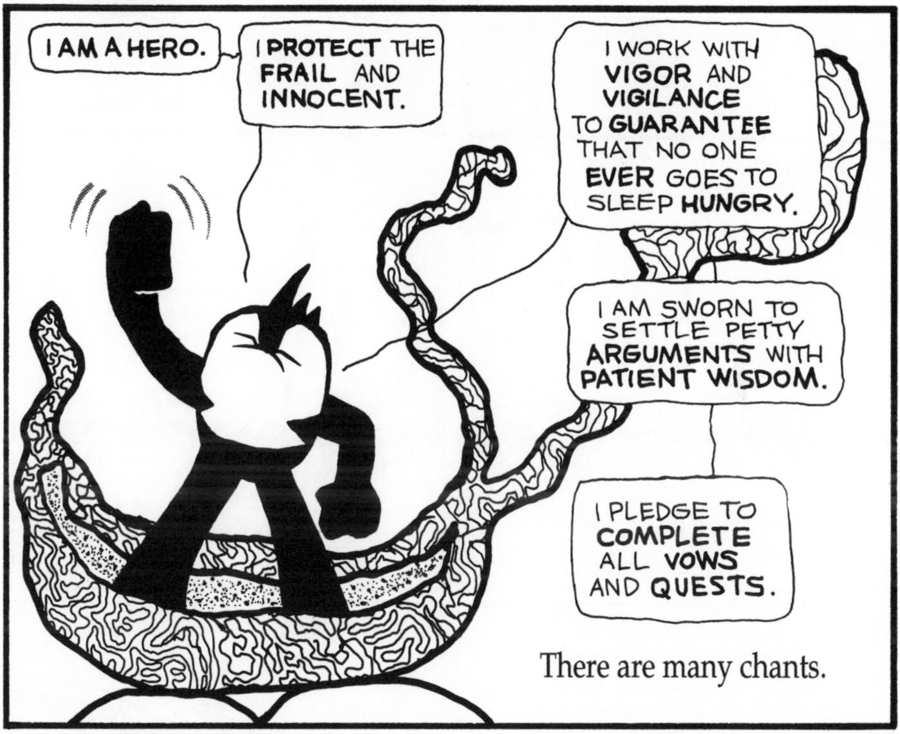
I AM A HERO.
I PROTECT THE FRAIL AND INNOCENT.
I WORK WITH VIGOR AND VIGILANCE TO GUARANTEE THAT NO ONE EVER GOES TO SLEEP HUNGRY.
I AM SWORN TO SETTLE PETTY ARGUMENTS WITH PATIENT WISDOM.
I PLEDGE TO COMPLETE ALL VOWS AND QUESTS.
There are many chants.

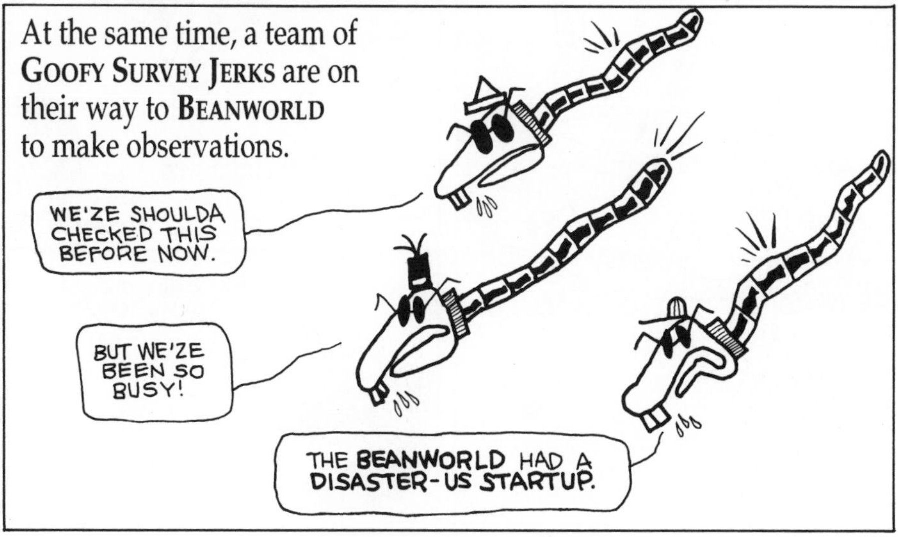
At the same time, a team of GOOFY SURVEY JERKS are on their way to BEANWORLD to make observations.
WE'ZE SHOULDA CHECKED THIS BEFORE NOW.
BUT WE'ZE BEEN SO BUSY!
THE BEANWORLD HAD A DISASTER-US STARTUP.

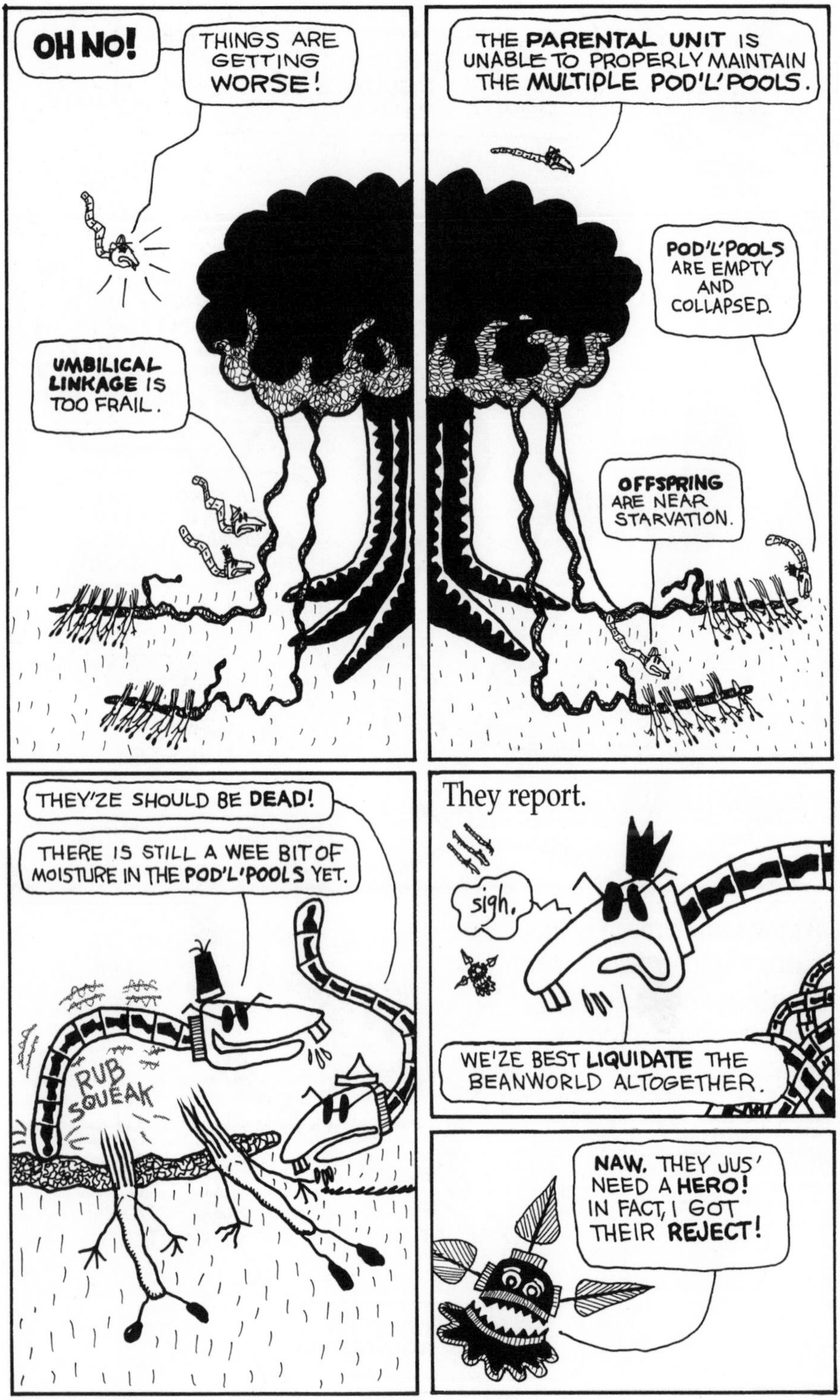
OH NO!
THINGS ARE GETTING WORSE!
THE PARENTAL UNIT IS UNABLE TO PROPERLY MAINTAIN THE MULTIPLE POD'L'POOLS.
POD'L'POOLS ARE EMPTY AND COLLAPSED.
UMBILICAL LINKAGE IS TOO FRAIL.
OFFSPRING ARE NEAR STARVATION.
THEY'ZE SHOULD BE DEAD!
THERE IS STILL A WEE BIT OF MOISTURE IN THE POD'L'POOLS YET.
RUB
SQUEAK
They report.
sigh.
WE'ZE BEST LIQUIDATE THE BEANWORLD ALTOGETHER.
NAW. THEY JUS' NEED A HERO! IN FACT, I GOT THEIR REJECT!

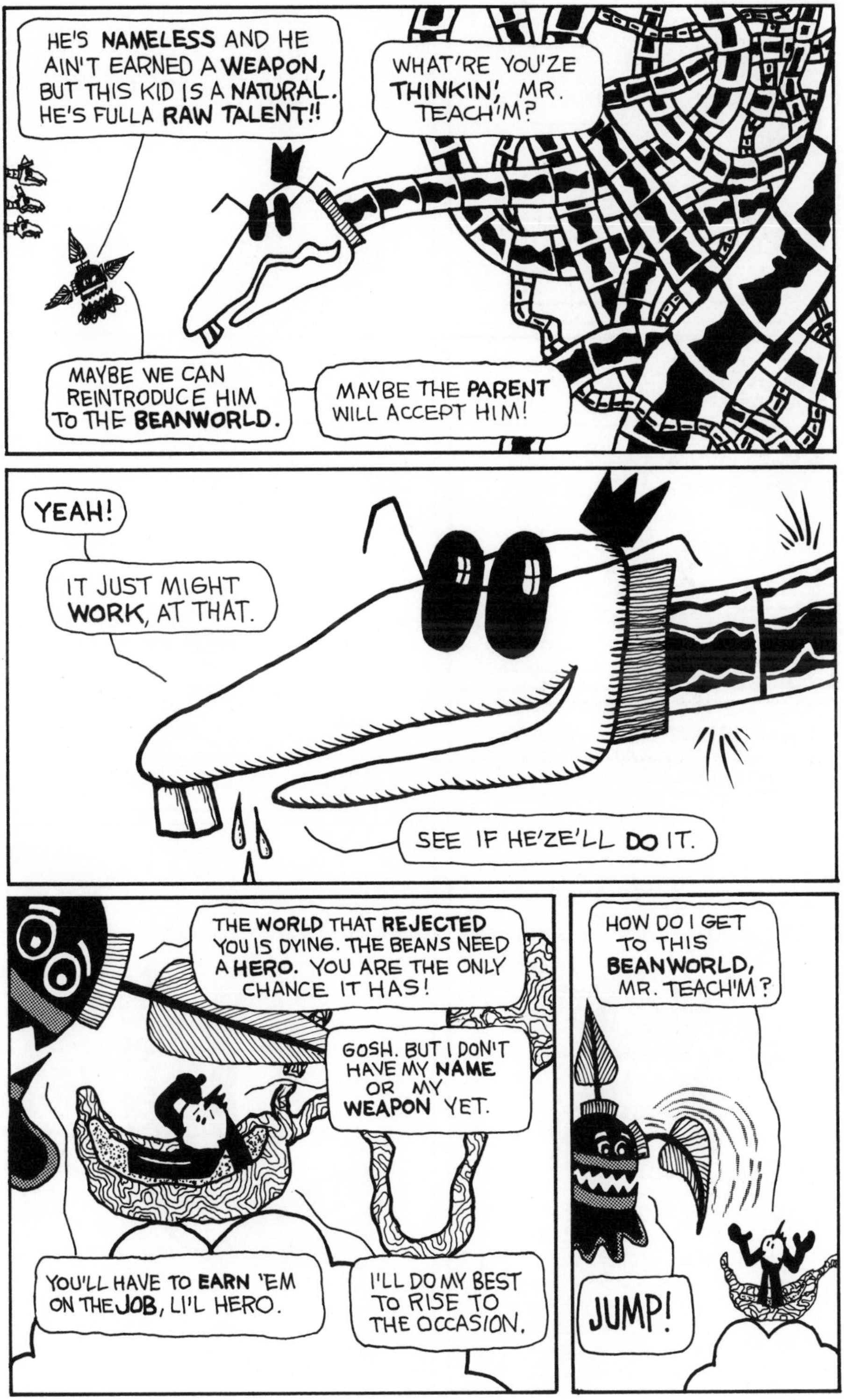
HE'S NAMELESS AND HE AIN'T EARNED A WEAPON, BUT THIS KID IS A NATURAL. HE'S FULLA RAW TALENT!!
WHAT'RE YOU'ZE THINKIN', MR. TEACH'M?
MAYBE WE CAN REINTRODUCE HIM TO THE BEANWORLD.
MAYBE THE PARENT WILL ACCEPT HIM!
YEAH!
IT JUST MIGHT WORK, AT THAT.
SEE IF HE'ZE'LL DO IT.
THE WORLD THAT REJECTED YOU IS DYING. THE BEANS NEED A HERO. YOU ARE THE ONLY CHANCE IT HAS!
GOSH. BUT I DON'T HAVE MY NAME OR MY WEAPON YET.
YOU'LL HAVE TO EARN 'EM ON THE JOB, LI'L HERO.
I'LL DO MY BEST TO RISE TO THE OCCASION.
HOW DO I GET TO THIS BEANWORLD, MR. TEACH'M?
JUMP!

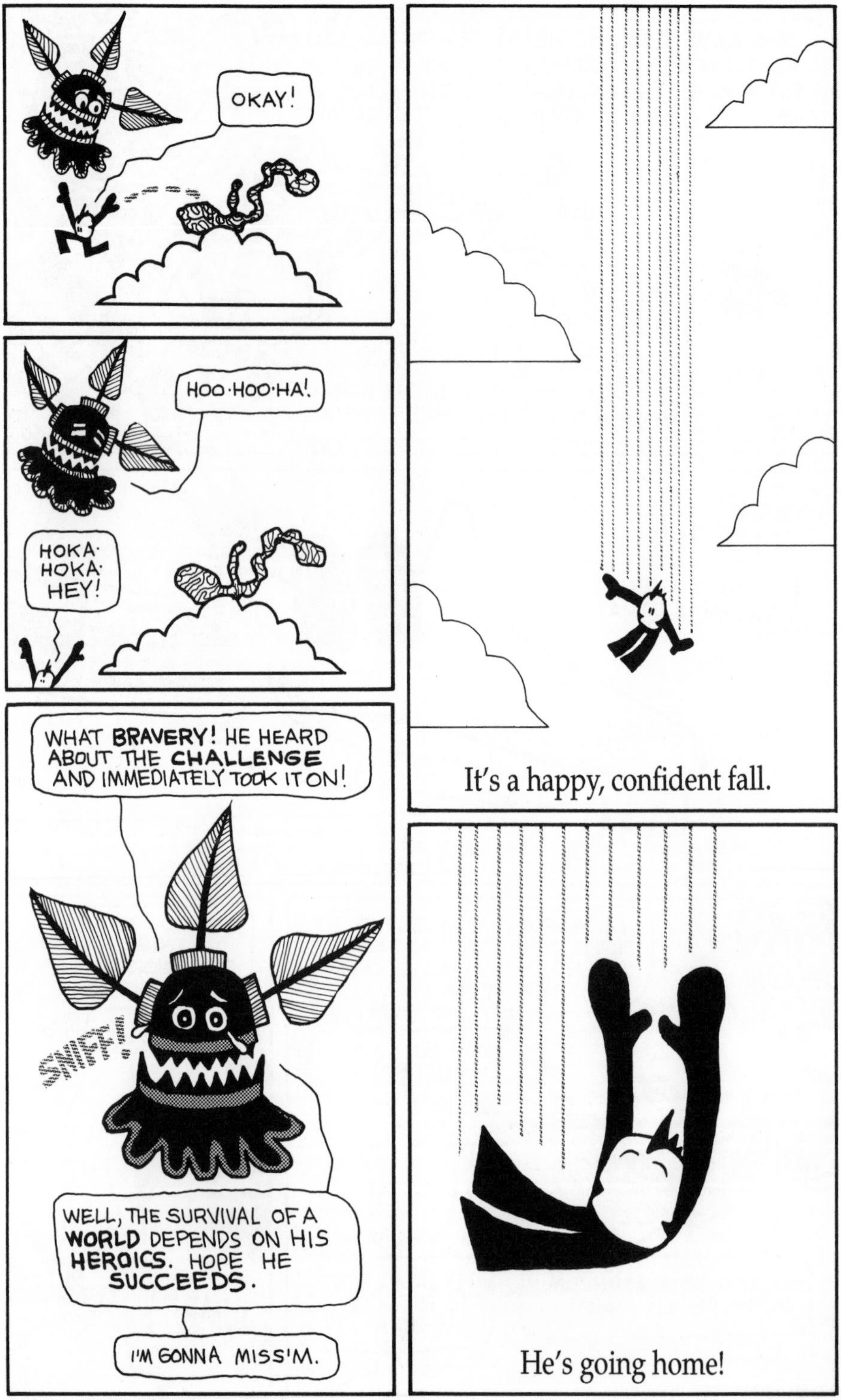
OKAY!
HOO·HOO·HA!
HOKA·
HOKA·
HEY!
WHAT BRAVERY! HE HEARD ABOUT THE CHALLENGE AND IMMEDIATELY TOOK IT ON!
SNIFF!!
WELL, THE SURVIVAL OF A WORLD DEPENDS ON HIS HEROICS. HOPE HE SUCCEEDS.
I'M GONNA MISS'M.
It's a happy, confident fall.
He's going home!

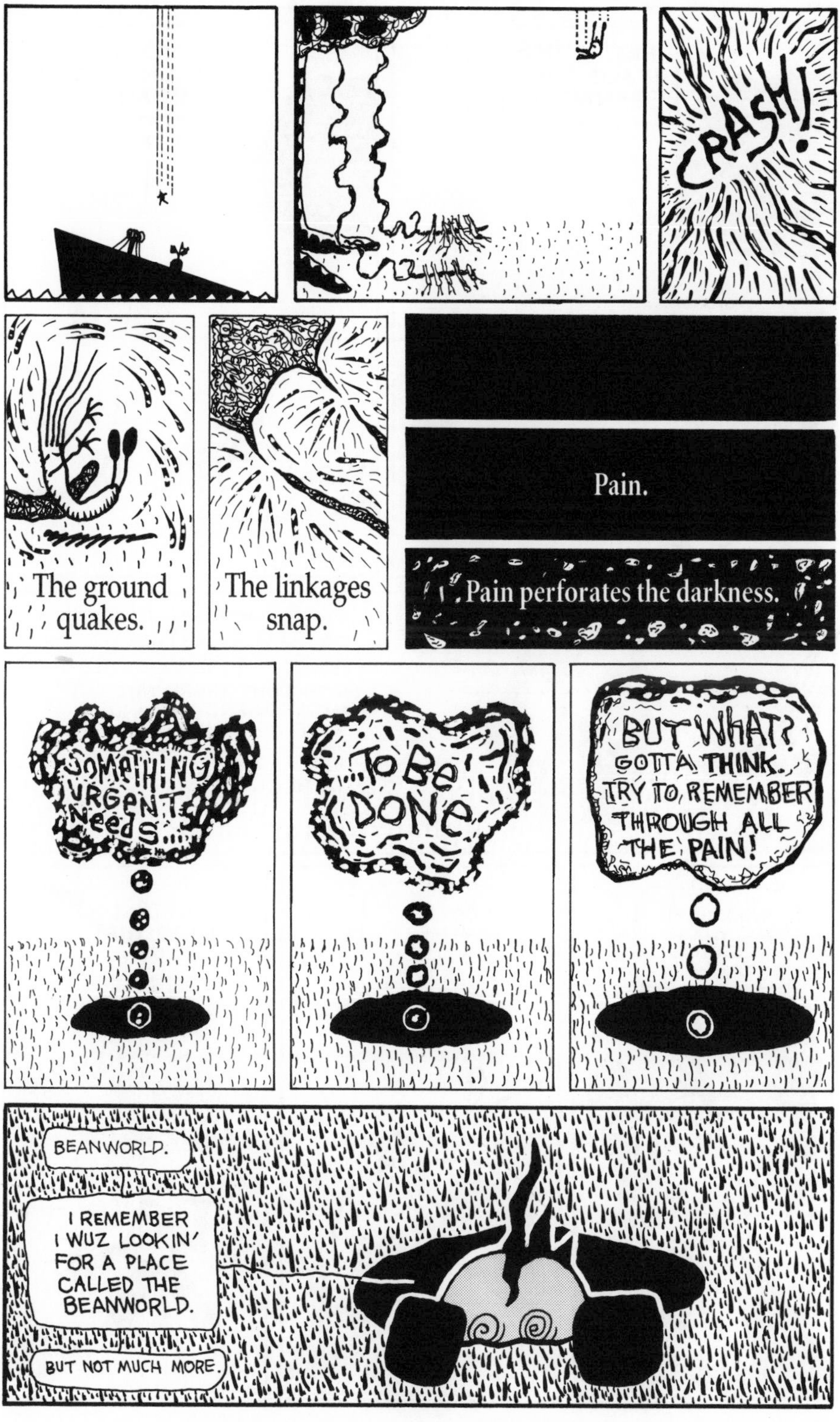
CRASH!
The ground quakes.
The linkages snap.
Pain.
Pain perforates the darkness.
SomeTHING URGENT Needs...
...To Be DONE
BUT WHAT? GOTTA THINK. TRY TO REMEMBER THROUGH ALL THE PAIN!
BEANWORLD.
I REMEMBER I WUZ LOOKIN' FOR A PLACE CALLED THE BEANWORLD.
BUT NOT MUCH MORE.

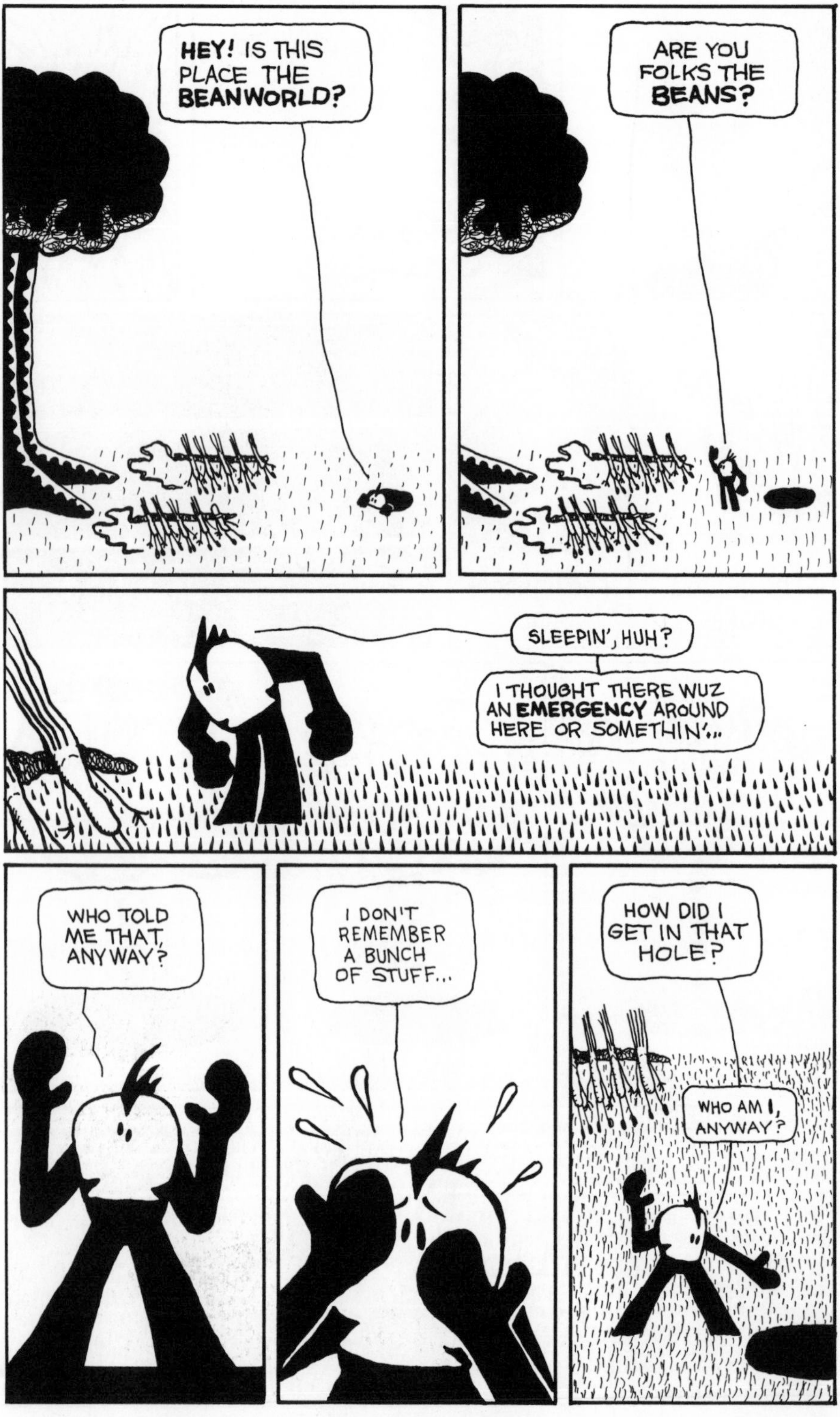
HEY! IS THIS PLACE THE BEANWORLD?
ARE YOU FOLKS THE BEANS?
SLEEPIN', HUH?
I THOUGHT THERE WUZ AN EMERGENCY AROUND HERE OR SOMETHIN'...
WHO TOLD ME THAT, ANYWAY?
I DON'T REMEMBER A BUNCH OF STUFF...
HOW DID I GET IN THAT HOLE?
WHO AM I, ANYWAY?

GRAN'MA'PA worries. Is this intruder a friend or foe? An investigation will be necessary.

GOTTA ASSESS MY CIRCUMSTANCES...

...FIGGER OUT WHAT I KNOW FOR CERTAIN.

HMMM.

I'M A HERO.

I PROTECT AND SERVE THE... THE...

AM I REALLY A HERO?

?

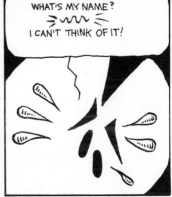

WHAT'S MY NAME?

I CAN'T THINK OF IT!

WHERE'S MY WEAPON?

MAYBE I'M NOT REALLY A HERO AFTER ALL...

YIPES!

GRAN'MA'PA recognizes this poison.

RUB! RUB!

It is the abomination. He's large and strong.

The poison has been transmuted into something noble and heroic.

He's the perfect candidate for **HERO** of this noxious new world.

GRAN'MA'PA accepts him with love.

They bond...for now and forever. Then **GRAN'MA'PA** withdraws.

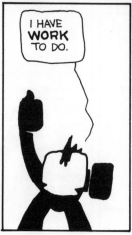

I HAVE **WORK** TO DO.

I HAVE TO FIGURE OUT WHAT'S WRONG WITH THESE BEANS.

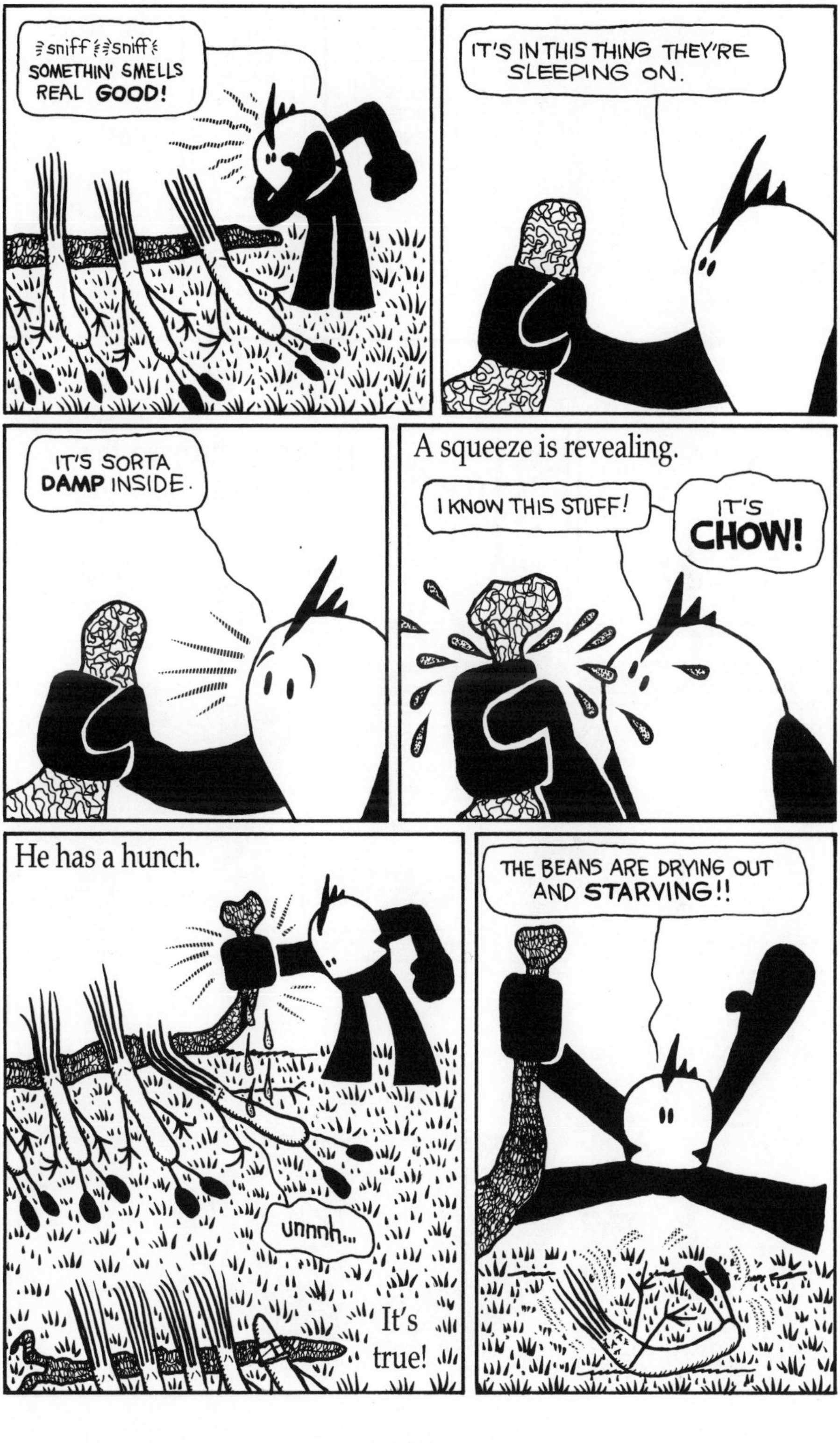
sniff sniff
SOMETHIN' SMELLS REAL GOOD!
IT'S IN THIS THING THEY'RE SLEEPING ON.
IT'S SORTA DAMP INSIDE.
A squeeze is revealing.
I KNOW THIS STUFF!
IT'S CHOW!
He has a hunch.
unnnh...
It's true!
THE BEANS ARE DRYING OUT AND STARVING!!

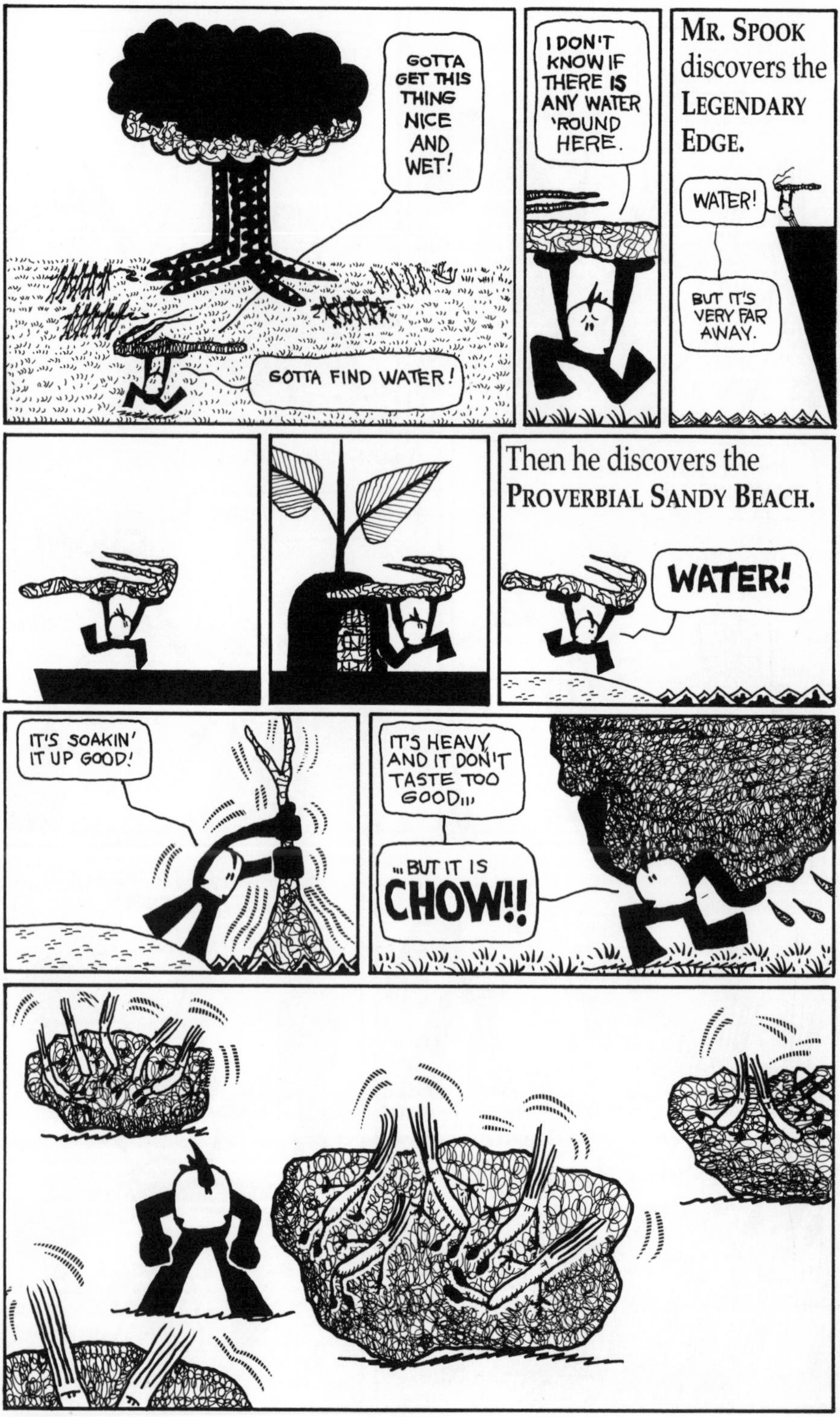
GOTTA GET THIS THING NICE AND WET!
GOTTA FIND WATER!
I DON'T KNOW IF THERE IS ANY WATER 'ROUND HERE.
MR. SPOOK discovers the LEGENDARY EDGE.
WATER!
BUT IT'S VERY FAR AWAY.
Then he discovers the PROVERBIAL SANDY BEACH.
WATER!
IT'S SOAKIN' IT UP GOOD!
IT'S HEAVY AND IT DON'T TASTE TOO GOOD...
...BUT IT IS CHOW!!

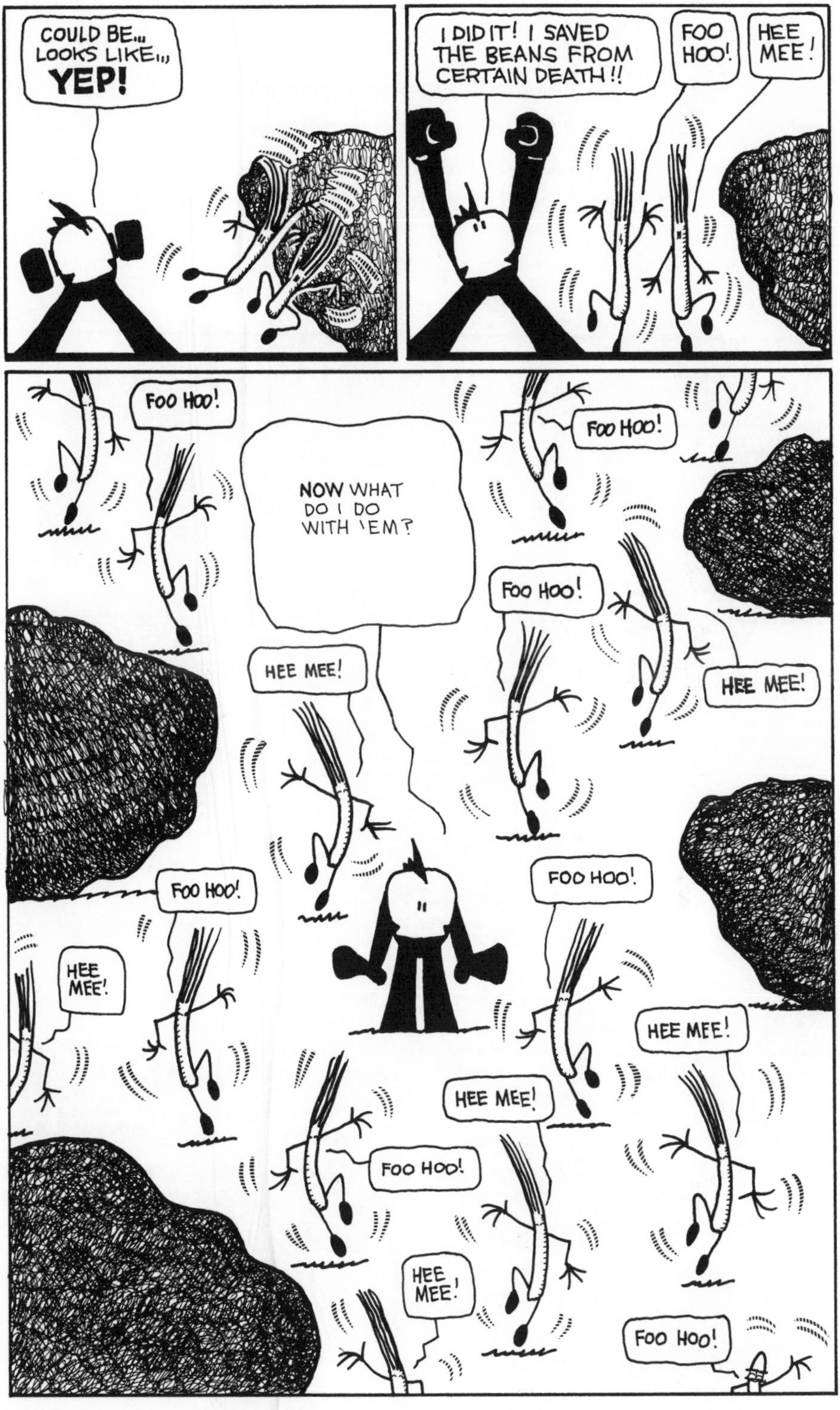

COULD BE... LOOKS LIKE... YEP!
I DID IT! I SAVED THE BEANS FROM CERTAIN DEATH!!
FOO HOO!
HEE MEE!
FOO HOO!
FOO HOO!
NOW WHAT DO I DO WITH 'EM?
FOO HOO!
HEE MEE!
HEE MEE!
FOO HOO!
FOO HOO!
HEE MEE!
HEE MEE!
HEE MEE!
FOO HOO!
HEE MEE!
FOO HOO!

And so the **BEANWORLD** crisis ends.
The young **BEANS** have their protector in place.
GRAN'MA'PA knows it's not the
ideal ecological system, but it'll do for now.

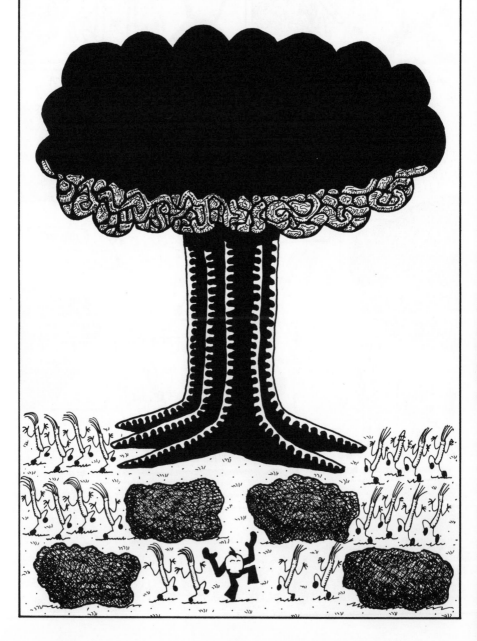

The First Time Professor Garbanzo Discovered the Four Realities.

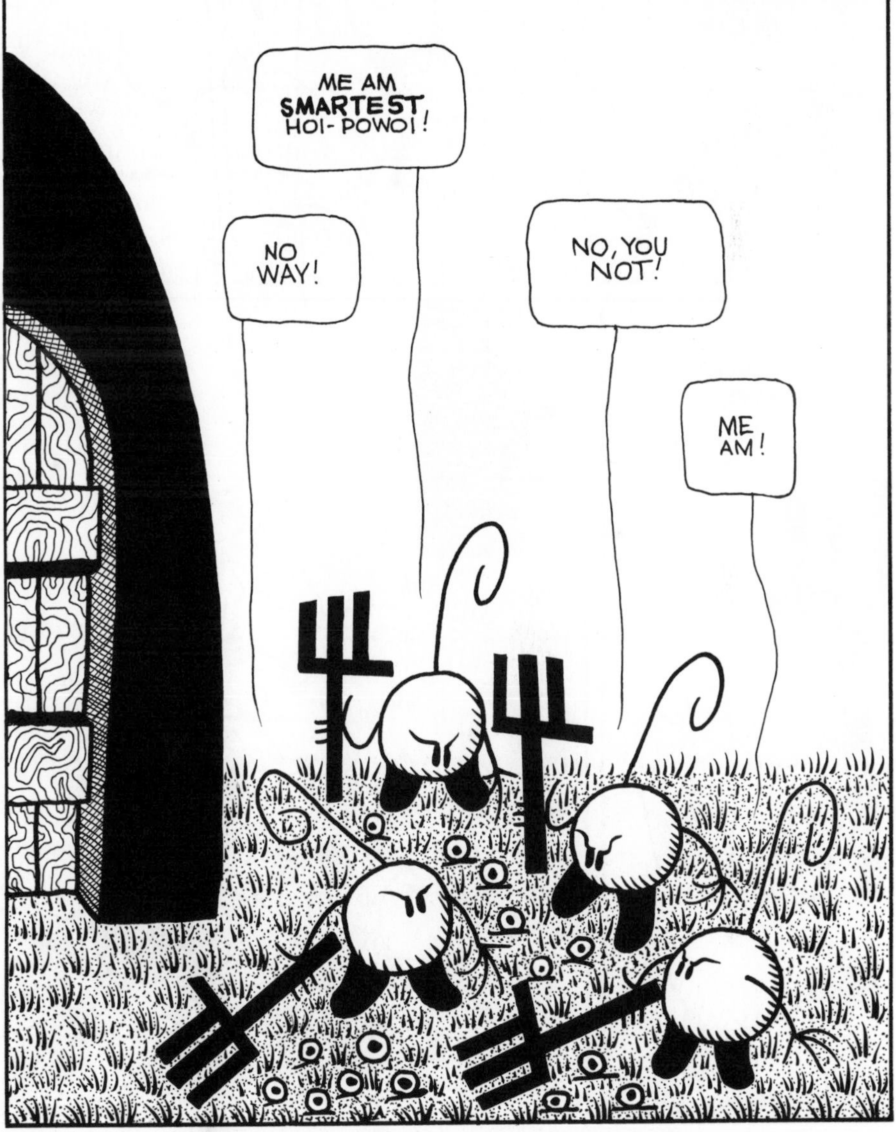
ME AM SMARTEST, HOI-POWOI!
NO WAY!
NO, YOU NOT!
ME AM!

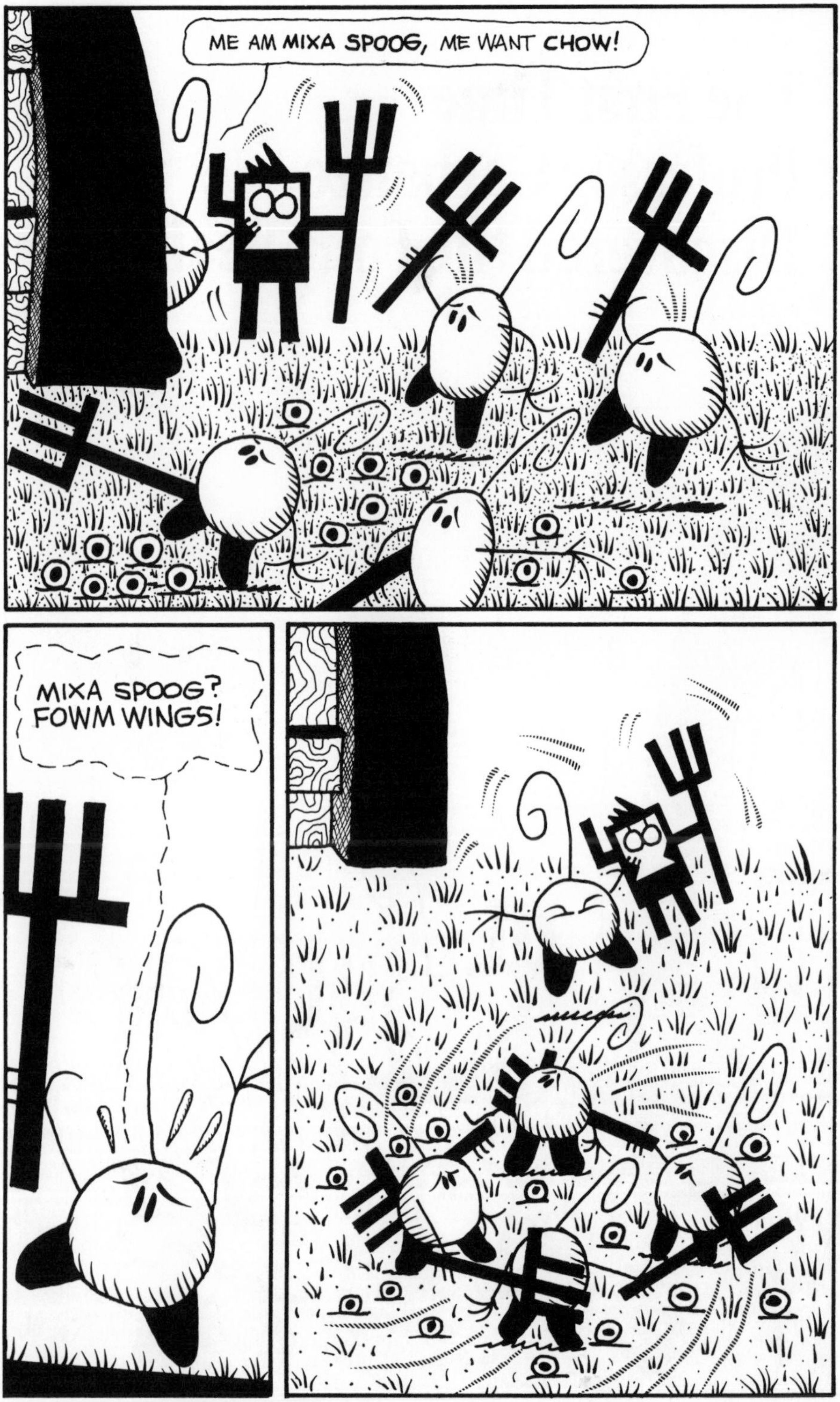
ME AM MIXA SPOOG, ME WANT CHOW!
MIXA SPOOG? FOWM WINGS!

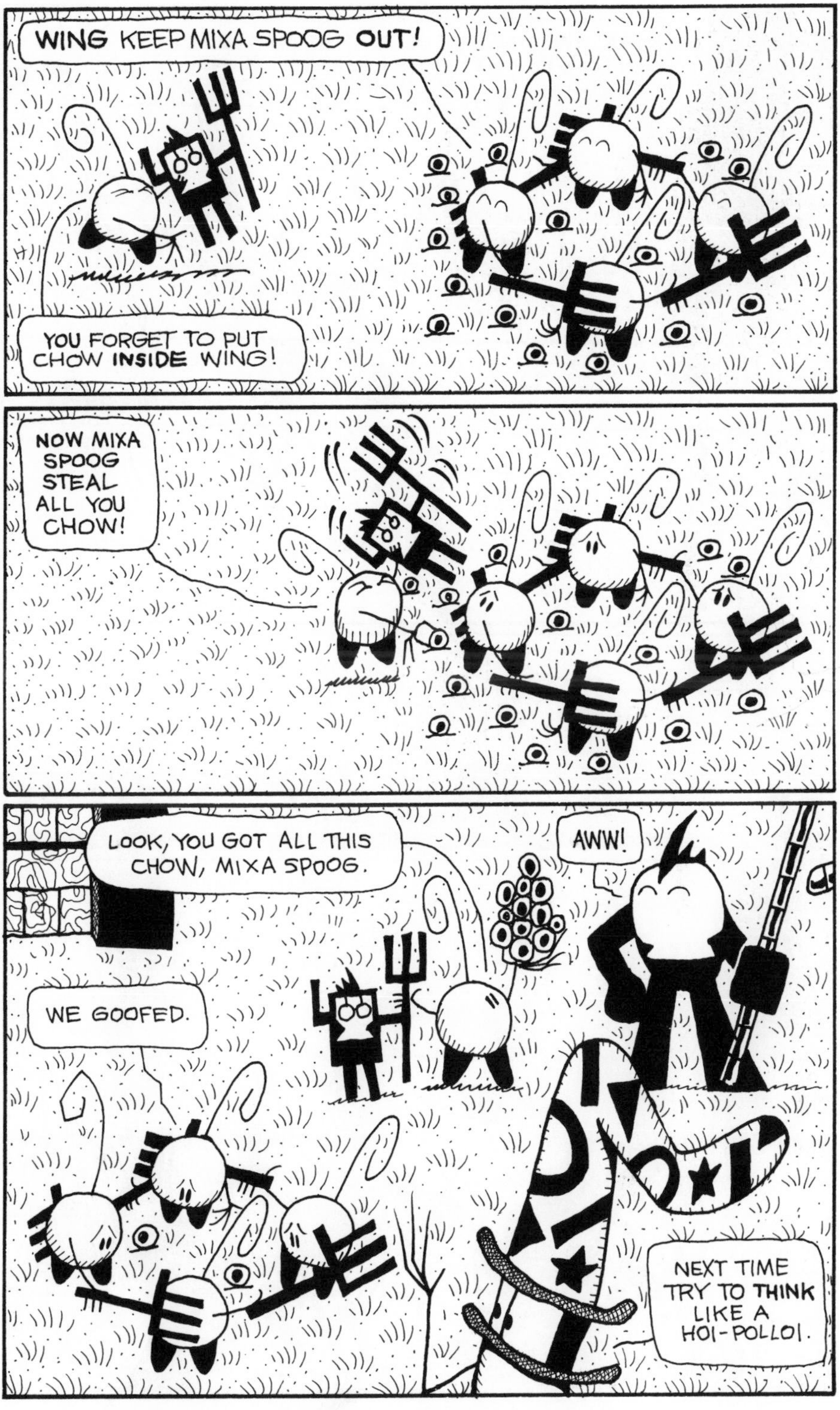
WING KEEP MIXA SPOOG OUT!
YOU FORGET TO PUT CHOW INSIDE WING!
NOW MIXA SPOOG STEAL ALL YOU CHOW!
LOOK, YOU GOT ALL THIS CHOW, MIXA SPOOG.
AWW!
WE GOOFED.
NEXT TIME TRY TO THINK LIKE A HOI-POLLOI.

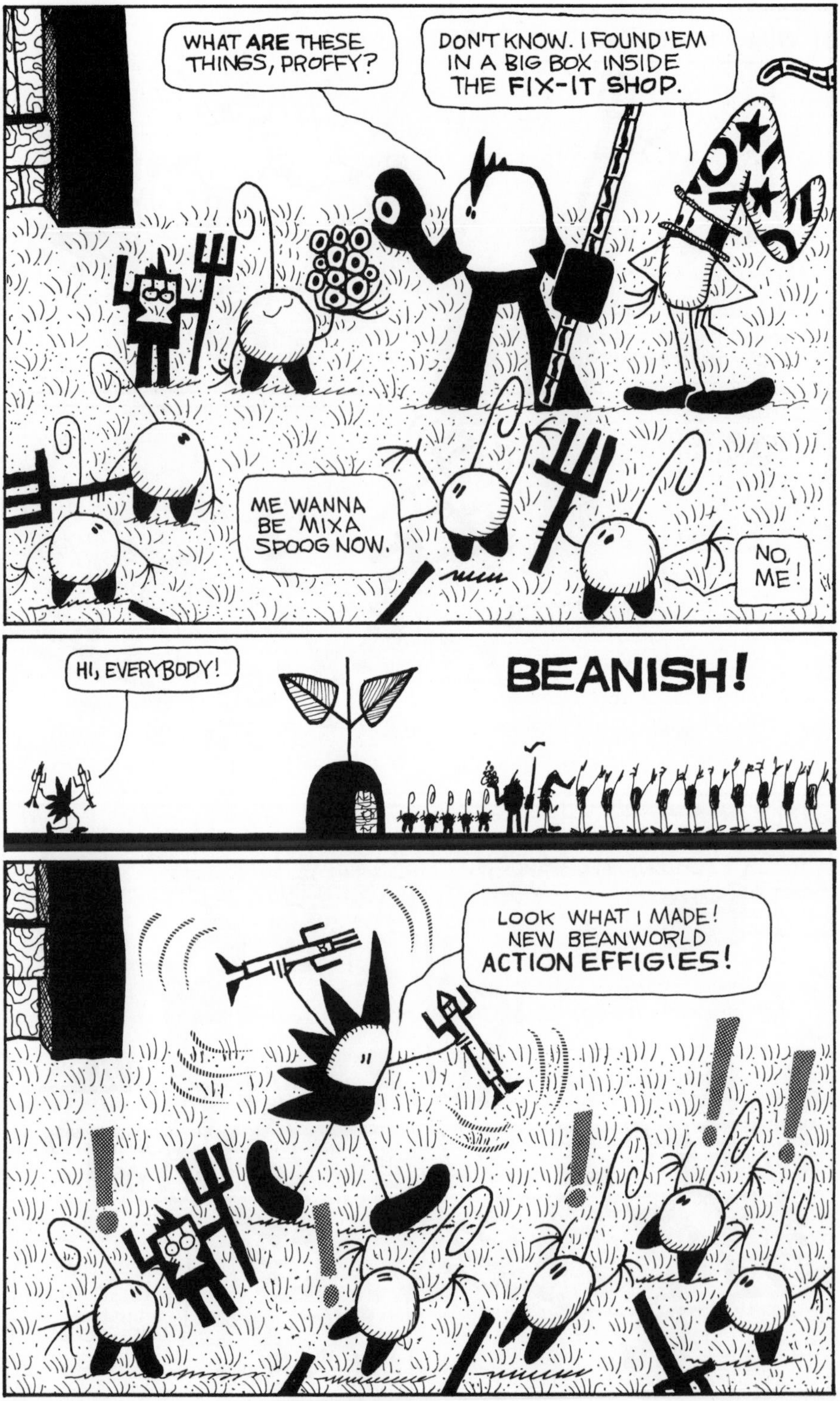
WHAT ARE THESE THINGS, PROFFY?
DON'T KNOW. I FOUND 'EM IN A BIG BOX INSIDE THE FIX-IT SHOP.
ME WANNA BE MIXA SPOOG NOW.
NO, ME!
HI, EVERYBODY!
BEANISH!
LOOK WHAT I MADE! NEW BEANWORLD ACTION EFFIGIES!

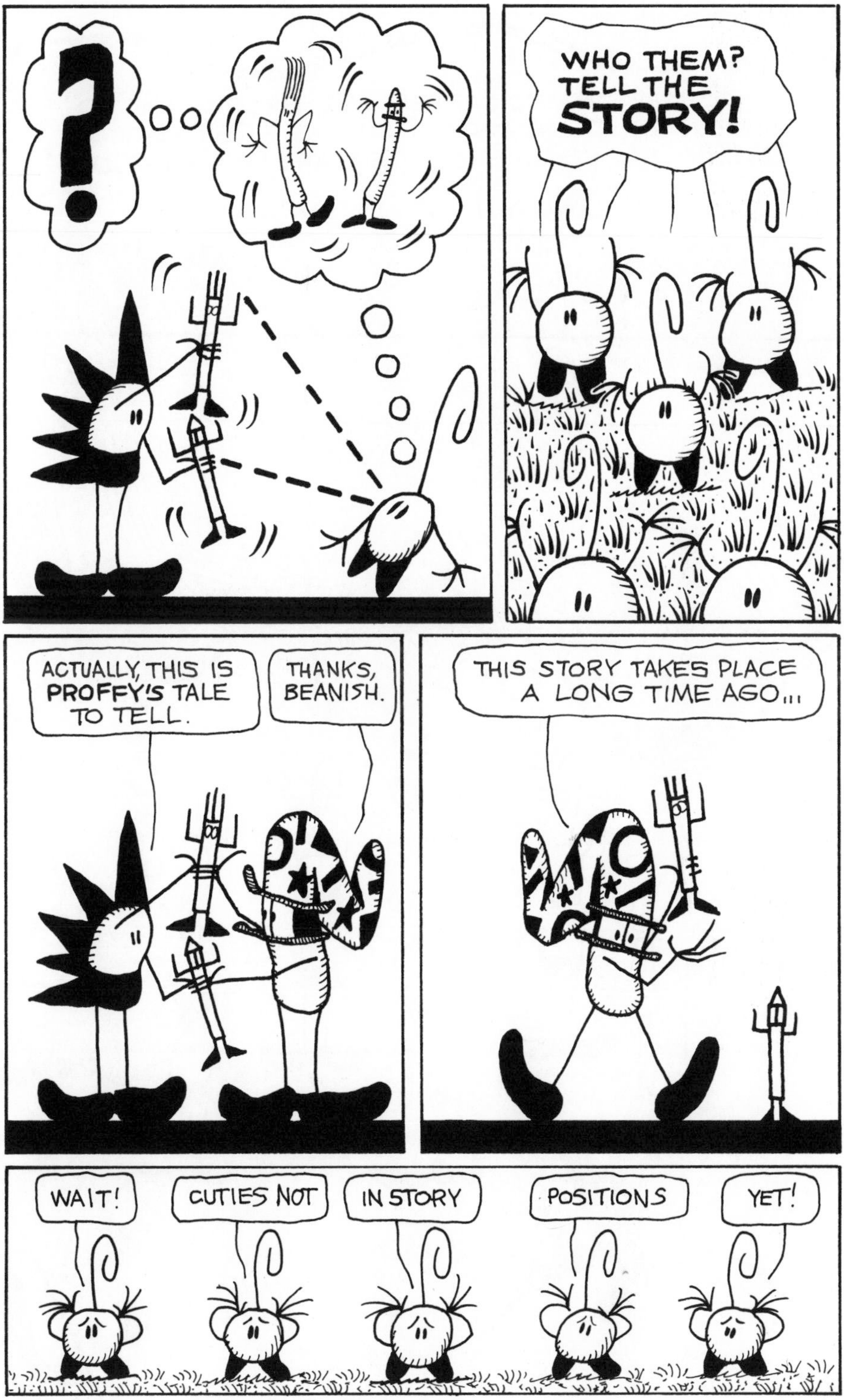
WHO THEM? TELL THE STORY!
ACTUALLY, THIS IS PROFFY'S TALE TO TELL.
THANKS, BEANISH.
THIS STORY TAKES PLACE A LONG TIME AGO...
WAIT!
CUTIES NOT
IN STORY
POSITIONS
YET!

That is remedied.

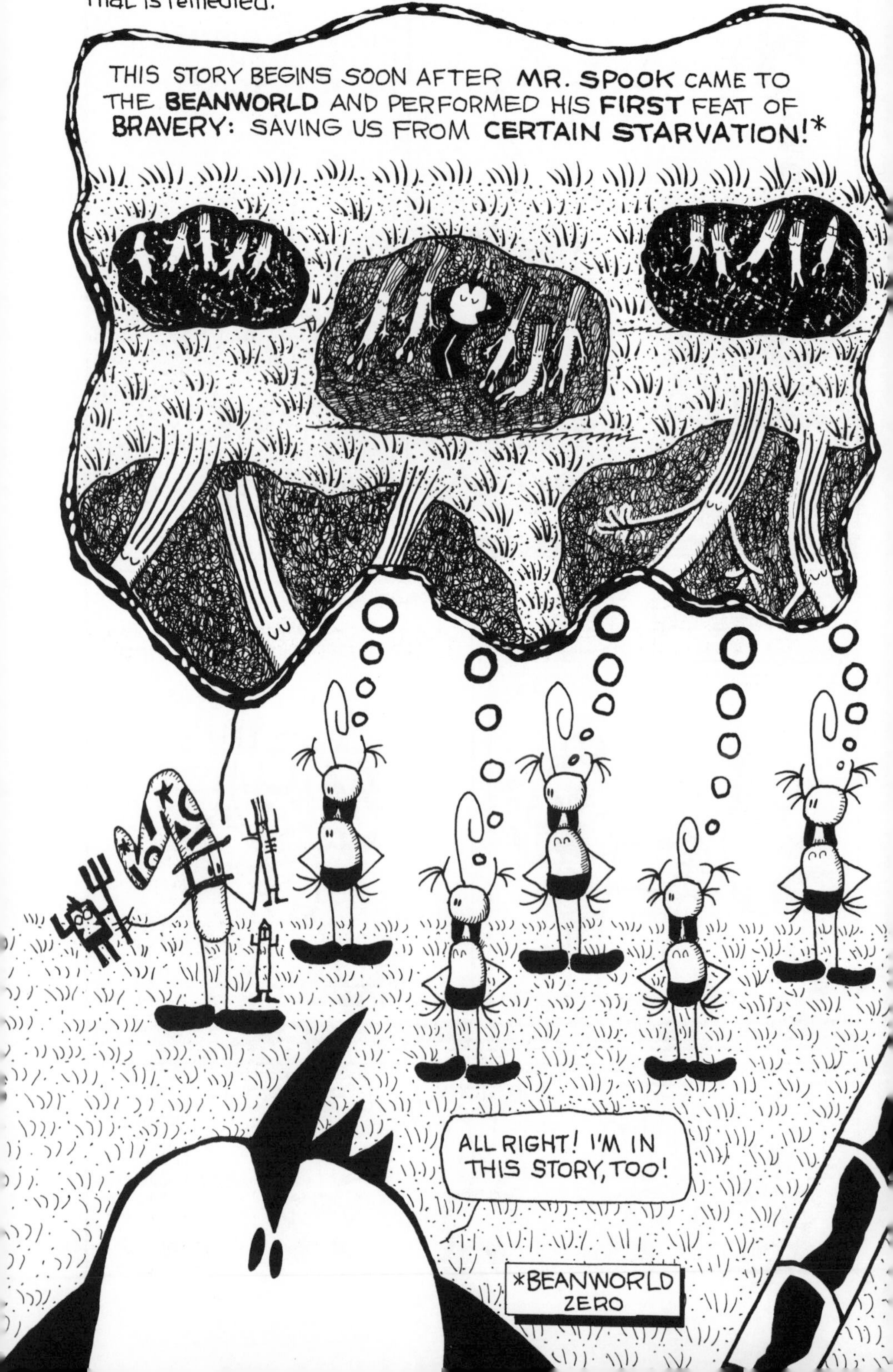
THIS STORY BEGINS SOON AFTER MR. SPOOK CAME TO THE BEANWORLD AND PERFORMED HIS FIRST FEAT OF BRAVERY: SAVING US FROM CERTAIN STARVATION!*
ALL RIGHT! I'M IN THIS STORY, TOO!
*BEANWORLD ZERO

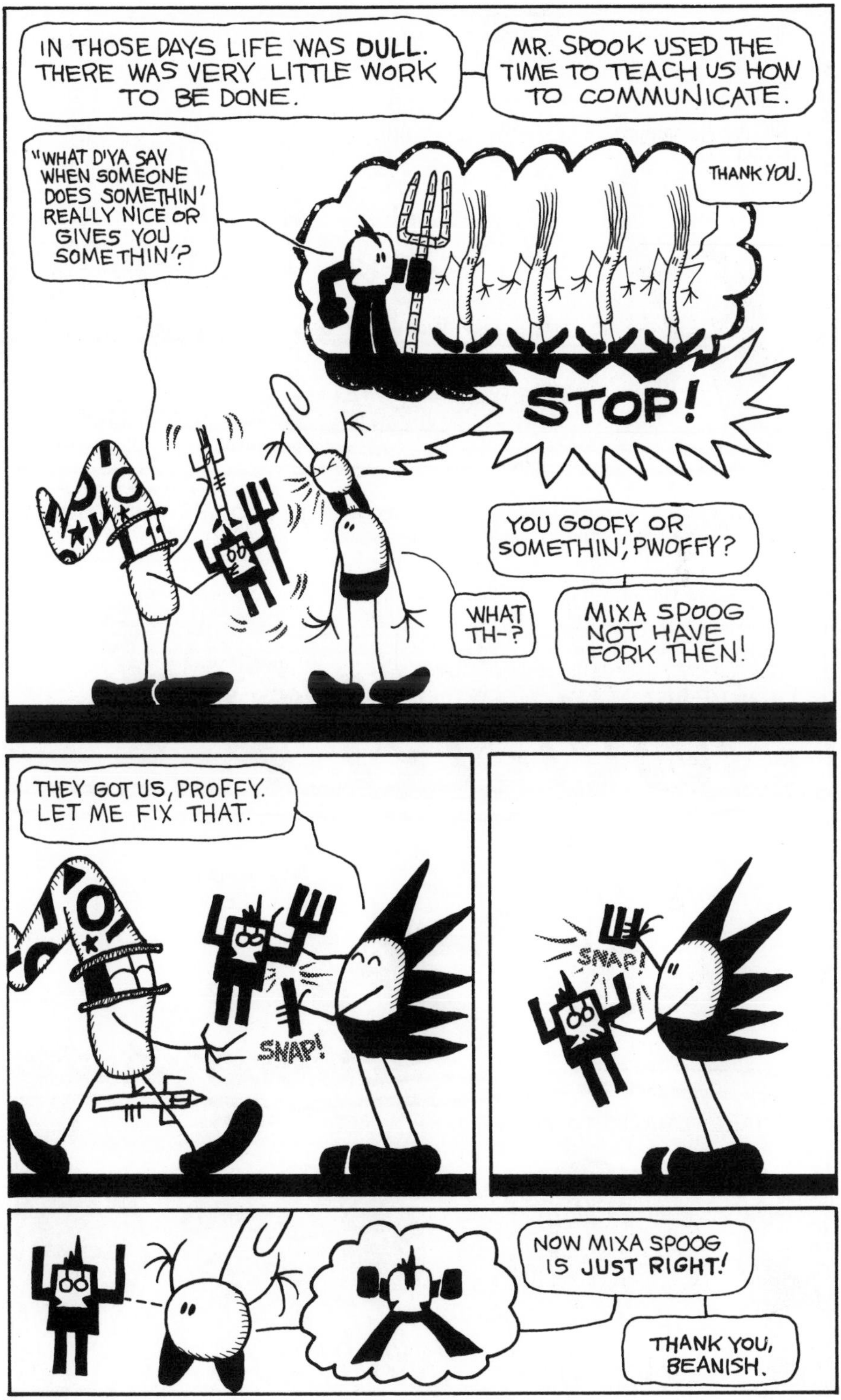
IN THOSE DAYS LIFE WAS **DULL**. THERE WAS VERY LITTLE WORK TO BE DONE.
MR. SPOOK USED THE TIME TO TEACH US HOW TO COMMUNICATE.
"WHAT D'YA SAY WHEN SOMEONE DOES SOMETHIN' REALLY NICE OR GIVES YOU SOMETHIN'?
THANK YOU.
STOP!
YOU GOOFY OR SOMETHIN', PWOFFY?
WHAT TH-?
MIXA SPOOG NOT HAVE FORK THEN!
THEY GOT US, PROFFY. LET ME FIX THAT.
SNAP!
SNAP!
NOW MIXA SPOOG IS **JUST RIGHT**!
THANK YOU, BEANISH.

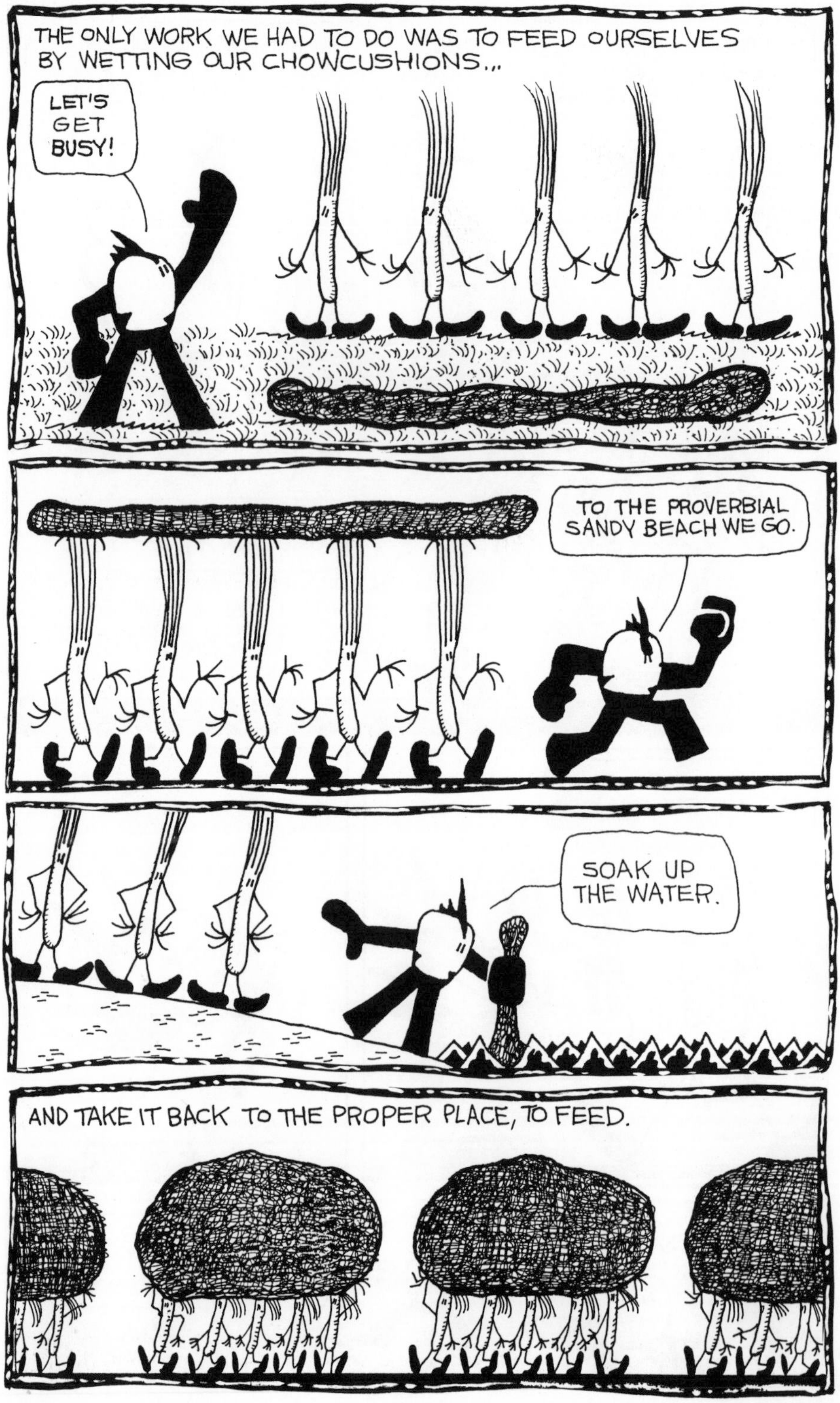
THE ONLY WORK WE HAD TO DO WAS TO FEED OURSELVES BY WETTING OUR CHOWCUSHIONS...
LET'S GET BUSY!
TO THE PROVERBIAL SANDY BEACH WE GO.
SOAK UP THE WATER.
AND TAKE IT BACK TO THE PROPER PLACE, TO FEED.

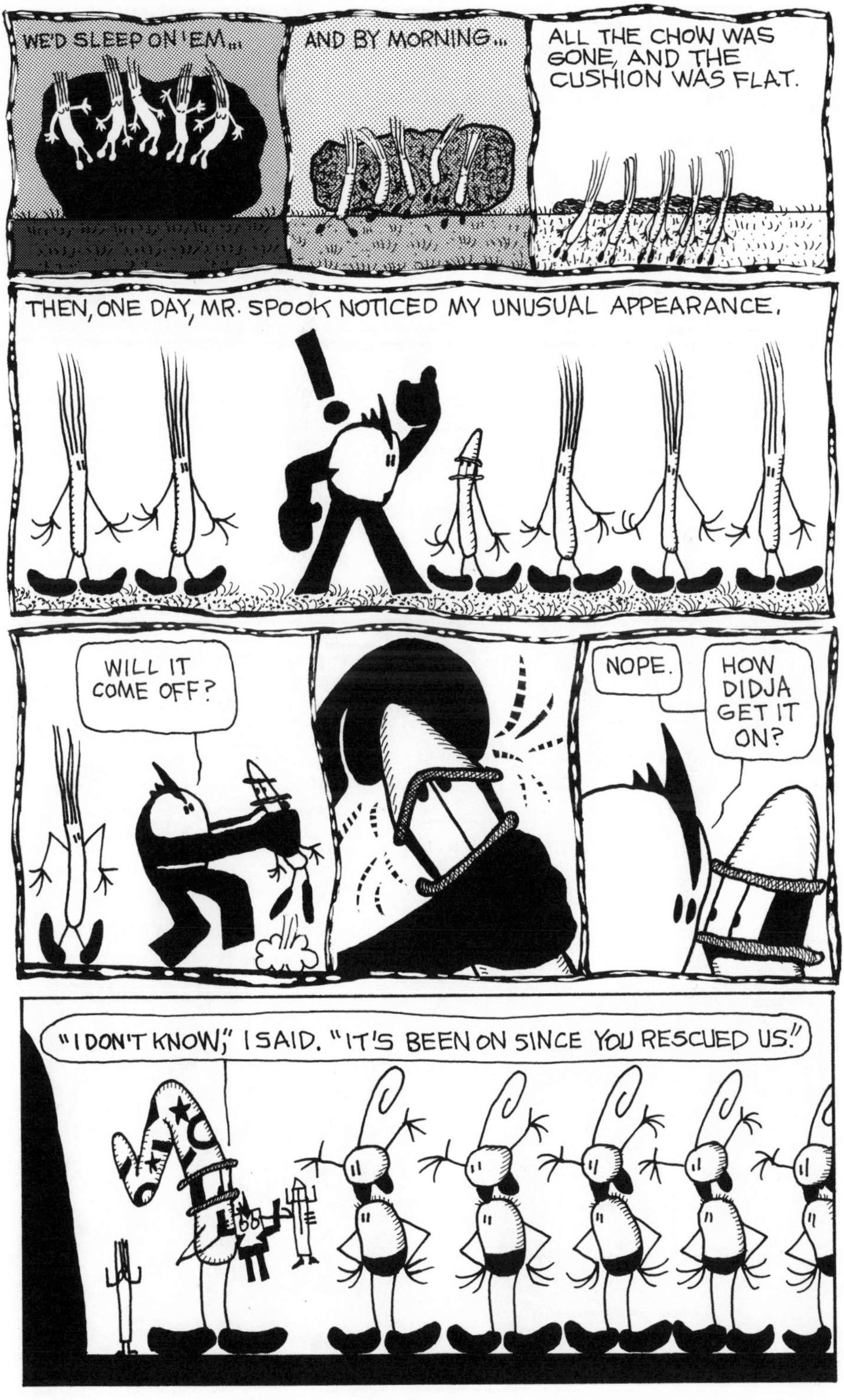

WE'D SLEEP ON 'EM...
AND BY MORNING...
ALL THE CHOW WAS GONE, AND THE CUSHION WAS FLAT.
THEN, ONE DAY, MR. SPOOK NOTICED MY UNUSUAL APPEARANCE.
!
WILL IT COME OFF?
NOPE.
HOW DIDJA GET IT ON?
"I DON'T KNOW," I SAID. "IT'S BEEN ON SINCE YOU RESCUED US."

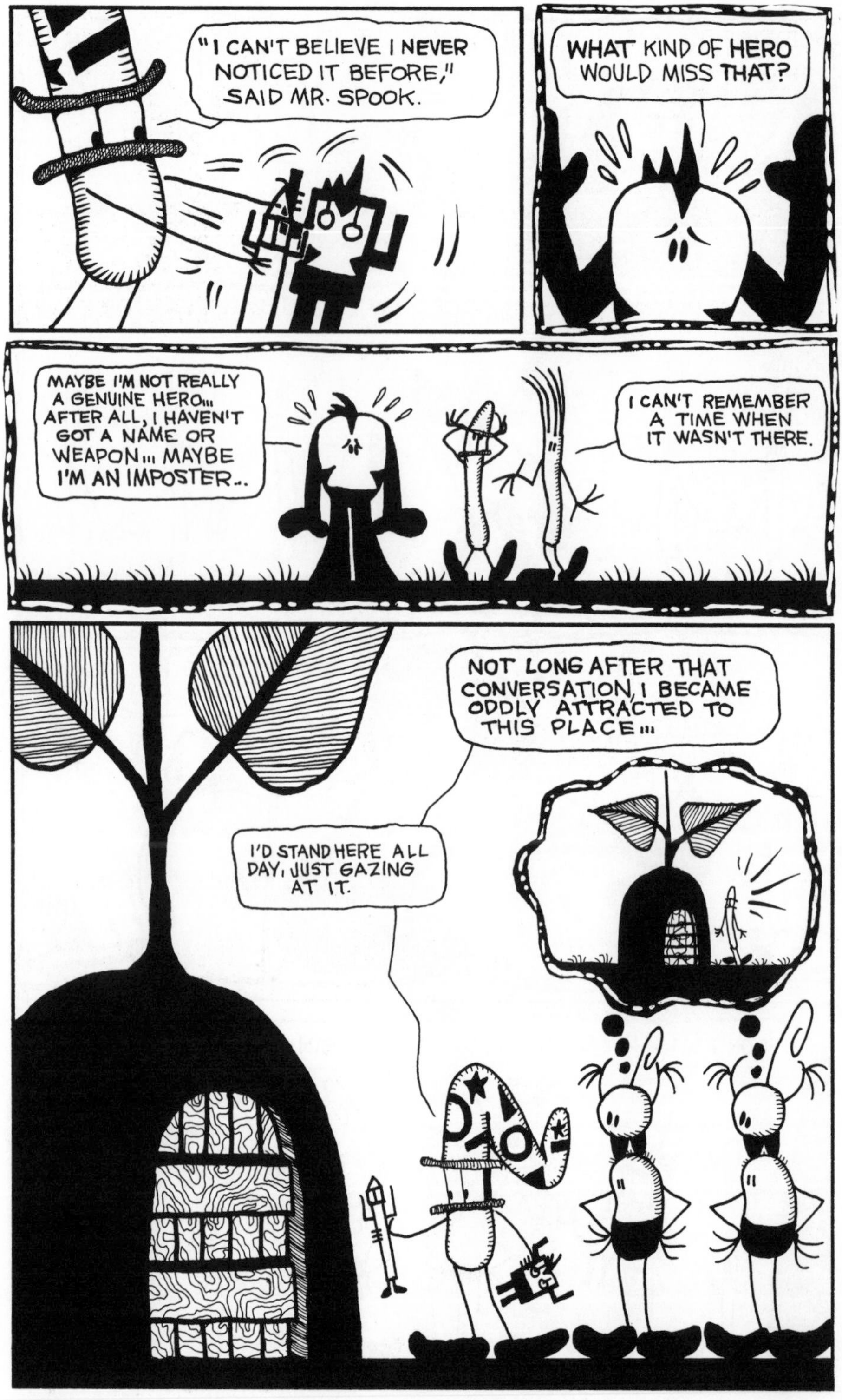
"I CAN'T BELIEVE I NEVER NOTICED IT BEFORE," SAID MR. SPOOK.
WHAT KIND OF HERO WOULD MISS THAT?
MAYBE I'M NOT REALLY A GENUINE HERO... AFTER ALL, I HAVEN'T GOT A NAME OR WEAPON... MAYBE I'M AN IMPOSTER..
I CAN'T REMEMBER A TIME WHEN IT WASN'T THERE.
NOT LONG AFTER THAT CONVERSATION, I BECAME ODDLY ATTRACTED TO THIS PLACE...
I'D STAND HERE ALL DAY, JUST GAZING AT IT.

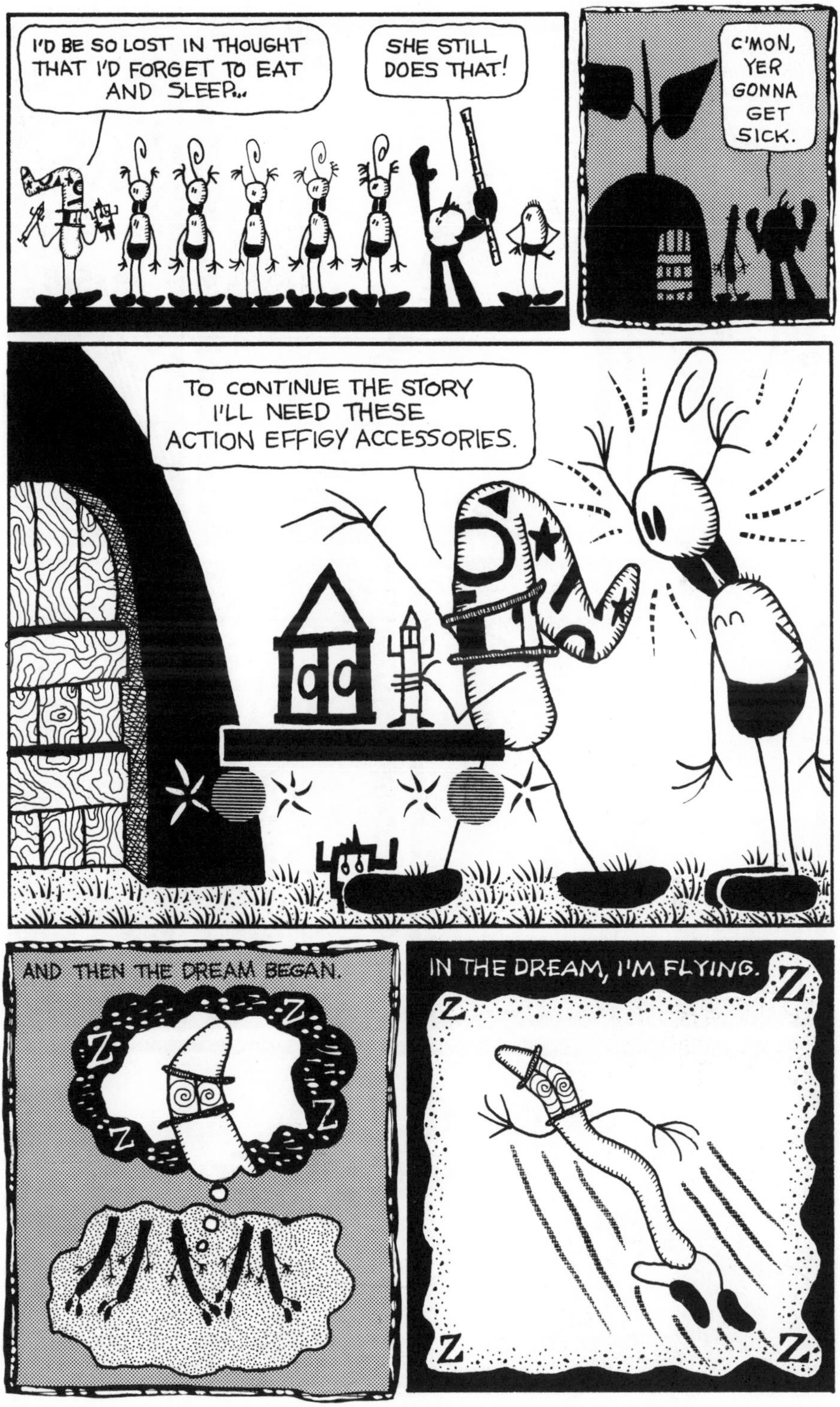
I'D BE SO LOST IN THOUGHT THAT I'D FORGET TO EAT AND SLEEP...
SHE STILL DOES THAT!
C'MON, YER GONNA GET SICK.
TO CONTINUE THE STORY I'LL NEED THESE ACTION EFFIGY ACCESSORIES.
AND THEN THE DREAM BEGAN.
IN THE DREAM, I'M FLYING.

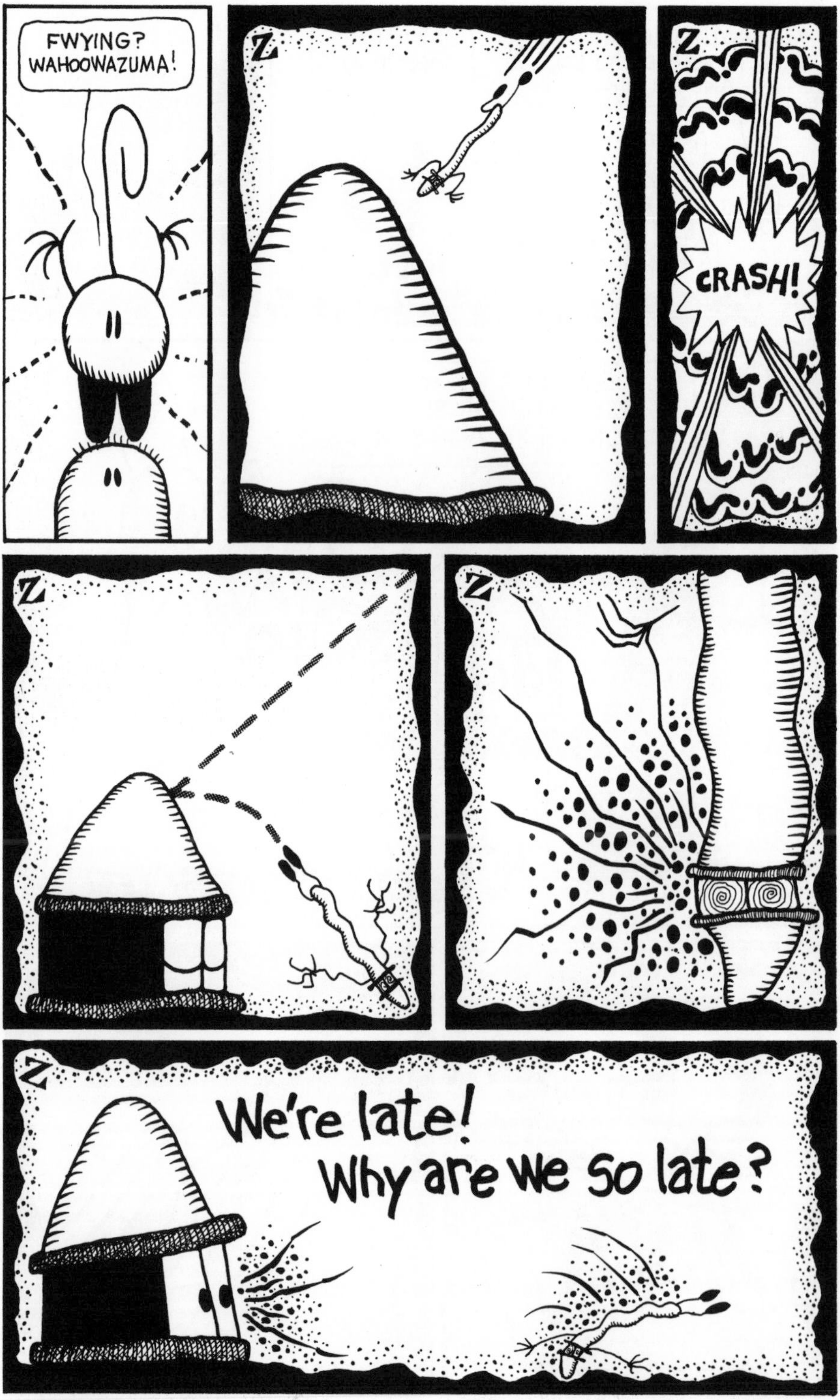
FWYING? WAHOOWAZUMA!
Z
Z
CRASH!
Z
Z
Z
We're late! Why are we so late?

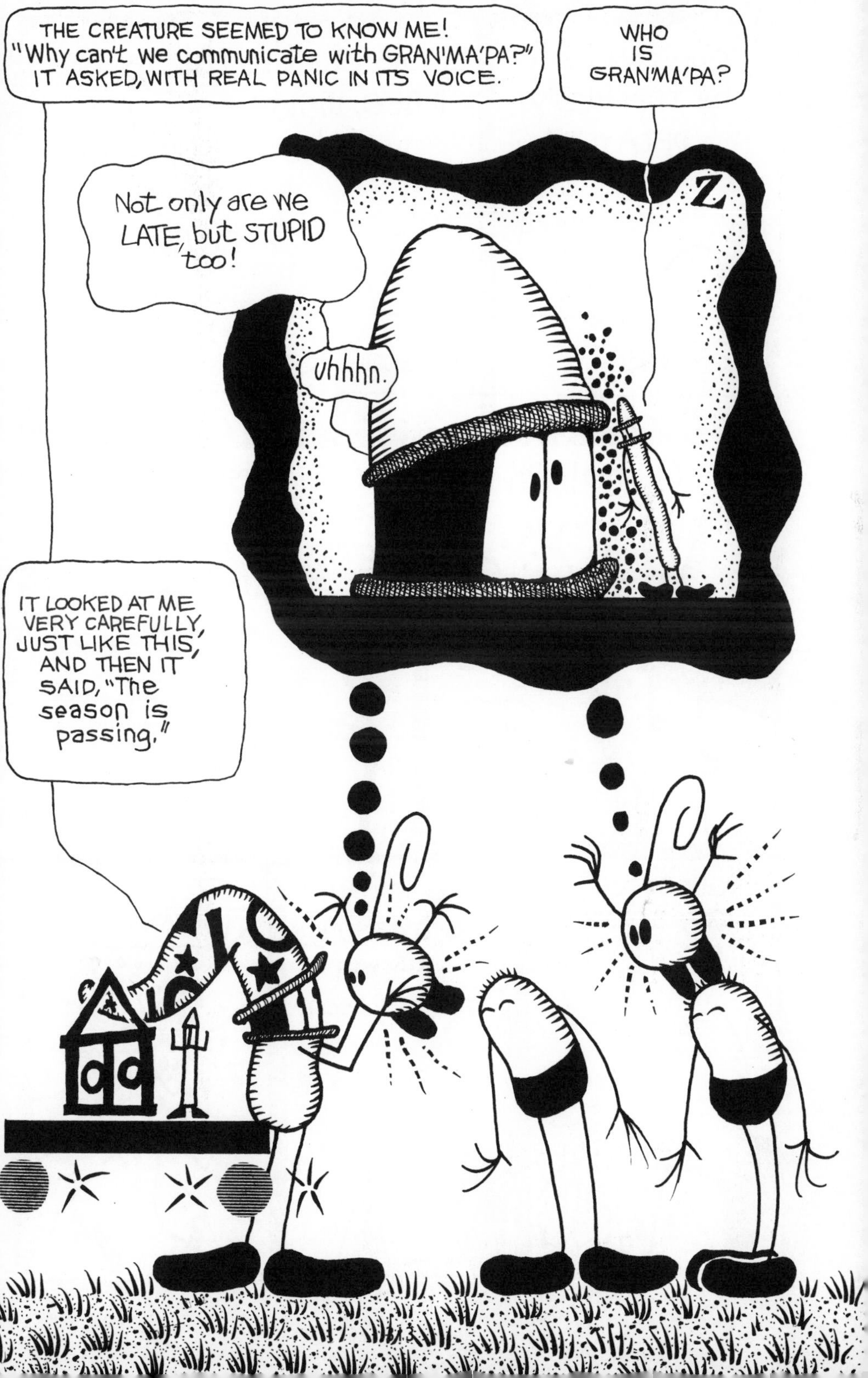
THE CREATURE SEEMED TO KNOW ME! "Why can't we communicate with GRAN'MA'PA?" IT ASKED, WITH REAL PANIC IN ITS VOICE.
WHO IS GRAN'MA'PA?
Not only are we LATE, but STUPID too!
uhhhn.
Z
IT LOOKED AT ME VERY CAREFULLY, JUST LIKE THIS, AND THEN IT SAID, "The season is passing."

Our tools will be hopelessly DELAYED!

WHAT'S A TOOL?

Tools are the things we make, inside. Just how stupid are you this year, anyway?

UH....

Oh no! Oh no!

WHAT? WHAT?

It's the worst case scenario. Your hat is blank! You've lost the FOUR REALITIES that open the door!

WHAT'S A DOOR?

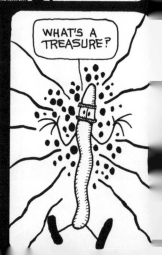

What's a door? What's a tool? Who is GRAN'MA'PA? It's all gone!

WHAT'S GONE?

You've lost all the treasures, except speech!

WHAT'S A TREASURE?

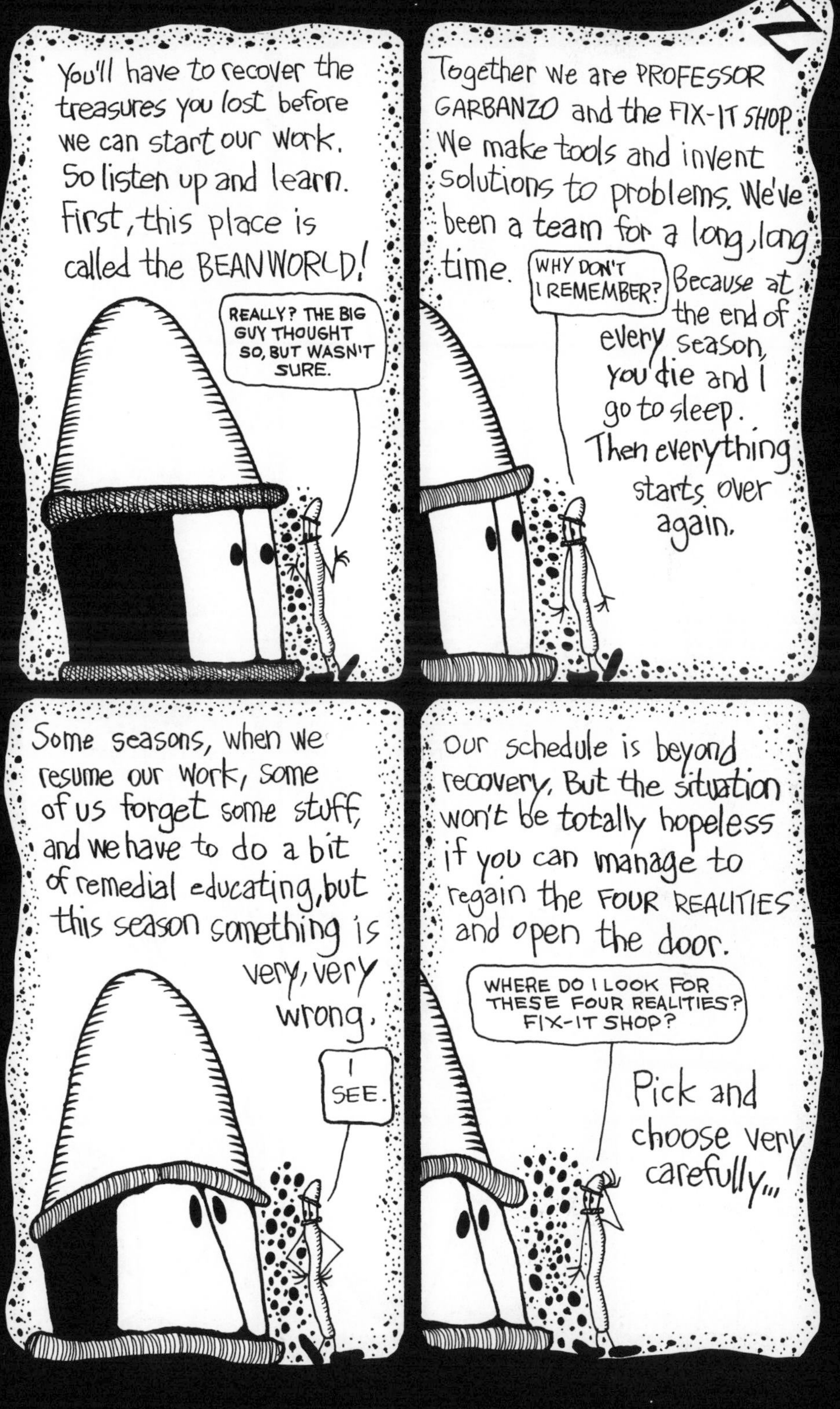
You'll have to recover the treasures you lost before we can start our work. So listen up and learn. First, this place is called the BEANWORLD!
REALLY? THE BIG GUY THOUGHT SO, BUT WASN'T SURE.
Together we are PROFESSOR GARBANZO and the FIX-IT SHOP. We make tools and invent solutions to problems. We've been a team for a long, long time.
WHY DON'T I REMEMBER?
Because at the end of every season, you die and I go to sleep. Then everything starts over again.
Some seasons, when we resume our work, some of us forget some stuff, and we have to do a bit of remedial educating, but this season something is very, very wrong.
I SEE.
Our schedule is beyond recovery. But the situation won't be totally hopeless if you can manage to regain the FOUR REALITIES and open the door.
WHERE DO I LOOK FOR THESE FOUR REALITIES? FIX-IT SHOP?
Pick and choose very carefully...!

AND THEN I WAS FLYING AGAIN.

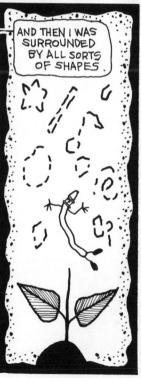

AND THEN I WAS SURROUNDED BY ALL SORTS OF SHAPES.

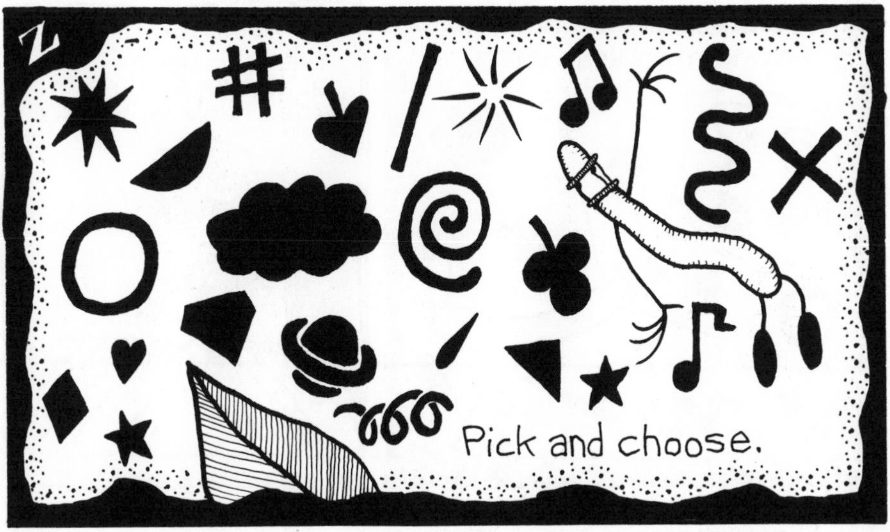
Pick and choose.

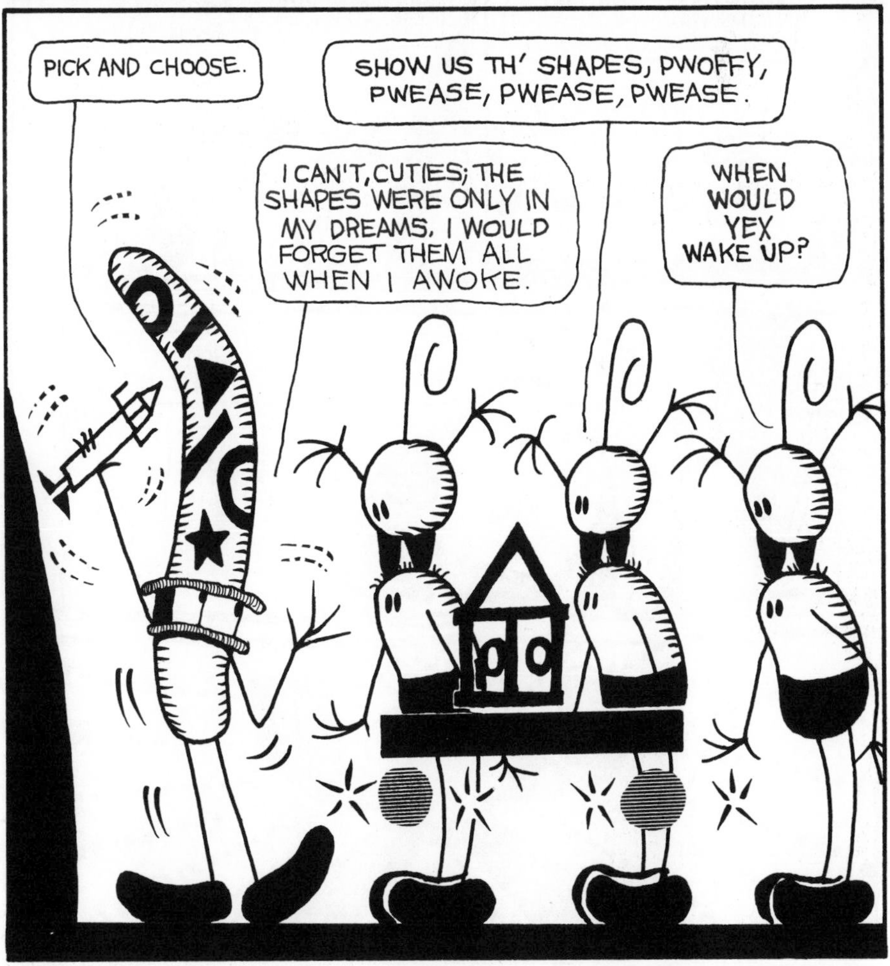
PICK AND CHOOSE.
SHOW US TH' SHAPES, PWOFFY, PWEASE, PWEASE, PWEASE.
I CAN'T, CUTIES; THE SHAPES WERE ONLY IN MY DREAMS. I WOULD FORGET THEM ALL WHEN I AWOKE.
WHEN WOULD YEX WAKE UP?

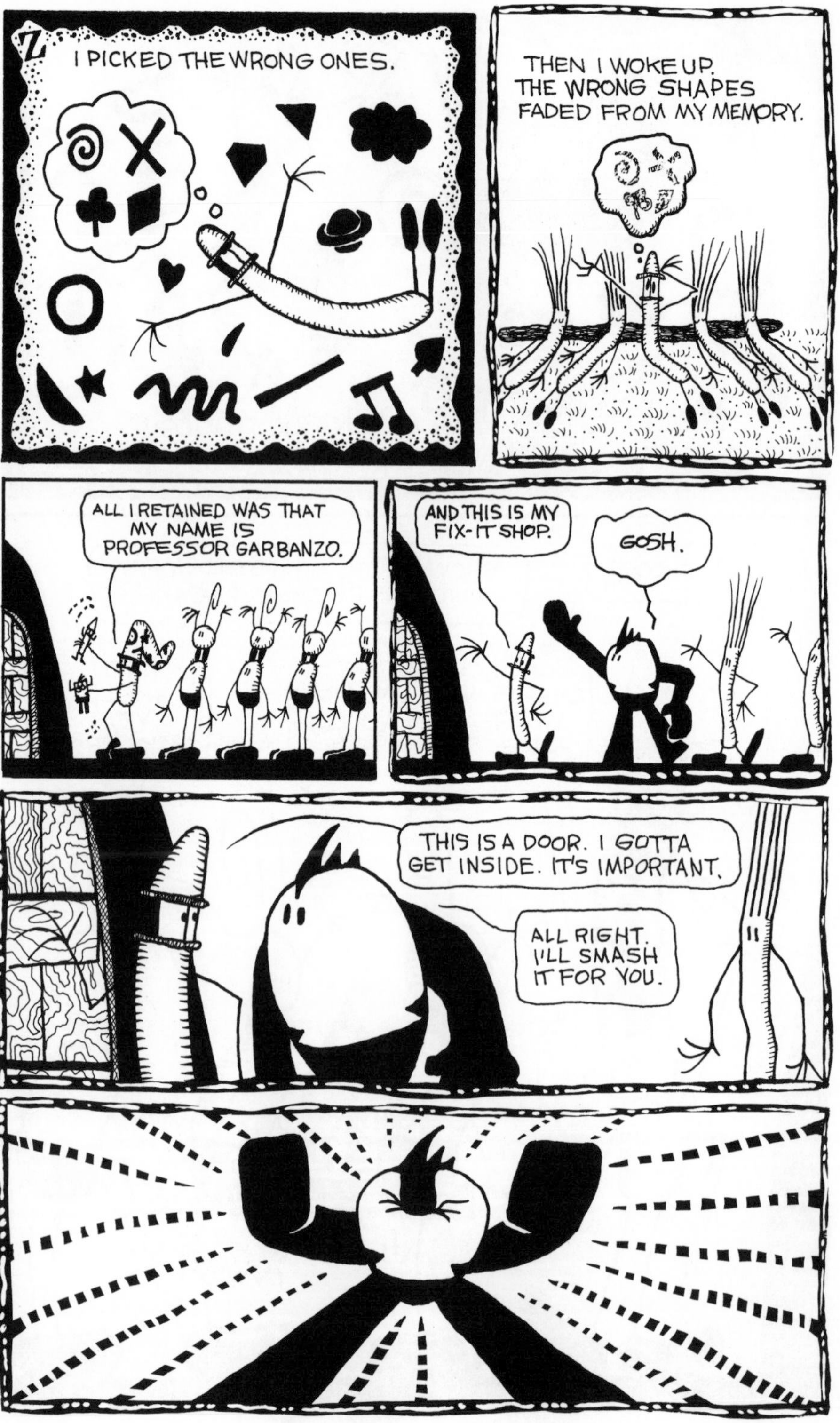
Z
I PICKED THE WRONG ONES.
THEN I WOKE UP. THE WRONG SHAPES FADED FROM MY MEMORY.
ALL I RETAINED WAS THAT MY NAME IS PROFESSOR GARBANZO.
AND THIS IS MY FIX-IT SHOP.
GOSH.
THIS IS A DOOR. I GOTTA GET INSIDE. IT'S IMPORTANT.
ALL RIGHT. I'LL SMASH IT FOR YOU.

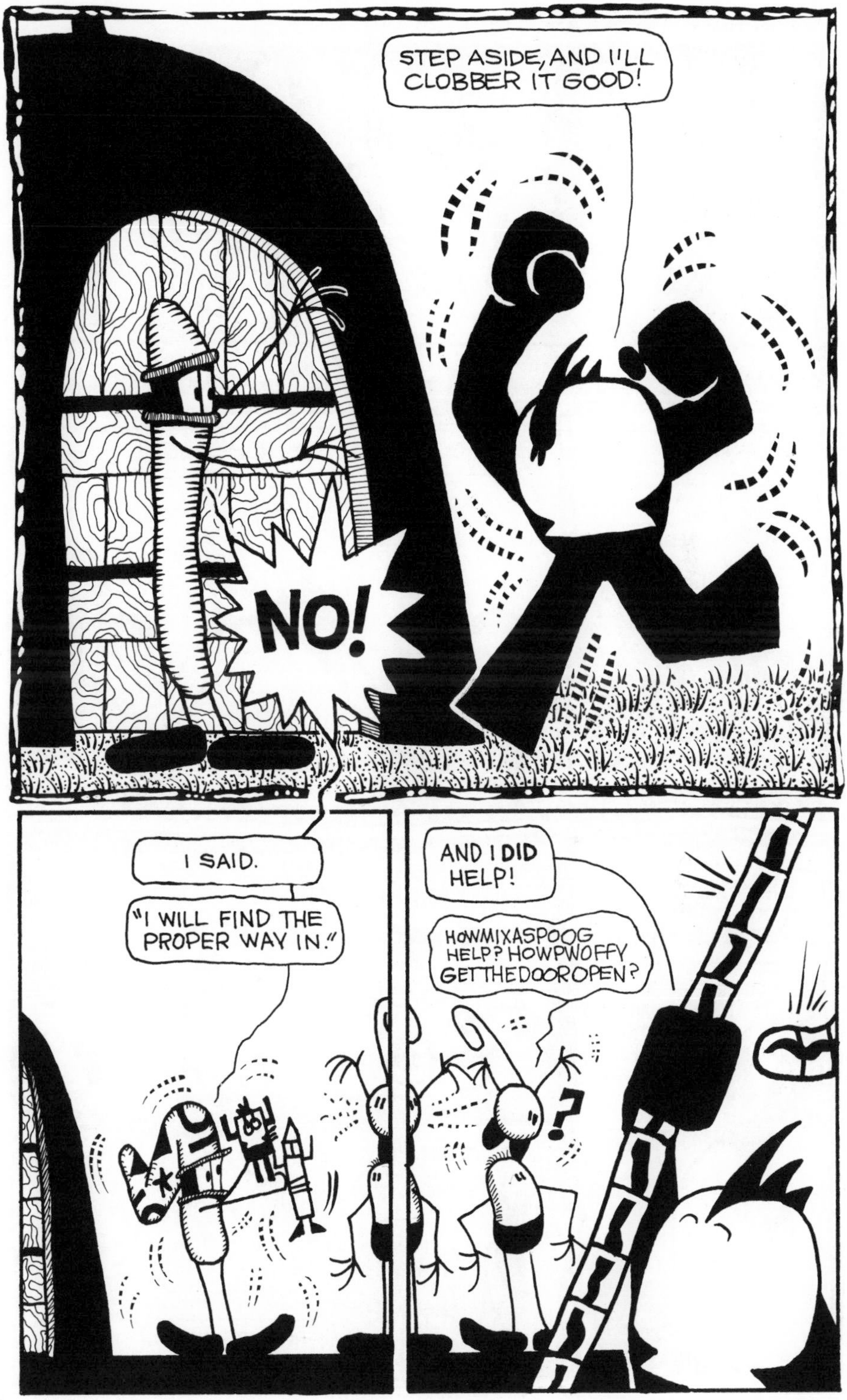
STEP ASIDE, AND I'LL CLOBBER IT GOOD!
NO!
I SAID.
"I WILL FIND THE PROPER WAY IN."
AND I DID HELP!
HOWMIXASPOOG HELP? HOWPWOFFY GETTHEDOOROPEN?
?

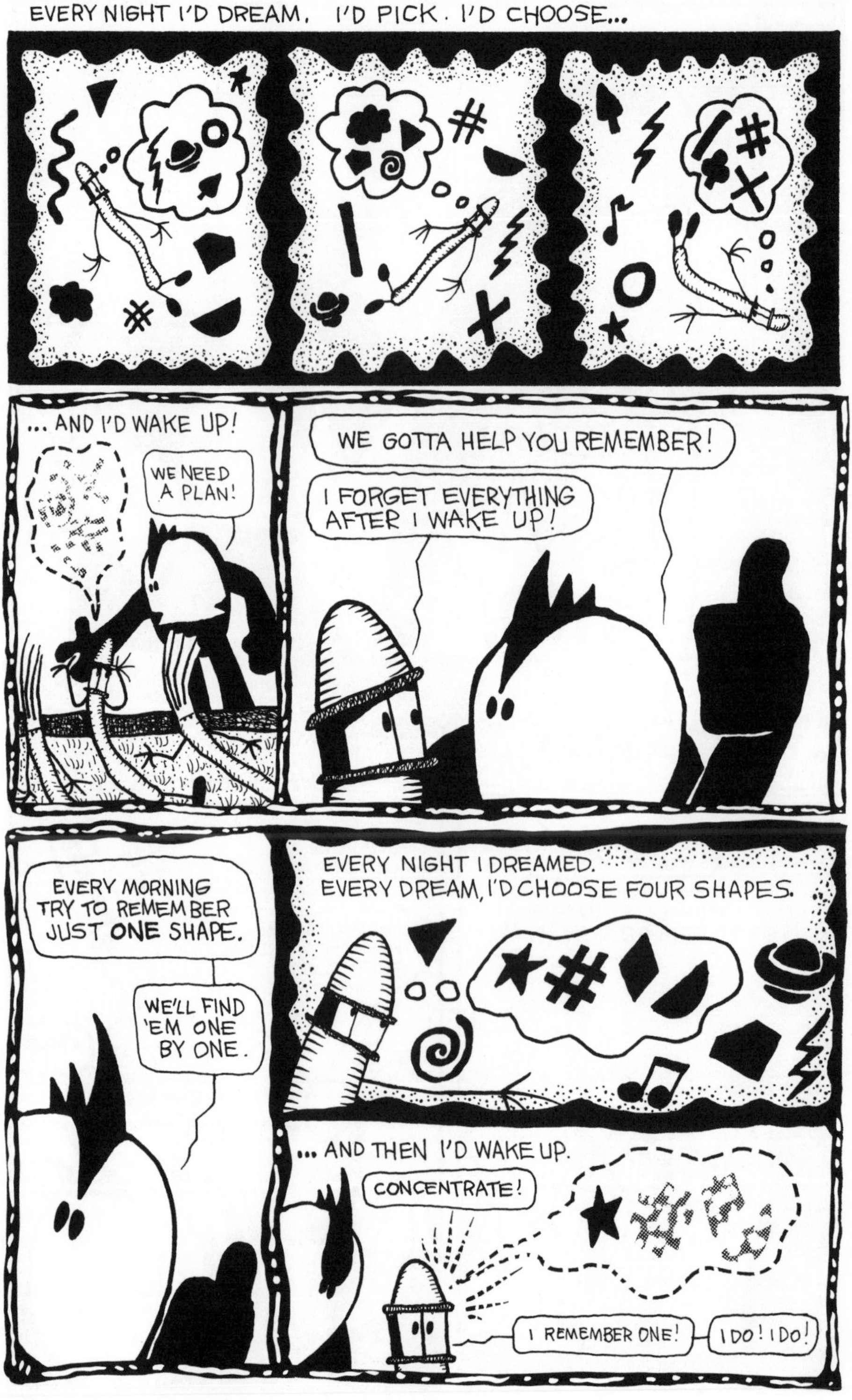
EVERY NIGHT I'D DREAM. I'D PICK. I'D CHOOSE...
... AND I'D WAKE UP!
WE NEED A PLAN!
WE GOTTA HELP YOU REMEMBER!
I FORGET EVERYTHING AFTER I WAKE UP!
EVERY MORNING TRY TO REMEMBER JUST ONE SHAPE.
WE'LL FIND 'EM ONE BY ONE.
EVERY NIGHT I DREAMED. EVERY DREAM, I'D CHOOSE FOUR SHAPES.
... AND THEN I'D WAKE UP.
CONCENTRATE!
I REMEMBER ONE!
I DO! I DO!

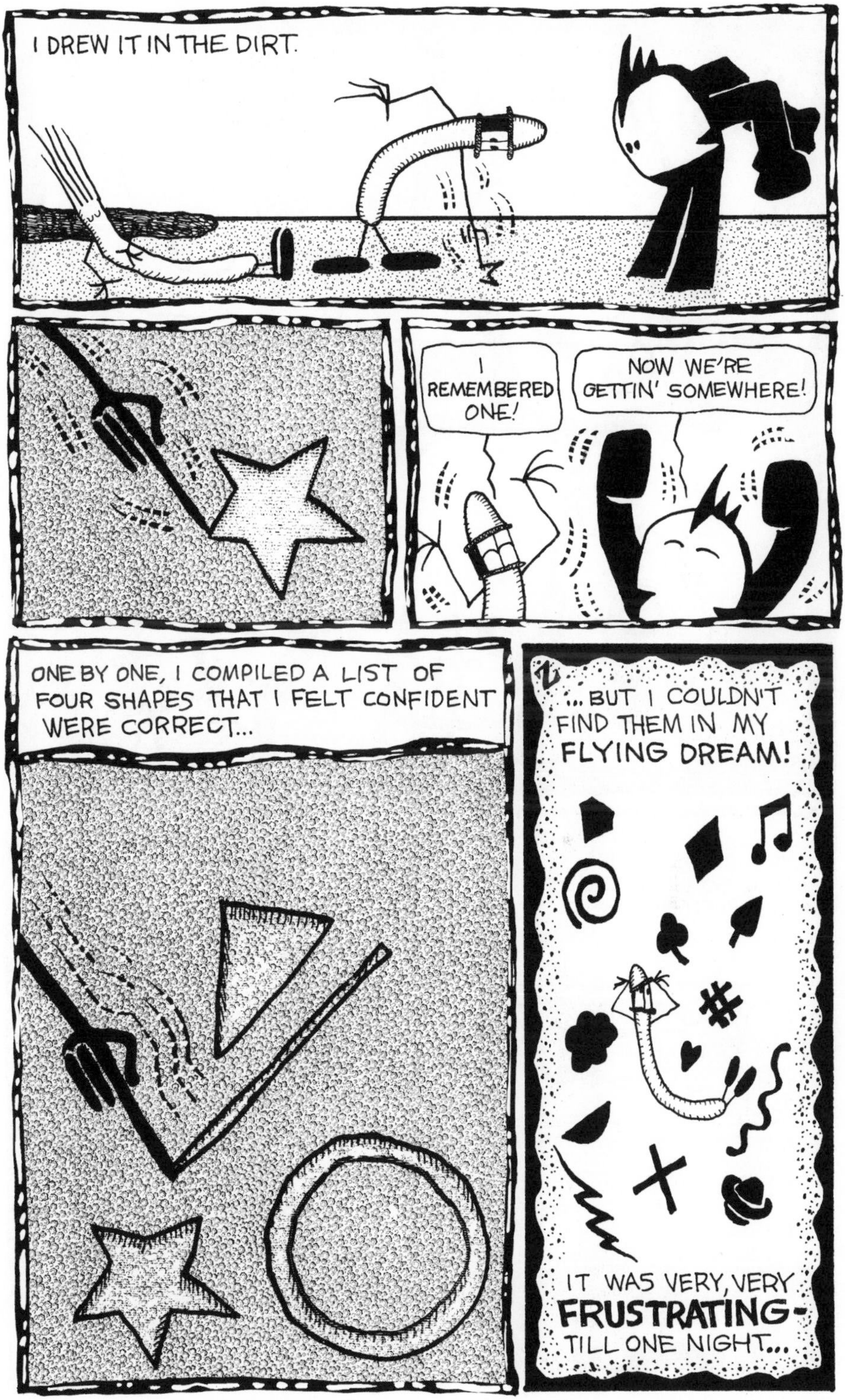
I DREW IT IN THE DIRT.
I REMEMBERED ONE!
NOW WE'RE GETTIN' SOMEWHERE!
ONE BY ONE, I COMPILED A LIST OF FOUR SHAPES THAT I FELT CONFIDENT WERE CORRECT...
...BUT I COULDN'T FIND THEM IN MY FLYING DREAM!
IT WAS VERY, VERY FRUSTRATING-
TILL ONE NIGHT...

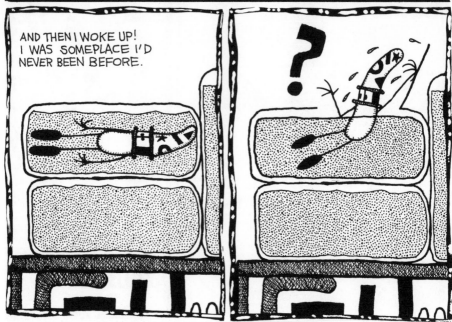

AND THEN I WOKE UP! I WAS SOMEPLACE I'D NEVER BEEN BEFORE.

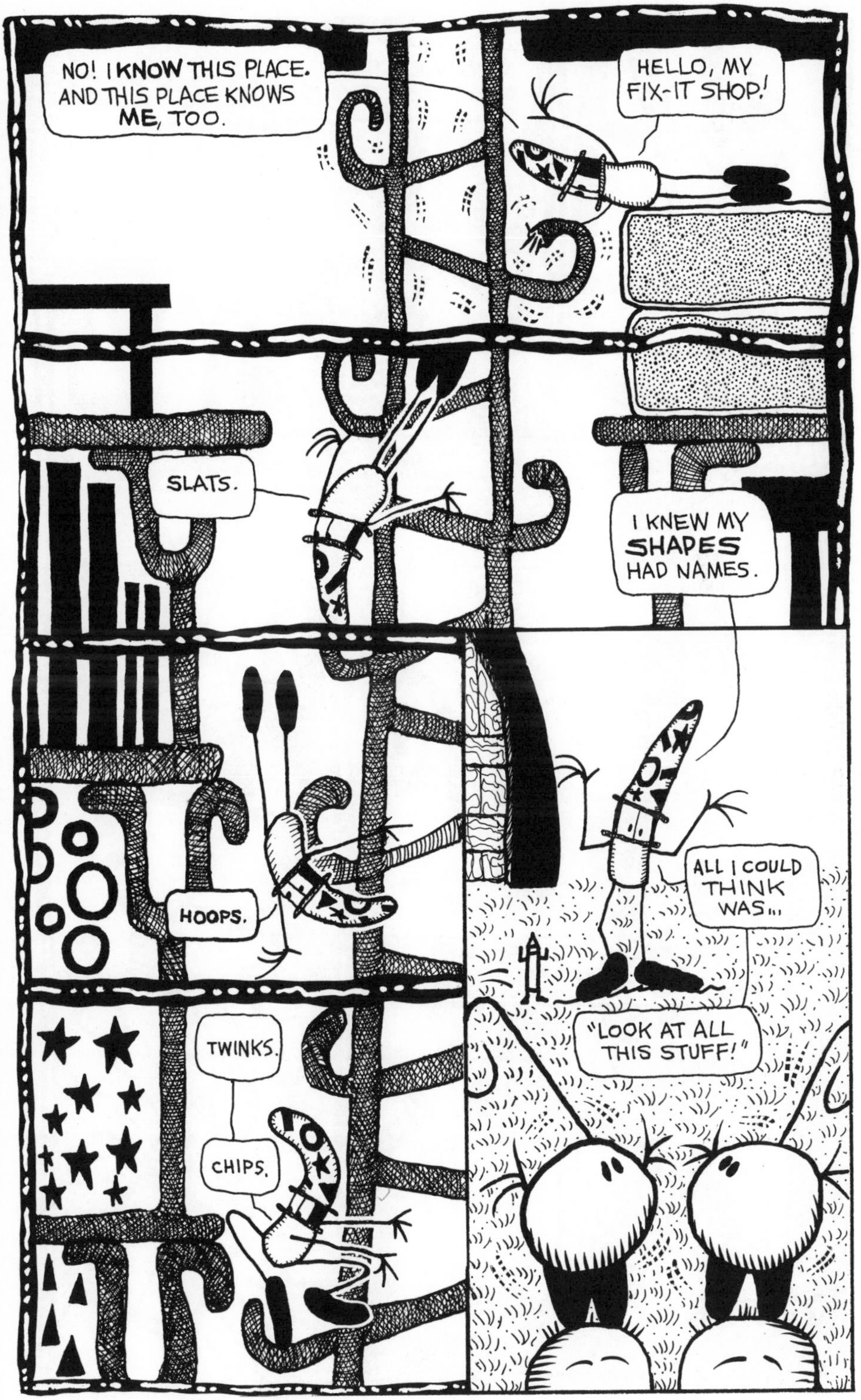
NO! I KNOW THIS PLACE.
AND THIS PLACE KNOWS
ME, TOO.
HELLO, MY
FIX-IT SHOP!
SLATS.
I KNEW MY
SHAPES
HAD NAMES.
HOOPS.
ALL I COULD
THINK
WAS...
TWINKS.
CHIPS.
"LOOK AT ALL
THIS STUFF!"

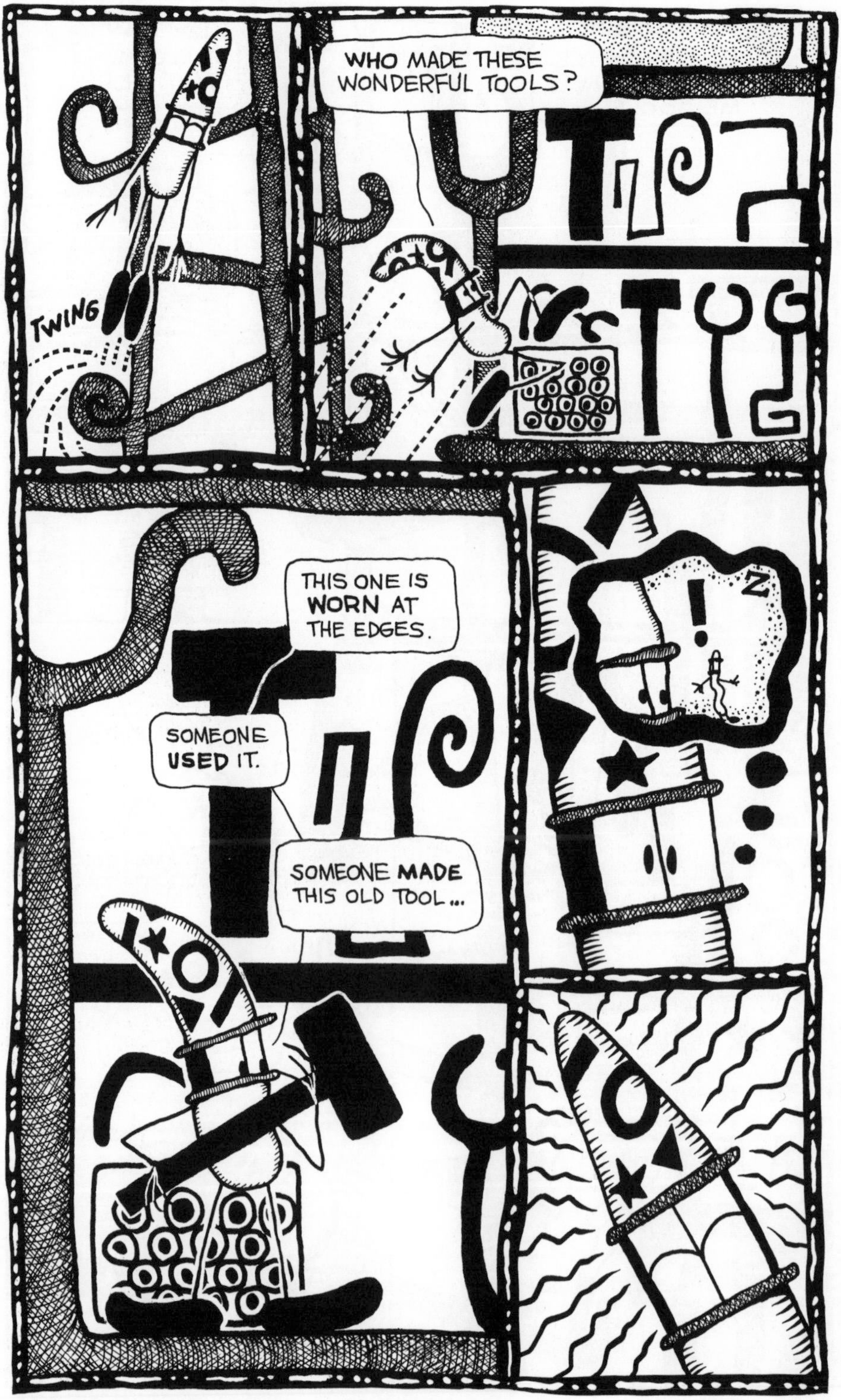
TWING
WHO MADE THESE WONDERFUL TOOLS?
THIS ONE IS WORN AT THE EDGES.
SOMEONE USED IT.
SOMEONE MADE THIS OLD TOOL...
!
Z

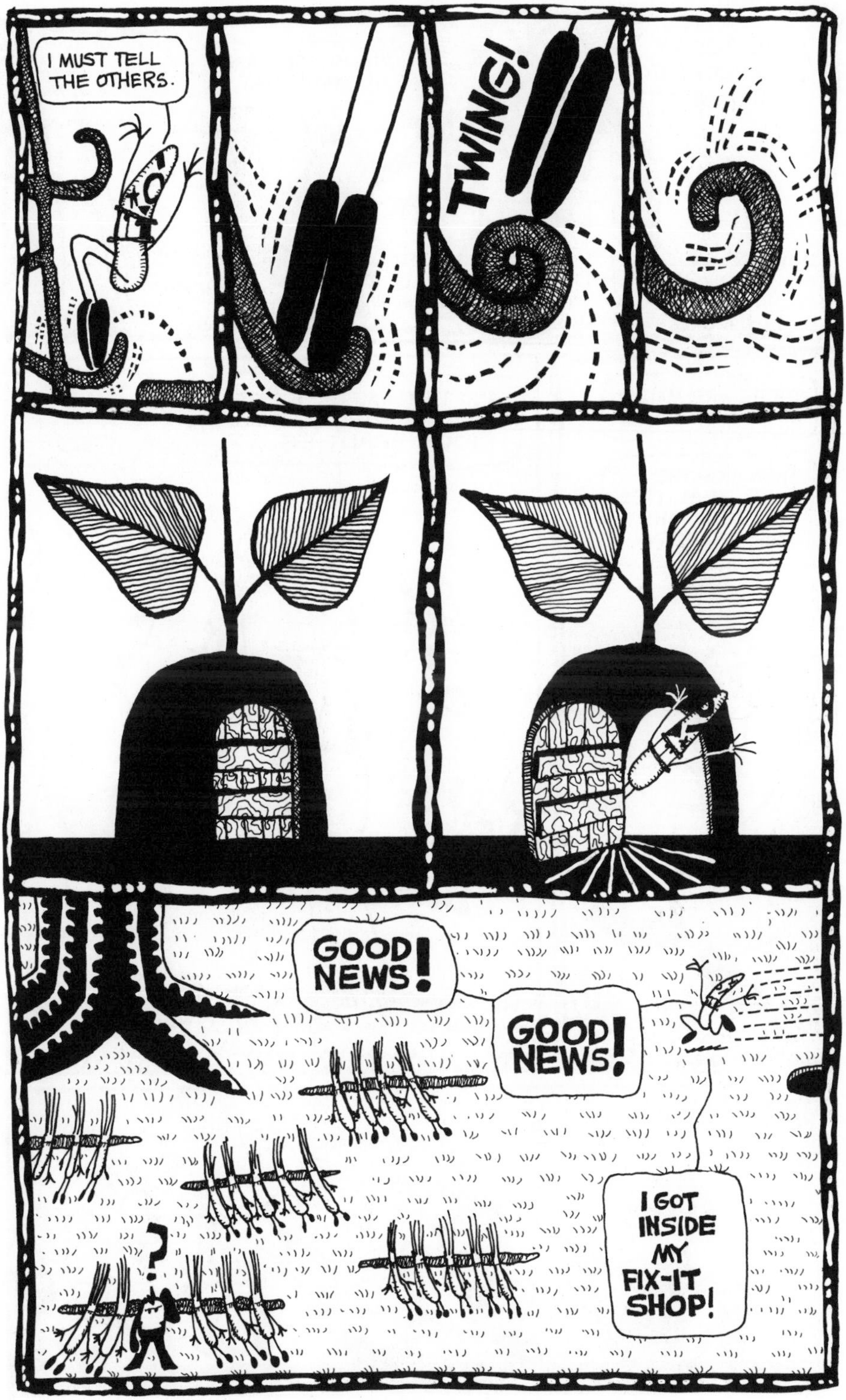
I MUST TELL THE OTHERS.
TWING!
GOOD NEWS!
GOOD NEWS!
?
I GOT INSIDE MY FIX-IT SHOP!

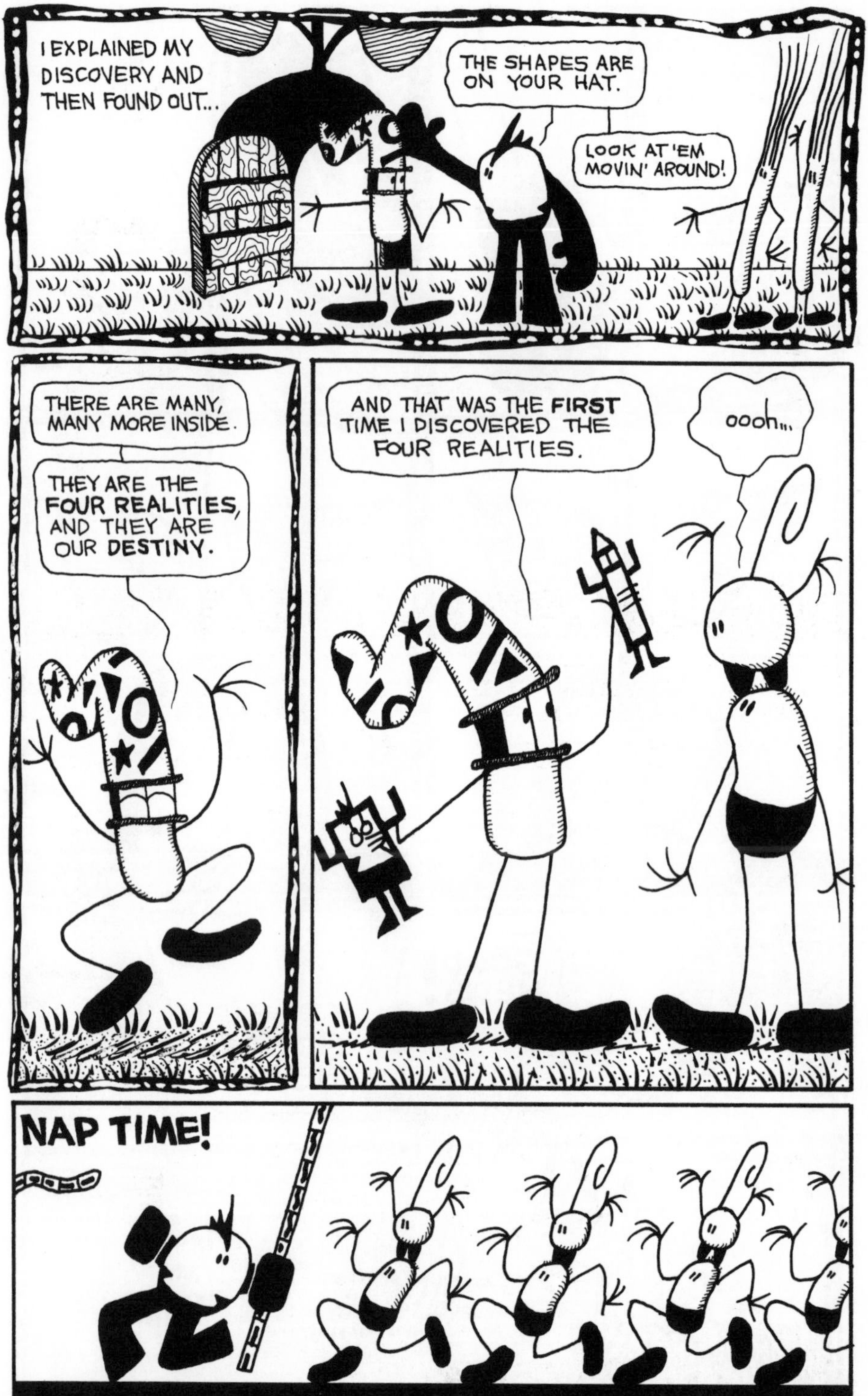
I EXPLAINED MY DISCOVERY AND THEN FOUND OUT...
THE SHAPES ARE ON YOUR HAT.
LOOK AT 'EM MOVIN' AROUND!
THERE ARE MANY, MANY MORE INSIDE.
THEY ARE THE **FOUR REALITIES**, AND THEY ARE OUR **DESTINY**.
AND THAT WAS THE **FIRST** TIME I DISCOVERED THE FOUR REALITIES.
oooh...
NAP TIME!

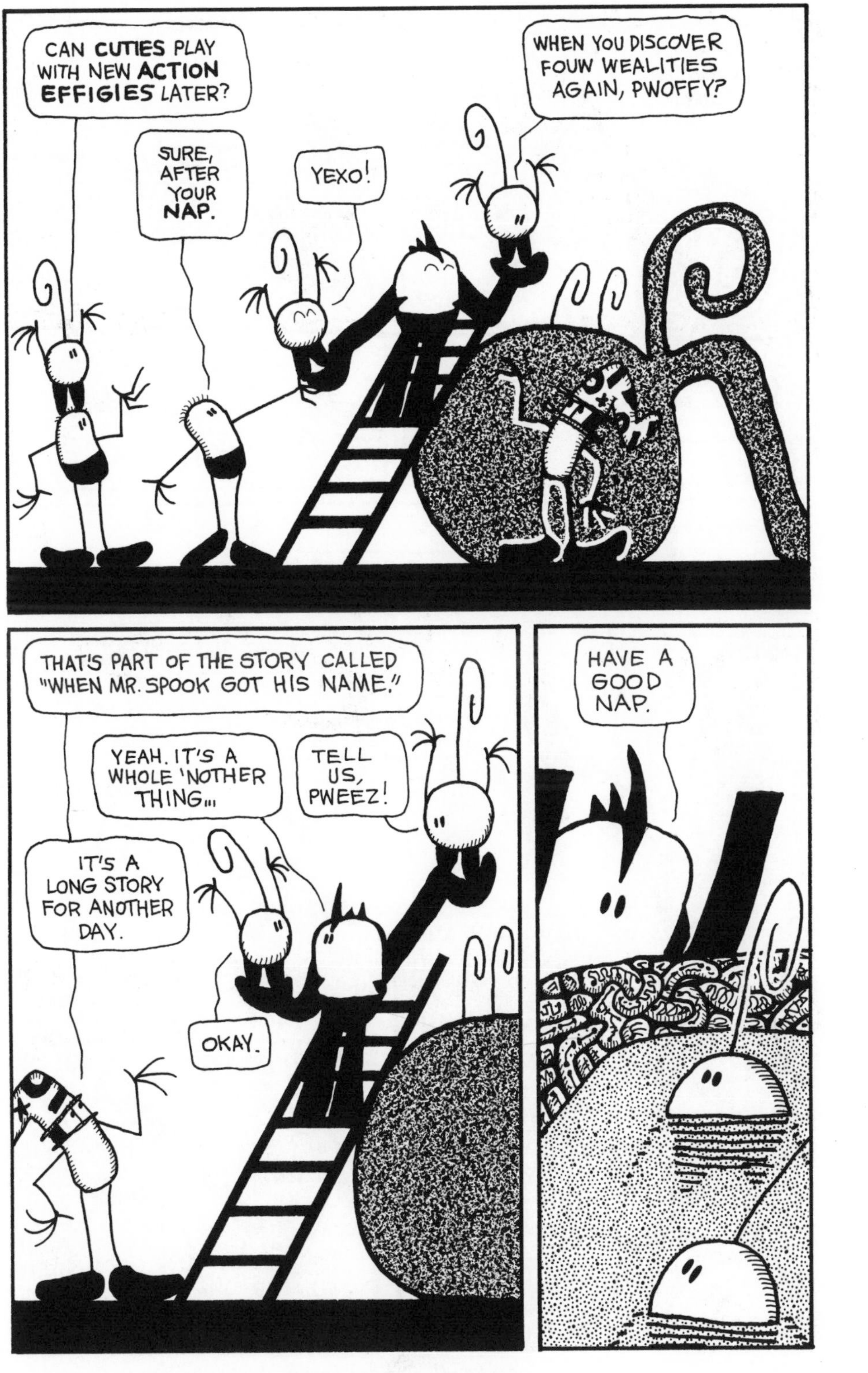
CAN **CUTIES** PLAY WITH NEW **ACTION EFFIGIES** LATER?
SURE, AFTER YOUR **NAP.**
YEXO!
WHEN YOU DISCOVER FOUW WEALITIES AGAIN, PWOFFY?
THAT'S PART OF THE STORY CALLED "WHEN MR. SPOOK GOT HIS NAME."
YEAH. IT'S A WHOLE 'NOTHER THING...
TELL US, PWEEZ!
IT'S A LONG STORY FOR ANOTHER DAY.
OKAY.
HAVE A GOOD NAP.

THAT WUXA WAHOOWAZUMA STORY.
YEXO!
Later.
AWWW.
ME FWYIN'!
ME SMASHIN'!
ME SMARTEST ONE THERE IS!
WANNA BET!

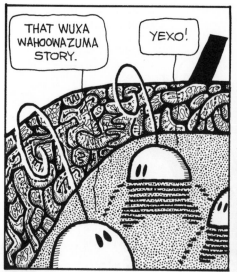

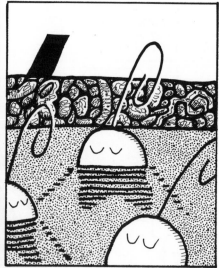

And so the legend grows, by beginning to fragment...

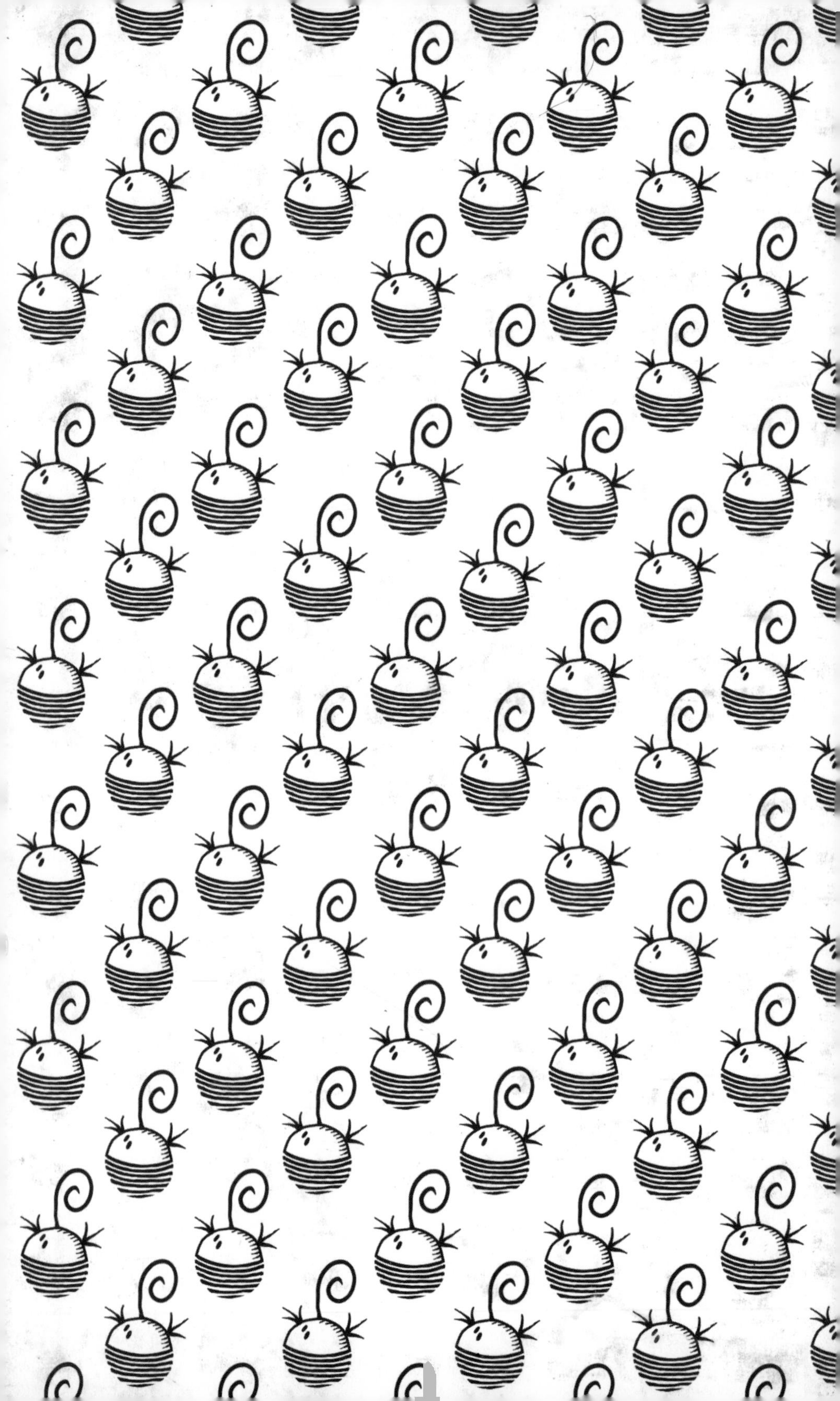